IT HAPPENED ON THE LAKE

Books by Lisa Jackson

Stand-Alones
SEE HOW SHE DIES
FINAL SCREAM
RUNNING SCARED
WHISPERS
TWICE KISSED
UNSPOKEN
DEEP FREEZE
FATAL BURN
MOST LIKELY TO DIE
WICKED GAME
WICKED LIES
SOMETHING WICKED
WICKED WAYS
WICKED DREAMS
SINISTER
WITHOUT MERCY
YOU DON'T WANT TO KNOW
CLOSE TO HOME
AFTER SHE'S GONE
REVENGE
YOU WILL PAY
OMINOUS
BACKLASH
RUTHLESS
ONE LAST BREATH
LIAR, LIAR
PARANOID
ENVIOUS
LAST GIRL STANDING
DISTRUST
ALL I WANT FROM SANTA
AFRAID
THE GIRL WHO SURVIVED
GETTING EVEN
DON'T BE SCARED
OUR LITTLE SECRET

YOU'LL FIND OUT
IT HAPPENED ON THE LAKE

Cahill Family Novels
IF SHE ONLY KNEW
ALMOST DEAD
YOU BETRAYED ME

Rick Bentz/Reuben Montoya Novels
HOT BLOODED
COLD BLOODED
SHIVER
ABSOLUTE FEAR
LOST SOULS
MALICE
DEVIOUS
NEVER DIE ALONE
THE LAST SINNER

Pierce Reed/Nikki Gillette Novels
THE NIGHT BEFORE
THE MORNING AFTER
TELL ME
THE THIRD GRAVE

Selena Alvarez/Regan Pescoli Novels
LEFT TO DIE
CHOSEN TO DIE
BORN TO DIE
AFRAID TO DIE
READY TO DIE
DESERVES TO DIE
EXPECTING TO DIE
WILLING TO DIE

Published by Kensington Publishing Corp.

IT HAPPENED ON THE LAKE

LISA JACKSON

KENSINGTON
PUBLISHING CORP.

kensingtonbooks.com

KENSINGTON BOOKS are published by

Kensington Publishing Corp.
900 Third Ave.
New York, NY 10022

Copyright © 2025 by Lisa Jackson, LLC

All Kensington titles, imprints, and distributed lines are available at special quantity discounts for bulk purchases for sales promotion, premiums, fund-raising, educational, or institutional use.

Special book excerpts or customized printings can also be created to fit specific needs. For details, write or phone the office of the Kensington Special Sales Manager: Attn. Special Sales Department. Kensington Publishing Corp., 900 Third Ave., New York, NY 10022. Phone: 1-800-221-2647.

KENSINGTON and the K with book logo Reg. U.S. Pat. & TM. Off.

Library of Congress Card Catalogue Number: 2025932703

ISBN: 978-1-4967-3703-8

First Kensington Hardcover Edition: July 2025

ISBN: 978-1-4967-3704-5 (ebook)

10 9 8 7 6 5 4 3 2 1

Printed in the United States of America

The authorized representative in the EU for product safety and compliance is eucomply OU, Parnu mnt 139b-14, Apt 123
Tallinn, Berlin 11317, hello@eucompliancepartner.com

IT HAPPENED ON THE LAKE

October 31, 1960
Halloween

Prologue

Harper knew better.

Of course she did.

Even though she was only nine.

She shouldn't leave the house and had promised Daddy she wouldn't.

But under the covers of her bed, she'd crossed her fingers. So it wasn't really a lie. She was sick, running a fever and coughing. Daddy had given her three big spoonfuls of the cough syrup with codeine, and she was drowsy.

Even so, she couldn't sleep.

Wouldn't.

It was Halloween.

"I'll be just downstairs, sweetheart," Daddy had said, leaning over her bed and pressing a kiss to her temple. "I'll pass out candy if anyone comes."

"No one ever does."

"That's okay. I'll watch Danny Thomas, okay? Zsa Zsa Gabor is on his show tonight."

"Who's she?" Harper had asked over a staged yawn.

"Possibly the most beautiful woman in the world." He'd smiled then.

Harper asked, "Isn't Mama the prettiest?"

Something had flickered behind his eyes, and his smile had seemed to waver a bit. "Of course she is. Now, Harper, you go to sleep. I won't bother you. Call if you need me. I'll be right downstairs."

But he'd lied.

She'd seen Bandit, her dog curled on the end of the bed, raise his scruffy head, his ears perking up as the front door had creaked open. Groggy as she was, Harper had heard the engine of Daddy's Aston Martin turn over. She'd seen flashes from its headlights as he'd driven away.

He'd lied?

To her?

She understood that he sometimes lied to Mama, but he'd never told her anything that wasn't the truth.

She wondered how long he'd be gone. But she didn't care, even though she felt horrible from a flu bug that had been going around school and her parents had decreed that she couldn't go out with her friends. Tonight. On Halloween.

It just wasn't fair.

*Every*one, including her jerk of a brother, was going out trick or treating. And even though it was a Monday, Levi Hunt's parents were letting him have a party!

Harper's only consolation was that her best friend had promised to share her candy. "I'll get two of everything," Beth had promised. "Even from Old Man Sievers!"

That had been another lie. Old Man Sievers was Beth's neighbor, a creepy old guy who kept to himself in a house surrounded by a huge fence and guarded by a massive dog that looked like a wolf.

Beth wouldn't go near his front door.

No one would.

But it didn't matter.

The plan had been for Harper to wait until she spied Beth crossing the lake in her mom's kayak and then meet her on the dock. That's where the candy switch was going to take place, Beth bringing over the duplicates she'd picked up and Harper giving her some of the candy that Gram always bought despite the fact that the mansion received no trick-or-treaters.

Ever.

Still, Gram bought dozens of big candy bars like Butterfingers and Big Hunks and Baby Ruths, all left in a huge bowl near the front door.

Harper knew just where to watch for her friend.

Even if she had to lie to her folks.

So Harper broke the rules.

And snuck out, leaving Bandit in her room.

Big deal.

It wasn't the first time.

She didn't bother with a jacket, just slipped silently down the stairs, out the back door and around the house. Then, glancing back only once, she dashed through the thick mist to the open gate where gargoyles huddled on their posts. Barely noticing them, Harper ran across the narrow, wet bridge leading to the private island where the huge house loomed.

Coughing as she opened the door to the garage, she slid inside and hurried to the staircase that curved upward to the attic space where the gardener sometimes lived. At the landing she stepped through a small door that opened to the second floor of the main house, an entrance used by servants. It was dark inside, only lamplight from the first level illuminating the narrow, winding staircase.

But she knew the way.

Already she had found and pocketed the extra key to the tower room, her grandfather's private domain. Armed with a weak-bulbed flashlight, she swept past the third floor where Mama sometimes stayed and wound her way up the narrow steps to the turret.

At the top step, her leg brushed against something soft.

"*Rrawr!*" one of Gram's cats shrieked.

Harper jumped back, her foot slipping.

She caught herself on the rail, dropping the flashlight. It tumbled down the flight, sending its yellowish beam reeling over ceiling, walls, and stairs. The wide-eyed cat, that miserable Diablo, crouched. Then, with an irritated hiss, he flashed his needle-like teeth before quickly scurrying away, his long gray tail trailing after him as he skulked down the stairs.

Harper froze. Afraid someone might have heard the commotion.

But the only sound was the thudding of her own heart, pounding loudly over the whisper of air in the heat ducts.

She blinked several times, straining to listen, disregarding the fact that she felt hot.

But there was no noise from the servants' quarters. They all had the night off. And Harper knew her grandmother was passing out baskets of candy at St. Catherine's Hospital and Orphanage, so Gram wouldn't be back for a while. Gramps was at his gentlemen's club in Portland.

She silently stole down the stairs to the third floor, retrieved her flashlight at the door to the room Mama claimed. Her "sanctuary" whenever she and Daddy had a fight. The door was ajar and Harper peered inside, caught a glimpse of the Bible on the night table and the crucifix with bleeding Jesus on the cross positioned over the bed where several of Gram's weird dolls had been propped. Another cat was curled on a pillow, a fat silver tabby who lifted his head briefly.

Harper left him where he was and mounted the stairs again. She was feeling worse than ever, but she used her purloined key and stepped inside a room that smelled of tobacco and English Leather cologne. She didn't bother with the lights, just made her way to the telescope mounted near the windows overlooking the lake.

Though this room had windows all around the turret, including the small bathroom, Gramps's leather chair was positioned near south-facing panes and the wide expanse of black water. Here, high above the trees, he had a wide view of all of Lake Twilight, illuminated tonight by a nearly full moon shrouded by the ever-shifting fog.

Seated on the edge of the chair, Harper ignored her pounding headache and adjusted the scope to peer through the eyepiece. The telescope was already focused directly across the lake to Beth's house. But she didn't spy Beth. Instead, through the rolling mist, she caught sight of Mrs. Leonetti in her bedroom. Alaina was taking off her blouse and bra before stepping out of her slacks. She'd been a model, Beth had confided in Harper, and a "Playboy Playmate" for *Playboy* magazine. The centerfold! Like that was a big deal or something. Harper's mother had overheard the conversation, and Mama's lips had pursed as she read from her *True Confessions* magazine. Her eyebrows had risen, and she'd muttered something about fake boobs and "falsies" in obvious disapproval before turning the page.

Harper didn't know about any of that, and she wasn't interested in Alaina's bare breasts, but she thought she might see Beth.

No such luck.

No sign of her friend.

So she turned her attention to the neighboring house where Levi Hunt was to have had his party. But she spied no kids on the dock, where grinning jack-o'-lanterns glowed, their ghoulish reflections barely visible on the dark water. Obviously the party was well over, the costumed kids let loose on the surrounding neighborhood.

Harper had thought she might spy her jerk of a brother at the Hunts' house. Evan was friends with Chase Hunt, Levi's older brother. Evan, Chase, and Rand Watkins, another neighbor, were always together. "Thick as thieves," Mama had said. Not that Harper cared what Evan was doing.

Where was Beth?

Still out with all their friends?

Beth had mentioned that she had to take her brothers out trick or treating in the neighborhood, three-year-old twins that Harper thought were cute and annoyed Beth to no end. But it was late. Shouldn't Bobby and Billy be in bed?

So . . .

She slipped off the chair and found Gramps's binoculars. They weren't as high-powered as the telescope, but she could search the dark water quicker standing on the window seat and swiveling.

She scanned the water, but she saw no boat through the rising mist. No sign of her friend.

Harper felt more lonely than ever.

And a little dizzy, her head thick and pounding, her legs a bit wobbly, her chest tight.

Weird.

She should go back to bed.

Before Dad got back and decided to check on her.

Besides, she knew Beth wasn't coming.

This was a dumb idea.

Now she crept down the staircase, her flashlight catching in the eyes of several of Gram's cats, who stared at her with unblinking gazes.

"I'm leaving," she told them, her throat raw.

But . . .

There was another telescope on the main floor in the parlor, and seated next to it was one of Gram's dolls. She had a million of them, and Harper had been warned not to touch them unless Gram supervised. As if she'd hurt any of the creepy things. Most of them were old, dressed in clothes from a different era. As Harper walked into the parlor, she picked up an ancient doll with a hard face and eyes that rolled up. If you pushed on its belly, it let out a pitiful "Ma-ma."

"Isn't she a beauty?" Gram had said with pride. "Her name is Maude."

Well, she wasn't all that pretty. One eye barely opened, the brushy eyelashes thick, her pinafore very old-timey. Harper listened as the doll wheezed, "Ma-ma."

The truth of it was that Harper didn't much like dolls. She was what Mama called a tomboy at heart, and she preferred being outside, climbing trees or swimming, or playing war with Evan and running along the trails that crisscrossed this island. What she really wanted was a horse that she could ride forever. So far, Mama and Daddy had refused to get her one, even though they promised Evan a motorbike when he turned sixteen.

It wasn't fair.

Again.

Angrily she tossed icky Maude back into her chair and was rewarded with a final "Ma-ma."

On the off chance that Beth was still coming, Harper tiptoed to the foyer with its marble floor, massive chandelier, and split, curved staircase.

She eased across the tiles to the center table where a huge bowl in the shape of a pumpkin was set, then stole a handful of candy bars before she made her way back to the parlor, where the calico cat was seated on Gram's favorite chair. It stood and stretched, as if hoping for Harper to pay it some attention.

Not tonight.

Not feeling as crummy as she did.

Instead she looked out the window once more, staring across the terrace to the black waters of the lake. But her vision was off, her own watery reflection seeming to wobble in the window. Steadying herself, she was about to peer through the telescope when she saw movement near the boathouse on the dock below.

Beth!

She had shown up!

But no.

Not Beth.

On closer inspection she realized the vision wasn't her friend.

Instead, a woman appeared through the fog.

Ghostly.

Dressed in white.

The mist climbing around her in the unsteady moonlight.

Harper blinked, trying to focus, the world seeming woozy.

The apparition remained.

With long dark hair curling down her back.

"Mama?" she whispered, blinking, a blackness pulling at her consciousness.

The ghostly woman looked like her mother. But Mama wasn't home, she remembered, her thoughts thick.

Why would Mama be on the dock staring out to the dark waters of the lake? The lake that had been called Lake of the Dead by the native tribe that had once lived on its shores. At least that's what Gram had told her. Only later when it was settled by white people like her ancestors had the name been changed to Lake Twilight.

"More calming, don't you think?" Gram had said with a raspy chuckle as she'd imparted what she'd called one of her little fun facts. "Though if you ask me Lake of the Dead is so much more intriguing."

But it was creepier.

And fitting for a night like tonight.

All Hallows' Eve. The night, according to Evan, where all the evil beings ever to exist returned to the earth in the forms of devils, ghosts, demons, and zombies. It was a night when those horrid, wicked creatures came to steal children before feasting upon them.

She didn't really believe him.

Evan was a big, fat liar.

But still . . .

Squinting, Harper saw that the woman was still at the edge of the dock and wobbling as she gazed into the water's dark depths.

Harper stumbled out onto the terrace, one of the cats slinking through the open door to dart toward the tram that was parked at the side of the house. The mechanical beast could scale the steep cliff from the house to the dock if you didn't want to bother with the stairs.

She made her way to the railing, where she heard the soft flutter of bats' wings over the gentle lap of the lake against the shore. Though her thoughts were heavy and scattered, she focused on the specter of the woman.

Something was wrong about this.

Very wrong.

Something evil.

Her hot skin crawled as she remembered what she'd learned about hell and the demons who resided there, as well as the dark fallen angel, Lucifer himself.

She shivered, though she was burning up inside.

Mama shouldn't be out there . . .

She leaned over the railing, the world spinning as she clutched the wrought iron.

The woman below teetered on the edge of the dock. "Mama," Harper mouthed, and felt her knees buckle. Her fingers slipped. Scrabbling awkwardly for the railing, she dropped the candy bars she'd forgotten were in her hand. She caught a glimpse of movement—a shadow darting through the fog, springing onto the dock, toward Mama!

One of the demons!

Let loose on Halloween night!

She tried to scream, but she could only croak out a raspy warning that seemed to die in the night.

The world spun.

For a moment she caught glimpses of the moon peeking between the branches of a fir tree as she fell shivering onto the wet flagstones, the candy bars scattered around her.

Though her mind was hazy, she heard it.

The sound of sobbing whispering through the night.

Tortured, ragged sobs.

Just before the splash.

October 1988
The Present

Chapter 1

The past is unforgiving.

The nagging voice just wouldn't stop. Harper set her jaw and kept driving, her eyes focused on the narrow, winding road, the illumination from her Volvo's headlights shimmering against the wet pavement.

You're not wanted.

She shifted down. The wagon shimmied a little as she took a corner too fast. Water splashed as she tore through a puddle.

You shouldn't be here.

"Stop!" she said, angry at her self-doubts as the mansion came into view. "Enough already."

This is a mistake!

Harper ignored the voice in her head that had been nagging her since she'd slid into her Volvo in Northern California about ten hours earlier. Her eyes were gritty, she needed a shower, and she did not need her guilty conscience pricking at her.

Not just a mistake, but a mistake of epic proportions!

"Oh, give me a break. I'm going back, dammit, and I'm going now."

Sometimes her inner thoughts, riddled with guilt as they were, bugged the crap out of her. Like now. On this dark, dreary Oregon night.

She stepped on the accelerator and her Volvo shot forward, hitting a pothole, the whole wagon shuddering. Harper's fingers tightened over the wheel.

You're going to regret this.

"I'm not going to be here long," Harper argued aloud. "I'm leaving again. Satisfied?"

Of course not.

Her deep-seated doubts were never sated.

"Pull yourself together," she told herself, but that had been nearly impossible lately with her recent divorce and estrangement from her daughter. And then there was her father's heart attack. Bruce Reed had survived, she'd heard, but she had yet to see him herself. As soon as she was settled in the cottage, she'd drive to St. Catherine's Hospital. Not that she and her dad were close these days, but she sure as hell hoped he would recover.

And really, who was she close to at this juncture in her life?

No one.

Not one damned person.

She set her jaw as her headlights reflected on the old deer crossing sign riddled with bullet holes.

Some things never change.

And some things always do, her nagging brain reminded her.

"Shut up!" She cranked up the radio, blasting U2's "I Still Haven't Found What I'm Looking For." "Me neither, Bono, me neither."

From the cat carrier on the seat beside her, Jinx gave out a low, irritated mewl.

"Almost there," she told the cat, just as she spied the edge of the drive, nearly hidden by untrimmed laurel and overgrown rhododendrons. "You're fine," she assured him, then added, "We're both fine," though that was a lie.

She eased up on the gas. *I'm home*, she thought hollowly, an emptiness invading her soul.

How many ghosts from her past lingered on the solitary island, that jagged stump of rock jutting from the dark, impenetrable depths of Lake Twilight?

Her heart squeezed when she caught sight of the caretaker's cottage at the edge of a parking apron, the place she'd once called home.

It had been a spot where she'd lived on and off during her adolescence, a place of solace and heartache.

She let the Volvo roll to a stop near the cottage, just in front of the huge gate leading to the mansion. Beyond the wrought-iron pickets, she saw the bridge that spanned a narrow neck of the lake, connecting the mainland to the island. Her island now. She was thirty-seven, the magical age her grandmother had thought she would be responsible enough to claim her inheritance. Thirty-seven. Was that midlife?

All signs point to "yes."

"Oh, shut up!"

And as far as crises went, she'd been through her share already.

She cut the engine and climbed out of her wagon. Flipping up the hood of her jacket, Harper stood at the gate, the Volvo's headlamps casting her shadow through the bars of the massive wrought-iron barrier beyond which the narrow bridge seemed to disappear into the darkness.

The island itself was blurry, a massive, indistinct shape with towering fir trees that rose from the cliffs and sheltered the mansion. No lamps were lit, no exterior lights glowed to highlight the ornate walls or the high turret that knifed into the sky.

"Welcome home," she told herself.

She'd thought as a child that the house was straight out of *The Addams Family*.

And she hadn't been wrong.

But it had been Gram's home, once upon a time, an architectural showpiece that had turned into a house of horrors.

Harper shivered and pulled her jacket tighter around her.

You can never go back.

Well, here she was.

Very much back.

At least for a little while.

She cast a disparaging glance at the stone posts that were not only fastened to the gate but also served as perches for the gargoyles her grandmother had loved so fervently.

"Tacky, I know, and possibly a tad macabre," Gram had confided in Harper one summer morning. They had stood just inside the gate, the bridge to their backs as they'd studied the carved beasts in the sunlight.

Harper had been in her teens at the time, and the monstrous winged creatures seemed to her as if they'd risen from hell, just like Sister Evangeline had warned in catechism. The gargoyles' lips were pulled back into snarls, fangs long and curved, each with a snakelike tail that coiled around its muscular body.

They were not identical. One was sculpted with reptilian eyes and scaled like a dragon. The other's skin was taut and smooth over visible muscles. Horns curved from its forehead. Huge eyes bulged above a pug nose, and sharp claws extended from manlike hands. The end of its tail was carved into an arrow's tip. A devil-creature.

To Harper, each sculpture appeared to be the epitome of pure evil.

"You want to scare people away?" she asked, studying the stone creatures warily as she sidled closer to her grandmother.

"No. Not really." Gram pulled shears from the pocket of her golf skirt and clipped off an errant bit of ivy that had dared wrap around the wrought-iron railing. "I just want people to think about it before they ring the bell. They might even consider me a bit eccentric. Wouldn't that be delicious?" She'd flipped up the sunglasses she referred to as her Audrey Hepburn *Breakfast at Tiffany's* pair, setting them into her perfectly coiffed hair.

Her blue eyes sparkled as she winked at Harper. "It's all kind of in fun, you know. But, yes, I do like my privacy. Grandpa, he wasn't fond of them." She hitched her chin toward one of the stone carvings. "He called them 'Ugly and Uglier.' Thought he was so damned funny." She sighed and for a second was caught in a nostalgic moment, her eyebrows pinching together. "I guess he would have preferred something more traditional. More regal."

"Like?"

"Oh, I don't know . . . lions, I suppose." She swatted at a mosquito, then snipped off another offensive sprig of ivy. She let the sunglasses drop onto the bridge of her nose again. "Come to think of it, he did mention lions, oh, and eagles. Yes, that's right. Too traditional." With a quick shake of her head, she added, "As if. Let me tell you, I nixed those ideas quicker than you can say Jack Robinson. *My* house, *my* choice, *my* gargoyles." She eyed the carved creatures and smiled. "You know, I think they protect me. Keep all of us safe."

"What about Mama?" Harper asked, feeling the heat from the sun beat against her crown and a coldness enter her heart. "They didn't keep her safe."

A shadow crossed Gram's face. Her amused smile faded. "No, I suppose not." Gram cleared her throat and scrabbled into her pocket, this time for a pack of cigarettes. She lit up quickly with a silver lighter. As she shot a stream of smoke to the blue, blue sky, she said, "Your mother, she didn't like them much either." Her voice had turned soft as she wrapped one arm around her slim waist, holding her cigarette aloft in her other hand as she squinted up at the scaled gargoyle, the dragon, the one Harper's grandfather had named "Ugly."

"When she was a little girl, about your age, or a year or two younger, maybe, your mother suggested we should replace them with race horses or unicorns." Another puff. "Can you imagine? Unicorns?" She said it as if it were a joke, but there was a sadness to her tone, as there always was when she mentioned Mama. Harper felt it, too. That sadness was like a shadow, always close, ready to grow if you thought too long.

"Well, that was Anna for you. Forever the dreamer." Quickly Gram took another draw on her cigarette, then dropped it onto the pavement and crushed it with her sandaled foot.

Harper had hazarded a glance up at Ugly with its scaly skin and folded wings. If it had been the gargoyles' job to protect the family, then they had failed miserably. Otherwise Mama would still be alive.

Now, of course, Evan, too, was gone and had been for years. But she wouldn't think of that tragedy. Nope. There was no time for melancholy on this miserable night.

The Volvo's headlights offered enough illumination for her to run up the uneven flagstones to the caretaker's cottage. While rain peppered the ground and dripped off the sagging eaves, she huddled on the porch and fumbled with the key ring—Gram's set of keys to unlock the door.

Stepping inside, she flipped on the light switch.

Nothing.

The house remained dark, cold, the emanating scent of mold evident. "Not good," she told herself and backtracked through the rain to the car where she searched in the glove box. All the while Jinx let her know he was still very unhappy. "I know, I know, it won't be long now," she said as she found the flashlight, snagged it, and headed back to the cottage.

Once inside again, she swung the weak beam over the interior and saw the soggy mess. Buckled stairs, peeling wallpaper, sodden carpets, and swollen hardwood. The brick floor near the front door was still intact, but everything else inside appeared ruined.

"Well, crap."

No way could she stay here.

Not until everything was repaired, which would take weeks—no, make that months. So why hadn't the attorneys in charge of the estate made the repairs? Why had they let the house erode to this abysmal level?

Carefully she stepped into the living room, felt the sponginess of the floor, and retreated to the front hallway again.

There was nothing she could do tonight.

On to Plan B.

Which she had hoped to avoid.

"Grow a pair," she told herself. For the love of God, she was no longer that desperate, wide-eyed girl who had fled this place half a lifetime ago. She was a grown woman now. A mother and a wife— *well, no, an ex-wife*, she reminded herself.

The hood of her jacket fell away, and November rain drizzled down her collar as she skirted puddles and made her way to the gate.

Which wouldn't budge.

The automatic keypad was ruined, the hinges rusted.

"Great." She shoved again, this time planting her feet, ignoring the pain in her leg and throwing her shoulders into the task. The gate was heavy and had, it seemed, been closed for eons. With an effort, using all the strength she could muster, she forced the damned thing open. Old hinges creaked, but she was able to clear a space wide enough for her car.

Good enough.

"We're in," she said to the cat as she settled behind the steering wheel and rammed the gearshift into first. "Even if we really don't want to be."

Then she tested the bridge, walking over it and deciding it was still sturdy.

Sending up a prayer as the wipers slapped the rain from the windshield, she drove slowly to the island.

She made it.

The old piers and abutments held.

For now.

She parked in front of the garage and glanced up at the mansion, a huge, three-story monster of a house with a towering turret above it all.

"Home sweet home," she said with more than a trace of sarcasm. "You're gonna love it." She glanced at the passenger side, where the cat carrier was belted tightly into the seat. Two gold eyes peered through the mesh, glaring at her suspiciously. "Trust me, this is gonna be heaven."

Or hell. Yeah, more likely hell. But she wouldn't utter those dark thoughts aloud. "Hang here for a sec," she said, before realizing she was having a conversation with a cat.

A cat!

Not even her cat!

She'd inherited Jinx when her daughter had taken off for college.

"Awesome," she muttered under her breath. Now she was stuck with the damned thing.

Well, so be it. This was her life now, and bringing Jinx here seemed only right. Cats had always been a part of this place. Gram had taken every stray that had ever wandered onto the island. "It's a huge house, so why not?" Olivia Dixon had said, upon "adopting" an obviously pregnant calico when Harper was twelve.

She reached into her pocket for the keys, found the one for the front door, and forced it into the lock of the massive double door. With a click, the dead bolt slid out of place, and she pushed the creaking door open.

Everything in the house was as Harper remembered.

Just falling into disrepair.

The split staircase still wound up on either side of the wide foyer to the landing twelve feet overhead. But the banister was now dull, the handrail no longer gleaming. Some of the marble tiles in the floor were cracked. The wallpaper that had intrigued her as a child with its brilliant peacocks and peonies was now faded and peeling near the ceiling where cobwebs collected and draped.

All in all, the foyer was a mess.

And it didn't bode well for the rest of the house.

Dropping her purse onto a dusty side table, Harper reminded herself that living here didn't have to be a permanent plan.

As if you've ever had a plan in your life.

Face it, Harper, you fly by the seat of your pants.

All the plans you've ever made are just reactions to the mistakes you've made.

Ignoring the doubts crowding through her mind, she walked quickly through the arched hallway and straight to the back of the house.

Again, she hit a light switch. Several lamps responded to cast a warm glow over the dusty antiques, period pieces, and just plain junk that still filled the room. Gram's things. Tiffany lamps and a fringed chaise longue straight out of the twenties mixed with club chairs and a sixties era console housing a TV/stereo combination.

How many hours had she spent in front of that thing watching *I Love Lucy* or Walter Cronkite reporting the news?

Too many to count, she thought as she spied some of the dolls Gram had collected still propped on the furniture and all the religious paraphernalia from her Catholic childhood evident in the bookcases and walls.

The dolls were still strategically placed around the rooms like little pudgy wide-eyed soldiers, guarding the place and now collecting dust. Though Gram had showered her with several Barbies and a Chatty Cathy that repeated recorded phrases like "I love you," or "I hurt myself" in a wheedling tone, Harper hadn't been all that interested.

Eyeing the room, it seemed as if time hadn't lapsed.

Harper half expected her grandmother to roll into the room in her wheelchair, though that was, of course, impossible. And there was no lingering scent of cigarette smoke or whiff of Chanel No. 5 perfume in the air, no rumble of the ancient Kirby vacuum cleaner being pushed over the patterned carpets by the maid. Nor, thankfully, was there a glint of cat eyes watching her or moving as the furry beasts slipped from one hidden alcove to the next. Even the grandfather clock had gone silent with the passing of time. So no, Gram couldn't appear from her room just off the parlor, the only bedroom on the first level.

Harper gave herself a quick mental shake.

That was then.

This is now.

She walked to the window and pushed aside the tall curtains before raising the shades. Staring across the terrace, she saw the dark waters of Lake Twilight shimmering restlessly. On the far shore the homes of people she'd known, those who had been close to her, those who had not. *Friends and enemies*, she thought, staring through the rainy night, remembering what might have been if tragedy hadn't struck.

But it had. And it had struck with a vengeance.

"Woulda, coulda, shoulda." She touched one of her grandfather's telescopes, this one still mounted in the area between his chair and the window. She thought of all the times she, as a kid, had peered through it, "spying" on the people on the other side of the lake. Just like Gramps with all of his sets of binoculars and the more powerful telescope in his private chambers in the turret where he'd focused on the Leonettis' bedroom. Harper had caught her grandfather once in that tobacco-scented room when he'd forgotten to lock the door and she'd followed one of Gram's cats upstairs. She'd peered through the crack between door and jamb to spy Gramps, his hand in his pants. His face was red above the bristles of his beard, and he'd been grunting and breathing hard as he'd stared through the lens.

She'd backed out, not understanding until much later.

Tonight, trying to dismiss the disturbing image, she walked directly to the sideboard near the butler's pantry, where the liquor had been kept. An array of glassware and several crystal decanters half-full of dark liquid were visible behind the glass doors. Good. Telling herself she deserved a drink after her long drive from California, she reached inside for a glass.

Instead she found a gun.

Chapter 2

"What the—?" she whispered, then picked up the revolver with its long barrel and pearl handle. It was heavy. And familiar. The last time she'd held it . . .

"No!" She dropped the damned thing as if it was hot. With a loud crack, a jagged line cut across the glass shelf. She backed away. "No, no, no!" But the memory she'd tried for decades to repress sliced into her brain.

Evan.

Oh dear God.

"Get a grip," she told herself. She'd been in the house less than ten minutes, and already her nerves were shattered.

This revolver wasn't the gun that had taken his life. The police had taken that one. This pistol was its twin, part of a set that Gramps had kept locked in his tower room.

So why was it here?

Setting her jaw, she picked up the gun again and examined it. Nearly an antique, the revolver was the kind she had seen in old TV westerns. One side of the mother-of-pearl handle was loose. The screw holding it in place needed tightening with a tiny screwdriver— she remembered that, her grandfather forever trying to fix it.

And Evan had been fascinated by it. She remembered seeing one of the pistols in her brother's hand as Evan had twirled it and pretended to be Roy Rogers or Wild Bill Hickok or some other TV cowboy she couldn't name.

She turned the gun over in her hands. Holding the grip, touching the cylinder and trigger, staring at the damned gun with its six deadly chambers, she remembered Evan as he'd been the last time. Eighteen, his blue eyes bright, pupils dilated, brown hair fanned around his face. Always full of "piss and vinegar," as Gram had said so often. But not then.

Her throat tightened and she refused, absolutely would not think about that hot summer night.

But she was still bothered to have found the pistol and wondered again why it had been left in the cupboard that had housed glassware. And by whom?

Questions flitted through her mind, but she had no answers and wasn't going to try and force them. "Not tonight," she told herself and put the damned thing back in the cupboard for now. Later, she would transfer it to Gramps's locked safe. If she could open the massive thing.

For now, she rooted through another cabinet, found a glass, and blew out any dust that might have collected over the years. She lifted one of the crystal decanters, nudged off the top with her thumbs, and smelled the peaty scent of Scotch.

Her first sip was strong and burned a bit but settled into her stomach. Two more long swallows, and the glass was empty. Soon she would warm from the inside out as the alcohol seeped into the bloodstream.

But first, she needed to unpack the car.

Starting with the cat.

Jinx complained mightily from his carrier as she hauled it, along with a small bag of cat food, to the kitchen. Again, she flipped the light switch. Only a few of the overhead lights winked on, illuminating the kitchen in a weird, almost sepia light. Then she made sure the three doors were closed before opening the cage door. Wide-eyed, all sleek black fur and white toes, Jinx slunk out.

"What'd'ya think?" she said as if the cat could answer. When he didn't respond, just eyed the new surroundings warily, she said, "I know. Me, too, but trust me, you're going to fit right in." She found two ramekins in a cupboard and rinsed them before adding water to one, cat food to another. "Morris loves this stuff, you know," she told him.

Jinx was unimpressed and didn't seem to care about the spokes-cat for 9 Lives. Ignoring the dishes, he crept around the perimeter of the large kitchen. "Get comfortable," she told him as he circum-vented the wide island between the stove and refrigerator.

As he explored, she slipped back to the parlor.

"Just one more," she said as if the cat could hear or understand. She poured herself another healthy shot from the open decanter, drank it in three long swigs.

Jinx was crying at the swinging door.

"I know," she said, letting the door swing open. "It's kinda strange being here, isn't it?" Picking him up, she confided, "It's weird for me, too." She left her empty glass on a side table and, stroking the cat, made her way to the window. Her stomach tightened a bit as she looked out across the terrace where she'd last seen her mother so many years before. She'd been just a kid, and her memory was as blurry as that foggy night, some parts completely obscured.

Her fingers tightened.

Jinx yowled!

He kicked hard, scrambling out of Harper's arm, scratching wildly.

"Ah, wow!" Harper sucked in her breath against the sting but took off after the cat before he could get lost in this huge mansion filled with nooks, crannies, and cupboards. He'd shot down the hallway to the back stairs. "Jinx!" She hit a light switch.

No light sizzled on.

And she saw no cat as she ran past the elevator to the staircase where one flight ascended to the upper floors and the other wound down to the basement.

Both doors were open.

"Jinx," she called into the darkness. She slapped at a light switch and nothing happened. Crap. "Jinx? Come, kitty." But her voice seemed to fade into the darkness.

She waited, calling softly. Coaxing.

He didn't appear.

But he would. He always did.

She tried the light switches for each set of stairs.

Again, the darkness remained.

"Great." Going down to the basement with its rabbit warren of hallways would be dangerous and fruitless. And searching the upper stories, three counting the tower room, would prove impossible. Her flashlight was weak to begin with, the batteries dying and she had no new ones, so it would be nearly useless.

She would just have to wait until he calmed down and returned.

As he had in the past.

Rubbing her arm, she felt the warm beads of blood that had risen when his claws had caught her wrist and forearm.

"Come on, Jinx," she said once more and told herself that losing the cat was the perfect end to a miserable day that had started at dawn in Santa Rosa before her drive north. All the way, as the miles had passed beneath her Volvo's tires, she'd told herself that returning here was no big deal, that all of the pain of the past might surface a bit but would eventually retreat again.

But she'd been wrong.

Dead wrong.

All the old pain was still there, the unanswered questions returning.

She found an ancient box of Kleenex, pulled out all the tissues and took several from the middle of the folded sheets to dab at her arm, then considered another drink but decided against it.

Instead, she gazed through the windows to a spot on the opposite shore. Fox Point, where the lake was narrowest. She remembered each of the houses and their inhabitants: Old Man Sievers's bungalow near the swim park and closest to town, then the Watkins' A-frame and the Hunts' cottage and—

"What the—?" she whispered. Something was out there. Something bright and swirling, seeming to grow more luminous and larger, as it bobbed on the surface and drew nearer.

A fire? There was a fire in the middle of Lake Twilight?

But—?

No.

Couldn't be.

Heart thudding, she swung her grandfather's telescope around and peered through.

"Oh God." Her heart sank.

Sure enough, a boat was ablaze, flames rising into the rain-washed night.

A woman was aboard, her tortured face turned up to the heavens.

Cynthia Hunt.

Chase's mother.

A woman who blamed Harper for all the heartache in her life.

A woman who wished Harper dead.

"No," Harper whispered. "No . . . no . . ." There couldn't be another tragedy on the lake.

Not after there had been so many.

And yet, once more Lake Twilight was claiming its own in its deceptively calm waters.

Fighting a searing sense of déjà vu, Harper ran straight to the bedside phone in Gram's room, a clunky dial-faced relic that had never been replaced.

Sweeping up the heavy receiver, she sent up a prayer that the line was still connected, that she could still reach someone. A dial tone hummed in her ear.

Thank God!

She jammed a finger into the 9 slot and waited for the dial to slowly rotate back into place. It seemed to take forever for the phone to spin out each digit of the emergency number. "Come on, come on," Harper said as the phone started to ring. "Answer!"

She stretched the cord and paced.

"9-1-1." A female voice startled her and started asking questions.

But Harper cut her off. "There's a boat on fire in the middle of Lake Twilight! Near Dixon Island! There's at least one person on board! A woman! Send someone now!"

"On Lake Twilight? If you could please identify yourself and—"

She didn't hear the rest. Just took off through the side kitchen door that was used as a service entrance. Sprinting around the side of the house, she dashed onto the slippery flagstones of the terrace to the stairs.

Slipping and sliding, her pulse pounding in her ears, she scrambled down the steep concrete steps, some crumbling, some slick with moss.

The fire was in full view if anyone was looking, a wavering blaze undulating on the choppy waters, three hundred, maybe four hundred yards from either shore. Surely someone else had noticed the flames. Surely someone had—

Her bad leg gave out.

She missed a step.

Twisting, she went down hard.

Bam!

Her chin bounced on the edge of a step.

Pain exploded through her jaw.

"Oooh. God." Stunned, Harper slid down the final two steps to the rain-soaked deck. She rolled onto her back. The warm ooze of blood mingled with cold raindrops to run down her chin and neck. She blinked to stay conscious. Thought she might be sick.

No! No! No!

Get up!

She took in a deep breath. *Damn it all!*

From the corner of her eye she caught a glimmer of orange. The flames. The boat afire. A woman—Cynthia Hunt—trapped on board. A woman who hated Harper's guts.

Gritting her teeth against the pain, Harper forced herself to her feet, swiped at her chin, and refused to feel the ache in her right leg as she ran across the deck, kicking off her shoes and peeling off her sweater.

Somewhere far off, she heard sirens wailing through the night.

Thank God!

Oh, please, please, hurry!

She sprang, diving deep.

Knifing into the water.

Feeling the lake's icy embrace.

Swimming faster than she'd ever swum before.

Toward the torch in the middle of the lake.

Toward Cynthia Hunt.

Before it was too late.

If it wasn't already.

Swim!

Swim, Harper, swim!

Faster!

Where the hell were the other neighbors?

As she swam, she thought she heard the motors of other boats.

Oh God, please . . .

And the cops. Could they hurry and show up?

Stroke!

Stroke, stroke, stroke!

The boat loomed nearer, a funeral pyre.

Aboard, surrounded by flames, Cynthia screamed horribly, her voice rising with the smoke and flames.

Harper thought she might be sick.

Stroke, stroke, stroke!

She knifed through the water. Hard. Fast. Toward the flames.

Closer.

Feeling the heat.

Smelling the smoke.

Watching Cynthia writhe, her face twisted in agony, her arms flailing as she tossed leather-bound albums into the water.

"Jump!" Harper screamed, treading water for a second. "Jump!"

Cynthia's dress caught fire.

She didn't notice. Just reached down and flung a thick album into the lake. What the—? "Cynthia, jump! Get out of the boat!" Harper yelled again.

But the woman ignored her and reached through the flames to grab a record jacket and send it skimming across the lake right at Harper.

She ducked. Jesus, was Cynthia aiming at her? The woman seemed blind to anything other than her mission.

Another record album shot across the surface.

Where were the police?

"For the love of God, Cynthia! Get out!" Harper screamed, panicked. "Jump!"

Wild-eyed, Cynthia tossed something glittering, a small statue—no, a trophy like the one Chase had earned in high school—into the water.

What was wrong with her?

Flames licked at Cynthia's face and caught in her hair, singeing the gray strands.

"Jump!" Harper yelled again, her voice raw. "Cynthia! Get out of the damn boat!" What was wrong with the woman? Treading water less than ten yards away, Harper heard the shriek of sirens and caught a glimpse of red and blue lights slashing through the trees on the south shore. *Finally. Oh God, please, hurry!*

But it seemed too late.

Fire crawled up Cynthia's robe.

She heard the sound of other motors, caught a glimpse of two boats approaching quickly, the men aboard yelling, motioning frantically for Harper to get out of the way.

Cynthia let out a soul-jarring scream.

A human torch, she picked up another leather-bound photo album.

"Get off the boat!" Harper screamed, looking for a way to get closer, to drag the crazed woman from the boat, but the flames were everywhere.

A man yelled, "I've got her!"

Harper heard a splash—the boater leaping into the water?—just as Cynthia hurled the album.

It skimmed fast across the surface.

What?

Harper ducked.

Too late!

Bam!

The thick book smacked into her face, a corner jabbing into Harper's eye socket. Knocked backward, she started to sink, the water a cool, soothing blanket. For a second the world swam before her eyes, orange and gold shimmering. Pages from the album floated downward. Photos swirled around her, old pictures of the boys she'd known.

Boys she'd loved.

Boys she'd touched.

Chase . . .

Levi . . .

Chase again . . .

Rand and Chase . . .

Stunned, blood whirling around her, she was lost . . .

"Harper," Gram said as surely as if she was whispering in her ear, *"Harper, you wake up! You wake up right now!"*

Harper blinked, floating as if in slow motion, the world spinning.

Her eyes opened and for a few seconds she couldn't determine what was up or down or remember where she was . . . and then she caught a glimpse of the orange glow seeming to float in the sky above her.

She blinked.

In a second, she was alert again.

Realized where she was.

She kicked upward.

She needed air.

Now!

As she broke the surface, she gulped water along with air. Coughing and sputtering, pain ricocheting through her face, the horrible night came into clear, sharp focus.

Cynthia Hunt's clothes were aflame, and she shrieked in agony, falling to her knees as another swimmer, a balding man, nearly reached the craft.

It was too late.

Gas had spilled onto the debris-strewn water. Flames surrounded the small craft. Burning, cracking, sending up a cloud of black smoke. The man kept trying to get to the Hunts' boat but was driven back.

Dazed, Harper floated.

Sirens screamed, closer now, echoing over the water.

Did she hear shouts?

The sound of another boat engine?

A large craft tearing across the water, a spotlight trained on the horror in the smaller craft?

She couldn't tell.

The world spinning.

The boat seeming to sink and the wild-eyed woman aboard pointed a long, accusing finger in Harper's direction. It seemed that through her lipless mouth, one ragged word escaped: "Bitch," just before Harper lost consciousness.

February 1968

Chapter 3

Her nerves were shot.

She couldn't sit still.

She paced back and forth across Gram's Persian carpet, from the window to the couch and back again. Sat down between some of Gram's dolls, then was on her feet again.

The sound of the grandfather clock in the hallway, ticking off the seconds of her life, only made it worse.

She checked her watch.

For the thousandth time tonight.

Because she was stuck "Gram-sitting," as her father called it, and it was making her crazy.

She'd already suffered through an episode of *The Lawrence Welk Show* followed by *Mannix.* She'd nearly gone out of her mind. All the while that she'd stared at the boob tube she'd been thinking of Chase and how she had to meet him tonight.

Alone.

Once Gram had fallen asleep.

If the old lady ever went to bed and began to nod off.

I don't have time for this, she thought, pacing back and forth in the parlor. Licking her lips, she made her way to the window and stared out at the dark night. No sign of life on the black water.

But it wasn't time.

Not yet.

Still, her nerves were stretched tight.

She had to see Chase. To tell him.

She heard the sound of Gram's wheelchair as she rolled into the room.

"Good Lord, girl, you're going to wear out the carpet!" Gram said. After her stroke last month she'd spent most of her days in a wheelchair, though with physical therapy she was determined to walk again. "Come over here. Sit. We can play a couple of hands." She was wearing her favorite kimono—red and gold silk decorated with wide-winged cranes. "It'll be fun!"

Great. Just what Harper wanted to do, square off in a gin rummy match against her wily grandmother. Tonight. Of all nights.

"Come on." Gram motioned awkwardly for Harper to join her at the small inlaid table Gram had picked up "outside of Tokyo," a lifetime ago. "Sit," she repeated.

Harper glanced out the window to the dark waters of the lake and pulled up a chair, startling the one-eared orange tabby who had been curled on the cushion. It hissed its displeasure before hopping to the floor and slinking into the shadows.

"Oh, Earline, you stop that," Gram said, amused as always by the cats she'd adopted over the years. She claimed there were only five, but Harper felt that there were at least a dozen. At least! And none of them liked her.

The feeling was mutual. "Okay," she said, hoping she sounded more interested in the card game than she really was.

*Any*thing to pass the time.

Again, she glanced at her watch as Gram tried to shuffle the playing cards—a deck she'd picked up in Malaysia.

"Here, you do it," she muttered, obviously irritated at being unable to perform the simple task.

Harper did as she was bid, shuffling the deck and dealing out the cards just as the grandfather clock in the hallway bonged out the half hour. Eleven-thirty. Past Gram's usual bedtime.

Unfortunately Olivia Dixon seemed wide awake tonight.

Silently Harper cursed her luck.

Why had Matilda picked this very night to suddenly take time off?

It was almost as if that wily caregiver had guessed what Harper had planned and was determined to thwart her. Miserable bitch.

In Harper's opinion, Matilda Burroughs was a pain in the backside. Harper lumped Matilda into the same categories as the cats: Disliked and Not Needed.

"What's wrong with you?" Gram asked, frowning as she picked up her cards and placed them in her card holder. "You're as nervous as a long-tailed cat in a room full of rockers."

"Nothing," Harper lied. Her grandmother might have had a stroke, but she was still sharp as a tack, could still read Harper like a book.

"Hmmm." Gram moved the cards around in the holder, adjusting them to her liking. "If you say so."

Harper wanted to argue. Yes, she was on edge. More anxious than even Gram guessed. The fact that, at the last minute, she'd been called to "Gram-sit" only made things worse. Lots worse. Harper scratched the back of her hand absently, then stopped when she caught her grandmother watching her.

"Seriously, Harper." Gram's voice had grown soft. "If something's bothering you, you know you can tell me." She smiled. "Trust me, I know how to keep a secret." One eyebrow raised over the top of her reading glasses. "I've kept my share."

"Nothing's wrong." Harper forced her most bland expression.

"If you say so," Gram repeated. Sighing when Harper didn't respond, Gram motioned to her pack of Salems lying on the table next to her favorite ashtray and Grandpa's lighter. "Would you be a darling?"

"Sure." Harper rounded the table, plucked a long cigarette from the pack, and placed it between her grandmother's lips before helping her grandmother light up. As Gram drew deep on the filter tip, Harper clicked the lighter shut and set it down.

Gram let out a cloud of smoke and sighed. "Ahh . . . A horrible habit, I know, but so . . ." She thought for a second and waved away the smoke. "Satisfying. In a naughty way, I suppose."

"If you say so."

"Don't ever start," she warned, taking another long drag and pointing a finger across the table. "Seriously, Harper."

No worries there, Harper thought as the seconds ticked by and she played cards distractedly.

"Oooh. Got that one!" Gram picked up a card from the discard pile, the cigarette dangling from her peach-colored lips. She stared at her granddaughter over the rims of her readers. "You're not on your game tonight, Harper. That was a sloppy move. Worse than a play by Louise Chilcote, the mayor's wife. And, believe me, she's the worst!" Gram snorted as if disgusted at the thought of the woman with the flaming red hair back-combed high on her head.

"I'm just tired, I guess."

"Umhmm." Gram sucked on her smoke and adjusted the cards on the tray in front of her. "I can smell boy trouble a mile away, you know."

"No trouble," Harper lied.

"Is it Craig Alexander?" she asked. "I can tell he has a crush on you."

A crush? Really? And ick, no! Not Craig, the groundskeeper's rangy son with his shaggy blond hair and cocky attitude. "I said, 'no trouble.'"

"Umhmm. Right. If you say so." Gram didn't push it. But she didn't hide the skepticism in her eyes when Harper made another stupid play. Gram swept up the discarded Jack of Hearts with some difficulty and said, "Gin!" with satisfaction. Then, "Another hand?" she asked, fumbling to stub out her cigarette in the ashtray.

"Shouldn't you go to bed?"

"You want me to?"

"No, it's not that, but Matilda said—"

"Oh, bah! Who cares what she said?" Gram's lined face twisted in irritation. "I'm a grown woman, not a four-year-old!"

"I know, but Matilda told me you should be on a schedule, you know, for your physical therapy and pills and—"

"Matilda can go stuff herself!" Gram let out a disgusted huff. "A drill sergeant, that's what she is!" She snorted, then softened a bit. "Besides, I so enjoy your company, Harper. I'm glad Matilda was called away, for whatever reason."

She rapped her knuckles on the table. "You give me a good run for my money in cards." Then she caught Harper's gaze. "Well, usually." She cast Harper a knowing look. "When you're not distracted."

"I'm not—"

"Oh, bull!" Gram pushed away from the table. "Go ahead, keep your secrets," she said, muttering under her breath as she spun the chair and rolled into the bedroom, the only one on the main floor. "Don't forget to leave the nightlights on in the parlor."

"I won't."

It was nearly midnight.

Chase would be coming.

Nervously Harper hurried into the kitchen, pushing through the swinging doors, then found the pills that Matilda had measured into two ramekins that were used to bake crème brûlée at Christmastime. One was clearly marked "evening," the other "morning." Easy enough. Harper ignited a burner on the oversized stove and heated water for Gram's chamomile tea. Matilda had it all set up.

With one eye on the clock, Harper impatiently waited for the water to heat. God, it was dark outside. Maybe Chase was already on his way. She hoped so. She had to talk to him. Tonight. It couldn't wait any longer.

The teakettle began to whistle, steam erupting from its spout. Good. Swiftly, she poured water into the waiting cup where Matilda had left tea in an infuser. Immediately the sweet scent of chamomile drifted upward.

Balancing the teacup in one hand and the ramekin of pills in the other, she backed through the swinging doors to the dining room. And tripped over a cat. "Shit!" Harper tried to catch herself and failed. The cup and saucer toppled, sloshing scalding water over her wrist before smashing into the floor. Pills scattered across the wood. A second cat scrambled out from under the table. "Shit, shit, shit!"

She tried like crazy to collect all the pills. God, how many were there? Seven? Eight? More? She scraped them up, as many as she could locate, even using Gramps's old weak-beamed flashlight to check under the buffet, chairs, and bar. She came up with eight, all covered in dust and cat hair, some wet from the tea.

Now what?

She hurried into the kitchen, heated more water, found the broom and mop, and while waiting for the water to get to temperature, she picked up the shards of the cup, mopped the floor, and swept it as best she could.

She heard the clock strike midnight.

Oh God.

She was out of time.

She was supposed to meet Chase. Right now!

She knew the other pills were locked in some cabinet that only Matilda and Gram knew about, and she didn't have a key, nor did she have time to explain to Gram about what had happened.

Quickly, she washed off the pills, feeling some of the tablets beginning to disintegrate, then dumped them all into the hot water. She swirled the infuser with its already-soggy tea inside it around in the cup and walked into Gram's room where that awful Diablo was waiting, seated at a chair at Gram's secretary-type desk and glaring at her with his hateful gold eyes. "Shoo," Harper said, sick of the felines, especially this long-tailed devil of a cat.

"Are you talking to me?" Gram, devoid of makeup, rolled out of the washroom where she'd brushed her teeth, something she still insisted upon doing by herself. She also managed to wrap a netting over her head to keep her short curls in place before her next visit to the hairdresser. As Harper helped her into bed, she complained, "Getting old isn't for sissies."

"So then, you're okay?" Harper said. "Because you're not a sissy."

"You always were a sassy one." But Gram managed a smile before, propped up on fluffy pillows, she reached for her cup. "Where are my pills?"

"I, um, I goofed. Added them to the tea."

"What?"

"I tripped, spilled everything including your medication, so I washed off all the pills and put them into the cup with the tea. Because they were disintegrating."

"Oh . . . my." Gram blinked. Hesitated. "All of them?"

"Yes." Harper sat on the edge of the bed and bit her lip. "I'm sorry, Gram. I broke one of your cups."

The old woman sighed and shook her head. For a second Harper thought she was going to be scolded, but instead Gram said, "Accidents happen. That's life." She lifted the cup to her lips and took a tentative sip. "Oh, Jesus, Mary, and Joseph, that's bitter!" Sucking in her breath on a whistle, she shook her head. "Though I guess I've tasted worse. That's the same thing I said about whiskey when your grandpa introduced me to it." Her eyes brightened. "Oooh." She sucked in a delighted breath. "Now, there's a thought. Be a dear and bring in the bottle—not the whiskey, though, get the gin. You know where it is?"

Of course she did. Harper was familiar with gin, and as a teen had tasted it on more than one occasion. From the very bottle Gram was requesting. "You sure?" she asked.

"Absolutely."

"I don't know."

"It's fine. Be a dear and go get it."

Harper retrieved the bottle, returning to the room just as Gram drained her teacup and made a sour face. Harper said, "I don't know if you should—"

"Oh, for the love of God, Harper, I've been drinking gin for fifty years—er, maybe even a little longer."

Harper hesitantly poured, and when she tried to pull back the bottle, Gram motioned quickly for more and coaxed, "Don't be shy."

Okay. Fine. Maybe a little alcohol would help Gram sleep better. Harper filled the cup to Gram's satisfaction and recapped the bottle as her grandmother sipped. "That's better," she said with a satisfied sigh as she leaned back on pillows where two of her favorite dolls, Raggedy Ann and Raggedy Andy, were nestled. "Thank you." Another sip and she added, "Listen, Harper, whoever this boy is who is giving you so much worry . . ."

"No, Gram, I—" Harper tried to cut in, but her grandmother held up a shushing finger.

"He's not worth it." And before Harper could say another word, Gram buried her face in her cup and took a very long swallow. Then Gram dismissed her. "I'll see you in the morning."

Harper started to leave, but Gram wiggled her fingers at the bottle. "Just leave it." The old lady winked. "In case I need a little nip in the middle of the night."

Harper was pretty sure that by-the-book Matilda wouldn't leave a half-full bottle of gin on the bedside table, but then Harper wasn't the nursemaid, and her grandmother, as she'd pointed out earlier, was a grown woman.

Chapter 4

Shutting the door softly behind her, Harper let out a long breath, then hurried up the steps, avoiding all the dolls Gram displayed on the staircase, to the turret bedroom on the third floor which had been her mother's room at times. From this little room with its high windows, she had a bird's eye view of the lake. It wasn't as expansive as the locked tower room on the floor above, but it would do.

In the darkness, she went to the lamp near the window and turned the light off and on three times in succession—their signal, then searched the darkness for a reply, an answering three short bursts of light.

Nothing.

She waited another five minutes and tried again.

Still no response.

Something was wrong.

Really wrong.

But she had to meet him.

Had to!

Have some faith, Harper. She hazarded a glance at the crucifix of Jesus with blood dripping from his crown of thorns. *Faith.* She sketched the sign of the cross and decided to trust Chase.

He would come.

If he could.

Using a small set of binoculars she found in the drawer of one of the bedside tables, she scanned the dark water, her eyes darting from the dock on the island across the lake to the far shore and Fox Point, where Chase Hunt lived with his parents and younger brother, Levi. One light was burning, a low glow from the kitchen. Probably the stove's hood light his mother always left on.

But no sign of Chase, and she couldn't see if the family's boat was in the boathouse.

She moved the binoculars a bit, to the Watkins' A-frame where Chase's best friend, Rand, lived. But the Watkins' home was dark, no signs of life.

"Where are you?" she whispered as she checked out the next house on the point, the bungalow close to the swim park and nearest to town. Old Man Sievers's place. Eyeing it was a long shot. There was no reason Chase would be anywhere near the bungalow where the crazy old coot lived with his guard dog. His place, next to the swim park, was visible under the glow of his security lights. An antigovernment loner, Edward Sievers was a one-man vigilante. A "nut job," according to Gram. He didn't get along with anyone, especially his neighbors. It was rumored he had motion detectors and booby traps installed around his house—even a bomb shelter where, according to local kid gossip, he hid the dead bodies.

Tonight Sievers's house was quiet, visible in the blue haze of a security lamp.

Finally she turned the binoculars on the house at the opposite end of the point, where the road petered out to a dead end at an old deer trail. She didn't know anyone who lived there at the cabin as it was a rental, with, again according to Gram, "a revolving door of hippie slackers. All they do over there is smoke dope and practice free love. Disgusting!" Gram didn't even believe they were students. But Chase had mentioned some of them. What were their names? Charla, maybe, and Ronnie and then some girl named Moonbeam and a guy who called himself Trick.

She searched for any sign of Chase. But the shades were drawn, a few silhouettes passing behind the closed curtains, people still awake.

There even seemed to be a small light emanating from the round window of the roofline, which had to be an attic or loft or something, but as she peered at it, the light disappeared.

Something was definitely wrong.

Harper bit at her already-chewed fingernail. "Come on. Come on. Where are you?" she whispered as she refocused the field glasses.

She glanced at her watch. Nearly twelve-twenty. Had Chase come early and left when she hadn't been able to meet him right at midnight? Had she missed him, as she'd been stuck dealing with Gram and her stupid pills?

Or was there another reason?

A more worrisome reason.

Had he been caught sneaking out? That was kind of ridiculous. He was nineteen, even though he was still living at home. He should be able to come and go as he pleased despite his strict father.

Or . . . she experienced another horrid thought. What if Chase had stood her up on purpose?

He wouldn't, would he?

But deep down, she wasn't certain.

He can't abandon me now, she thought as she glanced around this tiny bedroom that had once been her mother's. The quilt was still the same, the pictures on the wall, even the crucifix of Jesus over the bed hadn't been changed. Everything in this room was just as it had been the night Mama died. She felt a familiar darkness in her soul as she thought back to that night, so she closed her mind to it and held on to the bedpost, conjuring up her mother's fading image and trying to feel closer to her.

But her thoughts returned to Chase.

He was all that mattered now.

Mama and the rest of Harper's family were her past.

Chase Hunt was her future.

She loved him.

With all of her heart.

Are you sure? Her willful mind asked.

An awful question!

Of course she loved him, and she would prove it!

Hadn't she already?

Even done the unthinkable?

So why didn't you tell Gram about him? Why are Beth Leonetti and just a handful of friends the only ones who know you're still seeing him, even after breaking up after he went off to college?

Why the secret, Harper?

What are you afraid of?

She didn't want to think about that now, nor did she want to admit that it was Chase's idea to break up and then get back together in secret.

It had always bothered her.

But it was about to change.

Again, using the binoculars, she stared through the window, first focusing on the terrace off the parlor downstairs, then on the tram that ran from the terrace to the boathouse. It was quiet, as usual, the tram's car tucked into its small garage.

No one was outside. Not even a cat showing in the moonlight. She didn't see any sign of the bats that roosted in the boathouse— the "bat house"—as her brother Evan had called it, insisting it was filled with vampires intent on sucking every drop of blood from her body.

He'd thought it was a great joke.

Macho and full of himself as he was, Evan had always teased her, had thought he could get the better of his younger, more naïve sister.

Never had he fooled her. "Never," she whispered aloud and hated to admit how much she missed him.

Once more, she twisted the knob on her lamp, giving the signal.

She waited and watched.

Not a flicker of response.

"Oh, come *on!*"

She tossed the binoculars onto the bed in frustration.

On the window seat, staring through the glass, she waited as night turned to morning.

Eventually she dozed in that position.

Dreams of Chase sifting through her mind.

When the clock struck four, she awakened with a start, her neck cramped.

She couldn't stand the waiting a minute longer.

She had to find him. Talk to him. Even though it was still hours before dawn.

She considered calling his house, but if she did, she would wake the entire household. And his parents already didn't like her. Especially his mother. No, no, that wouldn't work.

After taking the back stairs to the kitchen, she snagged her rain jacket from a rack of coats mounted over a row of boots in the mud room. Then she slipped out the side door where deliveries were made. A soft February drizzle was falling, the clouds overhead obscuring the moon and stars. Hardly daring to breathe, she skirted the tram's garage and used the outdoor stairs to the dock.

Of course there was no sign of Chase.

If he'd made it this far, he would have used the key she'd secretly given to him and made his way inside. And his boat would be tethered nearby, most likely at the boathouse entrance, or beneath the willow branches of the tree near the only stretch of beach on the island.

She checked both places.

And came up empty.

Shivering, fearing the worst, she focused on the houses across the lake and the stretch of water that separated the island from the point. It was the narrowest span here. For a second she thought she caught a glimpse of something in the water, possibly some kind of craft floating on the undulating surface.

Squinting, she moved to the very edge of the dock and squinted. Yes! There!

A few hundred yards off the point! A boat!

Her heart jolted.

Finally!

He was coming!

Sending up a prayer of thanks, she felt a moment's relief before she realized she heard no rumble of an engine. The boat wasn't approaching. If anything it seemed to drift farther away.

What?

Was it someone else on the lake? Some early morning fisherman? No . . . no, no, no!

Swallowing hard, her heart beating with dread, she climbed back up the stairs and slipped noiselessly into the house to the parlor and the telescope. It was positioned as she'd left it, focused on the far shore.

She bit her lip, hoping beyond hope that Gram hadn't wakened as she sometimes did in the night. But the rooms were quiet. Even the nocturnal cats were hidden and hopefully sleeping. Throat dry, she focused the lens, then swung the telescope away from the Hunt house to search the blackness of the lake.

Yes! There it was!

The Triton!

The two-toned mahogany hull was distinct.

Tom Hunt's sleek pleasure boat.

Rocking in the water.

Silent.

No signal light flashing to her.

No one at the helm.

No movement on board.

Almost ghostly.

She went cold inside.

Where the devil was Chase?

Frantically, she moved the telescope over the dark craft, stern to bow, but saw no one aboard.

And the water surrounding the boat?

Black and silent.

No sign of Chase.

Chapter 5

"No." Harper let out a little cry as she stared through the telescope. She was certain it was Tom Hunt's boat . . . no . . . oh . . . God . . . She searched the surrounding area around the boat again, and with every beat of her heart her dread mounted. It was dark, far from a hint of sunlight in the eastern sky, but, as far as she could discern, the black water appeared unbroken. No person in the water. No Chase. Nowhere.

Call his house! You have to call and check!

Harper didn't. Instead, she raced to the back hallway where the keys to Gram's old Cadillac hung and pulled them from the hook.

Wait a second!

If she started the car and drove across the bridge, then opened the gate on the other side, she'd have to drive by the gatekeeper's cottage. Her father or stepmother would probably hear her. Even if she kept the headlights off so that the Caddy's beams wouldn't splash against the windows, there was no way they wouldn't hear the gears of the gate grind or miss the rumble of the car's big engine.

Her grandmother might be partially deaf.

Not so Bruce or Marcia Reed.

The canoe!

She could use it without waking anyone.

She scrabbled on the shelf above the keys for a flashlight, nearly tripping over her father's wet boots in the process and startling a cat that was perched on the shelf in the dark. "Shit," she muttered under her breath as that damned Diablo hissed, switching his long tail as Harper snagged the flashlight.

Silently praying that Gram wouldn't wake, she slipped through the side door and retraced her steps to the dock, where she found the canoe positioned upside down near the boathouse.

Heart in her throat, she pushed the craft off the dock and didn't care that it scraped loudly. She rolled it into the water, then slid inside and began to paddle feverishly around the old willow tree that jutted out over the water from the island's only small beach.

Maybe she'd been mistaken.

Maybe Chase was in the boat and she hadn't seen him. Maybe he'd fallen asleep.

She cast a quick glance over her shoulder to the island. For a second she thought she saw movement on the dock. A shadow slinking by the stairs—but no. It was just the willow tree, bare branches moving in the wind.

She turned her attention to Fox Point and rapidly began rowing, dipping her oar in and out of the water, pushing the canoe forward.

Closer to the boat rocking slightly on the water.

But it was empty; no one on board.

Circling the boat, she eyed the water. With each stroke of her oar, her fear deepened.

It was too dark to see below the surface, but even as she squinted and searched, she found it hard to fathom that Chase, an athlete and excellent swimmer, would have drowned. So . . . what then?

"Where are you?" she whispered into the night, and though she dreaded what she might see, she pulled the flashlight from her pocket and shone its yellow beam into the water. Heart pounding, she searched the depths and half expected Chase's bloated face to surface, blond hair floating around him.

She thought she heard an oar dip into the water and froze.

Was someone nearby?

She looked around quickly. "Chase?" she said, goose bumps rising on her arms. "Chase, is that you?" She spun the canoe around, but all was quiet now. She shone her light in the direction of the sound. "This isn't funny."

But the night remained still.

Only the sound of a frog croaking somewhere.

Maybe she'd just heard the sound of a fish jumping or a duck landing or . . .

She heard the noise again and swung her flashlight wildly, once more finding nothing.

Swallowing back her fear, telling herself that she was just jumpy, she started paddling again, faster and faster, to the far shore. She felt as if hidden eyes were upon her, that her every move was being followed, but she shoved her case of nerves aside and concentrated on Chase.

Maybe for some unknown reason, he had returned home or been forced to.

Without the boat?

She couldn't come up with an answer, not one that made any sense. Even if the engine hadn't started, it could be rowed . . . or not. Maybe that was the problem. The engine had died and Chase had decided to swim home and get help from his brother, Levi, or maybe his best friend. She'd heard that Rand Watkins was home on leave from the army, maybe . . .

Oh, please!

Emotions raw, fear raging, she kept rowing toward the south shore.

Hard.

Fast.

She spotted the Hunt house located at the very tip of the point, the "fox's nose" according to some locals. Weak light filtered from the kitchen window.

The neighboring two houses, the Watkins' A-frame and the Leonettis' split level, remained dark.

Good!

Those three families—Leonettis, Watkins, and Hunts—spent a lot of time together hanging out on their docks, having neighborhood barbecues and parties and such. Harper had always envied them their closeness. She knew the distance between the neighbors on the point and her family on the island and far shore was wider than the stretch of water physically separating them. The beach ran deeper. But she wasn't going to think about that now. She was too scared. Too worried.

She rowed the canoe along the shoreline and decided she couldn't risk tying up on any of the private docks. The chance of being seen or heard was too great.

Instead, she moved a little farther on, toward town and the community swim park. Less than a quarter of a mile from the point, it was easy to spot as a nearby street lamp gave off a faint, filtered illumination.

She moored the canoe at the public dock.

Using her flashlight sparingly for quick bursts of illumination, she jogged on a path that cut through the tall firs and past the now-closed snack shack. The gates were locked, but she scaled the fence easily, dropping onto the cracked asphalt of the parking area.

Then she ran.

Skirting the lamplight, she dashed to the fork in the street where Southway Road wound sharply up the hill while Trail's End edged along the shoreline. She ran past Old Man Sievers's place where the chain-link fence was plastered with handwritten signs warning off trespassers.

Through the mesh, she spied Sievers's dog, a huge German Shepherd that usually patrolled the yard. Tonight the beast was lying on the porch, a furry shadow in the golden glow of the exterior light. His ears pricked up as she passed, and his eyes followed her. Silent.

Don't bark! For God's sake . . .

Hackles raised, the dog growled once and kept his wary eyes on her as she ran past to the edge of the Watkins' yard, noting that Rand's Jeep was parked in the drive.

So it was true, he was back for a short leave.

Rumored to soon be shipped to Vietnam.

Rand was Chase's best friend. And he'd been drafted into the army soon after he'd turned eighteen.

Just as Chase would now be, since his college deferment was no longer. At that thought, she nearly stumbled. Chase had talked about going to Canada before. Would he? Abandon the boat in the lake to cover his tracks and then hitchhike or take a bus north to the border? Would he do that and not tell her? Leave her alone and . . . no, no, no! Not now!

Stop it!

There had to be another reason, and she just had to find him. That was all. But with each step, she felt a deeper fear, a darkness gnawing inside.

Whatever had happened tonight, it wasn't good.

She spied Chase's car parked at the side of the driveway.

Relief washed over her. He was home.

So why hadn't he met her?

Heart hammering, she crossed the small yard. On the porch, she eased along the floorboards to the window of Chase's room where she tapped softly on the glass.

Please be inside.

Please, please, please be okay.

Nothing.

She tried again with another series of taps—slightly louder this time.

Suddenly a shadow loomed on the other side of the glass.

Chase!

Her heart leapt for a second.

But no—

His brother, Levi, stood on the other side of the window.

Chapter 6

Harper's heart nose-dived.

Levi fiddled the window latch, and even in the shadowy night she noted how much the brothers resembled each other.

Chase was the taller of the two, his hair a lighter blond, his eyes a startling blue. Levi's deep-set eyes were a light shade of brown, not that she could tell now as he glared at her, his hair rumpled from sleep and a beard shadow evident. He put a finger to his lips as if she needed to be reminded to be quiet, then pushed the window open quickly and slipped through, shutting the sash softly behind him. Then she noted the small bandage.

"What happened to you?" she whispered.

"Cut myself," he explained, keeping his voice low. "I . . . um, fell against the jukebox downstairs in the rec room."

She reached out to touch it, but he jerked away.

"Don't. It's fine. No big deal. What're you doing here?" he demanded, and she smelled alcohol on his breath.

"I can't find—"

"Shh!" Levi caught her by the elbow and pulled her away from the house. Walking quickly, he shepherded her toward the far side of the road, where there were no houses and the wooded hill rose sharply.

"Looking for Chase."

He frowned. "I thought he was with you."

"He said so?"

"No, but since he's not in his room . . ." He acted as if one thought went unerringly to the next.

She yanked her arm away and rubbed her elbow. "No—no, he was supposed to meet me, but he didn't show up. His boat—your dad's boat—is in the middle of the lake."

"What? Oh, fuck! He took the boat? And he's not there? You don't know where he is?" he asked, his gaze boring into hers.

"That's what I said!"

"What happened?"

"I don't know! That's why I'm here," she whispered harshly, the panic she'd started to quell rising again.

"Tell me what you do know."

"Nothing. That's it!"

"But you must've had plans or something."

"Yes!"

"What were they?"

Her stomach knotted as he glared at her. She wanted to die a thousand deaths rather than explain anything to Levi.

"Harper?"

"Fine." She kept her voice soft and reluctantly filled him in. She told him that she and Chase had planned to meet on the dock on the island, but he hadn't shown up. She'd waited for hours, then spied his boat on the water, took the canoe, found the craft empty, then rowed here, and ended with, "I thought maybe he'd swum back home."

"And left Dad's boat in the middle of the lake?" Levi demanded, incredulous. "That's crazy. It's even nuts that he took it without permission. That boat cost Dad a butt-load of money. Dad used his inheritance to buy it. Jesus. It's his pride and joy."

"I know! But maybe . . . Chase left it there because something happened. Maybe it stalled, I don't know. But his car is here, and so I thought maybe he'd swum back or that the boat got away from him and drifted or . . ."

Levi scowled, and in the weak lamplight he looked more like Chase than ever. "He's not home." He half ran over to Chase's car and peered through the window as if he expected to find his brother within. He shook his head as he jogged swiftly back. "Shit, he's not there."

"So where is he?" Her voice was rising, and Sievers's dog was on his feet again, pacing in front of the old man's bungalow.

"Shh!" Levi pulled her farther down the street, past the Leonettis' house to a wide spot in the road, a turnabout across from the cabin that was rented out to college kids. Three old cars and an art-covered Volkswagen bus were parked haphazardly in the drive and on the curb.

Harper whispered, "We have to tell your dad."

Levi shoved his hair from his eyes, then shook his head. "Not yet."

"He's a cop, he'll know what to do."

"No!" He was vehement. "He'd kill Chase for taking out the boat."

If he's not dead already.

The horrid thought stopped her short. She let out a little squeak and blinked hard against a sudden spate of tears. She was so scared she was shaking. "We . . . we *have* to find him."

"I know. I know. We will," he promised, his voice softening. He awkwardly folded her into his arms. The drizzle was giving way to a fine mist, and Levi's body against hers felt warm and solid. Strong and safe. Familiar. Her throat clogged and she clung to him. "We will, Harper. We'll find him." His breath ruffled her damp hair, his lips moving against the wet strands.

She wanted desperately to believe him, to meld into him, to let down completely, to trust him completely.

But she couldn't.

Wouldn't.

She and Levi had their own rocky history and were no longer the friends they had been while growing up.

The rift that had widened between them had been her fault as much as his, but there was no going back, no bridge that could span that deep cleft.

She blinked back tears and pushed him gently away, noticing as she did, a shadow pass behind the shades of the rental house. The scent of marijuana drifted out of the open window, and she wondered if whoever was in the house, up and smoking pot at this hour, had heard them.

Well, too bad. Chase was missing.

"Maybe Rand knows something," Levi suggested.

"Like what?"

"I don't know. But he's Chase's best friend. I figure it's worth a shot." Levi started walking back down the narrow road.

She had to run to keep up with him when he broke into a jog past his own house. As they reached the A-frame, he stopped, then whispered, "It might be best if it's just me."

"But I'm the one who—"

"I know, but it might be best to keep you out of it now, ya know?" He looked at her and she understood. Rand's father, like Tom Hunt, was a policeman. She would have a lot of explaining to do, explaining she'd rather keep to herself. Levi said, "If Rand doesn't know where he is, then we'll have to tell Dad. But . . ."

"For now keep the cops out of it?"

Their gazes met, and he gave a curt nod. From the upper branches of the surrounding trees an owl hooted hollowly.

Levi said, "Until I talk to my old man."

"He'll go ballistic."

Levi's mouth twisted down at the corners, and he said, "Won't be the first time."

She knew that to be true. Chase's father tried to rule his headstrong sons with an iron fist.

"Stay here." Levi motioned for her to get into his truck, an old pickup parked on the street opposite the Hunts' house. As she climbed inside the battered Dodge, he jogged to the Watkins' scrubby yard.

From the other side of the fence, Sievers's dog gave off a sharp, warning bark.

Levi paid no attention to it. He stepped onto the concrete slab in front of the door and knocked.

Seconds later an interior light snapped on.

Next door, at Old Man Sievers's house, the dog started whining and growling, pacing the length of the porch. Harper rolled down the window and adjusted the big side mirror of the pickup so she could watch the Watkins' porch.

The door opened, and Harper held her breath, hoping that Rand answered. His father, Gerald Watkins, was known as a tough cop, one who never bent the rules.

Luckily Rand stepped through the door. His black hair was shorn in a military cut and he was barefoot, she noted, wearing only jeans and an army jacket thrown over a T-shirt. He and Levi stepped off the porch and talked in low tones beneath a towering fir tree.

The dog went nuts. Barking. Growling. Leaping on the fence.

Illumination suddenly flooded Sievers's yard.

The old man with his thinning long hair and bristly beard peered out the window. He opened the sash, surveyed his property through narrowed eyes, and focused on his guard dog. "Duke!" Sievers yelled. "Settle down!"

Harper didn't dare breathe.

Levi and Rand stepped farther from the fence.

With a snort the dog sat on its big haunches and continued to stare through the fence, but Sievers retreated, satisfied no one was trespassing on his property. Rand cast a narrowed gaze at the truck where she was hiding and she recoiled, then chided herself. She wasn't usually a coward. She should talk to Rand herself. Or Chase's parents. Or her own. Or have the guts to phone the police.

But here she was *cowering* in Levi's truck.

Because something bad happened.

Something very bad.

Something she couldn't face.

She caught sight of Levi returning and slid across the bench seat to open the pickup's door, the interior light winking on. She stepped onto the street, the damp air hitting her in the face. "Did Rand know anything?"

"No." Levi shook his head. "Nothing."

"Oh God." Again, the tears threatened as she shut the Dodge's door quietly and leaned against it. "I need to tell the police," she said. "Maybe I should . . . I could talk to your dad?"

"No—no, I'll do that."

"But I should explain—"

"Listen, Harper," he cut in, taking hold of her arm. His fingers were like steel. "You need to go home. Got it?" Then, more calmly, "Just wait. Okay? I'll talk to my folks and tell them that I knew Chase was going to meet you." He released her arm. "They'll probably come talk to you, and you can tell them that you were waiting for him and you saw the boat. Or whatever."

"The truth," she said in a barely audible voice. But not all of it.

"Well, yeah. Just let me break it to them. They're not all that crazy about you and Chase seeing each other."

"I know. They hate me. Especially your mom."

"No, no, it's just—"

"They hate me," she said again as a car approached, engine roaring.

Levi pulled her to the side of the road.

Headlights washed over them.

The car—a Chevrolet sedan—slowed, and the driver tossed a newspaper over the fence and into Sievers's yard. Along with cigarette smoke, music filtered through the car's open window, the organ intro to "Light My Fire" by the Doors breaking the quiet of the pre-dawn hours. The driver hit the gas only to slow for a group of mailboxes grouped together between two firs. He slipped copies of the daily paper into the accompanying yellow boxes.

"You have to go," Levi insisted, dark eyes serious.

The sedan's engine revved again, and the driver pulled a quick U-turn near the rental house at the end of the street.

"Now," Levi insisted. "Before my folks wake up." He was pulling her to the side of the road as the Chevy shot past again, music thrumming over the sedan's knocking motor. "I'll drive you."

"No. I can't just leave the canoe at the swim park."

"We'll take it with us." Levi was firm. Not to be deterred.

"I don't know—"

"Well, what about your grandmother? Didn't you say you were taking care of her tonight."

Gram!

Yes, she thought guiltily, *I have to get back*.

Harper had been so consumed with worry for Chase she'd forgotten about Gram. Her grandmother would be getting up soon and need help getting out of bed before demanding her first cup of coffee, her cigarettes, and whatever pills started her day. "Okay," she finally said. "Yeah, I have to get back. But what will happen? Will your dad come to the island?"

"Probably. I mean, I don't know. It depends when he finds Chase, I guess. And if not, yeah, he'll want to talk to you."

"Oh God."

"Look, once I get back and scope out the situation, see where we are, if anyone knows where Chase is, I'll call you," he promised, and she knew, deep down, she could trust him. Hadn't she before? "I'll phone your grandmother's place. That's where you'll be, right?"

"Yeah." She was nodding.

"Okay, let's go."

She climbed back into the truck and huddled against the passenger door as he slipped behind the wheel on the driver's side. She told him where she'd left the canoe, and he drove to the park, left the truck idling before scaling the swim park fence. Within minutes he returned. He managed to get the canoe over the fence and into the bed of his pickup, refusing her help as he strapped it down and left the tailgate open.

"We won't go through town," he said and turned up the hill, taking Southway past the viewpoint and around the far end of the lake to the north shore. They met a few cars, early commuters, and as his truck approached the turnoff to the island, Levi cut the lights.

The sky had turned flinty, clouds low, the mist forcing him to use his wipers. "You have to open the gate," he told her, "if you want me to haul the canoe back to the dock."

What were the choices? No matter what, she'd have to tell her parents what happened. She watched as a wavering V of geese flew over the mansion, seeming to nearly skim the top of the turret as they passed.

She opened the gate and Levi drove through, picking her up before driving across the bridge. Silence stretched between them. He parked near the garage, then carried the canoe down to the dock, she a step behind.

Once on the dock, he glanced across the lake. "They're up," he said, staring at his house before turning to leave and staring up the steps again. Harper followed, noting that Earline, Gram's one-eared tabby, eyed them from beneath the branches of an overgrown rhododendron. Once back at the garage, Levi shut the tailgate, then paused. "I don't know what's gonna happen," he said, catching her eye. "But I think it's gonna be rough."

"I know. Thanks," she whispered unsteadily.

He paused.

"Harper—" He seemed about to say more, holding her gaze for a quick second, the truck's engine softly ticking as it cooled. But whatever he was about to share, he thought better of it and climbed into his truck.

She watched as he started the engine, made a three-point turn, and drove back across the bridge, his taillights fading as he passed the gatehouse.

Bracing herself, she turned to go into the house to face the music.

Oddly, the strains of the intro to "Light My Fire" sifted through her brain.

There was something in the lyrics about being a liar.

So sad.

And, in her case, so true.

Chapter 7

The mansion was quiet.

Harper slipped off her shoes and looked in on Gram.

Still lying on her back.

Not awake.

Thank God.

Harper needed time to think, to plan exactly what she would say to her grandmother and her father. It was only a matter of time before the news was out and Harper would have to confide in her dad.

Confide?

Or confess?

She snapped on a few lamps as the gloomy morning did little to cast any light into the rooms. Unable to shake the feeling of doom that had been with her ever since she'd first seen the Hunts' boat floating in the middle of the lake, she walked to the window and stared out. The boat had drifted a little farther toward town.

Across the lake, lights were turning on, people facing the morning. Her chest was tight as she stared at the Hunt house. Suddenly light appeared in the windows.

She gripped the back of a chair, and her throat turned to sand.

People appeared on the dock, standing near the empty boat slip.

Even from a distance, she recognized Thomas Hunt and his wife, Cynthia.

Lamps in neighboring houses flickered on.

Harper picked up the binoculars and peered through.

Levi comforting his mother, who clung to him as they stood near the sliding glass door. Everyone was grim-faced, and Cynthia, Chase's mother, appeared to be fighting back tears.

Harper knew the feeling.

Thomas Hunt was nervously pacing near the edge of his dock, talking on a radio while his eyes scanned the lake. Soon he was joined by Rand Watkins's father, Gerald. Two friends, two policemen. Harper watched as they talked for a minute, then walked together to the Watkins' boathouse and disappeared inside.

At the next house Old Man Sievers, dressed in camo, leaned against the railing of his deck. A cap crammed onto his head, he smoked a cigarette and watched the action in the middle of the lake while his dog patrolled the perimeter of the backyard.

Cold to the bone, she noticed that Rand, too, had made his way to the Hunt home, where he stood, hands in the pockets of his jeans, his jaw set, his eyes narrowed on the drama unfolding in the middle of Lake Twilight.

He glanced up across the lake to stare directly at her.

Or so it seemed.

She drew back, away from the telescope and the window, and reminded herself she would soon have to deal with Gram.

Taking the stairs two at a time, she climbed to her mother's old bedroom. She stripped off her wet clothes on the way to the phone-booth-sized shower and turned on the water full force. She needed to wash away all her doubts, all her fears for Chase, to stem the tears that threatened to fall.

Twisting off the spray, she bolstered herself. *Get it together, Harper. Whatever happens, you have to pull yourself together.* Finally she was warm again. She dried off, scraped her wet hair into a ponytail, then dashed to the bedroom where she rifled through her small overnight case and threw on clean underwear, jeans, and a turtleneck sweater. Before heading downstairs, she looked through the bedroom window.

The sky was lightening to the east, the thick clouds reflecting a somber gray on the water. On the opposite shore, red and blue lights flashed through the trees. More people on the docks.

She couldn't help herself and picked up the field glasses on the window seat. As she focused on the far shore, she saw a police boat cross the lake, heading to the area where the Hunts' boat was adrift. But it wasn't the first boat to arrive. Gerald Watkins and Thomas Hunt had already motored to the middle of the lake in the Watkins' fishing boat and were idling nearby.

Harper saw their grim expressions as they scanned the area using bright flashlights to pierce the depths, as if searching for a body.

Harper felt as if she might throw up.

She sagged against the window and fought tears. This couldn't be happening. They couldn't really think that Chase was dead. "No," she whispered, swiping at her eyes, just as the police boat arrived and a diver plunged into the water.

Her heart turned to ice.

No, no . . . please God, no. He can't be dead. Not Chase! She glanced up at the crucifix. At Jesus. Sketching out the sign of the cross and silently praying, she turned back to the window. "Please, please, please, let him be safe. Let him be okay." Her throat was so thick she couldn't speak as she saw the cops watching from the deck of the police boat.

Surely, they didn't really think they'd find Chase at the bottom of Lake Twilight. No, no, no! The diver—he wouldn't find him, tangled up in weeds or fishing line or whatever it was that would keep a body from floating to the surface.

Other boats were joining the two already surrounding the empty craft, fishermen and neighbors nosing around, trying to see what was going on and probably trying to help. The police were keeping them at bay, but the curious were arriving in rowboats and motor-boats and canoes and skiffs.

She heard the clock strike seven and tore herself away from the window.

Gram was usually up by now, but she could be sleeping late. When she was on her regular routine with drill sergeant Matilda, Gram was in bed by ten and she did *not* get a couple of shots of gin before being tucked in.

But she would be awake soon, so Harper forced herself downstairs and into the kitchen, where she put the teakettle on to boil and found a bag of Earl Grey. She started filling the coffeepot with water in the chamber and several big scoops of Folgers in the basket, though she lost count of how many as her fingers were shaking and her mind was on Chase and the search party on the lake.

Maybe this was all for nothing. Maybe he would call her today and explain what had happened and . . . She clung to that hope.

"No need to borrow trouble," Gram had told her often enough. "It comes knocking on your door, so don't go looking for it."

Well, it had definitely knocked—no, make that pounded—last night.

The teapot whistled, and as Harper began pouring water in the cup, the coffee gurgled, percolating and visible in the clear knob on the coffeepot's lid.

Good.

Gram, who liked to bend the rules at night, stuck to her morning routine. First her tea with the pills, then a quick trip to the bathroom before she had coffee, an English biscuit, and a morning cigarette in the parlor. Gram ate her breakfast at nine, and hopefully Matilda would be here to take over by then.

Because Harper was going out of her mind.

She needed to be with Levi. With Rand. She needed to help.

As soon as Gram was up, Harper would walk across the bridge to the cottage to tell her father about last night and the fact that Chase Hunt had gone missing. She hazarded another glance out the windows to the lake and saw that even more boats had gathered, swarming near the police craft, but, from what she could tell, no sign of Chase.

Her stomach knotted painfully again, and for a second Gram's tea and pills were forgotten as she stared at the far shore. Levi stood next to his distraught mother, who was talking to Alaina at the rail of the deck while keeping her gaze fastened to the activity in the lake. From this distance, Harper couldn't read her expression but guessed that Chase's mother felt the same numbing fear that pressed her heart. She glanced at the telescope, tempted to peer through, but decided she had to deal with Gram first.

For the first time in forever, she didn't spy a single cat slinking through the parlor.

Not this morning.

This quiet morning.

She didn't even hear the furnace rumbling or Gram's soft snoring. Only the coffeepot gasping and gurgling in the kitchen. She peered in on her grandmother. Not moving, eyes closed, mouth open.

But . . .

She noticed Diablo crouching on the top of Gram's desk.

The big gray cat, gold eyes alert, long tail twitching, watched as she set Gram's tray on a side table and reached for the cord for the drapes. "Gram," she said softly, hating to wake the old woman, but knowing if she didn't, Matilda, when she arrived, would have a fit about Gram not getting her morning medication on time. So fine.

"Gram?" she forced out, though her gaze was riveted on Lake Twilight. Rain was falling again, drizzling down the window in thin rivulets. "It's time to get up." The window revealed the dismal day beyond. More boats had gathered on the lake and lights were flashing on the point, police cars visible in the spaces between the houses.

Harper's throat closed.

Levi was still huddled with Cynthia. He was bareheaded in the rain, the tie of Cynthia's robe flapping in the wind. They seemed oblivious to the weather.

She cleared her throat and forced her gaze from the window to the bed where her grandmother lay, red-haired Raggedy Ann and Raggedy Andy next to her. "Come on," she said, and as the window hadn't provided much light, she turned on a bedside lamp.

Gram didn't move.

Didn't so much as blink.

Or cough.

And her pallor was wan. Gray.

"Gram!" she cried, finally noticing that her grandmother's chest wasn't rising and falling, not one little bit. "Gram!"

Diablo leapt from the secretary and onto the bed.

Gram didn't respond at all. Not a flinch. No reflex.

Oh God. No, no, no! Harper touched the old woman on the shoulder and shook her.

Nothing.

She placed a hand under her nose.

Felt no whisper of breath.

And her pulse—Harper tried to find it but couldn't.

And her skin was cool to the touch.

"No!" Harper yelled, and the cat rocketed off the bed, sending the dolls to the floor. "No! Oh God!" She picked up the bedside phone, stretching the cord, her heart thundering a hundred times a minute. She dialed 0 and waited for the dial to slowly spin back to place. This couldn't be happening!

The operator answered.

Harper didn't wait. Panicked, she yelled into the receiver. "I need an ambulance! Right now. Do you hear me? Send an ambulance to Dixon Island off of Northway Road in Almsville!" Her voice was high-pitched, catching on the numbers as she repeated her address. "It's my grandmother. Olivia Dixon. She's not breathing! Oh God, she's not breathing! Send an ambulance!"

CPR!

She'd heard about it in health class.

She should be administering CPR!

However you were supposed to do it.

Harper had barely listened in health class, but there was something about pushing on the chest to get the lungs going, then forcing air through the victim's lips.

Freaked out, nearly hyperventilating, Harper slapped the receiver's cradle to end the call. Once she heard the dial tone again, she spun out the numbers for the gatekeeper's house.

Dad was there.

He will know what to do, she thought as the rotating dial took eons to return with each digit of the number.

Even though she sensed it was too late.

You didn't have to be a doctor to see that her grandmother was gone.

Even Harper knew it.

Marcia, Harper's stepmother, answered the phone. "Hello?" Her voice was groggy.

"Put Dad on the phone."

"What? Harper. Your dad's asleep and—"

"Just get him! It's an emergency!"

"What emergency?"

"Get Dad! Tell him to come to the house! Now!" She slammed down the receiver so hard the gray cat scrambled out the door. Harper collapsed into the chair near the bed and held her grandmother's cold hand. A million thoughts raced through her head, pictures of herself and Gram throughout her life, how delighted the older woman had been in her grandchildren, especially Harper, and now . . . Harper's gaze landed on the gin bottle. Now empty. She thought of the mix-up with the pills and Gram's insistence on having a drink and . . .

Oh. Dear. God.

Guilt sliced through her.

She shouldn't have messed up the pills. She shouldn't have let Gram have a drink. She should have been here.

If she'd just stayed, she might have heard Gram cry out.

If she'd checked on her, she might have stopped Gram from having another drink.

But she hadn't.

And now her grandmother was dead.

Chapter 8

"Harper!" her father yelled as the front door banged against the wall.

"In here!" Harper dropped her grandmother's hand.

Footsteps pounded through the hallway as Bruce Reed raced into the bedroom and Harper flung herself into his arms.

Her voice cracked. "I'm sorry," she said. "I'm so, so sorry."

"What's going on?" Marcia was holding her dressing gown closed, her hair in rollers as she followed her husband inside. "Bruce—? Oh Jesus!" She stared in horror at the woman lying in the bed. With a gasp, she took a faltering step backward. Turning wide eyes at her husband, she whispered, "Is she . . . ?"

"I don't know. I think so," Bruce said, releasing Harper and searching for a pulse at Gram's wrist, then her neck. He shook his head.

"Lord have mercy." Marcia stopped in the doorway and held on to the jamb as if she needed support.

"We need to get her to the hospital," Bruce said, listening at Gram's chest for any sound of a heartbeat.

"I already called for an ambulance." Harper could barely get the words out. Tears ran down her cheeks. Gram looked so tiny. So frail. How had she not noticed?

Faintly, but growing stronger, the wail of a siren could be heard.

"They're coming," Marcia said.

"You left the gate open?" Bruce asked his wife.

"Yes!" Marcia was turning toward the parlor when something in her peripheral vision seemed to catch her attention. "What in God's name?" she whispered, gazing out the window to the lake. "Something's going on. Bruce—"

But he wasn't listening to his wife. His gaze moved from Gram to the empty gin bottle on the side table. His eyebrows drew together. "What happened here?"

"She . . . she wanted a drink."

"And you gave it to her?" Marcia demanded, the siren loud now.

"She insisted."

"But she's . . . she was on medication! You shouldn't have—"

Harper wasn't listening. She was already running through the parlor as the siren's wail reverberated through the house.

Through the foyer where the February wind was racing into the house.

Headlights bright, single red bulb flashing, siren shrieking, the ambulance streaked over the bridge. The driver hit the brakes and cranked on the wheel, forcing the Cadillac to skid into a quick U-turn. As the big car shuddered to a stop, both doors were flung open and two men leaped out, both volunteers for the fire department. The driver was Beth's dad, Tony Leonetti.

The attendant who had been in the passenger seat was Craig Alexander, who had once lived in the attic apartment over the garage with his father. Two years older than Harper. He was the boy her grandmother had accused her of being involved with. "Your grandma, right?" he asked.

"Olivia Dixon," Mr. Leonetti said.

"Yes. In her bedroom."

The men rushed in, Craig leading the way through the hallway to Gram's room.

Harper followed, stopping at the doorway, her insides jelly, watching as her father stepped away from the bed and Marcia huddled near the windows. The two attendants performed a quick examination of Gram, going through much the same routine as Harper and her father had only minutes earlier.

Ashen-faced, her fingers twining in the curtain, Marcia asked, "Is she—?"

Mr. Leonetti shook his head. To Craig, he said, "Go get the stretcher." Then, as Craig hurried out, he explained that they were taking Gram to the hospital where a doctor would make the final call.

He didn't say the words, but they all knew it. Gram was dead.

Harper, fighting tears, wilted against the wall.

Marcia pointed past the rain-drizzled panes. "Do you know what's going on down there?"

"It's the Hunt boy. Chase. Gone missing," Mr. Leonetti said. "As I understand it, the Hunts' boat was found adrift on the lake. I was about to go out there when I got the call to come here."

"Dear Lord," Marcia said.

"Chase Hunt?" Dad asked, staring at Mr. Leonetti as if he'd misheard before turning to his daughter.

"Oh. No." Marcia's eyes widened, and she, too, stared hard at Harper.

Harper shriveled inside.

"Did you know about this?" Dad asked.

Harper squeezed her eyes shut and nodded. She felt as if she might faint.

Dad whispered, "Tell me," as he wrapped a comforting arm over her shoulders.

Harper's throat closed. She felt as if she were ripped in two. She couldn't get the words out.

"Wait a minute," Marcia said. "Are you telling me that they think Chase is—?"

"Unknown," Mr. Leonetti cut in. "But they called in a diver."

"A diver?" Dad said. "Harper? What's going on?"

Harper swallowed hard and closed her eyes and had trouble breathing. "I—" She forced the words out. "I . . . I was supposed to meet him last night . . . he was supposed to come here."

"Oh my God!" Marcia stared at Harper in horror. "You were supposed to be taking care of your grandmother. And you were meeting that boy?"

"Let her finish!" Dad ordered.

Marcia said, "She was planning to leave! And Olivia was here . . . dying?"

Dad's arm tightened over Harper's shoulders. "What happened?"

"Nothing!" Harper choked out. "He . . . he didn't show up." Her voice faded, and Marcia went off.

"That's it? End of story?" she said, her eyes narrowing. "You just what? Said your prayers and went to bed?"

"Marcia!" Dad warned.

"Well, I'm sorry, but her grandmother died on Harper's watch! She was supposed to take care of Olivia for one night! And now she's admitted to letting Olivia swill vodka—"

"Gin," Harper corrected.

"Whatever! The point is that you were planning to meet up with Chase Hunt while your grandmother died right here." She pointed emphatically to the bed. "And Chase will probably end up drowned. Two dead, because of you!"

"Marcia! Enough!" Dad said, releasing Harper and taking a warning step toward his wife.

"Don't you try to sugarcoat this, Bruce, you know that she's been sneaking around to do God knows what—"

At that moment, Craig returned with a stretcher, and the two men hustled Gram onto it. Harper's heart cracked. Gram looked so tiny on the stretcher, her thin hair mussed, her cheeks sunken as they hurried her out of the house and into the ambulance.

Harper stood in the slanting rain, staring at the taillights as the ambulance rolled over the bridge.

"It's ironic," Marcia said from the porch as she cinched the ties of her robe more tightly around her waist.

Harper didn't see anything ironic about it, but Marcia went on to explain. "She bought that ambulance for the hospital."

"Part of it." Dad, drink in hand, joined his wife on the porch. "The lodge started the fund."

"But she was the primary donor," Marcia argued, not that Harper cared as she shivered in the rain. "Before that the town used the funeral home's hearse. Not that long ago."

"When Anna died," Dad said. "After your mother . . . well, after Anna passed away, Olivia donated the rest of the funds that were needed."

"A lot," Marcia added. "The town couldn't have enough bake sales and car washes and spaghetti feeds."

At the thought of her mother, Harper felt a fresh wash of tears.

"No need to discuss this now. Let's go inside." He took a sip from his glass.

"Whoa. What're you doing?" Marcia demanded. "It's barely nine in the morning."

"Rough morning."

"Still. No. And . . . where is Matilda?" Marcia asked, frowning. "Wasn't she supposed to be here by now?"

Dad said, "We should call her."

"Maybe she's on her way." Marcia grabbed the glass from his hand and carried it into the kitchen.

Dad ushered Harper back to the parlor, where he motioned for her to sit. "You wanna tell us what happened last night?"

Obediently, Harper dropped onto the overstuffed love seat near the console that housed the stereo and TV. Cold from the inside out, guilt digging its painful claws into her soul, she said softly, "What do you mean?"

"Let's start with why you were planning to meet Chase when you were supposed to be taking care of your grandmother."

Marcia had returned to the parlor and stood, arms crossed over her chest, waiting for an explanation.

"We were just going to meet. That's all."

"Hmmm." Marcia tapped the window overlooking the lake with a long fingernail. "What do you know about what's happening down there?"

"Nothing."

"Wait a second," her stepmother said. "You're trying to convince us that you don't know anything when your grandmother is dead and Chase Hunt is nowhere to be found?"

"Marcia," Bruce said softly, "go easy. Okay? This—whatever the hell it is—is hard on all of us."

"I know. But something's going on down there." Waving a finger at the window and the scene beyond, she added, "Can't blame me for being curious."

"We need to get to the hospital."

"Because you think Olivia might pull through?" Marcia didn't bother hiding her skepticism. "Bruce, it's too late."

"No, no. I know she's gone." He scratched at the stubble on his jaw. "But we need to be there, to be certain and to make all the arrangements." He, too, glanced out the window, then said to his wife, "Come on, we'll get dressed and then, on the way to St. Catherine's, Harper can tell us what's going on." As he started for the door, he said to Harper, "Get your coat and come on down to the gatehouse. Oh. And leave a note for Matilda. Let her know she has the day off and she should call me. I'll explain what happened." Then he snagged an umbrella from the stand near the front door and wrapped an arm around his wife's shoulders.

Together they started walking quickly to the bridge, nearly stepping on Marilyn, Gram's beloved calico, who scooted out of the way and gazed at them with wide eyes, a dead rat hanging from her mouth. Marcia gave off a disgusted squeak accompanied by an exaggerated shudder as the cat scuttled away with her prize. "Oh God, Bruce. Yuck! Cats with rats. Disgusting!" Marcia said, loud enough for Harper to hear. "They have to go! Every last one of them."

Harper shut the door and leaned against it, sadness welling within her.

The big old house seemed empty.

Without life.

Without Gram.

Without Chase.

Oh God. She was crumbling inside.

Be strong. You have to be strong.

It was almost as if Gram were talking to her, but of course, she knew better. Just as she knew it was false hope to think the old woman had survived.

The mix-up of the pills. Too much alcohol.

On your watch and definitely your fault.

Nope.

She wasn't going to go there.

She wrote the note for Matilda.

As the grandfather clock ticked, she found her jacket and slipped it on. But before she started for the cottage on the other side of the bridge, she glanced back at the telescope. Unable to help herself, she took one more look across the lake. One last time. She swept the lens slowly along the water's edge on the far shore.

Old Man Sievers was still outside despite the drizzle, a baseball cap pulled low over his eyes.

Alaina Leonetti, Beth's mother, had joined Cynthia Hunt on her dock. Smoking cigarettes, the two women were huddled together under a large umbrella. Gazes trained on the middle of the lake, they watched the police boat and all the other small craft assembled between the island and the point.

Levi was standing away from his mother with Rand, but he glanced up as if he felt the telescope being leveled at them. His eyebrows drew together as he stared at the mansion on the island. Was he searching for her? Had he seen her in the window?

Possibly.

As she focused on him, he glared straight back.

He knows you're watching.

And he knows you lied.

She stepped back, away from the damning lens.

Because if looks could kill, she would be a dead woman right now.

Make that a dead, pregnant woman.

1988
The Present

Chapter 9

On days like this Rand Watkins hated his job.
He parked his Jeep in the hospital lot, pocketed his keys, and wished to high heaven that Harper Reed hadn't shown up in Almsville again.

Because she had always been trouble.

Most likely always would be.

Why couldn't she just inherit her fortune, sell the damned island, and stay in California? Or wherever.

He slammed his door shut and half ran past the life-sized statue of St. Catherine.

Inside, the hospital was a hodgepodge. Old and new. Redbrick and mortar from the turn of the century. Concrete and glass from the sixties. The most recent addition, now nearly twenty years old, was a modern wing of concrete and glass that had been erected in large part due to an endowment from the Olivia Dixon Foundation.

He made his way to the information desk, where a fussy-looking receptionist with teased hair and thick eyeliner was positioned in front of an oversized portrait of Olivia Dixon.

The receptionist pasted on a fake smile at his inquiry, then directed him to Harper Prescott's private room on the third floor. He already knew where the Intensive Care Unit was. He stopped there first to get an update on Cynthia Hunt. It wasn't good. With burns over fifty percent of her body, she was comatose and soon being transferred to a burn unit at a Portland hospital. What was left of her hair was singed, and she was wrapped in bandages, her chances for survival slim according to the doctor he spoke with. Rand hoped, for her sake, she never woke up.

He'd known her all his life.

She'd been his neighbor growing up, the mother of his best friend. He couldn't count how many nights he'd spent in the Hunts' rec room playing ping-pong or darts or just screwing around and playing records on their jukebox. Cynthia had always been there with pitchers of Kool-Aid or cans of soda and countless bags of potato chips. "You boys, keep it down," she'd always say with a smile.

Those had been the happy days.

Before all the tragedy.

And now . . .

Reduced to this. He sent up a rare prayer to a God he'd left behind in the hot jungles of Vietnam, then left the ICU.

He made his way to the elevator and got off on the third floor.

Minutes later he was rapping softly on the open door of Harper Reed . . . no, Harper Prescott's private room.

She lay in the bed, gazing out the window at the gray day beyond and obviously lost in thought.

The last time he'd seen her had been twenty years before, when they were just kids. He on his way to war, she still in high school, Chase Hunt missing.

"Harper," he said as he rapped his knuckles on the open door again, a little more loudly.

She turned on the pillow, her face older than he remembered it, of course, her skin pale, her cheekbones more defined, her blue eyes more serious than they had been when she was a girl. A bandage swathed her chin, and there was bruising on her forehead, another bandage near her eye.

"Rand?" Her voice was stronger than he expected. "Rand Watkins?" Her eyebrows pinched together. "What're you doing here?" She straightened in the bed and fussed with the neckline of her hospital gown.

When he flipped out his badge, she caught her breath. As if he'd startled her. Eyeing his ID, she said, "You're with the police?" She looked up to meet his gaze, and something inside of him shifted. Something he didn't want to think about.

"Yeah." He nodded. "For about a dozen years now."

"But I thought . . . I mean, didn't you hate the fact that your dad was a cop?"

"Guess I changed my mind."

Creases appeared on her forehead, and she let out a little sigh. "So, I guess you're here because of last night."

"I thought you might want to tell me about it."

Her eyes narrowed a fraction, as if she didn't quite believe him. But he knew the feeling. As a teenager he hadn't trusted the cops even though his dad was a detective. But he wasn't alone. Since he'd joined the force, he'd sometimes sensed that same distrust from both criminals and victims.

Harper was no different.

He had to remind himself of that fact as he heard a pager calling for Doctor Sanchez in the hallway outside the open door.

"How is Cynthia?" Harper asked.

"Don't know."

Again, that skeptical glance. More playing with the neckline of the drab gown. She swallowed, looked away, and whispered, "It . . . it was awful."

"You recognized her?"

She nodded, swallowed hard, and looked away, back to the window, but he guessed she wasn't seeing the ridge of bare-branched trees rimming the parking lot. No, she was caught somewhere else, in the memory of the night before. "I was at the house on the island," she said and he nodded. "I really had just gotten there, hadn't even unpacked. I saw the fire as I passed by the window, and I couldn't believe it. I mean a fire in the middle of the lake? So I looked through one of my grandfather's telescopes. At that point I wasn't sure what I was seeing. But then I saw the boat was on fire and someone was on board. I recognized Cynthia."

"So what did you do?"

"Called 9-1-1. And then, I took off down to the dock and swam. There was no boat, so . . . it was the only way I could get to her." Her eyebrows drew together, forcing little lines between them as she replayed the scene in her mind. "I yelled at her. Told her to jump. Screamed at her. But she ignored me and kept hurling things into the water. Pictures and albums and all kinds of stuff. It was bizarre . . ." She cleared her throat, her voice lowering. "Really, really awful." Her fingers were twisting the fabric of her gown. She paused, closing her eyes, reliving the horror.

He waited, and she drew in a long breath. Finally she said, "I think they brought her here, but no one's telling me anything."

"How did you get here?"

"Ambulance, I guess. I don't remember it." She motioned to the bandage over her eye. "I remember getting hit by something and kind of sinking, barely coming to. Someone pulled me out of the water. The next thing I knew I woke up here. I've asked about Cynthia, but no one's telling me anything."

He decided she needed to know the truth. "I talked to the doc. It looks like they'll be transferring her to a burn unit in Portland."

"But she's going to make it," she said eagerly.

Hedging, he said, "We can only hope." Then he changed the subject. "So what do you think happened out there on the lake?"

"You mean, why was she out there? Don't know." Harper frowned and shoved her hair from her face, the movement stretching the IV line attached to her wrist. "As I said, I'd just gotten back to the house when I saw her. You know the rest. I called for help, then swam out to her. Maybe it was stupid, but I just reacted, Rand. Didn't really think about it. Someone needed help."

"You knew she was down there?"

"As I said, I saw *someone*. A woman, I thought, then I recognized her. But she freaked out when she saw me. Even more than before." Harper closed her eyes and shook her head, her body shivering at the memory. For a few seconds there was silence in the room, then she whispered, "I can't do this." When she opened her eyes again, she met his gaze. "I can't. Not now."

He thought about pushing her a bit, but he backed off.

"I'll need a formal statement."

"Yeah, I know." Nodding, she wrapped her arms around her middle, again stretching the IV. "I'm supposed to get out of here today, I think. I don't know when."

"I'll be at the station most of the afternoon."

He tried to read her expression. Couldn't. He wondered if she was hiding something, masking her emotions. Not that he'd ever been able to read her and now, with a bruise forming under her eye and her chin and forehead bandaged, her hair stringy and face pale, he had no idea what she was thinking. "I'll see you then."

Once more, a shadow passed over her eyes.

For a quick second Rand remembered the night everything changed, when Levi Hunt was on his old man's doorstep and he'd caught a glimpse of Harper cowering in Levi's truck, the night his best friend had disappeared. Never to be seen again.

Harper's grandmother had died that same night.

A tragic coincidence?

He'd thought so. Tried to convince himself. After all, Olivia Dixon was old, her health deteriorating, and there was a chance that Chase had disappeared by choice.

Maybe. But he wasn't sure. That was the trouble with being a cop. There were always more questions than answers, more doubts than certainties, more lies than truth. And always, underlying it all, suspicion.

"I'll see you later then," he said and walked out of the hospital, memories of the tragedies twenty years ago tangled with the questions about the here and now. Connected? Probably not.

Cynthia Hunt had suffered in the past two decades, her mental and emotional stability seeping away. The story was probably just as Harper recalled.

But he had to make certain.

Like it or not, that was his job.

Chapter 10

The last person, the very last person Levi Hunt wanted to deal with was Harper Reed. Make that Harper Reed Prescott. She'd married since he'd last seen her twenty years earlier.

He'd kept track.

And had kicked himself for doing so.

Now, as a dreary dawn broke over the city and he stood peering through a small window into the ICU where he could view his injured mother, he knew he'd have to talk to Harper.

I should be thankful, he told himself. If it weren't for Harper spying his mother on the flaming boat, Cynthia Hunt might not have survived. Then again, if not for Harper, the entire Hunt family history could have been so much different and, he was certain, so much less tragic. Maybe Chase would still be around. Maybe his father would be alive.

Maybe.

But who knew?

He wasn't one for conjecture or "what ifs," but he couldn't help but think Harper Reed was a curse upon his family. He watched as a doctor with a shock of white hair and rimless glasses examined his mother. She was swaddled in bandages, unconscious in a hospital bed, IVs and monitors hooked up to her.

From his vantage point, Levi saw that the individual "rooms" of the ICU were just partitioned by curtains, fanned out so that anyone in the nurse's station could keep an eye on the patients. There were three that he could see, unmoving bodies on beds, hooked up to monitors and IVs.

Fuck.

Staring through the glass at the form on the hospital bed, Levi had trouble believing the comatose fire victim was Cynthia Hunt, the once-vivacious and happy-go-lucky woman who smoked and drank and told bawdy jokes and took in stray puppies. But that particular woman had been gone a long time, ever since Chase disappeared.

Now his mother looked much like a mummy.

Her face was covered in white gauze, space for her nose, eyes, and mouth left clear. Her arms and hands were also covered, no fingers visible, the rest of her hidden by a sheet.

He swallowed hard, and his jaw ached, it was so tight.

How had it all come to this?

Why had she been on the boat?

Why was it on fire?

Why had Harper been involved?

The police, so far, were being pretty mum on the whole situation, but he planned on talking to Rand. Now a detective with the department, Rand Watkins would have the inside scoop.

If he would share it.

The doctor, Frank Costello, was the town's oldest GP and had delivered both Levi and Chase. As he finished his cursory exam, Costello paused to say something to the nurse at the desk before walking toward the hallway. Levi watched as Costello pressed a button unlocking the secure area.

As the door clanged open, Levi approached the doctor. "How is she? My mother. Is she going to be . . ." He almost asked if she would be okay, but that would have been ridiculous. She wasn't okay before this last horrible fire and now . . .

"She's doing as well as can be expected, considering."

Meaning that she was alive. Barely.

"Walk with me," the doctor said, checking his watch. "We're transferring her to Mercy General," he said and went on to explain that St. Catherine's, in the small community of Almsville, didn't have the equipment, space, or staff that the burn unit in Mercy General could provide. "All the best care there," he was saying, "state of the art." He went on about the Portland hospital being newer, larger, and better equipped to care for burn victims. But it was just white noise to Levi. He had gone through so many other conversations like this about members of his family that they all ran together.

". . . She should be there in two, maybe three, hours or so. They'll need time to admit her, and Dr. Horn will want to examine her, of course." Dr. Costello paused and clapped Levi on the shoulder. "It's what's best."

Was it?

Keeping a woman alive who would never be herself again?

He had his doubts as they walked down the pristine hallway where the tile floors gleamed under the fluorescent lights and the smell of antiseptic was strong, masking whatever other odors existed.

"I would guess you could visit her again this evening, maybe sooner."

"Will she know I'm there?" Levi finally asked as they passed a nurse pushing a rattling cart of medications in the opposite direction.

"She's still comatose and . . ." Costello didn't finish his sentence, didn't state the obvious, that it was best for Cynthia Hunt to remain unconscious. At least for now. And inwardly Levi wondered what to wish for. Years of plastic surgery and physical therapy and pain for a woman whose mind had already begun to fail her? Or a quick and hopefully painless death? His jaw tightened, and he hated himself for his thoughts.

"Talk to Dr. Horn," Costello said. "She's the best Portland has to offer." He gave Levi a kind smile and walked away, past a nurse pushing a patient in a wheelchair toward the elevators.

Levi hesitated.

He should just go home.

Leave well enough alone.

But he couldn't.

Not knowing that Harper, too, had been admitted.

Earlier, posing as a relative, he'd called the hospital and managed to get the number of her room. So even though he told himself he didn't want to see her, he felt compelled. As a man pushing a walker, a rolling IV attached to him, inched by, Levi toyed with the idea of seeing her.

What good would it do?

More importantly, what harm?

It had been two decades since he'd seen her on the other side of the window of Chase's room. He remembered how panicked she'd been, how he'd driven her back to the island after their frantic, fruitless search to find his brother.

What had been odd, he thought as he pushed the elevator call button, was that she and he had been friends. Good friends. All through grade school and into junior high, they had ridden bikes and snuck out to swim in the lake under the moon at night, swinging on a rope over the water, or playing Truth or Dare. He'd taught her how to throw "like a boy," had shown her how to skim smooth flat stones on the lake's surface, and rolled them both their first cigarettes. The Prince Albert shag tobacco, papers, and matches swiped from his uncle's stash. They'd gagged and coughed their lungs out, then sworn they would never take up the habit so enjoyed by their folks.

However, once they'd entered the hallowed halls of Almsville High School, things had changed. Harper was no longer a gangly tomboy but had, over the course of one summer, blossomed into a beautiful girl.

One who had caught his older brother's eye.

And so their story had spun on its axis, landing on that rainy night Chase had disappeared.

Levi remembered her standing on the porch, her hair wet and curling, her eyes round with fear, her chin chattering.

Bedraggled.

Frantic.

Desperate.

And still beautiful.

Of course that had been years ago, before she'd disappeared from his life.

The elevator car landed, doors whispering open to allow a couple of nurses who were deep in conversation to step into the hallway. As soon as they passed, Levi slipped inside and, before he could second-guess himself, pushed the button for the third floor.

At the open door of Harper's room, he hesitated and noted that the bed was empty.

Thinking she may have already been released, he took a step inside and found her seated in a chair near the window, a blanket over her legs, bandages on her face.

She looked like hell. Pale skin, huge shadows under her blue eyes where blood vessels were visible. Her lips were cracked, a bruise blooming over one eye. Her still-damp hair had been pulled back into a limp ponytail. She appeared small and fragile in the chair.

But he knew better.

She was staring outside, only to glance over her shoulder when she heard him. "Levi?" she whispered, her voice raspy. She muttered something under her breath that sounded like, "Wow. Guess it's old home week." Her lips twisted ruefully when she caught his perplexed expression. "Rand was here. You just missed him."

"Rand?"

She raised an eyebrow. "Don't play dumb. You know why. He was here ostensibly to check on me, but really he had a lot of questions. You know, in his official capacity. Geez, he's a cop now. A detective. Can you believe that? I thought he hated cops. I mean I think he hated that his dad was one."

"That was a long time ago. We were kids. Getting into trouble. No one trusted the police."

"I guess."

"Time doesn't stand still."

"Doesn't it?" She looked at him hard then. "Maybe not for you."

What was this? "Not for anyone." He didn't add that years ago she had moved on pretty quickly. Jetting out of Almsville before she even graduated and marrying someone soon after in what he assumed was a whirlwind romance.

"If you say so." She met his gaze. "So how's your mom?" she asked, and her face softened with worry. "If Rand knew anything, he wouldn't say."

Levi walked to the end of the bed. "Not good."

"I didn't think so." She turned in the chair to face him full on. "I'm sorry."

"Me, too."

"So, let me guess. You're here because you want to know what happened last night, what I was doing on the lake, right?" Before he could answer, she added, "It's no big mystery, Levi. I just got home, noticed a fire on a boat in the lake." She went on to tell him about calling for help, then swimming to the middle of the lake in hopes of helping his mother. She told him how she'd begged Cynthia to abandon the boat, to save herself, to jump into the water. "I kept yelling for her to jump, but she was frozen. The boat started sinking, and it was too late. Thank God the police showed up." She rubbed her upper arms, as if she was still feeling the cold of the lake water.

"What was she doing out there?" he asked.

"As if I have any clue," she said, almost to herself, then raised her eyes to his. "Why don't you tell me?"

"I have no idea." Who knew what went through the fragile mind of his mother? Certainly not he. "I guess I should thank you for saving her life."

"Yes." She gave a curt nod, her bedraggled ponytail bobbing with the jerk of her head. "You should."

He hesitated half a beat and couldn't help but think again that it might have been better for Cynthia Hunt to have passed last night, that her future was grim at best and unthinkably pain-riddled at worst. "Well, okay. Thanks," he said tightly, the word tasting bitter on his tongue. Yes, Harper had saved his mother, calling 9-1-1 when she spied Cynthia on the boat, but aside from his mother's horrendous condition, there were other reasons he would never forgive her. If Chase had never met her . . . Shit, if *he* himself had never met her, things would have turned out differently.

But they hadn't.

He jammed his hands into his pockets. "So how about you . . . are you okay?"

She slid him a glance, then obviously lied. "I'm fine. A few cuts and bruises. Nothing serious. They just brought me in to check me out." And then she paused, looked him up and down. "Do you still live in Almsville? I thought you went away to school and were in the service or something."

"Or something." He didn't add that he'd been in Naval Intelligence and, once he'd gotten out of the service, worked for the FBI. And now . . . a private citizen with an investigative firm in Portland. "I've got a place across the river, in Sellwood. An apartment. But I'd already decided to move back to the house on Fox Point because it was obvious Mom wouldn't be back." He cleared his throat. "She's been at Serenity Acres for a while now."

"Really?"

"Yeah. A couple of falls. Sprained ankle and broken wrist." He rubbed the back of his neck and didn't really know how much to confide. That his mother hadn't always recognized him? That she'd left the stove on? That she wasn't eating right and had started to wander? "It's been better for her."

"So how about you?"

"I'm fine."

"Married?"

"Was. It didn't take." He didn't feel like explaining. Two agents with different careers, different personal goals. One who survived. One who didn't. "So now I work in Sellwood. Private investigator. It's a long story."

"I'd listen."

But as he looked at her, he felt something inside of him set off warning bells in his brain, a gut instinct he'd honed over the years. And what was the old saying? Once bitten, twice shy?

"Maybe some other time."

"Kids?" she asked, and he shook his head. "What about you? You're married, right?"

"Was." She grinned, and he remembered how infectious her smile could be. "It didn't take."

"Kids?"

Her smile seemed to freeze. "Yes. One. A daughter. She's—she's in college now."

"So you're an empty nester."

"Right."

A heavy-set nurse in a crisp white uniform stepped into the room. Her hair was gray, her smile cheerful. "Paperwork," she said, placing some forms on the side table before glancing at Levi through wire-rimmed glasses. Her practiced smile faltered. "It's not visiting hours."

"Just leaving," Levi said, backing to the door. He lifted a hand toward Harper. "Good seeing you."

"You, too," she responded.

He figured they both were lying.

Chapter 11

"I'll pick you up and give you a ride home!" Beth insisted from the other end of the phone line.

"You don't have to," Harper said. She was seated on the edge of her hospital bed and ready to leave. "I can call a taxi, or Marcia can probably take me."

"The step-monster? Forget it! It's no big deal for me to swing by. Besides, I can't wait to see you! I didn't even know when you were coming back here, and then I heard from Craig about what happened last night. For the love of God, Harper, what were you thinking? What was *she* thinking?" Beth asked, obviously meaning Cynthia Hunt. "So don't argue, I'm coming and I'll drive you back to the island. I would love to see it again! And to catch up. It's been too, too long."

"Okay," Harper agreed.

"Good! I'll meet you in the lobby."

"Okay, but give me half an hour, okay. I need to check on Dad."

"He's at the hospital?"

"Unfortunately, yeah. He had a heart attack. It's one of the reasons I'm back."

"Oh. I'm sorry. Is he gonna be okay?"

"I hope so." Harper crossed the fingers of her free hand as she explained what she knew, which wasn't much, but she had heard from Marcia that Bruce had suffered a "mild heart attack," whatever that meant.

"Me, too. I'll see you in a bit. Kisses!" Beth signed off with her signature farewell, which usually included blowing a kiss.

Harper had already signed all the release papers, so she headed down to the cardiac unit. Harper's return to Almsville had been prompted by her coming of age according to her grandmother's will, but she'd also recently been concerned for her father's health. Bruce Reed had always been a strong, virile man but just last summer had experienced some vague health issue that he'd told her was not a concern. Even Marcia had dismissed his case of dizziness as no real problem. But just two days ago she'd received the call from Marcia that Dad was in the hospital recovering from the slight heart attack.

So she'd packed up her car and driven north, leaving keys to her home with a neighbor until she decided if this was a permanent move. "Unlikely," she told herself as she took the elevator down a floor.

She braced herself at the door to his room, then stepped inside.

Bruce Reed lay on the hospital bed, his head propped by pillows. His color was off, his skin wan beneath three days' worth of graying beard shadow, and he was hooked to an IV and several monitors. He didn't seem to notice her as he stared up at a television poised high on the far wall. The sound was muted, inaudible, a golf tournament playing on the screen.

"Hey, Dad," she said and walked up to the bed, her fingers on the rail. "How're you?"

"Still kicking," he said softly and to prove his point moved his foot beneath the sheets. "How 'bout you?" He pressed a button to move the head of the bed up slightly. Eyeing her up and down, he said, "I heard you were some kind of hero last night."

"Hardly." She stepped to the bed and brushed her lips across his grizzled cheek.

"You okay?" he asked.

"Been better."

His lips twisted into a bit of smile. "Me, too." Then his eyes turned dark. "But Cynthia . . ." With an almost imperceptible shake of his head, he whispered, "She's been out of whack for a while now. Ever since . . ." His voice trailed off, but Harper knew where he was going because the path always led to the night Chase Hunt vanished.

"Where's Marcia?" she asked. "I thought she'd be here."

"In the hospital chapel, I think, praying for me and my sins." He actually smiled, a bit of a twinkle visible in his eyes. "That might take a while. Or maybe she's asking about last rites."

"I heard that!" Marcia's voice preceded her quick steps as she clicked into the room. "I'm doing no such thing." Her narrow face was devoid of makeup for once and visibly etched in concern. Wearing a mock-turtleneck sweater tucked into belted jeans, she walked to her husband's bedside. "It's not your time!"

"Is that what God told you?" he asked.

"It's what I'm telling you. Don't you think for one second you can die on me yet!"

"Just joking," her father said and chuckled.

Marcia shook her head and said to Harper, "I guess he's feeling better."

"Good."

"And you?" She eyed her stepdaughter up and down. "Shouldn't you be resting? Oh, dear. You look . . ."

"Bad, I know."

"I was going to say tired."

"I just wanted to check in on Dad."

"I see that, but I thought you'd been admitted, that you were injured." She motioned to the bandage on Harper's chin.

"I'm fine, just a little beat-up."

"I'll say." She frowned as she noted the bruises on Harper's face.

"You should see the other guy," Harper said, but the joke fell flat.

"And are you healed from the last time?" she asked, referring to Harper's previous hospital bout, one she didn't want to think about, the one for which she still blamed her ex.

"I think so, it's been a while."

"I remember. Good Lord, you scared us half to death with that fall!"

Absently Harper rubbed her hip where the scars from her surgery still bothered her every once in a while.

"You were in the hospital for what—a week?"

"Nearly," Harper admitted, then lied, "But I'm good now." Her broken ribs had healed as well as her punctured lung, but she had shattered her pelvis in the fall and her hip still gave her trouble when she overdid it.

"If you say so." Marcia didn't seem convinced as she waggled her fingers at Harper's clothes as if noticing them for the first time. "Dear God, what're you wearing?"

"Scrubs. Compliments of the hospital. Everything I wore here is wet."

"Seriously?" Marcia frowned. "Well, I guess . . . but I could have brought you something or . . ." Marcia started to say, then waved away whatever other thought had crossed her mind. "What in the world happened last night? We're just hearing bits and pieces here, that Cynthia Hunt was on her boat and it caught fire. Or something?"

"Or something." With a glance at her father, who was watching from the bed, Harper sketched out the events of the previous night.

"How horrid," Marcia whispered and made the sign of the cross over her chest. "I mean . . . My God." She shuddered.

Her father's expression had hardened. "It's too bad, but it was bound to happen. As I said, Cynthia's been you know . . ." With one finger, he made a whirling motion near his head.

"Crazy," Harper said.

"Bruce!" Marcia shook her head, permed blond hair brushing her shoulders. "That's not true. She was a fine, good Christian woman who raised those two hellions the best she could and—"

"Oh, come on, Cindy's a nut case. You and I both know it." Bruce's gaze landed on his wife as if he hoped to shut her up.

"I know no such thing," Marcia argued. "It was just, you know, losing Chase that was difficult for her. And then Tom. That fishing accident that made her a widow. On the damned lake, no less! It was just too much for her."

Frowning, Bruce pressed the call button on the bed. "I'm just tellin' it like it is. No reason to sugarcoat it."

"Geez." Harper backed up a step. The horrid memory of Chase's mother engulfed in flames flashed through her mind. "That's harsh," she told her father.

"Maybe. But it's the goddamned truth."

"Bruce, do not take the Lord's name in vain!" Marcia actually stomped a booted foot just as Harper heard the elevator ding.

"Not the point, Marcia," he argued stubbornly. "You and I both know it."

Marcia shot Harper a glance that silently said, *See what I have to put up with?*

From his bed, Bruce asked, "Where's the nurse? It's time for my pain meds."

Marcia's lips curved downward. "It's only been—"

As if hovering at the doorway, a twenty-something nurse bustled into the room. With short dark hair and glasses, she smiled brightly. "What can I do for you, Mr. Reed?" she asked, while pulling out a thermometer and placing it under his tongue.

Marcia spoke for him. "He wants his pain medication."

Harper could relate.

The nurse glanced at his chart and the clock over the wall. "Not quite yet," but to Bruce, who was starting to mumble a protest around the thermometer, she added, "Soon. Forty minutes."

While Marcia shot her husband an I-told-you-so glance, the nurse removed the thermometer and placed a blood pressure cuff over his upper arm. Once she was gone, Harper glanced at the clock mounted on the wall near the television. "I'd better go. Beth's probably waiting for me. She's giving me a ride back to the house."

"Beth Leonetti?"

"Alexander."

He frowned and ran a hand over his unshaven jaw. "That's right. She married that son of a bitch. They got married and somehow ended up with the house on the lake. Cut her brothers out completely."

Again, Marcia feigned surprise at her husband's assessment. "Ouch."

Harper said, "Craig's a contractor now."

"Yeah, yeah, I know." Still, he frowned, fingers scraping against his whiskers. "So he says. But if you ask me, it's not that much of a business and wouldn't exist without his wife supporting him. I just don't trust him. I knew him as a kid. You did, too," he said to Harper. "He and his father—what was his name, the gardener?"

"Martin," Marcia replied.

"Right. Martin. Didn't like him much. And his kid? That Craig is a sneaky son of a bitch. If you ask me, some of those cats that went missing when Olivia was alive? I think he shot them."

"What?" Harper said, horrified.

Her father was insistent. "That son of a bitch had a damned pellet gun and was always killing birds and moles and whatever. The cats would've made easy targets."

"You don't know what you're talking about," Marcia said. "Dear Lord, Bruce, just shut up about it, would you?" To Harper she whispered, "It's his medication talking."

"I heard that!" Bruce said. "It's *not* the medication. It's the damned truth," he insisted, shooting his wife a narrowed glance. "Craig learned it from his old man, a mean son of a bitch if there ever was one. Used to take a strap to his kid, for all the good it did."

"Enough!" Marcia pronounced.

Bruce snorted and looked out the window where rain was peppering the glass pane. "It's all a fact."

"Pure fiction, you mean," Marcia argued.

"The apple doesn't fall far from the tree. I wouldn't trust Craig— or Martin, for that matter—as far as I could throw them!"

Harper had taken a step back. Didn't want to think that Craig had purposely wounded or killed any of Gram's cats. But the truth was that some had vanished over the years. Earline, the ever-hissing one with only one ear, in particular had just disappeared. And another one—Long John, the silver tabby. Hadn't he hobbled home with a BB in his hip?

"The island was never safe with those Alexanders living there. Probably still isn't. Who knows? And that's a helluva big place. It's too much for you. You should sell it."

"I said, 'enough,'" Marcia warned her husband. "And Harper doesn't need to sell the island."

"Why not? It's a damned albatross around her neck! It would take years and hundreds of thousands of dollars, maybe millions, to fix it up."

"You don't know that," Marcia said. "Now sit up and I'll adjust your pillows." He obliged and Marcia straightened the linens. "No more arguing," she ordered.

For once, Harper agreed with her stepmother, wanting the argument to end before it exploded into an out-and-out shouting match.

"Let's just deal with the here-and-now, Dad. Craig's an adult, Beth's husband, he's got his own business and still volunteers with the fire department. Maybe we should give him a break."

"You give someone a break and you could end up falling into the crack." He scowled, turning away from the window. "Where the hell is my medication?"

"Coming," Marcia said.

"I should get going," Harper said. "You feel better, Dad."

"And you don't trust Craig Alexander or his wife. She's a real estate agent now. A crafty one. Part of the 'million dollar club' or whatever. A little on the shady side, if you ask me."

Harper held up one hand. "Dad—"

"You just wait. I bet you she's gonna want to wangle a listing for the island from you, gonna want you to sell the whole kit and kaboodle now that it's yours. Probably gonna insist that her husband do the work to fix it up for the market." The lines around the edges of Bruce's mouth deepened, and he picked at the tape holding his IV in place on his wrist. "Don't forget, I was in the business for years. Still have my license. If you were going to sell, I could do it for you. Much less commission." He scratched at the stubble on his chin. "I know what she's up to."

"Beth was my best friend."

"And a schemer," her dad said. "Always had her eye on the prize." He pointed a finger at her. "You be careful, Harper. You're a rich woman now. Everyone, and I mean everyone, will be gunning for you. Offering you sweet deals and new ideas and ways to invest your money. And those are the clever ones. Others will flat out ask you for loans." He pointed a finger at her, stretching his IV line. "That's the problem with money, Harper. When you have it, everybody else wants it. So be cautious, I mean it. You can't trust anyone."

Chapter 12

As promised, Beth was waiting for her in the lobby.

"Harper!" she cried and half ran across the tiled floor, her high heels clicking rapidly. Beth was as ebullient as ever. Her brown hair had been permed and feathered around her face, bangs nearly touching her eyes. She'd put on a few pounds since high school but was still on the petite side, just had a few more curves. "It's so, so good to see you." She gave Harper a bear hug before taking a step back. "What's this?" She motioned up and down with one finger to indicate the blue scrubs Harper was wearing. "Wait a second. Don't tell me. You're interviewing for a job here?" she joked. "Either as a patient," she motioned to the bandages on Harper's face, "or a nurse?"

"Yeah, right."

"You're kind of a female Dr. Jekyll and Mr. Hyde all in one."

"Very funny."

"Seriously, it would make a *great* Halloween costume. 'Tis the season, you know."

"If you say so."

"Just kidding! How are you feeling?" She eyed the bandages on Harper's face. "Not all that great, I bet."

"Been better."

"But you'll be okay?"

She wondered. "Loaded question."

They were walking out the door.

"I'm over there." Beth pointed to the spot where she'd double-parked in a zone where the curb was painted red and a sign warned against parking. "Let me take that." She grabbed the plastic bag from Harper and hurried around the front of her little BMW to slide behind the wheel.

Harper slipped into the passenger seat. Beth tossed her bag into the back just as a security guard hustled out of the main doors. He was jogging fast, raising a hand at them.

"Oops." With the radio blaring, Beth peeled out, cutting off a transport van and shooting for the exit of the parking lot.

"Whoa!" Harper said, buckling her seat belt quickly. "Some things never change." Beth, in high school, had been a lead-foot and had the speeding tickets to prove it.

"Oh no, no," Beth argued as Bon Jovi belted out "Bad Medicine" from the CD player and she tapped out the beat on the steering wheel. "I've slowed down. A lot." She caught Harper's skeptical gaze and turned the volume down, the song fading into the background. "Really." And as if to prove her point, she reduced the Bimmer's speed to a few miles over the limit as they wound down the hill on which St. Catherine's had been constructed.

"That's what having a kid will do for you." Sliding Harper a knowing glance, she added, "You know how it is. Your whole life changes. Including how you drive."

Harper did know. She thought of those first frantic years of motherhood when she'd been a child herself. Suddenly the whole world had turned dangerous, one booby trap after another—electric light sockets, laundry detergent, the front steps, speeding cars cutting through the neighborhood, asbestos, and Red dye #2, for crying out loud.

But Dawn had survived and grown from a happy-go-lucky child in pigtails to a recalcitrant teenager who embraced all things Goth before becoming a college student who no longer believed her mother was the enemy. Thank God.

At the base of the hill, Beth slid through a yellow light before cutting into a neighborhood filled with the oldest homes in Almsville. Turn-of-the-century Victorians interspersed with postwar ramblers, all with small neatly kept yards, birch and oak trees nearly bare, while fir branches waved in the breeze, pumpkins and corn stalks decorating the porches. "Bring back memories?" Beth asked as she cruised by the high school, a two-story building of redbrick, the rows of windows glowing in the gloom.

"A few."

"More than a few, I bet." She waited at a stop sign, then turned toward the lake. "So what do you do now, Harper? I mean, do you work?"

Harper slid her a glance. "No, I'm just a trust fund baby."

"Oh."

"Just kidding." It was true she'd always received a quarterly check, issued by Gram's attorneys, and the funds had kept her afloat, paying for college and rent, then later supplementing her income. She'd gotten her degree in California while Dawn was a toddler, then taught English in middle school for years while also freelancing with a newspaper when Dawn was in school. But after the dissolution of her marriage, Dawn moving to Oregon for college, and her inheritance coming due, Harper had quit her day job. And now . . . God now, she might actually write that novel she'd always talked about. How many times had she started chapter one? Just as many as she'd put it aside. "I quit teaching last June," she said. "You know, I finally think I'll try my hand at writing. You remember, I always talked about it."

But now she had time. No kid to raise. No husband to tend to.

Beth slowed for a corner, waited as a bicyclist sped past, then turned onto Northway, driving past the homes that were tucked between the lake and the shoreline. In the spaces between the houses, Harper caught glimpses of the lake, still and gray, reflecting the somber sky.

"So," Beth ventured, as she switched out one CD for another. "You're planning to stay?"

"Don't know yet. I've thought about selling—"

"Well, if you do, I would be thrilled, I mean *thrilled* to have the listing!"

"—but I'm just not sure. Haven't really figured out what I'm going to do." And that was God's honest truth, even though her father's recent warning about Beth angling for a listing still darted through her mind.

"I can't imagine you'd want to stay here with everything that happened, you know, Chase and your grandma . . .well and everything."

"I'm just not sure. Thought I would at least stay a while, fix it up some, and then make a decision."

Would she want to stay in the huge house with all of its memories, ghosts of the past, or would she want to move on? Make a fresh start. And yet, there were some good recollections that tethered her here, to the lake, and she wondered as she stared through the rain-splattered windshield if Dawn might want to live here someday?

"It's a seller's market now, and the low interest rates won't last forever," Beth advised.

Beth drove along the twisting road, taking the deadly S curve a little too fast, though the sleek car hugged the road. Finally she turned unerringly into the lane leading toward the island. "Oh Lord!" she said, eyeing the gate and the gargoyles perched on the support posts. "Are you kidding? I can't believe you've still got those hideous beasts at the gate! They're still creepy as hell."

"Worse than," Harper agreed, glancing up at the statues backdropped by roiling gray clouds. "But I kinda like them."

"Seriously?" Beth threw her a glance as they drove onto the bridge. "You and who else?"

"Gram."

"Well, she's gone and they should be, too."

The BMW slid to a stop in front of the house. "Wow. I'd forgotten how impressive this place is." She cut the engine and stared through the rain-spattered windshield to the brick mansion with its sloped roof and tall windows. "Can you believe you own a private island, for God's sake? How's that for exclusive?"

Beth tossed her keys into her purse. "You know I never see this side of the house from my place. I get the other view. From across the lake. It's impressive from there, too. Looks like a damned castle."

"You still live on Fox Point?"

"Craig and I bought Mom and Dad out years ago."

So her father had said.

"Craig said we couldn't let it go, you know. That it would be our only chance to live on the water, so we worked out a deal with Mom and Dad, who were looking to downsize."

"Your brothers were okay with it?"

"The twins were still in college, so what did they know?" She changed the subject. "We have so much catching up to do!" She reached into the small backseat and picked up Harper's bag of wet clothes. "Kinda weird, ya know? I'm in the same house I was growing up, Rand is just down the street in his dad's A-frame, and now you're here on the island. It's like the band's back together."

"Minus a few key players."

"Yeah. But the rental next to me has tenants again, and Old Man Sievers's place? His daughter, what's her name—?"

"I didn't know he had a daughter."

"Oh yeah . . . Uh, Frankie—Francine, that's it! She's in his place with two kids, teenagers—the girl is in Max's class, and the boy, oh, I don't remember, a year or two older, I think." Beth slammed the BMW's door shut. She backed up a few steps to the edge of the parking apron and craned her neck to gaze up at the pitched roof and high turret, visible just above the roofline.

Harper climbed out of the car and noted the rain had stopped, though the old asphalt shimmered with puddles. "What about the Hunts' house?"

"Oh-um, I guess Levi might move back. He's been talking about it, and now that his mother won't be returning, who knows?"

"You keep up with him?"

"A little," Beth said. "I haven't talked to him since last night. I mean what do you say to a guy who's lost his brother and father to the lake? And now his mom? Geez. It's like the whole family is cursed." Then she sighed. "Well, maybe we all are, you know? Maybe we're all cursed."

"I guess. You know that the lake was once called the Lake of the Dead."

"I heard that. Good thing they changed it, or I'd never sell a house around here." Beth laughed at her own joke and took another step back, the heel of her boot sinking into the wet mulch of Gram's rose garden, so she could get a better look at the upper story of the house.

"Be careful," Harper warned.

"Why?"

"That's the spot where Gram buried her cats."

"Are you serious?"

"Very."

"Jesus. Gross!" Quickly Beth moved to stand on the asphalt again and regarded the skeletal vines with horrified eyes. "Oh. My. God. You're kidding, right?"

"Nope. Every time a cat died, she buried it and planted a rose on it. I think you were standing on Long John's grave. You remember him? Silver tabby with a crooked tail?" *And the cat your husband might have used for target practice*, she thought, remembering her father's words.

"Take a look. There should be a little engraved marker by each of the rose bushes. Gram even planned elaborate funerals for each of them." Harper remembered having attended the "ceremony" for the calico with the striking markings. Gram had named that gorgeous cat after the screen icon Marilyn Monroe.

"Seriously?" Beth glanced down and saw the small headstone, no bigger than a baseball. "Oh man, that's sick!" She inched farther away from the garden. "First the gargoyles, now this?"

"She bought special roses, each one symbolic of the cat."

"I've heard enough! You have a strange family, Harper, and no, I didn't know any of your grandmother's damned cats. Just that she had a ton of them. Too many. It was odd. Way odd. Borderline wacko." She gave the rose garden another skeptical look. "You might want to keep that information—about the rose garden—to yourself, especially if you decide to sell."

"I'll keep that in mind."

"You know," Beth said. "Your family is even weirder than I thought."

Weirder than you'll ever guess.

"Okay, so let's get serious. Really, what're you going to do with this house and the island? I mean, the whole damned island! You own it outright now, right? Creepy kitty cemetery and all."

"Right." The terms of her grandmother's estate were pretty much public knowledge in Almsville, leaked years ago to the newspaper at the time of the scandal surrounding her death.

"And the guesthouse?" Beth asked. "Where you lived—well, most of the time. That's part of it?"

"The caretaker's cottage—that's what Gram called it—but yeah." Harper was already walking through the huge double doors and into the foyer.

Beth followed after her. "It's like being in a time capsule and teleported back to the sixties." Beth dropped the bag of wet clothes next to the cat carrier near the stairs. She left her purse on one of the bottom steps. "I'd forgotten about this staircase, how it runs up each side of the entry to meet on the top floor—so cool."

"I guess."

"For sure!"

Flipping on lights, Harper called for the cat as she headed into the parlor. "Jinx. Kitty? Come on, Jinx."

"You have a cat?" Beth asked, catching up to her.

"Yeah. Inherited."

"One that escaped the bone yard?"

"No, not from my grandma, those are long gone. Jinx was—is?— my daughter's cat, but then she went off to college so, at least for now, he's mine."

"Oh. I thought you were always a dog person," Beth said, running a finger over the edge of the liquor cabinet and eyeing the tall windows with their dusty curtains and the furniture that was decades old.

"All animals, but yes, growing up we had a dog. Bandit," Harper said, remembering the shaggy brown mutt with long ears and a black mask. Even now, years later, she felt a little pang in her heart when she thought of him. "Gone now." She cleared her throat. "A long time ago." She turned her attention back to searching for the missing cat. "I'm afraid Jinx may have gotten out." She walked to the door off the kitchen and found it ajar, just as she'd left it last night. "Damn." Though she and Jinx had never really bonded, she didn't want to lose him.

"He's gone?" Beth asked, as she pushed past the swinging doors and into the kitchen with its massive stove and double refrigerators, oversized sink, and marble counters.

Harper shrugged. "Dunno. I hope not." But what were the chances? If nothing else, the damned cat was an escape artist. He'd proved that time and time again in the past when she and Dawn had lived in

Santa Rosa. How many times had Joel had to climb into the lemon tree or onto the roof, or go searching through the neighborhood for the damned cat? Too many to count. Once Jinx had disappeared for three weeks, only to show up, thin and haggard, his collar missing, a new notch in his ear. And now? In this new place with an enormous house and an entire island? What were the chances that he would return here?

She didn't want to think about it. Nor how Dawn would react if the cat didn't show up again.

Harper checked on the food and water she'd left out earlier. Untouched.

"Great," she muttered under her breath.

This wasn't good. Not good at all.

"So what are your plans?" Beth asked.

"My plans?" She gave off a little huff. "If only I knew."

"No idea?"

"Well," she said, shutting the door. "I had thought I might live in the cottage while I fix this place up. I knew it would need work."

"To . . . sell?" Beth said, trying to keep the hope out of her voice.

"Probably. But I have to scrap that idea because it turns out the cottage is a total wreck. Literally falling apart."

"It can probably be salvaged."

"You haven't seen it."

"Yet," Beth said, looking through the window that opened to the front of the house and offered a view of the parking apron and garage. "Insurance might be able to help."

"Maybe." If Gram's incompetent lawyers had kept it up.

Harper went through the butler's pantry to the living room, caught a glimpse of the decanter of whiskey or whatever it was she'd left on the side table. *A shot of hard liquor would go down smoothly right now*, she thought. It might calm her jangled nerves and take the edge off the pain she felt in her jaw, shoulders, and hip, but she left it be. It may well be "five o'clock somewhere," but, she reminded herself, it was barely noon in Almsville, Oregon.

"This view is incredible," Beth said, catching up with her and peering out the windows.

"Yeah," Harper agreed, but in her mind's eye she witnessed Cynthia Hunt's tortured face, could hear her bone-chilling shrieks.

"I knew it was, but I'd forgotten. As a kid, you know, who cared? Anyway, if you do decide to put it on the market, talk to me." Beth's gaze swept over the tall windows, the worn carpet, the ancient furniture. "Of course you'd have to fix it up, but that shouldn't be a problem, right? You inherited more than the property?"

She was asking about money in the estate. A not-so-small fortune.

Before Harper could reply, Beth added, "Craig could fix this place up. I think I mentioned that he has his own construction company now, and he knows this place like the back of his hand from living here, you remember, when his dad was the groundskeeper?"

All too well. "Yeah."

Her father had been right about Beth suggesting Harper hire her husband, just as Dad had remembered how Craig was as a teenager. How many times had she caught him surreptitiously eyeing her as she sunbathed or swam in the lake? While trimming shrubbery or mending the gutters or painting the trim, Craig had often let his eyes stray to her bikini-clad body.

Not that it had been a crime. Just a little unsettling. And then, after graduation, Beth had married him.

Quietly Beth surveyed the rooms and grounds, biting her lip as she walked to the French doors and stared out at the terrace.

Assessing.

Evaluating.

Calculating.

Despite Harper's headache, exhaustion, and worry about the damned cat, she knew what Beth was doing. She felt a jab of disappointment that there was more to Beth's insistence on driving her home than just Beth's need to help out and reconnect. But really, what had she expected? Hadn't it happened before? Even when they were "besties" in school, hadn't Harper known that deep down her friend's interest in her was all because of Beth's crush on Evan, Harper's older brother?

"If you decide to sell . . ." Beth said again.

"Yeah, yeah, I know. You want to list it."

"Of course I'd love it! But only if you want to—"

"I'll think about it." Harper cut her off, suddenly weary, her headache pounding, her shoulder beginning to ache.

"Do. If you decide, I'll look around and give you a fair assessment.

The only private island on the lake! And it's yours!" she gushed. "Well, until it isn't. Until you sell it and make an absolute fortune!" She was beaming. "I'd like to look around, check out the bedrooms and garage and—" She stopped short, must've read the censure in Harper's eyes. "And you're tired." Though Harper hadn't said a word, Beth held up her hands, palms out, in mock surrender. "Sorry. I got carried away. I've always loved this island, you know. Envied you for being able to live here. In your own private Eden."

How ironic. Harper had always felt isolated on this side of the lake, had wanted to be a part of the crowd on the south shore.

Beth noticed the telescope, bent down, and adjusted the focus. "Oh wow," she said. "What a view. You can see everything going on in the lake from up here and . . ." Her voice drifted away. "And the houses on Fox Point." She moved the telescope slowly.

"I know."

"I guess I never realized how much you all could see from here . . . The point is kind of sheltered, except . . ." She let out a whistle. "Holy Mother Mary, you can see right into our bedrooms and bathrooms and . . ." She straightened, her eyes troubled. "I guess we should all pull our shades, or else you could become a Peeping Tom." She forced a smile that didn't reach her eyes. "Or a Peeping Thomasina!"

"Yeah, right." Harper tried to sound dismissive, but Beth didn't know the half of it. How many times had Harper stared through that very telescope hoping for even a quick glimpse of Chase?

How pathetic it seemed now.

Harper had been hopelessly, blindly in love with him. Of course it had been puppy love, but it had consumed her. She would have done just about anything for him, and now that thought made her uncomfortable. Looking through the linked prisms of age and wisdom, she realized how one-sided the love had been, how pathetic.

Beth peered through the eyepiece again. "This is *really* high-powered."

"My grandfather bought it a million years ago." So he could get off by ogling the women—and girls—across the lake. George Dixon, "Gramps" to Harper and Evan, had pocket binoculars, as well as this telescope and an even higher-powered one in the tower room on the fourth floor.

Beth would have freaked out if Harper had dared to share the extent of her grandfather's interest in the women of Lake Twilight while touching himself. Had he been watching Cynthia Hunt exercising? Or viewing Beth's mom, Alaina, the ex-model sunbathing in her tiny bikini? Or had he been focused on Beth, who was just starting to develop into a woman, or even some of the coeds who occupied the last house on the point?

Harper never knew.

She had backed down the steps, quiet as a mouse, when Gramps did his dirty spying.

Over the years, she'd steadfastly pushed the vision of her grandfather with his hands down his pants aside, just as she'd tried to forget the "girlie" calendars she'd found in the garage. Sensual images of Hollywood starlets, posed nearly naked, large breasts with pink nipples exposed, lips puckered in come-hither expressions. Despite the years passing, Gramps had kept the slick calendars and foldouts in a neat stack.

"Your grandfather could have been a pervert," Beth said astutely.

"No could have known about it. Well, almost no one."

"But you knew?"

"Gram did, too. Looked the other way. But it bothered her."

"It sure as hell would bother me, too." Beth straightened. "Oh well, he wasn't the only one. Unfortunately this town is filled with them. But I wonder how many lecherous old farts got their rocks off as they watched us . . ." Then, as if she were forcing it back on her face, Beth's ebullient mask was in place. "Water under the bridge, so to speak. Right?" She checked her watch. "Oh crap, I've got to run! Max is already late for his tennis lesson! I hope you find your cat. I'll call you or you can drop by the office. It's on Maple Street, part of the old theater—you remember. It was renovated into offices about ten years ago, and I snapped one up! Okay. Gotta run. Feel better."

And she was off, the heels of her boots clicking sharply on the marble floor as she hurried across the foyer, Harper right behind her.

Beth scooped up her purse, searched inside, and grabbed her keys as she hurried out the door and into the rain.

"Thanks for the ride!" Harper called.

"Anytime. Kisses!" Beth waved but was already slipping into her BMW. She fired the engine and completed a sharp, three-point turn, narrowly missing the back of Harper's Volvo. As she passed, Harper heard Bon Jovi again, this time singing "You Give Love a Bad Name" as the car sped onto the bridge.

Harper hoped to high heaven that Jinx wasn't anywhere near the Bimmer's path and told herself she was borrowing trouble. Until she caught a glimpse of black fur sliding through the bushes near the lane.

No, no, no!

"Beth! Watch out!" she yelled, squinting against the curtain of rain.

But Beth, head bobbing to the music, cranked the wheel at the end of the bridge and hit the gas.

Harper screamed, "Stop!"

But the creature had scurried out from beneath the bushes and started across the lane.

Thud!

Harper gasped and heard a pathetic little squeal.

Oh. God. *No!*

"Jinx!" Sick inside, she ran through the rain across the bridge, her heart pounding as fast as her footsteps. *No, no, no!*

Beth's car had disappeared by the time she reached the far side of the bridge, and she braced herself for the sight of the bloody, mangled body of her cat.

But there was none.

No crushed feline anywhere on the roadside or in the bushes. Relief washed over her, but the cat was still missing. "Jinx," she called, over and over as a wash of rain deafened her. "Jinx! Here, kitty, kitty! Goddamnit, Jinx, where are you?"

She wondered if she'd conjured the shadow darting near the BMW's wheels. A figment of her imagination, her own dark fears coalescing behind her eyes after the traumatic, sleepless night? Or . . . was it something worse?

Then out of the corner of her eye, she saw the lifeless body tucked under the dripping leaves of a rhododendron.

She froze, her stomach roiling.

Stepping closer, she recognized the matted, wet black fur, the long hairless tail and the snarled yellow teeth of a dead rat.

It didn't move.

Blood pooled from its mouth.

Her stomach heaved, but she didn't throw up.

A rat. It was just a rat. An unfortunate rodent that got caught under Beth's BMW's wheel.

Her stomach threatened again.

She leaned down, her elbows on her knees, and retched. At least it wasn't Jinx.

This time.

Swiping a hand over her lips, she straightened and swallowed back her revulsion as cold October rain washed over her. Blinking, she looked up at the gargoyles with their taloned feet curled on their perches and their stony faces ever menacing.

What was it that Beth had said?

That maybe they all were cursed?

As Harper walked across the bridge to the garage in search of a shovel, she knew there was no "maybe" about it.

They *were* all cursed.

Every last one of them.

Chapter 13

Detective Rand Watkins's day had spiraled from bad to worse. Cynthia Hunt had given up the ghost.

Just before she was to be transported to Mercy General Hospital in Portland, Cynthia had suffered a massive heart attack and died. Right here at St. Catherine's. On a standard-issue gurney.

Code Blue.

And it appeared there was a fuckup involved.

Shit.

He walked out of the hospital for the second time that day and told himself that his suspicions were way out of line, that he'd been shaken by the events of the past twenty-four hours because he'd been thrown back into a time he didn't want to remember.

Because of Harper Reed.

Because she was back in Almsville, which was now his jurisdiction.

And how off the wall was it that nearly the minute Harper showed up, Cynthia Hunt managed to put on a violent, self-mutilating display in the middle of the lake? One more tragedy for the Hunt family and another problem for Rand and his department.

And this one cut too close to the bone.

It didn't take a brain surgeon to realize that because of Cynthia's bizarre death, all the old scandals and secrets would be dredged up again. Already he'd received three calls from reporters wanting information about the Hunt family.

He climbed into his Jeep and started the engine. Waited. Letting the engine warm in the cold October air.

Why did he feel that this was going to be a shit show?

He spied his partner hurrying out of the main doors of the hospital and put the Jeep into gear. Michelle Brown was his latest partner. Green as the Chicago River on St. Patrick's Day but smart as hell. Flipping the hood of her jacket over her head at the imposing statue of St. Catherine, she glanced up at the sky, then hurried his way.

As she slid into the passenger seat, he turned on the windshield wipers.

"Get anything?"

She shot him a what-do-you-think glance. In her late twenties, she was athletic, with smooth mocha-colored skin, black hair pulled into a tight ponytail, hoop earrings, and an attitude that wouldn't quit.

He put the Jeep into gear and pulled away from the curb.

"The only person who checked in on her since her arrival, other than hospital staff, was her son. Levi Hunt," she said. "He was there this morning but left without actually going inside the ICU. Talked to the doctor in charge, a Dr. Frank Costello. People called in, inquiring, and I'll get those numbers from the phone company." As he pulled away from the curb, she asked, "Do you really think something's going on here? I mean, the woman had burns over half of her body. Don't you think nature just took its course?"

"Probably." The autopsy would show as much. But it was odd that Cynthia Hunt had been left alone in a hallway before the transport could pick her up. Worse yet, in that particular area, there were no security cameras.

Her heart probably stopped due to natural causes. Jesus, who could survive what she had been through?

Yet . . .

A coincidence?

Probably.

But it just didn't feel right.

He drove down the hill from where the hospital had been built and into the town where he'd lived most of his life. Almsville had grown in the past few decades. No longer a small town on the shores of a lake, it had become a larger bedroom community of Portland, more houses being built on the shores of the lake, newer businesses crowding into neighborhoods.

"So where's the crime?" Brown wanted to know.

"Don't know yet."

"Because maybe there isn't one."

"Maybe." He slowed for a stoplight, waited as cross traffic passed, and noted the Sold sign plastered over the For Sale sign in a window of the old Tastee-Freez where he and his buddies had biked for dipped cones and vanilla Cokes.

"You couldn't possibly think Cynthia Hunt was murdered. Everyone we interviewed so far says the same thing: she set herself on fire on her boat."

"I know." The police had talked to the boaters who had arrived on the scene and a few neighbors who had caught sight of the conflagration in the middle of the lake. Their stories had been much like Harper's.

But it didn't sit well with him. From what he'd pieced together, Cynthia had somehow escaped from the facility where she was being treated for her dementia, found a way back to the family home. Once there she'd retrieved the key to the boat, then driven it, along with all kinds of memorabilia she'd loaded into it, to the middle of the lake. Oh, and she just happened to have an extra gallon of gas and a lighter to set herself and everything in the boat on fire. And just after Harper Reed had arrived at her grandmother's house and looked out the window, she'd witnessed the fire. Harper had the common sense to call 9-1-1 but then tried to rescue Cynthia and ended up nearly drowning before being rescued.

He didn't like anything about it.

Brown cut into his thoughts as the light changed and he made the next turn to the tree-lined street where the station was located. "If you ask me—"

He hadn't.

"—I think Cynthia Hunt's heart attack is a damned blessing in disguise. I mean, what kind of a life was that woman gonna have? Jesus, did you see her? What do you think she looked like under all those damned bandages?"

Unfortunately, he would probably find out. He always visibly appraised the bodies of the victims in his cases. Cynthia Hunt's death wasn't yet classified as a homicide and hopefully never would be. Nonetheless, Rand viewed all of the bodies in the deaths he investigated. And already he was looking into the circumstances of her bizarre death. He knew some people thought him morbid or that he might even get his jollies by viewing cadavers, but that wasn't it. Not at all. It was a ritual he placed upon himself.

Ever since his tour in Vietnam, he'd forced himself to survey the grisly effects of man's inhumanity to man.

Just to remind himself. Keep his thoughts clear.

"There's a chance," she said, "that you're overthinking this. Because it's personal. I know your dad and Cynthia's husband were tight. Worked together, here," she said, nodding at the station as it came into sight. "And you were neighbors, right?"

"Yeah."

"So don't let it cloud your judgment."

He sent her a look meant to tell her to back off, but he wondered if she got the message. "I wouldn't. I just want to check things out."

"Okay. Fine. We just don't need to make more of it than there is."

"Agreed." But he wasn't going to let her tell him how, when, where, or why he was going to investigate. He parked in the lot adjacent to the station. It was a patchwork of a workplace, originally three separate buildings that had been linked together over the years as the town had grown. City hall, the police department, and the local jail were all connected by a series of hallways and staircases.

Brown was out of the car before he cut the Jeep's engine.

She didn't much like him, but he didn't take it personally. She was bristly and smart, a girl who had gotten into police work because her own father had been murdered, the case unsolved and now cold as an arctic winter. Nonetheless, she was young enough to believe that by sheer will and determination she would be able to solve the case and bring her dad's killer to justice.

He didn't blame her.

Probably would do the same if he were in her shoes.

A cold wind cut through the town, a promise of the coming winter as he followed her inside. He hung his jacket in the locker room, then walked along a hallway where pictures of officers lined the wall, his father's portrait included. As if the old man were watching his every move. Ignoring the picture of a much younger Gerald Watkins, Rand made his way through a rabbit warren of cubicles on the way to his office. Which, for the meantime, he shared with Michelle Brown. At least until Chuck Fellows retired this summer.

Neither Rand nor Brown much liked the situation, but for the foreseeable future they were stuck with it.

Brown had already shed her coat and was seated at her desk. It was slightly smaller than his own and had been pushed under the window next to a short filing cabinet. The windowsill was now covered with houseplants and pictures of Brown either hiking, riding horses, or canoeing on the lake. Beneath the trailing ivy or whatever the hell it was, her desk was strewn with empty coffee cups, Diet Coke cans, and messy piles of paper, some of which had migrated onto the filing cabinet.

His desk, set at an angle to hers, was neat, file folders stacked in one corner, his in-basket on the other, phone and computer in the center.

He settled into his chair, logged onto his email, a new addition to the department, and was scrolling through when the phone rang and he scooped up the receiver.

"Mrs. Prescott is here, Detective Watkins."

Mrs. Prescott, aka Harper Reed.

"She says she's here to give a statement regarding Cynthia Hunt."

"That's right. Give me five, then bring her back to Interview 2."

"Got it."

He gave Brown a heads-up about Harper Prescott giving her statement, then slid his arms through the sleeves of his jacket and grabbed a legal pad, pen, and pocket recorder as he made his way down the short hallway and around a corner.

He'd just sat down when Officer Suki Tanaka, the front desk officer, escorted her in.

"Come on in," Rand said, up on his feet again and noting that she'd changed into jeans and a sweater, her shoulder-length hair now down. Though she was still sporting a bandage covering her chin and one higher on her cheek, she'd applied enough makeup to partially disguise the bruise around her eye. But she hadn't been able to hide the swelling or the broken blood vessels. "Have a seat."

"Okay." She sat on one side of the small table, he on the other, as the officer closed the door behind her.

"How're you feeling?"

"Fine."

"Would you like something to drink? Coffee or a soda or . . . ?"

"Let's just get on with this."

"Okay." He pulled his recorder from his pocket and straightened the legal pad on the desk. "I want to ask you about last night."

Her lips tightened, and her good eye glared at him. "Fire away."

"I'm going to tape this."

She nodded as he hit the Record button. The little red lights started blinking as he made mention of his name and rank, the date, time, and that he was interviewing Harper Reed Prescott. Then he got down to it.

"You know that Cynthia Hunt died?"

"What?" A hand flew to her mouth. "No . . . what? Are you . . . no! When? Holy God. I—I—" She caught herself and took a long, audible breath. "I thought she was going to be sent to a burn unit at a Portland hospital."

"She was. Didn't happen."

"No," Harper whispered. She held up a hand, as if to push back on any other question he might have. For a minute she gathered herself. When she looked up at him again, all of the anger and fire he'd witnessed in her gaze earlier had diminished, replaced by confusion. "I didn't . . . I mean I knew she was bad, but I thought she was going to pull through." She was obviously stunned.

"They think she had a massive heart attack," he explained. "Just before she was transferred."

"At St. Catherine's? But I was there . . ." Harper let out a long, tremulous sigh and glanced up at the window mounted high overhead where the gray sky was visible. "Sorry . . . I just didn't know. I mean, I knew she was in bad shape and that she might not make it, but . . . it's still a shock." Then she cleared her throat. "Oh. Dear. God. Is—is Levi okay?" Her eyes shone with restrained tears, but she blinked them away.

"Don't know."

She looked at her hands and seemed to gather herself before whispering, "Maybe it's for the best."

"Maybe."

"Thanks for letting me know," she said, then seemed to give herself a mental shake. "So. You wanted to know what happened last night?"

"That's right."

"Okay. I came back to the house on the island, had driven all the way from Santa Rosa. Long trip. I was about to unpack when I looked out the window to the lake and saw the burning boat."

"And then?"

"And then . . . God, I just reacted." She told him about calling 9-1-1 before diving into the lake, swimming, and finding Cynthia Hunt tossing all kinds of things into the water as the craft was on fire. About how she'd gotten hurt from slipping on the wet stone steps on the island and from some flying shrapnel, courtesy of a raving Cynthia.

"Did she say anything to you?" he asked.

"Oh yeah." She bit the edge of her lip, as if she wasn't sure exactly what to confide and then added, "Out of the blue, while she was on fire, she saw me, recognized me, and started throwing things at me and screaming that I was to blame for Chase's death. Yelled out that I'd killed him, if you can believe that." Harper paused and shook her head. "I didn't even know that he was dead. I thought he was still missing."

"He is."

"But why would she . . . ?"

"Who knows? Officially he's still a missing person."

"But unofficially?"

"What do you think?"

She lifted a shoulder and frowned. "I've been gone a long time, but I thought someone would have let me know if his bod—if he'd been located."

"It would have been big news around here." He leaned back in the uncomfortable chair. "Did she say anything else?"

"No."

"Did you see anyone else in the lake?"

"No. Not until other boats started showing up."

"No one was in the boat with her?"

Staring at him as if he were mad, she said, "I just told you. No. She was alone."

"Did you see her pour gasoline or any other kind of fuel on the boat?"

"No."

"Did you see her light a match or use a lighter to—"

"No!" Her temper flared in her eyes. "I told you everything I saw, everything I did, everything that happened, okay? Look, Rand—er, Detective—I don't know anything else. Why am I down here anyway? Am I under some kind of suspicion? Because that's just ludicrous! I tried to help a woman in distress, and I didn't know it was Cynthia Hunt when I saw the boat, okay? Not at first. I just reacted to try and save her. And it looks like I did a damned piss-poor job of it, doesn't it?" She was upset, angry now, her pale face suddenly flushing. "Wait a minute. Are you accusing me of something here?" she asked in disbelief.

"No, just getting the facts."

But she was undeterred. "Do I need to call my attorney? Do you think—what? That I killed Cynthia Hunt?"

"This isn't a homicide investigation," he said. "You're not under suspicion."

"Oh, good." She didn't bother to hide her sarcasm. "What a relief. Because for a second or two, I thought you were going to say that me trying to save Cynthia somehow contributed to her death."

"That's not what I meant."

"You're sure?" she demanded. "Because this is feeling a lot more like an interrogation than an interview." Her gaze found his and held. "And it's not like I haven't been here before," she said, her lips flat. "The only difference is that the last detective wasn't someone who used to be my friend."

If that was supposed to sting, it didn't. Because she was pushing it. They'd never been friends.

"So," she said, her spine stiffening a bit. "Why don't you ask me what you really want to know?"

"And what's that?" he asked, not following.

"If I know what happened to Chase. Well, crap, Rand—er, Detective—I don't. I wish to high heaven that I did! That question has haunted me for twenty years."

"That's not what you're here for."

"No?" she said, on her feet. "Well, since I am here, maybe I should ask you the same question. What happened to Chase? You were his best friend. You saw him that night. For God's sake, why didn't he show up and meet me like he promised?" She was leaning over the table now, her bruised face only inches from his. "What do you know about that night?"

"What?"

"You and he—you knew everything about each other," she accused. "What did he tell you?" Her blue eyes were focused on him, her sharp gaze penetrating, as if she could see deep into his soul. Which was ridiculous.

"I don't know anything," he lied, refusing to flinch and irritated that she'd turned the interview around, so that she was asking the questions he didn't want to answer.

Angrily, she hit the Stop button on the recorder.

The blinking red light died.

"Hey, you can't do that!" he protested, shocked.

"So arrest me."

"What? Are you crazy?"

Her pale face was suddenly flushed. "You're a liar, Rand," she accused. "You know more about what happened to Chase. You have to! You and he were thick as thieves. We both know he would have done almost anything to avoid being drafted. He would have told you if he was planning to go to Canada or whatever. You probably knew if he had other girls that he was seeing. You were on your way to Vietnam and there was a chance you'd never see each other again, so he would've confided in you."

"You're wrong."

"I don't think so," she countered, then added, "and I think this interview is over. If you need to 'talk' to me again, I'll want my lawyer present."

"Jesus, Harper, you can't just—"

"Watch me." She threw on her coat, scooped up her purse, and swept out the door, nearly running into the desk officer who was about to enter.

The officer inquired, "Is there a problem?"

"Ask him!" Harper jerked her chin at Rand before breezing past the shorter woman.

"What the hell?" Tanaka asked. "Should I stop her?"

"No. Don't." Rand waved a dismissive arm. "Let her go."

"What was that all about?"

"The past," he said and glanced at her. Then picking up his recorder and notepad, asked, "Isn't it always?"

"If you say so." Tanaka seemed a little baffled as she watched Harper leave, her footsteps echoing down the hallway, hard and fast over the sounds of muted conversations and ringing phones.

"Trust me," he reiterated as he slid his recorder into his jacket pocket. "It's *always* about the past."

Chapter 14

*T*he past.

Thinking about it was a trap.

That's what Rand tried to tell himself as he walked back to his office.

But with Harper Reed back in town, escaping the past was sure to prove impossible. And she was still intriguingly beautiful. Even beaten to hell with a bandage across her chin and bruises on her face.

Or maybe he was just a fool.

Harper Reed came with a whole set of problems capped by a volatile temper.

But he didn't know the half of it. When he walked through the door to his office, he found Chelle Brown elbow deep in a dusty box on the floor.

"What's this?" he asked, tossing the file onto his desk and pulling his recorder from his jacket pocket.

"Cold case."

"Yeah? Which one?" But he had a nagging suspicion that he already knew.

"Olivia Dixon," she said, succinctly.

Harper's grandmother.

"It's not a cold case."

"No?" She cocked her head quizzically. "The way I see it, it was a case that was never really solved."

"As I remember it, an old woman died by an accidental overdose of medication. Not considered to be a homicide."

"A rich old woman."

"So?" He didn't like where this was going. "Is there a reason you're going through all this now?"

"Yeah. I'm interested. Another person dies on the lake just as Harper Prescott returns to the family home. It got me thinking about the other deaths related to her, to that island she calls home, and more specifically the lake."

"So you decided to pull out decades-old files."

"Yeah." A grin slid across her face. "It's what I do."

"When you're not working on active cases."

"This is related."

Chelle rocked back on her heels, came up with a file of yellowed papers, and tossed it onto her desk. "And it still hasn't been transferred to the computer records—everything about it is in here." She motioned to the box as she settled into her desk chair. "You know that Mrs. Prescott—then Miss Reed—was taking care of her grandmother that night but admitted to leaving the premises when her boyfriend didn't come and meet her."

Yeah. Rand knew it. Even now he remembered her as she had been on that long-ago night—ashen-faced and hiding in Levi's truck.

"I think there's more to it than was ever found out." She slapped the files onto her desk just as the furnace kicked in, warm air rumbling through the ducts. "Maybe it's time we took another look at what happened that night."

"You think?"

"Yeah, I do. I think someone killed Olivia Dixon, and I think it might have been her granddaughter, who was supposed to be caring for her on the night she died, and who, I just learned, inherited a fortune from the old lady." She added, "Who had a stronger motive to get rid of her?"

"Olivia Dixon's case wasn't a homicide," he repeated.

"Wasn't it?" She wiggled her flat hand up and down, in a maybe yes, maybe no gesture. "No one could really tell, could they? You're right. 'Accidental overdose' is what they came up with back in the day, but really, her demise could've been intentional." When he didn't respond, she said, "Isn't that right?"

"Harper was eighteen."

"Teens aren't known for their stability. Or great judgment," she countered. "Capable of all kinds of things. I say it's worth looking into."

He scratched his jaw. "You won't find anything."

"My time."

"Fine."

"Okay then. There were other suspicious deaths in the Reed family, right?"

"Hey, where're you going with this? Harper was just a kid when her mother died."

"What about the brother, though?"

"Jesus, Chelle, are you on some kind of vendetta here? Don't you have other, more important work to do?"

But she ignored him. "He died from a . . . self-inflicted gunshot wound."

"'Self-inflicted' being the important information."

Her expression changed, sobering as she picked up a yellowed bit of newsprint she'd dug up. "Harper found him."

"That's right."

"Huh."

Rand could almost see the gears turning in Chelle's brain. "And then there was the mother—what was her name?" She checked her notes. "Anna."

He nodded and heard a phone ring in a neighboring office.

"Suicide." Her expression turned thoughtful. "And again, in the lake."

He felt his jaw tighten. "Harper wasn't there."

"You're sure?"

"Yes. And I don't know where you're going with this."

"I don't either. That's the point. Maybe no one does. But Harper was found . . . let me see." She picked up another faded bit of newsprint. "On the terrace and rushed to the hospital. Had pneumonia."

He felt his gut tighten. "She was nine years old."

"I know." She twiddled her pen, still thinking, putting the jagged pieces of the Dixon Island deaths into place. "It's just an odd string of deaths, you know. And now they're all gone, and she inherited millions, right? Maybe even tens of millions."

"That's not a crime."

"I'm just saying it's curious, that's all. If it had just been the grandmother. If she'd died, you know, 'accidentally,'" Chelle said, making air quotes, "it wouldn't be so odd. But the other ones . . . let's see, the brother, Evan, he was eighteen and their mother just double that, dead at thirty-six." Leaning back in her chair, she studied him with slitted eyes. Quietly assessing.

"Coincidence?" he suggested. "Maybe just bad luck."

"Mmm." She glanced down at the list she'd made again, then her eyes were back on him. She finally adjusted her ponytail and asked, "Did you have a thing for her?"

"A thing?" He felt all his muscles tense.

"Come on. Don't play dumb. It doesn't fit. You know what I mean."

He did. But dodged it. "She was my friend, Michelle, Chase Hunt's girlfriend. Chase was my best friend."

"Yeah, I know. The dude who went missing. And it's Chelle. Remember?"

"Right."

"So," she asked again, "did you have a thing for her?"

"What?"

"Were you ever involved with Harper Reed?"

"Jesus. I said—"

"I know what you said, but it's not the first time a friend has the hots for his friend's chick. You know, a 'Jessie's Girl' kind of thing. You've heard the song, right?"

"It wasn't like that," he said, knowing it was a lie. How many nights alone in his loft bedroom had he stared out the window to the island and fantasized about Harper Reed?

"If you say so." Her eyes sparked with a naughty, knowing twinkle.

"I do." And he felt his jaw tighten to the point it ached.

She drummed her fingers on the desk and dropped that particularly sharp topic. But she wasn't done. "If you ask me," Chelle said, "all those deaths associated with that damned family deserve another look." Her eyes met his, as if daring him to argue, as if she was silently suggesting he was hiding something and that something had to do with Harper Reed. "I'm telling you, there's something off about all of this."

"I'll pull the files," he said. "See what's there."

"Maybe those cases, even if they're closed, could use fresh eyes," she challenged, and he could almost see the suspicious wheels in her brain turning. "You might be too close to it. The way I hear it, your family and the Hunts were thick as thieves, right? Your dad and Tom Hunt worked together, here. Were partners at one time."

Obviously she had already looked into this.

She suggested, "And you and Chase were besties."

What was she getting at? He said, "It was a long time ago."

"I know." She pinned him with her dark gaze. "So here's a question for you: If Harper Reed hadn't shown up here yesterday, do you think Cynthia Hunt would have been on that boat?"

"She didn't know that Harper was back."

"You think. But Harper's father had a heart attack—what, a few days before—right? And . . . if you kept up, you'd know it was about the time she was going to inherit. It was in all the papers way back when." She motioned to a clipped newspaper article from years before. "Not really a secret, so Cynthia could have figured it out. Or maybe Harper let people know. Or possibly, like the brother, Levi? He could've spilled the beans."

"I don't think he knew Harper would be back."

"But you don't know," she pointed out.

"Cynthia Hunt was in a care facility. She was mentally declining."

"But she got out, didn't she? On her own. Made her way from Serenity Acres to the lake and started the boat, so she wasn't mentally that far gone."

"She set herself on fire. Pretty far gone."

"You're taking Harper Prescott's word for it," she said and plucked a dead leaf from one of the vines running from her desk down the side of the file cabinet.

"There were other people on the lake. They saw it."

"Two night fishermen—is that even a thing? Anyway, they were out drinking for sure and fishing in the dark maybe. Neither guy is completely certain what actually happened. The other boats showed up later. So we're taking one woman's word for it, the same woman who gave us all the information on Chase Hunt's disappearance and

Olivia Dixon's death. I think it all deserves to be checked out again."
She raised her eyebrows as if waiting for him to disagree.

He wanted to argue, God, he wanted to. He'd hoped that particular chapter of his life when Chase Hunt disappeared was closed,
never to be reopened. Of course that wish was folly now. Harper
Reed Prescott had seen to that. "I was there," he reminded her. "I
saw the fire from the house when I heard the neighbor's dogs barking. I took my boat out."

"But after it all went down, right?"

He gave a curt nod and heard the fax machine down the hall start
spitting out pages.

"You and the rest of the neighbors," she said, crushing the dead
leaf in her fingers and tossing the bits into the trash under her desk.

"That's right."

She thought about it a second. "But the point is she came back
because her dad has a heart attack. And all of a sudden Cynthia Hunt
breaks out of some old people's home, manages to get to her old
house, takes out the boat, and sets herself on fire. All on her own?"

"Cynthia Hunt was in her room at the last bed check," he said. "I
talked to the general manager at Serenity Acres, who had verified
that with the night staff. So far no explanation, but we're on it."

"Don't they have cameras? Or alarms?"

"Apparently not. Or at least none that was working."

"Convenient." Her eyebrows pulled together as she picked up her
pen and started twirling it again. "I'll double-check."

"Good."

The phone rang, and she picked up the receiver. "Detective Brown."
A pause and then, turning her gaze to Rand, said, "Ms. Simms with the
Tribune?" She lifted her eyebrows in a question, and Rand shook his
head and held up a hand.

"I see. Well, for now, I'll transfer you to the public information officer and—"

Rand was already out of his chair.

"I can't comment at this time. As I said, I'll transfer you and—" A
pause, then, "No, I said—"

Rhonda DeAngelo Simms wasn't taking no for an answer. Not a
surprise. Rand remembered her from school. She, like he, had returned to Almsville, where she'd taken a job as a reporter with the

local paper. He had no interest in talking to her at the moment and left Chelle to deal with her.

He headed for the break room. In the hallway, he passed a uniformed officer ushering a disheveled man in cuffs toward the interrogation rooms. The guy was a mess, the smell of alcohol seeming to seep out of his pores while he argued loudly with the female officer escorting him in the opposite direction.

Rand turned a corner and stepped into the break room with its round tables, vending machines, microwave, and coffee station. It was quiet, no one inside, and the glass carafe in the coffeemaker still held a cup or two. Someone had strung black and orange letters spelling out HAPPY HALLOWEEN over the high windows and there were a couple of small pumpkins and a gourd nestled on the counter, Almsville Police Department's nod to the season.

He poured himself a cup and thought about his conversation with Chelle.

She was right, of course.

He wasn't objective when it came to Chase Hunt or Harper Reed.

Nonetheless, if she was going to start digging, he wanted to search through the old files before he handed them over to her.

Chapter 15

Finishing his coffee, Rand was about to head to the cold case files when Ned Gunderson, wearing a heavy jacket, walked from the outside and entered the break room. A heavy-set old-timer with close-cropped hair that was more salt than pepper, Gunn was only a couple of years from retirement, one of the few cops that had been on the force for over twenty years.

"Jesus, it's wet as hell outside and pretty damned cold, too. You'd think it was the middle of January." Gunn rubbed his hands together before pouring himself a cup of coffee, emptying the pot just as his partner, Eleanor Brady, joined him. Half his age and half his size, Brady was petite, blond, and a divorced mother of two who was blessed with a razor sharp tongue and had earned a black belt in karate.

"You gonna refill that?" she asked, eyeing the empty pot.

Gunn sent her an are-you-kidding look before tearing open several packets of Equal. Adding the sugar substitute to his cup before he doctored his brew with a shot of Coffee-Mate. "Looks like it's on you." Using a stir stick to mix the concoction, he took a chair at a round table where newspapers had been scattered while his partner sent him a dirty look.

"Fine. I'm doing it because I want a fresh cup, not because it's 'woman's work,'" she told him. "You got that?"

"I didn't say anything like that. Geez!" Gunn wasn't the least bit abashed as he glanced at Rand, as if expecting backup.

No way was Rand going to step into that dog fight.

Gunn muttered, "It's got nothin' to do with sex."

"You mean in my being a woman."

"Jesus. Word games." Tossing his stir stick into the trash, he grumbled under his breath. "Damned libbers. Everybody's so damned touchy these days."

"You got that right." A pissy frown in place, Brady swabbed the pot in a nearby sink and refilled the water chamber. She measured out fresh coffee for the basket, pushed a button, and waited, arms crossed over her chest.

Gunn shed his jacket, letting it fall against the back of his chair, and slid a pair of reading glasses onto his nose. After pushing aside a basket of sugar packets, he sifted through the scattered sections of *The Oregonian*, the state-wide newspaper. "Where the hell is the sports section?" he muttered. "If that goddamned Fellows took it— oh! Hello. Here we go." Snapping open the pages, he glanced up at Rand. "If you ask me, it looks like the Dodgers are gonna sweep the series. Got a good shot at it. The A's? Not so much. And don't talk to me about Canseco and McGwire." He shook his head. "Bash Brothers, my ass." He looked over the tops of his reading glasses. "Wait a sec. Don't tell me you're an Oakland fan."

Rand lifted a shoulder. "They've got a shot."

"Wanna bet?"

"Give it a rest, Gunn." Brady was still waiting on the coffeemaker as it heated. Empty cup in hand, she asked Rand, "So how's it going with the Cynthia Hunt case?"

"Looks cut and dried," Rand said.

The coffeemaker started growling and gurgling, scenting the air with the warm aroma of some kind of roast.

"Ya think?" Gunn said. "Word all over town is about Cynthia Hunt becoming a human torch."

Rand winced at the description. "We're still sorting things out."

Chelle had entered the break room and was slipping coins into the soda vending machine.

"Hi there, cutie!" Gunderson said as she retrieved a bottle of Coke from the machine. "What's a young thing like you doing working in a place like this?"

"Exactly that. Working," Chelle shot back, and if looks could kill, Gunderson would already be six feet under, even though he was still chuckling at his time-worn line. She headed for the door, and Gunderson watched her backside as she left.

"Oh, for the love of God, give it up, Gunn! Put your eyes back in their sockets," his partner said sharply. "No one wants what you're selling." The coffeepot gurgled a last gasp.

"You never know."

"Trust me, I do." Eleanor poured herself a cup, sat at the table near Gunn, and took a long sip. She sorted through a section of the newspaper, found the page she wanted, and smoothed it onto the table. After retrieving a pen from her pocket, she clicked it and started in on the crossword puzzle.

"In ink?" her partner asked.

"Always." Then she grinned at him. "What's a nine-letter word for dick? Oh, I've got it. G-U-N-D—"

"Very funny," Gunderson muttered.

"I thought so."

Gunderson scoffed and sipped from his cup.

"So what about Cynthia Hunt? What's going on there?" Brady asked Rand without looking up.

"Couldn't survive the trauma of the burns, I guess," Rand replied. "We'll know more once we see the autopsy."

"And Harper Reed? She's okay, right? I heard she was admitted to the hospital but was released and came in and gave a statement."

"Right." He didn't elaborate as he noticed Chelle loitering near the doorway, half hidden by a bank of lockers in the hallway but obviously listening to the conversation. He couldn't explain why her doggedness concerning Harper's family bothered him, but it did.

"Bet you had to twist her arm," Gunn said, not looking up as he scanned the headlines.

"She came of her own volition."

"Riiiight," he mocked. "You know that family, they have a habit of getting into trouble and skirting the law."

"The Reeds?" Eleanor asked.

"Dixons." Gunderson ran his finger down the sports page, checking scores. "Started with the old man. George. Piece of work, that one. Made his fortune during the Depression selling land to people who couldn't afford it, taking their money until they ran out, then foreclosed and sold the same piece to the next sucker who came along."

Rand had heard rumors to the same effect.

Gunderson added, "Old George ended up the richest man in town with a lot of property, including that island. Rumor was that he was some kind of sex freak. Is it okay to say that, or does that offend you?"

Brady scowled. "Get real."

"Anyway, he was a con man's con man, if you know what I mean." Gunn thought for a second, then added, "You know what? I'll give odds ten to one that his old lady did him in." Eleanor was about to interrupt, but Gunn said quickly, "Oh, I know all about the results of his autopsy report. That he died from something that gave him a heart attack or whatever. In a car crash. And he did have a bad heart. Once before, an ambulance was called for a heart attack, and the guys who took him to the hospital said his pants were at his ankles and there was—how should I say this? Uh. Evidence. Yeah, there was *evidence* that he'd been jack—" He caught his partner's sharp stare. "Uh. Pleasuring himself at the time. He survived that, but it was mortifying for his wife, you know. I'm thinking the old lady did something to induce the heart attack. So, later when he did cash in his chips, maybe he was driving and got himself so—uh—excited, you might say—that he gave himself another attack and crashed that fancy car of his." His lips curved at the thought. "Helluva way to go."

"While he was driving?" Brady said. "Oh sure. Gross, Gunn. And was it a heart attack at the wheel?" She didn't seem sure about it, but she shrugged it off. "It was before my time here. Anyway, what does this have to do with Harper Prescott?"

"Just that her family has a history of strange deaths," Gunn said.

"Strange how?" Brady asked, though she was carrying on the conversation while filling in the squares of her crossword puzzle.

"Unusual deaths. First the woman, Harper's mother."

"Anna," Rand said.

"Right, Anna. Then her old man and then a couple of years later, her kid. The son. Harper's brother." Gunn scowled and rubbed his head. "What the hell was his name?"

"Evan," Rand supplied.

"Yeah, that was it." Gunn nodded.

Rand asked, "What does that have to do with Cynthia Hunt?"

"Nothin', probably." Gunn took a long sip from his cup. "It's just that damned lake. You know what I mean. You live there. Lots of weird stuff goes on there, if you ask me."

"No one did," Brady said, shooting him a glance.

Rand heard muffled voices in the hallway just before two female officers walked to the locker area. The clang of metal doors shutting and locks clicking interrupted Gunn for a second.

As the women retreated into the hallway, Gunn picked up where he'd left off. "Money does weird things to people, you know."

"I'd like a little of that weirdness," Brady said. "Try raising a couple of teenage boys as a single mother. I swear they're gonna eat me out of house and home. When they're not eating, they're sleeping, but somehow they make insane piles of laundry and never leave gas in the car. That weird money you were talking about would help."

"So take your ex to court. Or play the damned lottery," Gunderson suggested.

As Rand refilled his cup, he noticed Chelle still lingering in the hallway. Sipping her drink, she was listening hard, not even trying to disguise her interest.

"You knew the Reed kid, Evan. Right? Aren't you about his age?"

Rand nodded. "I knew him." But he didn't elaborate on just how close they had been.

Gunderson actually sighed and shook his head, looking up from his paper. "God, that was a tough one. I was the cop on duty." His expression turned thoughtful. "It looked like suicide, but I never felt right about it." Gunn's gaze shifted to a middle distance only he could view as the memory caught him. "His sister found him."

"Harper?" Brady asked.

"Uh-huh. Just like she found her grandma. She has a way of doing that, doesn't she?" Gunderson said as Chuck Fellows wandered in and helped himself to a cup of coffee. Fellows was a big, athletic man with thick white hair and a bulbous nose.

Gunderson made his point. "I just think it's quite a coincidence that she was the one who discovered her brother, her grandma, and now Cynthia Hunt."

Even Brady had stopped working on the puzzle. "Was she with her mother, too, when she died?"

"No. She wasn't with Anna Reed, thank God. But she'd been outside."

"I remember," Chuck Fellows said as he cradled his cup and walked closer. He was one of the few cops who had been around at the time. "Halloween night. That poor little kid was traumatized. Ended up in the hospital, if I remember right. Had pneumonia or something."

"Right," Gunn agreed.

"And wasn't she involved with Tom's boy?" Fellows asked before taking a swallow of coffee. "You remember, the older son who went missing."

"Chase." Gunn nodded as he poured himself a fresh cup. "Yep. McKenna and I caught the two of them once, parked up at Lookout Point, while we were on patrol. They were, you know . . . doing what teenagers do up there. You remember—Chase Hunt—yeah, 'course you do," he said to Rand as he took his spot back at the table. "You were his friend, right?"

"Right."

"Anyway, the girl—Harper—claimed he was supposed to meet her the night he vanished. God, what a shit show that was," Gunderson said, nodding to himself before taking a sip and pulling a face. "The whole damned department was down there on the lake searching for the kid." He found another packet of Equal in the basket on the table, opened it, and added the crystals to his cup.

Brady said, "That stuff'll be the death of ya."

"Not yet." Gunn took a sip. "Chase and Tom were like oil and water, ya know. Couldn't get along. Not since the kid went off to college and got involved with the antiwar movement or whatever. Tom, he was a World War II vet, decorated and all, survived Normandy, but his kid didn't want to go to Vietnam, had a thing against that war, but flunked out of college, so was up for the draft. If you ask me, Chase Hunt turned tail and ran. Just took off."

Brady eyed him. "And left his family to wonder about him?"

Gunn shrugged as he drank from his cup. "Been known to happen."

"Maybe," Rand said, "No one knows for sure."

"That's right, but what I do know is that the boy was missing. Never heard from again." Gunderson's face crumpled, his lips pursing, his eyebrows nearly touching. "It just about killed his father, maybe did in the long run."

"Ancient history, Gunn," Eleanor Brady said as she turned her attention back to the open page in front of her, then glanced up quickly to pin Rand in her uncompromising stare. "But your dad should know all about it. He lived through it. Tom and he were tight, right? Isn't that what I heard?"

"Yeah."

"Had to be tough on all of them. All of you."

Amen, Rand thought, *more than anyone knows.* He kicked his chair back then topped off his cup.

Chelle had slipped away.

Good. Carrying his cup, he left the break room.

In his office, he found Chelle already at her desk. She was working busily on the contents of an old case file, as if she'd been at it for the entire time he'd been gone.

Yeah, right.

He caught a glimpse of Harper's name on a note pad and his gut twisted.

Chelle didn't know the half of what happened that night, he thought as he settled into his desk chair.

But she would. He read the determination in the set of her jaw.

What's the old saying? *The truth will set you free?*

Maybe, in this case, it was just the opposite.

1968

Chapter 16

Rand was going out.

No matter what his old man said.

Not that Gerald Watkins could say much.

Rand was in the army now, had completed a tour in Germany, and was, after this brief leave stateside, on his way to Vietnam. So his old man couldn't really tell him what to do anymore. Not that he wouldn't try. At six foot two, Gerald Watkins was all muscle. He'd been a sergeant in the army during World War II, and, as a reservist, had again served in the Korean conflict. Afterwards, he'd become a police officer. Gerald Watkins's adult life had all been about law and order.

So he'd been certain his son would be following in his footsteps.

Which, Rand thought, *was bullshit*. And yet here he was on his way to Vietnam.

But not yet.

In a black T-shirt and faded jeans, Rand yanked on his old pair of Converse high-tops and glanced in the mirror where he'd tucked a few pictures into the frame. He focused on the photo of himself in his football uniform from a couple of years back. A gangly boy then, not the man in the reflection tonight. He'd grown three inches and gained twenty pounds since his junior year at Almsville High. Now his hair was buzz-cut, his beard shadow beginning to show.

The kid holding a football helmet tucked under one arm, with pimply skin and wild black hair, was from another lifetime. An innocent, with free time before he'd gone through basic at Fort Lewis in Washington, then been shipped to a base in Germany where life had been regimented but relatively safe.

Now, though, it was a different story.

He jammed his Seattle Supersonics cap onto his head and headed downstairs from his bedroom in the loft to the living room, where the TV was tuned into *Hogan's Heroes*, one of his dad's favorite shows. These days, Rand saw nothing funny about war or POW camps, but he didn't bother to change the channel as he was heading out.

Over the conversation on the tube, Rand heard his father's voice, carrying from the back of the house. He stopped in the dining area and stared into the kitchen where the fluorescent lights overhead flickered on Gerald Watkins seated at the table. His back to the living room, he was talking on the phone, the cord stretched taut from its base attached to the wall between the cupboard and sliding door.

". . . I know, I know, but he'll be out in less than eighteen months now," Gerald was saying, receiver to his ear, a beer on the table near an unruly stack of bills and his open checkbook. A cigarette was burning unattended in a glass ashtray. A pause. Then, "Jesus Christ, Barb, sure, it's a hellhole. Don't I know it? But hey, it's his duty. If he plays his cards right, he could get Uncle Sam to pay for his college when he's out or train him to be a pilot or whatever while he's in . . . Listen . . . I know, I know . . ." His voice was getting louder. Terser. As it always did these days when Gerald was on the phone to his ex-wife, Rand's mother.

Barbara May Smith Watkins Eldridge.

"Fine. Fine. Hold on a sec. I'll get him on the line." But before he could call for Rand, he said into the phone. "Yeah, yeah, I said, 'I know.' Didn't I already say that it's a fu—damned hellhole?"

A long pause.

"He'll be okay . . . what?" He was getting mad now. His voice even tighter. His face red. He took a long swallow from the beer can, then crushed it. "How many times do I have to say, 'I know,' Barb, but shit—"

Rand had heard enough. Intent on leaving through the front door, he'd backed up a step when his father's voice stopped him short.

"That's great, Barb, just fu—effin' great! *You* talk to him about it. I'll get him on the line." He placed a hand over the mouthpiece of the receiver, "Hey, son—"

"Got it." Rand crossed the kitchen and snagged the receiver from his father's hand.

Gerald glowered. "How long you been there?"

Long enough. "Hey, Mom," Rand said, putting the receiver to his ear.

"You been listening in?" his father demanded before taking a long swallow of beer.

Rand turned his back and ignored Gerald as he heard his mother's voice on the other end of the line. She wasn't quite sobbing, but her voice sounded wet. "Hi, honey," she said. "I just want to say that I'm sorry I didn't come over earlier to say goodbye."

"It's okay."

"It's not," she said brokenly. "I should be there. And . . . and I could stop by later." He imagined her on the other end of the line, wearing her signature shade of pink lipstick, her newly blond hair teased into a perfect "flip," as she called it, the upturned ends at her shoulders.

"You don't have to. I'm heading out for a while anyway. See some friends, you know."

"But, really. As soon as Kent is back with the car, I could come over. It would be late, but I'm coming!"

"Mom, please, don't worry about it. Okay? I'll be back stateside before you know it." He didn't know if he could convince her. Once she got an idea in her head, it took a pickax to dislodge it. "I'll be fine."

"But it's dangerous! And I—I—I love you." Her voice broke, and she was sniffling now, and Rand's own throat tightened as he shifted from one foot to the other. He noticed, in the faint reflection of the back door, his old man stub out the forgotten Marlboro and light a fresh one, his face in the flicker of his match appearing older than his thirty-eight years. For a split second Rand wondered if this was how he himself would look, tired and angry at midlife? After all, how many times had Rand heard that he was the "spittin' image" of his father except his eyes were a couple of shades lighter than his father's deep brown?

"I love you, too, Mom," he said and saw his father scowl in the ghostly reflection, Gerald's visage blurred by smoke. Admitting you loved someone out loud was not on Gerald Watkins's play list. He didn't believe in it; instead he believed in being stalwart and strong without any emotion. "Just get the goddamned job done. Whatever it takes." That was his mantra.

Dad was angry these days, angrier than usual, and he was pissed about politics again, upset that Martin Luther King had been assassinated, and only two months later RFK gunned down and killed in California. Gerald Watkins let it be known that the country was going down the tube—the race riots and antiwar protests that even included the Democratic National Convention were proof of it. But as much as Gerald despised the war in Indochina, he was conflicted because he truly believed being a patriot to America and serving one's country was every man's duty. He'd served in the armed services and, by God, his son would, too.

"I'll write you—at least once a week if not more often," Mom was saying.

Rand turned his attention away from his father's angry reflection just as he heard another voice, a deeper one that was muffled. Her husband. Kent Eldridge. His stepfather must've arrived home. Great. Rand had no use for him. A local dentist whom Rand considered sadistic was the man Barb had "traded up" for with his thriving practice and steady hours. Her voice was muted now, and Rand guessed she'd placed her hand over the receiver. Still, he heard that she and Kent were arguing, then suddenly her voice was clear again. And rushed. "Okay, sweetheart, you take care of yourself. Be safe. I'll talk to you soon." And then she hung up.

He dropped the receiver into its cradle. "I'm going out," he announced to his father as Gerald shoved back his chair.

"Where?" Gerald asked, then frowned, drawing hard on his cigarette, obviously deciding it didn't matter where his son was heading. Soon Rand would be shipping out to a war-torn country halfway around the world.

"With friends." Rand was already out of the kitchen and striding across the living room with its orange shag carpet and BarcaLounger situated squarely in front of the TV where Bob Crane was playing a wisecracking POW.

"When will you be back?" His father called as Rand snagged his army jacket from a peg near the door, then stepped onto the front porch.

"What does it matter?" He pulled the door shut behind him.

Outside the night was cold and crisp, a hint of snow in the air. He ran to his Jeep, a '58 Willys that was his pride in high school and was now parked in the drive. Now—well, he still loved it, though not with quite the same ardor.

Life had changed.

Big time.

He slid behind the wheel and switched on the engine before cranking the radio up and reversing onto the street, gravel spinning beneath the Jeep's big tires. Jaw set, he hit the gas, pushing through the gears as he drove to the old logging road, fifteen miles into the surrounding hills. The rain of the days before had stopped, and the night was bitter cold, winter in full force, but the moon was visible through gauzy, slow-moving clouds.

He was out of town in minutes, winding upward on the old county road through the forests of Douglas fir and past the unlocked gate to the private road owned by a logging company. The gravel was sparse, the potholes many, and the dense old-growth trees knifed upward to the night sky. Eventually the access road ebbed into twin ruts where dry weeds scraped his undercarriage. He drove until he reached the wide spot in the road where Chase's '63 Chevelle was already parked. Once Chase's prize possession, now the metallic blue paint job was splattered with mud.

Chase sat behind the steering wheel, obviously waiting for him, but as the beams of Rand's headlights washed over him, Chase climbed out.

Rand parked and stepped into the dark night.

" 'Bout time you showed up," Chase said, shaggy blond hair visible in the faltering moonlight. He was wearing a fringed jacket and battered jeans. A string of hippie love beads was visible at his throat.

"My mom called," Rand explained. "I had to talk to her."

Chase mocked him in a boyish, high-pitched voice. "My mommy called."

"That's right." Without another word, Rand led the way, using a flashlight to illuminate the familiar trail that rimmed the canyon, where, far below, the river rushed. He and his friends had spent hours at this spot on the river, drinking beer, smoking joints, getting all kinds of high to skinny-dip and hunt and fish or just party.

But not tonight. Not this cold night in February where the earthy smell of the forest was all around, a brittle wind rustling through the branches overhead.

Chase had called, said he wanted to meet. Alone.

So here he was, and as they reached the rocky cliff overlooking the river twenty feet below, Chase reached out, catching him by the elbow. Rand stopped, and they faced each other in the darkness.

"What's up?" Rand asked, his breath fogging the cold air.

"I just wanted to say good-bye and tell you to keep your ass down over there."

"Bullshit. You could have said that on the phone."

A pause where all they could hear was the sound of the river. "I wanted to see you, man," Chase said, but there was more to it. Rand knew as much. He'd known Chase all of his life, and he could tell when something was bothering him. Tonight he thought it ran far deeper than concern for his best friend heading to war.

"Okay, so you've seen me."

"Fine." Chase reached into the pocket of his jacket, found a joint and a lighter, lit up. He handed the joint to Rand, who had a toke, held the smoke, and waited for the high, along with Chase's real reason for insisting they meet up here. Away from everything and everyone. He passed the joint back, and Chase took another drag before letting out the smoke slowly.

Rand waited. Waved off another hit. "Spill it."

"Okay." Chase nodded. "So, I know you're going to 'Nam and that's cool and all, but it's not for me."

"You've got a deferral." Chase was a student at the University of Oregon in Eugene. "There's a chance you can ride out the war."

"Nope. Not an option."

"Because—?"

"Because I flunked out."

"You're kiddin'." Chase was an A student, or had been in high school, as well as a big-time athlete, lettering in three sports. He'd been focused on his future and intent on not screwing up his life.

"No, definitely not kidding." He drew on the joint again and then added, "My old man is gonna kill me when he finds out."

That was a little extreme, but there was no doubt Thomas Hunt would be pissed as hell, and he wasn't afraid to take it out on his kid. "So what're you gonna do?"

"I don't know, man, that's just it. I can't go to Vietnam." Chase was shaking his head violently. "I really can't. I'd go crazy."

Rand bit his tongue as a gust of bone-cold wind swept through the forest, catching in Chase's hair.

"So . . . I've got some ideas," Chase went on. "I could say I've got flat feet or bone spurs or am still suffering from the time my shoulder was dislocated during that game against Jesuit, when we were juniors, but my old man won't go for it. And he won't buy into the whole conscientious objector, 'against my religion' thing as my family is a founding member of the Methodist church in town." He gazed out across the dark chasm of the river. "He'd disown me first. Shit, he was awarded a Purple Heart when he served and . . . well, no, saying it's against my religion won't fly." Chase took another toke.

"Canada?" Rand suggested as the joint was passed back to him. "I think that's what happened to Patrick Sullivan. I heard his uncle has a hunting cabin in Alberta, I think, or maybe B.C. Anyway, he hitch-hiked up there, then hiked across the border somewhere in the mountains."

"I've thought of that," Chase admitted as he let out his breath. "And . . . I've even thought of getting Harper pregnant." He was nodding slowly, as if the idea had merit, but Rand, the joint halfway to his lips, stopped.

"You'd do that?" Rand asked, feeling the chill of the night. "Have a kid?"

"Hell, yeah, I would."

"And Harper?" Rand tasted bile rising in his throat.

He lifted a shoulder. "She's into it."

"Really?" Rand didn't believe it. "She'd give up college?"

"The thing is, she'd do anything for me," Chase admitted. "Doesn't even mind the thought of being knocked up. I quit using rubbers a while back."

"Are you shittin' me? And she's not pregnant?" That seemed odd. If Rand were to believe his father, one time of not taking precautions and you were all but assured of getting a girl pregnant. He knew that wasn't necessarily true, of course, but still.

"Not yet. So . . ."

"But wait." He knew that Chase had been seeing other girls, down at college and even here in Almsville. "Isn't there some other girl in Eugene?"

"A couple."

Rand waited.

"So I've fucked around, so what?"

"But you want to get Harper pregnant?"

"Well, sure. But if some other girl happened to end up PG . . ."

"What? Are you crazy? That would be okay?" Rand couldn't believe what he was hearing. "Any girl would do?"

"It's not for the rest of my life."

"Isn't it? Hell, Chase, that's fucked up! I mean, really fucked up!" He threw up his hands. "How would Harper feel if some other girl claims you're her kid's father?" Was Chase nuts?

"Harper's not gonna get drafted."

"That's cold, man."

"Just tellin' it like it is." Chase actually looked thoughtful as he stared across the chasm, the sound of the river far below muted. "And yeah, I know it's fucked up. I like Harper. Crap, maybe I even love her. And I would marry her, I would." He rubbed the back of his neck. "But for now, I'm still single and those chicks at school or, Christ, right down the street here. You've seen them, right? At the house on down at the start of the deer trail? You know the one I'm talkin' about."

Of course he did. Rand had walked or biked past the cabin to the path that wound uphill through the scrub oak and firs. It led to the main road that rimmed the south side of the lake. Rand had seen the girls Chase was talking about. Even in the dead of winter they sometimes wore halter tops. "Yeah."

"Well, those girls in there are bitchin', I tell ya. Shit, they're stoned half the time and beautiful. I mean, drop-dead Marilyn Monroe gorgeous with racks like you wouldn't believe. There's one, Moonbeam, a redhead with tits like—like a goddamned Playboy bunny. Huge." He placed his cupped hand six inches from his chest.

"Moonbeam?"

"That's not her real name. I mean, I don't think so. I think it's Jan or something like that. Janet Van Something I think. Doesn't matter. I'm tellin' ya man, she's stacked." His smile grew evil. "I've seen those tits. Touched 'em. Fantastic. We did it."

"You and Moonbeam?" Rand asked, disbelieving.

"Yeah, yeah," he said. "We were both high and she was out on their deck, then grabbed me by the hand and went up those outside stairs to some kind of locked attic room. She had a key and led me inside. I had to duck to get through the door, and even then once I was inside I banged my head on a beam, but it was a cool spot, you know?"

Rand didn't but let Chase go on.

"I saw some equipment and first thought it might be a place to jam, you know, cuz I saw a guitar on the wall, but that wasn't it." He scratched his chin, remembering. "On one wall—the one with the window facing the lake—there was this long desk or table or whatever. Just a big sheet of plywood stretched over cinder blocks. And on top of it? All kinds of cameras and shit. I mean *expensive* shit. Cameras with zoom lenses. And . . . and . . . tape players and movie cameras and binoculars. I mean it was right out of a spy novel. Really tricked out." He glanced at Rand. "I even wondered if someone sat up there and got off watching everyone through that window that faced the lake. But the best part?"

He grinned, his teeth flashing white in the darkness. "A mattress on the floor on the other side of the room. That's where we got down to business and man, oh man, was she into it. Went down on me and then got on top of me with those big incredible tits in my face. I could've sucked on them for hours. Hours! Shit, if there's a heaven, that's it."

Rand was fascinated but wondered if Chase was fantasizing or just downright lying. It wouldn't be the first time.

"Bullshit."

"It's true. I swear! And . . . and get this! There were holes in the attic floor with little covers, and you could remove those little covers and bingo—you were looking down at the bedroom below, kinda through the light fixture so you could see who was getting it on. Can you believe that? They were spying on each other—well, hell, maybe on everyone on the lake. Anyway, Moonbeam, she was awesome. Knew what she was doing if you know what I mean—"

"Really?" Rand cut in. This sounded like a load of BS. "It happened? Between you and this girl? For real? When there were other guys at the house?"

"I know! That's just it! They're all cool with it."

"Bullshit." Rand didn't believe it.

"No! I swear!" He lifted his palms up to beside his head. "They share! Free love, you know? Free-fucking-love!"

Rand's stomach turned. Not so much about Chase fucking everything that moved. Who cared? But because Harper Reed thought she was in love with him. *And*, he thought, *she deserves better.* "And Harper's okay with this?"

"Aaah." Chase shifted from one foot to the other on the ledge, as if he finally felt some prick of conscience. "The thing is, she doesn't really know. If she found out, she'd go ballistic. You know about her temper, right? It's . . . well, scary sometimes. It's like she can't control herself."

"Really?"

"One time she was so mad at me, she practically ran me over with her Grandpa's boat. I was waterskiing with another girl and Harper saw me. She was in his Chris-Craft and turned that sucker around, then headed straight for me while I was in the water waiting to be picked up. She claimed it was an accident, that she didn't see me." He paused, took another drag. "But she was lying."

"Jesus."

"I know. Nuts. Doesn't matter anyway."

"But you're going to marry her?"

"Maybe. If I don't break up with her first."

"Shit. Seriously?" Rand couldn't make sense of what Chase was telling him. "What the hell? I don't get it. Either you're in love with Harper and you want to get married, or not."

"It's not simple."

"I think it is. It's sick, that's what it is. You're using her . . . like some brood mare."

"No!" Chase was suddenly angry. "I told you. I care for her."

"And a whole lot of other girls."

"You've got it all wrong," Chase bit out. "It's more complicated than that. The whole damned world isn't black or white."

"Does Harper know that?" Rand countered. But deep down, he was relieved.

"Not yet. She will." Chase chewed on his lower lip, thinking, as a night owl hooted from a tall tree nearby, then he passed the joint back and said, "I'm gonna talk to her tonight. Explain things. She'll get it."

"Oh sure." Chase was talking nonsense.

"She will."

"Like hell she will. You'd better figure out what you're gonna say, cuz if you tell her what you told me tonight, she's gonna freak out." Rand took a final toke and passed the joint back.

"She'll understand."

Rand didn't think so.

"Harper's cool," Chase insisted. "Look, man, I know you're a boy scout. Always trying to do the right thing. All gung ho army and all."

Rand didn't argue. Couldn't. He didn't mind serving, had signed up, but the war—that was a whole different thing. So, gung ho for a tour in Vietnam and getting his ass shot up? No. He was far from keen on going. Going AWOL had crossed his mind more than once, but those thoughts had been short-lived. A fantasy. No, he was in for serving the country. For now. Rand snorted his disbelief and jammed his hands into the pockets of his jacket.

"Listen, I get it. And if I could serve, man, I would, but I can't go, I just can't."

Chase was shaking his head, long hair shimmering in the moonlight. He drew the joint down to a roach, which he snuffed out between his fingers as he finally let out the smoke. "I'm just sick of my life, ya know? I'm tired of being told what to do. Teachers, coaches, and my dad. Jesus, my dad. Thomas Calhoun Hunt. I'm never good enough for him. No matter what I do. He's always on my case. So, no.

I'm not going to let some dick army sergeant start breaking my balls. I get enough of that shit at home. You know what I'm talking about."

Rand did. His father hadn't been afraid to pull out his belt and use it on Rand to keep him "in line." Gerald Watkins believed "Spare the rod, spoil the child," and his thin strap of a belt had been used to bring his point home and make his recalcitrant child obey. Thomas Hunt, too, was known to force Chase or Levi to cut a switch from the willow tree that hung over the lake, then bring it to him so he could use it on their bare asses. Not often. Just enough to remind his sons who was the boss.

"Shit." Chase was shaking his head. "It's time to live my own life." He reached into the pocket of his jeans. "And to that end, wanna go on a trip?" He pulled out a small packet.

"A trip to where?"

Unwrapping a sugar cube, Chase said in a low voice, "Anywhere you want to go, man. Anywhere at all."

Rand shook his head. "Not into acid."

"Your loss." Chase swallowed the cube and grinned in the darkness, his eyes gleaming in the moonlight.

"Where the hell did you get it?"

"Guy at the house at the end of the street. Goes by Trick. From somewhere in Texas. Near the border, I think." He grinned. "He can get you whatever you want. Any slice of heaven. I'm not kidding. You want me to hook you up?"

"No. Look, I should get going," Rand said. Let Chase trip-out by himself.

"Not yet." Chase grabbed him by the elbow. "I might need your help."

Rand didn't like the sound of that. "With what?"

"I've got to leave. My time is up, man. I'm thinking about leaving. Seriously. Get the fuck out."

"You're all over the place," Rand said and jerked his arm away. First he was going to knock up Harper, probably marry her, then no, he was gonna break up with her because she wasn't pregnant but maybe some other girl could be. Now he was going on an acid trip before talking about taking off. "Now you want to cross the border? Go to Canada?"

"I could hike up there, I guess . . ." His voice faded off, as if he wasn't sure.

"Or—?"

"Or, you know. Disappear."

"What?"

Chase reached down, picked up a rock, and flung it out into the darkness. It sailed into the ravine before plopping into the water, the sound barely audible over the river's rush. "I could fake dying."

Chapter 17

Rand froze, his friend's words echoing through his brain. Was Chase kidding? Was he really thinking about faking his own death? "You're not serious."

Chase shrugged, the fringe of his jacket rippling in the half-light of the moon. "Yeah. Kinda."

"Oh shit." Was Chase already tripping, the drugs talking? But the suddenly somber tone of his friend's voice convinced him that Chase had considered the weird idea. "How the hell would you do that?"

"I'm working on it," Chase admitted. "Just if, you know, I come up missing?" He paused, and for a few minutes all that could be heard over the rush of the river was the continued hooting of the owl. "I might need your help."

"What? My help for you to disappear? Are you crazy?" Rand pulled off his cap and ran his fingers over the short hairs on his head. "Shit, man, what're you saying?"

"You do nothing," Chase said, and he did seem more mellow, as if the LSD was working some kind of magic on him. "Don't say a word. And just don't look too hard for me."

"Are you nuts? I can't—"

"You can! And you will!" Chase was insistent as a breath of cold wind swooped through the hills. "You're leaving soon, right? This week? So, as far as we're both concerned, this conversation never happened. Got it?"

"Got it," Rand said as Chase dug into his pocket again and came up with a pack of Camel straights.

"Good." Chase plucked out a cigarette and offered Rand the pack. Rand held up a hand and shook his head.

Chase lit up and drew deep as he pocketed the pack and his lighter. "So, just to be clear," he said, in a cloud of smoke. "What're you going to do if I vanish?"

"Jesus, Chase, you're not serious."

"I am." Chase's voice was low.

"Then, nothing." This wasn't happening. The conversation had just gotten way too weird.

"And what're you gonna say?" Chase prompted as the owl hooted again.

"Nothin'. Nada."

"Swear?" Chase persisted.

"I swear," Rand said, knowing Chase wasn't going to go through with his nutso, drug-induced plan.

"Good." He picked a bit of tobacco from his tongue. "But you have to do something for me, okay?" Chase's voice was low. Somber.

"What?" Rand was wary.

"You have to take care of Harper."

What was this? No. "What the hell are you talking about? You're all over the place, dude. First you want her to get pregnant so you can marry her, then you're going to break up with her, then you love her, then . . ."

"I don't know, man!" Chase said and closed his eyes as if he were in pain. "I don't fuckin' know!" He took a long drag on his smoke, then flicked the butt into the river, the red tip arcing in the night before disappearing far below. "You'll do it, right?"

Rand didn't answer, and suddenly Chase snagged Rand by the neck of his jacket, strong fingers twisting the fabric as he pressed his face nose-to-nose with Rand. "Just say you'll fuckin' take care of her!" he hissed, smoky breath seeping from his suddenly tight lips. From deep in their sockets, his eyes reflected the thin moonlight.

Rand's fists balled. This was crazy. "You're what? Leaving? Disappearing, and you want me to take care of Harper? What about Levi? Can't he do it?"

"Not Levi!" Chase spat out.

"He's your brother—"

"*Not* Levi!" Chase repeated, his lips pulled back in anger, his teeth flashing. "Goddamn it, not Levi. He's a prick!" he said vehemently. Rand knew there was a fierce rivalry between the brothers but hadn't realized how deep it ran.

"Levi can't be trusted," Chase insisted. "It's got to be you!" He jerked on Rand's collar, almost pulling Rand off his feet.

Just like that, the scent of a fight crackled through the air.

Chase glared at Rand for a second. He was so close Rand smelled Chase's sweat, mingling with the cigarette smoke. In the moonlight, Rand saw the sheen of perspiration on his friend's face and noticed that his eyes were almost black, his pupils dilated to the point of obscuring most of the blue. On this near-freezing night when his own breath was fogging, Chase was sweating.

"You son of a bitch, you take care of her!" Chase ordered. Then, almost dismissively, "Shit, you're half in love with her already!"

Rand was stunned at how Chase had read his emotions. He'd thought he'd been so good at hiding how he felt about Harper.

Apparently not. And now Chase sounded desperate. His fingers clenched more tightly over Rand's jacket, and every muscle in Rand's body tensed. His own hands curled into fists. He was ready for a fight.

"Do it! Swear it, man!" Chase shook the bunched jacket, yanking Rand even closer. The air crackled between them. "Swear to me that you'll take care of her!"

"I'm leaving! Goin' to fuckin' 'Nam." Rand's own temper seethed, barely in check.

"Swear it!"

"She won't like it."

"Who the fuck cares?" Another shake, this time Rand was pulled off his feet, his hat slipping off.

Rand saw red.

His military training kicked in.

He caught the offensive wrist with one hand. Ready to swing with the other. "Let go of me," he ordered through lips that barely moved. Anger blistered through him, every muscle tense, ready to explode.

"Just promise."

"Let go!" Rand drew his arm back, fist cocked.

"Damn it—"

Rand swung.

Hard.

Bam!

His fist smashed into Chase's jaw with a loud crunch.

Pain burst through his knuckles.

Chase's knees buckled.

He let out a pained groan.

As he crumpled, his fingers loosened, releasing his grip on Rand's jacket.

As his feet hit the ground, Rand stumbled backward. His high-tops slipped at the edge of the ravine, kicking out gravel that tumbled over the edge, raining into the black chasm and the river far below.

Shit!

He teetered for a second.

Falling backward.

No!

In desperation, he flung his body forward, hitting the ground hard.

His fingers dug into the wet earth, finding weeds and shards of gravel.

The night seemed to close in on him.

Nearby, Chase, still stunned, was struggling to a sitting position. Breathing raggedly, he propped his back against a blackened stump. "Fuck." Rubbing his jaw, he focused on Rand still gasping for breath at the chasm's edge. "You little cocksucker." Zeroing in on Rand, he forced himself to his feet, swaying slightly. Even in the weak moonlight, Rand saw that Chase's face was twisted into a mask of rage, his lips pulled back, nostrils flared.

Oh shit.

This wasn't over.

Rand rolled over, forcing himself upright. To the balls of his feet. In fighting position. Ready to lunge.

If he had to.

"Chase," he warned. "Let's . . . let's not do this, okay?" Even though his blood thundered in his temples, nearly drowning out the roar of the river, and he knew that this fight was no answer, he wanted to hit Chase again. To pound some sense into him. To make him realize what he was doing to Harper. To wise him up to the fact that he was talking about options when Rand had none. To end this. Now.

Too late.

Head down and bellowing, Chase rushed him like a bull. He ran straight at Rand, ready to tear him from limb to limb.

"Fuck you!" Rand sidestepped the tackle.

Chase flew past.

Too late Rand realized his mistake.

Too late, Chase caught sight of the edge of the ravine.

Frantically, he tried to put on the brakes. "No! Shit! Rand!" The ground crumbled beneath his feet.

He tumbled forward.

Scrabbled wildly in the air.

No!

Rand threw himself at Chase and caught him by one arm. "You fucker," he said through clenched teeth, his hand on fire.

Pain screamed up his arm to his shoulder. For a split mind-bending second, he considered letting go. Just releasing his best friend and letting Chase drop into the blackness. In a heartbeat he remembered how Chase used and abused all of his relationships, including Harper.

He caught a glimpse of Chase's face, his features distorted by panic. "Son of a bitch," he said, "God, Rand, help me!"

Chase didn't deserve any kindness. Not after using and abusing so many people. But this—to let him drop into the roiling, frigid waters of the river? To be swallowed and dragged by the current to drown? No.

"Help me," Chase pled. "Jesus, Rand, help me!"

Pushing past the agony in his hand, Rand set his heels into the mud, trying not to be dragged over the edge by the weight of his heavy friend. Gritting his teeth, Rand pulled, every muscle in his back and shoulders straining, beads of sweat forming on his face from the painful effort.

Chase was swinging slightly, trying to get footing on the cliff face, clawing at the dirt with his free hand.

Rand strained, certain his own tendons would rip, his muscles tear. Pain tore through his arm and shoulder as he tried to save his friend.

Using all his strength, Rand pulled. Sweat poured off his forehead and ran down his arm. His grip was slick. His hand throbbing. His muscles screaming. His back bowing with the pressure. "Climb!" he gritted out between clenched teeth. "Climb, you son of a bitch."

Chase scraped at the dirt, sending rocks flying, frantically, catching hold of roots with his free hand, his feet finding something hard it seemed because suddenly the tension eased a bit.

With all of his strength, Rand threw his back into the task at hand. He leaned hard, straining, his shoulder aching to the point he thought his arm might wrench from its socket. "Come on, come on," he ordered through a locked jaw.

He saw the crown of Chase's head. Rand inched backward, afraid at any second his feet might slip.

But all of a sudden Chase was able to help. He quit swinging, got some sort of purchase. He flung his hand over the edge and grabbed hold of a rock. With a roar, he pulled his shoulder over the ledge and as Rand dragged him, Chase was able to pull himself away from the overhang.

Finally Rand released him. Chase crawled forward, then fell onto the wet ground beside Rand, the long fringe of his jacket slapping Rand in the face as he landed.

Breathing hard, Chase ground out, "Thanks, man."

Rand spent several seconds breathing hard and feeling the sweat cool on his body. Every muscle ached as he finally pulled himself into a sitting position, his knees bent. He was exhausted, his hand throbbing. He looked up at the stars as he took in several more deep breaths of the cold, river-scented air. "You're a fucking lunatic," he finally said.

"I know." On his back, staring at the night sky, Chase was breathing so hard Rand could hear it. Chase shoved his sweaty hair from his eyes. "Damn it, I know."

Good. Maybe his near-fatal fall sobered him up. Could it be the shock, the adrenaline rush of facing death that made Chase Fuckin' Hunt reevaluate whatever the hell it was that he'd been thinking? In the half-light of the moon, Rand looked over at his drugged-out, scared friend.

Athletic but no longer clean-cut, a bruise developing beneath his scraggly beard, his once-clipped blond hair now in disarray, long locks fanning around his face, Chase slid a glance in Rand's direction. "Holy Christ, that was a rush."

"What? Nearly killing yourself in the river?"

"Yeah, I know, but hell, it makes me feel alive now."

"You're wasted. Too high."

"Probably." He pulled himself into a sitting position, the love beads glinting beneath the collar of his jacket. "Definitely."

"Let me know when you land." *And get a cold dose of reality.*

He finally rested his elbows on his knees and held his head. "Okay, okay. It's cool. It's all cool."

Rand didn't believe it for a second. He let out a long slow breath. So this was what his last night stateside was going to be. But what had he thought? Too young to hang out at a bar with friends, no girlfriend to cling to, nothing but his one damned strung-out buddy who had talked nonsense all night. He kicked at a tuft of grass and wondered if he'd ever be back here again. His whole world was about to change. He didn't know if he'd ever see his old man, or Chase or . . . or Harper. He'd thought about calling her, saying goodbye, but it would have been awkward. Stupid. She was Chase's girlfriend, whatever that meant.

He stood. Time to get going.

"Just tell me you'll take care of her," Chase said, breaking into his thoughts. "Take care of Harper."

This again. Chase wasn't going to give up. "Shit, yeah. I swear," Rand said, just to shut him up. So that he wouldn't have to deal with his own conflicted thoughts. "But I'm shipping out. I won't be around."

"You'll be back."

"And if I'm not? I'm going to war, man! Remember? I might not come back." For the first time aloud, Rand voiced his own fears, and the night seemed suddenly colder.

"You will." Chase wasn't going to be denied. For the moment Chase was satisfied, but there had been something restless and off about him tonight, and Rand guessed it had less to do with the drugs and more with his off-the-wall mental state.

"I gotta go," Rand finally said and found his cap near the back tire of Chase's car. "You okay?"

Chase snorted. "Yeah. I'll be fine."

"You sure?"

"Who knows? Not your problem." Chase dug into his pocket for his pack of Camels. "But you—you keep your ass down."

"I will."

"Good. Countin' on it." He shook out a cigarette and lit up. "Be safe, brother."

Rand left Chase to contemplate the stars, universe, or his own damned fate and headed back to his Jeep. Disturbed, he got behind the wheel and jabbed his key into the ignition. The car was cold, the temperature having plunged.

He turned on the heater, backed up, then hit the gas, tires spinning in the gravel before the Jeep took off. His headlights cut through the night, illuminating the potholes and weeds and bouncing off the thick gnarled trunks of the surrounding trees. He fiddled with the radio until he heard Mick Jagger singing "Ruby Tuesday" over the crackle of static. But his thoughts were swirling with Chase and Harper. Shit, he had to get her out of his mind.

Except that he'd promised Chase he'd take care of her.

Oh sure.

How the hell was he supposed to do that? As if she would even let him.

As he shoved the gearshift into third, he caught the reflection of a deer's eyes at the side of the road.

"No!" He stood on the brakes.

The Willys fishtailed.

"Don't!" he yelled. As if the damned deer could understand him. "No!"

The blacktail leapt in front of the Jeep.

Rand cranked on the wheel and braced himself for the impact. The Jeep shuddered to a stop.

The doe's eyes found his as it flew across the road.

It touched down just beyond his front fender, missing the headlight by inches, only to bound into the surrounding thicket. "Holy crap." His heart was pounding, adrenaline surging through his blood from the near miss.

For a few seconds, he didn't move. Just stared into the forest and let out his breath as the Rolling Stones kept on playing and his heartbeat slowed. He barely heard the lyrics about losing dreams and losing your mind, but somehow they seemed to fit with the night.

At least I didn't hit the deer, he thought, then admonished himself. It was only a deer, for Christ's sake. He was on his way to hunt other men, or boys probably younger than himself, in Southeast Asia.

The enemy.

Charlie.

A deer was nothing. "Shit." He ground his teeth together and started again, shifting through the gears as the ruts widened into a gravel lane.

Glancing in the rearview, he didn't spy any other headlights cutting through the night.

Chase hadn't gotten into his car and followed.

Yet.

Maybe that was a good thing, considering how out of his mind Chase had been.

But then Rand worried. For half a heartbeat he wondered if he should pull a 180 and make certain his friend, hopped up on grass and acid, could drive himself home. Or wherever Chase was planning to go, even if it meant to break up with Harper.

Nah, this was Chase's life.

Let him deal with it.

Rand's conscience pricked a bit as he slowed, then turned onto the asphalt of the county road.

But Chase was his own person these days and Rand didn't want to risk another fight. Besides, he didn't believe Chase would go through with a half-baked plan to fake his own fuckin' death.

No way.

No how.

Chase was just confused.

And scared.

And blowing off steam.

He wasn't that off the rails.

Rand hit the gas again. He adjusted the radio again. The sound of Ben E. King singing "Stand by Me" filled the interior of the Jeep.

The lyrics hit hard.

He'd almost lost a friend tonight.

And all Chase had asked him to do was take care of Harper. How hard would that be? Impossible while he was in the service, but he could write her. Possibly call her. Do the best he could while Chase was . . . was what?

As he drove out of the hills and the lights of Almsville appeared through his windshield, Rand tried to convince himself that Chase wasn't serious about disappearing.

That was just too nuts.

Right?

Well, it was his problem now. Rand had his own. He was going to fuckin' Vietnam. So tonight, he decided, he'd celebrate freedom in the good old U.S. of A. Get shit-faced, if he had to.

He cranked up the radio, heard Jimi Hendrix wailing on his guitar.

A good start.

1988
The Present

Chapter 18

It was barely three in the afternoon, but already the sky was darkening, cloud cover thick though sunset was still a few hours off.

Harper was still pissed. She left her car on the street near the station, then walked several blocks to tamp down her temper and stopped at a café where once there had been an Italian restaurant.

Thankfully the café was nearly empty, the lunch crowd having dispersed. But it was warm inside and smelled of hot coffee and fragrant spices. Music was playing softly, and the café was decorated for the season with pumpkins on the counter, twinkling lights around a large chalkboard menu on the wall, and a life-sized papier-mâché witch on a real broomstick that swung from the high ceiling.

Unfortunately, Harper hated Halloween and anything associated with the holiday. She found it macabre rather than lighthearted and fun. Ever since that awful night on the terrace . . .

Don't go there.

She found a booth in the back corner and turned her thoughts to the present, such as it was. She needed time and space to cool off after her heated exchange with Rand Watkins—oh, excuse me, *Detective* Watkins—whatever that was all about.

Dealing with Rand had never been easy, not since grade school. Now that he was a cop—a full-fledged detective, no less—one with obvious suspicions about her, she was certain that dealing with him wasn't going to get any easier.

Well, too bad.

She'd given her statement.

She was done.

She did feel horrible about Cynthia Hunt, though. The woman may have despised Harper, even blamed her for Chase's disappearance, but the way Cynthia had died had been horrendous. And there was Levi, now having lost his brother and both his parents. Alone in the world.

Her heart was heavy at the thought. She ordered a glass of Chardonnay from a passing waitress, a slim redhead whose name tag read TAMI.

The wine came, and when pressed, Harper ordered the first thing she saw on the menu, a Caesar salad and cup of soup.

She was still thinking about Chase and his family when her order was delivered and, though she ate, she barely tasted anything. Her thoughts moved from the Hunt family tragedies to the interrogation—because that's what it felt like—with Rand Watkins. She was still bugged by their heated exchange.

So, really what had she expected when she'd gone to the station? That it would be all hearts and flowers? "Rand was right," she had to admit as she dipped her spoon into the clam chowder. They'd never been friends. Not twenty years ago and obviously not now.

But back then, in high school, he hadn't been an enemy.

Now, she feared, that had changed.

She conjured up images of Rand as a youth, when he'd hung out with Evan and Chase, then later became a soldier.

You can never go back.

The wayward thought echoed through her mind.

"Oh, shut up," she muttered and saw the approaching waitress react, suddenly backing away from the table.

"Sorry," she said quickly. "I was just . . . talking to myself." Geez, she probably looked like a mental case. Her face was bruised and bandaged, and here she was muttering to herself.

"You want another glass of wine?" Tami asked.

Though it was tempting, Harper shook her head. One more might well lead to another. "Just the check, please."

Dear God, she needed to turn her head around.

She had to deal with real life, and the day had nearly slipped away.

She planned to pick up much-needed groceries, go back to the island, find the damned cat, shower the day and night off, then call Dawn and bring her up to speed.

Tomorrow she would tackle the unpacking and start organizing the house. There were utility companies to call, repairmen to find, and housekeepers and gardeners to contact.

She left enough cash on the table to cover the bill and a tip, then stepped outside to find a fine October mist falling on already damp sidewalks, wet leaves collecting in the gutters, the day gloomy and cold, the night creeping in. Her head was bare, so she flipped up the hood of her raincoat, her boots splashing through small puddles. As she rounded a final corner, she spied the police station, a conglomerate of three buildings that took up half a city block, windows bright in the gathering night. Near the glass door in the front of the building stood a flagpole, Old Glory drooping in the drizzle, lit by surrounding street lamps.

Spying her car in the adjacent lot, she fished her keys from her purse and headed straight for her Volvo. As she unlocked the car, she caught her own reflection in the window of the driver's door, a shimmering image distorted by raindrops sliding down the glass.

And behind her, over her shoulder, something moved.

A person?

She turned just as she heard a female voice say, "Harper? Harper Reed?"

"Yes?"

"I thought so!" the woman said. She was small and compact, a long wool coat cinched at her tiny waist, a hood covering her head. "Wait a minute. It's Harper Prescott, right? You're married now."

"Was," she said, thinking the woman was vaguely familiar. "I'm sorry. Do I know you?"

"Oh yeah, you do! It's me!" the woman said, offering a wide toothy smile. "Rhonda!"

"Rhonda?" Harper repeated, trying to place the name and face.

"Rhonda Simms—well, now, but you knew me as Rhonda De-Angelo."

"Rhonda DeAngelo." Faint bells were ringing in Harper's mind: warning bells.

"Yeah, yeah! We were in chemistry together as juniors. Remember? Seventh period? Mr. Latham's class? I cheated off of you all the time," Rhonda admitted, stepping into the light. Suddenly her features—big, Kewpie doll eyes, rosy cheeks, and pointed chin came into clearer view. Harper's gut tightened. She did remember. But the girl she recalled was a dishwater blond with straight hair, braces, and a bad case of acne in high school. She'd worn cat-eye glasses and had been quiet, a listener.

This was a newer version. With straight teeth, blue eyes, clear skin, and platinum curls sprouting out from beneath the rim of her hood, this Rhonda was definitely more confident and forthcoming. "Sorry about the cheating, but I just didn't get it. At all!" She flashed Harper what was clearly meant to be an abashed smile.

"Doesn't matter now."

"No, I suppose it doesn't, but I'd love to talk to you. Maybe get a drink? Or coffee? Catch up?"

"Now?" Harper asked, remembering the petite little girl who slithered around corners, listening to gossip, pretending she wasn't trying to overhear what anyone was saying. Harper had always considered her a bit of a snake. So what was she doing lurking in the parking lot of the police department?

"Now would be great!" Rhonda enthused. "I mean if you're up to it. Are you okay?"

"I'm fine. Oh." She was talking about the bandages. Inadvertently, Harper touched her chin.

"I heard what you did last night," Rhonda was saying.

Already. "Did you? How?"

"Oh, come on, you know. Almsville might have grown in the last decade or so, but it's still a small town. Gossip spreads like wildfire."

And you're probably holding the gasoline can. Harper didn't say it, but she was getting the gist of what was going on here. Rhonda had been the editor of the school newspaper back in the day. So now? "Let me guess, you're a reporter."

"Well . . . yes!" she said, unable to keep the enthusiasm from her voice and her gaze from the gauze on Harper's face. *The Twilight Tribune.*"

Crap! The local paper. And Rhonda had either followed her here or somehow discovered that she would be at the police station. Had Rand spilled the beans? Unlikely. He'd been closemouthed in high school, and as a cop he had an obligation to keep things private. But who knew?

"And I'd love to do a story about the island," Rhonda said, gearing up. "And about your family and how they ended up with it. There's just so much interesting history there, so I thought a series about it, and your family and you, of course, now that you've inherited it."

"How do you know that?"

"Public knowledge."

That much was true, so she shouldn't have been surprised. There had been a lot of talk about the dispersal of the Dixon fortune at the time of Gram's death. Some of her assets had been donated to the university, some to St. Catherine's Hospital, and the bulk, including the island, left to Harper.

And of course Rhonda would want to dig further. She'd probably probe about what had happened the night Chase disappeared and her grandmother died. All part of the island's "interesting history." At the time her father had shipped Harper off to California to live with a second cousin of his so that she would avoid excessive and seemingly unending interviews by the press and possibly the police and somehow, hopefully, regain her anonymity. He and Marcia had arrived a few weeks later.

But she refused to dwell on all that now. And she certainly wasn't going to discuss it with a reporter, any reporter. "Wait a minute. How did you know I'd be here?" she said, motioning toward the police station.

Rhonda ignored the question. "There's talk that you might put the island up for sale. So a feature on it would be great publicity, you know. That island's got a lot of history, and it's unique, the only one on all of Lake Twilight."

"How long have you been waiting here for me?"

"A while."

"You didn't answer my question. How did you know I was here?"

Rhonda started to hedge. "Well, I—"

"From Beth Alexander?" Harper guessed.

"No, she didn't tell me you would be here, but she did mention that Detective Watkins had tried to talk to you at the hospital."

"And—?" Harper was getting angry.

"Your car has California plates."

"That you checked somehow? Ran my plates somehow?"

"No. No. It was just a lucky guess."

Harper couldn't believe it. Nor could she believe that she was standing in the rain discussing it. "So you waited for me?"

"I figured you needed the car."

"We're done."

"No wait. The article would be good publicity for you, for the island."

"What? No."

"Just listen. So much has happened there! And just last night you saved Cynthia Hunt from drowning."

Uh-oh. So this is where all the interest is coming from, Harper thought as the rain peppered the ground and pinged against the Volvo's roof and hood. "I don't know what you heard, but I didn't save anyone. Look, it's raining. I've got to go."

"But you got hurt," Rhonda said. Again, she was staring at the bandage on Harper's chin.

"Doesn't matter."

"And Cynthia Hunt—"

"I didn't save her," Harper cut in angrily. Would this woman never quit? "I really have to go."

Rhonda wasn't taking the hint. "I know, she passed on earlier and God rest her soul, but you're the one who saw her last, who tried to get her off that boat before it burned to a crisp or sank. Dear God in heaven, I *can't* imagine."

Harper opened the car door. "As I said, I'm leaving."

"But wait!" There was a strident edge to Rhonda's voice. "Isn't that what happened?"

"Something like that." Harper slid behind the wheel.

"I'll call you," Rhonda said, a little bit of panic in her voice. "We can have lunch. I'll buy. Or dinner or drinks. Here's my card." She forced a business card into Harper's hand.

Dear God, she really wanted this.

"I really don't have anything to say." Harper tried to pull the door shut, but Rhonda held it open.

"You know, Harper," she insisted, "people would love to hear your story."

"My story?" Harper repeated, her anger rising.

"You were the last person, or one of them, to see Chase Hunt and he's still missing, and now his mother is . . . well, gone, and who knows what happened there."

"I don't," Harper said, peeved as she jerked the car door closed, slamming it hard and swearing under her breath. Rain still dripping from her hood, she dropped the wet business card onto the passenger seat and started the engine. "What a pain," she murmured as she shoved the gearshift into reverse and hit the gas, driving backward around the tiny woman just as Rhonda found the good sense to back off.

Thankfully.

Harper hadn't liked Rhonda in high school, and so far her feelings hadn't changed. In fact, her dislike had definitely sharpened.

At the edge of the parking lot, she slowed to let a passing bus go by and checked her rearview mirror.

Rhonda was jogging to a dark sedan.

Once the bus had passed, Harper gunned it. She didn't need the local reporter following her, had experienced enough of that years before when her boyfriend went missing and Harper's grandmother, the wealthiest woman in all of Almsville, suddenly died on her watch. There had been incessant phone calls and photographers collecting near the gate. They'd been relentless as they snapped pictures of the gargoyles, the long bridge, and the house on the island. Some of the more aggressive reporters had come by boat, docking and taking pictures of the back of the house, trying to get shots of Harper, the teenaged girl somehow involved in her boyfriend's disappearance and grandmother's death. Hence, the decision to send her to California.

At that time the tragedies of her family had been unearthed all over again—stories in the papers and on the local television stations revisiting her mother's early demise and her brother's accident.

It wasn't going to happen again. Not from Rhonda Frickin' DeAngelo or whatever her name was now!

She drove through the town's streets, past the Nazarene church and the town square, a city park three blocks off the lake. Many of the businesses had changed. The Rexall Drug Store was now a pizzeria, and the auto parts store housed a garden center, but some of the mainstays survived, and she had to smile when she saw the marquee for Van's Groceries, a friendly mom and pop corner shop that had been in Almsville forever.

She and Beth had ridden their bikes to Van's for ice cream bars and popsicles when she was in grade school. They would prop their bikes on the bench outside the screen door of the shop, buy their treats, and eat them on that same bench as they swatted yellow jackets away and watched the traffic slow for the Stop sign at the crosswalk.

Evan had sometimes deigned to ride with them, though he'd been always screwing around, riding his bike in front of theirs, usually with no hands, showing off and sometimes throwing firecrackers. Beth had always been enthralled with his antics. Harper had thought he was a pain until their lives had been turned inside out.

Evan had been her rock when Mama died . . .

Her throat closed, and she blinked back tears as she cut the engine. She didn't know, nor had she ever gotten any real answers regarding her own mother's death.

Her family had always been tight-lipped about it.

Harper had only been a child when tragedy had struck and Mama had "gone to heaven" as Gram had insisted, but she'd seen her. That night on the dock. Through the haze of a fever and codeine, she'd witnessed what she now knew was her mother, wavering on the edge of the dock, a ghostly figure on Halloween night.

But her father would never speak of what happened.

And Gram, until her death, had been tight-lipped, as if she were protecting Harper somehow.

From what? she wondered as a child.

But the answer was simple: They hadn't wanted her to know the truth.

Chapter 19

Before she got out of the car, Harper checked her rearview mirror to make certain Rhonda hadn't followed her. It seemed unlikely. Rhonda was a reporter, not a stalker. But who would've thought she would have tracked Harper down by her license plate number and then sat in her car waiting for Harper to show up?

Seeing that the coast was clear, she dashed into the store, which, of course, had changed in the past two decades. But the old wooden floorboards still creaked, the apples and oranges were stacked in the woven baskets, even the oversized ice-cream freezer was still in its spot, next to a wall of newer glass cases. The deli counter displayed a selection of cured meats and cheeses in the case while a huge, silver meat slicer was at the ready on a table behind the counter.

Though the merchandise had changed over the years, the old grocery seemed familiar. Like home.

She bought some basic necessities, including some microwave dinners and paper products and a six-pack of soda before returning to her Volvo and climbing inside. She checked the parking lot and the cars on the street, as she half expected to find Rhonda DeAngelo Whatever tailing her.

As if she were in some spy movie.

"Get over yourself," she said aloud when her wagon rattled past the gargoyles and crossed the bridge. Night had fallen, and the drizzle had turned to rain.

"Jinx," she called, scanning the paved area and the bushes as she juggled the two grocery bags to the house. Where was the damned cat? She hadn't spied him on either side of the bridge or near the house but told herself he would show up, if only to get out of the rain. He was a California cat, used to basking in the sun and climbing lemon trees. That said, if felines really did have nine lives, Jinx had only given up one or two that she knew of.

Not that she believed all that nonsense. Nonetheless, one could hope.

Inside the old house, she unpacked the groceries, then ran a cloth over the inside of the refrigerator before shoving items inside. The whole place needed a thorough, professional cleaning. A.S.A.P.

With an eye out for Jinx, she opened a bag of Doritos and checked the countertop microwave, an Amana Radarange, one of the first on the market. Luckily, it still worked.

Eating chips from the sack, she walked through the butler's pantry and turned on lights to search the rooms. *There are a million places a cat could hide in this house*, she thought, walking into the parlor. Her gaze traveled over the couches and chairs and her grandmother's favorite chaise longue.

Nothing.

The cat wasn't curled on one of the cushions, nor was he hiding between the legs of a table or lurking between the damned dolls propped everywhere. She glanced over to the curio case, tables, lamps, and bookcases but found no hint of Jinx.

He'll come back.

He always does.

But this was a new place. Unfamiliar.

Determined not to dwell on his fate, she walked to the window. She had no reason to look through the telescope but found herself sitting in the chair next to it and swinging the eyepiece close to her face. As she ate the chips, she peered through the high-powered lens and concentrated on the houses across the lake, all five on Fox Point.

She started with the Hunt cottage, which was at the tip of the point. Dark. No one inside. And no boat peeking out of the open garage door of the boathouse. Of course. Most of the Hunts' cruiser was now in charred pieces at the bottom of the lake. Her stomach twisted as she thought about Cynthia again. Still holding a triangular chip, she crossed herself and sent up a little prayer for the woman who had cursed her own soul to hell.

She wondered about Levi. He'd surprised her by showing up at the hospital, and for a second she'd been thrown back to that long-ago winter. He'd been the one who had helped her that night when Chase disappeared, even tried to keep her secrets. But they ran deeper than he knew. She didn't want to think about him or his brother or their complicated lives, so she moved the lens to the Leonetti place where Beth was living with her husband.

Unlike the two dark houses, the split level with its bank of windows was lit as bright as a Christmas tree. On the main level, Beth was in the kitchen, hovering over the sink, a phone pressed to her ear, and at the opposite end of the house, a light was on, though Harper saw no one, only recognized a poster for the movie *First Blood*. So this was probably Beth's son's room now. Max, she remembered. The window to this room was high, cutting her visibility.

What was wrong with her? Why was she spying when she was dead tired, her stomach growling, her face aching?

She was about to turn away when she noticed movement in the lower level, a shadow slinking through the dark recesses of the house.

Harper adjusted the focus as the figure stepped from the back of the house, beyond the staircase. She remembered that area. It had been Mr. Leonetti's work space, a windowless, concrete bunker of sorts, cut into the side of the hill under the garage. Mrs. Leonetti had always sworn she was going to make the area a wine cellar, but her husband had insisted he needed a place for his tools and workbench.

The shadow slipped through an open doorway to what had once been the Leonettis' rec room.

A light snapped on, flooding the room with illumination from the same fluorescent fixtures Harper remembered.

The room was still walled in the wood paneling from the 1960s, but the long, low couches surrounding the stereo/TV console had been replaced by a huge desk with a personal computer, a drafting table, and filing cabinets. Even the ping-pong table and super-cool foosball game were no longer front and center by the slider. Instead, she saw a rack of hand weights in varying sizes tucked into a corner with a rowing machine and stationary bike positioned closer to the windows.

Obviously the space had become Craig's office and personal gym.

He had put on muscle since the last time she'd seen him on the night he'd wheeled Gram out on a stretcher. Now his shoulders, thick neck, and biceps suggested he used the rowing machine and free weights. Instead of a floppy Beatles' cut from high school, he now sported a curly mullet, cropped short on the sides but long enough in the back to brush his shoulders.

He closed the door behind him and took the time to lock it, all in full view due to the floor-to-ceiling windows and wide sliding door that opened to the exterior deck.

Intrigued, and telling herself she should turn away, Harper instead adjusted the viewfinder for better clarity.

She expected him to get onto the bike, but instead he double-checked that the door was locked, then crossed the room to a dartboard mounted on the wall. With a flip of a switch, the cover slid to one side to reveal a safe. Again, he glanced over his shoulder as if double-checking that he was alone. Then he spun the safe's dial several times.

The safe opened.

He reached inside.

And came out with a pistol.

What?

Harper stopped eating.

It's not that unusual, she told herself, but she still kept her eyes riveted on Craig. And the gun.

Furtively, he glanced toward the glass doors, as if he'd sensed her. He tilted his head, staring upward at the mansion.

For a second she thought he was staring straight at her. As if he'd felt her hiding in the darkness, observing his every move.

Which, she supposed, she was.

Her heart dropped, and she told herself that nothing he was doing was any of her business. So he had a gun? So what? Didn't she, after all?

She should look away.

But couldn't.

Mesmerized, her eye still glued to the telescope, Harper watched as Craig reached inside once more and retrieved something—she couldn't tell what—that fit in the palm of his hand. A packet of ammo, maybe? Or something else? He closed the safe and replaced the dartboard, setting the gun and other item down before retrieving a black sweatshirt from the handlebars of the exercise bike. He yanked the sweatshirt over his head, adjusted the hood, and scooped up the pistol and smaller item.

With one final look at the door to the room, he moved to the slider and stepped barefoot onto the wet deck where unused patio furniture, boxes, and firewood were stacked. As if he were expecting an ambush, he advanced slowly, half crouched, easing stealthily across the wooden planks, the long-barreled pistol raised in both hands as his gaze swept across the dark water.

The gun.

She recognized it.

It looked similar to her grandfather's handgun, but it was too dark to see the grip, to confirm its pearl handle.

Like the one in the cabinet?

Or was she imagining things? All guns were similar, and from this distance in the dark, even with the high-powered telescope she couldn't tell. Just because she was missing one didn't mean that Craig Alexander had it.

"What're you doing?" she whispered as a light flicked on upstairs, in the room with the poster, the bedroom she assumed belonged to Max, Craig and Beth's son. She even caught a glimpse of the top of Max's head in the high windows. Curly blond hair flopped over a high forehead as he walked across the room, then disappeared as if he'd either sat down or flopped onto his bed.

Fascinated, though she couldn't explain why, Harper swiveled the telescope.

Beth was still in the kitchen, chopping something on the kitchen counter and watching a nearby small black and white TV. She seemed oblivious to her husband's surreptitious movements.

What does it matter? Why do you care?

She couldn't explain why she was intrigued, but she couldn't stop and turned her attention to the dock, but Craig had disappeared. She swung the lens to his office again, expecting he'd gone back inside, but no, he wasn't visible and the slider was still closed, the room as he'd left it.

So?

Big deal.

But her stomach tightened as she searched the darkened dock and water.

"Where are you?" she whispered aloud and was about to turn away when she caught a small beam of light at the edge of the Alexanders' dock. A flashlight? She couldn't tell. As quickly as it appeared, it died.

Squinting at the area, she could barely make out a man—Craig, presumably—stepping into a canoe that was tied to his dock, then shoving off. For a second or two she had trouble following him in the night-shrouded lake, but in a heartbeat she caught sight of him again as he turned on the flashlight for a second before cutting the light once more.

"What the hell are you doing, Craig?"

As the canoe passed behind the houses, she caught sight of his silhouette, a dark image cast against the vaporous incandescence of the street lamp on the other side of the Hunts' house. In the soft bluish glow, she watched him as he stepped lightly onto the Hunts' dock. He looped the canoe's mooring rope around a cleat, then hopped onto the wooden planks.

Silently, her Doritos forgotten, she followed his every movement.

Stopping at the edge of the back door to the house, he reached up along the sill and her heart nearly stopped. She knew he was searching for a key, the same key she had used decades ago when she and Chase had met in secret. Her stomach nose-dived at the memory. "Oh God," she whispered as he let himself in and didn't bother with lights.

The flashlight flickered on again, and she followed its shifting beam from the kitchen through a short hallway before it vanished. The house was dark for a few seconds, then the bobbing light reappeared in the upstairs bedroom. Tom and Cynthia's room.

Why?

He cut the light again, and before her eye could adjust to the darkness, the flashlight flickered briefly downstairs once more. He slipped out the back door, locked it, and seemed to replace the key on the ledge above. Then, quick as a cat, he hurried across the deck, dropped into the canoe, untied it, and was lost in the darkness once more.

Odd, she thought.

Maybe more than odd.

Something dark . . .

She checked the Alexanders' house and caught sight of the kid's head as he left his room. Beth was still in the kitchen. She took a bottle of beer from the refrigerator, then headed toward the stairs.

Oh God, Craig was going to get caught.

Good.

Harper tightened the viewfinder just as Beth met her son at the top of the stairs leading to the basement. She paused to say something to the kid.

Craig was still outside, tying up the boat.

Beth started down the stairs.

Harper's pulse jumped, and she bit her lip. She couldn't imagine that Beth knew what her husband was up to. He'd been so furtive as he'd left.

Craig hopped onto the dock and hurried to the door.

His wife was out of sight, descending the stairs.

Harper's pulse elevated.

Was Beth going to find him coming inside and ask what he'd been doing? Or did she know already?

Somehow Harper wanted that confrontation.

Under the bright lights, Craig was already at the door to his office, unlocking it, before nearly leaping to his desk. He managed to tear off the sweatshirt and stash it in a drawer as he settled into his desk chair.

Beth opened the door just as he was picking up a file folder and pen, pretending to be reading the contents of the folder while leaning back in his chair, clicking the pen as if distracted.

He wasn't.

In an instant Craig Alexander transformed from clandestine cat burglar to concerned businessman and loving husband. He looked up from the manila folder and grinned as Beth held up a beer. Nodding in appreciation, he set the folder aside and they talked a bit—though, of course, Harper couldn't hear any of the conversation. She watched with bated breath as Beth gestured toward the outside, and for a second Harper was certain Beth had caught him coming and going, but as they stepped onto the deck, that didn't seem to be the case. Instead, Beth directed his gaze across the lake, to the island. Harper didn't move a muscle.

Beth motioned toward the manor, her hand moving from one side to the next, as if discussing the finer and lesser points of the place. She was a real estate agent, after all, and appeared to be giving her would-be contractor/husband the details of a possible job. Craig hooked one arm over her shoulders and, with his free hand, sipped his beer.

There was a chance that they were not discussing the pros and cons of the island. Harper wasn't certain Beth was lobbying for him to make repairs to this house. Maybe they were talking about Harper's return to Almsville and the horror of the night before, though it didn't seem so.

After a few minutes, Beth took her leave. Harper watched as Beth returned to the kitchen, opened the oven door, then checked her watch. Their son was nowhere to be seen.

But Craig was at his desk again, leaning back in his desk chair while he took a long pull from his beer.

The telescope was so strong she could read the bottle's label, as well as catch the headlines of the January edition of *Field and Stream* in a nearby magazine rack. A buck with a large rack of antlers was the cover photo.

So where was the pistol he'd retrieved from the wall safe—the one that might be the twin of the one she found?

Was it in the pocket of his sweatshirt, now wadded up beneath in a desk drawer?

Or left in the canoe?

Or planted somewhere at the Hunts' house?

If so, why?

She bit her lower lip and swung her telescope, sweeping Craig's office/gym again.

Yes, the telescope caught all the minute details of the room, but it sure didn't explain what he'd been doing.

"Nothing good," she told herself as she saw him peer through the glass door again, angling his head so that his gaze swung upward and across the lake. To the island. To the house she was in. To the very room where she sat in the dark.

Craig reached for the phone, then wedged the receiver between his shoulder and ear. Still staring, he punched out a number.

A second later, the house phone began to ring.

Chapter 20

Harper's pulse pounded, and her stomach ground nervously. Had Craig seen her spying?

Was he calling to warn her to mind her own business?

What would she say?

Could she deny it?

Or maybe he was going to ask her about fixing up the place?

She hurried into the kitchen, her hip protesting as she snagged the receiver from the wall phone. "Hello?" she said breathlessly, her heart in her throat.

"Mom?" Her daughter's voice stopped her cold.

It was Dawn.

Dawn was calling.

Not Craig Alexander.

No one had seen her spying.

"Hi, honey," she said, sagging against the wall in relief.

"Jesus, Mom, what the fu—hell is going on?"

Harper's relief was short-lived as she heard the angst and the anger in Dawn's voice.

"Why didn't you call me and tell me that you were in the hospital?" Dawn demanded. "Holy shi—crap, Mom! You should have called me immediately! Instead, I get this call from some lame-ass reporter!"

"Rhonda DeAngelo." The woman worked fast. What had she said her name was? Smith or . . . "Simms. Her name is Simms now."

"Like I care! It doesn't matter, Mom," Dawn snapped. "God!" Then she took in a deep breath before adding, "Maybe. Maybe that was it. I don't remember, but she told me. Yeah, maybe, Rhoda or Rhonda Something. I'm not sure. I didn't really catch her name. I was too freaked out! I wasn't thinking straight. She told me something about you and a woman who died in a fire *on* the lake and I couldn't say anything. I just hung up on her and called the gatehouse, but there was no answer. Nothing, just some dead-sounding voice saying the number was no longer in service."

"Oh, honey, I'm so sorry—"

"So I tried this one for the lake house that you gave me like a million years ago. I didn't even know if the phones there still worked. You know it was really embarrassing for some random reporter to be the one to tell me you were in the hospital!"

"I was going to call you."

"When?" Dawn wanted to know, and Harper could imagine her eyebrows slamming together in frustration. Brown eyes peeking out from dyed black hair, skin as white as alabaster, black lipstick—all part of the whole Goth thing she'd been going through. "Jesus Christ, Mom, if—"

"Hey! Language!"

Dawn let out an audible puff of disbelief. "Like you're religious or never swear!"

"Okay, that's fair, I do swear, but I am religious, it's just my own personal religion, my thing with God."

Dawn huffed, "If you say so."

"I do."

"The thing is," Dawn went on, "I shouldn't have had to hear from some stupid reporter that you were involved in some kind of boat fire or something! I mean I could have come up there. It's only a couple of hours, you know. It's not like I'm still in California."

That much was true. Dawn was now at the university in Eugene.

Dawn added, "Isn't it bad enough that Grandpa's in the hospital, but now you?"

"I'm fine, and obviously out, or you wouldn't have reached me here. And I saw Grandpa today," Harper said, trying to calm her daughter. "He's going to be okay."

"And I should take your word for it?"

"Why would I lie?"

"You tell me, Mom," Dawn shot back. "There are lies of commission and lies of omission, isn't that what you always say?"

"I guess."

Silence from the other end of the line, but at least she hadn't hung up.

"I'm sorry. Okay? You're right. You should have heard it from me. Not a reporter. I just got home about an hour ago, and I was going to call you. I just hadn't gotten around to it yet. But, as I said everyone's fine—"

"Except for the dead woman!"

"Well, yeah. Of course." Harper sighed and refused to think of Cynthia Hunt's horrid demise. "I know. It's sad. Tragic."

"And weird!"

"Very." But Dawn didn't know the half of it. The history.

"So what happened?"

If she only knew. Leaning a hip against the kitchen counter, Harper tried to ignore the headache that was starting to pound behind her eyes. It didn't help that her gaze landed on the untouched ramekins she'd positioned near the back door for Jinx. As best she could, she told Dawn about the day before, how she'd barely gotten here when she spied the fire on the lake. She downplayed her own horror at recognizing Cynthia Hunt.

"You knew her?" Dawn demanded.

"She was the mother of one of my friends." Two actually, but she didn't need to go into details.

"Why would she do that? I mean . . . it's awful and crazy and . . ."

"Who knows?" Harper said, wrapping the coils of the phone cord around her wrist. "I think she was ill."

"No duh! And you weren't even going to call me?"

"Of course I was. I told you."

"When?" Dawn demanded.

"Tonight. After I went through the shower and had dinner."

A pause.

Harper relented. "I should have called you first. I just didn't want to worry you."

"Well, you did."

"I'm sorry."

Mollified somewhat, her ruffled feathers smoothed, Dawn asked, "And you're sure you're okay?" She actually sounded concerned.

"Beat up and bruised, but yeah, I'll be fine. No permanent damage." Again, that was a bit of a lie. After witnessing the horror of what happened to Cynthia Hunt, Harper doubted she'd ever be the same. She changed the subject. "So, how're *you* doing?"

"Oh, fine, I guess."

"School?"

"I said, 'fine.' But you know, it's school."

"College. More fun than high school."

"If you say so. How does Jinx like it on the island? I bet he loves it."

Harper's stomach knotted. Oh God, no. She forced a lilt to her voice. "He's getting used to the place. Exploring." Not *exactly* a lie.

"Is he making friends with any of Great-Grandma's cats?"

Dawn had heard stories.

"Oh no. Those cats are long gone, I'm afraid," Harper said and glanced out the window to the front of the house and the rose garden where so many of Gram's favorite felines had their final resting place.

"So sad."

"It was a long time ago. So," Harper said, "are we good now?"

"You and me? I guess. But I'm still pissed off—er, ticked off that you didn't call me when you ended up in the hospital. And you would be, too, if it were the other way around. It's not like I'm five, you know. I'm a grown-up."

Not quite, Harper thought but nodded to herself and said, "Point taken."

"And I told Dad."

Harper froze at the mention of Joel. "You didn't."

"He has the right to know."

Did he? Harper didn't think so. She suddenly wanted to throttle her kid. She closed her eyes and mentally counted to ten. "We're divorced," she reminded Dawn.

"I know. But he still loves you."

Harper bit back a sharp response to that. Dawn, of course, didn't know the ins and outs of her parents' marriage and wasn't privy to the lies and truth of it all. She probably never would be.

"We're still a family," Dawn said a little more loudly. "That's what you told me."

Harper winced at that. "Yeah, I remember."

"So he should know."

Even though he's with his girlfriend? Harper bit her tongue. There was no reason to bring Melanie into the conversation. "I just don't want him, or you, to worry. Nothing serious happened to me last night," Harper insisted with conviction, despite the fact that the headache was thundering and her chin was throbbing and she was dead on her feet.

"Sure." Dawn didn't sound convinced. "I'll talk to you soon. And you can call me anytime. You don't have to leave a message on the machine. I've got a pager, and the number is—"

"Wait! A pager?" Harper repeated. "Like what doctors use or . . . or drug dealers?"

"No! I mean, well, yeah, probably. I don't know. But everyone's starting to get them here at school. And they work great. Through a service, but it's cool."

"You pay for the service?"

"Dad does. He knows. He's got one, too."

Of course. Joel always had the latest gadgets, anything bright and shiny that caught his eye. Including women.

"So, this way you can reach me anytime. So, like, if I'm out of town, you won't have to wait for me to get home and go through my messages and call you back. I'll know you want to talk to me when you call—your number will show up on the screen."

"I don't know."

"You want the number or not?" Dawn sounded exasperated.

"Yeah. Yeah. Of course. Hold on." Harper stretched the phone cord so she could reach the junk drawer. "I'm looking for a pen." She opened the drawer and pawed through paper clips, old lists, keys, cat collars, and even several books of S&H green stamps, which her grandmother, like everyone else in the sixties and seventies had collected. "Just a sec." She tried several pens that didn't work before she located a pencil that was more than a stub. "Go ahead," she said, cradling the receiver between her shoulder and head as Dawn rattled off a number. "Got it," she said, scratching the digits onto a book of matches from a steak house that no longer existed.

"You really should get one."

"A pager?"

"Yes!"

"I'll think about it."

"Good. I'd like that." A pause. Then, "Hey, I just saw the time. Oh God. Sorry, Mom. Gotta run."

"Love you," Harper said, but the line was already dead, her daughter having hung up.

She held the receiver in her hands, then finally replaced it. A pager? Really? She found a bottle of Anacin in her purse and walked back to the parlor, where she tossed back two tablets and washed them down with the left-over drink from the night before. It burned on the way down again, but she poured herself another, which she drank far too quickly. On her third drink, she reminded herself to sip.

She told herself *not* to pour another as she felt like warmed-over crap and eyed the telescope again. Looking through it would only get her into trouble. She had no right to peer inside other people's lives.

And yet . . .

She couldn't help but lean down and train the telescope in the direction of the Alexanders. They were seated around the table, the three of them in the nook off the kitchen. Nothing going on there. And the Hunts' place was dark. She moved the telescope again to focus on the Watkins' A-frame. The lights were on, shining brightly from the peak of the windows at the top of the A-frame and down the back side to the floor below to the bank of windows that illuminated the kitchen area and part of the living room.

She wondered if Rand was home, and just as she did, she saw the top of his head and then his body as he climbed the stairs into the loft. He'd pushed a desk up to the glass, so that he could sit and stare out at the water, and though he didn't know it, he was facing her as well. His features seemed less harsh in the soft glow of the desk lamp, and she observed the brush of his eyelashes against his cheek as he opened an accordion file folder that seemed ancient. Slowly, he pulled out a sheaf of papers tucked inside. The pages were yellowed, obviously very old.

"What're you up to?" she whispered, watching the man who had questioned her at the police station, the detective who had once sworn he hated the fact that his dad was a cop, the one person she suspected of knowing what really happened to Chase Hunt.

How ironic.

As she viewed him, she saw Rand frown and sit on a corner of his desk as he began to read, and she watched him sort through the pages slowly, his eyes scanning the yellowed sheets.

Funny, she'd never noticed his eyelashes before, though earlier today she'd been reminded that his eyes were golden brown, his cheekbones as sharp as they'd been in his youth, only his jaw darker from beard shadow. Also he bore a tiny scar above his eyebrow that she was certain he hadn't had in high school.

There had been a time in junior high when she'd been teased mercilessly that he had a crush on her. They'd even shared a kiss, compliments of a taboo game of Spin the Bottle at a seventh-grade party. Her first kiss. Maybe his, too. She didn't know. Didn't care.

A smile touched the corner of her mouth as she focused and caught sight of the newspaper clipping he'd been reading, holding up to his face. As he spun in his chair, she was able to barely make out the headline over his shoulder. Then he tacked the article to a bulletin board, and she could see the headline clearly. although she remembered it.

TEEN GIRL SUSPECTED IN GRANDMOTHER'S DEATH.

She gasped, her heart turning to stone. "You son of a bitch," she muttered, all kind memories of Rand Watkins withering quickly. There were other articles and notes tacked to the board, most of which she could read due to the intense magnification of the telescope.

He rotated back to the desk and glanced up then, to look out the window as he ran a hand through his black hair. His eyes narrowed, and she wondered if he could see her through the panes and across the distance, but she doubted it. She didn't think he was focusing on anything nearby, anything real. No, he seemed caught up in his thoughts, staring into the middle distance but searching inwardly, possibly returning to the night when his best friend vanished and the only person he could blame was Harper.

Angry, she backed away from the window and told herself to let it go. Rand was only doing his job.

"Really?" she asked aloud, then forced herself to turn away. The events playing out on the other side of the lake were already plaguing her thoughts. She couldn't quite forget that Rand appeared to be investigating her, and Craig Alexander was doing what? Hiding a weapon he didn't want his family to find? Planting evidence of some crime in the Hunt house? Returning a gun he'd stolen or been given?

And what about Levi?

Hadn't Beth said he might be moving back to the house on the lake? She knew so little about him. Only what he'd divulged when he'd come to the hospital. The truth was she hadn't kept up with him, had thought it for the best.

But she'd probably been wrong about that, just as she'd been wrong about so many things.

"Get out of the past," she told herself. She needed to leave the telescopes and binoculars and such alone.

She wasn't a voyeur, for God's sake!

She spent the next few hours finishing another couple of drinks while unpacking, making lists of things she needed, and searching for the elusive cat, which was nearly impossible. There were so many hiding spots, nooks and crannies, attics and basements, three staircases, the turret and apartment over the garage. Then there was the island itself with its myriad of paths crisscrossing through overgrown landscaping and towering fir trees. Not to mention the boathouse, tram, and dock. She could hunt for the elusive feline from here to eternity and never find him. Though she didn't like it, if Jinx didn't want to be found, she probably would never see him again.

That thought sat like a stone in her heart, and no matter how many times she admonished herself to "buck up," as Gram had often told her, she was still worried. She went to the kitchen where she opened a can of tuna and added the flakes of fish to Jinx's bowl as extra enticement for the cat to reappear.

But no amount of searching, calling, and coaxing could convince the sly feline to show himself. For now, she gave up and concentrated on unpacking the car.

Harper brought the last load inside, adding to the pile at the base of the back staircase. Once the car was unloaded, she took several trips up and down the stairs with her suitcases.

On the last trip down the stairs for her sleeping bag and pillow, she considered a final nightcap. Why not? It had been a long, nerve-wracking day. "Just one," she said and sipped the drink while slowly walking through the rooms, hoping to get a glimpse of Jinx, though she now believed he wasn't inside. Otherwise his food would have been touched.

Unless he somehow got locked into a closet or behind the door of the staircase or inside a cupboard.

But she hadn't opened any.

No, he had to be outside. Tomorrow, when it was light, she would go on an all-out search for him, and if he didn't come back in another day, she would start knocking on neighbors' doors. She looked out the window, willing him to be on the terrace, but there was nothing but the dark, cloud-covered night, not a star visible, the lake a wide, black expanse, the houses on the far shore looking distant.

The old timbers creaked, and she felt a little shiver.

She wasn't afraid of being alone. Never had been. And the dark didn't frighten her. This house, massive as it was, with all its dark corners, myriad of rooms, and winding staircases had never felt foreboding or unwelcoming, but tonight it seemed cold. Unnerving.

Maybe it was because she was on her own for the first time in her life. Her separation and divorce from Joel had transpired over the last two years, the final papers signed just last July after she'd visited him at his home in Bend with the thought that they might give the marriage one more try. It hadn't worked out, and she had the pain in her hip to remind her of that fact.

Then, just last month, after two years at a junior college in California, Dawn had transferred to the University of Oregon in Eugene, the very college Chase had attended two decades earlier.

So she was alone.

In this huge house with all of its ghosts.

"Memories," she reminded herself. "Not ghosts." She closed her eyes for a second and gathered herself, then decided she could use another drink. She ended up restraining herself. No reason to get wasted, right?

As she capped the decanter, she wondered if she could ever really live here again.

All by herself?

In this huge mansion?

She would have to hire housekeepers and gardeners just to maintain the place.

It seemed beyond ridiculous.

So why not sell? She could rebuild the cottage.

It all sounded overwhelming tonight.

Better to tackle it in the morning, as she was tired, the drink hitting her a little harder than expected, and she wasn't in any condition to make life-changing plans. "Tomorrow," she told herself and headed upstairs, nearly stumbling over one of the dolls propped near the lowest step. She almost kicked the baby doll with its curly brown hair and outstretched arms out of the way, but she thought better of it when she recognized Toodles. She remembered Gram had told her how special the doll was.

"I bought this one because it reminded me of you," she said once, when Harper was about six. Delighted, Gram pointed out the plump doll's features. "See here, she's got brown hair and blue eyes, just like you."

Now Harper looked the doll over. "I don't see the resemblance," she admitted, then plopped Toodles down on a side table between a Tiffany lamp and a heavy glass ashtray. "Stay," she said, before starting up the stairs and wincing at the pain in her hip.

It would have been far easier to camp out in Gram's room, but no way could she sleep in the bed in which her grandmother had breathed her last. In her mind's eye, she saw her grandmother as she had been that last night, pasty-skinned and unmoving. Lifeless. Nope, that was way too disturbing.

Yet curling up in the room where her mother had grown up wasn't exactly calming. Harper wondered if she should settle into one of the guest rooms on the second floor. But those rooms, too, held their own particular ghosts. "Let it go."

She unrolled the old zippered bag over the double bed and tossed her pillow to its place near the wooden headboard where, years before, she had carved Chase's initials surrounded by a heart.

How silly, she thought now. How over-the-top in love she'd thought she'd been. Love at seventeen and eighteen was something far different than it was when another twenty years had passed.

Or so she imagined.

It seemed like eons since she'd been in love. Really in love.

If she ever had been.

In the adjoining bath she stripped and tossed on an oversized black T-shirt from a KISS concert she'd attended years before, then ran a damp washcloth over the parts of her face that weren't bandaged. Brushing her teeth was more of a chore than normal. Since the pounding in her head hadn't subsided, she opened the medicine cabinet to see an ancient thermometer, a rusted pair of scissors, Band-Aids from the sixties, and an old bottle of aspirin. She picked it up, looked for an expiration date, but it was too old to even list one.

Twenty years and degraded?

Probably not a good idea.

She dropped the bottle into the empty trash can near the toilet.

As she closed the cabinet door, she caught her reflection in the mirror.

The phrase "death warmed over" came to mind. Her skin was sallow, the bandage over her chin no longer bright white, the one near her eye beginning to fray. Deep circles were visible under her eyes, one of which was swollen a bit, a major bruise developing over her cheekbone. Even some of the blood vessels in the white of her eye had broken. "Lovely," she said. No amount of makeup would improve her much. Well, too bad.

Yawning, she rubbed the strain from her neck, then unzipped the old sleeping bag she'd had since the first years of her marriage. From its depth she pulled out one framed picture she'd brought to Oregon, her favorite snapshot of Dawn, at about eight. Her front teeth were too big for her slim face, her brown eyes wide and sparkling in the Southern California sunlight, her hair a deep gold at the time and seeming to sprout from a black mouse-eared hat. It had been their first trip to Disneyland, and Dawn had been over the moon.

How long ago it all seemed now.

Crrreaak.

The sound echoed through the house.

Again.

Her heart stilled.

She didn't move a muscle.

Waiting.

Did she hear rustling? Something moving? A door quietly opening? Or was it a step protesting against someone's weight?

She swallowed hard and told herself that she was imagining things, that whatever she heard wasn't out of the ordinary and was probably amplified by the simple fact that she was alone. She just wasn't used to the sounds the old house made.

Quietly, she set the framed picture onto a night table.

Old houses settled.

Still . . .

"Hello?" she called from the landing outside her bedroom door, and her voice seemed to echo down the well. Heart suddenly pounding, she glanced up at the dark turret, then down the winding stairs. She saw nothing but darkness.

Anyone could be lurking in the shadows.

"Is anyone—?"

No one answered.

Of course. No one was here. What was wrong with her?

Yet she couldn't shake the feeling that someone was watching her.

Ridiculous.

Ears straining, she listened but heard only the thudding of her heart in her ears and the soft rush of warm air being forced through the ancient heat ducts.

She slipped back into the bathroom where she'd seen an old pair of scissors. Once she had them in her grip, she decided to check the house.

One more time.

Holding the shears in a death grip, she headed first up the stairs to her grandfather's crow's nest and held on to the banister for support. She had, after all, had several drinks, and she wasn't as steady as normal. Once at the top of the turret, she flipped on the light and blinked, muscles bunched, ready to spring if an attacker was inside.

But no.

She found no one lurking in the shadows or hiding in the shower stall. Down she went, past the floor she'd claimed for her bedroom, then lower to the second floor. Cautiously, every muscle straining, she searched the bedrooms and bathrooms, opening closets and expecting someone to leap out at her at any moment.

No one did.

Don't freak yourself out!

On the landing, she paused, again listening hard.

Could Jinx have nudged a door open? One that hadn't quite latched? "Kitty?" she called. "Jinx?" But her voice seemed to die in the darkness.

Down another flight she went, switching on lights. Through the foyer and kitchen, parlor and Gram's bedroom and everywhere, every damned room she encountered the dolls, all of them staring sightlessly at her.

Plastic faces unmoving.

Rubber arms limp.

Lips set in forever pouts.

Unnerving.

She'd get rid of the damned things tomorrow. Every last one of them.

Still clutching the scissors, she moved through the butler's pantry and dining room, then peered out to the terrace where anyone could hide in the darkness. The lake beyond was a black abyss, only a few lights on the opposite shore winking.

Get a grip, she told herself but knew she'd never go to sleep unless she double-checked the doors.

So she went through the same routine she'd done with Gram years before: front door, kitchen door, terrace door off the parlor, door to the basement, and door to the garage. Five. "Like the points of a star. Remember that," Gram had told her when she'd been a child and they had counted them off together. Then, later, when Gram was unable and Harper had spent some nights with her, she had gone through the ritual.

Tonight, all the doors were secure.

Berating herself, she returned to her room, her heartbeat returned to normal, though she was still unsteady and her damned hip was hurting again.

Well, so be it. At least she was safe here.

After snapping off the bedroom light, she slid into the flannel-lined bag and told herself not to be such a goose—and to cut down on the drinking. She needed to keep her wits and be at the top of her game.

No one else was inside this huge house.

Yet, despite everything, she kept the shears at her side in the sleeping bag.

In the pale light from the window, she caught one last glimpse of the crucifix in the room, Jesus appearing to look down on her.

"Don't judge me," she mumbled to the ceramic son of God hanging on the faded wallpaper. Then absently made the sign of the cross over her chest, a habit left over from childhood. As she was drifting off, she told herself she was being ridiculous. She hadn't been to mass in ages.

But so what?

Right now, considering everything that was happening, Harper needed all the help she could get.

A small dose of divine intervention wouldn't be such a bad thing.

Chapter 21

While nursing a bottle of Budweiser, Rand sifted through the old files in his home office, the loft of his A-frame, a room that had once been his bedroom. The workplace was makeshift at best. His old man's battle-scarred desk was situated beneath the windows that overlooked the lake—a spot where his twin bed had once resided.

Four old, pre-computer files were stacked on the desk. The important information he tacked to the old bulletin board, again from his father, so he could glance at the facts while working. Along with the folders Chelle had dug up on Olivia Dixon and Chase Hunt, he'd added Anna Reed and her son, Evan. His one-time friend. What had his mother said about Evan Reed? "Spoiled rotten and whip-smart. A deadly combination."

Barbara Watkins had been right.

As he skimmed the thin files, he had the uneasy feeling that they were incomplete, as if whoever had investigated the cases hadn't been thorough, or at least not as thorough as police procedures and practices were today. He reminded himself these were not homicide files. None of the deaths had been the result of murder. Just deaths that were investigated. As he read the reports, he made notes because each file brought up more questions than answers.

Worse yet, his old man's name was listed as the lead investigator in every case. Gerald Watkins's slanted handwriting and signature were on all of the files. Other officers were listed as taking down information, of course. Thomas Hunt, Dorothy Thiazine, and William McKenna, who were no longer with the department, had taken eyewitness reports. However, Chuck Fellows and Ned Gunderson were still on the force and might have some answers.

Sipping his beer, he read each of the statements twice.

From what he pieced together, it seemed that Olivia Dixon's death had been ruled an accidental overdose of sleeping pills and booze. Specifically barbiturates, chloral hydrate, and gin.

That Harper had administered.

Accidentally.

He believed that much.

Harper was many things. But not a killer. At least not in his estimation.

But what did he really know about her? He'd pledged to his best friend that if anything happened to Chase, he would take care of her. That had proved impossible. He'd shipped out, she'd moved to California, and before his next leave to the States, she'd gotten married to some guy he'd never heard of. Joel Prescott, he now knew. Once she was married and had a baby, he figured his promise to Chase was no longer valid. By the time Rand's tour of duty was over and he'd been discharged, Harper was a wife and mother.

Now she was divorced.

And a rich woman who didn't need his help in any way, shape, or form. He had witnessed that himself earlier today.

She had a temper.

No doubt about it.

And some people, Cynthia Hunt included, had been vocal about Harper's guilt. Cynthia had been certain Harper had killed her grandmother with a mixture of pills and alcohol and had been somehow involved in Chase's disappearance.

Thinking, Rand drummed his fingers on the desk. He located and read the statement of Matilda Burroughs, Olivia Dixon's caretaker.

In it Matilda swore that she left the right dosage of medication for Harper to give to her grandmother. All the girl had to do was be careful and *not* allow the old woman to drink alcohol.

While Harper had insisted she gave her grandmother the amount of pills the caretaker left in the kitchen, Matilda had said confidently that she hadn't made a mistake in dosage. In the side notes taken by his own father, Gerald noted that the caretaker was visibly distraught and affronted. Gerald also wrote that the woman called Harper "a self-involved little whore who had left her grandmother to die while out doing the nasty with her boyfriend!" That phrase was left off her official handwritten statement.

He found another note stating that after her oldest daughter's graduation from high school a few months later, Matilda had packed up her family and moved to Canada.

He snagged his longneck, nearly draining the bottle, and wrote himself a reminder to track Matilda Burroughs down. As he set the near-empty bottle on the desk again, he glanced up and stared through the window and across the lake. To Dixon Island, where lights shone from some of the windows in that behemoth of a house. He wondered how long Harper would stay in Almsville. Probably just long enough to sell the whole kit and caboodle, pocket her fortune, and leave.

Not that it mattered to him.

As he stood, his shoulder twinged again, a pain that never quite went away, compliments of the shrapnel still buried there. He'd tried and failed to convince himself that the soreness was all in his head, that the continuous ache was like the nightmares that sometimes plagued him, part of the war that would forever be his mental companion.

Shaking the feeling off, he drained his beer and carried his empty downstairs. He left the bottle in an empty six-pack carton in the laundry room where like six-packs were stacked before walking barefoot outside, the boards of the deck wet and cool.

Clouds moved slowly over a quarter moon, and the air was heavy and damp, but no rain was falling at the moment. Even the breeze had died to a whisper.

Next door, the Hunt house was dark. Now that Cynthia was gone, he wondered what Levi would do with the cottage. Rand had heard he might move back; that had been his plan before his mother's demise.

Rand stuffed his hands into the pockets of his jeans and eyed the cottage with its large daylight basement. He'd spent a lot of time over there, hanging out in Chase's room listening to records or talking sports.

A ravine with a creek separated the properties, and when they were both on the team, Chase and Rand had spent hours tossing a football back and forth over the stream.

And then things had gotten complicated.

The irony wasn't lost on him that he'd become exactly what he'd railed against as a youth. Though as a boy he'd admired his dad and had thought he'd become a cop just like his father, that had changed with adolescence, when the police were no longer heroes but the enemy.

And now here he was.

Living in the old man's house.

Using his desk.

Doing the same job at the Almsville Police Department.

How had that happened?

Rand had asked himself that same question a hundred times over and had never come up with an answer. His gaze dropped to the Hunts' empty boathouse before he looked to the middle of the lake and wondered again about Cynthia. What had driven her to the lake and her ultimate horrific demise?

He shoved a hank of hair from his eyes and heard a cricket chirping nearby.

Rand reminded himself to talk to Levi, as well as with some of the staff, possibly nurses and a social worker at Serenity Acres, the care facility from which Cynthia Hunt had wandered. Somehow she'd gotten through the facility's security and made her way five miles to the Hunt home. Once there she'd gathered mementos of her life and carried them along with a gas can and lighter to the boat, then motored to the middle of the lake.

Less than an hour after Harper had returned.

What were the odds of that?

He was headed inside again when he noticed lights on at the Sievers' home. The old man no longer lived in the house, but his daughter, her kids, and two small mutts had taken over the home. The chain-link fence was still in place, but the warning signs and security lights had been taken down, fresh paint making the bungalow more welcoming.

The dogs seemed friendly enough, though they tended to bark whenever the ducks and geese that lived on the lake got too close. And they'd put up a helluva ruckus last night.

He'd heard the neighbor dogs barking and going out of their minds about the time he'd been called from the station. While on the phone he'd looked out the window and seen the boat in flames.

He hadn't waited for the fire department but instead had dashed out the back door and climbed into the old motorboat, heading straight for the flames where a woman was screaming and writhing aboard. As he got close, he'd recognized the boat as the Hunts' Triton. Sick inside, he'd arrived just as the crew on the department's boat had cleared the area, firemen trying to save her.

Even then he'd known it was too late.

The horror on the sinking craft had consumed his attention while others saw to a lone swimmer, getting her to the hospital, a woman he hadn't recognized. Only later had he learned her name and was struck that Harper Reed was back in town.

And once again involved in a tragedy.

Coincidence?

Unlikely.

Of course all the neighbors on the point and along the lakeshore had been interviewed, asked about what they'd seen the night before, and most of them were in concurrence. No one had noticed anything unusual until they'd caught sight of the fire on the water or heard the commotion and looked outside.

Francine Sievers O'Malley had said the same. She'd been watching television, an episode of *The Wonder Years,* when her daughter had said she saw "something weird" on the lake and soon thereafter the dogs began barking their fool heads off.

Walking inside, he contemplated another beer and battled against it. His family had a history and a complicated relationship with alcohol, not the least his own father's entanglement, which had really taken root around the same time that Chase Hunt had gone missing and Rand had left for Southeast Asia.

But one more wouldn't hurt. He opened the fridge, grabbed another longneck, and opened it. With the same damned church key his old man had used. Frowning, he told himself he *wasn't* his father as he climbed the stairs to the loft. With a long swallow he settled back down in his chair and glanced down at the report on Olivia Dixon's death.

Accidental overdose.

And not the only one, he thought, rubbing his chin as his gaze moved to Anna Dixon's death certificate. Again, those words: Drowning caused by *accidental overdose*.

Like mother, like daughter?

He took a big pull from his bottle and went over the coincidences again.

Harper had been found outside on the night Anna had died.

She'd discovered not only her grandmother's body but her brother's as well.

And she'd been the woman who had first reported the fire the night Cynthia Hunt had died.

A weird connection.

If it was one.

He scratched the back of his neck as he wondered again about Harper being the one who had called 9-1-1 and risked her own life to save Cynthia's. There were houses scattered all around the lake, and yet Harper—who, according to her, had just arrived at her grandmother's house—just happened to see the fire.

What were the chances?

Since leaving Almsville two decades earlier, Harper had married, had a kid, and divorced. She hadn't been back to that house, as far as he knew.

He'd kept track as best he could.

For Chase.

His once-upon-a-time best friend.

Still missing.

His jaw grew tight as he remembered what Chase had told him the night of his disappearance. That he needed to vanish. Before Uncle Sam claimed him.

And Rand had kept his silence. Most of it.

Shit! He shoved his hair away from his face and kicked back his chair so hard it careened across the small space and slammed against the railing.

What a mess.

And he was in the middle of it.

In more ways than one.

Frustrated, he stood and rubbed the back of his neck, guilt riddling through him as it always did when he considered the consequences of keeping his promise to his drugged-out, confused friend.

He should have spilled his guts the minute he learned that Chase had gone missing. However, he'd kept quiet, hoping his friend would show up, as he left the next day, on his way to a camp in the middle of a jungle thousands of miles away.

But there had been other opportunities.

And if he had told everything he knew? Maybe then Chase Hunt wouldn't be an open file on his desk.

He took a long swallow from his beer and looked down into the living area of this cabin he'd called home for most of his life. The sloped, wooden walls and plank floors looked much the same as they had all those years ago. Although the orange shag rug had been replaced years ago, and his father's battered recliner and the small black and white TV were long gone, the freestanding wood stove still dominated the room and the avocado green stove still worked in the kitchen.

Just as it had when Chase had come over and they'd made Jiffy Pop on the coiled burners.

Leaning against a post, he thought back to the cold night high above the river. What had Chase confided?

That he would marry Harper to avoid the draft. If she was pregnant.

Or that he would find a way to leave the country—probably make his way into Canada and cross the border, like Patrick Sullivan had.

But there was also the allure of the free sex and drugs at the little house at the end of the street. He remembered his father calling them "no-good dope-smokin' hippies, on the dole, if you ask me. Student deferments, my ass. President Johnson should draft 'em all."

Maybe so, but those "no-goods" might just know something.

Rand thought back to the night Chase died. Hadn't he said something when Rand had suggested his brother might watch over Harper. ". . . not Levi. He's a prick! . . . Can't be trusted."

What was that all about? Simple sibling rivalry? Or something more? Something darker?

Recalling that night, he also remembered Chase's damning accusation about Rand's feelings for Harper: "You're half in love with her already."

That much had been true.

And seeing her today? He didn't want to go there. Some emotions just never die.

Turning his thoughts from Harper, he rubbed his knuckles, almost remembered the pain he'd felt in his hand when he'd slammed his fist into Chase's jaw. From that fight and Chase's desperate attempt to save himself from plunging down the cliff face, Rand knew that Chase would never have committed suicide. Not only had no body ever been discovered, but the truth of the matter was that Chase Hunt was all about Chase Hunt living the good life.

He wasn't about dying.

So how was his disappearance tied to all the rest of this mess, newly exacerbated by his mother's bizarre death?

He kicked his chair back into position at the desk, sat down, and took another swallow from his bottle. As he flipped through Chase's file, he once again found his father's signature as lead investigator.

Rand's own statement was there. Short and to the point. He'd been with Chase earlier up at the logging road, where they said their good-byes over beers as Rand was leaving the next day. He'd told the cops—not his father—a cleaned-up version of what had happened, leaving out the drugs, Chase's crazy talk, and the fist fight that had nearly taken Chase's life. Then he'd explained that he'd stayed out until closing time at the local watering hole, which he assumed the bartender had verified. He'd been so intent on drowning his own sorrows, he'd even missed his mother's visit. He'd learned later, from a letter he received on the other side of the world, that she had, as promised, stopped by the house, but Rand hadn't been there.

If his dad had noticed Rand's bruised hand and split knuckles, he hadn't asked about it, but probably Gerald Watkins had been too busy dealing with Olivia Dixon's death and Chase's disappearance to notice.

Or he hadn't wanted to know.

That thought ate at him as once more he eyed the pages on Chase's missing person's file. The statements were old and faded, the notes short and inconclusive, a list of names and phone numbers of people associated with Chase. He recognized a few, his own home phone number as well as the Hunts' and the Dixons', the number for the main house on the island. The digits he didn't recognize had names attached to them.

He read the familiar names: Harper Reed. Tom and Cynthia Hunt. Levi Hunt. Rand himself. A few other people, including Chase's high-school coach, a couple of friends, his college roommate, and a few people Chase had befriended at the university. No one had a clue. No one had thought Chase seemed troubled. No one had been involved in his disappearance. No one knew if he had plans to leave.

Except Rand, and he hadn't admitted as much.

"Well, hell," he muttered, guilt creeping up on him as he paged through the notes.

Chase's Chevelle had been left at the house. If he'd decided to head for the border, he'd taken off on foot, hopped a bus, or hitched a ride from a stranger. Unless he had some secret accomplice who had later lied.

Then what about the boat found in the middle of the lake?

A decoy?

Left adrift to put the police and his family on the wrong trail?

Possibly to buy time?

That damned boat, Rand thought.

He leaned back in his chair.

There were also statements from the other residents' houses on the point, including Ed Sievers, the recluse next door; the Leonettis, who lived on the other side of the Hunts; and a few others from the rental house at the end of the block: Charla Lopez, Ronald Mayfield, and Janet Van Arsdale—ahh. Moonbeam, as Chase had called her. He noted her given name. But there was no mention of the kid from Texas who seemed to be the dealer. What was his name? God, it had been so long. He had a weird name. Like . . . what? Trip? For the LSD? Or Tripper? No—Trick! Chase had said, "*A guy from Texas, Trick, he can get you whatever you want. Any slice of heaven. I'm not kid-ding.*" Unless Ronald Mayfield had been given the nickname of Trick, the guy wasn't listed.

Harper's and Levi's statements echoed each other: Harper showed up at the house in the early morning hours. She knocked on the window, waking Levi. Together they looked for Chase. They stopped to talk to Rand. Then Levi drove her and her canoe back to the island before driving home and telling his parents that Chase was missing.

So all the information jibed.

And yet it seemed off. Shallow.

Harper had been questioned, of course, with her attorney present. Her statement included information about how she'd been caring for her grandmother and how she, after allowing the woman to have alcohol with her medication, had waited for the old woman to fall asleep, then taken off in the canoe in search of Chase. She'd admitted to dropping Olivia's pills on the floor and scrambling to pick them up, perhaps screwing up the dosage, but it had been an accident. And she'd been a minor, not quite eighteen, so no charges had been filed. In fact, there had been no further investigation into Olivia's death.

Accidental overdose.

He glanced through the window to the night beyond and, across the lake, the island with its heavy gate, private bridge, and imposing manor where a few lights burned. The isolated house with its turret and gargoyles, peaked roof, and rooms filled with antiques from another era seemed almost Gothic.

Or maybe he'd seen one too many vampire movies.

He glanced down at his notes again as he finished his beer.

What had his partner said?

If you ask me, all those deaths associated with that damned family deserve another look.

Anna Reed's file lay open on his desk.

Before her death, Rand, Chase, and Evan had been close. "The Three Musketeers," Cynthia Hunt had called them. They'd hung out, riding bikes through the woods and on deer trails or playing board games for hours on the weekends in the winter while spending as much time as possible swimming, skinny-dipping, and boating during the summer. They'd snuck cigarettes and even some beers from their parents and camped under the stars on the banks of the river. *We had the world on a string*, he thought, rubbing the thin white scar that ran across the palm of his left hand.

Until all their naïveté, bravado, and innocence had been shattered as easily as thin glass.

1960

Chapter 22

Rand crouched by the edge of the spillway in the dark, the misting rain running under the collar of his jacket, the smell of the wet leaves and earth filling his nostrils. Squinting, he peered through the large culvert, then clicked his flashlight three times, its yellow beam reflecting on the undulating surface of the creek. The water was running fast for October, almost deafening as it rushed through the huge cement tube beneath the bridge.

He waited for an answering signal and hoped his friends were on the other side of the bridge as planned.

"Chase!" he yelled, though the current was so loud that even he couldn't hear his echoing voice over the roar of the running water. For the twentieth time he told himself he shouldn't be here. If his dad ever found out, he'd be a dead man. Gerald Watkins would kill him. Or at least ground him like for*ever*.

"He won't find out. No one will," Chase had assured him two days earlier when they'd met at the sand lot behind the school and hatched their plans. "You're just chicken."

"Am not!" Rand had protested.

"Then prove it. Don't be such a candy-ass." Evan, always the instigator, was all-in on the plans.

"Fine."

"Show up!" Evan had said, backing up toward his bike and pointing his finger at Rand. "Do it."

"I will," he'd vowed.

So now here he was, proving his courage, crouched on the slick, mossy rocks and wishing he hadn't been so bold. "You're a moron," he muttered under his breath just as he caught sight of three responding flashes of light from the other side of the culvert.

So Chase was in place.

Returning the signal.

Rand's pulse jumped, and he wondered if he should just leave. Before they really got into trouble. He'd shown up as promised. That was good enough, right?

No.

Of course not. They were blood brothers, a fact Chase never let Rand nor Evan forget. The three had sworn allegiance to each other in a ceremony two years ago on the island. They'd convened at midnight, in the boathouse that had been cut into the rock walls of the island and was connected to the huge house by a series of tunnels.

The perfect place.

With the smell of water and oil in their nostrils, while bats flew overhead and the old boat creaked on its lift, the three boys had sliced their palms with Chase's dad's hunting knife.

"Make it deep enough to count," Evan had said in the flickering light of an old kerosene lantern he'd brought from one of the storage rooms.

Rand had gritted his teeth but made the cut. After a red line had bloomed on all three palms, they shook hands, all around, smearing and mixing their blood in the ritual uniting them, wiping their hands on their T-shirts once the process was finished.

What a stupid thing to do, Rand now thought as he hid on one side of the abutment, armed with a dozen eggs.

Once more, he considered ditching the others, climbing onto his bike and feigning getting sick or something, anything to avoid getting caught and having to suffer through his old man's wrath.

Then he heard it. Over the roar of the creek, he heard the rumble of an engine—a large truck from the sounds of it, on the road above and fast approaching the bridge.

Too late to back out now.

"Go!" Chase yelled loudly, his voice reverberating through the culvert. "Go, go, go!"

Rand sprang into action, clambering up the rocky bank and reaching the road just as two headlights cut through the darkness, the pickup rattling across the span, headlights burning through the darkness, illuminating the road.

"Fire!" Chase yelled.

Rand reached into his pocket and loaded up. He hurled the first egg just as the front wheels of a red and white pickup reached the edge of the bridge. *Splat!* His egg landed on the Ford's windshield. Its shell, yolk, and clear goo splattered.

He fired two more, zinging them in rapid succession, eggs smashing on the hood and windshield, the wipers smearing the egg gunk over the glass.

With a squeal of tires, the truck skidded to a stop.

"Hey!" the driver, a big burly man shouted, opening the door, the interior light flooding the area.

From the other side of the road, a bevy of eggs assaulted the truck.

Splat! Splat! Splat!

"You fucking kids!"

The driver leaped from the cab, his bald head shining under the dome light. He reached back inside.

To the gun rack mounted across the back of the cab.

To the rifle with its scope resting in the rack.

Holy shit!

Rand didn't wait. He just started running. No prank was worth being shot at! He sped through the trees lining the side of the road, then vaulted across a low fence. He cut through a leaf-strewn backyard, tripping over the edge of a sandbox. Catching himself, hearing the bark from a dog inside the house, he slipped through a side gate just as he caught a glimpse of the bald guy leaping over the fence.

Crap.

Scrambling to his feet, he beelined for the empty lot and forest beyond.

There was a trail that cut through these woods, a shortcut back to his house.

His heart was thumping as he glanced back. Seeing no one. But hearing heavy, fast-moving footsteps closing the distance between them.

Oh. Please.

"You!" a deep, male voice bellowed, seeming to ricochet off the thick trunks of the Douglas firs and vine maples.

Crap!

"You stop, you little fucker!"

No way.

He rounded a final corner and nearly tripped over his bike where he'd left it propped against the trunk of a gigantic fir tree, their meeting spot. He heard his friends running through the forest, rushing footsteps, all three of them trying to get away from the bald man.

Rand grabbed the handlebars of his Schwinn. With a running start, he flung his leg over the seat and started pedaling along the trail that ran in a zigzag pattern along the edge of the access road.

Faster and faster.

The world was spinning by, branches slapping at his face.

Where were his friends?

They had been close—

"Stop!" The man yelled, his low voice booming.

Oh God, how close was he?

Close enough to aim and shoot?

Already in third gear, Rand pedaled as if his life depended on it.

He didn't know where his friends were.

Didn't care.

He just had to get away from the bald guy with the gun.

Shit! Shit! Shit!

What had he been thinking, letting Chase talk him into this crazy-ass scheme. So it was Halloween. So what?

He sped across fallen limbs, dirt clods, and dips in the path, each bump jarring him, yet he was able to keep his three-speed on the familiar trail.

The night was dark, but this section of woods that stretched between the lake and the road above had a bit of illumination as street lamps offered feeble blue light, just enough so that he could see the path ahead, where it cut through the thickets, where it was crossed by other trails.

Rand heard the sounds of branches snapping, footsteps running, and his friends' voices.

Nearby.

Somewhere in the surrounding trees.

Chase yelled, "Go, go, *go*!"

Rand went.

More shouts.

But no shots.

Yet.

He prayed they hadn't been caught. Oh, Geez, what if they had? His heart was pounding like crazy, his blood pumping wildly, his thoughts spinning as fast as the wheels on his Schwinn. Evan wouldn't be in trouble. He never was. A rich kid whose parents thought he could do no wrong—"the little prince," as Rand's mom called him—always skated when it came to punishment. But Chase? And him? Sons of cops? Holy shit, they'd be skinned alive.

And he couldn't be found with the eggs.

No.

So riding with one hand, pedaling like crazy, keeping his balance, he emptied his pockets. He flung eggs into the underbrush, hearing them crack and splat as he strained to listen for the sound of his friends on their bikes. Where were they? Why hadn't they caught up with him?

As he hurled the last egg into a clump of ferns, he saw movement on the trail in front of him. Something big and black. A dog? A deer? Or a man crouching and waiting?

The path curved.

His front tire hit a rock.

The bike shuddered, tire slipping.

Rand went flying, his momentum hurtling him forward.

Through the air in a split second.

Thud!

He slammed face first into the rough bark of a fir.

All of the bones of his body seemed to crush together.

Pain burst through his face.

"Oof!" He landed on the soggy ground.

Dazed, he blinked and tried to regain his bearings. Something warm was trickling from over his eye, and one arm, where his sleeve had bunched up, was scraped raw. The world swam for a second.

Shit!

Pain was everywhere.

But he *had* to keep going.

He *couldn't* get caught.

Despite his injuries, he knew that much.

He blinked, staggered to his feet.

His bike . . .

It lay, wheel still spinning on the trail. He prayed it wasn't wrecked.

Swiftly, with pain throbbing in his face, he righted the Schwinn and heard noises on the trail behind him.

Not the whizzing wheels of other bikes but the guttural swearing of a man. *The* man from the pickup.

And he was close.

So close!

Dazed, Rand swung his leg over the seat and—

A huge, gnarly hand grabbed the collar of his jacket.

"You little prick," the guy growled, yanking him from the bike, hot beer breath and sour sweat assailing Rand's nostrils. "What the fuck did you think you were doing? You could have caused an accident, killed someone. Killed *me!*"

Rand tried to shrink away, but the steely fingers held fast.

The man gave him a rough shake. "I'm gonna—"

"Hey, chrome dome!" a voice called from somewhere in the darkness.

Chase?

The man froze. "What the—?"

Phssst!

Smack!

The guy jerked as an egg caught him between the shoulders.

"What the fuck?" He whipped around, his fingers still gripping Rand's collar.

Crack! Another speeding egg hit him square in the face.

He yelped, stung, his grip around Rand's jacket loosening.

Splat! Another egg to his head, the gooey mass sliding down over his nose.

"You sick little fucks!" he roared as more raw eggs pelted him and his grip loosened.

Chase yelled, "Run!"

It was all the urging Rand needed. He wiggled away from the guy who was roaring his outrage.

"Oh no, you don't! Come back here, you little shit!"

He lunged for Rand and tripped.

Rand ran, snagged the handlebars of his bike again, flew onto the seat. He hit the pedals. Hard. And took off. Not looking back. Adrenaline firing his blood, clearing his mind.

He sped crazily along the path, his heart pumping so hard he thought it might leap from his chest. Again, in his peripheral vision in the watery light, he caught sight of a shadow moving through the trees.

He didn't slow.

Just kept riding as if his life depended upon it.

Because it did.

Skidding around corners, flying over rises, splashing through puddles, and bouncing over rocks and roots, he rode.

As freaked out as he was, he had a prick of conscience that told him he should go back and make sure Chase and Evan were okay. He didn't. He knew enough about the other boys to feel that they were safe. Evan could talk his way out of anything, and Chase never stuck his neck out far enough that he was in danger of losing his head.

Except that if Chase's dad ever found out . . . that would be bad. Then Chase would be a dead man. Tom Hunt was of the "spare the rod, spoil the child" mentality.

He saw the road through the trees. Blue light filtering through the branches. Right past the hairpin curve of the trail.

Pulse pounding through his brain, he hit the curve, put down one leg and skidded his bike around the tight corner, then headed to the berm, faster and faster where the trees gave way to pavement.

Fortunately, there wasn't any traffic at the moment.

No headlights cut through the night.

At the berm, he lifted his handlebars and shifted his weight as he'd done a thousand times before.

His bike soared over the berm.

Then landed with a bone-jarring jolt against the cracked pavement of the street.

One more corner to Trail's End, the street where he lived. Leaning hard, he again skid-turned, not far from the swim park where the lake glistened between the trees.

He was almost home!

But he heard the rumble of an engine behind him.

No!

Shit, shit, shit!

Hazarding a look over his shoulder, he saw the beams of headlights cutting through the drizzle.

A truck!

Probably the bald guy.

Sweating despite the cool night, he raced even faster on the pavement to the V where the road forked, one route heading upward and continuing around the hills overlooking the lake, the other, Trail's End Road, leading downward to Fox Point where he and his dad lived.

Legs pumping, he veered downward and sent up a prayer that the truck behind him would keep driving on the main road, ever upward.

Nope!

He wasn't that lucky.

The truck bounced down the narrow lane behind him, bearing down.

Jesus.

Faster! He stayed just outside of the headlight beams, using the sharp downward slope to increase his speed. His hair was flying, the wind harsh against his bruised face.

No way could he stop and turn into the A-frame without being caught, so he just kept riding, past the Hunts' and Leonettis' houses and beyond the rental house at the end of the street. He didn't stop there either but jumped the curb and hit the trail that led to nowhere, just more woods past a trickle of a waterfall from the cliffs above.

At the end of the path, he slid to a stop. His heart was hammering, his panic growing, as he stashed the bike behind a huge fallen tree. Breathing hard, he crawled to the edge of the root wad, peering between the exposed, broken roots and limbs to squint through the thickets. From his hiding spot he was only able to catch a glimpse of the street in the distance.

He saw the vehicle.

Not the truck the old man had been driving.

Instead Rand watched a DeSoto station wagon pull into the driveway of the house at the end of the street. Pink and gray, just like his mother wanted. She commented about it each time it passed the house. The family of five piled out, mom and dad and three blond girls wearing eye masks and carrying bags of candy.

Not the bald man who'd been chasing him.

Rand let out a long breath.

No sign of the guy in the massive two-toned pickup.

Maybe he'd lost Baldy.

Could he have gotten that lucky?

Or maybe the guy was dealing with Evan and Chase.

He waited a few more minutes, half expecting his attacker's pickup to roll down the street, but the road remained quiet.

Slowly Rand began to breathe normally, and after what seemed a lifetime, he got onto his bike again, always on the lookout for his friends. Thankfully his old man was working tonight, a cop on patrol, making certain there were no juveniles causing trouble, no pranksters. And his mother was working at some church Halloween party, on the clean-up crew, so she'd be home late.

Rand swallowed hard. If his dad even guessed what his only son was up to, Rand would be dead meat.

He hid his bike behind the wood stacked at the side of the house and heard a growl from Sievers's place. He didn't really mind the dog, had even managed to pet Duke a couple of times through the fence, but the owner was bat-shit crazy, one of those vigilantes who didn't trust anyone, especially the government and cops. Sievers's whole house was booby-trapped, according to Chase.

Just last summer when Rand and Chase and Levi had been swimming but were taking a break and eating Fudgsicles on the deck, Old Man Sievers had been spreading gravel in his side yard. Nodding toward the older guy, Chase had said, "I've seen him with sticks of dynamite. He puts 'em in that shed of his, and it's got a basement. That's where he keeps kids hostage."

"No way," Rand had said, just as Duke started barking from the other side of the fence.

"Scout's honor." Chase wasn't backing down. But he kept his voice low so the neighbor couldn't hear him. "I saw him with chains and locks going in there."

"You did not," his younger brother, Levi, had argued while Sievers ordered his dog to quiet down.

Levi accused, "You're a liar."

"And you're a snot-nosed little shit," Chase said, tossing aside his Fudgsicle stick before tackling his younger brother. He wrestled Levi to the ground and forced him to say "Uncle," before finally letting him up.

Tonight, after his initial warning growl, the dog was quiet.

Rand slipped inside and was about to hurry upstairs when he heard voices on the dock and headed to the kitchen. Peering through the window, he saw Chase near the back door. Evan, tossing his dark hair from his eyes, was just stepping onto the deck.

"You okay?" Chase asked as Rand walked onto the deck, closing the door behind him.

"Yeah. Fine." Rand wasn't sure he was okay at all, but he wasn't going to admit to being scared shitless.

His friends were huddled near the boat slip. Their jacket collars were turned up against the mist, their faces barely visible in the gaseous light cast from the street lamp at the front of the house.

"He had you, though, didn't he? That old chrome dome had you," Chase said in low tones.

Evan, his cheeks still flushed, added, "We saw it all go down."

"I know," Rand agreed.

Chase was amped up. Agitated. His eyes wide. "I thought he was gonna kill you."

"Me, too," Rand said. "But he didn't."

"That's cuz of me and Evan, we got him good! Did you see his face when that egg smacked into him?" Chase asked, laughing at the image. "Egg dripping down his nose. I thought he was gonna have a heart attack."

"Or shit himself." Evan let out a nervous chuckle.

Rand was nodding. "You saved my life."

"Hell yeah, we did." Chase clapped Evan on the back.

Rand nodded. "I owe you."

Chase said, "I'll remember that."

"Do."

"You know you're lucky he didn't recognize you," Evan cut in, and his gaze slid across the lake to the island, his face suddenly sober. "Do you have any idea who that guy is?"

Rand felt a new dread. Hadn't his attacker seemed faintly familiar? "No."

Chase said, "Martin Alexander."

Oh. No. "Craig's dad?" Rand whispered, his stomach sinking.

"Yeah, and he's a mean son of a bitch," Evan put in. "Beats the crap out of Craig. I know. I've seen it. He's got a thick black belt that he whips out of his pants whenever Craig messes up."

"Which is a lot," Chase added.

Rand couldn't believe his bad luck. Craig Alexander was a year younger than he but already bigger and tougher, just like his old man.

Evan was saying, "I'm lucky he didn't see me cuz he works for my grandma, at the house on the lake."

"He *knows* you?"

"Yeah. Kinda. He's living on the island now. With Craig. There's like this apartment in the attic over the garage, and they moved in when Craig's mom took off."

"Oh crap," Rand said. He knew that Evan and Harper lived at the gatehouse, a cottage near the bridge to the island. But not all the time. Sometimes they spent weeks or months living *on* the island in that massive house with their grandmother.

"Don't worry," Evan told him. "He didn't see me. Or Chase. Just you. And even then it was pretty dark." He glanced across the lake. "Look, I gotta go. I have to ride all the way around the lake and make sure that Harper tells my folks that she saw me leave to go trick or treating."

So now Evan's sister was being dragged into it. Rand didn't want to think about her having to lie for them.

"Later." Evan ran back around the house to the front yard where he'd ditched his bike.

"Rich kid," Chase said under his breath.

Chase had always envied Harper and Evan and their family's wealth. It didn't matter that they were all friends. Even though Chase, Evan, and Rand were close—even "blood brothers"—there was a divide between them that was wider than Lake Twilight when it came to social status.

Not that Rand gave it much thought. He liked Evan for the most part.

Then there was Harper.

But Rand didn't want to think about her at all. It was too confusing.

Chase looked across the creek to his house, where jack-o'-lanterns had been placed around the perimeter of the dock, their distorted faces reflecting eerily in the lapping water below. "I'd better get home and wait for my dumb-ass brother. He's out trick or treating or whatever, and when he gets back, I need to be there. He's my alibi, y'know? Mom and Dad think we're out together. And I want to make sure he says I was with him the whole time."

"*We* were with him," Rand reminded him as he felt a bat swoop close, then skim over the water.

"Right."

"Will he?"

"Yeah. Levi's a dick, but he'll do it."

Chase was already heading home. "I'll catch you tomorrow," he yelled over his shoulder as he took a running leap across the creek, splashing as he landed near, but not quite on, the far shore. He always thought he could jump the creek but never quite made it.

Rand waited until Chase disappeared into his house before going into his own home. Inside, he stripped off his wet clothes and surveyed the damage to his face in the mirror over the sink. Not too bad. The cut over his eye had stopped bleeding, and his face was scraped and maybe a little bruised, but it would heal. His arm hurt, and he saw that the skin had been scratched, but there wasn't much he could do about it.

In his bedroom, he changed into a pair of pajama bottoms he'd left on the floor this morning, then grabbed a T-shirt from his dresser, a hand-me-down from an uncle. He kept a stash of Necco Wafers, Hershey bars, candy cigarettes, and Pixy Stix, whatever he could buy at the five-and-dime with his extra lunch money, but tonight he was too keyed up to think about snacking and slammed the drawer shut.

What if Craig Alexander's dad had recognized him?

Would he call the cops?

Tell Rand's father?

And how did Evan know the guy hadn't figured out who he was?

Regret ate at him. He never should have gone out on his bike with Chase.

He slid into bed but wasn't able to sleep.

Still tossing and turning, he heard his mom come home, her light footsteps downstairs. He feigned sleep as she climbed the stairs to check on him, then returned to the main floor.

The phone rang, and she answered.

Rand froze. This was it! Martin Alexander was calling to tell her what Rand and his friends had done. He rolled out of bed quietly and crept partially down the stairs, listening.

But his mother kept her voice low, and he could only hear part of the conversation.

". . . I know . . . Yes . . . I'll try . . . but you know how he is . . ."

Rand was certain the bald guy was ratting him out.

Or was he?

Why was Mom so calm?

". . . I've really got to go . . . I will . . . I promise . . . oh, me, too. You know I do."

Click.

But she didn't come up the stairs. She spent some time in the bathroom and went to bed. Later, his father came home. Still wide awake, Rand braced himself. Expected to hear his father's heavy footsteps on the stairs. Even if Martin Alexander hadn't recognized any of them, what if he had gone to the station and made a police report? What if he'd given a description of Rand or his bike? His throat went dry, and he listened, barely breathing as his old man opened the refrigerator, rattled around in the kitchen, and, from the sounds of it, cracked open a beer.

After what seemed like an eternity Gerald Watkins finally turned off the lights.

Only then did Rand relax.

Only then did exhaustion take over anxiety.

Only then did sleep finally find him.

Chapter 23

Rand was facing a firing squad of one.

The bald guy was dressed in army fatigues and pointing a machine gun at him.

He couldn't move!

"Got you, you little shit!"

"No!" he yelled, but no sound came out. He was gagged! And tied to some stake.

With a nasty chuckle, Chrome Dome pulled the trigger.

Rat-a-tat-tat!

Bullets sprayed all around him, hitting hard and fast and loud.

Rapid-fire explosions.

Rand's eyes flew open.

The sound of the bullets striking furiously didn't abate.

He bit back the urge to yell.

Then he realized he was in his own bed. The plaid comforter was on the floor. His sheets were twisted all around him.

But the sound of the bullets striking continued.

A woodpecker rat-a-tat-tatting noisily against the house. "Oh man," he whispered, blinking, his racing pulse finally beginning to slow. He glanced at the nightstand near his bed. Five after seven, according to the clock radio.

Feeling sore all over, he remembered the night before and closed his eyes, trying to block it out, hoping for a few more minutes of sleep. But the alarm blared before he could doze off. He groaned and rolled over, then forced himself to get up. It was Tuesday. A school day.

Yawning, he carried clothes down the stairs and went into the bathroom, where he got ready, stepping through the shower and brushing his teeth, tossing water into his dark hair and slicking it away from his face. His battered face. He was bruised where his nose and cheeks had hit the rough bark of the tree, and one of his eyes was already red, a shiner on its way.

There was no way to hide it.

No lie he could think of that would explain it.

Crossing his fingers, he hoped his parents would sleep in.

No such luck.

Mom was in the bathroom. Rand heard the water running in the sink. And his dad had already poured himself a cup of coffee. He was standing at the back door, staring out at the mist-shrouded lake as he sipped from his mug. His T-shirt stretched tight over his shoulders, his slacks still without a belt, the worn moccasins he used as slippers on his feet. The newspaper already open on the table, his pack of Pall Malls near the ashtray.

Dad barely glanced over his shoulder as Rand stepped into the room. "Mornin'." Holding his coffee cup in one hand, he opened an overhead cupboard with the other, pulled out a box of Trix, and shook the box. "Not much left, probably just a bowlful. That do?"

"Sure." Rand, face averted, walked to the refrigerator, opened the door, and found a jug of milk. It, too, was nearly empty, but he grabbed a bowl from the shelves, a spoon from a drawer, then poured himself cereal as Gerald lit a cigarette and sat at the table, perusing the morning paper.

Rand barely looked up as he dug in, though he wasn't really hungry. He placed the cereal box between himself and his dad and, keeping his face down-turned, pretended to be fascinated by his tricolored breakfast.

The woodpecker went to work again, rat-a-tat-tatting against the siding.

"Holy Kee-Rist! Do you hear that? Damned woodpecker! You got your slingshot?"

Automatically, Rand glanced up.

And Gerald Watkins got a look at his son for the first time that morning. He zeroed in on Rand's bruised face. "What the hell happened to you?" Cigarette dangling from his lips, he was out of his chair in a second, examining his son's face. "You get in a fight or something?"

"No, I just fell off my bike, into the gravel and rocks."

Gerald noticed a scrape on the side of Rand's hand. "Holy Mother of—" He didn't ask, just rolled up his son's sleeve and looked at the slight abrasions. Pall Mall clenched between his teeth, he said, "That's one hell of a raspberry. You sure you didn't get into a fight?"

"I told you, I just fell off my bike."

"Really?" His dad gave him the stink eye and sucked hard on the cigarette. That was the problem with his old man being a cop. He was always suspicious. Frowning, Gerald asked, "You okay?"

"Yeah. Fine."

Still unconvinced but not able to call Rand a liar, he said, "Well, put some Mercurochrome on all the cuts, okay? I think there's some in the medicine cabinet. If not, we've got iodine." He backed up and sat down, leaned back in his chair, and squinted at his son through the smoke. It was as if he was sizing Rand up and weighing how much he could believe his son. And just how much BS was being shoveled his way. "No need for infection to set in." Still seeming unconvinced, he took a sip of his coffee. "You be careful on that bike."

"I will."

"Is it okay?" he asked, suddenly, his eyes dark with a new concern. "The Schwinn, it's not wrecked, is it?"

"No. No. It's good." The three-speed had been last year's Christmas present, and Rand had overheard his dad claim it had cost "a pretty penny" in more than one conversation. Rand scraped back his chair, left his bowl in the sink, and quickly started for the bathroom. The less he said to his father—and mother, for that matter—the better. If the old man ever got wind of what he'd done with his friends and then *lied* about it, there would be hell to pay. He wouldn't be able to sit for a week.

"Election's next week, you know." Dad rapped his fist on the newspaper. "You know about it, right?"

"Heard about it in school."

"It's a big one. Kennedy, he might just beat old Tricky Dick."

Like he cared. "Who?" Rand asked.

"Nixon. The vice president. Never liked the guy, not when he was a senator from California and not as Ike's V.P. Just don't trust him. Kennedy's young, and he's Irish Catholic. And ya know what? He might just beat Nixon."

"Good," Rand said, though he didn't care. Right now, he had bigger worries. What if Craig Alexander's father had recognized him? The old guy had been drunk last night, yeah, but maybe when he sobered up, he'd put two and two together.

"Don't they teach you this stuff in school?"

"What?" Oh, his dad was still talking about that boring election stuff. "I guess." Who cared? Stomach in knots, he met his mother in the living area as she was coming out of the bathroom.

"Good morning—hey, what happened to you?" she asked, catching him by the sleeve as he tried to pass. "My God, Rand." Her gaze moved across his face, and she tried to touch his cheek, but he jerked away.

"I'm okay. I just fell off my bike."

"How?"

"Hit some gravel last night. It's no big deal. Dad told me to take care of it."

"You were riding in the dark? I thought you went trick or treating."

"We did. This was after. Just here on the street. Slid on some gravel. Old Ma . . . Mr. Sievers had a pile of it in his yard. I mean, I guess that's where it came from. Don't know."

"But your face."

"It's okay."

"Doesn't look okay," she said, still viewing him with a critical eye. "Let me help you bandage it up."

"Nah, I'm good." He yanked his arm away, slipped into the small bathroom, and locked the door. He didn't want to answer any more questions. He didn't want to lie.

In the medicine cabinet, he found the Mercurochrome bottle,

opened it, pulled out the stopper, and swiped the glass applicator over the cut above his eye. Then he attended to the scrapes on his arms and hands. The medicine stung. Not like iodine, but still. He sucked in his breath with each application until the burn slowed. Now he really looked like shit, his cuts discolored.

Great.

When the pain subsided a bit, he recapped the bottle and jammed it onto the shelf next to the tin of Band-Aids and Mom's jar of night cream.

Just as Old Man Sievers's dog started barking his fool head off.

Again.

"That miserable mutt!" his father muttered, scraping his chair back loudly on the linoleum as Rand came out of the bedroom and headed for the stairs.

"It's irritating, but just a dog," Mom countered, as Rand started up the steps.

Gerald scoffed. "Been a helluva morning. First the damned woodpecker and now—"

A frantic pounding on the front door stopped him short.

Bam. Bam. Bam!

"Watkins! You in there?" a gruff male voice yelled as the dog kept up his crazed barking. The incessant pounding continued.

Rand paused midway up the flight.

The voice came again. Insistent. "Watkins!"

"Yeah, yeah! Hold your horses." Irritated, Gerald walked straight to the front door and opened it wide.

Old Man Sievers stood wild-eyed on the doorstep. He was unkempt as usual in camo pants and a battered army jacket, his graying hair standing straight up, his face white, his eyes wild.

"Can't you get your damned dog to shut up?" Gerald said.

"No!"

"There are laws—"

"She's dead!"

"What?" Gerald Watkins froze. "Who?"

"Don't know," Sievers said. "But she's out in the lake."

"What?"

Mom had come out of the kitchen. "Gerald?" she said weakly.

"What's going on?" She eyed the wild-eyed man and clutched the tie of her bathrobe.

"I'm tellin' ya," Sievers said to Rand's father. "There's a dead woman in the lake! Jesus H. Christ! You're a damned cop, right? Go look for yourself!" Through the still open front door, Sievers's dog kept up the incessant barking and growling against the fence.

"Oh dear God," Mom said as Rand came slowly down the stairs.

The whole scene was surreal. Never had Sievers shown up at their door. The way everyone told it, the old man held a grudge against the police and had a reputation for hating cops. But that didn't matter now.

Dad was already sprinting to the back door and flying outside. Rand was right on his heels, the cold air hitting him hard in the face. Then Rand saw it—the body—a woman—floating face down.

Rand's stomach turned over.

"Shit!" Kicking off his slippers, Gerald yelled over his shoulder, "Rand! Get Tom. Go get Tom! Tell him we need backup! And transportation to the hospital! Go!" Fully clothed, he dived into the cold water, then swam toward the body lying face down thirty yards from shore.

Rand stood frozen for a second. He thought he might puke.

A dead woman?

Holy shit! He blinked, then took off, nearly bowling over Sievers, who had followed them to the yard.

He pushed past Mom, who stood, hands to her mouth, in the doorway. She was pale as death herself as she kept her eyes on the body in the water. "What—who? Oh dear Lord." Rand didn't stop. Just raced through the house and out the open front door, not bothering to close it. He darted across the yard and jumped the creek without breaking stride. He reached the Hunts' house within seconds.

Lights burned bright through the windows. As he pounded on the door, it swung open. Levi, pale-faced, hair disheveled, stood in his pajamas.

"I need to see your dad—"

"He's outside," Levi told him. "Out back."

Rand brushed past his friend, running fast down the hallway to the back of the house and the open sliding door off the kitchen. Levi followed him, stride for stride. Outside, Chase, in boxer shorts, was leaning over the rail of the deck, staring into the water. Cynthia stood closer to the house. Her hair was wrapped in brush rollers, her bathrobe cinched tight, her face pale as death as she tried to light a cigarette with shaking fingers.

Rand skidded to a stop, his gaze glued on the lake.

Levi didn't slow down. He leaped over the few steps to the dock. "Dad? You need help?"

But Thomas Hunt was too busy to answer. He was already swimming to aid Rand's dad, who was dragging the woman's body to shore.

"Did you—did you call for an ambulance?" Rand asked.

Eyes wide in horror, Cynthia nodded blankly. But she was finally able to put the flame from her lighter against the tip of her trembling cigarette.

From the other side of Rand's house, Sievers's shepherd was still barking and growling, pacing on the old man's deck, sending up a racket. Other dogs around the lake joined in, a cacophony of barks and yips. Beyond the point, lights from other houses flicked to life. In neighboring yards, neighbors appeared, some in jackets, some in pajamas, all serious and huddled in family groups. All eyes were trained on the drama unfolding on the lake.

Together, holding the woman's head above the surface of the water, Dad and Tom swam toward the Hunts' dock. The woman floating between them was dressed in a long white nightgown that floated around her. Her eyes were wide, seeming to stare at the charcoal sky, her dark hair drifting around her head.

"Who is it?" Levi asked. He was standing next to his mother on the deck, Rand a few feet away.

Cynthia Hunt whispered, "No . . . oh God, no." She dropped her cigarette.

Chase was staring at the woman as his father hauled her onto the dock and Tom Hunt yelled, "Stand back! For Christ's sake, Cyn, get the kids inside!"

"It's Evan's mom," Chase said, dumbstruck as Cynthia began to sob.

"Cynthia! Go inside! Take the kids!" Tom ordered as he dragged himself out of the water, his hair plastered to his head, his breathing labored. "Did you hear me? Get the boys inside!"

"Oh no . . . oh no, no," Chase said as the two men hauled the woman onto the dock and her ashen face was visible, her features defined, her blue, blue eyes lifeless.

"What?" Shocked, Rand didn't want to believe it. And yet he knew Chase was right. It was Anna Reed.

Not just Evan's mom but Harper's as well. His stomach revolted.

"Anna?" Cynthia gasped, disbelieving.

"Go inside!" Tom bellowed.

Rand doubled over at the edge of the dock and heaved, vomiting into the dark impenetrable water, his body cramping.

From the corner of his eye, he saw Cynthia shepherding her sons inside the house while his dad and Tom tried feverishly to revive the woman on the dock.

But it was too late.

They knew it.

Old Man Sievers knew it.

And, Rand, only eleven years old, knew it.

But, he guessed, Evan didn't yet know his mother was gone.

Nor Harper.

But they would.

And when they found out, Rand surmised, everything would change.

Everything.

1988
The Present

Chapter 24

L evi sat in the dark car.
He hated being here.

This place that he'd once loved, where he'd grown up.

He stared at the exterior of the cottage with its once-white clap-board siding and black shutters. At night, with no lights on, it looked abandoned. And maybe it was. But not for long. He planned to move back, had given up the lease on his apartment weeks before his mother had given up her life.

He didn't understand why she'd done what she'd done or how she'd done it. Her mental capacity had been limited at best, and she had been on that crooked, dangerous path to insanity.

Or she'd arrived at its doorstep, her self-induced flaming destruction testament to how far gone she'd really been.

The muscles in his jaw tightened, and he told himself not to be maudlin or blame himself. It was over.

Surveying the wrap-around porch, he remembered growing up in this house, the good times and the bad. And the horrible.

He'd fought with himself.

Sometimes he'd wanted to move back in, make it his home again.

Other times he'd wanted to burn it down.

For now, though, he'd decided to move back.

At least for a while. *Nothing in life is permanent*, he reminded himself, and God, didn't he know it?

He climbed out of his Ford, walked up the overgrown path to the front porch, and unlocked the door with his own key.

The house was quiet.

Lacking any signs or sounds of life, smelling of disuse.

The police had come and gone, so it wasn't as musty as it had been the last time he'd walked inside, yet tonight it felt dead. Things weren't all that disturbed, as this place wasn't officially a crime scene, but he noticed that some of his mother's Early American-style side chairs had been moved a few inches, the drawers of side tables left slightly open. All in all the interior was the same as he remembered, down to the amber ashtray sitting front and center on the maple coffee table within easy reach from the floral-print couch that his mother loved.

In the dining area, he ran a finger through the dust on the oval table where they, as a family, had played raucous pinochle matches or never-ending Scrabble and Monopoly games. Smiling, he recalled a time playing Risk when Evan, losing badly, had gotten so angry that he'd upended the board, sending the tiny colored "army" cubes scattering all over the shag carpeting. Cynthia had watched the ensuing wrestling match and, after ordering all the players to pick up the pieces, had burned the game that night in the fireplace. "Play nice or don't play at all," she'd admonished her sons, as well as Evan and Rand.

Those were happier times, he thought now as he walked to the sliding door overlooking the lake and caught his reflection in the glass.

Twenty years had passed since his mom and dad had left him and his brother alone on their "date" nights.

Mom had always left them with Swanson's TV dinners and bottles of Nehi soda and said, "Be good," before she and Dad rumbled out of the drive in the Oldsmobile. Those evenings, the two brothers would wait, Levi standing guard at the living room window until he saw the taillights of the Cutlass disappear while Chase hurried downstairs to the rec room. Using the tiny key hidden high on a shelf behind a dusty vase of fake roses, he'd open the liquor cabinet and return to the kitchen with the purloined bottle of booze. Judiciously they'd add the liquor to their drinks and lock the bottles back in the cabinet, leaving the key where they'd found it.

While Mom and Dad were out, they had sat side by side on the floor, backs propped against the couch, the coffee table filled with their foil trays of fried chicken, vegetables, and mashed potatoes with a glob of butter. Sipping their doctored bottles of grape soda, they watched *Daniel Boone* and *Star Trek* on the TV console while getting a little buzzed until the folks came home.

Usually laughing and teasing, smelling of cigarettes and beer, neither Tom nor Cynthia seemed to notice that their sons weren't completely sober.

The good times.

Along with the bad.

His jaw tightened at the thought of the worst night, one he would never forget.

One he'd lied about.

One that had haunted him for twenty years.

Rubbing the back of his neck, Levi walked to his brother's bedroom.

It, too, was silent.

Lifeless.

A dusty shrine to another lifetime.

Chase's double bed nearly filled the small space, and his hand-me-down dresser was covered with trophies. On the walls were several awards along with teen art from the sixties. Levi eyed a psychedelic *Skeleton & Roses* poster for the Grateful Dead along with the poster Mom really hated for the movie *One Million Years B.C.* in which a scantily clad Raquel Welch stood warrior-like in the foreground while ferocious dinosaurs battled cavemen in the background.

"Isn't she the sexiest?" Chase had asked Levi as he'd taped the poster to the wall, then pressed tacks into the corners. "I mean, man, look at her! Those legs. That rack. And her hair. She's the whole package."

Levi hadn't been able to argue the fact. Not then, and not now.

Mom had threatened to rip the "indecent" poster off the wall.

But she never had.

Ever.

Levi glanced at the array of trophies on the dresser and picked up the one that was a small statue of a football quarterback, leaning backward, arm aloft, football in hand, ready to throw a pass. Chase's name and the date were inscribed on the block on which the player was mounted.

Levi ran a thumb over the inscription and remembered the night Chase had won the award that went with it. *Best All Around Athlete, Chase Hunt, 1966.*

Sitting on the edge of the bed, he stared at the trophy and whispered, "What happened to you, brother?"

There were no answers in the silent bedroom, but his gaze moved to the window overlooking the front porch. That night, he'd heard the tapping from his own room and had walked in to investigate. Harper Reed, her expression concerned, had stood on the other side of the glass pane. His heart had beat wildly at the sight of her upturned face and the worry in her dark eyes. He'd wanted to take her into his arms, to tell her that everything would be all right, but he hadn't. Because nothing about that night had been all right. In fact, it was the night that everything had gone wrong.

1968

Chapter 25

"You sneaking, ungrateful son of a bitch!" Tom Hunt roared, his anger seeming to palpitate through the house, though really it was echoing through the dusty floor vents. Any conversation that took place in the basement drifted up to Levi's bedroom. So, lying on his bed, Levi heard every word.

And when Dad was like this, all hell broke out.

"Where in Christ's name have you been? Out carousing? Drinking? Doing drugs? What're you into now? Pot? Speed? Maybe acid? What the hell's gotten into you?" Dad roared. "What in the world are you thinking? Flunking out of school? Throwing your life away!" A pause. No answer from Chase. "I've seen you sneaking around down the street, too. Don't tell me you're fucking one of those hippie sluts!"

"Thomas," Cynthia interjected, her voice faint. "If you could just calm down and—"

"You want me to calm down?" Dad yelled. "While our son is out whoring and doing God only knows what?"

"I don't think it's any of your business what I do," Chase challenged.

Uh-oh. Not good.

Levi rolled out of bed quietly to crack open his bedroom door and peer across the short hallway to the empty living room bathed in warm light from amber-colored lamps.

The conversation was now muted, seeping up the open stairs from the basement. Levi, careful not to make a sound, eased down the carpeted steps.

"Getting angry isn't going to help," Mom was saying, her voice louder as he rounded the corner near the bottom of the staircase.

Levi dared to peek into the room. They were all squared off; Dad and Chase facing each other, Dad's face red and sweating. Chase, too, was flushed, his body coiled, ready to spring.

And Mom stood behind the couch, her hand on its velvet back.

"Are you out of your mind?" Dad obviously didn't believe what his eldest son was peddling. "Didn't you read the letter from the university?" he demanded, glancing at his wife. "See his grade report? He's flunked out of college, Cindy! *Flunked out!* Our all-state academic athlete! He's thrown it all away! Flushed his future down the toilet. No scholarship. No fucking deferment. For the love of Christ, what a mess!"

"It's my life," Chase argued, blinking hard, his jaw set. "Not yours!"

"Oh yeah? Who do you think paid for all your tutors?" Dad demanded. "Your private coaches?"

"That was *your* choice, Dad. You loved every minute of it! Bragged about it. How *your* son was so great." His eyes shone. Jesus, Chase was near tears.

But what Chase said was true. Hadn't Dad always shone in the reflection of "his boy's" achievements, especially on the football field and basketball court?

"So now you're gonna waste it all? All that effort? All that time? All that money?" Dad wasn't letting it go.

"I never asked for any of it!"

Still in the shadow of the staircase, Levi stepped closer to the archway of the rec room where his brother and father were facing each other, fists clenched, jaws tight, gazes locked. The low-ceilinged room ran the length of the house, with a pool table on one end, the jukebox at the other, a few old chairs and lamps in between.

And father and son right in the middle, looking to tear each other apart.

Dad's face was so red as to be almost purple, his teeth bared, a vein throbbing at his temple. His usually neatly combed hair was a mess, exposing the bald spot growing beneath the graying strands.

Wild-eyed, Chase looked like he was hopped up on something.

Dad wasn't wrong about that.

Mom had moved to the sliding door, her face a mask of worry, her chin wobbling as she shredded a tissue between her hands. "Stop this now," she said, her voice trembling. "We can talk about this in the morning. When you're, I mean when we are all calmer."

"Nothing to talk about." Dad's eyes were focused solely on Chase, his feet planted on the checkerboard tile floor, the zebra-skin rug between them. "So, what now, boy?" he taunted. "I guess you'll be hauling your ass down to the recruiter's office cuz sure as shootin' Uncle Sam is on his way."

"I'm not signing up," Chase said. They were circling each other.

"You won't have to."

"I'm not going."

"The hell you're not. Any son of mine is damn well serving his country. And proudly."

"Bullshit! You can't tell me what to do!" Chase yelled. Now the tears were flowing. He dashed them away with the back of his hand.

"My house. My rules," Dad said.

"If I have to, I'll be a conscientious objector."

"No, that's not an option."

"Then I'll get Harper pregnant."

"What?" Mom gasped, the tissue in her fingers forgotten. "No, no, no. Don't even think that way. Who knows what would happen with that rich little . . ." Apoplectic, she was shaking her head violently. "I mean, she could trick you! You wouldn't even know if the baby was yours. Do *not* go there, Chase Thomas!"

Levi couldn't stand it a second longer. His mother's sharp words cut too close to the bone. "Hey!" he said as he stepped out of the shadows and held up his hands, palms out. "Stop! Okay? Just *stop!*"

"Stay out of it, Levi," Chase warned, sniffing loudly. "This is between me and him."

"Go back to your room!" Dad was talking between clenched teeth, and the air in the room seemed to crackle. "Go. Now! You, too,

Cindy! Go." With a glance at Levi, he ordered, "Get your mother out of here!"

"Tom, please, don't," she said, stepping forward, the destroyed tissue drifting to the floor.

"Stop!" Levi ordered again and caught the warning in Chase's eyes. He ignored it and pled, "Just freaking stop!"

Chase turned on his brother. "You little pansy-ass! Butt the fuck out!"

"Chase!" Mom gasped. "Don't!"

But Chase wasn't listening. Muscles coiled, face twisted in fury, he turned on his brother. "This is none of your damned business, Levi."

"It's all of our—"

Chase sprang.

Across the rug.

Hitting Levi in the midsection.

Entangled, they flew into the jukebox.

Levi's head crashed against the sharp corner of the Wurlitzer.

Hot pain burst across his forehead.

The jukebox skidded, slamming against the wall, blood smearing across the glass cover, distorting the numbered list of songs on display.

Mom screamed, "Stop! Chase, don't!" Then turned to her husband. "Tom! *Do something!*"

Together they tumbled over the rug, careening into the coffee table. It upended, the ashtray and box of tissues flying.

Chase hauled back to punch Levi's face.

With a roar, Levi kicked upward, flipping Chase onto his back and pushing him away.

"Stop! Boys, stop!" Mom yelled.

Chase lunged.

Dad caught his elbow and yanked Chase back. "You little prick!" he growled. "Stop this, now!"

Mom skirted the upside-down table and hurried over to Levi. "You're bleeding," she said.

"Get him out of here," Dad ordered, notching his chin toward his younger son.

"You're hurt," she whispered, finding another tissue in the pocket of her housecoat and dabbing at his eyebrow.

He jerked away. "I'm fine." Breathing heavily, the scent of blood and a fight still in the air, he wanted a piece of his brother.

Undeterred, she reached for him. "No, honey, you're—"

"I'm fine, Mom!" he repeated, afraid the tears stinging the back of his eyes might fall, further humiliating him. He threw off her arm. "Screw it!"

"Levi!" she whispered, but he didn't care.

Let his dad and brother tear each other limb from limb. Holding a hand over the wound near his eye, he got to his feet, and with one last glowering look at his sack of shit brother, he climbed up the stairs, straight to the bathroom where he slammed and locked the door. Holding onto the edges of the sink, he dropped his head and let blood fall onto the pink basin. Every one of his muscles tensed, and he wanted, oh how he wanted, to smash his fist into Chase's always smug face. Well, this time Chase was in big trouble. Major trouble. He'd finally gone too far. The golden boy losing some of his shine.

Fool's gold. That's what it was.

Damn his brother. Damn his father. Damn his whole family.

He looked up to find himself in the reflection, his face still flushed, his nostrils flared, his lips pulled back as he took short, fast breaths.

Chase didn't know how good he had it. He was such a dick! Levi turned on the faucets, leaned over again, and sluiced water over his face.

Then, slightly calmer, he washed the sticky blood from his hands and found a Band-Aid from the metal box in the medicine cabinet. He tore off the wrapper, then had to retrieve a second Band-Aid as the first was immediately soaked through.

All in all, it took four of the stupid bandages to cover the wound and stem the blood flow. In that time, his shame at being taken down by Chase had been replaced by anger at the entire situation.

Not that Levi blamed Chase for wanting to leave. But he could have found a better way than flunking out of school and then trying to dodge the draft. And he should *never* have said anything about getting Harper pregnant. Once-upon-a-time A student Chase had proved himself to be a moron.

As for Harper getting pregnant? That was just plain nuts!

Nonetheless, he felt a jab of jealousy at the thought of Chase and Harper together. She had been *his* friend, and then Chase had noticed her. And then, oh crap. He closed his eyes. Couldn't go there. "Fuck," he said under his breath.

He heard his mother's hurried footsteps as she rushed up the stairs to her bedroom on the upper floor. A door shut forcefully before he heard a series of muffled sobs.

Great!

Now Dad was pissed as hell.

And Mom was crying.

He took a deep breath and stepped out of the bathroom. His mother's broken sobs were louder out here in the hallway, and he started for the staircase. There was a chance he could offer her some comfort, say something to smooth things over, but no words came. He didn't know what to say. Maybe it was best to let things settle. Sleep on it.

He went into his bedroom. But behind the closed door, he could hear the fight still raging downstairs, his heat vent a speaker.

He stripped and fell into bed.

"You'll never amount to anything!" his father accused.

Smack!

The sound of flesh hitting flesh.

Levi cringed.

"It's my life!" Chase insisted again, his voice breaking.

Crash!

Levi reached between his mattress and box spring to withdraw a flask he kept hidden there. He opened it quickly and took several swallows of the whiskey he'd swiped from the bar downstairs. It burned his throat on its way to his stomach, but he hoped it would calm him, quiet his jangled nerves, and mute the sounds emanating from the basement.

It didn't.

Even the throbbing over his eye and the alcohol seeping into his bloodstream couldn't drown out the voices and sick sounds of violence.

"I'm not joining up!"

Thud.

A body crashing against something hard.

Tom said, "Try it, boy."

Oh God. Levi imagined Chase ready to pounce—maybe with a weapon, and Dad with all his police training, standing across the room, bloodied and battered and waving his fingers in a "come-on" motion, waiting for Chase to charge blindly, like an enraged bull.

It happened.

As Levi squeezed his eyes shut, he heard Chase say, "I hate you!"

Then, running footsteps.

Another thunderous crash.

A wail from his mother's bedroom.

Then, the most damning words from his father. "You're not my son any longer, Chase. From this day forward, you're dead to me."

Levi closed his eyes, took another sip. For once, Chase was in trouble, when Levi was usually the one who didn't measure up. An evil little part of him liked the thought of shining, perfect Chase getting what was due him because Levi, more than anyone, knew what his brother was really like—at his center. But he felt guilty immediately and rolled over, pulling the covers over his head.

No good.

Levi still heard the soul-jarring cursing. Groaning. Fists smashing. Furniture crashing. Wood splintering. Walls shaking. His head felt as if it might explode. He couldn't stand listening to the fight, feeling the rage simmering through the house. Not one second longer.

He had to get out.

Leave.

Now!

He flung himself off his bed. In the dark he found his clothes on the floor, threw them on, and grabbed his jacket from the back of his desk chair. Mom was still upstairs weeping, Dad and Chase going at it in the basement, so he slipped out the front door and across the wide porch.

As he started jogging, faster and faster, getting away, he heard Sievers's dog bark. A cold breeze slapped his face, and it felt good. Running forced his thoughts away from his brother and father.

He kept up his pace.

Toward town.

Past the deserted swim park.

Around the lake.

He hugged the side of the road, dodging the few headlights that passed. He didn't have a plan, but he just kept moving around the lakeshore, observing the dark water, looking up at the stars when the clouds thinned.

As he approached Almsville, he skirted the main streets, avoiding storefronts with their security lights and circumventing the blue pools of illumination cast by street lamps. He took back alleys and quiet, familiar lanes, spying a scraggly cat traipsing along a fence line and later a possum scuttling through the hedge of a manicured lawn. As it was still an hour or so before midnight, windows glowed in the dark, casting patches of light on the lawns, playing upon fountains, trees, and even a bicycle left on a front porch. The houses appeared serene, as if each and every one was home to a perfect, happy family.

But who knew what went on behind closed doors?

He wondered if anyone suspected that his own house was often one of chaos, that even when Mom decorated it with Christmas lights or Easter baskets, there was darkness behind the door with its welcome mat.

Everyone has their troubles.

He'd heard that somewhere, and the thought certainly came home to roost tonight.

He kept moving. Step after step, dashing around the lake.

Though he hadn't had a destination in mind, he ended up at the road leading to Dixon Island. Probably his subconscious leading him here, he thought as he made his way down the lane to stand at the closed gate flanked by its cool gargoyles. He stared through the bars and across the bridge toward the old mansion where, these days, Harper was living, he knew, most of the time.

He'd like to talk to her.

That was the problem.

Always.

He'd had a crush on her for all of his life. It was bad enough when you fantasized about a friend's girlfriend, but what did it say about him that he ached for his brother's chick? How sick was that?

He closed his eyes, his pulse accelerated as he remembered . . .

Oh God, he couldn't go there!

Gripping the rails, he stared through the gate to the big house, barely visible though the tower lights were on.

He thought of Harper inside.

Pining for Chase.

His insides turned cold.

He expected that Chase, after the fight with their dad, would seek Harper out. He'd probably take the boat out and "go dark" without running lights, skimming across the water, as he had in the past. A reckless, dangerous ride.

Levi's gut twisted a bit at the thought, and his hands clenched over the bars of the gate. He told himself he was being stupid, that Harper was off-limits, but they'd been in the same class in school, known each other since kindergarten. Chase hadn't paid any attention to her until he was a senior and she a sophomore in high school, when she'd blossomed from a long-legged coltish kid into a beauty. They'd started dating the end of her sophomore year, and even though they'd had their share of breakups, they were together, she willing to do anything for him, it seemed.

But maybe not for long.

Chase had confided to Levi that he'd been seeing other girls at college and he'd spent more than a little time at the house at the end of the street, a place where cars came and went at all hours. A spot where drugs and booze were plentiful and sexy girls hung out.

Harper deserved better.

If she were Levi's girl, he would do better by her.

But she was out of reach.

Turning away from the gate, he shoved his hands in his pockets and kept walking. Mixed with his conflicted feelings about Harper was the memory of the horrid fight, still replaying in his mind. Dad had been madder than ever and Chase had pushed it, maybe still was.

He walked several miles on Northway before crossing the west-end bridge and making his way along the road that wound along the hillside, where the houses were built on pilings that stretched out over the chasm and offered expansive views of the water far below. He caught glimpses of the lake through the trees and met a handful of cars on the high slope, their headlights bright and stark in the night, their taillights winking red.

The rain started again just as he reached the summit. From there it was only a hundred yards or so to the trail that wound downward through the trees to the end of his street. It was darker in the woods. He stumbled a couple of times over dirt clods and fallen branches. Cussing himself for not bringing a flashlight, he had to remember how angry he'd been when he left. Fired by a little booze and a lot of testosterone, without a plan, he'd just started walking. Now, though, the alcohol had worn off and his fury had subsided by leaps and bounds. He was still upset, but he could handle his emotions now.

He picked his way down the familiar path, guided by the dim street lamp near the Hunts' house.

As he was about to step out of the woods, he heard the slap of footsteps. He froze. From the shadows he saw a tall man running down the street as if Satan himself was chasing him. As the runner reached the rental house at the end of the road, he cut quickly into the yard. Not breaking stride, he ducked around the corner to the back near the dock and out of sight.

Levi had just taken a step forward when the guy reappeared, closer, on the near side of the cabin.

Levi watched as the guy raced up the outside stairs. At the doorway he paused and gave a quick knock. A door cut into the roof opened. The guy's hood fell back, and Levi caught a glimpse of pale blond hair as he greeted whoever was inside, then as the door opened wider, dim light from inside exposed his face—a man in his twenties that Levi didn't recognize.

But the guy greeting him? On the inside? Levi had seen him before—a guy with long hair, thick sideburns, and John Lennon glasses. His teeth were a little crooked, one front tooth overlapping the other. Levi had seen him sometimes in a green Corvair with a bad muffler. Sometimes in a rattling VW van with a peace sign painted on it. Didn't matter which vehicle. Every time he drove down the street, Old Man Sievers's dog would go ape-shit.

Now he had a pissed-off look on his face. He let the blond guy inside and shut the door.

Levi figured there was probably a drug deal going down. He'd heard that there was a guy who was dealing out of the place. He studied the cabin for a minute. Behind the window shades, lights flickered. The porch light was glowing and casting light over the cars and vans that littered the driveway and street, all parked haphazardly, the Corvair among the rest.

He wondered what exactly went on inside and cast one last look to the attic door. It hadn't opened again.

Time to head home.

He stepped onto the street, hands deep in his jacket pockets.

As he was almost past the cabin, a girl slipped out the front door only to close it behind her. Her red hair was wild, held in place by a headband, a fringed vest barely covering her breasts as she sat on the steps.

"Hey!" She waved to him and smiled. "Whatcha doin'?" she asked, standing near a macramé hanger where a near-dead plant hung from a hook screwed into the roof's overhang. "Want a hit?"

He paused as she lit a joint and sucked hard.

When he stepped closer, she froze, a small stream of smoke exiting her parted lips. Sensual lips. "Oh. I. Uh." Her eyebrows drew together and she was clearly confused. "I, um, I thought you were Chase."

Levi wasn't surprised. Aside from their differences in hair and eye color, he and Chase resembled each other. A lot. Chase was bigger, an inch taller, but even that might change as Levi grew older.

"Yeah, I'm his brother," he said.

"Really? Uh. Yeah. I've seen you." Nodding, she got to her feet. Approached. "The offer still stands. Wanna toke?" She smiled, more broadly to show off white teeth.

"Sure." He took the joint and acted as if he smoked pot all the time, which he didn't, but he needed something to distract him from her massive breasts, swinging freely beneath the scrap of a suede vest with its long fringe.

Somehow he avoided coughing and asked her name.

"Moonbeam."

"Moon—?"

"Moonbeam. Everyone calls me that." At his skeptical look, she said, "Yeah, I know," and rolled her big expressive eyes. "It's kinda crazy but it's waaaay cooler than Janet."

"If you say so."

"For sure!" she said with a tinkling laugh, her eyes twinkling in the porch light.

"Okay. Moon, er, Moonbeam."

Giggling, she said, "I think I like you, Chase's brother, even if you are jail bait."

"Jail—?"

The front door opened and the strains of "White Rabbit" wafted out on the woody scent of patchouli. A muscle-bound guy with a huge Afro nearly filled the doorway, his big frame silhouetted by shifting light from lava lamps that were visible just beyond his shoulders. "Who're you?" he demanded gruffly.

Janet/Moonbeam hurried up the steps and placed a hand on the guy's bare chest. "He's cool," she assured him. "He's Chase's brother."

"Shit. A kid?" His dark gaze landed on Levi. "What're you doin' here?"

"Just walking."

"It's late. Ain't it past your bedtime?"

"Hey, Ronnie, don't," Moonbeam said in a soft voice. "I said, he's cool. No need to give him a bad time."

"I don't like kids hanging out. Isn't he the son of a cop or somethin'?"

"So is Chase and"—she shrugged—"the cops don't bother us."

"Yet," he said, skewering Levi with a suspicious glare.

"You worry too much." She kissed one of his bare pectoral muscles, and he let out a sigh. "Someone's got to."

"Give it a rest."

"Okay. This time. But I don't like kids hanging out here." To Levi he said, "You'd best be gettin' home." Then to Moonbeam, "What're you thinkin'? Now, come on." With a possessive arm around Moonbeam's slim waist, he drew her inside and shut the door. A second later Levi heard the distinctive sound of a dead bolt slamming into place.

But the shade wasn't completely drawn.

He took a chance, peeking beneath it. Inside the black dude and Moonbeam finished the joint, then started kissing and touching. He pushed her onto an orange couch, his big hands working upward, past that tantalizing fringe to squeeze a suddenly exposed nipple.

She arched her back, and he took the nipple into his mouth.

And damn it, Levi felt himself get hard.

He pulled away, disgusted with himself and more disgusted with Chase, who had mentioned the chicks and free love at this little house more than once.

Levi wanted no part of it.

He walked quietly home, then slipped inside the house, which was much quieter now. Just the furnace rumbling and rain on the roof.

Was it odd that Moonbeam knew Chase? Was she always so free with her body? Had Chase been down there and actually screwed her?

Their mother was always ranting and raving about "that awful place filled with free love and who knows what else?" But despite the rumors of drugs at the small house, the cops, including his father and Rand's dad, had pretty much turned a blind eye to the comings and goings.

As Moonbeam had alluded to.

The cops don't bother us.

What was that all about?

Not that he really cared.

Suddenly bone-tired, he kicked off his clothes and slipped wearily between the sheets. He was closing his eyes when he heard the sound of bedsprings beginning to squeak. Rhythmically and slow, and then faster and faster. Shit. His parents were doing it! His father, all hyped up on anger, was . . .

He wouldn't think about it!

Nor would he think about Moonbeam's supple body.

He felt an erection swelling again and tried to ignore it when he heard movement.

Over the squeaking mattress and his mother's stifled moans, he heard Chase leaving the room next to his. Quick, light footsteps hurrying toward the basement stairs.

Man, Chase was pushing it.

He strained to hear the sound of the slider opening downstairs and thought he heard the click of the lock, but he couldn't be certain. Nonetheless, Chase didn't return to his room.

He must've made it out.

Within seconds, the dog two doors down began to bark ferociously. Old Man Sievers's shepherd. Forever on patrol.

The dog probably caught wind of Chase.

Overhead, the squeaking suddenly ended. For a second Levi expected his father to come racing down the stairs after Chase.

Levi waited, counting off the seconds.

It didn't happen.

Good.

As at odds as Levi was with his older brother, he didn't go along with some of Dad's rules. It was stupid that Chase, almost twenty with over a year of college under his belt, was forced to skulk around like a pre-teen.

But that's the way it was in Thomas Hunt's house.

As Dad had said earlier: his house, his rules.

Well, fuck that!

Levi reached under his mattress again and pulled out the flask. He'd get drunk. Why the hell not?

He downed what was left in the flask, and then exhaustion overtook him. He closed his eyes and within seconds slept the sleep of the dead.

1988
The Present

Chapter 26

Scratch!

The grating sound was coming from somewhere far off.

Scratch! Scratch! Scratch!

Someone clawing . . . but how? Harper stood on the small boat in the middle of the lake, the wind snatching at her nightgown. It was dark, the stars hidden by low-hanging clouds, the surface of the water choppy with white caps.

Scratchhhhh!

Was something or someone scraping and tearing the hull?

Something large, with sharp claws or teeth, ripping at the wood?

The boat buckled on a wave, and she scrabbled to grab onto a mast with tattered sails to keep from being thrown overboard.

"Jump!" She heard someone yell at her, a faint voice over the rush of the wind. "Jump! Jump!"

Craaack! Beneath her bare feet, the wood began to splinter.

"No," she whispered. "No, no, no!"

Water rushed into the craft.

"Jump!" she heard again, before realizing it was her own voice, drowned out by the loud, horrifying cry of a banshee as a giant wave rose.

As the scream continued, the boat split.

Flung into the water, she was engulfed, the dark void surrounding her.

Swim, she told herself, forcing leaden legs to kick. Up, up, up to the ever-distant surface. *Swim! Kick!*

She flailed upward. Past photographs that sank into the darkness. *Kick! Swim!*

She rose slowly, and just as she broke the surface, she saw two great taloned beasts rise to the heavens, one was scaled, the other with smooth skin, both winged. The dragon and the devil, gargoyles come to life, teeth bared as they screamed, their wings opening in flight.

She gasped, horrified, sinking back into the water.

But she found no safety in the depths, as through the dark water a body appeared, little more than a hideous skeleton with fish and eels floating through its eye sockets and ribs.

"I love you," it seemed to say, and in that second, she saw him as he once was, a tall athletic boy with blond hair and an easy smile.

"Chase," she tried to whisper, but the words wouldn't come and his visage disappeared into the rotting skeleton. She screamed then, echoing the banshee's cry.

Harper's eyes flew open.

She sat bolt upright on the bed in her room.

Moonlight streamed through the window, casting the crucifix in relief against the wall. It was a dream. Just a bad, bad dream. She breathed deeply, calming herself. "Get over it," she said aloud as vestiges of the nightmare, like ashes from a dying fire, still floated in the air.

Once more, the headache that had been with her most of yesterday reappeared, and she chastised herself for having too many drinks the night before. Today—none, she vowed. She needed to be clearheaded.

But the nightmare. Wow.

She shoved her hair from her face with trembling fingers and mentally castigated herself for being such a ninny. After struggling out of the sleeping bag, Harper snapped on the bedside lamp, winced at the light, but checked her watch on the night stand. Four-thirty in the morning.

Too early to get up.

Make that *way* too early.

And her head was pounding.

Great.

Yawning, tamping down the memories of the dream, she walked to the bathroom, turned on the tap, and dipped her head under the sink, taking a long drink in the hope it might stave off or lessen the hangover. But that was just wishful thinking, she knew as she splashed water over her face and felt the bandage on her chin shift. She'd have to put on a new one as she doubted the cut had healed.

As she reached for a towel, she caught her wan image in the mirror, the slipping bandage, dark circles under her eyes.

And a tiny, evil face.

Just over her right shoulder.

What?

She bit back a scream and whirled to find Maude, wide eyes open, sitting on a shelf on the opposite side of the room.

The lifeless doll with her brush-like eyelashes and plastic face seemed to stare straight into Harper's soul.

"You—you little freak!" Harper spat, her heart racing. She knocked the doll from its perch. It landed on the tile with a thud and a faint, "Ma-Ma."

"Oh, shut up!" Harper kicked the doll again. It bounced against the door frame with a pitiful "Ma-Ma."

"Sweet Jesus." Heart knocking, head thundering, adrenaline pumping through her blood stream, Harper glowered at the inanimate toy, head drooping downward. "What the devil?" Harper shoved her hair from her eyes and glowered at the doll. How had it ended up here? Who the hell had put the damned thing up on the shelf positioned just so?

Maybe it was you. Maybe you did it. You locked all the doors last night. And face it, you were pretty wasted.

"No."

No one else has a key.

Or do they?

The damned doll didn't march up the stairs and hop up onto the shelf by herself.

Harper breathed deeply, trying to piece together the night before. She remembered seeing all the dolls downstairs—including Maude.

Right? Her memory was fuzzy from the alcohol, but she was pretty sure . . . and then she'd nearly stumbled up the stairs and half-tripped over that other stupid doll, the one Gram called Toodles. Once she'd landed on the third floor, she'd flopped straight onto the bed and struggled into the sleeping bag.

Right?

No—no. She'd changed in the bathroom. To confirm, she glanced down at her KISS T-shirt and pile of clothes left near the shower. She hadn't seen the doll then, nor did she recall carrying it up here and placing it on the shelf. No, no, no, she wouldn't do that. She didn't even like touching any of the old things.

She'd been really tired, and her headache had pounded.

Wincing against the pain building behind her eyes, she tried to think, to remember. Though the night before was a little blurry, she was certain there had been no dolls in this suite. Zero. And she didn't remember carrying any of them up here.

No, she wouldn't have.

No reason.

And yet, somehow, someway Maude had ended up here.

Goose pimples crawled up the back of her arms.

Hadn't she heard the creak of a door opening last night?

Had there been footsteps? A groan of the old steps?

Hadn't she, rusted scissors in hand, checked? And she'd looked at her reflection in the mirror and seen no evil little face in the reflection.

To confirm her memory, she went back to the bed, felt inside the sleeping bag, and sure enough the shears were where she'd placed them.

And nothing had happened.

The doll was in the wrong place, but she hadn't been assaulted last night. So why would anyone go to the trouble of putting Maude on the shelf? It didn't make any sense.

Now that her racing heartbeat had slowed, she was thinking more rationally. She picked up the doll. No, she didn't remember even touching her. So . . . why? Turning it over in her hands, she heard the weak little "Ma-Ma" sound again.

"What are you doing up here, Maude?" she whispered, turning the doll over and catching sight of something red showing beneath the dingy pinafore. She lifted the once-white hem. A single word was scrawled in dark red across the doll's belly: *ICU*.

"What the—?" She dropped the doll as if burned.

It hit the floor with a thud, sputtered a pathetic little "Ma-Ma," and lay crumpled, its head twisted at an unnatural angle, its eyes wide and condemning.

"No," Harper whispered, backing up until her hips hit the cold porcelain sink in the bathroom.

Had the red message scrawled on the doll's belly been recently added, or was it old? Maybe Gram had loaned it to the hospital and it was marked with ICU. No, no, that didn't make any sense. Harper was pretty sure toys weren't allowed in Intensive Care.

So obviously the message was left for her. And obviously someone had been in here last night.

Who? Who would do this to her?

How? How did they get in?

Her blood turned to ice as she thought of someone creeping past her bed as she lay sleeping, someone pausing to watch her, someone sick.

Get a hold of yourself.

Don't lose it.

For the love of God, Harper, do not *lose it!*

With trembling fingers, she picked up the doll gingerly, as if she expected it to come to life.

Pull yourself together. It's only a child's toy. Old and slightly creepy, but just a damned doll.

She managed to examine the message more closely.

ICU. Again, she thought of the Intensive Care Unit in a hospital. St. Catherine's. Where Cynthia Hunt had been taken. And where she'd died.

Was this some kind of warning? Was she being blamed for Cynthia's death?

Or . . . she read the message aloud. "I. C. U." She paused, then came up with "I. See. You." Well, no shit. Anyone who had put the doll in the attached bathroom had definitely seen her. An extremely unsettling thought. "They're telling me I'm being watched?" Her insides curdled at the thought. What was to say that the intruder had left? What if he were still in the huge house, hiding in a myriad of dark corners and hidden spaces?

Her throat went dry. Swallowing back her fear, she listened. Hard. Did she hear the creak of a floorboard over the rumble of the furnace? Was that the sound of a door clicking open, or was that her overactive imagination?

Get a grip, Harper.

Every instinct on high alert, again she armed herself with the scissors. She moved quietly, carrying the disgusting doll with its disturbing message down the stairs.

No sound over the whisper of the October wind buffeting the windows.

No door softly closing.

No rushed, padded footsteps.

No open window banging against the shutters.

Everything was calm.

Too calm.

Any night wind had died in this pre-dawn hour.

Nerves stretched tight, she dropped Maude into the trash can in the kitchen and checked all of the locks on the doors, like the five-pointed star Gram had told her about when she was a girl.

Everything appeared to be locked up tight.

She felt no disturbance in the air.

There's no one here. Not now.

Still, she went through every room and made certain the latches on all the windows were secure. One by one she tested them. Kitchen, dining room, foyer, den, and parlor . . . all the windows were closed. Until she felt a breath of cold air. A draft? Her heartbeat accelerated as the whisper of cold air crawled up her nape.

She backed up and felt the icy breeze seeping from beneath a window overlooking the terrace from the parlor. Though the latch appeared locked, it wasn't. The window had swollen. When she pushed on the window sash, the pane slid upward with some difficulty. "Son of a—" She tried to shut the window, but despite throwing all of her weight into it, it wouldn't completely close.

She hadn't noticed last night.

She peered through the rain-dappled pane to the darkness beyond. Of course there was no one visible. Stepping backward, she tried to find a footprint on the floor and even reached down to feel the carpet.

No wet print.

But this had to be the point of entry.

"You bastard."

She rummaged around in the kitchen until she found a flashlight, which, of course, wouldn't light. But she located one of the new packs of batteries she'd picked up at the grocery, loaded up the flashlight, and headed to the terrace. Outside she tried again to lower the window. It didn't budge. It would have to be fixed, along with the dozens of other repairs this old house needed just to function properly.

Sweeping the flashlight's beam over the flagstones, she walked to the steps, the very steps she'd flown down in her desperate attempt to save Cynthia. So anyone could have approached by boat. Silently. Without a motor running. But who? Why? Unerringly, she stared across the lake to the point and the five houses directly across. Every home had a boathouse or slip housing some kind of watercraft and docks protruding from the shore, the largest belonging to the last house on the street. Some of the homes had canoes or kayaks on their docks. Also, hadn't she witnessed Craig Alexander using a boat when he was creeping into the Hunts' house?

Could he have rowed silently across the lake, climbed the stairs, found the unlatched window, and climbed in?

Her blood ran cold at the thought.

Or could it have been someone else? There were several hundred houses all along the shores of the lake. She was only fixated on those located at Fox Point because it was the shortest distance to the island. And she knew some of the people who lived there.

More importantly, they knew her.

But who would do this horrifying but childish prank? Why?

And really, couldn't someone have come from the road, through the open gate? Or by boat from one of the other houses or public accesses around Lake Twilight? She scanned the dark shoreline that stretched for miles.

But again, who? And why?

And why break in and try to terrorize her rather than harm her?

Finding the doll scared her, yes, but whoever was behind the sick deed could just as easily have attacked her in her sleep. Even killed her. But he hadn't. His intent was to freak her out, intimidate her, or play mind games with her.

She walked over to the open garage housing the tram, the car still in place. Running her flashlight's beam over the interior, she wondered if the tram still ran. The inside showed wear, a little rust, and it seemed as if it hadn't been used in years. Like everything else. Outside the car, she ran the flashlight's beam over the rails onto which it was attached. She expected fir needles and leaves, even clumps of dirt on the rusted track that ran zigzagging down the hill from the house to the dock.

But it was clear.

Not so the path. The steep trail of switchbacks was covered in soggy leaves, broken boughs, and dirt. She walked slightly uphill to the spot at the back of the house where the path forked, one trail winding around the side of the house to the garage and parking area, the other leading to the kitchen door. With all the wet yard debris, it was impossible to see any footprints, but she shone the light along the ground as she made her way behind the garage to the front of the house. And in the back of her mind, she hoped she would spot Jinx, out prowling.

She didn't see any eyes reflecting from beneath the fern fronds and rhododendrons, neither feline nor those of a raccoon, possum, or rat.

She thought of the intruder.

Whoever had come here had been stealthy.

In the parking area she aimed her flashlight down the length of the bridge, but the beam faded into nothingness before reaching the gate at the far end. And the grounds at the front of the house, including the roses in the garden that doubled as a cat cemetery, didn't so much as shiver as there was no breeze. The blooms were long gone now, the skeletal canes growing wild along the tiny headstones where Gram's pets had been buried to much fanfare, towel-draped corpses laid to rest in the soft loam of the garden.

Now quiet.

Almost eerily so.

Again, no live cat.

She kept searching for hints about the person who had broken into the house.

Her panic had subsided, thankfully. By nature, she wasn't nervous or afraid, not a shrinking violet. If anything she was often times too forthright and vocal, her temper too quick to flare, her tongue sometimes razor sharp. And right now she felt a surge of anger. Who would dare do this ridiculous, childish prank? And why? To scare her off? To frighten her into selling?

Well, she wasn't about to be intimidated.

Still, the next time she went to bed, she would sleep not only with the scissors but also with the hunting knife she'd seen in Evan's jacket, still hanging in his closet. And she'd even take down the crucifix, use it as a weapon.

Just in case.

"Go ahead," she said aloud as the clouds scudded over the moon. "Bring it on. Give me your best damn shot."

At the sound of her own words, she thought of the gun she'd found when searching for liquor. The pearl-handled revolver.

She'd find some ammo.

Then take the gun.

Chapter 27

The last person Harper wanted to talk to, the very last, was her ex-husband, but here she was on the phone, winding the cord nervously in her fingers and listening to Joel tell her that he'd be "right there." He reminded her that Bend, Oregon, was only a little over a three-hour drive to Almsville and the island.

Right.

Just what she needed.

Joel riding in on his white steed—or in his case a red Camaro—like the damned Lone Ranger to save her.

He'd done that once before, and look where it had gotten them. She wasn't about to make that mistake again.

He was saying, "I'm packed—already on my way."

"Look, Joel, no," she said for what seemed the dozenth time. "I'm all right."

There was a pregnant pause, and she knew what he was thinking, that she'd never been "all right," not in the past twenty years.

"Seriously," she insisted. "Don't come."

"Okay," he said, and she pictured him, standing at the phone, rubbing the back of his neck, his hair rumpled. "But you were in the hospital, Harper. Injured. Again. Jesus, you've barely gotten over that leg injury from falling through the deck."

She bit her tongue rather than remind him again that it was his faulty step that had caused the tumble that had sent her to the hospital in Bend.

He added, "And you've been through a helluva thing with that woman drowning and all."

"I said, I'm fine," she stated more firmly. "There's nothing for you to do here." Stretching the kitchen phone cord, she looked into the foyer, then down the hallway to the parlor and couldn't imagine Joel poking around the place. He was tall, six foot two, his eyes blue and scrutinizing. His blond hair had grown darker than it had been when he was growing up near Malibu, when the California sun had bleached it nearly white. Not that she'd known him then, of course. But she'd seen pictures. Even when he'd moved to Oregon in his early twenties to go to college, he'd been far more blond than now.

If he showed up here, he'd be curious about the island, the house, the gatehouse, and all within. He'd be sizing the place up, mentally taking note of the value of everything while still trying to play off his once-upon-a-time surfer dude vibe.

No, she didn't need him.

Not anymore.

Hadn't for a long time.

He's served his purpose, she thought, cringing a little at the thought.

"Tell you what," he said, still pushing, "I have to be in Portland in the next couple of days on business. I might be staying awhile. I'll stop by."

"Call first." She'd get the gate fixed and make sure it was locked. "I'm in and out." And maybe she'd change the phone number, too. That wasn't such a bad idea.

"Harper," he said, finally getting it. "I could—"

"You *could* remember we're divorced."

"We have a kid."

There was that. She had a sharp retort but held her tongue. And said instead, "And you have a girlfriend."

A pause. "Melanie and I broke up."

Oh, boo-hoo. But she didn't say it, didn't want him to hear her sarcasm. Nor did she care one way or another about her ex's love life. Except that now he was calling her. Feigning interest. Not because she'd been in the hospital, but because now, finally, she'd come of age and inherited her family's fortune. She knew that much.

"Listen, Harper. You and I—we agreed to get along. For Dawn," he reminded her. "She wants to see you. She said so."

Harper's stupid heart twisted. Damn Joel. He knew just how to manipulate her. And using her daughter as bait was cruel enticement.

"I talked to her," she said finally. "Again, I already told her I was okay."

"She didn't believe you."

"I'll tell her again. Or she can come up, she's got a car. Or I can drive to Eugene in a couple of days, see her apartment—"

"I'll bring her over."

"No!" she said sharply. Then, knowing a fight wouldn't help things, said more calmly, "Just let me settle in."

Before he could argue, before he could work on her emotions, before he could remind her *You owe me*, she hung up.

She couldn't deal with him. Not now. Joel Frickin' Prescott wasn't her only problem, unfortunately. There was Rand, once Chase's best friend and now a damned detective of all things. Worse yet, he was obviously looking not only into Cynthia Hunt's accident but also into her grandmother's death and Chase's disappearance.

It didn't take a rocket scientist to figure out that she, once again, was a suspect.

Which was just what she didn't need.

As if she wasn't edgy and stressed enough already. Although she'd thought she would sleep like the dead the night before, she hadn't. Sleep had been elusive, and she'd spent hours tossing and turning in the sleeping bag before waking up to the whole weird doll thing and the knowledge that someone had been in the house.

So, no, she didn't need Joel calling her or Rand questioning her or Levi showing up in her hospital room.

Despite her headache and her preoccupation with the fact that someone had actually gotten into the house, she'd spent some time with an out-of-date yellow pages but had yet to connect with a cleaning service that wasn't out of business. She also found an old toolbox and hammered stops in the broken window frame so the pane couldn't be opened more than two inches. She cleaned a little, concentrating on dirty fixtures and dusty countertops. All the while, of course, she searched for the cat and nursed her hangover.

Then Joel had called.

"Get over it," she told herself now and heard a scrape. The sound of a footfall.

But no one was here.

Oh, for the love of God, she was freaking herself out. "Don't do this," she warned, but felt the hairs on the back of her neck prickle.

It was as if she could feel someone in the house or at the very least someone watching her.

It wasn't anything she could name, just a slight shift in the air and the soft sound of someone creeping through the rooms, but, of course, she had checked all of the floors again this morning.

Found no one.

She thought about the broken window latch. She thought about the doll she found in her bathroom, with the warning scribbled across her panties.

How?

Who?

Why?

"You're a basket case," she said, checking her watch and noting that now it was officially afternoon.

Though she knew it was a mistake, she went back to the liquor cart and poured herself a stiff shot of vodka that was probably twenty years old. "You need therapy, not a drink," she mocked, and remembered Joel saying just those words to her. The prick. She downed the drink, contemplated another, and reached into the cupboard for the bottle again, before she realized that something was off.

Something was missing.

The revolver.

Gone.

But she'd left it here. Remembered handling it and putting it back.

Had it been here last night, when she'd poured herself the drinks?

Yes? No?

Had she noticed it?

She couldn't remember. Nor could she recall seeing it when she was creeping around the house, her fingers clenched around a pair of scissors. The hairs on the back of her neck prickled as she searched through the glassware.

No gun.

Of course she remembered Craig Alexander with a similar pistol, one that he left at the Hunts' home. "Not obviously," she reminded herself. It might have been another gun altogether. Or he may not have left it there. All she knew was that she hadn't seen it again that night.

She rocked back on her heels and told herself she was not losing her mind. Someone was in the house last night, moved the doll and took the gun. That had to be the explanation.

The doorbell chimed just as she was reaching for the vodka bottle.

Belatedly she remembered that she hadn't closed the gate.

Shoving the bottle into place, she walked through the parlor and down the hall to the foyer, where she peered through the sidelights of the massive front doors.

Beth was standing outside. In a red jumpsuit with oversized sleeves and a wide silver belt that matched her wedge heels, Beth held a huge wicker basket.

She was definitely put together. While Harper in her ratty jeans and a dirt-streaked sweatshirt was not.

Awesome. Just frickin' awesome.

Catching sight of Harper in the window, Beth waved frantically, her wide smile in place.

Great. Just what Harper needed. Cheery, well-dressed Beth carrying an enormous gift basket.

Forcing a smile she didn't feel, Harper opened one of the doors and a cool October breeze scooted inside, bringing with it the promise of rain. "I didn't know you were stopping by," she said, as Beth stepped into the foyer.

"Compliments of Alexander Realty," Beth said brightly. "I thought I'd swing by and officially welcome you back to Almsville." She motioned to the basket laden with small bags of cookies, coffee, cups, candles, and miniature pumpkins all wrapped in cellophane and tied with a huge black and orange bow. "All of these items are made in

Oregon, most of them around here actually." Her grin just wouldn't quit as she passed the basket to Harper. "But—" She checked her watch with its large bejeweled dial. "—I can't stay all that long. I've got a showing later today, and I want to get there early to make sure the house is presentable. The owners have two dogs, and they *need* to be locked up. Little barkers, both of them. They're friendly enough but jump up and demand attention and so—off they go to the kennel in the garage!" Then her smile faded slightly, and her eyebrows knitted in sudden concern. "So how're you doing today?"

"I'm okay." That was a bit of a stretch. Harper's headache had just about disappeared after two doses of Advil, and her whole body ached. Not to mention she'd been up long before dawn and was anxious about the doll and someone breaking into the place. And then there had been Joel's call. And now, the missing gun.

"You've been through hell! Oh. My. God. I just can't imagine the trauma of seeing Cynthia on the lake on fire!"

"I try not to think about it." Which was true.

"Oh right, right. Sorry. It's just that I'm concerned."

"I think I said I'm okay."

"I know, but . . ." Then she caught the look in Harper's eye and whatever she saw there made her voice trail off.

"Rhonda DeAngelo—er, Simms caught up with me when I left the police station the other day," Harper said. "In fact, she was waiting for me."

"She's a pain. Remember how mousy she was in high school?" She didn't wait for Harper to agree, just went on. "Well, you saw her, she's definitely not a mouse anymore! More like a rat with fangs and fake boobs. Man, has that girl had some work done! I mean, really? How could she go from like a minus A to a double D?"

"Ouch! Harsh!"

"Who cares? It's just the truth."

"She said you told her that I was back in town."

"No, no . . . she already knew that, but yeah, I guess I confirmed it. She had heard you were back, I don't know how, maybe she has a leak in the police department or something and so she was going to visit you in the hospital and saw you getting into my car." Beth shrugged. "No big deal, Harper. People are going to find out. But avoid her, if you can."

"I will."

Beth was already casting an appraising glance at the stairs and chandelier. "You know, if you want to sell this place, you really need to fix it up, make a few updates. Not too many, though, because the place has a certain charm."

"Haunted house à la Transylvania?"

"No!" Beth laughed, ran a finger along the curved railing, and stared up at the high ceilings and the landing where the split staircase met. "More like one of a kind, authentic turn-of-the-century Queen Anne with original fixtures and incredible views." She raised an eyebrow as she walked toward the back of the house, high heels clicking on the marble floor. "How many homes come with their own private island?"

"And their own unique, slightly macabre history?" Harper asked.

Beth reached the parlor and did a quick spin, surveying the room. "Well, we might not tell the buyers *every*thing, you know."

"Hey, remember? I'm not sure I'm selling. I think I made that point when you drove me back from the hospital."

"I thought you might be a little more clearheaded by now."

"Not yet." On one hand, Harper couldn't get rid of this place fast enough; it held too many painful memories. But on the other hand, Dixon Island had once been her home and sanctuary.

"Well, I wouldn't wait too long. Who knows where the market will go?" Beth said. Then, as if sensing Harper's reluctance, "Okay, so let's just assume you are going to sell," Beth went on, peering into Gram's bedroom, then the butler's pantry, and even walking through the kitchen. Once back in the parlor she said, "First things first. If I were you, I'd deep-six the dolls. God, they're everywhere and creepy as hell." A pause, and then, "Oh, hello—seems like you're already on my wave length." She'd caught sight of Maude's legs dangling out of the trash can. "See, that's the idea. This is what you should do with all of them!"

Before Harper could stop her, she plucked the doll from the can. "Dear God, this one is pretty awful, but an antique, I guess." She turned the doll over. "What's this?" she asked, eyeing the message under Maude's pinafore.

"Not really sure."

Beth was shaking her head. "Nothing good. What does 'ICU' mean? Like you're going to end up in the ICU? Shit, is it a warning of some kind?"

"Don't know."

"Tell me this," she pointed to the red letters, "is *not* blood."

"Red marker, I think."

Beth dropped the doll back into the trash, but her gaze was fastened to it, and she visibly flinched at the sound of Maude's weak voice. "Who did that?"

"Again, don't know."

"Was it meant for you?"

"Maybe, but—"

"You don't know." Her eyes finally met Harper's again. "And so you just found it and thought 'oh well, I guess I'll just put it out with the garbage?'"

"Something like that, yeah."

"Come on, Harper. Really? Instead of going to the police?" Her eyes rounded.

"And say what? That I found a doll with a weird message on it in my bathroom? Don't you think that they have better things to do?"

"But—that!" Beth pointed at the doll. "It's . . . way beyond creepy. Way beyond! Don't say it doesn't bother you, because it would freak the hell out of me." She eyed the doll speculatively. "It was in your bathroom?" Beth bit her lip. "When did you find it?"

"Early this morning."

"You didn't see it before?"

"No. It wasn't there."

"Wait. You think someone put it there since you moved in?" she asked, obviously dumbfounded.

"I don't think I would have missed it." She thought about telling Beth about the missing gun, but Beth would only freak out more. Besides, with all she'd been drinking, Harper wasn't really sure what she'd done with Gramps's pistol.

"Jesus God, I'd move out immediately!" Beth said.

"I'm not going to let some stupid prank scare me away." Harper was surprised at the conviction in her voice. But it was true.

"I would. The next time it might not just be a doll." She eyed the nearby window. "How did he get in?"

"Over here." Harper headed through the parlor, and Beth followed. As she did, she eyed the room with its antique furniture and dozens of dolls. "Oh my God. There are more of them. Like a doll army."

"You remember that Gram collected them."

"I don't remember there were this many, and I sure don't remember how creepy they all are. I probably thought it was cool and, well, the point is just because your grandmother collected these old things doesn't mean you have to. Seriously, I'd get rid of every last one of them. I mean, some might be valuable, I guess, but either dump them in the trash or take them to a dealer or something." She touched Harper on the arm. "I know you were close to your grandmother and all, but it's time to clean this place out."

Harper had reached the window and showed Beth how she'd secured it.

"But how did whoever did this know about the window or that you'd be back . . . and you think they were in here while you were asleep?" Her brow furrowed. "That's really scary."

"And you're not helping me feel any better about it. Look, just in case this isn't the way whoever it was got in, I've called a locksmith. New keys for all the doors. He's coming this afternoon."

"But the windows?"

"The locksmith is going to go over each one. He's a handyman, too. And if he finds any he can't repair, he's got the name of a window company."

"Look, while I'm here, why don't you show me around?" Beth suggested. "You know, in case you decide to sell. I don't have time to do a full assessment. But we can do that later. You've got a basement, right?"

"Two floors below this one, but—"

"Okay, then let's start there and work our way up."

"It's got to be a mess," Harper argued. "I haven't even gone down there and who knows what we'll find."

"Don't worry about it. You can't believe what I see in my business." Beth rolled her eyes. "Rats. Squirrels. Mice. Wasps' nests, rot and mold, even a dead raccoon once." She flashed a smile. "You can't scare me off that easily."

"But the dolls freak you out."

"And how! Especially weird-looking ones with cryptic messages," she said. "Now, come on, let's see this place. It's been years!"

"Fine, but remember: I'm not sure I'm going to sell."

Chapter 28

Windshield wipers swiping at the thickening mist, Levi turned off the county road and drove into the long, tree-lined drive of Serenity Acres. Last April, the cherry trees had been gorgeous, blooming pink, a bright spot on somber spring days, but now, with winter soon arriving, the branches were shedding their leaves, looking barren and bleak, a reflection of his own feelings.

He wanted answers, and he wanted them now. How the hell had his mother gotten out of the facility and ended up in the middle of Lake Twilight with the means to set herself afire?

Even now, his stomach churned at the thought of it.

But he had to know what had set her off.

Couldn't stand the unanswered questions.

He'd always been this way. Had never been able to let things lie. His mother had called him "curious." To which his father had replied, "He's goddamned nosy if you ask me. Remember the old saying about curiosity killing the cat?" With that he'd skewered his son with a hard glare. "So, Levi, you keep *your* nose clean and out of other people's business."

Well, screw that.

Especially now, he thought as the facility came into view, a huge structure sprawling over gentle hills, parking lot to one side, sloping lawn on the other.

Then there was the matter of Harper. He believed that somehow suspecting Harper was returning to Almsville had exacerbated his mother's mental state and pushed her into the chasm of insanity. Not that Cynthia hadn't been teetering on the brink for years. But something had propelled her to find her way to the middle of Lake Twilight with family photo albums, a can of gasoline, and a book of matches.

But how the hell had she gotten to the lake in the first place? How had she known about Harper. *Had* she known?

He parked in the near-empty lot, where only a few cars and trucks were scattered. He cut the engine, noting that a large white van was leaving as another sedan pulled into the lot, a dark Toyota.

People coming and going, visiting loved ones, some of whom were shut-ins.

He climbed out of his Fairlane, locked it, and pocketed his keys. Turning his collar to what was becoming a steady drizzle, he jogged to the front door and walked into the reception area with its pale blue walls, industrial-grade carpet, and potted palms.

"Mr. Hunt!" Patty, the petite receptionist, greeted him from behind a massive desk. She had a wild mane of permed brown hair and wore oversized glasses. Behind her, a large poster decorated with smiling jack-o'-lanterns invited residents and family to a Halloween social promising hot apple cider, donuts, a raffle, and "fun for all."

No thanks.

Not that he had any connection to the place any longer.

"I'm, um, terribly sorry for your loss," Patty was saying. "Your mom was a sweetie."

Doubting that anyone here would think his often sarcastic mother was sweet, he nodded and paused at the desk. "I've got a meeting with Allison."

"Yes, I know." Patty was nodding rapidly, her mountain of brown hair barely moving. "Sign in." She pointed to the clipboard on the desk. "She's expecting you. It'll be just a sec. She's with someone—"

At that moment the door to Allison Gray's office opened, and Rand Watkins strode out. He was beelining for the doors but stopped at the sight of Levi. "Hey."

Levi nodded. He'd been friends with Rand years before, if you could call it a friendship, but they hadn't been around each other for a couple of decades. Who knew what the guy was like now? He extended his hand by rote, and Rand shook it.

"You find anything out?" Levi asked. "About Mom?"

"Workin' on it."

"You know anything more?"

Rand's expression showed no emotion. "Not yet."

A non-answer. Levi said, "Keep me informed."

"I will. We need to sit down. For your statement."

"Okay. I'll stop by the station later."

"Call first. To make sure I'm there."

"Okay."

They locked eyes for a moment, and Levi got a hint that Rand—make that Detective Watkins—was all business. The firmness of his handshake and the way he held Levi's gaze suggested that Rand took his duty as a cop to the letter of the law. Which Levi understood. He figured Rand was one of those rules-are-rules guys. No breaking nor bending them. He expected that Rand's world was made up of black and white, no shades of gray. The law was the law. There were good guys and bad guys. Right now Rand hadn't decided on which side of the dividing line to place Levi. Friendships in high school, loose as they were when you were the younger brother of a best bro, didn't figure in.

But that worked two ways. Rand had been close to Chase, closer than anyone, and Levi had always suspected that Rand knew more about his brother's disappearance than anyone else. It just so happened to coincide with Rand shipping out to Vietnam, so . . .

He told himself to let it go.

Rand was a cop now.

Trustworthy.

Sworn to protect and serve.

But beneath it all, he was still just a man.

And everyone had secrets, even a decorated war vet who'd become an officer of the law.

"See ya around," Rand said and was through the door.

Levi didn't bother signing in but walked through the still-open door and found Allison Gray behind her wide desk, just picking up the receiver of her phone. She glanced up sharply as he arrived.

For a second panic rose in her eyes, but it was quickly disguised.

"Oh." She dropped the receiver into its cradle and rose. "Mr. Hunt." With sharp features, wispy Debbie Harry hair, and bright red lips, she forced a smile as she stood and offered her hand. "So good to see you, even though I know this is a hard time for your family. I'm so, so sorry for your loss. Cynthia was . . . was a character, a fixture around here if you will, and we all loved her."

At least Allison didn't call his mother a "sweetie." Still, this was all corporate cover-your-ass bullshit.

He took her hand for a brief second but then didn't mince words. "I just want to know how the hell she got out of here—walked right out and no one seemed to notice."

Her confidence faltered for a heartbeat, but she found it again. "Please, have a seat." She motioned to the two chairs facing her desk. "I have to be honest with you—"

In his world those words were usually a hedge if not an out-and-out lie.

"—we're not really certain how she was able to leave undetected. But we're working on it."

"It's your job to know."

"Of course, and as I said, we're launching our own internal investigation to find out how to prevent—"

"My mother died," he said flatly. "As the result of your incompetence—"

"Sometimes, if a resident is determined to leave, it's impossible to deter them," she interrupted, cutting off his threat.

"This place is supposed to be secure." He wasn't backing down. Not an inch.

Allison tensed visibly. Her practiced smile tightened. "As you know, and as it's spelled out in the contract you signed, Serenity Acres is not a lockdown facility."

"It should be! I was led to believe—"

"As I was saying, our policies are written into our contract," she said, her chin notching up a fraction. "Now, as I said, I'm deeply sorry for your loss, Mr. Hunt. If you could be so kind as to take your mother's personal belongings, say, by sometime tomorrow? I'll have all of the paperwork ready."

"Don't the police have to go through her room?"

"That's happening as we speak." Her smile was brittle. "I've asked them to be quick about it, as it's disturbing for the other residents."

"Tomorrow, then?"

"Yes, in the morning if you can manage it. We're a very sought-after facility, and we have a waiting list for our units. So, the sooner you can arrange to take her things, the better." She scraped together a few loose pages on her desk.

"Really? Is that all you can say when a woman died on your watch—that you need to turn over the room?" he asked, and when she didn't respond, he realized that Allison Gray dealt with death on a monthly or often weekly basis. One way or another, this was the last stop for a lot of people.

But not under conditions like this.

"I would hate to have to charge her estate for another month," she said firmly.

"My mother died a horrible, grisly death."

"Yes. I'm aware. It's awful. As I said, my condolences." She managed a quick, insincere smile as she slipped the pages into an envelope and handed the packet to him. "Please bring these back with you when you clean out her belongings." Her icy smile was back in place. "And again, Mr. Hunt, I'm truly sorry for your loss."

"As you've said a couple of times."

"Yes, well. Your mother was—"

He didn't hear the rest. Didn't want to. No amount of platitudes would suffice. And if they charged him for another month's services, so be it. He'd take his own damned time.

In the reception area again, he turned away from the exit and reception desk, passing by the wide dining room with its plastic-covered chairs situated around an array of tables. The dining area opened to a veranda. Through the glass doors was a calming view of the well-kept lawn and trees with bird feeders swinging in the breeze. Two elderly women, one of them in a wheelchair, were deep in conversation near a huge coffee urn.

He wondered if they'd known his mother but left them to their conversation as he entered Hallway C and ignored the faint smell of pine cleaner as he walked to room C-112. His mother's name was listed on a placard on the door: Mrs. Cynthia Hunt. Above the plac- ard someone had hung two decorative ears of Indian corn, dry husk open, colorful kernels exposed. A nod to the season.

His jaw tightened, and for a second he remembered his mother as she had been when he was growing up, a tall, willowy blond with an affinity for Virginia Slims, fake fur coats, and dry martinis. She'd been a smart woman, wily in her youth.

Mrs. Cynthia Hunt had an infectious laugh and a naughty twinkle in her brown eyes, and a sharp tongue that her husband often dulled.

That was until her eldest son vanished.

Then everything changed.

Everything.

The sparkle. Gone.

The sarcastic wit. Disappeared.

Even her perfectly coiffed blond hair had dulled and become un- kempt, her gray roots often showing.

Their family had been gutted, and rather than growing closer, the three had been driven further apart.

And then her husband, too, left her. In the very boat that he'd cherished, the Triton that somehow had been left idling in the lake when Chase had vanished.

After that, Mrs. Cynthia Hunt had lost the ability to distinguish be- tween reality and fantasy. She'd told him of conversations she'd had with "Tommy" and that Chase had visited her on occasion. He'd sug- gested that the visits and conversations had been in her dreams, but he couldn't convince her of the truth, so a few months ago, he'd stopped trying.

Even when she called him Chase.

He'd let it go, rather than argue and confuse her more.

He pushed open the door and was met with a mess. Yes, the po- lice had been here. Though his mother hadn't been the neatest homemaker on earth, and certainly whatever skills she'd once pos- sessed had declined over the years, she wouldn't have left drawers open and belongings scattered throughout the two rooms.

He braced himself.

Going through her things was going to be tough.

But maybe, just maybe, he'd find something the police had overlooked. Something that would give him some inkling as to what had gone on the other night. He hoped to God he was right.

He had an appointment later today with a woman who was certain her husband was cheating on her and needed proof. He was the man for the job these days, even if some tasks cut a little close to the bone. But he'd come back another time with boxes and figure out where to donate her belongings. Again, he was plagued by the same questions that had haunted him since he'd first heard the unthinkable news. How? Why? How did she manage it?

He caught sight of a picture on the wall—the family at the Seattle World's Fair in 1962. They stood on the revolving observation deck of the Space Needle. Dad in his narrow tie and sport coat, Mom wearing a sleeveless pink dress. Chase, at thirteen starting to lengthen out, while Levi was at the age when he'd thought he'd never grow. In the photo his brother and father towered over him while his mother's hands rested gently on his shoulders, her fingernails painted frosty pink to match her lipstick.

Happier times, he thought now and abruptly left his mother's room at the nursing facility. He nearly ran over a gray-haired septuagenarian bent over a walker.

"Sorry," he said and tried to skirt the guy.

"You a cop?" the man almost yelled.

"What? No. I'm . . . Cynthia's son." Levi hooked his thumb and motioned to the door. "Cynthia Hunt."

"Her boy?" The old man eyed Levi suspiciously, his brow furrowing, his unruly eyebrows lifting over thick glasses. Frowning, he shook his head. "Her boy disappeared. Years ago."

"My brother." Did he know this man?

"Oh! Let me see." Eyes thinning in appraisal, the stooped man asked, "You're the younger one?"

"Yes. Levi." Levi stuck out his hand and introduced himself as the old guy lifted a gnarled palm.

His grip was like iron.

"Yes," the old guy said. "Yes, you are. You were a troublemaker in your youth. Looks like you maybe straightened up. She said so."

Levi assumed the man was talking about his mother.

"I'm Ed," he said. "Ed Sievers, we were neighbors."

Old Man Sievers. With the barking dog and rumored bomb shelter. His long hair was little more than white stubble over a pink pate these days, and his face was lined with deep wrinkles. Thick glasses bridged his nose, and rather than camouflage gear he'd picked up at the army surplus store, he was now dressed in an oversized robe and striped pajamas.

Sievers looked over his shoulder and whispered, "This is a hell-hole. Yep. That's what it is. Don't let anyone tell you any different." He paused and added, "Sorry about your mother." He clucked his tongue and shook his head. "A shame. That's what it was. A damned shame."

"You knew her?"

He pointed a big-knuckled finger to the door across the hall. "We were neighbors here, too."

"Do you know why she—?"

"Why she lit herself up like a Christmas tree on the lake? Nope. Not a clue. But I know she was upset that the girl was coming back to town." His head was bowed as he adjusted his walker, and he looked up at Levi over the rims of his glasses.

"The girl? You mean Harper Prescott?"

"That her name now? She's Livvie Dixon's granddaughter," he said firmly. "You know, her mother died in the lake, too. Years ago. I saw her. Had to run over to that cop's house—Watkins. Bah! Never cared for him. You remember?"

Levi had never forgotten that night. His gut twisted at the memory of his father and Gerald Watkins retrieving Anna Reed's body.

Sievers was hitching his walker across the hall. "Come on in," he said as he unlocked the door and a sudden burst of yapping greeted them. As he opened the door, a tiny terrier shot out—a scruff of mottled black and brown fur that bounced at Ed's feet.

"Shh. Jake. Shh. You'll get me in trouble." But Ed chuckled as he bent down and picked up the perky-eared pup, which rewarded him by washing his face with his tongue. "Come in, come in," he said, looking over his shoulder at Levi. "I've got something for you."

He set the dog on a carpet worn with the tracks of his walker, then opened a drawer in the small kitchenette within the studio unit that held a tiny table, large recliner, and twin bed. "Let's see . . ." He pulled out a wallet, some receipts, a bottle opener, a book of stamps, and finally a small sealed envelope that Levi recognized as his mother's personal stationery, embossed with CLH, Cynthia Larsen Hunt.

A lump grew in Levi's throat as the old man handed him the small envelope with his name written in his mother's hand. *Levi.* His throat grew tight. "She gave this to you, when?" he asked.

The old man rubbed the stubble on his chin. "That night," he said, as if Levi should have guessed the truth. "Just before I helped her get out of here."

Chapter 29

Since Beth insisted on seeing "everything" from the lowest level of the manor on up, Harper complied, starting with the boathouse. Cut into the stone of the island, the boathouse was really a cavern that had been fitted with heavy crossbeams and a boat lift decades earlier.

Inside, the air was heavy and smelled dank, the odors of water-logged rot and decay pervasive.

"Dear Lord, no one's been down here in a while," Beth observed.

A long while, Harper thought as she reached for the light switch. Just one of the two dim lights fizzled on, casting more shifting reflective shadows onto the rough stone walls, offering little illumination. Gramps's old wooden Chris-Craft was raised on the lift, dangling awkwardly above the water, the boat's hull obviously moldering, the straps supporting it disintegrating.

"Oooh, that's too bad," Beth observed, glancing around the dark cave-like room that echoed with her voice, lake water lapping at the rotting planks of the decking. "Someone would have loved that boat. It was a classic, I remember."

"I guess." Harper noticed the rafters, some covered by rat droppings, and the holes in the rock walls, easy enough for a rat to slide through. She remembered the one Beth had killed after dropping

Harper off from the hospital. Where there was one, there was likely to be two, or ten, or a hundred. She only hoped that Jinx, wherever he was, had started culling the herd, or in the case of rats the mischief, which was what a group of rodents was called. She remembered it from some biology class she'd taken.

Beth, too, was surveying the boathouse/cave with a critical eye. "It would take a lot to clean and fix this place if you'd even want to, and the boat lift is ancient . . . I'm thinking the buyers might want to build a boathouse off the dock and maybe even seal this place off . . . I'm not sure it could be brought up to code if a building inspector even looked at it. Oh shit! Are those bats?" she said and nearly shrieked as she squinted up at a crossbeam over the boat.

"Probably."

"Oh God, oh God, oh God," Beth said, backing up and nearly falling into the murky water. "No . . . oh God, no."

"I thought you'd seen everything."

"Everything but bats."

"Okay, let's go this way." Harper took Beth by the elbow and opened a door to an area that cut farther into the island. Again, Harper flipped a switch and a light came on to expose a small room where out-of-date boating equipment was lodged. In one corner, a tiny bathroom had been added.

Beth still hunched down and, looking over her shoulder as if she expected a bat to come swooping down, took the time to peer inside. "This just gets worse and worse," she said, catching sight of a dry, stained toilet and shower with broken tiles and rusted fixtures, its pan chipped away by time and neglect, rat and bat droppings evident.

"Oh God, I think I'm going to be sick." Beth backed away.

Harper explained, "No one's used this in years."

"I can see that. For good reason. It's a dungeon." She cast another worried glance over her shoulder. "Let's get out of here. I've seen enough."

"This way." Harper pointed to a door leading to a long tunnel that wound up shallow steps. It opened to a wide area of the basement where small windows had been cut into the brick walls, allowing in some light, while two huge furnaces dominated the low-ceilinged room. Once they were fueled by wood, but they had been converted to electricity years before. Remnants of that day and age, in the form of stacked firewood, still remained, though the huge bins themselves were empty, the fuel chute no longer used.

Harper ushered Beth past the chute where the firewood had once been dumped to the stone steps leading upward.

"This is slightly better," Beth said. "Emphasis on slightly." Eager to get out of the "dungeon," Beth hurried ahead, only to glance back as Harper lagged behind.

"You're limping," Beth said, her forehead furrowing. "From the other night, huh? God, that was awful!"

"It was, but it didn't happen then. Months ago I tripped on a broken step." But she didn't add that her husband had told her the stairs were fixed, that he'd personally nailed the broken board back into place. *Liar!* Though all that remained of her injury was pain in her hip, the accident had been far more serious, and she had ended up with a fractured pelvis and three broken ribs, one of which had punctured her lung. She'd been in a hospital in Bend for nearly a week, then recovering at home while seeing a physical therapist for months.

That trip to Bend had been part of a fool's mission, Harper now knew. She'd driven to Bend, to Joel's mountain-view home, to see if they could piece together their broken marriage as once again he and Melanie had broken up.

But the effort was as doomed as Humpty-Dumpty. And Harper had ended up taking the fall.

From the get-go things had been tense, made worse by the fact that her father and Marcia had driven from Portland and come for dinner one night. Then, on day two, Harper had taken the tumble. On her way down to the pool, she'd stepped on the broken stair and tumbled half a flight, her foot twisting in the railing.

It turned out that her marriage had been more damaged than her body. Her broken bones eventually healed. As for wedded bliss? Not so much. After her hospital stay, she'd discovered that he was still involved with Melanie, the woman with whom he'd had an affair while still married. So—no, there was no reconciliation. The minute she'd been able to fly, she'd left her two-year-old Acura for her daughter to pick up, then flown back to California and her older Volvo wagon. A week later, she'd signed the divorce papers that had been put on hold.

"Sorry about the hip. Ouch!" Beth was saying. "That's why you have to maintain your property. It can be dangerous."

Amen, Harper silently agreed as they made their way through a short hallway to a set of stairs that led to the garage with its gun cabinet, long workbench, shelves, and closets. "Okay, okay," Beth said, nodding to herself as she observed wide bays where Gram's pink Cadillac and Gramps's convertible, a 1959 Corvette, were parked, backed into their individual bays.

Beth was so intent on the cars that she didn't seem to notice the dust that had collected everywhere in the space nor the papery hornets' nest in a dark corner near the workbench nor the grime that coated the floor and windowsills.

Harper switched on the lights.

"Oh wow! These are classics," Beth said with a low whistle. "I'm surprised they're still here." She ran a red-tipped finger over the Corvette's smooth fender. "And in such good shape. Does it run?"

"It's supposed to."

"Craig will flip out when he sees this," she mused, then glanced at Harper. "I assume it's for sale, too? Either independently or as part of the listing?"

"Maybe, *if* I decide to sell."

"Hmmm." Beth squinted at the vehicles, making mental notes and appraising them. "The bike?" she asked, motioning to the third bay where a motorcycle stood upright on its center stand.

Harper's heart twisted a bit as she looked at it. Evan's pride and joy.

"It's a Honda, right? I kind of remember when your brother got it. New at the time, like maybe 1966?"

"Yeah." Harper nodded, thinking back, remembering Evan literally jumping for joy when he saw the bike for the first time, a huge red bow tied to one of the Honda's grips. All smiles, he took off on the motorcycle, speeding across the bridge, then onto Northway, where he disappeared, though Harper could hear the bike revving through its gears as he pushed the speed limit. He returned fifteen minutes later, the bike speeding over the bridge to skid to a stop in front of the garage where she was waiting with Gram and her parents. Harper said, "He got it for his birthday."

"And every boy at Almsville High was jealous." Beth bit her lip. "So it was barely driven, then?"

"Right." The smile that had been teasing Harper's lips at the memory faded away.

Beth touched the bike's seat. "You know I had *such* a crush on him back then."

"I did know." It wasn't like Beth had ever been anything but transparent or that she hadn't whispered her feelings to Harper on every sleepover or lit up like a Christmas tree whenever Evan was around.

Beth sighed dramatically, just as she had as a lovelorn teen lying on Harper's bed, staring at the ceiling, pouring her heart out. "But, of course, I had to get in line. A very long line."

That much was true. In high school Evan had an extended list of girlfriends and an even longer one of wannabes. Good-looking and charming, with a "bad-boy" attitude, he charmed more than his share of girls, some older, some younger, and all, Harper suspected, with an eye on his bank account.

Pushing an errant strand of hair from her face, Beth added, "You know, I always thought that he'd found someone who caught his attention at that house next door to me, growing up. The yellow one. Remember? At the end of the street and owned by the Musgrave family. I checked on its ownership once, as I had a client who was interested. Anyway, they, the Musgraves, never sold and own it to this day. It's still a rental, I think, but I haven't seen anyone around for a while, so I'm not sure.

"But back in the day all kinds of college-age kids lived there. Kind of a commune, if you ask me. Before communes were even a real thing. But the hippie movement was kind of just getting started." Harper had known as much. Chase had told her something similar.

"Trust me, something was going on there. Free love. That sort of thing. And they were dropping acid, smoking pot, and I think, or I heard, using peyote. Brought up by one of their roommates, a kid from Texas."

"They were students."

"If you say so," Beth said, lifting a shoulder as a fly buzzed around her head. "Get out of here," she muttered, swatting at it. "Where's a spider when you need one?"

"Oh, I think we have our share." The corners of the garage were draped in cobwebs and spiders' nests.

The fly got the hint and buzzed off to crawl around the edge of a window.

Beth focused on the conversation again. "I don't think all of the kids that lived in the Musgraves' house were going to college, or at least not full time."

"You know this, how?" Harper asked, though it didn't really matter, and she was ready to end this tour.

"Chase told me."

"Chase?" Harper tensed, just as she always did when she thought of Chase, which, before she returned to the island had been less and less over the years. But now that she was back in this house, the memory of the night he went missing, the night Gram died, seemed ever-present, exacerbated by the tragedy of Cynthia Hunt's hellish death. "When did Chase tell you that?"

"I don't know. It's been so long . . ." Beth thought for a moment, her fingers tapping lightly on the edge of the Corvette's windshield. "A week, maybe two, before he vanished." She cleared her throat as if in so doing she could rid her mind of the memories of Chase and that awful night. Then she quickly changed the subject. "So these classic cars and the bike. Would you be interested in selling them?"

"I don't know. I just haven't got that far yet."

Yes! Damn it! The answer is "yes." Why can't you just admit it? You need to sell this place, Harper, and everything in it. Get away A.S.A.P. Before the past swallows you, or what's left of you. Somehow, she found her voice. "I'll think about it. So, do you want to see the rest of the house?"

"Yeah, but I've got to make it quick. I've got that showing."

Good.

Harper gave her a quick tour of the apartment in the garret over the garage. It was connected to the second floor of the house through a door that was now locked, the other access being an outdoor staircase running up the side of the garage.

"Now this is great," Beth said, eyeing the interior with its sloped ceilings and paned windows. Decades before it had been retrofitted with a kitchenette and a small, private bath. "It would be a nice mother-in-law space or maybe for a college kid, or even as a rental unit."

"I guess."

"I think Craig lived here for a while. Didn't he? After his mom and dad split up?" She bit her lip and looked around. "Yeah, I remember. For sure he did."

Harper nodded. "Uh-huh," she said and recalled how uncomfortable it had all felt. Not at first, but as she'd grown from a gawky tomboy into a teenager with curves she had caught him watching her as she sunbathed. He'd helped his dad with yard work, trimming the grass and shrubbery, washing the cars, or cleaning out the gutters, whatever odd job was needed. But more than once he'd set down his gloves and shears to stare at her as she lay on the dock while she rifled through copies of *Seventeen* or *Teen* magazine. She also perused *True Confessions*, which her grandmother deemed inappropriate—which, of course, made reading the taboo copies all the more exciting.

Harper wondered now how much Craig had witnessed back then. Had he seen her skinny-dipping at dawn or sneaking out of her room to moon-bathe those summers? Did he know that she sneaked out of her room to meet Chase at the dock?

Did it matter?

Probably not, she thought, again remembering Craig on his solo mission with the pistol under the cover of darkness, when he thought no one was watching. What the hell was he up to? Was it one of her grandfather's matching revolvers? Should she bring it up? And how could she do it without admitting that she'd been spying, seated at the damned telescope while snacking on Doritos?

"Let me know if you want to sell the cars and the bike," Beth was saying. "Craig would love any or all of them!"

"I'll keep that in mind. Is he a collector?" she asked, trying to sound nonchalant. "I mean guys collect all kinds of things."

"Like your grandma?"

"Well, not dolls and teacups and green stamps, but, you know, cars and equipment and guns, hunting gear, that kind of thing. Guy stuff."

"Yeah, Craig's into all of that," she said as they went back to the house through the front door.

Beth was familiar with the main floor of the house and the terrace, so she passed on the living quarters. "I'll check these out more thoroughly next time. And by then—no dolls."

"Got it. *If* I decide to sell."

"I know, I know. You keep reminding me. But even if you don't. For your own damned sanity. They would drive me crazy! But let's see your grandmother's bedroom. It's on this floor, right? I was never allowed in as a kid."

"She liked her privacy."

"Don't we all?" Beth said as she walked through the parlor and into Gram's room.

"I guess." But Harper winced, thinking how she'd spent time observing Beth and her family through the telescope, like a voyeur hiding in the shadows.

"This is like walking back into 1950—make that 1930!" Beth said as she noticed Gram's Victorian vanity with its oval mirror and tufted bench. Gram's bed had been stripped and draped, but a few of the dolls were in evidence, Raggedy Ann and Andy tossed into the chair that the cat Diablo had once claimed as his own.

Beth opened the drapes and stared out at the lake, then noticed the rag dolls. "Those two," she said, motioning to Ann and Andy. "No messages scribbled on them?"

"No."

"Good! In the trash with Maureen."

"Maude," Harper corrected.

"Whatever. They're all history!"

"I'll see. I have a lot to do here."

Beth nodded. "I'll say."

Harper let it slide. She wasn't sure she could just throw away her grandmother's favorites. Some things she would keep, but most, of course, would have to be sold, donated, or tossed.

Beth poked her head into the bathroom, then they quickly headed upstairs to the second floor. "You'll want to fix the elevator," Beth said as she quickly scanned some of the rooms while Harper remained on the lookout for the cat and now the missing pistol. There were four large bedrooms in all, the two facing the lake separated by a long corridor to the bedrooms that overlooked the parking area and bridge.

"Man, we spent hours in here," Beth said as she entered the room where Harper had stayed so many nights in the canopy bed with its matching curtains and full-length mirror. Now dust covered everything, turning the mint green coverlet dingy. "How I envied you."

"Funny, I envied you. Being down at the point where all the action was."

"Really? When you lived in a mansion? You remember my bedroom? It was about the size of this walk-in closet," she said, stepping through the open doorway and snapping on the light. "The twins got the bigger one . . . oh God, what's this?"

"What?" Harper hadn't even been inside any of the closets yet.

"I think maybe these are Chase's things?"

Harper had followed Beth into the closet and saw the letterman's jacket hanging on an old wire hanger.

Her heart clutched.

She'd forgotten.

On a shelf was a small album filled with Polaroid pictures. Next to it was a broken jewelry box that her grandmother had given her one Christmas. Tentatively she opened it and saw several forgotten necklaces, their tiny links twisted and knotted together, alongside two bracelets and Chase's class ring. "Oh." She felt a tug on her heart as she picked up the ring and remembered the hot July night Chase had given it to her, the summer before he'd taken off for college. They'd been on the lake, in his parents' boat, insects humming, the moonlight from a half moon glistening on the water.

"Oh, Geez," Beth said as Harper turned the ring over to where dental floss covered with nail polish had been wound so that it would fit on her smaller finger. "What're you going to do with this stuff? It has to be cleaned out of here, if you're going—"

"I know. *If* I'm going to sell." Then she took a deep breath and ignored the dull ache in her heart. "And even if I'm not." She returned the ring to the jewelry box and then opened a little compartment where another necklace lay, the large diamond winking bright.

"What's that?" Beth asked, picking it up. "Oh my God. This looks valuable. Is it real? Well, of course it is, if it belonged to your family."

"It's an heirloom."

"From your grandmother? Good Lord, if this stone is real, it's worth a small fortune and needs to be locked in a safe somewhere. It's amazing that it's still here."

"No, um, not Gram's. Chase gave it to me," Harper said as she replaced the necklace in the jewelry case.

"From Chase? Really?"

"I know." But she didn't elaborate, remembering that when Chase had given the necklace to her, he'd sworn that he would have the stone fitted into an engagement ring. Her throat turned dry at the thought, and she remembered him kissing her temple softly and telling her he loved her for the first time before placing the fine chain around her neck and slowly untying the shoulder straps of her sundress.

Swallowing hard, she pushed aside the memory. "I guess I'll talk to Levi," she said, over the nostalgic lump in her throat.

Because there was no one else.

Chapter 30

"You helped my mother escape?" Levi asked as he held the cream-colored envelope in his hand.

"Shh. Keep your voice down." Sievers glanced around his small apartment furtively. "The walls have ears."

"You think Serenity Acres is bugged?"

The old man placed a finger to his lips, then reached into the junk drawer again and came out with a folding knife. With a press of his finger, the blade shot out.

"They let you have a switchblade?"

"Contraband." He held the knife out to Levi as the dog danced near the door. "Open it," he said to Levi. "I gotta take Jake out for a piss."

Heart in his throat, Levi used the sharp blade to slice open the envelope.

"Wait. Maybe you want your privacy," the old guy said. "Seeing as your mom's gone and all."

"How did you help her get out?"

Sievers's gaze darted around the room, as if, again, he was searching for a tiny listening device.

"Let's go outside," he suggested and snagged a leash from a hook by the door before snapping it onto the dog's collar. Jake started straining to get out, paws scratching the door.

"Hold on, hold on," Sievers said as he slipped on an oversized parka, then led the way out of his room, pausing to lock the door and say to Levi, "You can never be too careful." With Jake leading the way, and Sievers pushing his walker, they made the long trek to the end of the hall. They passed other residents, a man in a plaid bathrobe and using a cane, and two women, both gray-haired, one in a prim suit, the other a housedress, both fussing over Jake as he tugged on the leash.

As the women went on their way, the old man whispered to Levi, "Damned dog's a chick magnet."

If you say so, Levi thought but held his tongue.

It took several minutes to make it out through a door at the end of the hall. "Never locked," Ed said, "and no alarm bells, neither."

Levi frowned at the lack of security.

"The prison guards look the other way. Hell, they come out here and join us for a smoke now and again." The small garden area was fenced, with benches, standing ashtrays, and a gate that led to the side parking lot. A man who'd been smoking beneath the overhang stubbed out the butt of his cigar, and as Levi held the door, he slipped back inside. "The thing is, the door *is* locked. You can get out, but you can't get back in."

"So someone has to let you inside."

Ed stared at him as if he were a moron, and Levi understood why. A brick lay next to the door, and just before the door closed behind the mustachioed cigar smoker, Ed toed the brick into the opening and the door stayed ajar. "So what happened—with Mom, I mean?" Levi asked as they stood beneath the portico and watched the drizzle turn to rain, the afternoon so gloomy as to be nearly dark.

With a shrug, Ed said, "I gave a lady a lift home. She asked and I couldn't say no."

"You have a car?"

"Not exactly." Ed looked over the chain-link to the lot where a row of vehicles was parked in the resident and employee lot. He smiled as Levi focused on the old rusting Volkswagen Microbus, its hippie art faded, the same vehicle he'd seen parked at the house at the end of the street when he was a kid.

"That thing's still around?" he said.

"And runs like a top. Bought it off one of the kids who lived there, about the same time your brother went missing. They all wanted to split, and I bought the van for a song," he said proudly. "Helluva deal."

Levi's mind was spinning. He watched Jake nose around some of the small bushes near the patio before lifting a leg. "So wait. You drove my mom back to the lake in her housecoat and just dropped her off? You didn't think to tell anyone what she was planning?"

"I didn't know what she was planning, son. I just gave her a ride." He nodded toward the envelope still in Levi's hand. "Maybe that will explain it all. I doubt it, but maybe. Come on, Jake," he said to the dog and turned to go back inside.

"Wait. Who did you buy the van from again? I mean, you said the kids but surely one of them had their name on the title."

Sievers halted and looked over his shoulder. "The kid's name was Trick. That's what he went by, but the name on the paperwork was different. Real name was Tristan something or other." He bit his lower lip. "I think it started with a B, no wait, a V—Geez, what the hell was it?" He thought for a second, scratching his chin. "Uh, Vargas, I think it was. Yeah, that was it. Tristan Vargas. Does it matter?"

"Probably not," Levi said, still piecing things together. Any information was worthwhile. "Did you ever have the van cleaned?"

Sievers snorted, "Why would I?"

"You didn't find anything in it?"

"For what?" the old man asked. "I bought it, no questions asked. That's the way I do things."

Sievers had made his way to the door, Jake leading the way.

"Hey, hold up a sec!" Levi said.

Sievers paused, the dog inside, he and his walker out. "What now?"

"Why didn't you tell the police? About taking Mom to the house at the lake? About this?" He held up the note.

"No one asked."

"But you could have volunteered."

"Don't think so." The old man's smile twisted. "Your mom asked me to keep it to myself."

"But that was before she . . ."

"Look, son, I don't trust cops," Ed said, shooing his little dog ahead of him. "Never have. Never will. Your mother asked me to keep her secret and I have. 'Til now."

"But Detective Watkins was here."

He snorted. "The neighbor? Never liked him. Didn't trust him. Duke didn't neither. Duke, he was my dog. Lost him a year or two after all the hubbub about your brother."

"I remember Duke. But that was years ago. That was a different Detective Watkins."

"Gerry. Yeah, I remember."

"His son, Rand, is the detective in charge now. He was just here. I saw him on my way in."

"Did ya now? Well, let me tell you somethin'. In my experience, the apple don't fall far from the tree." He gave Levi a hard look. "And you're Tom Hunt's boy, now, aren't ya? I don't like to speak ill of the dead, and I think your mom was a good, decent woman. But your old man? The cop? Not so much. So, that's all I got to say to you. Come along, Jake." He turned away and slipped through the door, leaving the brick steadfastly in place.

Levi saw that he was tarred by the same brush as his father, just like Rand was. But there was no arguing with Sievers, who'd said all he was going to say. Levi left through the unlocked gate rather than going through the interior and dealing with Patty and all her sign-in sheets. He'd take the cold October rain instead. He dashed along a sidewalk that curved sharply to the front of the building and the visitors' parking lot.

And ran into a woman holding an umbrella, a woman in a long coat who seemed to be scrutinizing the building. "Levi," she said, and his stomach dropped as he recognized Rhonda DeAngelo or whatever her name was now.

She happily supplied it. "It's Rhonda. Rhonda Simms. You remember me, from high school. Way back when, when I was Rhonda DeAngelo."

He nodded. "Yeah."

"I had *such* a crush on you," she admitted, rain dripping from her umbrella.

What do you say to that? Was there anything? "Oh, I didn't know."

She waved his embarrassment away and turned the conversation on a dime. "Look, I'd like to talk to you. I'm a reporter with *The Twilight Tribune* now . . ."

That much he did know.

"And I'm doing a piece on your brother's disappearance and your mother's demise. Oh, I'm so, so sorry for your loss."

A little too late. An afterthought. But then he knew Rhonda, or he had in high school. She'd been a sneak who idled around corners listening to gossip and always turning on a thousand-watt smile for the teachers. What they'd called a kiss-ass back then. But that had been twenty years ago. People changed as they became adults. At least some did.

"Thanks," he said blandly. He didn't want to think about dredging up all the scandal. He'd lived through it. And once was enough. He started for his car, but she kept step with him. "I'd like to know what you think."

"What?"

"You know, about your mother's . . . accident and your father . . . I mean he died on the lake, too. And Chase disappeared there."

He decided to cut to the chase. "You want to interview me for a story, is that right? And you want to put my family's tragedies in the paper?" Before she could answer, he asked, "What're you doing here, Rhonda? Why did you come to Serenity Acres?"

"This is where your mother lived."

He thought about Ed Sievers and his little dog. Ed had just been doing his mother a favor, but if the truth came out, no doubt he'd be kicked out of the facility, and not only would other reporters pick up the story but the police would come calling. What would happen to him then? Yeah, Levi was pissed that the old guy had snuck Mom to the lake house, but what was done was done.

"So, I'd love to buy you a cup of coffee or a beer or whatever, if we could talk about what happened."

From beneath the canopy of her umbrella, she smiled up at him. Friendly. Kind. Compassionate. At least that's the aura she wanted to convey.

"I'm busy."

"Later, then. You pick the time."

"I'll think about it."

Sensing she was getting the brush-off, she persisted. "Well, the sooner the better."

"I told you I'm busy."

"And I think you're trying to avoid me."

He didn't argue, sensed her anger, but kept walking.

She grabbed his arm, and he paused, rain collecting on his bare head. "Consider this a heads-up. I'm writing this story, Levi. With or without talking to you. In fact, it's going to press tonight, but I still have a little time. I would think you would want to give me your perspective, your side of what happened." Beneath the empathetic façade, he heard a glimmer of steel and noted that there were still just a smattering of cars in the lot, one of which was a dark Toyota sedan, the car that had rolled into the parking lot right after he arrived.

"Did you follow me here?" he asked.

"No!"

He thought of all the messages she'd left on his recorder, messages he hadn't returned, and he kicked himself for not realizing she'd been tailing him. He was a PI, for God's sake, and knew all the tricks of the trade. It was one of the reasons he'd bought this car, big and boxy, several of them in the town of Almsville alone, thousands across the nation, a family sedan that would blend in, not be noticed. Unless you were looking. Like Rhonda Simms. And not only had he not been expecting her, but he'd been caught in the web of his own thoughts. About his mother. About his brother. And about Harper.

He'd let his guard down.

"You did," he accused. "You followed me."

"Of course not . . ." She started to argue, then backed off. "Okay, fine. I did. You weren't returning my calls."

"Because I have nothing to say. Mom is dead. It's awful, all right? A horrible tragedy. And I would appreciate my privacy in my time of grief."

She blinked.

"You can quote me on that."

"Anything else?"

"No." He stood in the rain, water dripping down his nose as he stared at her. She finally got the message, let go of his wet jacket sleeve, and backed up a step.

"If you change your mind," she said, "give me a call."

He didn't respond, and she finally backed off, droplets of water flinging from her umbrella as she turned away. She strode to her car, the navy Toyota parked on the far side of the lot.

He couldn't believe he'd missed the fact that she was tailing him and he didn't catch her. But then, usually he was the hunter, not the prey. In the future, he'd be more vigilant.

He walked to his car and sat behind the wheel. He waited until he saw her headlights wink on and then watched through the fogging windshield as she drove out of the lot, her taillights disappearing as the car crested the small rise.

Only when he was certain she was not returning did he start the engine, letting the car warm, before he slid the two sheets of paper out of the embossed envelope.

He read the short note on the stationery in his mother's flowery script:

> *They killed him.*
> *They killed Chase.*
> *Make him pay.*

"What the devil?" he said, not understanding. He unfolded the second piece of paper. It was a cumulative bank statement showing cash deposits and withdrawals, all in the name of T. C. Hunt. "Thomas Calhoun Hunt." His father. The deposits had accumulated until February 1968. Then, abruptly, in March things turned around, and monthly withdrawals were made. Sometimes when the account was getting low, a deposit was made, but the withdrawals continued until May 1986, when the balance was zero, the account closed.

That was two years ago, the month of the fishing accident that took his father's life and just about the time his mother had started her ever-increasing descent into dementia.

Chapter 31

Beth was looking at the items in Harper's closet. "You really think Levi wants this stuff?" Beth asked. "Chase's class ring and jacket?"

"Maybe the necklace." Harper offered Beth a weak smile. "I'll find out."

"Well, okay. But if everything, including the necklace, were gifts?" She lifted a padded shoulder. "I don't know if they need to be returned. I mean, the only one left in the family is Levi, right? And he doesn't have any kids—no son or daughter—that we know of, so maybe you don't need to bother."

"I'll check anyway," Harper said, thinking it better to leave Levi's family situation out of the conversation.

Beth frowned. "If I were you, I'd keep the diamond—well, all the stuff—but then I'm not an heiress." There was a bit of a bite to her words, a little sting that Harper had felt throughout the years, not just from Beth but others who had envied her family's fortune. It always made her uncomfortable, but today she decided not to dwell on it.

Beth was already walking into the next room, the bedroom once occupied by her brother. Evan's things were just as he'd left them, neither Gram nor Harper having had the heart to get rid of his slingshot, records, books, skateboard, and baseball mitt, the twin beds still covered in matching nautical-themed quilts. All, like everything else, dusty from years of neglect.

Even bubbly Beth quieted when she walked through a room filled with the long-forgotten possessions a teenaged boy would covet, including his beat-up Converse high-tops and a hunting jacket that still held bullets in its pockets. A .22 rifle was propped against the wall of his closet, a Bowie knife on the shelf above.

"Wow, this is like a time capsule," Beth whispered, running her finger along the dusty edge of the bureau as she looked at a bulletin board where ticket stubs for concerts and events from the sixties were displayed. She eyed the stubs. "Geez, I don't remember most of these bands, but he saw the Beatles *and* the Stones?"

"Yeah."

"I would have killed to see them," she said. "I was *so* into the British bands at the time. What a trip." Then she stepped away from the board. "All of this, though, as cool as it might be, has to be cleaned out."

"Eventually."

Beth eyed the room quickly and turned toward the hall. "Let's get out of here. What's upstairs? I forget."

The third floor was similar to the garret over the garage, once a living space for servants, now an attic filled with junk, aside from the turret room—her room—which Beth observed with a jaundiced eye.

"The door needs rehanging," she said.

"I know."

"And not to be sacrilegious, but the crucifix, this one and, well, all of them have to go." Then hearing herself, she said, "Well, maybe one or two can stay, but the rest should be donated."

"With the dolls?"

"Wherever. Just . . . well, at least packed away if you want to keep them."

"I don't. Got it."

"Good. You're gonna need help. This is a huge place, and there's so much to be done. Even with Craig doing the repairs, the clean-up is going to be massive. Look, I know a couple of women who do this kind of thing—under the table, mind you, so cash only—but they could put this place in order, wash linens and dishes, and mop floors, shampoo carpets, and even tackle most of the windows. Whatever you want as long as you keep it on the down low, if you know what I mean."

Harper nodded. She did need help.

"Even so, it's going to take weeks, maybe more, and that doesn't touch the big stuff—like plumbing, electricity, refinishing the floors, and . . ." She let her voice trail off as she motioned to Harper's sleeping bag. "So this is where you're camping out?" she asked. "When there are all those other bigger bedrooms with larger bathrooms?"

"So far, yeah. I haven't really settled in."

"I guess." Beth shrugged. "Well, to each his, er, or her own."

"Right."

"There's another floor, right?" she asked, pointing toward the ceiling.

"Yeah. Well, just one room." Harper had mixed feelings about the unique area at the top of the turret—she hated it and loved it, sometimes dreaded going up there again, other times was lured to its incredible view. She led Beth up the narrow, curved staircase to the tower room, which her grandfather had called his "crow's nest," and unlocked the door with another one of Gram's keys.

This was the place where, she knew, he did private things. Dirty things.

But George Dixon had been dead for years—twenty-three years to be exact—and yet, as she stepped into the loft area, her skin crawled and it was almost as if he were here, as if she could smell the smoke from his pungent cigars. He'd bragged about still being able to get Cubans, though those imported cigars had been banned in the early sixties. But he had the boxes on the bookshelf in here to prove it.

The room was circular, windows all around, which allowed for a 360-degree view of the lake. The bathroom was partitioned off near the staircase, and it, too, had a wall of windows, so that even from the shower, one could look outside.

"Oh wow," Beth said, her breath taken away. "This . . . this is incredible. Your grandfather's sanctuary."

Harper was nodding, trying not to remember how Gramps would come up here, lock the door, smoke his cigars, pour a drink, and pleasure himself while looking across the water and ogling the women sunbathing.

It was more of a lair than a sanctuary.

"I didn't like him, but this is . . . well, it's a selling feature for sure. What's this—blueprint?" She unrolled large, yellowed pages with schematics of the house and outbuildings on Gramps's desk. "Oh wow," she said. "Look at this. Plans for when this house was built. Check the date. 1901. How cool. You should frame them," she said with a wink. "You know, for the new owner."

"Right."

"And since you'll probably remodel, these will save you having to start from scratch."

"I guess so."

"I *know* so. I live with a contractor, remember?" Beth rolled the plans up again, then peered through the telescope. "Holy Mother of God, with this, you can see . . . Geez, right into all of the houses on the point!" She swung the telescope left to right. "This is even more incredible than the one downstairs. There's the Sievers' place. Remember that old coot and his nasty dog? That German Shepherd. It was always on patrol around the perimeter of his property. You know, I wonder if there are still booby traps there? I told you his daughter owns the place now. A single mom, she moved in with her kids—I think they're teenagers."

"Right, you did tell me. Until then, I didn't know he had a daughter."

"None of us did. Never really saw her before he fell and broke his hip. He ended up in an assisted care facility. The same one where Cynthia Hunt lived. Serenity Acres, the only game in town." She was still bending over the telescope. "And there's the Hunts' place. I still can't look at it without thinking about Cynthia. Dear Lord, what was she thinking?"

"Don't know. I don't think we'll ever know."

"I guess . . ."

"Didn't you say that Levi plans on moving back?"

"Mmhmm. Soon. Maybe this weekend? He has a studio over his business in Sellwood, but he let his lease go."

He hadn't mentioned that when he'd visited her in the hospital. She asked, "He told you?"

"Yeah." Beth was still staring through the eyepiece of the powerful scope.

"Have you been there?"

"To his place?" A bit of color rose in her cheeks. "Yeah. I heard he might be interested in selling his house on the point, so I tracked him down."

"Oh." It seemed innocent enough, though Beth avoided her eyes, kept slowly moving the telescope.

"And is he? Interested?"

"Mmm. Who knows?"

"When he stopped by the hospital, he said he was a private eye."

"Yeah, I think he worked for the government for a while. FBI or CIA, maybe, something like that," she mused. "Then something happened—he got a divorce or . . . no! His wife died. That was it!"

"Died? How?"

Beth straightened away from the telescope. "I don't know all the details, or many of them really, but he came back to the Portland area a few years back."

"From where?"

"All around, I guess." She shrugged. "Washington, D.C., Seattle, and somewhere in California, I think. I don't really know." She turned her attention back to the telescope. "This could be addictive," she said.

Harper bit her tongue, but Beth didn't notice, she was too enthralled by what she could see. "This is so fantastic, you can see into Almsville. The Catholic church spire and city hall. Yep, there's the flag. And the water tower near East Bridge." She was slowly moving the telescope. "And all along the south side of the lake, the open spaces between the trees for houses and the road. Talk about a bird's-eye view! I mean, the view downstairs was spectacular, don't get me wrong. But this panorama? Wow. I had no idea." She straightened and dusted her hands, then slowly walked around the suite, all the while looking through the grimy windows. "Hey, there's St. Catherine's," she said, and it was true, from the north side of this room one could see the hospital's second and third stories rising on the hill over the tops of the trees. "So . . . at night—do you see the city lights? Can you actually see Portland?"

"Just the glow from the city. The hills are in the way."

"Doesn't matter. This—" Beth swung her arms wide and turned slowly. "This is incredible!" Frowning, she looked at the windows. "And when the glass is cleaned—God, I can't imagine what you can see."

"So it's better than the bat cave?"

"Don't remind me."

She peered through the telescope once more, training it on the opposite shore. "What a view! Just look at what you can see. It's . . . it's almost too clear. I mean, I can read Oster on my blender." Suddenly she lifted her head and backed away from the telescope. "It's a little creepy, if you know what I mean. How much is visible, especially if the blinds aren't drawn." She worried her glossy lip. "So you think, I mean, could maybe your grandfather have watched us? I mean, a long time ago, when he was alive, you know. When I was living there with Mom and Dad and my brothers?"

There was no reason to lie, no reputation to protect. "Yes, sometimes, I think so," Harper had to admit. It was obvious. "He spent a lot of time up here."

"Oh. Ick. And my bedroom . . ." Once more, the exaggerated shiver. "Do you think he watched my parents . . . you know . . . doing it?" Her expression turned to disgust.

"I don't know," Harper said quickly as the image of her grandfather jerking off filled her brain again. "Look, whatever he did, it's . . . it was a long time ago. He's been dead for ages." Dear God, was she making excuses for Gramps now? Or maybe for herself? Of course she didn't touch herself or fantasize while looking through the lenses, but even as a teen she'd stared through binoculars and telescopes hoping for a glimpse of Chase and felt a thrill run through her blood just at the sight of him.

Stupid.

Beth leaned down and put her eye up to the telescope again. She fiddled with the focus. "Anyone looking through this"—she tapped the metal optical tube—"could observe us and—oh God—videotape us . . . or . . . or . . . blackmail us if we were doing anything illegal." She looked up sharply. "Not that we are. No way. But from here you can watch us and . . . well, all of the houses on the point."

Harper thought again about Craig and the gun. "Good thing you're not criminals."

"For a lot of reasons," Beth said, peering through. "Oh, look, there's my husband now."

"Oh? What's he doing?"

"Paperwork, it looks like." She straightened suddenly. "I—I don't want to spy on him. That's not my thing. Lots of wives, they want to know what their guy is doing every second of the day, but that's not the way it is with us."

"So what is your deal?" Harper asked. "I mean, I didn't even know you were dating, and suddenly you were married."

"That works two ways, you know," Beth said. "I hadn't even heard of Joel Prescott, and then suddenly you'd eloped."

"I was pregnant," Harper said matter-of-factly. Why try to hide the obvious? "But you knew that."

"I can count," she said. "So your daughter? Is she Chase's?"

"Joel is Dawn's father," Harper said firmly, not wanting to go into details. She held her friend's gaze, and the room seemed to close in on them.

"That's what Dawn thinks?"

"She's never asked."

Beth raised a knowing eyebrow. "And when she does?"

"I guess we'll cross that bridge when it starts crumbling."

Beth let out a low whistle.

"But what about you?" Harper asked, changing the worrisome course of the conversation. "Why Craig?"

"Because he asked," she said, and a sadness stole over her face. "And because the boy I loved killed himself."

1967

Chapter 32

"I love you," Chase whispered against her ear again.

"I love you, too." Cuddling closer to him on the small beach of the island, Harper gazed up at the stars, glittering like diamonds in the sky overhead. She heard the quiet chirp of crickets over the sough of a warm breeze as it ruffled the dark water, and somewhere not far away a bullfrog was croaking in the quiet summer night.

Across the lake a few lights burned in the windows of houses near the shore, but tonight the Hunt house was dark.

She was just getting her breath back, Chase lying beside her, an arm around her shoulders as they lay naked on the sand.

"I want you to know that I'm serious." He levered up on an elbow, his pale hair falling over his eyes. "When I get through college, and you do, too? We'll get married."

"Is this a proposal?" she asked, hardly believing his words. Chase wanted to marry her? "Really?"

"No, no, no. Not yet. But a promise." He kissed her cheek. "Okay?"

She smiled at the thought of it. "Okay." She was gonna be Mrs. Chase Hunt. Someday. They would be married and happy forever!

He asked, "You'll wait for me?"

"If you wait for me," she teased, ruffling his hair.

"I will," he vowed, and kissed her between her breasts, on her skin just below where the cold diamond lay. "You're okay? I mean. I, uh. I didn't hurt you?"

"No, no, I'm good." That was a bit of a lie. She felt a slight burn between her legs, but she kinda loved it.

"You're sure?"

"Yeah. I'm sure." What she couldn't tell him was that it was a good hurt, a stinging but worth it. Some people said a person "lost" their virginity. She hadn't lost hers; she'd given it willingly. Eagerly. To the only boy she would ever love. "I'm fine." She pushed herself up so that her face was close to his and kissed him, softly at first, and then with more urgency.

He was quick to respond, and soon they were clinging to each other again, making love, joining their bodies in a fast, feverish rhythm, crying out in the night, the diamond necklace the only object between them.

When he came again, it was with a roar, and then he fell against her. She hugged him fiercely and felt the pain pulsing between her legs, a perfect pain. Evidence of what they'd shared.

She was left gasping as the cool night air whispered across her skin.

On a long breath, he whispered, "I—I have to go."

"No." She didn't want the night to end. "Not yet."

"I have to. Really." He was already disentangling himself, looking across the water to Fox Point and his house. Dark now. "They'll be home soon, and Dad will check on the boat. He always does. The Triton. It's his baby." He was already pulling on his jeans, standing over her.

"I know, but I'll miss you," she pouted.

"You would miss me worse if I was grounded." He tugged his T-shirt over his head and slipped his arms through the short sleeves. "Or it could be worse than that."

"What's that supposed to mean?"

"Just that he's tough. Doesn't like it when I break *his* rules. Oh, and maybe you should only wear the necklace when we're alone together. Okay? It's our secret."

"Sure, okay."

"Promise?"

"Promise," she vowed and crossed her heart.

"Good." Chase found his shoes but didn't bother with them, just bent down and gave her one more quick kiss. "You're sure you're okay?"

"Didn't I say so?"

"Okay, then." Carrying his high-tops, he ran across the sand and splashed into the water and under the overhanging branches of a willow tree where he'd hidden the boat. A few seconds later she heard the sound of the boat's motor and then saw him at the helm, driving the boat across the lake.

She sighed, caught in her love for him.

Some day they would be together.

Forever.

No more stolen moments, she thought, as he disappeared from sight and she saw a fish leap from the water, its silvery body arcing in the moonlight, the water rippling as it slipped under the surface.

The night was perfect, the softest of breezes caressing her skin as she pulled on her panties and slipped the sandy sundress over her head, then removed the necklace and slipped it into her pocket. It wasn't an engagement ring, but—

Bam!

The crack of a gunshot split the night.

Echoing against the water.

She jerked as if hit.

What was that?

She froze. One strap of her sundress tied, the other dangling. The area went deathly quiet. No noise from the bullfrogs, no buzzing of insects. Just the thudding of her heart.

Clunk!

Sweet Jesus!

The noise came from above her. Here, on the island.

From across the lake, a dog barked. Then another. And she didn't hear the motor of Chase's boat, but he was probably far across the lake by now and . . . or had someone shot at him? From here, from the house or terrace above?

No, no, no!

Her mind spun to horrible scenarios. All involving a bloody, gunshot chase. She let out a little mewl, then stopped short. *Don't freak out, Harper! Do not freak out!*

Her heart was beating so fast she thought it would fly out of her chest. She had to move, to do something.

Screeeecch.

What the hell was that?

The horrid grinding of metal on metal was, again, coming from above.

The tram? Starting its downward descent?

Sure enough, she heard the car clunking its way down the sharp hillside and caught a glimpse of its single headlight shining through the trees. She squinted, tried to see who was inside. Was it someone with a gun descending from the house?

Why?

Who?

Frantic, heart pumping wildly, her dress sliding off one shoulder, she ran barefoot to the path leading up the hillside.

Thud!

Dear God, what was that?

Footsteps?

Did she hear footsteps?

She flattened against the side of the cliff and hardly dared breathe. What was going on? Who had a gun? Or was it a gun? Had a car back-fired? Or some kid set off firecrackers left over from the Fourth of July?

No, no, no! It was too close, and she knew a gunshot when she heard it. Had gone with her father for target practice at the gun club when she was younger.

Hadn't anyone else heard the gunshot?

Of course not!

You're all alone.

Remember?

No one is at the gatekeeper's house. Dad and Marcia are at the Hilton in Portland for some sales conference. Evan is out with friends. Even the gardener, Martin Alexander, and his kid, Craig, are out of town on a camping trip.

Gram's in the hospital recovering from a gall bladder attack, her caretaker off duty. That's why you met Chase tonight, so you could be alone with him.

Blood pounded through her ears.

Panic threatened.

Over the whir of the tram's motor and the thudding of her own heart, she thought she heard footsteps. Running footsteps? Or was that her imagination? Oh God, was there a gunman on the island?

In the tram?

Or . . . ?

Her blood turned to ice, and she searched frantically in the darkness. *No, no, no!* Starlight and illumination from a crescent moon were weak. Still, she saw no dark figure scurrying furtively away. No bushes moving as a person skulked past.

With a squeal, the tram suddenly stopped.

Oh crap!

Don't freak. Do not freak out!

She waited, her mind whirling. Would someone get out of the car? Or was the gunman still inside the tram? Had he ever been inside? Why was he here? Was he still here? Had someone been shot? Oh dear God. She was sweating, freaking out, beginning to full-on panic.

Pull yourself together!

She gave herself a sharp mental slap.

She had to stay calm despite her racing pulse and gut-grinding fear.

Ears straining, she stayed flattened against the stone wall and tried to think of a way to get out of being trapped down here. The fastest, surest way back to the house was the stairway that ran parallel to the tram's rails. But she would be exposed.

Other than that, she could swim across the lake or to a neighboring dock on the north shore or possibly round the island and climb up the bridge. But who was to say he wouldn't be waiting there?

She could swim across the lake . . .

Her eyes were drawn across the water to Fox Point.

Security lights were visible at Old Man Sievers' bungalow, of course, but the Watkins' A-frame was dark, and the Hunts' cottage only showed the night-light that shone eerily from one window. The Leonettis' split level was devoid of any kind of illumination. Only the rental house's windows glowed with its weird pulsating light behind the blinds. No. Wait. Was there a light on in that round window cut into the roof? She squinted, almost imagining someone at the window, staring back at her.

But that was crazy.

And yet . . . there was the glint of something, like a small reflection of light from another source. A mirror? Or a telescope—maybe field glasses?

The thought that someone could be staring at the mansion, keeping track of what was happening, was unnerving.

But everything was.

Including the freaking gunman.

She didn't have time to think about a Peeping Tom now. She had to get back to the gatehouse somehow. It would be safe there, right? If nothing else, she could call Chase to come and get her. Yeah, that was what she would do. She took several deep breaths, then inched her way to the dock.

She saw no one.

So far, so good.

She stepped onto the dock and to the stairs and was about to start climbing when something shot across her feet, and she let out a tiny scream. Earline, Gram's orange cat with only one ear, turned and hissed before shooting toward the boathouse.

Shit! Damned cat!

Had the gunman heard? Been tipped off by her scream?

Oh. Dear. God.

Her pulse pounding in her ears, Harper melted onto the first step. Her scream had been stupid. The gunman could've heard her startled cry or the cat's hiss.

And yet there was silence, just the sound of water lapping at the dock and her own frantic heartbeat.

She waited, mentally counting off the seconds, nervous sweat running down her back.

Insects began to buzz again, and a bat swooped close.

Still no sound of anyone nearby.

Even the cat strolled past again to take up her favorite spot on the edge of the dock near the boathouse.

But why had the tram clanked its way from its garage to the dock? She studied it with its one glowing eye, no movement within its small compartment.

Maybe whoever had pulled the trigger was gone. Had left.

So far, there had been no other disturbance. No other gunshot. No more footsteps real or imagined.

Telling herself she was a moron, every nerve standing on end, she searched for a weapon—just in case—and grabbed the first thing she saw, an oar that had been left on the dock. It was a weak attempt at defense against a gun, but it was something. Heart in her throat, she swallowed back her fear.

Slowly, she made her way to the bottom of the steps where the tram's car sat, its motor still running, its single headlight glowing bright.

Just run by it.

Climb the steps fast and whatever you do, don't look.

Get up to the house!

Holding the oar in a death grip, her pulse pounding in her ears, she started up the stairs. She told herself not to look into the car, but her eyes didn't obey her.

And the door to the tram wasn't completely closed.

Someone was inside.

Someone lying down and . . . unmoving. Jean-clad legs visible.

She stumbled.

Saw the Adidas shoes with their three distinctive stripes.

Evan?

Whaaaat?

Her eyes widened. Dread pounded through her.

Oh Jesus! NO!

Dropping the oar, she peered through the open window of the tram.

"No," she choked out. "No. Oh God."

Evan lay sprawled across the seat. A pearl-handled revolver was in his right hand. A bullet hole at his temple was red, blood dripping through his brown hair and down the seat of the tram to the floor.

She shoved the door open further and flung herself at him. She tried to get him to move. This had to be some horrible, sick joke. He couldn't be . . . She wouldn't believe it. "Evan!" she cried, shaking him. But he didn't respond. "Evan! Stop this!" He didn't so much as flinch. Tears rained from her eyes, her throat raw, her body shivering. Blood on her hands. Oh God, no . . . *Please* no! But even as she sobbed through her silent prayers, she knew in her heart of hearts that he was gone.

1988
The Present

Chapter 33

"Look, I'm sorry, I shouldn't have brought up Evan's death." Beth was backpedaling quickly, as if reading the shock and horror on Harper's face, the telescope in the tower room forgotten. "It was tough for you, too. I mean you were there when it happened."

"No!" Harper said so sharply Beth took a step back.

"But I thought . . ."

"I mean I wasn't really there. I found him, but I'd been on the beach that night. I didn't see him do it. I just found him." That was the story she'd stuck with all these years, and she'd never mentioned she'd been with Chase.

No one had ever known about their meeting on the beach, and it didn't seem the time to tell all now, about how she'd lost her virginity and ended up with the necklace. It had remained their secret.

As to the tram incident, she didn't want to think about the gruesome scene the last time she'd seen her brother. So she spun the conversation around again. "I was just asking how you settled on Craig."

"It was a quick decision," Beth said, obviously glad not to dwell on Evan's death, either. "Not much thought went into it. Everyone was going off to college after graduation, and I couldn't afford it. My dad was of the opinion that girls didn't need an education to get an

M.R.S. degree. He actually said that, so I was on my own. I really didn't want to leave Almsville, though the twins were driving me crazy. They were *such* pains. I wanted to move out as I'd become my mom's go-to babysitter." Beth was walking around the room, eyeing the artifacts and landing on a vintage French edition of the Kama Sutra. "Geez, this was your grandfather's?"

"Yeah," Harper admitted and sat on the arm of her grandfather's leather chair that she imagined still smelled slightly of tobacco.

"He really got off on the sex thing?" Beth rifled through the pages.

"I guess."

"How old were you when he died?"

"Fourteen," she said uncomfortably. "Right before I started high school."

"I remember. It was really hot that summer."

Harper nodded, remembering. More than she wanted to. "You were talking about your brothers," she said, changing the subject.

"Oh. Right." After a peek at another illustrated page, Beth closed the book. "Bobby and Billy were into all kinds of sports—football, basketball, baseball—oh, and Bobby took karate. And guess who got to drive them back and forth? Not to mention breaking up their fights—those were really brutal. Have you ever tried to pull apart two twelve-year-old boys intent on killing each other? God, it was scary. So I figured it was past time to find a place of my own, and I ran into Sharon Burroughs—you remember her—she dated Evan briefly—well, who didn't?—and she was involved in school government, I think, and was on the track team—or was she? Doesn't matter."

"She was." Harper thought about Sharon, a bright, outgoing girl with wild red curls who just happened to be Matilda's daughter. Sometimes, when Matilda was working, taking care of Gram, she brought Sharon with her.

"Anyway, Sharon and I got an apartment in Southeast Portland right after graduation. That's when I got a job at a title company, and from there I kind of leapfrogged into becoming a Realtor. I knew Craig, he was working in construction—framing, at the time—and we hit it off. As I said, the boy I loved was gone."

"But didn't you go out with Levi?"

Harper knew as much. She'd seen them together, if only briefly.

"Oh. Yeah. I thought maybe I would make Evan jealous." She gave a sarcastic snort and ran her finger over the top of Gramps's desk. Coming up with a dusty fingertip, she frowned and rubbed her fingers together to clean off the grime. "But of course, Evan barely noticed. And then after Evan died, it was kind of a rebound thing, I guess," Beth said on a sigh. "But Levi was just being nice to me, I think. After Evan, I was a wreck . . . well, we all were. And so I cried on Levi's shoulder, but it just didn't go anywhere. Not then." She seemed wistful as she grew thoughtful. "I wasn't really over Evan, and I think Levi was in love with someone else. Levi never said so, but I could tell. I wanted to be with him . . . maybe anyone at the time, and we made out, you know, but . . ." She shrugged and gazed out the window where, Harper could see, a flock of geese were flying high in the sky, their wavering V heading south. "Levi's heart wasn't in it. He wouldn't even . . . well, you know."

"Wouldn't what?"

Beth looked at Harper as if she were stupid. "Go all the way. Duh!" She rolled her eyes. "It doesn't matter. Not now. We were just dumb kids."

"Right," Harper said, though she wasn't sure she meant it. "So are you friends now?"

Beth's eyebrows rose, and an enigmatic smile touched her lips. "Yeah, I think so." She seemed on the verge of saying something more about it but cleared her throat and said, "Anyway, I was talking about moving out after graduation, with Sharon." Beth glanced at the telescope again, then added, "But the apartment thing with her didn't last long, not even the six months for the lease. Her mother moved away, and Sharon went with her."

"I heard they went to Canada," Harper said.

"Right. Somewhere . . ." Her eyebrows drew together. "I think it's that place where they have the rodeo or whatever it's called."

"The Calgary Stampede."

"That's it!" Beth nodded.

"So, out of the country."

"Umhmm—they had family there or something. Maybe her mom's brother. Not sure, but I heard that Sharon got married and has a bunch of kids. Four or five or something. Can you imagine? After helping out with the twins growing up, I wasn't going to have any. Billy and Bobby were brats! Nightmares, both of them. Mom always just said, 'Boys will be boys,' but they were horrible. *Horrible!* And I *always* had to babysit. So I wasn't keen on the idea of having a kid, but Craig talked me into it. And I'm glad he did. Max is great." She smiled, her eyes bright. "To tell you the truth, I can't imagine life without him."

Harper knew the feeling about her own child.

"As for Sharon? More power to her, if that's what happened. I don't really know. We lost touch after the first couple of years. We each got married, and life went on."

"Do you have an address?" Harper asked, rising from the over-stuffed arm of her grandfather's favorite chair.

"Mmm . . . maybe, but it would be like, what? Fifteen years old. Maybe more? But I'll check my Rolodex, if you want."

"I think so, yeah."

"You got it." She glanced around the room once more with a critical eye. "Okay, I think I've seen enough. Let's get out of here. But seriously, I'm sending Craig over to give you an estimate to fix up the place." Beth started down the stairs, holding onto the rail as she wound her way down.

Harper followed, the pain in her hip nagging at her.

Once they were on the main level again, Harper said, "Look, I'm not sure I'm selling, but I do have to do at least minor repairs to the place."

"At least—and let's call them major repairs."

"Fine, if I can afford them."

Beth threw her a disbelieving look as they walked to the foyer.

"If you say so." Beth didn't sound convinced.

As they reached the door, Harper decided this was the chance to find out more about Beth's husband. What made him tick. "So tell me about Craig's construction company. How did he even get into it?"

"He's a bit of a one-man band," Beth admitted and opened her purse to retrieve a business card, which she pressed into Harper's hand. "He works with subcontractors—plumbers and electricians and the like—and has one guy who is kind of an extra handyman, I guess you'd say. I, of course, am the bookkeeper, but he pretty much runs the show. Things are slower right now, but there are times when he barely has any time off—even during hunting season, and that about kills him."

"He's a hunter?" Harper pressed.

"Oh yeah." Beth was nodding. "Major hunter. And he loves fishing and camping. Anything the least bit outdoorsy."

"He has guns, then?" Harper asked, trying not to sound too interested.

"Guns?" She let out a little laugh that echoed in the tall foyer. "Oh yeah. It's *way* beyond that. He has himself a damned arsenal. *Loves* any kind of weaponry. Knives, rifles, shotguns, you name it. And, let me tell you, if there's a gun show anywhere in the tri-county area? He's there! Like that!" She snapped her fingers. "I swear if it was legal to have machine guns and bazookas, he'd be at the front of the line to buy one." She laughed at the image.

Harper thought about viewing him with the handgun on his nighttime canoe ride to the Hunts.

"So what about pistols?"

"Sure. He inherited a lot of that stuff from his father. But I don't know the particulars as he's always buying and selling and trading with other gun nuts." Beth was already fishing in her purse for her keys.

Harper pressed, "What about cowboy guns, you know, pearl-handled revolvers?"

"Pearl-handled?" Beth asked, shaking her head. "Are those things for real?"

"Yeah."

Beth shrugged. "I really don't know. I leave all that weapon/army stuff to him. And I keep Max out of it, you know. Just because his father is a big gun nut—excuse me gun *enthusiast*—doesn't mean he has to be. Nuh-uh."

Once again, Harper wondered if she should tell Beth about seeing Craig on his night journey with the canoe, but that would mean she'd have to confess that she, like her grandfather, viewed the comings and goings of the houses across the lake, that she'd watched Beth cooking dinner, seen Max in his bedroom, and followed Craig's activities. All when they didn't know they were being observed.

She decided to hold her tongue.

For the moment.

Harper opened the door.

As Beth stepped onto the porch, she said, "And whether you do repairs or not, get rid of all those dolls and the other collections that your grandmother kept. Freshen the place up with some new furniture and curtains. It's a cool house, very cool, but . . ."

"But what?"

"I don't know how you can stay here all alone. It's so big and empty, and there are ghosts here, you know. A lot of people have passed. And now, you think someone is getting in and moving ugly dolls around. I don't know. I wouldn't stay here."

"I fixed the window."

"You temporarily fixed one. And there are dozens! And all the doors. You don't even know if he came in through the broken window." She eyed the exterior of the house, gloomy in the rain. "I just know I couldn't do it. I'd be a nervous wreck. I mean, what if he comes back? And this time he's not just messing with those repulsive dolls? What if, God forbid, he attacks you? You could be killed, Harper. Murdered."

"You're not making me feel better."

"I'm just trying to talk some sense into you," she said as a gust of wind rattled across the parking area, so fierce it blew wet leaves across the puddled asphalt. "You could live in the gatekeeper's house."

"Unlivable. Probably needs to be torn down."

"Then . . . then a hotel or rent a place. The house next to us is empty right now, and I have the Musgraves' phone number. We'd be right next door. Neighbors. Or wait a sec! What about spending some time with Craig and me? We've got an extra room!"

"Thanks, but it's really not so bad," Harper lied, thinking about how tightly she'd clutched the scissors as she lay in the sleeping bag listening to the huge timbers creak.

"Well, as they say, it's your funeral. Oh God, look at the time!" Beth said as she glanced at her watch, then the sky. "Damn it all, my hands were full, and I left my umbrella in the car. Well, too bad. I've *really* got to run."

And she did, dashing through the rain and slipping into her car. As she slid into her BMW, she turned on the ignition and rolled down the window. "You know, while you're at the fixing-up and cleaning-out stage, you should really consider getting rid of those." She pointed toward the gargoyles at the far end of the bridge. "You can put up planters on the pillars filled with flowers or large carriage lights, or anything a lot more welcoming."

"I'll think about it," Harper called. "And hey, be careful. I've still got a missing cat I don't want you to run over."

"As if!" With a wave, she called, "Kisses!" And then she was off in her BMW, hitting the gas to race across the bridge.

Harper watched as the sports car streaked past the gate where the large, hulking gargoyles stood watch.

If she decided to sell, maybe Harper would get rid of them.

Because, regardless of what her grandmother had confided ages ago, they were doing a piss-poor job of guarding the island.

Chapter 34

Levi knew there were no cameras in the parking lot of Serenity Acres. He'd asked when he'd learned his mother had gotten out of the facility and he wanted to know why. But still, he couldn't stay in the lot too long, or someone would notice. He stuffed his mother's note and bank statement into the envelope, then placed it in his glove box and withdrew a small flashlight and his set of picks, including his favorite slim-jim.

Would he be able to unlock the old VW bus?

He wasn't sure, but he was going to give it a try. According to Sievers, the Volkswagen had been sold to him by Tristan aka "Trick" Vargas. Levi remembered Trick as being slick and cocky, with a toothy smile that seemed to indicate he was certain he held one over on you. "Arrogant son of a bitch." And he'd been dealing. All the while neither his dad nor Gerald Watkins seemed to care. Unlike each man. Both stand-up cops. Or so he'd thought.

So this was Levi's opportunity, possibly his only opportunity, to search the van in the hopes that Vargas, in his quick escape away from the lake, might have left something in the van.

But twenty years?

What were the chances?

Not good. Nonetheless, opportunity only knocks once. Right? Wasn't that the saying? He locked his own car and dashed through the rain to the spot where the van was parked. It was a sorry-looking vehicle, faded and rusted, the peace sign that had been so vibrant two decades earlier now appearing dull, as forgotten as the movement it so proudly once touted.

He knew Sievers, who'd been the king of security on Fox Point back in the day, would have locked the vehicle, and he was right, but the old locks gave way easily. Without much effort he was in the passenger area of the van, now devoid of any seats, simply a cargo hold.

He caught sight of a car approaching, headlights cutting through the gloom, and he waited for the Chrysler K Car to pass. He watched as a young woman parked, then opened the back side door and put a baby in one of those collapsible umbrella strollers. She strapped a child of about two into it before pushing the stroller at a jog into the facility.

Once he was inside, he turned on his flashlight and started searching. It was a futile job. Though the interior was stark, it was dirty, with bits of trash, foil gum wrappers and a couple old newspapers, a pair of boots, and not much else. He shone his light under the dash, around the stick shift and upright steering wheel.

Nothing. Except wads of chewed gum left jammed on the doors and dash.

Probably there was never anything here. And he had no idea what, if anything, he was looking for. Maybe nothing. Tristan Vargas could have been a two-bit drug dealer who was long gone, maybe walking the straight and narrow right now, an insurance salesman with two kids living somewhere in the suburbs of Duluth, Minnesota, or anywhere else.

He shone a light once more under the front seats. Nothing on the floor, but he did catch sight of a bit of paper tucked onto the seat itself, as if it had been pushed there. Probably nothing. And yet . . . He stretched, barely able to reach it and wiggle it out while he held the flashlight with his free hand. The paper was stuck, as if it had been wedged there for years and might have been adhered to an ancient wad of gum. Slowly, he was extracting it, hoping not to tear it, telling himself it was probably useless and sweating with the effort.

Somewhere off in the distance, he thought he heard the yip of a small dog, but he kept working, easing the paper until suddenly it came free, tearing a bit beneath the gum.

Just as the sliding door to the van opened and there, hunched over his walker, backlit by tall security lamps, his hair plastered by the rain, was Edward Sievers.

"You little shit! What the hell do you think you're doing?" he demanded, Jake pulling at his leash and, sensing his owner's disapproval, growling menacingly.

"I thought Mom might have left something in here," Levi lied.

"Under my goddamned driver's seat?" he huffed. "I don't think so. Get out of there! Jesus Christ, I thought I was doin' you a favor!" Some of his bluster was disappearing. The dog, hackles raised, was still growling, and when Sievers looked down to reprimand him, "Stop, Jake, it's okay," Levi rolled over, tucked the paper into his pocket, and slid out of the van.

By now the dog had calmed and even Sievers appeared less irritated. "If you wanted to search the damned car, all you had to do was ask."

"I guess I should have."

"No guessing about it," Sievers said as Jake, calm again, sniffed at Levi's shoes. "Find anything?"

"Gum wads. Lots."

"Not mine. Those kids who had it before me. I cleaned out most of their crap, but the gum . . . that takes elbow grease."

As Levi straightened and faced him, Sievers looked up at him through the foggy lenses of his glasses. "You know, your old man was a prick. I hate to speak ill of the dead, but I know he took a strap to you boys. No wonder the older one took him on. I saw it. Heard it." He clucked his tongue as he glanced up at Levi. "Now go on, get out of the rain." With that, he slammed the door of his van shut, locked it, and headed back the way he'd come.

Well, he blew that.

So much for being a stealthy private eye.

But he'd found something—even if it turned out to be nothing.

What about his mother's note, though? Cynthia Hunt, if she'd been thinking straight, seemed to think that Chase had been killed by a team, or at least more than one person. But she was only seeking revenge on one? What did that mean?

Clearly she knew something.

And she thought Chase was dead. When had that changed? He remembered the days after his brother's disappearance, how she'd clung to hope that he was alive. How she'd believed he would return. She'd spent hours putting up flyers and talking to reporters, trying to keep the interest in his case in the news. She encouraged her husband to make certain that Chase's case didn't go cold, though over time it had.

But still she'd been his champion.

Her ardor for the case had faded over time, but she'd clung to the belief that he would return, that he'd either been kidnapped or left on his own, but that someday she would see him again.

Until . . . until her husband had taken his boat out into the middle of the lake and fallen overboard and drowned.

Chapter 35

Rand noticed lights shining from the windows of the Hunts' house next door as he pulled into his drive. A big, boxy car was parked in the Hunts' driveway, a Ford Fairlane from the looks of it. It looked like Levi really was moving back. So they'd be neighbors again, and Rand wasn't sure how he felt about that. He'd always gotten along with Levi. They'd known each other forever. But Chase had always thought Levi was a pain in the ass, not to be trusted.

Then again, Chase wasn't exactly a paragon of virtue.

Inside the house, he tossed his keys on a side table and shed his jacket. His stomach rumbled, and he considered his options for dinner.

Frozen pizza?

Mac and cheese?

Leftover takeout from Alberto's?

Rand's choices for dinner weren't exactly epicurean delights, but he didn't much care. He opted for the pizza, pulled the box from the freezer, and let the "Pepperoni Supreme" thaw a bit as the oven heated.

Stepping outside, he felt the chill of February work its way into his bones as he gathered firewood and kindling from the pile of cordwood he'd stacked behind the garage. He glanced across the water, to the island, and wondered about Harper. As he had every day since she'd returned. Hell, he'd even taken the boat out and motored over there, compelled in some way.

"Idiot," he muttered. Yeah, he'd had a crush on her as a teen, and even as he'd turned twenty, but that was long over. He turned away and headed back inside.

In the living room he stacked paper and kindling beneath a chunk of fir in the old fireplace and started a fire. The newsprint caught quickly, kindling starting to crackle just as the stove dinged, indicating temperature had been reached.

The fire started to give off a little heat. Rand cracked a beer and was just about to shove the pizza into the oven when he heard a knock on the door.

Snapping on the porch light, he saw Levi through a sidelight and opened the door. "You got a minute?" he asked without any kind of greeting or a smile. He was tense. Something on his mind.

"Sure. Come in. Thought you might be next door. I saw the lights."

"I'm moving back."

"I heard."

"Already started."

"Good." Rand didn't know if it was a good idea or not, but time would tell. "Want a beer?" He held up his bottle of Sam Adams.

"Yeah, sure. Why the hell not?" Levi gave a quick nod, and for a second Rand imagined offering a bottle to Chase. He wondered if they'd still be friends. If Chase would have settled down here, in Almsville. If he would have married Harper—even had a kid or two. Then would Tom Hunt still be alive? Would Cynthia have avoided her descent into madness?

Who knew?

"Have a seat," Rand said. As he stepped into the kitchen, the oven beeped and he slid the pizza into the oven, then set the timer all the while wondering what was going on with Levi?

He returned with the beer and saw that Levi hadn't sat down. Instead, he was standing in front of the fire staring off into space. He accepted the bottle from Rand and clinked the neck of his beer with that of Rand's, then took a long pull.

"Thanks."

"You want to take off your jacket?" Rand asked.

"Nah. I can't stay." He retrieved an envelope from his pocket and handed it to Rand. "Take a look at this."

"What is it?"

"A note from my mother. She left it with another resident at Serenity Acres. For me. You remember Old Man—uh, Edward—Sievers."

"My neighbor? Sure."

Levi explained how he'd run into Sievers when he'd gone to look through his mother's things at the care facility. "So he gave it to me. Look inside."

Rand slipped a bit of embossed stationery from its matching envelope and read the simple message.

They killed him.
They killed Chase.
Make him pay.

"Wait a second. *They* killed Chase, but make *him* pay? So is it one person, or several?"

"I don't know," Levi admitted. "It could have been a mistake. In the last few years, Mom wasn't always . . . you know. Not always there. So maybe she wasn't thinking straight."

Rand didn't think so. The note was too perfectly written, too carefully put together. "Did Sievers read this?"

"He said no. The note was sealed. And there's more. This was with it." He reached into the pocket of his jacket and came up with a piece of paper,

"What is this?" Rand asked, perusing the document as the smell of warming bread dough emanated from the kitchen. "Bank statement."

"Right, and check the date. All of the withdrawals, cash, on a monthly basis, until the month Dad died. By then the account was drained."

"Just your dad on it," Rand said, eyeing the figures. "He was making payments."

"In cash."

"No record," Rand said, starting to get a bad feeling. "You don't know of anything he was buying on time?"

"I don't think that's it. I think . . ." Levi paused and stared into the fire, where the flames were crackling. "I think he might've been paying someone off."

"For—?"

"That's the part I don't understand. I've been handling Mom's accounts, paying her bills, collecting Dad's retirement and social security for her, and there was nothing outstanding. The house is paid off, and I sold her car. The boat—it was bought years ago." He took a long swallow from his beer. "It could be some kind of personal note, I suppose, for something I don't know about."

"Gambling debt?"

"Never was into that, at least that I know of. It's the timing that worries me. And then there's the note from Mom."

"Have any idea what it means?" Rand said, turning the note over and studying it.

"Obviously she thought that Chase was killed and that whoever did it, whoever 'they' were, got rid of his body."

"But make 'him' pay."

"Right." Levi took another pull from his bottle and finally sat in one of the side chairs across from the fire. "So somehow one or more of the people she thinks killed Chase is gone, but there's one left and I'm supposed to make him pay."

"How?"

"You're the cop," he said. "You tell me."

The timer dinged. "Just a sec." Rand set his half-drunk beer on a nearby table and went into the kitchen. Using a pair of ratty old oven mitts his mother had once worn, Rand pulled the pizza from the oven and left it on the top of the stove. Cheese ran over the sides of the pan, but he didn't care and stripped off the mitts. "You want some pizza?" he yelled from the kitchen.

"Nah. Thanks." Levi shook his head. "Go ahead."

"I can wait."

Returning to the living room, he saw that Levi had a torn piece of paper in his hand. "Look at this. I don't know if you know it, but Sievers bought the old hippie van that was parked down the street when we were in high school. The one painted with flowers and a peace sign."

"I remember."

"When I got the note, I looked in the van and I found this." He handed a scrap of paper to Rand. "It's part of an old registration for the van, from years ago. Sievers said he bought the van from Tristan Vargas, the dude who went by Trick. Everyone said he was from Texas. That's where he claimed to have come from. But the VW was registered in Sierra Vista, Arizona. To Larry Smith."

"Who's Larry Smith?"

Levi actually smiled, though it wasn't all that warm. "I did some checking. Saw the driver's license pictures of Larry Smith and Tristan Vargas."

"Let me guess. They're one and the same." Rand took a swig from his beer. Levi as a private investigator had his own way of getting information. Rand didn't ask about how, didn't want to know.

"You got it. An alias. And it looks like Larry from Sierra Vista also became Conrad Nelson from San Bernardino in California in the seventies, after he split from here."

"After Chase disappeared."

"Right. He's been in and out of prison. Once for dealing and the most recent time for assault. Both in California. His record in Oregon is clean as far as I know."

"And where is he now?"

"That I haven't been able to figure out. Released from prison eighteen months ago."

"And you think Larry or Tristan or whatever he goes by now is somehow involved in this?" Rand held up Cynthia's cryptic note.

Levi shrugged. "I don't know. This is as far as I got. But he sure took off fast after Chase went missing."

"He and the rest of them."

"He seemed like the ring leader, but who knows? I thought you, or someone with the police, might want to look into it." Levi scowled into the fire. "Maybe you can figure out who Mom was talking about. That is, if she knew what she was doing."

"Did you find out how your mother got out of Serenity Acres?" Rand asked, studying Levi's face.

"No." Levi shook his head.

Rand pointed to the papers strewn over the coffee table. "Can I keep these?"

"Yeah." Levi drained his beer. "Sure. I mean, do what you want with it. I don't know what the hell she expected me to do. If she knew what happened to my brother. If she thought he was dead, why didn't she name names?" He raked his fingers through his hair in frustration, then set his empty on the table. "Oh hell, who knows if she even knew what she was talking about? She was so crazy."

Rand pinned Chase's brother in his gaze. "What do *you* think happened to him?"

"I don't know." Levi rubbed his jaw, as he thought back. "But after he got back to the house, after seeing you up at the river. That's where you were, right?"

"Uh-huh. The old logging road."

"Right. Well, Chase came home all hopped up, almost looking for a fight. He and Dad, they got into it. I mean, really got into it. It got physical. You know, Dad had a temper and so did Chase. They were downstairs. Mom, too. I went down to break it up, but they were both seeing red. I got in the middle of it but ended up taking a punch or two and getting Mom out of there. Then I left. I thought 'fuck it' and walked around the lake. When I got back, things had quieted down, so I just went to bed. I thought Chase was in his room. His car was there."

"But he took the boat out to meet Harper," Rand said and noted that Levi's statement hadn't changed over the years.

"I think I heard him leave. I thought my old man would follow, but he didn't, at least not that I know. I fell asleep—just before midnight, I think."

"Did you hear him take the boat out?"

"No," Levi admitted, apparently lost in thought. "I didn't hear anything more until Harper woke me up later. You remember. She rapped on the window of Chase's room, then we came over to your house."

Rand did remember. He'd just gotten home when there was a knock on the door. His old man was already in bed and hadn't wakened. Or had he? Now Rand wasn't sure. The night had been a blur due to the amount of alcohol he'd consumed in a short period of time.

As Levi took his leave and from the porch Rand watched him return to the house next door, he had an uneasy feeling that everything they knew about that night might be a façade.

Chapter 36

Contrary to Beth's dark prediction, Harper wasn't attacked in her sleep that night, or over the next two nights.

No one had snuck into the house and hacked her to pieces.

Nor had they shot her at close range.

Nope, Harper was alive, her brother's Bowie knife under her pillow, while the scissors and crucifix were in the sleeping bag with her, as they'd been for the past two nights. She would have loved to keep Gramps's pistol with her, but despite searching the house over, she hadn't been able to locate it.

Even with her lesser weapons around her, she'd slept fitfully, the noises of the old house piercing her brain. Creaking timbers, rattling windows, the sound of the train on the tracks just on the other side of Northway Road had caused her to wake with a start each time she'd dozed off.

Still no intruder had attacked her.

"Count it as a win," she said to herself and stretched in her bed. It was still dark, only a little after six, dark enough to feel like midnight.

But she needed to get up. Face the day.

From the time she'd seen Beth drive across the bridge, she'd worked at getting this behemoth of a house in order. First she'd gone to the phone company and ordered a repairman to put in two new lines, one for her fax machine, the second for her computer. She'd picked up new copies of the white and yellow pages and had let her fingers "do the walking," as the old advertisement had suggested.

She'd also called the two veterinarians in town and a cat shelter, each time asking about an unclaimed tuxedo cat. Unfortunately, she'd come up empty.

More and more she worried about Jinx, but she'd pushed her concerns aside for the moment.

As she was in and out of the house, most of the phone calls that had come into the house had gone directly to her answering machine, which turned out to be a good thing as she was able to avoid Rhonda Simms's calls. Rhonda had left three messages, each one a little more terse than the one before, each asking for an interview.

"In your dreams," Harper had said, erasing them all.

There had been hang-ups as well, which she'd attributed to the pushy reporter.

She'd hired a gardening crew to clean up the grounds and called a local housekeeping company. The manager had sent over two pairs of housekeepers. One set had started on the kitchen and main floor, while the second set began cleaning from the top floor turret room and worked their way down. They had worked long hours, and by six o'clock yesterday, the house was as clean as it was going to get for a while.

As soon as the turret had been scrubbed, vacuumed, dusted, and polished, Harper had been able to haul all of her equipment to her new office on the top floor. She'd boxed up her grandfather's magazines, books, and cigar boxes and had them taken to the garage by one of the gardeners.

She'd made her appointment with the doctor at his office near the hospital and had all of her sutures removed. She'd found the time to call Dawn, leaving a message on her pager, and checked in on her father. Although she hadn't actually talked to him, Marcia had conveyed that they were home at their condo in Portland and that Bruce was resting but would call her back.

So far she'd heard from neither her daughter nor her father and was running on the principle that no news was good news.

Fingers crossed.

Yesterday morning a locksmith had arrived to re-key all the doors and secure every window. She had a call into someone to check out the elevator and dumbwaiter, and a crew was set to come and clean the roof, gutters, and chimneys next week.

In a house this size, it was just a start, but she was feeling better about living here. She would learn more about what repairs were needed after her meeting with Craig Alexander later today. Beth had arranged it all, calling and confirming that Craig would come over this morning. When Harper protested, Beth had insisted. "It won't hurt to get an idea of what you're dealing with," she'd said. "Craig will check everything out and give you an estimate. That's all. It's not like it's written in stone. Oh, I've got another call. Talk later. Kisses!" And she'd hung up.

So Harper was meeting with Craig, and she decided maybe she'd learn a little from him, see if she could get any information about his nocturnal visit to the Hunts' house.

She rolled out of bed and walked into the bathroom, where she found no menacing doll staring at her.

Thank God.

But her own reflection wasn't much better. The bruising around her eye was turning a sickly yellow color, and though her stitches had been removed, Harper could see the spots where the sutures had been. "Good morning, bride of Frankenstein." She decided to forgo any kind of makeup again. What was the point?

After showering, she dressed in worn jeans and a long-sleeved T-shirt, then, because it was still dark as midnight, picked up the knife. Just in case. Gripping the hilt, on the lookout for some intruder or, more likely, the cat, she made her way down to the main level.

She wasn't accosted.

Nor did she spy Jinx.

"Crap." This was getting serious. "Come on, Jinx," she said to the empty hallway. In the kitchen, she checked his food dish and water. Untouched. "Where the hell are you?"

He should have come back by now.

Today she'd make some calls. Not only did she want to ensure that all the bills for the property came to her rather than to the attorneys, but she needed a repairman for the dryer, which took forever to get anything dry. Thankfully, all the other appliances seemed operational, if a little quirky.

She made coffee, nearly burned a couple of slices of toast, then walked to the parlor window and stared out past the misting fog that was creeping over the water to the far shore where a few lights were visible.

She spread butter on her toast and sipped the hot coffee, then took a peek through the lens of the telescope, still trained across the lake. For two full days she'd refrained from peering into the lives of those on the point, but this morning she couldn't resist.

"Some people read the morning paper, but you, Harper Prescott, you watch the neighbors, just like Gladys Kravitz," she chided herself, remembering the nosy neighbor on *Bewitched*, one of her favorite TV shows as a teen.

Lights were on at the Sievers' bungalow, and next door at the Hunts' place she spied Levi without a stitch on. Standing at the sliding door, drinking coffee, and naked. She couldn't help staring at him, noting how he'd changed in the years since she'd lived here.

A shadow passed behind him, and Harper froze.

He wasn't alone?

Maybe someone helping him move in? She'd caught glimpses of Levi moving boxes into the house in the last couple of days and some of the existing furniture moved around. But would someone be helping him move at this hour?

Of course not. He was a man in his late thirties. It shouldn't surprise her that he had a lover. Yet it was unexpected and surprisingly unwanted. Which was ridiculous. She had no tie to Levi.

Not that she would admit.

She tore herself away from the damned telescope and told herself Levi Hunt deserved a life. A life without Harper poking around in it.

Besides, she had a lot to do today, and she couldn't waste any time putting her nose into someone else's business.

Today she planned to start by boxing all of Gram's things that she planned to donate or throw out. Or keep. No matter what Beth said, Harper didn't see any reason not to preserve at least some of what Gram loved, her most precious belongings. In a house this size, Harper could dedicate a room, maybe even a floor, to Gram's things. She picked up Toodles from the love seat and stared at her cracked face. "You, for sure, have to go," she said, her eyes moving to the window and the houses across the lake.

A few lights were winking on. The loft in Rand's A-frame with its triangular window. The hand binoculars were resting on a side table, and she couldn't resist lifting them to her eyes. Sure enough, she spied Rand in a black T-shirt doing something—oh, possibly riding a stationary bike. The desk was in the way, but she was certain he was exercising.

She moved the binoculars to the Alexanders' split level. Still dark. Harper was about to turn away when she saw the front door open, the entry hall visible through the windows on the lake side of the house. Backlit by the street light, Beth entered, closed the door, and hurried up the stairs.

She'd been out?

And wasn't turning on any lamps?

Harper raised her binoculars so she could look into the master bedroom, no curtains or shades obscuring her view.

"None of your business," she told herself, but she noticed headlights flashing through the trees and between the houses as a pickup drove down Trail's End Road. For a second she thought it might be someone delivering newspapers, but the pickup must have stopped at the Alexanders'. The beams of the headlights went out.

Within a minute Craig walked through the front door and flipped on the lights.

A black bag was slung over one of his shoulders. He dropped it as he kicked the door shut, then shed his jacket. Working the kinks out of his neck, he walked to the kitchen, where he was in clearer view. He took a bottle of orange juice from the refrigerator and drank from it.

Harper couldn't tear her eyes away.

So both he and Beth had been gone in the wee morning hours?

Possibly overnight?

But, seemingly, not together.

You don't know that. They could have gone somewhere in separate cars.

But she hadn't noticed Beth's headlights. Only the dark street.

What does it matter? It is NONE of your business!

Harper started to put the binoculars down, then talked herself out of it. Adjusting the focus, she observed Craig scoop his bag from the front hallway floor and then start up the stairs. He opened the bedroom door, his silhouette visible because of the hall light filtering up the staircase.

A bedside light turned on. Beth's doing. She levered herself up on an elbow and yawned. Craig said something to her from the doorway, then walked to the bed. Stretching, her hair mussed, Beth acted as if she'd been asleep for hours. Craig pulled off his T-shirt and stepped out of his jeans before sliding under the covers.

Don't watch! Don't be like your grandfather. These people deserve their privacy.

Still, she stood at the window, binoculars glued to her face.

They kissed, Beth's arms wrapping around Craig's neck as he rolled atop her.

Finally Harper walked away from the window and realized she was still holding onto the doll.

The doll that she'd found on the sofa.

Not on the side table by the Tiffany lamp. Where she'd left it a few days ago.

Hadn't she seen it, still propped against the lamp just last evening, after the cleaning women had been in the house? They hadn't moved it.

Or had they?

The hairs on the back of her neck rose in warning. Something was wrong here. Or maybe she was mistaken. A lot of people had been in and out of the house in the days since she'd nearly stumbled over the damned doll. Someone could have moved it and she hadn't noticed.

But she thought back to the night before, when she'd sat on the sofa with a glass of wine and a paperback she hadn't been able to get into. She hadn't had to move the doll. It hadn't been there.

So Toodles had to have been moved *after* the locksmith had been inside and changed the locks.

But that couldn't be.

She tried to think, to come up with a different scenario, but couldn't.

And then she lifted Toodles's pink gingham dress. There on the white gathered panties were three red letters: *ICU*. Worse yet, when she lifted the dress, she'd realized there was something hung around the doll's neck. A necklace of sorts.

Something hidden by her clothes.

Something coldly familiar.

Her heart stopped for a beat as she saw the silver disc, engraved with the name *Jinx*.

She bit back a scream.

Toodles was wearing Jinx's collar?

Her blood turned to ice.

Fear curdled her stomach as she turned quickly around in the room, her heart in her throat, barely able to breathe. Her heart was drumming as fast as a hummingbird's wings and she had to fight the swell of panic rising within her.

Someone had Jinx?

And they were toying with her?

Taunting her?

Playing into her worst fears?

Who?

Why?

Frantically she eyed the room, looking for she didn't know what. A clue as to who was behind this sick little joke? A reason to believe that Jinx was still alive?

"Oh God," she whispered and realized she was still holding the offensive doll, the one Gram had said looked like Harper as a child. Her skin crawled from touching it, but she removed Jinx's collar and stuffed it into her pocket. Then she carried Toodles into the kitchen and the trash bin. She stomped on the pedal to open the lid and expected to see Maude staring up at her.

The can was empty.

A new frisson of fear swept up her spine. And she looked around sharply, as if the doll were somewhere else in the kitchen, staring down at her. Mocking her.

That was impossible, and she saw no evidence of Maude.

Anywhere.

Then she remembered the cleaning people. They'd taken out the trash, doll and all. "Calm down," she told herself as she turned on the exterior lights. "Don't give into them. They're playing mind games, that's all. Games you can win." Despite her verbal bolstering, she wasn't sure of her chances of winning against this hidden, maleficent enemy and fear was very much her companion. "Get a grip," she reminded herself. Whoever was behind these parlor tricks was a twisted individual and a coward, hiding in the shadows, watching from afar. She couldn't, wouldn't give him the satisfaction of cowering, but oh, oh, oh, she was worried sick about Jinx. Surely whoever had him, if they did, wouldn't hurt him. So far, the loser who had done this to her had just tried to scare and intimidate her.

But she couldn't trust he wouldn't escalate.

Shakily she turned on the exterior lights, then walked outside to the cool morning, dawn still not breaking. She went to the large cans by the garage and opened one. Junk and dirt was piled high, but she didn't see the missing doll. Nor was Maude in the second can.

Well, too bad. She dropped Toodles into the trash and said, "Sorry, Gram," as if her grandmother could see her and was silently scolding her. Then, still extremely unnerved, she went inside, her eyes sweeping the ground for any sign of the cat, or an intruder.

Of course she saw nothing.

"Great," she muttered, then went to the garage, found her grandfather's tool kit, dug through it, and, as luck would have it, found two hook and eye latches. They weren't all that strong but offered some security for now, since she hadn't thought to have the locksmith install a lock on her bedroom door.

She carried the tool kit up the stairs to the third floor and, using hammer, screwdriver, screws, and nails, fastened the latches to her door and frame.

It wouldn't keep a serious intruder out.

But it might buy her some time.

This was crazy.

Someone was playing with her.

Trying to frighten her.

But who?

And why?

By the time she replaced the toolbox in the garage, dawn was crawling across the eastern sky. Inside the locked house, she reheated a cup of coffee in the old Radarange and tried to keep her mind from spinning with questions she couldn't answer. She did think about calling the police, but again, what could she say?

Someone was sneaking into her house just to scare her?

That didn't make any sense.

Yes, they had left a weird message on the dolls and possibly stolen her cat, just to taunt her? Would the police even care?

Certainly they would think that whoever was doing this wasn't seriously dangerous.

Yet.

Otherwise she would be dead or maimed and back in the hospital. It was almost as if some ghost of the past was trying to intimidate her, wanting her to leave.

Except she didn't believe in such nonsense.

"This isn't Amityville," she reminded herself as she carried her cup into the parlor and then, noticing that the door to Gram's bedroom was ajar, she went to close it. As she did, she caught a glimpse of the bed.

There, wedged perfectly between Raggedy Ann and Raggedy Andy, sat Maude.

Chapter 37

Forget the historical society.

Forget any other place that might want the dolls for donations.

"You sneaky son of a bitch," Harper muttered as she dropped the trio of dolls she'd found in Gram's room right into the garbage can in the garage.

Maude and Toodles, lumped together. Of course, there were lots more dolls throughout the house. Tons of them. Harper planned to round them up and dump them, too. But for now, at least the worst of the lot were out there.

Until they crawl back in the middle of the night.

"Nope," Harper said aloud. She wasn't going there.

The garbage would be picked up tomorrow. She'd already confirmed that when she'd made her calls to the utilities.

Who was behind the stupid prank?

And why?

Someone was obviously trying to scare her off.

Names ran through her head as she breathed in the pre-dawn air, so cold her breath was visible. Lou Arista, the sleazy attorney Gram had hired, wanted her to sell. He might be worried about a lawsuit against him for the way he'd handled Harper's trust. But the childish antics with the doll were beneath him. And he no longer had a key.

Then there was her ex-husband. He'd always talked about her in-heritance and how she could sell the house for a fortune. "Not a small fortune, mind you," he'd advised on more than one occasion. But he was out of the picture. And again, without a key.

What about the people who lived across the lake on Fox Point? They were the only people who were connected to her or the island. Taking off her jacket, she forced herself to calm down. The thought of a drink sifted through her mind, but she resisted. Good God, it wasn't even eight in the morning.

Just to be certain she was alone, she grabbed a butcher knife from the block on the kitchen counter, then searched the house top to bottom, as best she could. She found no one hiding in the closets or cowering in the shadows. She checked the doors as her grandmother had taught her, the whole points of the star routine, and found all en-trances buttoned up and locked.

But someone had gotten in.

Someone evil had broken through Gram's feeble line of defense.

Nonetheless, she believed she was alone despite the ever-present feeling of hidden eyes watching her. How could she ever be certain? There were just so many nooks, crannies, entrances, and staircases in this old Victorian. And some lowlife had found access.

Nonetheless, for the moment, she told herself she was alone, that the intruder, whoever he was, had gone, that all her lingering fears were only manifested in her head.

For now.

She thought about Jinx again, still had his collar in her pocket, but tried to push her worries about him aside for the moment.

As she walked into the parlor, she picked up the pair of field glasses she'd left on a side table, then peered through the lenses.

The sky was beginning to pale.

Across the lake one window in the Sievers' bungalow was lit, a small upper window, possibly a bathroom. The rest of the house was dark, unlike it had been years before with all the security lamps. But no one there had any interest in gaslighting her.

Next door was the Watkins' A-frame. A few lights glowed. She couldn't help but wonder about Rand with his hard jaw, keen eyes, and military bearing. She had a feeling he didn't miss much, that he was suspicious by nature. He was far harder-edged than she remembered him, any hint of boyishness long eroded by time and experience and yet, as in the past, she found him much more layered than Chase had been. Or Joel, for that matter.

Now he was a police detective, had almost literally stepped into his father's hated shoes, and, it seemed, was a detective looking to solve a cold case or two. But even if he was digging into the past—her past—why would he stoop to such childish/terrorizing tactics of defacing dolls and using them to menace her? What would be the point?

Unless he knew more about Chase's disappearance than he'd ever let on?

Unless he thought she might somehow blow his cover?

Maybe he wasn't digging through the past looking for answers.

Maybe he wasn't digging at all, just shifting the sands, covering up.

But did that make any sense? She didn't think so. And knowing Rand, she couldn't believe he was behind any of this. No, scratch him off the suspect list.

Also, how would he get in?

He'd never had a key that she knew of, and even if he did, it wouldn't work now.

Sipping from her cup, she saw him walk through his kitchen in boxer shorts and battered T-shirt that stretched across his shoulders. He was muscled and fit, as if he kept to a regular exercise regimen. She saw him drink what appeared to be a glass of water, then disappear. The bedroom light switched on, but the shades were drawn and she had no idea what he was doing. A minute later she saw him again, in a sweatshirt and running shorts. He retrieved a rain jacket, slipped into it, and then was out of sight again.

Running?

Probably.

Maybe changing up his routine from the stationary bike to a jog?

But who cared?

The point was that there was no reason she could think of that he would try some parlor trick to get her to leave.

She wondered about him as she turned her attention to the Hunts' cottage. Now dark.

Was there a reason Levi would want Harper to leave? Did he blame her for Cynthia's death and all the other tragedies that his family had endured?

But the dolls? Nah. Wasn't his style. She and he had been friends a long, long time ago, and she couldn't imagine that boy stooping to sneaking into her house and messing with the stupid dolls. To scare her? To punish her?

No, she didn't believe it.

He's no longer a boy now but a man.

A man who has reasons to distrust her.

A man who could have blamed her for so many things.

A man who has more reason than you might know to want her far, far away.

She swallowed hard, her fingers tightening on the cup as she thought back to the nights she'd used him. Betrayed him. How she'd known that he was in love with her and how wickedly delicious that knowledge had been at eighteen. How she'd used it. How she'd used him.

She bit her lip and felt more than one jab of guilt.

Don't go there. Don't even think about it. That was all long, long ago. Think about the here and now.

She blinked at an unexpected burn of tears. As if regrets now could change anything. As she looked through the lenses, across the calm water, she asked herself how, even if he wanted to, would he have access to the inside of this monster of a house?

It was locked.

But he might have a key, right? Didn't you slip one to Chase when you were so crazy about him? Didn't you take it off Gram's key chain and later that night, when you were alone on the dock with him, offer it up? Didn't he willingly take it?

She felt her color rise. She'd never gotten the key back from Chase, didn't know what he'd done with it.

And then he'd disappeared.

But back to square one, she reminded herself. The key she'd given Chase would no longer fit.

Unless the locksmith missed one.

What about the basement? The access from the boathouse and

tunnel? And wasn't there some kind of connecting door between the second floor and the attic over the garage?

"Damn," she whispered. This old creaking house had more than Gram's "points of a star," so many almost forgotten entrances, any of which might have been accessed by an old key.

She moved her binoculars to the Alexanders' split level. Still dark.

But what about Beth? Could she really be behind the doll desecration and—what? Cat stealing?

No. That was crazy. Harper had witnessed how she reacted to Toodles. She'd barely been able to pick up the doll and throw it in the trash. True, Beth had motive. Harper's best friend from high school had always been envious, even jealous, of Harper's family's wealth. She'd said so herself. And she was pushing Harper to sell the entire island and no doubt counting on what her commission might be, but still, the idea was far-fetched.

Then there was Craig.

He was the dark horse in all of this. Her father didn't trust him; Bruce Reed had said as much in the hospital. And hadn't Harper always had an innate aversion to him? She remembered him creeping around when she was a teen, always eyeing her from a distance.

Oh, and now you're watching him, observing him across the lake, from afar but still doing the same thing he used to do. Only he was a horny teenager, and you're a grown woman. And remember: He's Beth's husband. Get a life, Harper!

But there was the gun she'd seen him skulking around with the other night. How could that be explained?

She had no answers as she turned her attention to the end of the street. The rental house was dark and, according to Beth, unoccupied.

She set the binoculars on a nearby table and told herself she was chasing ghosts, nothing tangible.

Maybe the residents across the lake had nothing to do with what was happening here on the island. Yes, she knew some of them. And yes, any one of them could paddle across the water unnoticed, climb onto the dock or the beach, and somehow get into the house.

But there were other people who had keys. People who had worked for Gram. Matilda Burroughs, her housekeeper who had moved to Canada soon after Gram's death, or Martin Alexander, Craig's father who had once been the gardener and lived on the property. Any one of Gram's bridge group friends, possibly, or even Harper's father or his wife.

What about other servants as well, or repairmen who had come and gone over the years?

And what if Evan, like she, had "loaned" a key to one of his friends or girlfriends and never gotten it back? Harper knew that he'd sneaked girls into the manor. She'd seen the backside of a brunette hurrying down the back stairs one night. It had been dark, and the image was fleeting.

It happened when Harper stopped in one night while Gram was away for a "girls' getaway" with some of her friends who had not been girls for several decades, and Harper was supposed to feed the cats one afternoon. She'd forgotten and remembered late that night, near midnight, so she'd come over to the house and slipped in the side door by the kitchen. She'd just reached for the cat food in the pantry when she heard quick footsteps and peered through the window to see a slim woman with long hair pass through the parlor and onto the terrace. Evan was right behind her. He caught up with her, and they embraced before disappearing. Seconds later she'd heard a boat's engine cough, then start.

She'd never found out who the woman was.

It hadn't mattered then. There were too many to keep track of.

But now she wondered if that girl, or any others, or some of Evan's friends had a key.

It didn't matter now.

Or did it?

Jinx's collar heavy in her pocket, she wondered. Someone was getting in. Somehow she had to secure the place and call the locksmith back, then, this time, seal up any forgotten access points.

If she could find them all.

Chapter 38

His pre-dawn run cleared Rand's head. As his Nikes slapped the wet pavement and the bracing air filled his lungs, he found some much needed perspective. He thought about the embossed card that Levi had given him along with the bank statement and bit of paper that had led Levi to find out a little more about Tristan Vargas aka Larry Smith aka Conrad Nelson. Then there was the cryptic note. *They killed him. They killed Chase. Make him pay.*

He turned the words over and over in his mind as he ran, sweating up the steep road of Southway and down to the bridge before he turned sharply and headed back, halfway home, veering off the road to the deer trail that cut sharply down the hillside. He had to slow to a jog through the fir trees and ferns, using his small flashlight and wending his way along the path. Who were "they," and who was "he"? Why didn't she give names? Was Cynthia's note the fantasy of a woman who had lost touch with reality? The results of a grief-addled mind? Or was she sane when she penned it but didn't name names for fear of repercussions?

And how, if at all, was Tristan Vargas involved?

He hit the curb at the end of the street and slowed to a walk, past the rental house which had been dark for weeks, then the Alexanders'. It, too, was dark, as was the Hunts', where Levi's car sat in the drive.

He wondered about the relationship between Levi and Chase, always strained. Levi had never quite lived up to his older brother's achievements while they were in school. He had never been as brilliant in the classroom or as athletic on the football field, though he had been an ace pitcher, his fast ball swift enough to gain him a walk-on position at Oregon State. But Chase, at one time the favored son, the golden boy, had always considered his younger brother a pain in the ass. "Baseball," he'd sneered when Levi made the high school varsity team as a freshman. Then again, Chase had never trusted Levi.

Why? Just the male rivalry thing?

Rand, who had no brother or sister, never really understood the acrimony between them.

From the outside Levi appeared to be a stand-up guy. But Chase's warning about having Levi watch over Harper still rang in his ears: "Not Levi . . . he can't be trusted."

Once home, Rand showered, shaved, and dressed. He made certain he had Cynthia's note along with the other information Levi had given him in his pocket, then drove to the station.

It was early when he got to the office, long before his shift officially started.

Waiting for him on his desk was the autopsy report on the woman who he'd seen floating face down in Lake Twilight nearly thirty years earlier. He remembered witnessing his father and Thomas Hunt trying to revive her. Gerald Watkins kneeling beside her body, water dripping from his hair as he gave her mouth-to-mouth resuscitation.

All to no avail.

Her cold blue lips never moved.

Her open eyes never blinked.

Anna Reed was dead.

His jaw tightened at the memory. He'd gotten sick, Cynthia Hunt had screamed, Chase had turned away from the horrid spectacle, and Levi had just stared, his own face ashen. And the sounds. The dog barking, others joining in, sirens splitting the night, and the horrid beating of his own heart. All thoughts of the night before when he'd been out on his bike, plastering Martin Alexander's truck with eggs, had been forgotten.

According to the toxicology report, Anna Reed's blood-alcohol level had been sky-high and there had been excessive amounts of diazepam in her bloodstream. Anna had been prescribed Valium for anxiety and insomnia, and she'd somehow overdosed, either accidentally or intentionally. The combination of booze and medications had caused intense drowsiness, and in the end, she'd drowned. The cause of death on the death certificate was listed as accidental drowning.

But why had she been in the lake?

At the time, he'd never questioned why she'd ended up in Lake Twilight. But then he'd been a kid at the time, only eleven. As best friends with Evan, Harper's brother, another one of "the Three Musketeers," Rand had always known Anna Reed was different. Distant and a little out of it.

With Anna's death everything had changed. Evan, once cocky and irreverent, had turned quiet. Dark. Introspective. He'd become a different person after losing his mother, but then who wouldn't? Hadn't Rand, himself, suffered a different kind of loss when his own mother had taken off?

But back to Anna Reed's death.

The question that had been on everyone in Almsville's lips that cold November morning—had Anna Reed accidentally taken too many sleeping pills and somehow ended up on the dock and fallen into Lake Twilight? Or had her death been intentional? No one understood why the heiress to Dixon Island would take her own life. Wasn't it perfect? A husband, two healthy children, and eventually enough money for herself, her children, grandchildren, and generations to come? Had she been mentally unbalanced? Emotionally unstable?

Or had she been the victim of homicide?

Had someone taken advantage of her drugged state and tossed her into the lake to drown, or even loaded her up with pills and then dropped her into the dark water? Or had she, for some private, unknown reason, taken her own life?

He wondered, clicking his pen and thinking back.

The gossip had been rampant, burning through the town.

That much Rand remembered.

But the subsequent investigation of Anna Reed's death had turned up no evidence of either suicide or homicide.

No suicide note left at her bedside.

No calls to loved ones to say goodbye.

No evidence of recent depression.

No suspicious activity by anyone close to her.

No witness to anything untoward.

Ergo, he remembered the conclusion based on the autopsy report: accidental death by drowning.

He leaned back in his chair and rubbed his eyes.

Like it or not, he'd look into it again.

As he would Olivia Dixon's death and Chase Hunt's disappearance, all part of a twenty-year-old mystery. He didn't expect there to be anything unusual about Harper's grandmother's death; the woman was old, with health issues, and as he looked over the yellowed paperwork, he found that the department had come to the same conclusion.

Yes, the granddaughter had been negligent with her medication by allowing the older woman to drink, but Harper had not been found culpable.

No charges had been leveled.

He read the names of the officers who had filed the report: Detective Thomas Hunt and Detective Gerald Watkins. He recognized each man's signature, though the ink had faded over time.

Rubbing the back of his neck, he eyed the report. He would never forget seeing a dead person emerge from the lake.

Even now, thinking about it, he felt his stomach twitch.

So he turned his mind away from that disturbing image.

He glanced at the clock. Almost eight in the morning, and the station was coming to life. Over the rumble of the furnace and chunk of some printer disgorging papers, the sound of ringing phones, fax machines, and footsteps were audible. Several conversations were going at once with occasional bursts of laughter.

Rand kicked out his desk chair, then headed for the break room for a cup of coffee before they convened the short morning meeting run by Sergeant Katz, who was fortyish, on the uptight side, and a stickler for detail.

Several cops had gathered, some shrugging out of jackets, others filling cups. Gunderson looked over Brady's shoulder as she was already working on the crossword puzzle at one of the tables. "You could give me some space," she said, scowling up at her partner, "or make yourself useful and grab me a fresh cup."

"I got it," Rand said as he was already at the coffeemaker. He poured two cups from the glass carafe and was carrying them to the table when he saw Chelle arriving. After coming through the back door, she unbuttoned her jean jacket and hung it in her locker, one of the few visible from the break room. She found her way to the coffeepot and poured herself a cup.

Of course Gunderson was watching her.

"Put your eyeballs back in their sockets, Gunn," Eleanor advised, glancing up from her puzzle and accepting the steaming cup from Rand. "Thanks." She blew across the rim and took a sip. "What's a twelve-letter word for wife?" she asked loudly. "Maybe more than one word. Second letter is an a."

Gunderson smiled at Chelle and raised his eyebrows. "How about ball and chain?"

"Just stop," Brady said. But Gunderson didn't.

Chelle didn't bat an eye, just said, "Don't know, but maybe another name for husband is dick and wad."

"Ouch," Eleanor said as Chelle breezed out of the room, Gunderson still watching. "That's gotta burn."

"She's a sassy one," he said, his eyes glinting as he nodded at Rand. "Lucky you. I like my women with a little spark."

"You'd better like being kicked to the curb," his partner said, "because women are tired of putting up with your kind of crap. There's a thing called sexual harassment these days, you know."

He shrugged. "I was just flirting. She likes it."

"Does she?" his partner asked. "Don't think so. And she's not the kind to put up with your shit, so knock it off."

Rand took it all in but pointed to the paper. "Married woman. I think that's the answer to the wife clue."

"By God, you're right," she said and filled in the letters while Rand said to Gunderson, "Listen to Eleanor. Times are changing. You can't get away with that kind of crap."

"Oh, so now you're the authority on what was it called—sexual harassment? Yeah, right." He snorted, then drained his cup. "It's all bullshit if you ask me."

"Just warning you, man," Rand said, then made his way back to the office.

As he expected, Chelle was at her desk and she was seething, her coffee ignored and cooling on the corner of her desk.

"He's a douche bag," she said, and before Rand could get a word in edgewise added, "And don't make apologies for him."

"Wouldn't even try."

"Here's a crossword clue for you: What's another name for partner of Eleanor Brady? Two words."

"Chelle, I don't—"

"Bing. Bing." She pretended to push a buzzer. "Too late. You lose." She glared up at him. "The answer is *Sick Prick*."

He started to argue but couldn't. He didn't blame her for being furious.

Poking the air angrily, as if Rand were to blame, she spat, "He's gonna lose his job and his retirement!" Her near-black eyes glittered. "I wonder what the old 'ball and chain' would think about that?" So livid her mocha-colored skin had darkened, she closed her eyes, balled her fists, and took a deep breath.

As he rolled his chair back to the desk, she slowly relaxed, letting out her breath and allowing her hands to unclench. Then, another prolonged breath, part of an exercise regimen he'd witnessed before when she was frustrated.

"Does that work?"

"The breathing?" She expelled more air and nodded. "Most of the time. But with Gunderson? No. Not yet." And she repeated the exercise another three times before her normal skin tone returned and she seemed calmer again, more in control.

"Okay," she admitted and took the time to pluck a couple of dead leaves from a trailing plant. "Now I can focus."

"Good."

She crumpled the brown leaves and tossed them into her trash can. After a sip of coffee, she picked up a stack of papers on the corner of her desk. "I've started looking for anyone Chase Hunt was associated with, going over their statements."

"And?"

"The kids who lived at the end of the street in the Musgrave family's rental, they're all scattered to the wind. I'm running down Ronald Mayfield. Looks like he moved to Mississippi, but that may not be current. I've checked with the Jacksonville PD. Charla Lopez is in the Seattle area, and I'm waiting for a call back. I think I have a lead on Janet Van Arsdale. She's the one who went by Moonbeam?"

Rand remembered, suppressed a smile.

"They all lived just a couple of doors down from the Hunts and you, right?"

"Yep."

"You know them?"

"Not by name, no. But I saw them coming and going. I'd heard about the house being a potential place to score pot or LSD or whatever."

She leaned back and eyed him. "Seems like a bad place to deal out of," she observed. "Dead end street, two cops as neighbors."

"I guess. But there were trails leading down through the woods from the street that runs above the cul-de-sac, if that's what you want to call it. Southway."

"I know it. Rims the lake on the south side."

"Right. And there was always the lake access if anyone wanted to meet their dealer and not have their car near the place."

"Huh." Little lines appeared between her eyebrows, and she looked about to ask another question but didn't. Instead, she contemplated the dark depths in her coffee cup.

He asked, "What about Trick, Tristan Vargas? I have a little info on him."

"Such as?"

He pulled out the information Levi had given him. "Take a look at this." He explained about Levi stopping by and the information he'd gathered, then handed her the note. "Cynthia left it with Edward Sievers, who also lives at Serenity Acres."

"Your neighbor, way back when? The guy who first saw Anna Reed's body in the lake?"

"The very same." He handed her the note.

"So she expected to die," Chelle mused, opening the stationery and reading, her eyebrows drawing together. "Weird. 'Make *him* pay,' but '*They* killed him.' Like two or more people actually killed her son and she kept it quiet, even though she knew? And now, what? One or more of them are gone? What happened? Did they move away? Did they die? I don't get it," she said, but the wheels were turning in her head when he gave her the bank statement and torn vehicle registration for the van. "More?" she asked. "What's this?"

"From Levi Hunt. The bank statement came with the note from his mother. He got hold of the van's registration from Sievers and did some checking on his own."

"Yeah, he's a PI. I know that much."

"Right." Rand relayed his conversation with Levi including, when she asked, that Levi didn't know how Cynthia got from the care facility to the lake. She bit her lip, lost in thought as she returned the note to Levi. "Do you have any theories?"

"Nothing solid. Just bits and pieces," he said. Over the course of the fitful night and the run this morning, his thoughts had gone down dark alleys to blind corners and blank walls and doors that he was going to force open. But his ideas were half-baked at best, worrisome and dark at worst, and certainly not ready to be shared.

She perused the pages, her eyebrows drawing together. He thought about what he'd known about Vargas and decided the guy made up personas with his aliases. No way could someone named Larry Smith pull off the cool hippie vibe Trick exuded.

"So you think this is all connected?"

"Don't know. But possibly."

"So we need to find Trick."

Chelle, bothered, set the page of stationery aside. "Strangest suicide note I've ever seen." She glanced up at Rand. "As for our friend with the multiple aliases, I haven't nailed his whereabouts down yet. But I'm hoping good old Moonbeam can shed some light on where he might have landed." She smiled at her own joke. "Van Arsdale— she's Janet Collins now—still in the area. Milwaukie—well, really the Oak Grove area—divorced with two teenaged sons. I've got a call in to her." She eyed him speculatively. "You didn't have any dealings with them growing up? Moonbeam and Trick/Larry?"

"Are you asking if I scored drugs there? No. I knew about it but wasn't into it."

"What about girls?" Chelle asked. "Did you score with any of them?"

He scoffed. "Give me a break."

"Hey, I was just asking." She blew across her cup before taking a swallow and eyeing him over the rim. "Wasn't it the Summer of Love or something?"

"Not that year," he said. "Not for me. I was in the army."

"If you say so." Chelle slid out of her chair and walked to his desk. "So you're reopening the Olivia Dixon case?" she asked, motioning to one of the case files on his desk.

"Just looking it over."

"Maybe find some connection to Chase Hunt's disappearance?" she suggested, leaning back in her chair. "Both happened on the same night. With Harper Reed at the center of both investigations."

"Don't think there's a connection," he said, noticing the papers strewn on her desk. "You've got Anna Reed's file out, too."

"I figured another look wouldn't hurt." Taking a sip from her cup, she said, "Too many deaths around the damned lake. All with connections to Dixon Island and Harper Reed."

"You still think Harper's involved?" he asked, disbelieving.

"I can't make the connections," Chelle admitted, "but she's always there, on the fringes."

Much as he'd like to, Rand couldn't argue the facts.

"Not only did she mess up her grandmother's pills and it killed her but she was there when Anna Reed ended up in the lake—"

"She was a kid," he reminded her.

"And then there was her brother, too. She found him." Chelle held his gaze. "Kind of a lot of trauma for one girl, wouldn't you say?"

"Evan's case was open and shut."

She reached for a file on her desk, flipped it open, and scanned the old pages. Her brow furrowed and her lips puckered.

Rand read Evan Reed's name typed in bold letters.

His insides squeezed. No way did they need to look into Evan Reed's death.

"Maybe it's not so open and shut," she said, lifting a page and scanning it, though he sensed it was for show, that she'd already read the case notes and autopsy report at least once. "The strange thing is that I checked the evidence room, hoping to find anything associated with the case."

"And?" he hated to ask. Something in the gleam in her eye warned him.

"And the weapon's missing."

Rand felt the muscles in the back of his neck tighten.

"Missing?"

"Uh-huh. No pearl-handled revolver anywhere to be found." She took a long swallow of coffee. "What do you think about that?"

"You're sure?"

"I am." She cocked her head. "You don't believe me?"

"No, no, it's not that."

Her gaze told him she didn't buy it.

"But there's a record of who checked it out," he said, his mind spinning. He didn't want to think about Evan's death. Ever.

"Yeah, I know. That's just it. Back then, all the records were on sign-out cards. The card for Evan Reed's case is missing."

"Missing?"

"Yep."

His stomach clenched.

"I talked to the officer in charge. Of course she's as baffled as you are. But she's only been at the desk for three years. And the officer before her?"

"Dead," Rand said, remembering Fred Chambers and the stroke that took him out. "So what you're telling me is that there's no way to find out who was the last person to look in the file?"

"That's about the size of it. It was way before we had cameras mounted near the evidence room." She asked, "What about the old man's death? What's the story there?"

"What old man? You mean George Dixon?" he clarified.

"Yeah."

"I think he died in a car crash. Single vehicle. The story was that he was drunk and had a stroke or something, driving home." He thought back. "I was a teenager at the time, about to get my license, and my father sat me down, told me about it, and warned me about drinking and driving."

"1965." She was nodding.

"You think Harper was involved in that one, too?"

"No, that's not what I'm saying. And this time she didn't find the body. But, big surprise here, Gunderson didn't have all of his facts straight. Yes, alcohol was involved. But it wasn't a stroke but shock. Anaphylactic shock."

"He was allergic to something?"

"Severely. Venom hypersensitivity. In layman's terms, insect sting allergy," she said, nodding, then glanced up, checking the clock. "Uh-oh. We're already late for the morning briefing. Katz won't like that. Let's go." But she didn't wait for him, just finished her coffee in one swallow, then shot out the door as gung-ho as ever.

Rand tried to pull himself together.

Evan Reed's death? She wanted to look into that, too?

Damn.

But it made sense, he supposed, because all the people she was talking about were connected. And at the center of the web?

Harper Reed.

Evan's sister.

Olivia Dixon's granddaughter.

Anna Reed's daughter.

George Dixon's granddaughter.

And, of course, Chase Hunt's girlfriend.

He leaned back in his chair and closed his eyes, didn't want to re-open all the old wounds.

Not so Michelle "Chelle" Brown. Nu-uh. She was eager to rip off all the bandages, reveal the scars, dig deep, and excise the truth.

I suppose it's time, he thought as he got out of his chair and headed into the hallway.

But it was gonna sting.

It was gonna sting like a bitch.

Chapter 39

"Hey. I got your message but don't have a lot of time," Dawn said from the other end of the telephone connection.

Harper couldn't help but smile at the sound of her daughter's voice. It was so good to hear from her. "I'm in between classes," Dawn rushed on, "but I wanted to know that you were okay."

"Still hanging in there." Harper was cradling the phone receiver between her shoulder and chin as she washed out the ramekins she'd left out for Jinx. They hadn't been touched, and she didn't want to attract any rats, especially now that she knew they were lurking due to Beth's maniacal driving skills.

"I'm trying to find a time to come up," Dawn said. "To see you and Grandpa. He's out of the hospital now, right?"

"Yes. I talked to Marcia. I offered to stop by, but she discouraged it. At least for the time being. She thought he needed his rest."

"What did he say?"

"I don't know," Harper admitted, placing the cleaned dishes on a towel near the sink. "I didn't talk to him."

"Isn't that weird?"

"A little, I guess, but you know Marcia." Even after all these years, she couldn't refer to her stepmother as Grandma, even though Marcia had been around all of Dawn's life. "I asked her to have him call me. So far, he hasn't." She dried first one of the small dishes, then the other.

"Do you think she even told him?" Dawn asked, not masking her suspicion.

"I hope so."

"Yeah, well. If you ask me, she has him on a pretty short leash."

Harper cringed at her own words being repeated by her kid. "I guess that's the way he likes it."

"More like the way *she* likes it."

True enough, Harper thought. Marcia had always been in charge, and it ticked Harper off that her father let his wife run his life. She changed the subject. "The good news is that his 'mild' heart attack can be handled with a pacemaker."

"And that's a good thing?"

"Yes."

"Okay. Cool. And you're okay?" she asked.

"I said so. What about you?"

"Me?" Dawn repeated. "Fine. Yeah, fine. Just busy."

"When you're not so busy and I get this house together a little more, I'll come down to Eugene and take you to lunch or dinner. You can show me your apartment. I'd love to meet your roommate."

"Uh . . . well, that would be hard," Dawn said, and the tone of her voice made the muscles in the back of Harper's neck tighten.

"Why?"

"Katie moved out about two weeks ago," Dawn admitted.

"Moved out."

"Well, in with her boyfriend, but, don't worry, she's still paying half of her rent."

"Because her parents don't know," Harper surmised.

"Right, and she might come back, you know. She's only known Ryan for about two months."

"And she's already living with . . ." Harper let the rest of the sentence fall away. Who was she to judge? How crazy in love had she thought she'd been around that age?

"Yeah. It's no big deal, but you don't need to come down here yet. I've got a jillion things to do, like two major papers due next week, and I really need to study."

There were probably other reasons her daughter didn't want her to just show up, but Harper didn't press it.

"I thought I'd come up and visit you and Grandpa," Dawn said. "I just don't know when."

"That would be great." Harper faked her enthusiasm. Until she figured out who was sneaking into the house and leaving macabre messages, she didn't want her daughter anywhere near the place. "Just give me a heads-up, so that I'll be sure to be here and not out running errands."

"I'll try to figure it out. But maybe over the weekend. Or the next one. When I figure it out, I'll call you back. Look, I gotta run, I'm late already."

"Sounds good," Harper said, but Dawn had already hung up. She held on to the receiver for a minute and leaned a hip against the kitchen counter.

The thought of her daughter showing up here was a worry. Much as she'd love to see her kid, it wasn't a good time. When she considered the disturbing message left on the dolls, the continued harassment from the reporter, and the fact that wily Jinx was still missing, Harper decided it would be best for her to drive to Eugene and catch Dawn on campus. Despite the whole "no roommate" thing. Harper suspected there was more to Dawn not wanting her mother to show up and interrupt her new, independent life. Too bad.

With an eye out for the cat, Harper slipped on a jacket, then walked across the bridge to the cottage and through the unlocked door. When she'd first landed back in Almsville—oh God, was that less than a week ago?—she'd stepped inside the house, then quickly backed out. Today she wanted to see just how bad the damage actually was.

Though the rain had stopped, there was a constant dripping noise inside the cottage, and the whole place smelled damp and moldy. The carpet was squishy, the paneling peeling, the wallpaper streaked by rainwater. Several windows leaked, and drawers in the kitchen no longer closed tightly, while a couple of the cupboard doors hung drunkenly, half off their hinges.

"Lovely," she muttered, climbing the stairs. Two of the steps had buckled, and she silently prayed that they held. She'd already fallen through one staircase within the past year and didn't want to do a re-peat performance.

Upstairs held two bedrooms—hers and Evan's. Both rooms had been cleared out as they'd moved to the main house years before. After their mother's death she and her brother had spent more time with Gram than they had with their father and his new wife. Bruce had been forever out of town on business with Marcia glued to his side. She wasn't going to miss out on the travel, nor was she going to play the dutiful stepmother and sit in this little cottage to raise his son and daughter. Not when she could live in a Portland penthouse with views of the mountains and city lights and a security guard. With an in-house spa and restaurant, the building was steps away from the boutiques and shops.

No room for Bruce's kids in the two-bedroom condo.

Gram, as always, had stepped up.

"This is what happens when you don't trust your spouse," Gram said once while watching Bruce and Marcia climb into a taxi headed for the airport on a cool summer evening. She and Harper had been standing at the gate, Bandit at their side as they looked through the wrought-iron rails to watch the taxi's taillights disappear around the corner of the lane. Harper had been about eleven at the time, and the fragrance of honeysuckle filled the air. "What happens?" Harper had asked.

"You don't dare let them out of your sight."

Harper had looked up at Gram in the gathering dusk. "But you trust Gramps, right?" she'd asked.

Gram's smile had twisted. "Not on your life."

"Really? Why?"

Her grandmother had sighed. "Oh, honey, it's complicated," she'd said and brushed aside a bumblebee that was buzzing near the fra-grant blossoms.

"How complicated?" Harper wanted to know.

"Oh, like so many things in life. You'll see."

Her grandmother tugged on her hand. "Come along now, let's go inside."

"Wait." Harper stopped, gazing up at the pillar where the dragon gargoyle crouched. "What's that?" She pointed a finger at the overhang on which the statue rested and the papery mass beneath it. Tucked beneath the shelf it looked like gray cotton candy with a dark, narrow hole at its tip.

"Oh, a nest." Gram said. "Hornets."

Harper studied the shiny creatures crawling on the nest and took a step forward until Gram's hand held her shoulder. "Don't disturb them," she warned. "Their stings are painful. And in a nest that size, there are enough of them to do real damage." Her voice trailed off.

"We should tell the gardener to get rid of it," Harper had said.

"Yes. Yes. I suppose we should. Don't worry about it, okay? I'll take care of it." With that, Gram whistled to the dog as she tugged on Harper's hand and started walking back across the bridge.

"I've got a new board game for you," Gram confided, squeezing her hand. "Have you ever heard of Stratego?"

Harper shook her head and glanced over the side rail to the darkening water far below. "No."

Bandit, ears flopping, shot past them, startling Marilyn, the pretty calico cat who had been sunning herself on a flat rock near the garage. Arching her back, she hissed at the dog, then scrambled up the rough trunk of a fir tree.

"Oh, Bandit, don't scare the cats," Gram mock-scolded with a chuckle.

As the dog wandered off, sniffing at the rose bushes in her garden, Gram explained, "Stratego is kind of a military war game, but you'll like it, I think. What you do is root out the spies of your enemy. Use logic. It's easier than chess but can teach you a lot about your opponent's strategy—hence the name, I suppose—and knowing your enemy's mind-set is always important. Not just in game play, but in life." She sighed heavily and glanced up at the heavens just as they reached the parking apron.

The house loomed before them, the first stars of evening visible in the sky. "Your mother, she never learned that lesson," Gram admitted sadly, then looked down at Harper and touched her on the nose. "Boop," she said as she always did. "We won't make the same mistake with you, though. Not on your life."

Today Harper felt a pang, missing Gram, but rather than allowing herself to get caught up in nostalgia or, worse yet, melancholy, she stared at the interior of her childhood home, taking stock and wondering if this cottage was even worth repairing. Maybe it would be better to raze the building and start over.

She'd find out more when she had her meeting with Craig Alexander, she supposed.

She didn't have to wait long.

Just as she was about to leave the cottage, a Ford pickup flew past, Craig Alexander at the wheel. A big woolly dog was on the front seat beside him while lengths of lumber protruded beyond the bed, a red flag tied to one of the boards and flapping.

He didn't catch sight of her as he drove across the bridge. She followed, jogging for the first time since she'd fallen through the steps at Joel's and feeling her hip protest in pain. She was only halfway across the span when he parked in front of the garage. Wearing a baseball cap, worn jeans, and a sweatshirt, he climbed out of the truck.

"Didn't see you," he said as she neared, then into the cab he added, "Rambo. Stay!" He shut the door, and the dog's head appeared through the open window. "Don't do it," Craig warned, then turned back to Harper. "Rambo, here, has a tendency to jump out. But he's a good boy. Calm. Mainly Newfoundland." Then he caught sight of her face and sucked in his breath. "Beth said you'd been in the hospital after trying to rescue Cynthia." Thick eyebrows slammed together. "You okay?"

"Getting there." Then she changed the subject. "Rambo?" she asked, petting the dog's broad black head.

"Yeah, Max named him. My son. He's seen that movie a dozen times, I bet."

She remembered catching a glimpse of the movie poster of *First Blood* in Max's room when she was looking through the telescope but, of course, kept that bit of knowledge to herself.

"Max is a big Stallone fan."

"So is half the country. Probably more."

Craig was nodding, but he'd quit sizing up her wounds to squint up at the house. "Beth says you need some work done."

"A lot, I'm afraid."

"Okay. Yeah, I wouldn't doubt it." He nodded and squared his hat on his head. "Let's take a look."

He started for the front door, but she said, "First you should see the gatekeeper's cottage. See if it's even worth repairing. Lots of damage. I just looked it over and it's bad, but—"

He grinned then. "My specialty." Grabbing a clipboard from the front seat of his truck, he gave a second command for the dog to stay, then followed her back across the bridge. All the while she thought of his nocturnal activities with the gun, then of someone breaking into her house. Despite the fact that he was Beth's husband, she needed to be careful around him.

He eyed the cottage as they reached it. "You probably want to save it," he said, "since it's where you grew up."

"For the most part." She and Evan spent most of their time at the lake, at the big house on the island with Gram. Rarely were they at the penthouse in Portland with Dad and his new bride, Marcia, whom he'd married less than a year after Mom died.

"A lot of the time, I lived with my grandparents."

"Yeah, I remember." Craig grinned again, and this time there was an edge to it—or was that her overactive imagination?

"But you're right, I'd like to save the gatehouse if it can be salvaged. And won't cost me an arm and a leg."

He laughed. "The way I hear it, you have lots of body parts to spare."

He was talking about her inheritance and thought he was being funny or clever. Forcing a smile, she bit her tongue. Though she really wanted to argue, she let it slide. She didn't want to do battle with him, needed him to believe that she trusted him completely so that maybe he would open up to her.

And tell you that he had one of Gramps's pistols and snuck it over to Cynthia Hunt's house after she set herself on fire in the middle of the lake? Get real, Harper. He's not that stupid.

Or is he?

"So everything is insured, right? I would think your homeowners would cover some of the damage. But man, who the hell was in charge?"

"Attorneys handled it," she told him, remembering the slick attorney she'd met on her last trip to Oregon. "A Portland law firm Gram used."

"Let the insurance company and the law firm battle it out. Someone's responsible." His eyes narrowed as he surveyed the exterior of the cottage. "Let's see what we've got."

She walked him through the cottage, and flashlight in hand, he poked around, looking into cabinets, testing the electrical panel, trying to turn on the water, checking the furnace, and eyeing the rooms. He even checked the attic, using an old chair he dragged from the kitchen up the stairs to hoist himself up.

"Lots of water damage," he said, hauling the chair down the uneven steps again.

"Tell me something I don't know."

He scratched the beard stubble on his cheek as he took one final look around. "It's a big job. I'll run the numbers, get together some estimates from the subs. So don't panic if you see a plumbing or roofing or electrician's truck parked out front." He paused for a second. "Listen, I'm not going to bullshit you, Harper. This will take a lot," he said, replacing the chair in the kitchen and eyeing the wood-soaked paneling. "You know, I remember being here. With your brother." Lifting his cap and running his hands through his hair, he shook his head. "Man, that was a long time ago."

He seemed caught up in a memory, so she said, "You were friends with Evan?"

"Well, yeah. Kinda. You remember. Right? We hung out as kids when Dad and me lived over your garage. Evan and me, we got along but we weren't real buds, if that's what you mean. Not like he was with Chase and Rand."

"So, do you still have a key for the attic?"

"What?"

"Since you lived here."

"Nah." He shook his head and stared at her. "Maybe my old man still does, but I doubt it. It's been years." His eyes narrowed. "Why?"

"Just trying to round up any that Gram may have left."

He shrugged. "I'll ask Dad."

She wanted to ask more questions, a lot more, but she didn't know exactly how to dig further without coming right out and asking about the gun. And the way he cocked his head, as if sizing her up, gave her pause. She either had to be up front and tell him what she saw or keep quiet and wait, rather than tip him off that she'd been aware of his late-night venture into the Hunt house.

For now, she held her tongue as they toured the main house together and he did the same kind of inspection he'd done at the cottage—taking stock, making notes on his clipboard, asking questions about the house and grounds.

Outside at the tram, he wondered aloud if she wanted it repaired and thought maybe the same mechanic who worked on elevators might be able to fix it. He thought all of the kitchen and laundry appliances should be replaced, and she might want the broken dumbwaiter converted to closet space on all the floors it serviced, which included the basement and up to the tower room.

"I mean, would you ever use it?" he asked, studying the service panel on the first floor.

"Yes." It would have come in handy when she moved her equipment to the tower room, and she explained as much.

"So you're really gonna live here? Beth says you were thinking of selling."

"Beth is thinking I'm selling," she clarified, and he let out a snort.

"That's my wife, always looking for the next listing." He eyed the furniture. "I remember this place. Looks the same. But, what, no cats?" he said as a joke, his eyes glinting.

"Only one and he's missing. Black and white. Be on the lookout."

"You got it."

She led him up the stairs and told herself not to be nervous even though they were alone in the massive house. He was Beth's husband, and his wife knew he was here.

Besides, he might not be the intruder.

Nonetheless, she was on edge as she opened the door to the tower room.

One step behind, he let out a low whistle as he surveyed the room. "Now this is something. I can see it from our place—the tower, I mean—but I had no idea of the view." Like his wife before him, Craig peered through the eyepiece of the telescope and slowly viewed the far shore. "Man, you could see a flea on a dog with this thing," he remarked. "This was your grandfather's room, right? I heard about it from my old man. Never was up here myself," he said, straightening and surveying the tufted couch in one corner. "I think Dad referred to it as 'Old George's study,' then he would wink at me and say, 'and what he is studying, son, is the opposite sex.'"

"Is that right?"

"Uh-huh." Craig checked the light switch, turning the overhead fixture on and off. "Dad said he'd sneak girls up here and show off this place, then, you know . . . score."

Harper bristled. "Girls?"

"Well, they were girls to him. I think I saw one of them once. A brunette in real high heels, and he was sneaking her in." Craig was nodding as he watched the light flicker off and on. "She wasn't a girl to me. Probably in her early twenties." Moving on from the switch, he added, "But definitely a *lot* younger than him." He smiled then, almost a leer. "I say, more power to him. If the old guy could still get it up . . . well, sorry." He held up his hands, palms out. "Nothing you want to hear." Then he gestured to the room as a whole. "But this place is awesome, you know."

She did know, and though he offered her a self-deprecating smile, she wasn't put at ease. No. She was still on edge, reminded of the unnerving message scrawled on the dolls and the fact that she'd thought she'd heard someone in the house before discovering Maude in the bathroom. Not only had she witnessed Craig skulking around at night, seemingly behind his wife's back, but also he lived just across the lake and had access to the island. Having lived on this property, he knew this place like the back of his hand. But what would be his game? She had no answer but couldn't help being nervous. Edgy.

Just ask him! See his reaction. Why the hell not?

But she waited, hoping he would trip himself up.

She held her tongue as they did a quick tour of the rest of the property, including the boathouse and basement. All Craig could mutter was, "A helluva lot of work," as they made their way to the garage, where he stopped short the second Harper opened the doors.

"Holy shit, would you look at that?" Eyeing Gramps's Corvette, he shook his head. "Jesus. The '59! Still here." Walking around the car, he added, "Frost blue. White accents. Blue interior. All fuc—frickin' original. Wow." Awestruck, he opened the driver's door and slid inside. "I can't believe you still have this." Hands on the blue steering wheel, he checked out the gauges in the dash, then touched the gear shift. "And in perfect condition! I heard it was wrecked, nearly totaled."

"Gram had it restored."

"But the old man—George—your grandpa, he died in the crash. Right?" he asked, his big hands almost caressing the steering wheel.

"Uh-huh," she said, recalling that hot summer night when she'd learned her grandfather had been killed in the single-car crash. "But Gram wanted to preserve the car. She figured it would become a classic."

"And man, oh man, was she right!" He slapped the steering wheel and gave a long whistle. "Tell me this baby is for sale."

"I'm not sure yet," she admitted.

"God, Beth will probably want to sell it with the house, kind of a bonus for the right buyer, but forget that. If you're going to sell it, let me know first, okay?"

"Yeah, sure, I guess," she agreed, though it could well be a lie.

"Don't let her talk you out of it. I'll make sure Beth knows the deal." He was nodding to himself. "I'll tell her I want it. God, can you imagine cruising around the lake with the top down? Hell yeah, that would be so awesome." Stretching out of the low-slung car, he took stock of Gram's Cadillac with a practiced eye, then walked to the motorcycle. "This was Evan's," he said, lost in thought. "I used to watch him ride it." He threw a leg over the Honda and placed his hands on the grips, then, like a ten-year-old boy, leaned low and moved his heel as if he was actually shifting through the gears. "He even gave me a ride once, down to the far end of the bridge and back, but never let me drive it." He swung off and rubbed his chin as he stared at the bike. "You know, I'll buy this, too. Max will be getting his license in a couple of years, so yeah," he was thinking aloud. "But as for the Caddy, I'll have to think about it."

"I'll think about it, too," she said, irritated that he just assumed he could buy the vehicles.

But why not? What're you going to do with them? Store them here, so they can continue gathering dust?

"While you're thinking about it, didn't your grandpa have a gun collection?"

Bingo! Harper couldn't believe her good luck, that she didn't have to initiate the conversation. "I think so. But, you know, I wasn't allowed to be around any firearms. With Evan, it was a different story. He was a boy and he hunted and . . ." She let her voice trail off.

"Right, right." He pulled a face. "Sore subject, I know, but if you want to get rid of any of the guns? I'm into them." His eyebrows lifted, and he glanced around the garage. "I thought there used to be a gun closet in here. I remember that sometimes it was my dad's job to clean the rifles and shotguns."

"Right. In the back corner." They walked behind the vehicles to a storage space tucked beneath the stairs leading to the garret. The door was locked. She pulled her grandmother's key ring from her pocket and tried each and every key. Nothing.

"Let me try." Even though he'd watched her try the keys, Craig shouldered past her and, as if she'd been too stupid to get it right, ran through them all again. No luck.

She snagged the key ring from his hand. "I guess Gram wasn't allowed in. These were hers."

"Huh." Beneath the brim of his cap, Craig's brow furrowed. "Do you have another set of keys that belonged to your grandfather?"

"If I did," she said with measured calm, "wouldn't I have tried them?"

"Ouch." He held up his hands. "Just asking."

Well, it was a stupid question.

"I'm thinking he had another set." With that, he walked back to the convertible. "Where are the keys to this?" he asked, and then started looking through the car, under the mats, in the glove box, and under the hood but came up empty. "Crap." Scratching his nape, he said, "If you find them or get into the gun closet, let me know. He had a Parker Side by Side that I'd be interested in."

"Okay." She didn't remember the gun.

"That's a shotgun," he explained, "and I think my dad said it was made in the 1800s."

She nodded. Knew what kind of firearm it was. Had seen Gramps oil it enough to know. Had never shot it but had gone to the rifle range with her father and Evan. She knew about guns. And how to use them. "So you just want the shotgun. No pistols?" she asked.

"Oh, I want to see the whole collection. Hell yeah, I do. Shotguns, rifles, pistols, bows, knives, any kind of weapon—I mean he could've been into all sorts of army stuff." His eyes lit up. "Maybe something from World War II or I? Boy, that would be cool."

"Okay," she agreed, though he was getting under her skin, really starting to irritate her. Nonetheless, this might prove to be her only chance to find out what he knew.

"I think I remember my grandpa having some old revolvers with mother-of-pearl grips or something." She feigned innocence, played the dumb girl card, which she abhorred. "You know, like cowboy guns."

Did she see just the hint of a muscle twitch near the corner of his eye? Did he stare at her a little harder? "Yeah, I remember my dad cleaning a pearl-handled pistol when he worked here." He was nodding, attempting to look nonchalant.

"There were two."

"Were there? I only remember your Dad with one, but maybe he cleaned one, then the other, and I thought they were the same gun. I was just a kid." He flashed a smile as if that explained it all. And he was lying. When he lived here, he was more than a kid, more like a horny teenager. "And didn't Evan use one, you know, when . . ."

The image of her brother, pistol in hand, lying in a pool of blood flashed through her mind. "Yeah. That's right."

In the suddenly awkward silence, he said, "Hey, look, I gotta run. I'm supposed to be at a job site in—" He made a big deal of looking at his watch. "—uh-oh, ten minutes ago. And it's fifteen minutes away. Damn." He frowned. "I'd better roll."

With that, he jogged to the truck, where his big, shaggy dog waited. He climbed in, then said through the open window, "I'll get to work on an estimate as soon as I get back to the office." He started the Ford's engine. "Let me know if you find those keys. And promise you won't sell the cars or guns until you talk to me!" Then he put the pickup into gear and cut a tight circle in the driveway before hitting the gas, his pickup rattling across the bridge, oversized boards hanging over the tailgate, red flag flapping behind.

The image of Craig with the gun, secretly slipping into the Hunts' house, skittered through her mind.

I wouldn't trust him if I were you, she heard her grandmother say as clearly as if she'd been standing next to her.

"I don't." She was shaking her head.

But then you don't trust anyone.

"Not anymore, Gram," she admitted and pulled down the garage door. "Sometimes I don't even trust myself."

Chapter 40

"...and since you haven't called me back, I thought I'd give you one last chance to add to the first installment of the series that will start running tomorrow. So just in case you lost my number, you can reach me at—" Harper erased the message before she heard Rhonda Simms leaving her damned phone number. The gist of the message was that the reporter had the green light to run a five-part series on the tragedies that had occurred on Lake Twilight, much of which involved Harper and her family.

"Not happening," she said to the empty kitchen. She waited for the next recorded call to play while searching through a nearby cupboard for a glass. Cradling the receiver between her shoulder and ear, she turned on the tap and filled the glass with water. She was thirsty and tired from putting her things away and trying to make the manor livable. She'd spent the day organizing her bedroom and office, removing old things, replacing with new, then as items had shifted since the major cleaning, rearranging a bit. Once the new phone lines were installed, she'd be ready to work. At least she had a bed with clean sheets, and her closet and the old bureau were filled with her clothes.

She used her grandfather's desk for her computer, a "portable"

Compaq in its suitcase-like case that she'd lugged up the stairs, cursing the broken elevator at each landing where she'd taken a break. She set her printer on a large side table. For now, the computer sat on a too-small stand near the telescope. Her grandfather had used the tall table for his cigars, matches, and ashtray, and it wobbled a little with the weight of the typewriter. But it would do. For now.

During all the hours she'd spent upstairs, she'd ignored the phone, leaving the answering machine to pick up her calls. *No way am I going to call Rhonda back*, she thought, sipping from the glass as she eyed the floor, her eyes stopping on the untouched dishes she'd left out for the cat.

She'd cleaned them and refilled them, but to no avail.

Still missing, she thought, eyeing the collar she'd left on the kitchen counter when she'd cleaned out her pockets earlier.

And it had been a week since the cat had gone missing.

Not good.

And someone found his collar.

Or had her cat.

That thought made her stomach churn. Surely no one would hurt him. Surely not. Dear God, she prayed so.

As she listened to the next message, she looked out the window, her eyes scouring the bushes for the dozenth time and coming up empty.

"Hello, Harper," a deep male voice said as the recorder started to play and all the muscles in her body tensed before he identified himself. "This is Lou Arista calling again. I left a message at your number in California, but since I didn't hear from you, I thought I'd call the old house number and check in."

"Oh, shut up, you slimy bastard," she said, though, of course, he couldn't hear her.

"I think it would be a good idea if we get together. We could set up a meeting at the office, or if it's more convenient I could visit you at the estate."

Over my dead body!

"I know the last time we spoke, things got a little off track—"

"You mean fucked-up."

"So now that the trust is complete, since you've reached the age your grandmother chose for it to be disbursed, I thought we should talk things out and I could explain how the final payments will be handled. We could go over the tax bill, then I'll let you know about the services our firm could offer. There are a few outstanding bills that we'll handle, but then there's the matter of your ex-husband's claim."

Joel.

So that was his "business" in Portland. Harper should have known. Well, she would deal with him. "Delete," she said aloud, then erased the lawyer's message and stopped the recorder. "Jerk-wad!"

Oh, she remembered Arista all right. Gram's slick attorney. She had visited his offices not long before moving up here and had found him self-serving and patronizing and barely able to hide the fact that he thought he was more knowledgeable, more educated, and well— just damned smarter than she was.

"Bullshit."

She still held the ace.

Her grandmother's estate. What was left of it, due to his mishandling. Somehow a good share of the money had been siphoned off for her own care and schooling by her parents, or, as he'd explained, "For taxes, management fees, estate management, and adjustments due to economic downturns," and blah, blah, blah. She suspected it was all BS.

He was a big man with an even bigger personality. His dark hair was thick and brushed back, his near-black eyes sparked with a calculating intelligence that felt almost sinister.

When his father, Louis, had died in a hunting accident Lou Junior had inherited his father's business, which included Gram's account, the estate and trust his father had orchestrated. Within a year of his father's death, and only six months after Gram was laid to rest, Junior had left the modest office space in a historic Almsville building and joined two other attorneys, Frank Bartlett and Joseph Connors, to become the founding partners of Arista, Bartlett, and Connors, Attorneys at Law, *The ABCs of Legal Services*, according to their local television ads.

Over the years, the firm had expanded and moved to its current location in a high-rise in downtown Portland. Arista's glassed-in office offered views of the Willamette River and the city stretching east to Mount Hood in the distance.

She'd been there once, to sign papers that started the process of distributing the remainder of the trust. She told the lawyer that she would be in the market for a new attorney. He'd just nodded, his smile not touching his eyes as he'd tried to convince her to change her mind about dismissing the ABC legal team.

She had assured him she wouldn't.

He frowned and said something about her being a single woman, as if that were some kind of disability.

She remembered him saying it was a mistake for her to leave.

She hadn't thought so then, didn't think so now. As far as she was concerned, Arista had lived off her grandmother's estate far too long.

She'd walked out of the law firm's offices that last visit, had her parking ticket validated by the sweet-smiling receptionist who'd tried valiantly to copy Princess Diana's layered hair style, then ridden the elevator sixteen stories down to the parking garage.

No, she wasn't calling Arista back unless it was, as Craig Alexander had suggested, to sue the bastard for neglecting the property.

Or unless Joel decided to get nasty.

Just let it go.

"No," she said aloud, then drained her glass and placed it in the sink with some other dishes. She was still waiting for all the account records. When they arrived, she'd go over the statements with a fine-toothed comb and hand copies to a CPA or financial attorney. Let the lawyers duke it out in court.

She hit the Play button again, and her heart twisted as she heard her daughter's voice on the recording. "Hey, Mom. Sorry I missed you again. But it turns out I have to stay in Eugene longer than I thought. Nothing big happening, just have plans with some friends, but I thought I'd drive up next week. And, like I said, see Grandpa, too. Look, I've got class in twenty minutes, so call me back on my pager and let me know you got this message. Okay?"

Harper phoned her daughter's pager and hoped Dawn would call her back.

Rubbing her hip, she hoped the cable company could run a connection to the tower and was reminded of Gram's philosophy: "Where there's a will, there's a way, and if there isn't a way, then there's always money."

Usually Harper didn't subscribe to Gram's ideology, but she was beginning to see some merit to it as she made herself a snack of cheese and crackers. She grabbed a Diet Coke from the refrigerator and popped the top. After taking a long swallow, she considered adding a shot of rum to the can. Why not? It was after five and she'd worked all day—but decided against it. Since the first few days when she'd landed back in Almsville, she'd tried to avoid too many drinks and too much fascination with watching what was going on across the lake. The snifters and crystal decanters were tempting, as were the multiple telescopes and pairs of binoculars on each floor, but she'd resisted.

For the most part.

After bolting down cheese and crackers, she told herself to get busy.

Today she'd tackle Gram's room, but as she passed through the parlor, she saw lights burning across the lake at the Hunt home. In the upstairs bedroom. Cynthia and Tom's room.

She thought of Cynthia Hunt and the deadly inferno on the water. The woman had seemed hell-bent to kill herself in a horrific and agonizing way.

Why, she wondered again, touching her chin that still itched where her stitches had been, a constant reminder of that awful night, *Why was Cynthia out in the middle of Lake Twilight?*

Because her life was crumbling, her mind deteriorating with the sadness and tragedy of her life.

Once Cynthia had been a willowy blond, a smiling mother of two who sometimes substitute-taught at the high school. Then had come the tragedies surrounding her family and Lake Twilight.

Decades-old guilt seeped into her blood, and she tried to disregard it. Nothing could change the past, as her grandmother had always claimed. Her voice rang in Harper's ears even now. "No use crying when you fail or fall down, Harper-dear. Just learn from it. What's done is done. Pick yourself up, dust yourself off, and step forward. Yesterday's gone, but tomorrow holds a whole new day of promise."

She walked into Gram's room and imagined her grandmother as she'd last seen her, unmoving in the bed, her skin a sickly gray color, her eyes open and fixed. "I'm so sorry," she whispered and picked up the rag dolls, intent on throwing them into the trash.

But she hesitated, her throat closing as she glanced down at Raggedy Ann and Raggedy Andy with their faded red hair and broken smiles and round eyes. Andy in blue pants and a checked shirt, his bow tie askew, Ann wearing a pinafore over striped socks.

"Oh, Gram." Harper didn't have the heart to throw them away. Not yet. Instead, she put them onto the bed, pressed into the pillows just as Gram had always placed them—without Maude wedged between the pair. "Another day," she promised, and looked around the room.

She took a seat at Gram's dressing table and remembered her grandmother brushing Harper's hair when she was still in grade school. Gram would stand behind her, meeting Harper's gaze in the oval mirror. "Such pretty hair," she would say as Harper fidgeted on the stool. Gram had always let Harper wear pieces of her jewelry while Harper sat trying not to cry as Gram struggled with the knots and snarls that were ever-present in her long hair.

"If you weren't such a ruffian, your hair would stay nice," she'd say, as Harper had spent most of her days climbing trees or riding her bike or playing war with Evan, chasing him and some of the cats through the myriad of trails that crisscrossed the island. "Maybe we should just cut it. A buzz-cut, how about that?" Gram had asked once, pausing to take a drag from her cigarette burning in the ashtray on the dresser. Harper had glanced up sharply, catching Gram's gaze in the reflection and seeing the mischief in her eyes through her smoke.

Harper recalled the long strand of pearls and matching clip-on earrings she loved to wear and how Gram had confided, "Those were your mother's favorite, too, when she was a little girl."

Now she turned toward the mirror, remembering her visage at six, all dimples and crooked teeth, and today—well, she was healing but still looked bad. Tomorrow, she might get up, wash her hair, and even add a touch of makeup, join the real world.

She opened several drawers in the dressing table and was surprised to find a bottle of Chanel. A twist of the cap conjured up more memories of Gram. "My sweet Number 5," she had called it. Harper studied a box of talcum powder along with bottles of makeup and tubes of Gram's favorite lipsticks, all still arranged neatly. She picked up a tube of Revlon's Cherries in the Snow, Gram's favorite, and opened the tube to see it was half used.

After replacing the tube, she tried to open one of the bottom drawers, but it wouldn't budge. She tugged harder before she realized that both bottom drawers, on either side of the small desk area, had locks. The one on the left opened smoothly, while the one on the right didn't budge. She found Gram's key ring and located several small keys. On Harper's second attempt, she was able to unlock the drawer, and it slid out with some difficulty. "So what've you got in here that you want locked up?" she asked as she pulled out a stack of personal letters to discover another set of keys, two of the attached keys bearing the Chevrolet logo. The keys to Gramps's Corvette, she guessed. A smaller one, probably for the gun cabinet in the garage, and several more that she couldn't identify but would try out.

The last item, wrapped in an embroidered hankie, was a small glass jar with a screw-off lid, in which a dozen tiny holes had been punched. And inside the glass itself, the bodies of six desiccated bald-faced hornets lay crumpled, their small bodies curled in death.

She eyed them with a sense of revulsion and curiosity.

Why would Gram have kept them, hidden away with her secret treasures?

Why would anyone?

Perfume, keys, makeup, jewelry, and hornets.

An unlikely combo.

And a mystery she couldn't solve now, or maybe ever.

She left the jar in the drawer with the other items and thought she should burn the letters. She would. But she would probably read them first. What would be the harm? Gram and almost everyone she loved was long dead.

"Not tonight," she said, recalling sadly that her grandmother had buried her husband, only daughter, and grandson before she, too, had left this world with the help of her granddaughter.

At that thought, Harper walked straight to the liquor cabinet and, despite her earlier convictions, poured herself a stiff drink—vodka again, to vanquish the spirits that haunted this island—or more precisely crept through her mind.

"There are no ghosts," she told herself before she took a long swallow and made her way to the parlor windows and the night dark beyond. A specter appeared in the watery glass—her own ghostly reflection, pale and wan.

From out of nowhere she heard Cynthia's curse: *You fucking bitch! You go straight to hell. You killed my son!*

"Not today," she said and finished her drink. "Not going to hell today." After all, she'd been there already, about twenty years ago.

1968

Chapter 41

Harper couldn't get out of bed.
Devastated and heartbroken, still wearing her nightgown, she stared at the ceiling in her room at the cottage. Bandit lay on the pillow beside her, the bedside lamp turned low, the February wind rattling the panes of the windows.

With effort, she forced herself to roll from beneath the covers. She was cold from the inside out, testament to her grief and the gray winter day. She peered out the window, wondered if it might snow, and without thinking, plucked at a spot near the window frame where the wallpaper was stained and pulling away from the casing.

Her mother would never have allowed the discoloration or the tiny tear. When Anna was alive, this room was awash with light, the woodwork was a bright white, the curtains crisp, the rug a thick shag.

But after Anna died, the room had seemed to fade and Harper had spent more and more time at Gram's big house. The books and toys still on the shelves were still the same as they had been for years. The only nods to her becoming a teenager were the portable record player that was set up on her desk, a scattering of 45s on the floor, and a small television with rabbit ears that had once been Evan's.

She flopped back onto the bed and heard her father and stepmother downstairs, smelled coffee brewing, and closed her eyes. She knew Marcia was angry that Dad insisted they stay here, at the cottage, rather than the condo in downtown Portland. She'd overheard several fights between them.

Didn't care.

Hadn't cared about anything since the night when Gram died.

Somehow a week had passed.

All in a blur of police interrogations, reporters' calls, funeral preparations, and lawyers' visits. The "big house," as Dad called it, had been crawling with cops, reporters at the gates. The whole town of Almsville and the world beyond were caught up in the scandal and mystery.

Another weapon in Marcia's arsenal in her fight to move back to their penthouse.

"We'd be protected there, Bruce. There's a doorman and security. We could be away from all of this madness. It would be good for us, you and me, and for Harper as well."

"Not yet," her father had replied. "I'm not uprooting Harper. She's been through enough trauma as it is."

The fight had ended with the bedroom door slamming so hard the whole cottage had shuddered. But they'd stayed.

Absently, Harper petted Bandit, barely feeling the dog's rough fur.

Her heart ached, not just for Chase, wherever he was, but for Gram as well. Harper couldn't imagine life without her grandmother.

Never had Harper felt so all alone. Even when her mother passed, Gram had remained stalwart, just as she had when Evan, too, left them.

But now?

Now?

Who was she left with? Her father and his wife. She let out a sigh. Daddy had always been somewhat distant, he'd been closer to Evan. Then there was Marcia, a stepmother who was only ten years older than Harper but one of those women who acted and appeared a generation older. Marcia's taste in clothes, hairstyles, music, makeup, you name it, was part of an older generation. More Marilyn Monroe than Twiggy. Just like Dad was more Dean Martin than Mick Jagger— but then he could be excused. He *was* from another generation. An older one.

And now there was a new one—or would soon be.

Harper swallowed hard and her hand went to her abdomen where, she knew, a baby was growing. She hadn't been to a doctor, it was too early for that, but she'd skipped not just one period but two. She'd have to tell Dad and Marcia before they guessed the truth. It should have been a time of joy. With the baby's arrival, Chase would be safe from the draft. Or something like that. But now, it was a time of worry. Fear.

"I'll take care of you," she promised her unborn child.

She squeezed her eyes shut tighter against the hot tears that were always there.

Marcia suspected the truth and had confided as much to Harper's father, a few days earlier. Harper had heard the conversation wafting up the stairs and had crept down to a spot where she could surreptitiously peer through the railing and watch what was happening in the kitchen.

"Something's up with Harper," Marcia stated. She was at the kitchen sink, her back to the room.

Dad looked up from his paper. "What do you mean?"

"I think she might be pregnant."

Harper's heart went still. She *knew*?

"What? Oh, for the love of Christ, Marcia, why would you even think such a thing?"

From her hiding spot, Harper hardly dared to breathe as she listened to more of the damning conversation.

Marcia was saying, "I'm the one who cleans out the trash in the upstairs bathroom, and there hasn't been any evidence that she's, you know, having her period."

"Marcia!"

"I'm just saying that girl was pretty regular and I could tell, not just by her moods but by what I found, or more precisely didn't find, in the garbage."

"That's ridiculous!"

"Is it?"

"You shouldn't snoop."

"Not snooping, Bruce. Being ahead of the game." Marcia went on spinning so quickly from the sink, Harper was certain she'd be seen.

But Marcia hadn't looked through the archway, instead pinning her husband in her glare. "She spends half her time, maybe more, over at that huge house with all of its rooms and a doting grandmother who has no rules. It probably happened there!" She snapped a terry-cloth towel from a peg near the sink and furiously dried her hands.

"You don't know that." Dad laid down his paper.

With a sigh, he said, "She's going to Olivia's tonight, and it's not to meet Chase. She's taking care of her grandmother. Matilda has the night off."

"Why?" Marcia demanded.

"No idea. I figure that's between Olivia and Matilda."

Marcia asked, "But does Harper know that she's on grandma duty?"

"Yes. It's all been decided," Dad assured his wife. "Harper's spending the night."

Harper's mind was already spinning ahead. Tonight would be the perfect time to meet Chase on the dock because he could boat across the lake.

Marcia scoffed. "I'm just telling you your daughter's boy crazy, and right now she's all over that Hunt kid. It's 'Chase this' and 'Chase that.' When she isn't with him, she's talking about him. As a matter of fact, he's *all* she thinks about."

"It'll pass. You remember how things were in high school. Everything was overblown. High drama. So don't worry about Harper. She's a smart girl. What's going on now, it's just a crush. Besides, Chase is at college, surrounded by other girls. He'll outgrow her."

"Maybe," Marcia allowed, not sounding convinced. "But it might already be too late."

"I don't want to hear this, Marcia," he warned, scooting his chair back. "Don't borrow trouble."

"There's no borrowing it. Trouble's brewing. Coming our way. In fact it's already here."

"You don't know that."

"Don't I?" she threw back at him, her voice rising. "Just don't come whining to me when you find out you're going to be a grandfather!" She threw the towel down and Harper scurried quietly up the stairs.

"Enough!" Dad reprimanded. "That's just crazy."

"Is it? I guess time will tell." Harper heard Marcia's clipped footsteps retreating from the kitchen.

She'd felt sick inside. Why hadn't she been more careful about hiding her pregnancy? Not that she'd expected her stepmother to be tracking her every move. But it didn't matter, she'd told herself. Because she was going to tell Chase that she was pregnant, and they'd find a way to get married and have a baby and . . . Even to her own ears, it sounded like a dream, but she'd closed her mind to all her negative thoughts. Tonight would be perfect. She'd set up a time to meet him and tell him the news. Even if she had to twist the truth a little.

Now, nearly a week later, as Harper lay on her bed, she heard the drone of the television downstairs. The phone rang. Again. Her father's voice drifted up the stairs as he said succinctly, "No comment!" then slammed down the receiver.

One day, when the phone had rung incessantly, Dad had even taken it off the hook, leaving the receiver to hum loudly, reminding them that no one could get through.

That had been a temporary solution because they couldn't be without a phone for any length of time. There were important calls from the police and the accountants and the lawyers and friends who needed to speak to them, funeral arrangements to be made. Oh, she'd heard bits and pieces of the conversations rising to the second floor. Her father's stern messages to the reporters who called, and then Marcia's whispered concerns to whatever friend had phoned: "We don't know what to do . . . she won't eat . . . no, no, won't come out of her room . . . nearly comatose, if you ask me . . . oh yes, yes, very concerned and the police won't leave us alone. It's a nightmare. Bruce is beside himself . . . oh, I don't know. I wouldn't think so . . . no, no, she *adored* her grandmother . . . yes, I know . . . Umhmm . . . if you ask me, he bailed, left his family high and dry . . . no, no, I don't have any proof, of course . . . no one knows what really happened . . ."

That was the truth.

Chase was still missing despite multiple attempts by divers to locate him in the lake. Since the water was up, it had been hypothesized that he'd drowned and floated down the spillway to the river. If not located soon, his body could be swept toward the ocean.

Hope was fading that he would ever be found.

Harper was devastated.

Sniffling, she climbed out of bed and walked to the window to stare outside through the cold window panes again. It seemed it was all she did besides sleep. The landscape was stark, snow threatening in the heavy clouds. In winter, after the oak and aspen trees had dropped their leaves, Harper had a bird's-eye view of the mansion. As a child she had watched the cars come and go through the gates and across the bridge when Gram entertained.

Now the house was dark and looming. Where once she'd thought the grand home almost a castle, now she considered it a tomb.

A week ago the world was filled with promise.

Now all she felt was doom.

She dropped down on the bed again, disturbing Bandit and hoping that somehow she could block everything out. She closed her eyes, hoping to drift off, intending to block out the world.

The doorbell chimed and the little dog leapt from the bed, yipping wildly and scratching at the door.

"You're an idiot," Harper scolded, reluctantly rolling off the comforter, "but join the club." She opened the door and he streaked down the stairs, a rush of brown and black fur as she heard the door open. The dog barking a greeting and Beth's voice insisting that she just wanted to see Harper.

"She's not seeing anyone," Dad said.

"Oh, let Beth try," Marcia said, an edge to her voice. "We have to do *some*thing to get her out of her funk, Bruce. Beth's her best friend."

Dad wasn't having it. "She said—"

"It's okay," Harper called from the upstairs landing and peered down to see the tops of their three heads. Marcia in her favorite angora sweater and slacks, Beth wearing a jacket over her miniskirt, tights, and knee-high boots. At the sound of Harper's voice, they all looked up and Beth, not needing any more encouragement, dashed up the stairs, her ponytail wagging behind her.

"Oh my God, how are you?" she asked, wrapping her arms around Harper so fiercely they almost fell over.

"Good Lord, Harper," Marcia said from the bottom of the stairs. "Could you at least get dressed?"

"It's okay. Leave her be." Dad placed an arm around his wife. "Come on, let's finish breakfast."

As they disappeared from view, Beth disentangled herself. "So?"

"I'm—I'm okay."

"Are you?" Beth arched her eyebrows suspiciously. "I don't buy it." But she bustled Harper back into the room and shut the door behind them. "It's been pretty crappy, hasn't it?"

"Real crappy."

"I know, I've seen everything on TV. They've crucified you!" There was a scratching at the door and Beth let Bandit in. He bounded onto the bed as Beth closed the door. "Okay, tell me everything!" she said, but Harper held up a finger, and before she said anything else, she put an LP onto the turntable and cranked up the volume so that the songs from *Beatles '65* filled the room. Harper aimed the speaker at the door to drown out her conversation with Beth because she figured if she could hear the conversation from downstairs in her room, then her parents could most likely hear what she said as well. For added security she placed hard-backed copies of several Nancy Drew books over the heat vent.

"Did you see Chase's parents on TV?" Beth asked.

"Yeah." She nodded. "But I turned it off." She couldn't stand the news and she'd caught glimpses of Cynthia and Tom Hunt's tortured faces as they'd been interviewed along with Levi. The family of three had been clustered together outside their cottage, huddled in thick jackets on the porch of their home while making pleas for Chase to come home. Cynthia had been fighting tears, Tom stiff and tight jawed, Levi appearing pale as a ghost.

Once the short interview was over, the camera had panned the lake as the news anchors at the station had catalogued the tragedies that had occurred on the somber gray waters.

"Cynthia blames you for whatever happened to Chase," Beth admitted, plucking a burr from Bandit's coat. "She told my mom."

"Tell me something I don't know." Harper sat cross-legged on the bed. "And everyone thinks I poisoned Gram." Her heart turned cold. "I would never."

"I know." Beth lay down beside her and they both stared up at the ceiling while the final notes of "No Reply" faded.

While music filled the small room, Beth spilled what she knew of the local gossip.

There had been some people who hypothesized that Chase and Harper had actually met, that there had been some kind of altercation, and Harper had either accidentally or intentionally driven him away. Maybe Harper had actually even killed the Hunt boy. Then, after somehow hiding the body so that no one could find it, Harper had set his boat adrift before canoeing across the lake to coerce Levi into helping her and establishing her alibi. And did anyone think that a girl who was capable of poisoning her own grandmother wouldn't go so far as to kill a boy who had been seeing other girls?

It was far-fetched. How could anyone have managed all that?

As for Cynthia Hunt, who knew what she really thought? But she hated Harper and somehow, no matter what happened, Harper Reed was to blame. At least that's what she'd confided to Beth's mother, Alaina. Cynthia had observed Chase with some of the girls who lived down the street and she was certain Chase had "outgrown" Harper.

"Mrs. Hunt really believes I would do anything to hurt him?"

"I don't know," Beth said, over the music. "She never said that directly. At least I don't think so."

"Did you hear anything else? What about Levi?"

"I—I don't know. I think just basically that you came to the house and the two of you went looking for Chase. Something like that. Is that what happened?"

Harper nodded, closing her eyes and leaning her head back against the headboard.

"What about Rand, does he know anything?" But she had little hope. She and Levi had spoken with him that night.

Beth told her what she'd heard, putting together bits and pieces of what her parents and the Hunts had confided in each other. The long and the short of it was that Rand Watkins had given the police a statement to the effect that he'd met with Chase up at the river earlier in the evening and that Chase admitted to Rand that he had intended to break up with Harper or marry her.

"Marry me or break up with me?" Harper said, disbelieving.

"The way Rand told it was that Chase had been confused that night. Maybe drunk, too. Rand admitted to having a beer or two. Anyway, Chase was real clear that he wasn't going to get drafted and end up in Vietnam even though he'd flunked out of school."

Harper felt miserable.

"It's all so crazy," Beth said as the next track on the album started and John Lennon began singing "I'm a Loser." A fitting song considering Harper's mood. "I mean who could think of you as someone who could . . . well, you know . . ."

"Everyone." At least that's the way it felt. It wasn't as if she were as pure as the driven snow by any means, but she certainly wasn't capable of any of the things people were saying.

"Did you see the news?" Beth asked tentatively.

"Yeah. Dad tried to keep me from watching it, but I've got Evan's TV, so I turned it on."

It had been bad. One clever reporter had gotten Cynthia to admit on camera that she believed Olivia Dixon wouldn't have died if not for her neglectful, selfish granddaughter. Cynthia had also pointed out that with her brother and mother dead, Harper was set up to inherit all of the Dixon estate as she was the only living heir. "You think that's a coincidence?" she'd asked the reporter. "And even if she didn't do it on purpose, she planned to leave that night to meet my son. Harper Reed admitted as much. So she would leave her own feeble grandmother alone when she was supposed to be caring for her. Tell me, what kind of person would do that?"

"She hates me," Harper said miserably.

"Who?"

"Chase's mom."

"Oh no, she's just upset. You can understand—"

"She *hates* me," Harper said and sat up against the headboards, pushing her pillow to the side. "She tried to get Chase to break up with me." It was all coming back to her, how much Cynthia was against their relationship. "She thought I would hold Chase back, that he wouldn't finish college and I would ruin his life!"

"You don't know that."

"I do know. We were coming out of the police station, my dad and me, and they were going in and Cynthia stopped and accused me of killing Gram. She said that with my mother and brother gone, the only thing that stood in my way of inheriting everything was my grandmother." Tears began running down Harper's face as she re-called Cynthia's twisted, hate-filled face, her husband trying to usher her up the steps to the front doors of the station in the rain. But Cynthia had stopped and spewed her vile accusations, letting her umbrella get caught in the wind as she'd turned and yelled at Harper. A reporter had been at the station at the time and snapped a picture of Cynthia's tortured face and Harper's stunned reaction. A second after the picture was taken, Cynthia spat, missing her target, as Dad had quickly shuttled Harper to their car.

Beth said, "So you've talked to the police?"

"What do you think?"

"Okay. Dumb question."

"The cops have questioned me three times. Once with my dad and twice with an attorney. And that doesn't count the first night, when they came to the house."

"Do they think—?"

"I don't know what they think!" Harper snapped. "And they've talked to everyone close to Gram and Chase and . . . *every*body. Including Old Man Sievers, who swore his dog went 'bat-shit' crazy around midnight and he thought there was an intruder. Later, the dog was at it again and Old Man Sievers heard a boat's motor or something nearby. At least that's what Dad told me."

"That's weird. We're only a couple of houses down, and we didn't hear anything until the sirens."

"What about the people in the house at the end of the street, next to yours?"

"They left. Like fast," Beth said, levering up on an elbow as Bandit scratched at the coverlet before rotating and settling down again. "I was there when the police showed up, and within minutes after the cops left, everyone in that place scrambled to pack up their cars and vans and took off. We're right next door and I saw it all."

So no one knew anything. None of Chase's friends had any idea where he was, nor had he been admitted to a hospital.

He was just gone.

Vanished into thin air.

"So what're you going to do?" Beth asked as the music stopped and she found another album, this one by the Supremes.

"I don't know!"

"Knock, knock!" Marcia's voice called as she rapped on the door. Without waiting for an answer, she pushed it open.

"Watch out!" Harper yelled.

Too late.

Carrying a tray, Marcia tripped on the record player.

The phonograph's needle screeched loudly across the LP, Diana Ross's voice gone.

Marcia's tray spiraled into the air.

Mugs of cocoa went airborne.

Hot chocolate and melting marshmallows sloshed onto Marcia as she tripped.

Oreos and Nilla Wafers flew.

The tray landed on the rug with a soft thud. Cups and cookies followed.

"Oooh, what . . . Holy . . ." Marcia landed on her knees, chocolate splashing onto her sweater and splattering on the rug while Bandit went nuts, barking wildly on the bed.

Marcia leveled her gaze at Harper.

Beneath the thick bangs of her bleached beehive, her eyes were ice. "What," she said through clenched teeth, "is going on here?"

"Nothing." Harper had been frozen on the bed, propped against the headboard. "Hush!" she yelled at Bandit. The dog leaped from the bed and scarfed up a wafer that had landed near the nightstand.

"Nothing?" Marcia repeated, her face flushed.

Harper scrambled from her bed.

"Yeah," Beth interjected as Harper tried to pick up the cookies and ignore the fact that a glob of melting marshmallow goo was dripping from Marcia's teased hair and onto the shoulder of her angora sweater. "We were, um, just listening to music."

"With the record player facing the door?" Her eyes narrowed even as Beth found some tissues and began dabbing at the rug.

Marcia felt the sticky marshmallow on her face, touched it with a tentative finger, then appeared about to explode. Her lips pursed as she tried to wipe away the goo, only making it pull into strands. "You don't have to lie to me. The music wasn't for you two now, was it? It was for us. Your dad and me." She was eyeing Harper now, while

Harper frantically tried to pick up the cookies before Bandit could gobble them all. "It was so that we couldn't hear what you were talking about or know what you were doing."

There was no need to argue. Harper had tried that before. It would only infuriate her stepmother more.

Marcia drew in a deep breath and closed her eyes as Harper scrabbled up the last soggy Oreo and Beth said, "I think we'll need a towel."

"Got one." Harper scrounged in her laundry hamper and withdrew a damp hand towel that she tossed to Beth, who began working feverishly on the rug where chocolate had oozed.

"Let me have that!" Marcia snagged the towel to dab at her sweater and hair. "Oooh. This is probably stained!" She gave up and angrily tossed the towel back to Beth. "I was just trying to be nice. You know? Bringing you some kind of snack." She rotated her palm toward the tray where Harper was piling the cups, saucers, and remaining cookies. "And this is the thanks I get?"

Harper bristled but held her tongue as her stepmother gained control of herself again.

"Next time," Marcia warned, "since the loud music was all for my benefit, you might consider playing something decent. Something I like—I don't know. Elvis, maybe? Or . . . or . . . Bobby Darin? Even Connie Francis, for God's sake. Not this British invasion or Motown crap!" She paused for effect and rolled her eyes before sinking onto a corner of Harper's bed. "Really?" She took in several deep breaths while Beth watched wide-eyed and Harper chased an errant Oreo that had slid beneath the bookshelf. Slightly calmer, Marcia said, "Look, Harper, I know you've been through a lot. Lord have mercy, I understand, but you have to see that you're not the only one affected here. We're all grieving for your grandmother and . . . and what happened to her and with Chase missing . . ." She paused and looked out the window. ". . . it's all too much. For all of us."

"What's going on up there?" Bruce Reed's deep voice traveled up the stairs.

Oh no. Harper died a million deaths. She didn't need Dad, too. But another round of questions and accusations couldn't be avoided because she heard his heavy footsteps as he climbed quickly up the stairs.

Great. Just fabulous, she thought sarcastically as she brushed off the dust bunnies and tossed the last cookie back onto the tray.

"Marcia? What's happening?" He stepped into the room and took one look around, his gaze landing on the record player, scooted to the middle of the floor, and the rest of the mess, including his usually neat-as-a-pin wife with gunk spilled all over her and Bandit, sniffing in a corner. "Harper?" he asked, finally looking at her as she stood. "I don't understand—"

"Neither do I," Marcia cut in, "but I think *your daughter* wants her privacy."

"For what?" He seemed genuinely puzzled.

Marcia gazed at her husband as if he were as dumb as a stone. "Who knows? Girl talk," she said, surprising Harper that she didn't tell him.

Marcia quickly shooed him out the door and closed it firmly behind her.

"She doesn't seem so bad," Beth whispered, eyeing the soggy Oreos on the tray.

Harper mouthed, "Step-monster."

That was the trouble with Marcia. She ran hot and cold. Cool and nice—even sweet—at times, and at others? A full-blown bitch who would explode for seemingly no reason.

She'd heard the fights between her dad and his wife.

When they thought she was asleep or far enough away not to overhear the harsh words and accusations. Marcia didn't trust Dad, and at times, it seemed the reverse were true. Accusations of "carousing" or infidelity when he'd come home late. Questions about phone calls and where the other one had been, though outwardly they appeared ever the loving couple.

But now, since Gram's death, the cracks were showing.

Marcia wanted to move into the main house.

Dad was against it, at least for now.

And then there was Harper's pregnancy.

She had to tell them.

But not today, she thought.

And probably not tomorrow.

1988
The Present

Chapter 42

"Bitch."

Cynthia's final accusation, one hurled in agony from a burning, sinking boat, still rang in Harper's ears.

So she decided to pour one more drink. "Why not?" Harper drained the remainder of the bottle into her glass, reminded herself to stop at the liquor store the next day, then walked up the stairs to the tower room. She didn't bother turning on the light but made her way to the telescope and brought her grandfather's chair closer to it. Ignoring the sense that she might be invading someone's privacy, that she wasn't much better than Gramps, she took a swallow from her glass, then bent down to look through the eyepiece. She, as was her custom, started with the Sievers' bungalow where lights shone from the windows.

A noise interrupted her.

Muted but audible.

A quiet footfall?

No.

But she didn't move a muscle and listened.

Was there another—just the softest tread of a footstep?

She swung around.

Nothing.

No one.

Get over yourself.

Yet she was certain she'd heard something. She walked to the top of the stairs and looked down the dark spiral to the light from the hallway below.

No furtive shadow passed on the landing.

No blood-thirsty monster jumped out at her.

No killer appeared holding a knife or gun.

Whatever she'd heard—or thought she'd heard—was gone. She strained to listen but heard nothing but the rumble of the old furnace and the sough of the wind as it swept around the tower.

Don't be a goose.

Yet her skin crawled, icy pimples on the backs of her arms, and she remembered the dolls, moved and desecrated.

Everything was quiet.

Still.

Maybe she'd been mistaken. Maybe what she'd heard was all her imagination. She took another sip from her glass, told herself to calm down, then settled in her chair again, but her nerves weren't calmed. Despite the warmth of the liquor running through her veins, she was still edgy, her ears straining for any unfamiliar sound, her muscles tense.

Pull yourself together.

She finished her drink and poured another, then spied the telescope and decided to check things out. Already it was pointed across the lake to Fox Point, so she leaned into it and focused on the houses across the lake. The night was clear, moonlight visible and a gaseous blue light from the lamp post on the street in front of the row of houses offered some visibility.

She started at the house closest to the swim park and town. Harper already knew there were people in the Sievers' place. She adjusted the focus and sipped from her glass until the images on the other side of the lake were crystal clear.

From her vantage point, she saw glimpses of a round woman as she walked in and out of what appeared to be a kitchenette. A teenaged boy with a mop of reddish hair sat at a table and scowled at the open books and notebook open in front of him. In a gray sweatshirt and jeans, he twiddled with a pen as he read the books and every once in a while stopped to take a note or sip from a Big Gulp on the table near his homework.

He didn't look up as the woman, his mother, presumably—Francine, according to Beth—opened the slider and walked onto the back deck. Short, with curling auburn hair, pulled into a topknot, she switched on an exterior light. Immediately her deck and dock were illuminated, and the light was bright enough to light several neighboring yards.

Harper watched and sipped, her glass draining, a buzzy feeling settling warm inside her, her frayed nerves finally calming.

In faded jeans and an oversized sweatshirt, Francine pulled on a pair of kitchen gloves, then carrying two buckets, she stepped onto the dock and sat on a plastic chair that was positioned on the dock's edge. She adjusted her topknot before using a knife and cleaning the buckets of crabs.

All the while, the kid worked at the table inside. Supposedly he had a brother or sister. Beth had mentioned two kids, but Harper saw no one else in the house, and as the kid picked up his drink, she hoisted up hers. "Cheers," she said, then swung the telescope to Rand's house again.

Tonight the A-frame was dark, no light emanating through its sharply angled windows, and she felt a little pang of disappointment.

Oh, puh-leez, Harper. Just how pathetic are you?

She moved the telescope to focus on the Hunts' cottage. It, too, was dark, showing no signs of life.

Another letdown.

Are you serious? Is this how you're going to get your jollies, by watching people you knew twenty years ago? For God's sake, get a life.

"For God's sake, shut up."

She took another long swallow and swung the telescope to the Alexanders' split level. No lights there. She didn't even see the dog that sometimes ambled out onto the deck.

"Strike three."

As for the last house on the point, there were no lights on and the shades were drawn, just as they had been twenty years earlier when it had been occupied by the rotating group of college students. Then she'd seen silhouettes of people backlit by the shifting, eerie light from the lava lamps and candles they had throughout the house.

Tonight? Nothing.

She took a long, final swig from the glass and was about to go downstairs in search of dinner when she took one last peek at the dark Hunt house. For a second she thought she saw someone on the deck but, after staring at it long enough, decided it was just a trick of light, a shadow cast by some of the tall trees surrounding the area.

Then the figure moved, catching a wink of light. A tall man. Broad shoulders. Light hair catching in the breeze.

"Chase," she whispered, her heart soaring.

In the wispy, foggy light she saw the sharp features of his profile.

She dropped her glass and fell to her knees. A small sob escaped from her throat.

He was alive!

After all this time—oh my God—Chase Hunt was alive!

Her heart skipped an elated beat, before she realized she was wrong.

Of course she was.

Her imagination had got the better of her.

Chase wasn't at the Hunts' house.

The man walking across the deck was Levi.

But, here in the dark, he could have been his brother's twin.

As kids, the two boys had resembled each other and as teenagers even more so. Now she couldn't help but wonder. If Chase were still around, would they still look so much alike? Or would they have grown into men who only slightly resembled each other? Their coloring was slightly different, of course, but other than that . . .

It was a moot point now.

Chase was long gone.

Living?

Dead?

She doubted anyone would ever know.

She picked up her glass from the carpet and went downstairs where she considered another drink. Deciding she was already slightly tipsy, she set her glass in the sink. She told herself to quit spying—who cared what Levi was doing, she was tired and should go to bed—but she couldn't resist and went to her bedroom where the binoculars were stashed.

Then, from this lower angle, she adjusted the lenses and noted that lights were coming on at the Alexanders' house. Feeling as if she were somehow betraying her friend, she trained the glasses on the kitchen where Beth dropped her purse and slipped out of her long coat before kicking off a pair of shoes. Craig and Max came in after her, the boy disappearing up the staircase with Beth following. Craig emptied his pockets of keys and wallet, setting both on a side table near the front door, then shrugged out of his jacket.

Lights snapped on upstairs and in the master bedroom, Beth shimmied out of a silvery jumpsuit, then disappeared into the adjoining bath, while in the bedroom down the hall Max had snapped on his bedroom light. Harper saw the top of Max's head and the messy upper shelf of his closet as he opened the closet doors.

Meanwhile, Craig had descended into his office/workout room and dropped into his desk chair. He rubbed a hand around his face, checked his watch, and then went back to the door to lock it.

Odd, Harper thought, and wished she had another drink.

Once back at his desk, Craig settled into his chair again and picked up the receiver before dialing the phone. All the while his gaze was drawn to the door, almost as if he expected someone to burst in. He seemed agitated, drumming his fingers on the desk, then snapping to attention as if whoever was on the other end of the line had picked up. But he didn't say a word, still waited, his face set and hard, then speaking for a few seconds—maybe leaving a short message—before he slammed the receiver down and dropped his head into his hands.

After a minute or so he looked up, muttered something, then stood and stripped off his polo shirt and tossed it onto the floor. He opened a drawer to retrieve a Walkman into which he slipped a cassette before fitting earphones over his head as he strode to the exercise bike in the corner. He swung onto the bike and started peddling fast, as if he were trying to run away from something but was going nowhere. As if demons were chasing him.

Harper moved the glasses. Though the shade was partially drawn in Max's room, she noticed light flickering as if a television had been turned on. In the master bedroom the lights were on and the bathroom door open.

No Beth.

So what?

She was probably somewhere on the street side of the house, areas that weren't visible from Harper's vantage point.

What the hell are you doing, spying on your friend?

Are you nuts?

And then in the dark kitchen, the refrigerator door opened, casting a soft glow on Beth's face as she quickly pulled out a green bottle of . . . champagne? She'd changed into jeans and a loose sweater with a boatneck. Not pajamas. Well, maybe it was too early for her to get ready for bed.

Stop it! You're spying. Intruding. Why do you care what other people do in the privacy of their own homes?

She started to back away from the telescope when out of the corner of her eye, she caught a glimpse of light go on in the Hunts' boathouse. She focused on Levi, peering inside as he stood in the doorway, his body cast in relief from the weak shifting illumination of lamplight on the water.

As if he'd sensed her watching him, he turned sharply toward the lake, his gaze focusing on the island.

She bit her lip.

Told herself to put down the binoculars.

Felt her heart begin to pound as she shrank back behind the curtains.

Even though she knew he couldn't see her. Nor did she think he sensed her watching. Yet she picked up the binoculars and stood near the curtains to stare at him through the glasses. As she did, she felt a little rush and swallowed hard, just as he whirled quickly to face the house, as if he'd heard something.

And sure enough, the side gate swung open and Beth, carrying the backpack, slipped into the backyard. Beth held a finger to her lips as she hurried onto the dock.

Though the light from the boathouse was feeble, it was enhanced by the Sievers' bright porch light. Harper saw that Levi was surprised, maybe even apprehensive, but that could have been her imagination because Beth quickly pulled the bottle from her backpack and handed it to him, before digging into the side pocket of the backpack once more and retrieving two champagne flutes.

"What're you doing?" Harper whispered, now engrossed in the scene unfolding across the lake.

For his part, Levi didn't move.

Beth stood on her tiptoes and said something to him, then took his hand and led him to the slider.

Once they were inside the dark house, the glass door closed behind them, she could see nothing more, none of the interaction, be it innocent or not. Were they popping the cork off the bottle of champagne? Watching the frothy liquid bubble over the sides of the bottle? Pouring two glasses? Celebrating? But toasting what? His mother had died only days before in a horrible, mind-jarring death. It seemed an unlikely time for any kind of celebration.

Fascinated, she stared through the lenses and told herself that the rapid beating of her heart had nothing to do with what she was trying to observe. Were they in the kitchen, toasting each other? Or . . . did she see movement in the bedroom on the upper floor—Cynthia and Tom's room, the space where she'd thought Craig might have hidden the revolver?

Then she remembered Craig.

She swung her field glasses back to the Alexanders' house where he was still on the bike, sweating now, his legs pumping fast, up and down, his face red, really going at it.

What the devil was going on over there?

Did he know that his wife had slipped out of the house?

Had she sneaked, or was her visit innocent?

Harper's mind raced faster than the wheels of the stationary bicycle.

Beth had seemed to surprise Levi.

And yet he'd followed her all too willingly into the house.

She'd brought champagne.

Maybe Levi had agreed to sell his house and list it with Alexander Realty.

Was this a clandestine meeting? If not, why no lights in the house?

Were Levi and Beth lovers?

But even if they were involved with each other, would they take a chance while Craig was in the house and—

Craig's workout was suddenly over. He stopped pedaling rapidly, the wheels of the bike continuing to spin of their own accord. He dashed across the room to pick up the receiver of the phone. Standing, stretching the coiled cord, he paced back and forth. Listening. Speaking. Obviously agitated.

Then he slammed the receiver down, stalked to a tall closet, grabbed a towel from within, and swiped it over his face and neck.

He reached for his discarded shirt, yanked it over his head, and started for the door leading to the hallway and staircase.

Harper caught her breath.

Beth and Levi were about to be found out.

Whatever was going on was about to come to a head.

She turned the field glasses to the Hunt cottage.

Still dark.

"Oh God."

Back at the Alexander house, Craig had left the basement. He appeared in the kitchen, where he went to the refrigerator and pulled out a beer, cracked it open, and took a long swallow. Then another.

"You'd better get home and fast," Harper whispered, as if her friend could hear her.

Still nothing happening at the house next door, at least nothing she could see.

Back in the Alexanders' kitchen, Craig took two more long pulls on the bottle, finishing his beer. He set the empty bottle on the counter and walked outside to the deck.

Harper watched as Craig, backlit by the kitchen lights, reached into his pants pocket and withdrew a pack of cigarettes and a lighter. A second later his face was visible as he lit up. His features were hard and set. He drew deep, snapped the lighter shut, then turned toward the lake as their big, shaggy dog wandered through the open door and headed down the exterior stairs. He wandered under the deck, pausing to sniff at the boxes and junk piled there until he finally made his way to the backyard.

Craig didn't seem to notice Rambo and continued smoking, staring across the dark water, watching as a solitary boat, running lights glowing, cut across Lake Twilight.

And then Harper saw it.

A flicker of light on the main floor of the Hunts' home, a shaft of lamplight from somewhere in the front of the house. Chase's bedroom? Levi's? From her vantage point, Harper couldn't tell. But it worried her as she felt in her bones that Beth was on a clandestine mission, one she didn't want her husband to be aware of.

And she was about to get caught.

Down near the dock Rambo started barking, low and loud enough that the deep sound rippled across the water. He was near a row of bushes separating the Alexanders' property from the Hunts', his head down, his body stiff, his tail straight up.

"No, no, no," Harper whispered. "Shhh." As if the big dog could hear her.

Craig flicked his cigarette into the yard below, peered down, presumably at his dog, then turned his attention on the Hunt property.

Oh. God.

Where was Beth?

This was going to be bad.

The slider door of the Hunt house opened, and Harper's heart nearly stopped.

"Here we go," she whispered, eyes glued to the unfolding scene.

Rambo was still making a racket when Levi appeared on the deck.

Harper swallowed hard. "Don't come out," she said, as if Beth could hear her. "Don't!"

But Levi stepped out of the house alone. He closed the door behind him and the dog quieted, pacing near the line of shrubs.

Where the hell was Beth?

Harper trained the binoculars over the back of the Hunts' house but saw no movement. Levi actually raised a hand at Craig, who nodded.

But no Beth.

This is no good, she thought, and then while Craig was facing the back of the Hunts' place, possibly engaging with Levi, Harper noticed the front door of the Alexander house open enough to let the filmy street light in. Not thirty feet from where Craig was standing at the deck's rail.

Harper felt every one of her nerves tightening.

Beth slipped through the door and closed it, in plain view of her husband. All he had to do was hear the softest noise, feel the slightest bit of air, and turn to catch her.

Harper's teeth sunk into her lip. "Be careful."

Beth scurried up the stairs just as Craig glanced into the house, as if he'd heard something. He started to go inside.

Upstairs, Beth didn't turn on any lights. Harper was left to imagine her stripping out of her clothes, tossing on pajamas, and sliding quietly into bed to feign sleep.

Or was she reading too much into this?

Maybe it was nothing furtive at all.

Maybe it was all innocent, Beth either sympathizing with Levi or possibly welcoming him back to the neighborhood. Hadn't she mentioned that Levi might return to the lake house? She could have spied his car and gone over to welcome him with champagne, kind of like she did with Harper a few days earlier—all "compliments of Alexander Realty." So what if there weren't chocolates or candles or a cheery basket involved? This could have been a spur-of-the-moment thing.

But it didn't seem so.

Craig had reached the stairs and was starting up. Quickly.

A cold feeling settled in her blood.

Her pulse had kicked up a notch.

Any second now . . .

And then Craig returned to the main floor, walked outside, and whistled sharply—Harper heard the quick blast. The dog. Harper had forgotten about him, but now he lifted his head, wagged his tail, and came bounding up the exterior steps to the deck.

Harper let out her breath. Didn't realize she'd been holding it.

And as she watched Craig, dog in tow, walk to the staircase again, she thought of Craig hiding a gun in the Hunt house not more than a week ago. And now this apparently clandestine meeting between Levi and Beth at the same house. She couldn't help but feel that something malevolent was going on, something she couldn't put her finger on, but something bad. Something very bad.

Chapter 43

For once, the house was quiet, thank God, even out here, in the garage.

Janet Collins unloaded the dryer, hauling towels and sheets into her basket. Afterward, she moved the load of jeans into the dryer, set the timer, and started the old Speed Queen tumbling again. It was loud, probably on its last legs, but for now, it had to work. God knew she couldn't afford a new one.

Carrying her basket, she headed up the three short steps into the kitchen. Her sons weren't home. Well, David had moved out and was working at a car wash in Northeast Portland while taking a few classes at the community college. Rory, now a rowdy senior in high school, was barely skimming through and was currently spending the next few days with his father.

Finally, peace and quiet!

Bliss!

She loved her kids, she reminded herself as she set her laundry basket on the kitchen counter, but she was sick to her back teeth of messy rooms, trash, and underwear left everywhere, and the fact that both of them, with their ravenous appetites, were bottomless pits. She figured she should have become a franchise owner at McDonald's. That would have been a helluva lot cheaper.

And the loud music! Enough with Michael Jackson, Guns N' Roses, and whoever else they were listening to. Well, to be fair, she'd cranked the bass up and listened for hours to Iron Butterfly's "In-A-Gadda-Da-Vida," back in the day. But she'd been stoned, of course, and hadn't changed her ways even when, before she'd moved out, her dad had yelled at her to turn down the phonograph because, "That god-damned hippie music makes my fillings vibrate!"

So maybe her kids were high, too. She hated to think that. But if they listened to the Doors or the Stones or Led Zeppelin for hea-ven's sake, that would be different. Besides, Jim Morrison, Robert Plant, and Mick Jagger? Oooh. Those men were gods!

Humming to herself, she put her ratty terry-cloth dish towels away and caught a glimpse of the video game console hooked up to her TV in the adjoining living room. Between MTV and all those damned video games, her kids were going to turn into zombies!

Worried about Rory, she wondered if she should give in and let him do what he always threatened and allow him to move in with his dad. She would give it about three days, a week at the most, before Rory came crawling back. And she'd let him. Of course she would. Unfortunately he reminded her of her own rebellious self in her late teens.

Lately, because she'd seen in a local news broadcast that Chase's mother had died on a flaming boat on the lake and that there was banter about some of the cold cases surrounding Lake Twilight being reopened, her thoughts had turned to those crazy days of her youth, where everything revolved around the whole peace, love, dove phrase. Back then she protested the war. She hated the establishment. She didn't trust the entire military industrial complex. She took a bus to Washington, D.C. and demonstrated after Martin Luther King was as-sassinated. Later she participated in Earth Day and joined an antiwar sit-in and burned her bra for women's rights, for God's sake. Looking back, some of that time in her life was a blur, some happening before she'd moved onto the lake, some after she moved away from Alms-ville.

But it was all a part of her identity, from the fury of the race riots to the serenity of the sit-ins.

Now, though, she had to admit, she'd been high a lot of the time or making candles or love bead jewelry or screwing her brains out.

Blushing, she remembered one night in particular when Chase had stopped by and she'd been involved with him and Charla, a threesome that had blown his mind. Chase had been an animal. An all-star athlete who could go for hours. But of course back in her "Moonbeam" days, she had no trouble keeping up with him. That had been a long time ago, when her hair had been long, her hips slim, her waist tiny, and her breasts not daring to sag.

Humming "We Shall Overcome," she pulled out a huge king-sized fitted sheet from the basket. Lord, she hated trying to fold these things. As she struggled with the sheet and caught the reflection of her middle-aged self in the plate glass window over the kitchen table, she remembered the events of the night Chase had gone missing. Everyone who lived in the house had split after a quick visit from the cops.

She, Moonbeam in those days, had been out on the covered deck, smoking a joint, staring across the water, listening to the rain gurgling in the gutters of the little house. She'd found a pair of small army grade binoculars on the railing where Trick had left them, probably by mistake. He loved to use them and spy on the houses nearby. Ronnie had accused him of blackmailing the people he spied upon, but Trick, as usual, blew him off.

That night, high on grass, she peered through the binoculars, focusing on that big house on the island. The curtains were open, and she noticed a blinking light in one of the upper windows. It went on for a few seconds, then stopped. Rhythmically, almost to the beat of a song that ran through her brain. It was kinda cool. As the mansion had grown dark again, she was about to turn away. But then the blinking started up again. Cool. But the house went dark. She kept watching and smoking.

She was just about to put down the field glasses when she spied a shadow outside the big house, like someone hurrying to the stairs that cut down the face of the island to the dock, near what looked like a cave but, Trick had informed her, was actually a boathouse. It was dark and misting so hard it was difficult to see. On top of that she was feeling the marijuana kicking in. Nonetheless, it sure looked like someone was now on the dock and wrestling with something large—maybe a kayak or a canoe. Crazy!

She caught another light and movement in the house, on a lower level. Most likely in the room that Trick had told her was the old lady's bedroom where the shadowy figure of someone was moving throughout the room. "Nothing goin' on in there," he'd confided when he'd told her about the mansion a few weeks ago. "That's the old lady's bedroom, and she's a wrinkled old prune, let me tell you. I bet she's dry as a bone inside. Probably farts dust."

"That's crude," Moonbeam had countered. "And cruel." Sometimes—make that often times—Trick's crassness really got under her skin.

"Just tellin' it like it is." He'd been standing on the deck with her, his glasses fogging a bit, the scarf holding his hair in place slipping.

"And how would you know?" she'd asked, bothered.

"Oh, I have my ways." His smile had been smug, not hidden by his beard.

"You've been there?"

"Maybe." But his sly grin had confirmed the obvious.

"But how?"

"My secret," he'd said, so proud of himself. "My 'tricks,' you know." He'd made air quotes and laughed. "You should see inside," he'd said. "So many places to get lost. So many places to hide. So many treasures to lift."

"You stole from them?"

"Moi?" he'd intoned, his eyebrows raising over the round rims of his glasses as he motioned to his chest and feigned affront. "Never!"

Man, she'd wanted to slap that self-satisfied smile off his face. And she knew he'd been lying. Trick was capable of just about anything if money was involved.

And looking through the binoculars this night, she wondered if she was even focusing on the right room.

Still trying to figure out what she was viewing on the island, she heard a door opening behind her. She turned to see Ronnie stepping onto the covered area. "Hey, Moon . . . wanna go for a ride?" He offered her a tab, and she dropped acid. And that was that. *Everything got a lot more fuzzy after that*, she thought now, as she gave up on folding the sheet neatly and picked up a pillowcase.

She did remember the cops, though. Down the street they'd roared. Screaming sirens. Flashing lights.

Panic had ensued.

Someone came—Jesus, had it been a policeman?—and told them to get the hell out.

They all did. In one big hurry. Scrambling away, not bothering with some of their things. Only staying long enough to say, "I didn't see anything," to the other officer who stopped by before they tore out.

It seemed surreal now, but through her haze she had recognized them. Weren't they the cops who lived down the street?

"But you're no longer a tripped-out flower child," she said aloud. Nope. Now she was a mother, with sons of her own. And a new respect for the law. As a kid all she wanted to do was avoid trouble, save her own skin, but now . . . should she call the police? Tell them what she knew? Her memories were foggy at best, drugged. And maybe it was unimportant now, wouldn't make a difference. She'd had feelings of guilt ever since she'd fled the house that night, been conflicted over the years, more so once she became a mother. She bit her lip and couldn't shake the feeling that she should make an old wrong right.

Probably because of the tragedy the other night. Chase's mother on that burning craft? There certainly was no connection.

Nonetheless, telling what she knew was probably the right thing to do.

She was a mother trying to set a good example for her two sons who seemed hell-bent to mess up their lives. "Do it," she told herself.

Then she dialed information, rather than 9-1-1, and asked for the detective division of the Almsville police where she was instructed to dial the emergency number for immediate assistance or leave a message. She opted for the voice mail and was surprised to hear a man's voice that identified himself as Detective Watkins.

Wasn't that the name of one of the cops down the street when she'd lived on Fox Point? One she'd seen that night? She froze for a second, her resolve crumbling a bit before she bolstered herself. She left her name and number, and a longer message than she'd intended. Then she figured she'd done her civic duty for the day. Now it was her free time. She placed the folded laundry back in the basket and carried the sheets to the bedroom.

Humming again, Janet wondered if what she witnessed that night, or what she *thought* she witnessed would be of value now. Probably not. She'd been drug-impaired. Make that *very* drug-impaired. And she'd have to admit that painful fact.

She scowled. If either of her boys ever used LSD or anything stronger than weed, as they referred to it now, she'd kill him.

After putting the sheets in the closet, she walked into the kitchen again. She found a half-full bottle of Merlot on the counter, the bottle she'd opened just last night after learning she was getting a raise. She'd celebrated alone and hadn't wanted to kill the bottle. Which worked out well for tonight. "Time for a nightcap," she told herself as she poured herself a healthy glass and took a long, smooth sip.

Perfect.

Kicking off her shoes, she headed for the pantry and grabbed a box of Cheez-Its on a low shelf from the back of the pantry where she'd hidden them from her tall sons who didn't seem to have the brains to bend over and look on the bottom shelf. She planned to settle down and watch a show or two she had taped on the VCR. As she headed to the living room, she took another long swallow, felt the wine begin to mellow her out, and smiled to herself. She'd snagged the VCR along with the king bed and an imported duvet in the divorce, despite her ex's complaints. "Too bad, Jeff," she said to the empty house. She had episodes of *Roseanne* and *L.A. Law,* along with her favorite guilty pleasure, *Days of Our Lives,* which she could never watch during the day as she worked as a Girl Friday at Ole Olsen's Used Cars on Eighty-second Avenue in East Portland.

Tonight was all hers, and she only hoped that the gods of storytelling had beefed up Bo and Hope's storyline in *Days.* That couple was her favorite, and they put Felicia and Frisco of *General Hospital* to shame. Not that Janet didn't tune into *GH* when she had the chance.

Before she could sit down, she heard the dryer's timer buzz. It seemed early, but it would be best to get her son's battered Levis out now. Leaving her wine and crackers on a side table with the VCR cued up, she snagged her empty basket from the bedroom, then walked through the house to the garage and reached for the light switch.

Click.

Nothing happened.

No sizzle and wavering illumination from the aging fluorescents.

Damn it, the bulbs had burned out again!

How many times had she asked Jeff to fix the lights?

Or better yet replace them?

Well, that was then, when she was still married. This is now. She'd do it herself tomorrow, though she found it odd that all the tubes had burned out at once.

Just her luck!

She could still see, at least a little bit. Light from the inside of the house seeped past her and reflected off her car, parked on the far side. Also she knew this little ranch house like the back of her hand, as she'd lived here for the past fifteen years.

Three steps down to the garage where the washer and dryer were nestled together in a back corner next to the utility sink.

She took one step down.

And then the toe of her shoe caught.

She tripped!

Tumbled!

Flailed wildly, her empty laundry basket flying out of her hands to skid across the oil-stained floor where her ex had parked his pickup during their marriage.

She caught herself barely, then her foot hit the rake that had fallen over the second step.

"Wha—?"

She lost her balance and the rake clattered noisily away.

This time she couldn't catch herself.

She fell, face down, on the dirty concrete.

Bam!

Her head hit.

Face-first.

The cartilage in her nose crunching.

Pain exploded in her face.

Blood gushed from her nose.

The world swam in a wash of pain and she cried out.

Tried to get her bearings.

Stunned, she blinked. Tried to focus in the darkness.

What the hell had happened? The stairs had been clear earlier, and no one was home, and . . . and she couldn't think. Her heart was pounding in her ears. Blood was running down her face, salty and warm on her lips. And the pain already throbbed.

"Ooh," she groaned, trying to get her bearings and mentally chastising herself for being such a klutz. She needed to get up, go into the bathroom, clean her wounds, and survey the damage. When was the last time she had a tetanus shot? Did she have any antiseptic? Neosporin?

So much for her cozy night alone with a glass of wine in front of the television.

Testing her arms, she started to push herself upright but paused.

Did she hear an unlikely noise?

The sound of rapid footfalls?

But she was alone. Maybe it was just the fact that she'd had her bell rung—Geez, she might really be concussed. She had to get up and—

Strong hands clamped over her shoulders.

"Hey!" she cried.

From the corner of her eye, she caught a glimpse of her attacker. Someone all in black.

"Stop it!" she sputtered. "Who the hell are you?" She struggled, twisted, throwing punches, kicking wildly. But the man was strong. "Let me go!" Jesus God, he meant to hurt her, or kill her or—

She screamed as loud as she could. Loud enough to wake the dead.

"Stop that!" he commanded gruffly.

But she didn't. He placed a gloved hand to shut her up, and she bit with all she had. Tasting the leather. Cutting through. Her incisors meeting flesh. Sinking deep enough that she gagged.

He yowled, his grip releasing, and she squirmed, trying to get away, now on her hands and knees. But he snagged a hank of her hair and twisted it while she screamed and writhed and kicked.

"You always were a bitch," he growled, wrestling her down, face first.

She knew that voice, she thought wildly, thrashing and still wrestling frantically to get free.

But his weight on her back forced her down.

She bucked.

To no avail. With his handful of hair, he drew her head back and then, with one forceful shove, slammed her face onto the concrete edge of the step.

Bang.

Pain burst behind her eyes.

Her body convulsed.

She tried to scream again but only managed to gasp and drag in air.

Her voice wouldn't work, her vision distorted.

The world began to disappear in the darkness.

She felt him, breathing hard, climbing off of her back. From the corner of one bleary eye, she saw him bending over her, his wavering silhouette caught in the light from the open kitchen door and strangely familiar. And then as he lifted her head once more, intent on banging her face against the cement, everything went black.

Chapter 44

Something moved.

Harper's eyes flew open.

She was lying in her makeshift bed and told herself she'd imagined it.

But, no, she sensed air moving when it should be still.

That's crazy. You double-checked the doors and windows. Points of a star—remember.

She turned on the bedside light.

There was nothing . . .

She had gotten the locks changed. No one could get in.

And then she felt it again, a movement. A disturbance in the air. Something very wrong.

Slowly, she climbed out of bed and grabbed the knife lying on the bed beside her but left the crucifix and scissors. She needed one hand free.

Carefully she opened the door to her room and felt it again, the change in the atmosphere. The hackles of her neck raised. What was wrong with her? She eased into the hallway, and yes, there was definitely a breeze, cold and shifting.

Shit!

She flipped on the switch for the staircase. The light was dim, but she saw nothing. Barefoot, one step at a time, she descended, her heart pounding, her fingers in a death grip over the hilt of the hunting knife.

Pausing at the landing, she listened.

No footsteps.

No heavy breathing.

Nothing but the weird whirring sound that came and went. A few moments and then a pause.

Mechanical?

She didn't think so.

On the main floor, she hesitated at the landing of the staircase, where it split in the foyer.

Nothing.

But the cool air. Where was it coming from?

Silently gripping the knife, she padded down the remaining steps and turned back toward the parlor but stopped as she passed the doorway to the kitchen, where she flipped on the overhead lights.

And discovered the side door ajar, cool air seeping in.

What the hell?

She crossed the cold tile floor and examined the dead bolt.

Unlocked. She tried it, and it functioned perfectly.

So had she not shut the door and twisted the lock, but no—she usually tried the door after she locked it. Just to make certain it was secure.

Had she?

Or had alcohol impaired her judgment?

She hadn't been drunk, but . . .

"Damn it all." She locked the door and double-checked the others. All locked. Satisfied that the house was as secure as she could get it, she started up the stairs, then heard the whizzing sound again.

"What?" she said, whipping around to eye the foyer just as a bat swooped down from the ceiling. She let out a startled scream. No. No, no, no!

Now what?

It flew up the stairs, and her heart sank. "No. Oh God." Quickly she rushed back to the kitchen, found a broom in the closet near the pantry, and eyes turned upward, flew up the stairs. She was moving fast and felt a twinge in her hip but ignored it.

The bat, of course, was nowhere to be seen. She paused at the second level, breathing hard, straining to listen. Dear God, there could be a million places for it to roost and hide, and as long as those spots were *not* in her bedroom, she would be alright. Except that her door was off its hinges a bit and bats, like mice, could slip through the tiniest of openings.

"Where are you?" she whispered and realized she was now holding a broom as a weapon and she'd left the knife in the kitchen—not that the blade would do any good against a bat, but she'd have to retrieve it.

After she'd dealt with the irritating flying pest.

She eyed the ceiling and in the dim light caught sight of a myriad of spots where it could conceal itself. Through the bedrooms and bathrooms on the second floor and then she heard the whirring again. In the hallway. She dashed out to see the thing fly upward to the third story and her bedroom. "No," she cried, as if she could control it. "Don't you dare."

Armed with the broom, she mounted the stairs and eyed the hallway. All the doors to the servants' quarters were closed tight, and sure enough, she heard the distinctive sound of the bat's wings as it flew in dizzying circles around the ceiling. "You can't stay here," she said. "No way."

But right now, there it was, flying as high as it could, in frantic circles.

Remember, it's more scared than you. It wants out as badly as you want it gone.

Heart pounding, adrenaline screaming through her bloodstream, she left the door open and mounted the stairs to the turret room at the top of the manor. Once inside, she went straight to the window farthest from the desk. She slid it open, feeling a rush of night air, then yanked out the screen and hoped to heaven that the damned bat would find its way out.

Setting her jaw, she made her way back to her room.

Silence.

"Where are you?" she whispered, and though it was against her most basic instincts, she turned out the lights and stepped into the hallway. "Come on, come on," she urged, though why she was talking to a bat made no sense at all. She didn't really fear them, but their quickness and the way they darted startled her, put her nerves on edge. And there was rabies to consider. If it decided to attack, which it wouldn't. Still, either the bat found its way outside or she would have to trap it, maybe kill it.

Where was the cat when she needed him?

Not that he'd ever caught a mouse, much less a flying bat.

But she couldn't think of Jinx right now. And she wanted the bat to take off, fly away, it didn't need to die.

She waited.

Nothing.

The seconds turned into minutes.

Why was the damned thing quiet now?

"Just leave," she mouthed.

Maybe it could sense her. Smell her or use echolocation? She had to move, to let the damn thing fly out of her room and hopefully up the stairs and out the window. Otherwise she would have to actually trap it or kill it.

She left the upstairs dark and went to the main floor, where she poured herself a drink. One surely wouldn't hurt, especially since her very last nerve was frayed.

She waited.

Ten minutes.

Fifteen.

Finally, at nearly half an hour, broom in hand, she mounted the stairs again and stopped at her room. Turned on the light.

Nothing.

She scoured the room with her eyes and waited, her gaze moving over all the nooks and crannies near the ceiling and saw no evidence of the bat. Relief! Then she checked her bed.

Her sleeping bag was unzipped and she tossed it, half expecting a tiny winged beast to fly into her face.

Didn't happen.

She was breathing hard, nervous as hell, certain the damned thing would fly out.

But nothing.

O—kay.

Maybe—just maybe—the room was clean.

Barely daring to hope and fingers clenched around the broom handle, she ascended to the top floor and her grandfather's refuge. Heart knocking, she flipped on the light. "Please," she whispered as she shut the door and scanned the room.

Saw no little bat cowering in a corner or hiding on the doorjamb.

"Where are you?" she wondered.

At that second the bat darted from behind the ornate frame of a picture, diving down and flying crazily around the room.

"Get out!" she ordered and swung the broom upward. "Get out!"

The little bastard cut past her, soaring in a panic as she swatted at it. "Get out, get out . . . get *out!*" she cried, as frantic as the bat. Flailing with the broom, she hit a lamp. It teetered, then fell, shattering against the floor.

The bat swooped again.

Harper spun, twisting her hip, then stepping backward and feeling a shard of glass from the lamp pierce her foot. "Shit!" she spat out but watched as the bat finally got the message and flew out the window and into the night. Quickly she hobbled across the room and slammed the window shut. "Thank God," she whispered, sagging against the sill and spying the splotches of blood she'd trailed across the old carpet. "Great."

At least the stubborn little creature was gone.

She only hoped he didn't have friends in the house.

Down the stairs she hitched, stopping off at the bathroom and opening the medicine chest she found the tin of Band-Aids, circa 1965. She picked out the small fragment of glass from her heel, cleaned the cut as best she could, dried it, and slapped two plastic strips over the wound.

Good enough for one in the morning.

Then, too hyped up to sleep, she limped her way down the stairs to the liquor cabinet and poured herself another drink. Just a short one. To steady her frayed nerves.

As she poured the last of the vodka into a glass, she told herself that she'd have to refresh the supply soon.

But tonight . . .

She took a long swallow of her drink and felt the alcohol warm her stomach as she made her way to the telescope in the parlor. It was late, probably no one was awake, and yet she couldn't help but peer through the eyepiece to observe the lives of the people across the lake. Visibility was hampered by the mist that crawled across the black water, but she fiddled with the focus and was able to bring the homes on Fox Point into some kind of clarity.

Most of the houses were dark, she noted. Only the Watkins' A-frame was illuminated at the very peak, where the triangular window offered a view of the loft and the desk where she'd seen Rand work before.

He was at his desk again, and she had to remind herself that he was the enemy. He thought her capable of murdering her grandmother and knowing about Chase's whereabouts. Didn't he remember that she and Levi had come to him that night to ask about Chase? Did he think it all part of some elaborate ruse she'd concocted at eighteen? An act?

"Who cares?" she said aloud, taking a sip. She watched as Rand stood and stretched, rotating his muscles and twisting his neck as if hours in the desk chair had cramped his muscles. Well, good. Fine. Harper hoped he ached all over. Unable to turn away, she observed him walking out of the loft to disappear, presumably going downstairs.

She focused on the lower level, but it remained dark.

About to give up, she took a final swallow of her drink and noticed a shadow. On his dock. Near his boathouse.

She leaned in closer as he disappeared inside the boathouse. A few minutes later his boat slipped onto the dark waters of the lake.

"Where are you going?" she wondered aloud as the boat, running lights visible, moved slowly around the point, then made a wide arcing turn to cross the lake and cruise toward the island.

He's coming here?

No.

Why? The muscles in the back of her neck tightened. This wasn't good.

They'd left on such harsh terms, she challenging him to arrest her and calling him a liar. "Not smart," she reminded herself. "Not smart at all."

And still she kept her eye on the boat as it slowed near her dock. She no longer needed the telescopic lens to watch as the boat crawled, slowly circling the island as if he were trawling for something.

Why?

From this vantage point she couldn't see the boat as it moved closer to the mainland and under the bridge, but she could hear the churn of its engine.

"What're you doing?" she whispered and hurried, wincing, into the kitchen, but the view of the water was obscured by trees, so she entered Gram's shadowy room and waited, pushing the sheer curtains aside and counting off the seconds. When he didn't appear, she imagined him stopping . . . but why? Of course there was the myriad of paths that crisscrossed the island, but they were overgrown and steep and rarely used these days. Besides, there was no reason for him to get out of his boat and climb the rocky cliffs. She strained to listen, wondering if she heard the sound of an idling boat engine, or was it just her imagination?

Time to find out.

She wasn't about to hide up here and peek out of windows.

She found a flashlight and walked back through the house just as the prow of the boat appeared.

Good.

May as well have it out.

She wasn't going to cower here in her own damn home.

He might be a detective, but he was Rand Watkins and she'd known him most of his life.

But she thought of the dolls with their weird message.

And she remembered how he'd stared at her during the interrogation, how his mistrust for her was evident.

And she knew that he was looking into her grandmother's death again.

So what?

She had nothing to hide!

She should confront him. Ask him what he wanted. Invite him in for a drink. See how he'd like that!

You'd be dancing with the devil, she heard her grandmother say.

Too bad. She wasn't going to be a wuss about it. If Rand had something to say to her, something he wanted to see at the house, then fine. Flashlight in hand, she walked to the French doors off the living room, and as she stepped onto the terrace she caught sight of his navigation lights, heard the purr of the boat's engine fading. He was already leaving.

"Hey!" she yelled, swinging the flashlight. "Hey! Rand!"

He kept motoring.

"Detective!" she screamed.

To no avail.

Well, fine.

"And good riddance," she added, not wanting to examine why he bothered her so much. It was more than the fact that he was looking into her grandmother's case or that he'd once been Chase's best friend. Something deeper. And something she didn't want to consider.

She went back inside, had one last drink, and was a little wobbly as she climbed the stairs to her room, then glanced up at the stairway to the turret room. She should clean up the mess from the broken lamp. At least sweep up the sharp pieces. She could find a hand vacuum and clean the rest tomorrow.

The broom was already in the room, so she trudged up the remaining flight, put the shade and base on the chaise, and began sweeping the big shards into a trash can.

She was just about finished when she noticed one piece of glass winking from beneath the skirting of the chaise longue. Bending down to reach it, she used the bristles of the broom to pull the jagged piece out of its resting place and peered beneath the fringe.

And stared into deep, black eye sockets.

She let out a gasp and scooted away.

Before she realized she was looking at the remains of a crouching skeletal cat.

"Oh God. Jinx," she whispered, her heart cracking, her insides shredding. Tears touched the back of her eyes. Her stomach turned over.

Dear God, who would—

Wait.

Something was off.

She looked again into those black eye sockets set deep in bone.

Barely any flesh on the graying bones.

Only a few thin tufts of fur.

No rotting smell.

Jinx had only been missing a week, and no way would he be this decomposed. No. Not at all.

Gritting her teeth and forcing back the urge to throw up, she forced herself to use the broom and drag the bones out from under the chaise. Her stomach turned over again when she saw the bits of orange fur. No, this wasn't Jinx, her black and white tuxedo cat. This long-dead feline was probably Earline, her grandmother's one-eared yellow tabby long buried in the rose garden/cat cemetery in the front of the house, across from the garage. The bones were dirty and gray, and there were a few fir needles caught between the cat's ribs.

"You sicko."

She rocked back on her heels, felt a bit of pain where she'd cut her foot, but stared at the skeleton and wondered who the hell had left it here.

Whoever he was, he was upping his game, trying to terrorize her.

"Bring it on," Harper said under her breath, her fear having morphed into a new, growing anger. Her blood, which had turned ice cold at the sight of the dead cat, was now running white hot.

She threw the broom across the room in frustration. It landed with a thump against the floor. She was tired of all this idiocy, sick of running through her house, *her* damned house, like a frightened schoolgirl.

No longer, she silently vowed.

She stood and kicked at a remaining shard of glass.

Dead cats.

Dolls with cryptic messages that moved around.

Bats flying through the house, probably let in by the same twisted loser who thought a dead cat would be a funny joke.

Does he have Jinx? she wondered, fear jabbing at her again. How else would he have left the collar on the doll? Next time, would she be dragging Jinx's remains from beneath a bed or table or whatever?

She felt a new fear and steadfastly tamped it down. She'd deal with that when the time came, which, she hoped, was never.

Harper was sick and tired of it all.

She wasn't going to sit around and wait for some twisted son of a bitch to play another sick prank on her.

No way.

Next time, she'd be waiting.

Chapter 45

"I have a bone to pick with you," Rand said, irritated as he slapped a copy of *The Twilight Tribune* onto the table where Gunn was seated in the break room. Gunn was sipping coffee and picking at the remains of a cinnamon roll.

"About what?" Gunn looked up, then down at the front page of the newspaper with the headline: LOCAL WIDOW DIES IN MYSTERIOUS LAKE FIRE. "Oh."

"Yeah, 'Oh.'" Rand twisted a chair around and sat on it, leaning over the back. "I thought all this information was supposed to come from the chief. Either directly or indirectly. He's hired a public information officer, you know."

"Yeah, well, I didn't say anything that really wasn't public knowledge."

"It's my case. You could have checked with me."

Gunn had the decency to frown and nod. "Yeah, I guess, but that reporter? Rhonda? I knew her dad. We were on the same softball team back in the day, and she was just this awkward little kid who hung out. You know the kind I mean? She didn't seem to have any friends. Anyway, when she saw me at the auto parts store a couple of days ago and offered to buy me coffee, I thought, what the heck? She said she wanted to talk about Chase Hunt, and I didn't think that would hurt anything."

"No?"

"No." Gunn scowled. "I know he was your friend and all, but that case is colder than a witch's tit."

"Geez, Gunderson," his partner said, walking into the room and heading straight for the vending machines. "Do you always have to be so crass? Can't you just say 'cold as hell' like a normal human being?"

"Hell isn't cold! And fine." He rolled his eyes. "And the case is cold as hell. Anyway, she asked questions and I was glad to answer. I mean, it wouldn't hurt to have some public interest in the case."

"Cases." Rand thumped his finger on the paper. "She asked about Olivia Dixon."

"Well, yeah, it all happened on the same night." He lifted his shoulders in a what're-ya-gonna-do expression.

Rand felt the cords in his neck tighten as he thought about Harper and what would happen once she read the article. But he was overreacting. Something he seemed prone to do lately. "What you're gonna do, Gunn, is keep your mouth shut."

"And what you should do, Watkins, is look at the case like a real cop." Gunn glared up at him, the folds of his face growing taut.

"Meaning?"

"You're just like your old man."

That cut a little too close to the bone.

"I remember he didn't want anyone else involved in his cases." Gunderson shoved his plate aside as Brady fed change into the soda machine and the coins rattled down the slot.

She looked over her shoulder, took one glance at the situation, and snorted. "Put your foot into it again, didn't you, Gunn?" She withdrew a can of Diet Pepsi and walked to the table where she read the headline. "Oh. Geez."

Rand got out of his chair. "Occupational hazard."

"Hey, can you leave the paper?" she asked as she popped the top of her can. "Someone took the office copy."

Rand nodded. "Yeah, fine." He didn't need it. He'd seen enough.

"Suki," Gunn said.

"Suki?" Brady snapped up the copy with her free hand. "Suki took the paper?"

"Yep." Gunn dabbed at the last crumbs and bits of icing on his plate. "I think she takes copies of recipes or something."

"Well, it's the office copy. Meant for everyone."

"Except for the crossword," he suggested with a sly wink. "That's yours. You think you own it and go ballistic if anyone starts filling it in before you."

"Oh, give me a break."

Rand left them arguing as he tried to shake off his irritation about the article and Gunn's remarks about his father. He considered calling Rhonda Simms at the newspaper's offices and reading her the riot act but decided against any conversation with her until he cooled off.

Because the truth was, whether he wanted to admit it or not, what most concerned him about the article wasn't the department's reaction so much as Harper's. Simms couldn't compromise a case that was stone cold, at least he didn't think so. Well, unless she had Gunn's help.

He remembered Chase's plea the last night he'd seen his friend. "Just tell me you'll take care of her. Of Harper."

Which Rand hadn't. Despite his promise.

And now wasn't the time to start. Not that she would allow it, as evidenced by her response during her interview here at the station and how angry she'd become. Hell, she'd shut off his recorder and dared him to arrest her. And then there was last night, when he couldn't sleep and had taken the boat out, steering close to the island, circling it, and remembering how many times he'd done the same as a teenager. Maybe he should have docked and gone up and pounded on the door, had a real conversation with her. But he hadn't. He'd hoped that getting on the water, being close to the island and the nexus of all that had happened, would make things clearer. He'd been wrong. He should've gone for a run. A long run.

"Fuck it," he said under his breath, then made his way downstairs to the windowless evidence room where he double-checked the records on the missing gun in the Evan Reed suicide case. He ended up spinning his wheels. Just as Chelle had said, there were no records, no card indicating who had last handled the evidence or ever looked through the locker.

Another dead end.

The officer in charge, Alicia Jefferson, had only been with the department for three years, and she could offer no explanation as she sat at her desk outside the locked door.

"Who knows when it could have happened?" Jefferson asked. She was a no-nonsense Black woman with half-glasses and big hoop earrings. "It's been over twenty years, hasn't it? 1967? And the way I understand it, things were pretty loose in the department back then. No cameras. It just wasn't a thing. People came and went as they pleased."

"Not people," Rand corrected. "Police officers. And they were supposed to sign in and out."

She looked at him over the tops of her reading glasses. "That's the operative word, isn't it? 'Supposed' to. I'm just tellin' you, not everyone goes by the book."

"And no one noticed the sign-out card was missing?"

"No one cared until just a few days ago." She leaned back in her chair and eyed him. "Your partner, Detective Brown? She came down here a few days ago. Didn't she tell you about the missing gun and card and all?"

"That's why I'm here."

Her eyebrows raised. "Double-checking?" Before he could answer, she shook her head, dark eyes serious. "Don't you trust her?"

"Of course."

"Then why are you all down here? If she told you, believe her. That Chelle? Detective Brown? She's one smart cookie."

"I know."

"Then?"

"Fine. Got it," he said, taking the stairs up to the main floor. It wasn't that he didn't trust Chelle. Sure, she was green, but smart as all get-out. It was just that the cases involving the entire Reed/Dixon clan were like a spiderweb, woven together, and when you touched one silken thread it pulled on another. The deaths in the family were years apart but all out of the ordinary, accidents in one way or another.

Or so it seemed.

He, like his partner, was starting to wonder about that.

Then there were the Hunts.

Three people gone.

All tragically.

All on the lake.

Coincidence?

He was beginning to think not.

Back in his office, he shuffled some papers, placed a couple of calls, and waited for Chelle to return. She'd been at the hospital, checking records and talking to the staff about Cynthia Hunt's death.

Within the hour Chelle returned, slipped off her jacket, and before she could settle down, pressed a fingertip to the soil in one of her plotted plants. "Oh damn." She left the room again and returned with one of the lunchroom carafes, then began drizzling water over the plants on the corner of her desk as well as those with trailing vines lined up on the windowsill.

"What did you find out?" he asked.

"I double-checked the hospital records on Cynthia Hunt and talked to several people on the staff. Everything seemed to be just as reported. A mess-up in that she died in the hallway, but nothing suspicious. At least that's the general consensus."

"Okay, good."

"And . . . I've got an *address* for Camille Musgrave. She and her husband, Victor, owned the rental house where all the students lived when Chase Hunt went missing."

"I thought you were looking for Matilda Burroughs," Rand said. After they'd decided to take another look into Olivia Dixon's death and Chase Hunt's disappearance, they had split up the work.

Chelle nodded, setting the carafe on a vacant corner of her desk. "I'll get to that. But first the Musgraves. I found out that Camille and Victor originally moved up to the Seattle area. Well, Bellevue to be precise. Victor died a few years ago, and Camille is now living back in Oregon, in Aloha, with her daughter, Lynette, and her family. I'm going out there later today.

"As for Matilda Burroughs, Olivia Dixon's caretaker, who had the night off when the older woman died? She still lives in Calgary. I tried calling her earlier and left a message. If I don't hear back from her in the next hour or so, I'll try again. Oh crap!" She noticed one of the pots was leaking, a trail of dirty water running down the window ledge and wall. In one quick movement she grabbed another tissue and leaped up to stem the flow. "Damn it all."

She was still blotting the drizzle as Rand said, "I'm on my way to see the officer in charge of these cases back then."

Chelle glanced over her shoulder. "Your dad."

He nodded.

"Need company?" She wadded up the tissue and tossed it into a nearby wastebasket.

"I think I should handle this one myself."

"If you say so."

"I do. See ya later." Chelle was still grumbling to herself as she found another tissue and started swabbing the windowsill.

Rand started down the hall only to sidestep Chuck Fellows lumbering in the opposite direction. In Chuck's wake was a twenty-something man, thin as a rail, three days' growth of beard covering his jaw, eyes wide, pupils dilated, stocking cap pulled low over his ears. His flannel jacket was unbuttoned, beneath which Rand noticed a faded T-shirt printed with *Go Ahead, Make My Day!* Scratch marks were apparent on his cheeks, and his wrists were cuffed, no shackles on his legs. Despite the fact that Fellows was strong-arming him down the hall to the booking area, he shuffled as if he could barely move.

"I didn't do nothin'," the cuffed guy protested, the smells of alcohol, cigarette smoke, and sweat permeating from him.

"Yeah, yeah, I know. Just like you never do." As they passed Rand, Fellows grabbed the guy by the elbow to shuffle him along and muttered under his breath, "I'm gettin' too old for this."

"I swear, she was lyin'!" the guy argued. "You know she's a liar! You know it!"

"What I know is that she has a restraining order. Jesus, Curtis, just shut up, would ya? You know the drill. You'll get your chance to talk."

"I want my attorney," Curtis insisted.

"On his way."

"*Her* way! I got a woman this time!"

"Fine, fine, then she's been notified." A door opened and closed with a thud, and the rest of the conversation was cut off.

Rand stopped at his locker for his sidearm, though he told himself he didn't need it; he was interviewing his dad, for God's sake. He packed the Glock anyway.

When he left, it was raining, hard enough that he had to flip his wipers on once he started driving. He hadn't told his father he was coming, wanted to see Gerald's reaction face to face.

Even with the rain beginning to sheet and traffic snarling, Rand made it to his father's duplex in less than half an hour. He and his wife, Dorie, lived on a golf course in Oregon City, and when Rand knocked on the door, his latest stepmother answered. She was a bit of a thing, less than a dozen years older than Rand, her oversized glasses and curling blond hair reminiscent of Charlie, the love interest in *Top Gun.*

"Rand," she said with a wide grin as he stood dripping on the porch. "Come on in!" She held the door open.

"Is Dad here?"

"No, he's golfing at the country club." Then she looked past Rand to the wet day beyond, where rain was pounding the brick walk. "Well, he was, it's his regular day, you know, the morning men's group, but I don't know with this weather. He's probably playing cards. Most of the time he's an all-weather golfer, but this is pretty bad." She turned her head to look up at the gray clouds. "He's usually back by one or one-thirty." She teetered one hand to indicate maybe less, maybe more.

"Maybe I'll catch him there."

"Or you could wait if you want." She was stepping aside, allowing him into the living room where the television was tuned to some game show and the paper lay open on a side table, the front page headlines visible from the porch.

"Thanks. Another time." He couldn't imagine trying to make small talk with Dorie, nor did he want to discuss what he planned to ask his father in front of the third Mrs. Gerald Watkins.

"Do you want me to give him a message, in case you don't connect with him?"

"No. I'll call." With a wave, he turned back to his Jeep.

As he slid inside, the words Chuck Fellows's prisoner had shouted sliced through his mind. "She's a liar. You know it."

Lies, that's what these cases always were about, and he knew, deep in his gut, that his father was lying. Or covering up. The notes on Chase's disappearance and Olivia Dixon's death weren't up to Gerald Watkins's usual clear, concise, and complete standard. No, something had been off. And it was more than the fact that his best friend's son had gone missing.

But who would know?

How could Rand prove it?

Confront his father?

That was his plan, but now, thinking about it, he decided he needed a little more ammunition, and he knew where he might find it.

Chapter 46

It looked like his mother was home.

Rand parked in the driveway behind her yellow AMC Pacer with a Reagan bumper sticker from the last presidential election still proudly displayed. Probably Kent's doing. Kent's influence on Rand's mother was ever-present.

When Rand knocked on the door, his mother answered. "Rand?" she said, obviously surprised, "I didn't expect you, but come in, come in." She stepped out of the doorway and let him pass into the living area, which smelled of lemon oil and furniture polish. "I can offer you a cup of coffee, unless you'd like something else. All we have is Diet Coke and Fresca, I think. Kent's death on anything with sugar. Claims it's bad for your teeth, and he should know, right?" She was heading for the kitchen.

"Coffee's fine," he said, following her through an immaculate house with modern furniture, long low couches, and chairs situated around a round teak coffee table. Probably twenty or so years old and still looking new. The art on the walls was original, all splashy modern pieces.

In the kitchen, she poured two large cups of coffee and motioned for him to sit at a white Formica-topped table. It was situated in front of a sliding glass door that looked out to a small yard where several bird feeders were surrounded by towering arborvitae and shrubs, most notably the heavy-blossomed hydrangeas with their fading blooms. "You still drink it black?"

"Right."

She placed the cups on the table, then sat across from him. "Well, this is a nice surprise," she said, smiling over the rim of her cup. Her hair was blond and cut in a short curly shag. She was still trim and fit, a dedicated Jazzercise enthusiast, now wearing acid-washed jeans and a coral sweater with wide shoulders that narrowed to her waist. "I thought you would be working."

"I am," he said.

"So this isn't just a friendly drop by." Her eyebrows arched.

"Afraid not this time." He glanced around the room. "Is Kent here?"

"At work, but only a half day. He has tennis and a massage later. Why?"

"Just asking," he said, sipping from his cup. "You know about Cynthia Hunt, right?"

"Oh, dear, yes. The poor thing." Barbara set her cup down. "A tortured soul."

"Right."

"You're looking into what happened?"

"That and a few other things."

"Like what?" she asked, and she played with her wedding ring, a nervous habit he remembered from the years when she was still living at Fox Point, still married to his father.

"Let's start with the night Chase Hunt disappeared," he said, and she looked away sharply, to the window where a hummingbird was flitting around a hanging feeder.

"You remember?" he asked gently.

She swallowed. "Yes. Of course. Who wouldn't?"

"You came to the house. You said you wanted to say good-bye as I was shipping out."

"That's right." She returned her gaze to his. "But you weren't there."

No, he'd been out getting drunk as hell after his fight with his best friend and before Levi had shown up on the doorstep. "Did you talk to Dad?"

She paused. Her pale pink lips compressed.

"Mom?"

Barbara let out a tremulous sigh. "No, I didn't. He wasn't there, either."

"Where was he?"

"I don't know, he never said." She played with her cup, spinning it slowly in front of her on the table. "I thought he was there because his car was in the drive, but no one answered. So I walked around back, thinking he might be on the dock, you know, having a cigarette or something, but it seemed like the place was empty." She hesitated, and he waited her out. "I asked him about it later, and he said he'd gone for a walk, but . . ." She stopped twirling the cup.

"But what?"

"The boat," she said, biting her lip. "It wasn't in the boathouse. I looked, thinking that maybe, you know, he was working on it or something, but it wasn't there. He wasn't either. I thought maybe you'd taken it out or something." Her face had turned pale as death. "And then? Later? I heard that Chase Hunt was missing and Olivia Dixon had died because Harper had left her to meet Chase . . . oh, I don't know what I thought." She swallowed hard.

"Did you give a statement to the police?" he asked.

"No one ever asked."

"Because you didn't live on the lake any longer and no one knew you'd been at Dad's?" he guessed.

"And . . ." Once more, she looked out the window, but the hummingbird had flown off. "And I wanted to stay out of it. I didn't want to get anyone in trouble."

"So you never went to the station to make a statement."

She was shaking her head, fighting tears.

"And Dad never asked you anything."

"No." She sniffed and cleared her throat. "Kent told me to stay out of it, that it was none of our business." She pushed a curl behind her ear. "If your dad would have been suspended or called on the carpet, it would have been bad. For all of us . . ."

Rand's gut tightened.

She went on, "Gerry had a career, was a good cop."

Was he?

Always.

"But you didn't trust him," Rand accused.

"That worked two ways," she whispered, and Rand felt his gut churn, remembering their fights, the accusations, the anger and tears before they'd split up. He'd ended up with his father because Kent Eldridge hadn't been interested in a stepson. They'd tried it for a few months. It hadn't worked out.

"You get half of Dad's retirement," he said flatly.

"That had nothing to do with it!" she said, offended, but he remembered that Kent had been buying his practice at the time, so it was a possibility that the thought of a steady paycheck would have been tempting. He saw it on his mother's face. The shame.

Jesus.

"I've got to go," he said, scooting his chair back and standing. He'd learned what he needed to know.

"Oh. But . . ."

He saw the regret in her eyes as she walked him to the door. "I'm sorry," she said, touching him on the arm, and their gazes locked.

"For?"

"Everything."

His jaw grew rock hard, but he managed to say, "Yeah. Me, too."

And then he took off, striding through the drizzle to his Jeep.

Bothered, his thoughts moving in dark directions, he drove directly to Lynx Hills Country Club located south of the city. Set on rolling hills in a cleared area that had once been a forest of old-growth timber, the course offered views of the wide Willamette River beyond which the Cascade Mountains rose in the distance, though today their craggy snowcapped peaks were obscured by the low cloud cover.

He parked in one of the guest slots, dashed through the rain, and walked into the clubhouse. No one was manning the desk, and no golfers were visible through the floor-to-ceiling windows overlooking the course.

He found his father in the men's bar, a cozy room complete with a huge fireplace, views of the first tee, and a smattering of tables over an industrial-strength plaid carpet. Several men chatting about the Portland Trail Blazers basketball team were crowded over sandwiches and beers at the long bar that separated the kitchen from the card room.

He saw his father with three other men at one of the designated card tables. After asking for a card from the dealer, Gerald received it, frowned, tossed his hand down, and finished what remained in a short whiskey glass. "I fold," he said and glanced up just as Rand approached. "Deal me out."

He finished his drink and scooted back in his chair. He must've read the grim expression on his son's face because he motioned Rand away from the table where the game continued. "What's up?" he asked, stepping away from the table. "Did someone die?" Then before Rand could answer, Gerald guessed. "This is about Cynthia Hunt."

"To start with."

With a glance at the table where his friends were still playing cards, Gerald suggested, "Let's talk outside," then led Rand through a locker room to a side entrance.

They stood under the striped awning near the locker room, the wind buffeting them, the rain still coming down.

"A bad thing, that. The fire. Cynthia in the boat." Gerald shook his head. "A damned shame." Lighting a cigarette, he asked, "What's going on?"

"I'm looking through some old cases."

"Homicides?" He blew out a cloud of smoke and looked Rand in the eye. "Are there that many?"

"Not homicides. Not even cold cases. Just odd deaths that are connected."

"To Cynthia Hunt? I'm not following."

But Rand thought his old man was bluffing.

"I'm starting with Chase. He disappeared and was never found."

"And he probably never will be." His father shook his head. "It's a mystery, yeah, but it's long over. I don't know why you're dredging it all up again." He looked pained as he blew out a stream of smoke. "I saw the paper this morning. Some damned reporter thinks the public is interested in ancient history."

"Because Cynthia Hunt died a horrible death."

"Yeah, well." He sighed. "That? What happened to her? A shame." His dad drew deep on his Marlboro and shook his head. "A real shame. God rest her soul," he said in a cloud of smoke. "But she's gone now. Mucking around what happened twenty years ago isn't going to help anyone."

"Maybe Chase."

Gerald glanced up sharply. "You really think you're gonna find him?"

"I'm going to try."

"Well, it's a waste of time, if you ask me. If he was alive, and that's a mighty big if, don't you think he would've shown up by now? There's no more war to dodge, and yeah, he might have to straighten things out with the government, but I'd be willing to bet that if he was alive, he would've come home after his dad died." He squinted through his smoke. "Don't you think so?"

"I don't know what to think. I'm trying to keep an open mind," Rand said as he watched a sleek Porsche swing into the parking lot, its headlamps reflecting the driving rain. Seconds later, a man in rain gear climbed out and hurried toward the front door of the club-house.

"You probably knew better than anyone what was on Chase's mind," Gerald reminded Rand. "You saw him that night. The last person to see him as far as anyone knows."

Was there an unspoken question in that statement? An innuendo? Rand ignored it and plowed on. "There are also some other things we're looking into."

"Such as? What? Olivia Dixon's death?" Gerald guessed. "Because it happened on the same night? Is that what you're thinking?"

"Maybe."

"Oh hell no! She died because of a screwup. The granddaughter messed up her pills. But it wasn't intentional. You're not thinking she tried to kill Olivia."

Did he sound unsure?

"Well, that's one case." Rand waited, measuring his father's response.

"There's more?" Gerald sucked hard on his cigarette as rain peppered the awning and splashed on the asphalt of the parking lot.

"A lot of unexplained deaths in the family."

"The Reed family? Is that what you're talking about?" Gerald demanded. "Holy Kee-Rist, Rand, you know what happened! Evan got stupid, high on LSD, and decided to play Russian roulette. And as for Anna, you were there when we pulled her out of the drink. That whole family had a problem with drugs and alcohol, and they paid the price. Those cases are closed. Plain and simple." He took a final drag, then jabbed out his cigarette in a standing ashtray near the door.

"You and Tom were the lead investigators."

"Hell yeah, we were. We were the *only* investigators."

"Chase was the victim," Rand pointed out. "His father shouldn't have been involved in the case."

"The department wasn't what it is now. It was much smaller. We made do."

"Even so."

Gerald glared at his son. "What the fuck is this all about, Rand? Don't you have enough to do, trying to keep the peace? Protect and serve and all that? Why the hell are you doing this?"

Two men pushed open the door from the locker room. They were deep in conversation but glanced up. The bigger guy, in plaid pants and windbreaker, raised a hand. "See ya next week, Gerry."

"Yeah." Rand's father gave a chin-up nod. "Sure."

The other guy, skinnier and wearing rain gear, sketched a salute.

Then as the two men dashed to their cars, Gerald took hold of his son's arm and propelled him out of earshot. He pushed him under the canopy of branches of a huge fir tree where the smell of damp earth reached his nostrils. "Why don't you just let sleeping dogs lie?"

Rand yanked his arm from his father's punishing grasp. "Because they're not sleeping, Dad. Not only are they waking up, they're fucking barking."

"Then what? You came out here to . . . what're you saying here, boy?" But he'd already guessed. "That I didn't do my job? That Tom and I did what? Screwed up the investigations?" His eyes thinned to slits, his face was shadowed, all blades and angles deepened by the dim light coming from a few high windows of the locker room.

"I'm saying that we're taking another look."

"We're?" Gerald repeated, scrabbling in his pocket for his pack of cigarettes. "Who else is in on this, whatever the fuck it is?"

"My partner."

"That little slip of a thing?" He scoffed and lit up again, shooting a geyser of smoke from the side of his mouth. "Well, good luck!" Gerald said, disbelieving. "Tom and I, we did everything by the book."

"Did you?" Rand tossed out. "Because I'm not so sure."

Gerald pointed to the bulge beneath Rand's jacket. "Jesus, Rand, are you packin'? To talk to me? What the hell?"

"I talked to Mom."

Gerald was about to take a draw on his cigarette, but he stopped for a second, just long enough to confirm Rand's worst suspicions. "Oh, did ya?" his father said, as if it was no big deal. "How is she?"

"Clearheaded," Rand said, watching for the telltale tic near his father's eye, a pulsing throb that always appeared when he was agitated. So far, Gerald was calm. "She remembers. About the fact that you weren't home when Chase went missing. That the boat was gone."

"And—?"

No tic. "Levi told me that Tom and Chase got into it that night. Both of them tearing into each other. The fight got out of control."

His father took another drag as a gust of cold wind swept through the branches overhead, causing them to groan and sway. "Is there a point to this?"

"Cynthia left a note for Levi."

The tic appeared, a tiny pulse beside his father's left eye. "Is there a point to this?"

"The note said, 'They killed him. They killed Chase. Make him pay.'"

"Sounds like gibberish to me," Gerald said. "Doesn't make any sense. You know she'd lost her marbles."

"And when did that start? With Chase's disappearance?" Rand asked, every muscle in his body coiled. "Or with Tom's suicide?"

"Shit, son, where are you going with all of this?" Gerald was irritated. "You're pulling things out of thin air. You sound as batty as Cynthia was!"

"*They* killed him. Make *him* pay. As if the others involved in Chase's death were already gone."

"Jesus Christ, no one knows for certain that Chase is dead! I don't know what you're getting at, but this—what's happening here?—is lunacy!"

"Is it?" Rand asked, his insides churning, the truth slicing through him like a machete. "How about this, Dad? How about Chase and his old man have it out and Tom, he decides he can't have a kid who's a draft dodger, the golden boy tarnished beyond repair?" Rand was watching his father. Gerald was tense, the tic full blown now, his lips thin, his jaw tight, his cigarette forgotten and burning in his hand.

Somewhere nearby a crow cawed and flapped noisily. Rand kept his eyes trained on his father.

"You think Tom and I—we killed Chase, is that what you're getting at, boy?" His face was getting redder, his tic really going to town.

"Why don't you just tell me what happened that night. Right here and now!" Rand jabbed at the ground, furious. How many times had his father alluded to the fact that Rand might know more about what had happened to Chase when all along, it had been the other way around? "What the hell happened to Chase?"

Gerald didn't answer.

"Dad? It's time. What the fuck happened?"

"Shit if I know!" Gerald exploded, then took a long drag on his smoke, the ash falling off as he did. "It was so damned long ago."

But like yesterday.

"You weren't where you said you were. Mom knows. You were in the boat that night, not home. What the hell were you doing?"

Finally, he flicked his cigarette onto the ground where it sizzled out with the rain. He closed his eyes and let out his breath slowly, smoke seeping from his nostrils and mouth. "I'm gonna need an attorney."

"I'm your son. Chase's friend. Just tell me."

"You're a cop now, boy. So was I. And a good one. I know the routine. If you want to do this, then run me in and let me have my goddamned attorney." He drilled his son with disappointed, accusing eyes, then said, "And for the record, I didn't kill Chase. Of course I didn't. What the fuck are you thinking? We're done here!" He started walking away.

Rand grabbed the crook of his elbow and spun him around. "No, Dad, we're not done! Not by a long shot!"

Gerald's muscles tensed.

His fist clenched.

He hauled back.

Swung fast.

Feinting, Rand caught his father's wrist. With all his strength, he twisted up and backward, forcing Gerald's arm behind his shoulder.

"Fuck!" Gerald cocked his free arm ready to strike, but Rand increased the pressure on his father's wrist.

Gerald landed hard on his knees. "Jesus! What the hell do you think you're doing?" he said through teeth gritted in pain.

"Getting the truth."

"You'll be up on charges!"

Rand jerked his father's arm hard. He didn't care about any of the ramifications and deep down, there was satisfaction seeing his old man squirming on his knees, getting his khakis wet. How many times had Gerald Watkins taken a belt to him when he was just a kid? He gave the arm another yank, stretching tendons to the breaking point.

Gerald yowled.

Rand demanded, "Tell me what the fuck happened that night."

"I told you."

Another jerk, and this time he thought he heard something pop in his father's shoulder.

"Stop! Shit!" Gerald ordered.

"You tell me, right here and now, what the fuck happened to Chase," Rand ordered. "You know, damn it, and you covered it up for twenty damned years."

His father's face was turning white, pain etched in the lines near his mouth.

"And you kept insinuating I knew what happened," Rand charged. "When all along it was you!"

His father looked up at him and closed his eyes for what seemed an eternity, inwardly wrestling with his need for secrecy and the fact that his son was about to literally wring the truth from him.

"What the fuck happened?" Rand demanded.

Nothing.

"Twenty years is a damn long time to carry that secret. A burden. Give it up, Dad. Tell me, or I swear, I'll run you into the station, you know, the one that still has your picture on the wall?"

Something inside of Gerald Watkins broke.

Rand could feel it, the tension leaving Gerald's taut body, his pale face going slack.

Voices could be heard from inside the building, deep, raucous laughter exploded. "Fine," his father said, breathing hard. "But not here." His gaze found Rand's, eyes pleading. "This is . . . where I hang out. My friends are here."

"Then right now. At the house. You ride with me."

"My car is here."

"I'll bring you back."

His father gave a short nod, and Rand let go, Gerald standing and rubbing his arm. "You about popped my arm out of its socket."

"I think you'll be okay. Work it out."

His father glanced up sharply, remembering the words he'd always told his son when Rand had complained of an injury.

"Let's go. My Jeep's over here." Rand started walking to the parking lot.

"I'll drive myself," his father insisted. "What do you think I'm going to do? Run away? Fuck that." He scrabbled into his pocket for his crumpled pack of Marlboros.

"I'll follow you."

Rand warned, "Don't fuck with me."

"I said I'll follow you!" Gerald said in another burst of anger.

Rand decided to trust him. For now. Jamming his hands into his pockets, he jogged through the rain to his Cherokee and slid inside. As he started his Jeep, he knew he was stepping through a door that could never be closed again.

Well, so be it.

He shoved the gearshift into drive. As he pulled out of the parking space, Rand caught sight of his father, his features distorted through the rain-spackled windshield.

He wondered if he'd ever really known the man who had sired him.

No.

Not at all.

But he was about to find out.

Chapter 47

Rand stood, his back to the fire, his legs warming while his dad sat on the couch, a cigarette burning in an ashtray on a side table, a short glass of rye whiskey nearby. Spread on the coffee table was the damning evidence, such as it was: Cynthia Hunt's note, Tom Hunt's bank statement, and part of the registration for the Volkswagen van once owned by Trick Vargas or Larry Smith or whoever the hell he was now.

Gerald Watkins looked suddenly old. He winced as he picked up his glass, ice cubes clinking. Taking a long swallow, he studied the papers in front of him.

"Let's start with Chase." Rand skewered his father with his gaze. "He's dead, isn't he?"

"No surprise there," Gerald said, nodding, finally giving up the secret that he'd carried for two decades. "But Cynthia got it all wrong. I had no part in killing him."

"His father did?"

"Yeah, but an accident." He set his drink down, then took a long draw on his cigarette. "Chase came home that night, all hopped up on who knows what, but out of his mind. He'd flunked out of school. Lost his scholarship. Was aimless, into drugs and all sorts of things, I guess. He was going to be drafted and was talking all crazy about getting his girlfriend, Harper Reed, pregnant and getting married to avoid the draft or go to Canada or whatever. He was a mess."

So far, that lined up.

Gerald took another pull on his smoke and looked past Rand and into the fire, as if lost in the flames. "That night they got into it. A big fight, the way Tom told it. Physical. Even Levi got involved, but anyway, Tom was not about to let his son become a draft dodger."

Rand was wary, but it seemed his dad was finally telling the truth.

"Anyway," Gerald said, turning away from the fireplace. "Tom thought it had all calmed down when he heard the kid sneak out."

"Sneak out? Chase wasn't a kid."

"Yeah, I know, but you get it. So Tom goes to confront him outside, and they get into it again. This time, Tom clocks the kid and, like I said, Chase is out of control and drunk and—anyway, Chase slips, goes down, and hits his head on the rail. And that's it."

"He dies?"

"Yeah. Tom tries CPR, but it's too late. The kid's gone. Tom came over to the house, here, and was out of his mind. Didn't want to call for an ambulance cuz it was too late and Tom would pay the price. Levi and Cindy, they had seen the fight earlier. As I understand it, Levi even got caught in the crossfire."

Rand remembered Levi's bandaged face. Remembered his own aching shoulder.

"Tom would've been up for manslaughter at the least. His wife and kid saw the fight, heard the threats, and both Chase and Tom had the bruises to prove it. If they testified, and maybe if they didn't, Tom was looking at going to prison."

Rand waited as his father nursed his drink.

Finally Gerald spoke again. "The long and the short of it is we came up with a plan. Tom said he knew what to do with the body, and he wanted to make it look like Chase disappeared, so all I ever knew is that he took Chase out in the boat and twenty minutes later, I met him in the middle of the lake in mine—ours. He climbed out of his boat, and I brought us back to shore."

"So what happened to Chase's body?"

Gerald scratched at the stubble on his jaw. "I don't know, son, and that's the God's honest truth. Tom stashed him somewhere around the lake or in the water and told me he would take care of it later. By that I think he meant dispose of the body. He was pretty broken up about it all."

But not broken up enough to come clean.

"Hold on a second. You don't know where he hid his son's body?" For the first time tonight, Rand doubted his father. "But the lake was searched. Dredged. People combed the shoreline as well as the town."

"You forget that Olivia Dixon died that night, too. Almsville was rocked by both deaths, and the department was stretched thin. And Tom knew this lake better than anyone. Had grown up here." Gerald looked pointedly at Rand. "My guess? He stashed the body in a place only he knew about, then, in the next week or so, once things had died down a bit, he took his boat, loaded the body into it, and towed it to the coast. Maybe Astoria, there at the mouth of the Columbia, or some other spot where the tide would wash it into the open sea." He took another thoughtful drag, then added in a puff of smoke, "But whatever Tom did with the body, he never said a word to me or anyone else that I know of. He took that information to his grave." Gerald hesitated, thinking, and finally said, "For the record, I never bought the whole idea that Tom had an accident on the lake."

"You think he committed suicide?" Rand asked.

"And covered it up, so that Cindy could still collect the insurance money."

"Jesus," Rand said under his breath. He couldn't believe what he was hearing. It was too bizarre, too far-fetched, and yet on the other hand it made perfect sense. Explained a lot. Except as to where Chase's body ultimately ended up. That part was still a mystery.

But now he knew Chase was dead. He remembered promising his friend that he would "take care" of Harper. He hadn't. Now, though, he could inform her, and Levi as well, that Chase was truly gone. He paced to the stairs and back again, and more questions arose. "So you think Cynthia blamed you and Tom for Chase's death?"

Gerald picked up the note she'd sent and winced at the pain in his shoulder. "Not originally. She wouldn't have spent so much time trying to find him if she had. And I don't think she would cover up for Tom or me." He took another long draw on his cigarette, then jabbed it out in the tray. "Doesn't make sense. No. She must've put two and two together when she saw this bank statement. Why else would she include it with the note?"

Rand walked into the kitchen, found a bag of frozen peas in the freezer, and took the package back to the living room. "What do you make of the bank statement?" he asked, handing the frozen peas to his father, just as the old man had offered a similar bag to him after particularly rough games on the football field.

Gerald placed the makeshift ice pack on his shoulder. "Looks like a shakedown to me."

Rand had come to the same conclusion. "By this guy?" he asked, pushing the bit of the registration toward his father. Gerald glowered at the name. "Vargas? I wouldn't put it past him. He was a snake if there ever was one." Gerald's eyebrows slammed together as he eyed the old papers again. "The shakedown happened right after Chase died."

"Until Tom's death," Rand said, his thoughts spinning. "I'm thinking Vargas knew something or saw something and he was holding it over Tom's head."

"Possibly. Tom said something about that. Pictures or some kind of home movie. But he wasn't clear, and I really don't know."

Rand looked hard at his father. "What about you? Did Vargas get to you, too?"

"What?" Gerald was taken aback. "You mean did he try to blackmail me?" He shook his head. "Nah."

"You think he knows where the body is?"

Ice pack balanced on his shoulder, Gerald was reaching into his pocket for his pack of cigarettes but stopped. "Don't know."

"But you do know that they were dealing out of the house down the street?"

His father's shoulders slumped. "Yeah. An open secret. Mainly just marijuana. Maybe some speed."

"More than that. Coke and acid, and whatever. Why didn't you bust Vargas and the rest of them back in the day?" Rand asked. "Why did you and Tom turn a blind eye?"

Gerald plucked the last bent cigarette from the pack. He lit up, drawing hard and letting out a cloud of smoke. "Because we were told not to."

"By whom? The captain?" and when his father didn't respond, he said, "Wait, the chief? You're kidding me!" Rand dropped into a side chair.

"The way I heard it, the word came down from the mayor, but who knows?" Cigarette clamped between his teeth, he shifted the icy bag on his shoulder. "Chilcote. He was the mayor back then, and the word in the department was that was where he got his supply."

"The mayor?" Roger Chilcote was long gone but had been the mayor of Almsville for nearly a decade during the sixties. "He was what? A pothead?"

"As I heard it. He lived right across the lake on Northway. Could've boated across in the dark of night. No one would be the wiser, so we—Tom and I—were advised to let sleeping dogs lie. So to speak. As long as the peace was kept. If anyone ever got out of line down there, any kind of serious disturbance, then we would deal with it, but, as far as that went, all those hippies kept their noses clean. Except for what they were snorting."

Rand didn't say a word, just let his father go on. Now that he'd admitted the truth, Gerald Watkins seemed eager to unload.

"And that Vargas," Gerald said. "He was a smart one, just slippery as hell. He knew a good thing when he had it and milked it for all it was worth." He finished his drink and found his son staring at him.

"What? Don't look so shocked. You think you kids had the corner on getting high?" Gerald scoffed. "I saw people of all ages going in and out of that place." He grinned without any joy. "So now you know Almsville's dirty little secret."

Gerald crumpled his empty pack and tossed it into the fire, igniting the glowing coals in a short burst of flame. "If there's nothing else, no more sins you want me to confess, then I'd better get goin'. Dorie will be looking for me." He stood and dropped the package of peas onto the couch.

"There is one more thing," Rand said before his father reached the door. "What do you know about a missing gun from the evidence room?"

"What?"

"The revolver Evan Reed used when he died in the tram on Dixon Island. What happened to it?"

His father's spine stiffened, and for a second Rand thought he was going to lie. Then he released a tired breath. "That's on Tom, too," he admitted. "I caught him with it and asked him about it. All he said was that it was better off if I didn't know."

"And you let it go."

"Yeah, son," Gerald said, his jaw set. "I did."

"You think Evan killed himself?"

"Open and shut."

"What about Anna Reed, his mother?" Harper's mother. "You think that was suicide, too?"

Gerald frowned, his dark eyes sober. "You were there, Rand. You saw Tom and me haul her out of the water. Do I think she killed herself? Yeah, I sure do. Do I think it was intentional? No, probably not."

"An accident then."

"As far as I know." And with that he was out the door.

1960

Chapter 48

Anna Reed thought of all the ways she could kill her husband. Fingers gripped around the steering wheel, she considered her options.

There was poison, of course, but where would she get it?

Nope.

So, maybe an accident. But how? A gun? Her father kept all kinds of guns in the garage and the manor. Rifles, shotguns, pistols. A bullet through Bruce's adulterous heart would do the job.

But could she do it? Actually pull the trigger?

She thought so. But maybe that was just the alcohol talking. She'd had three—or had it been four?—martinis at the cocktail lounge in Portland where she'd been stood up by her husband. Oh, he'd called the maître d' at the expensive restaurant and told the man to search out his wife, to pass on the message that Bruce couldn't make it. After all their plans. He'd gotten hung up. Harper was sick or something. Harper couldn't go trick or treating with Beth. Excuses, excuses, excuses!

She didn't believe it for a second.

There had been too many other times when she'd been left waiting in a restaurant, nursing a drink, knowing deep in her soul that her husband wasn't going to show. Tonight, she'd sensed, was no exception.

Well, Anna wasn't about to have dinner alone, so she'd ordered one last drink, nursed it, feeding her anger, then left the restaurant.

This wasn't the first time that son of a bitch had stood her up, but it would damn well be his last.

Maybe he wasn't out with another woman. Maybe he was home taking care of their sick child as the maître d' had confided to her. But she wasn't buying it. Yet.

Blinking back angry tears, she pushed the speed limit on the two-lane highway that followed the course of the river and connected South Portland to Almsville.

She drove recklessly, her concentration shot, the misting rain dampening her windshield and the tears forming in her eyes not helping her vision. She sniffed as the tires of her Thunderbird sang on the pavement and tried like hell to keep them from straying over the center line.

From the radio, Roy Orbison's voice crooning "Only the Lonely."

"Oh, shut up!" She snapped off the radio.

It's a miserable night, perfect for Halloween, she thought, trying to concentrate, to keep her mind on driving as the Thunderbird sailed into Almsville. Perfect for a murder. What could be more fitting?

Almost unseeing, absorbed in her own heartache, she passed groups of kids in rubber masks and overcoats, sacks of candy swinging from their arms as they splashed through puddles on the sidewalks.

You're not a murderer.

You cringed when you saw your father shoot a squirrel or a crow.

Do you really think you could point a gun at Bruce, then pull the trigger? The father of your children? The man you swore you'd stay with forever? Remember, "'Til death do us part"? Do you really think those vows meant, "'Til I kill you"? Get real.

Angry, she nearly missed the stop sign and almost plowed into a group of pre-teens racing across the street. They were shouting and laughing, calling to one another and not yet realizing the pain of being an adult.

"Jesus." She had to be more careful! With the car idling, she reached into her handbag, pulled out an engraved handkerchief and a bottle of pills. Barbiturates. Her doctor had prescribed them for her anxiety and insomnia. Boy, could she use them tonight. She unscrewed the cap, tossed a few into her palm, then threw them into her mouth and wished she had another martini to wash them down.

Not that she really needed another drink.

As it was, the world seemed a little off-kilter. Driving a challenge.

Through the downtown of Almsville, she stayed within the speed limit. She drove past storefronts festooned with Halloween decorations in their windows.

Once outside the city core she saw houses with leering jack-o'-lanterns, their crooked smiles glowing on porch steps, while hay bales and dried cornstalks leaned against doorways. Outdoor lights were glowing, inviting trick-or-treaters to knock.

All the little perfect houses with perfect families and perfect husbands, she thought, wrinkling her nose. "Phoneys. All phoneys." Knowing she was way past tipsy and now that some of her rage had cooled, she reminded herself to drive as carefully as possible. Tons of kids were out roaming the streets.

She thought fleetingly of her own two children. They were out here, too.

Well, no. Not if Bruce's message was to be believed.

Evan was out with his friends, probably raising hell. Her son was hard to read as a preteen. Even harder to rein in.

As for her daughter? It seemed Harper had been sidetracked from her plans of a party at the Hunt family's across the lake and then trick or treating with her friend Beth. The sniffles and scratchy throat that had kept her home from school had developed into a cough and fever, again, according to the note she'd been handed.

The lying son of a bitch!

How would her kids feel when they didn't have a father? What if they figured out their own mother had killed him?

"Stop it!" she said aloud and flipped on the radio again. Melancholy songs were better than her own painful, murderous thoughts.

Elvis was crooning "It's Now or Never."

"You got that right," she said to the empty car as she turned onto Northway and headed home, through the dark, along the shoreline of Lake Twilight. The pills—or was it the booze?—were starting to take root, her bones starting to melt, her brain coated in something warm and fuzzy.

As she neared the drive, she thought she saw someone dive into the bushes. A fleeting shadow that passed quickly.

She stood on the brakes!

Her Thunderbird shuddered, bouncing over a pothole.

Anna's fingers slipped, the steering wheel sliding through them.

Her car swiped the mailbox, knocking it over and shattering a headlight.

"Shit!"

Metal crumpled.

Jostled, heart in her throat, Anna grabbed the wheel again, then clenched it in a death grip as the Thunderbird finally slid to a stop.

Her heart raced, adrenaline firing her blood.

That was close!

Dear God, she had to be more careful. Driving in this condition was lunacy.

What if she had hit a child?

She let out a long, unsteady breath, her heart still knocking wildly, the one remaining headlamp illuminating the gate to the manor and the gargoyles crouched atop their pillars. "Your night to howl," she told them.

Then, as if the monstrous stone beasts could hear her, she yelled loudly, "Go! Fly away! Terrorize some of those damned trick-or-treaters."

Giggling, she fell back on the seat and was surprised at her reaction. Inappropriate. Probably the pills really taking hold. Well, good!

"Get a grip," she told herself, while noticing that her vision was more than a little blurred, her hands unsteady.

Shoving her hair away from her face, she tried to breathe deeply. She consoled herself with the fact that she hadn't hit a kid tonight. Thankfully.

Then her thoughts returned to her husband, and she tried to decide whether she'd kill him, as she'd been contemplating, or divorce him. Or could she? Murder was a mortal sin, of course, but the church really, really frowned on divorce. Didn't recognize it. Could she get an annulment? If she could prove that Bruce was cheating, wouldn't the church grant one?

And then what?

Her kids would be bastards.

She didn't like the sound of that.

No matter what, she had to be more careful. She'd wrecked her car. A gift for her birthday last year. From her dear hubby. And bought with *her* money. What a prick! Nonetheless, he was going to be sooo angry with her. Well, too damned bad.

Anna reached for the keys to kill the engine, and it took two swipes to catch hold of them. Again, they slipped through her fingers. As she tried once more to snag them, she thought she caught a movement out of the corner of her eye. Something in the greenery by the front gates causing the rhododendron leaves to shiver.

A raccoon?

Or a possum?

Maybe a deer or . . . stray dog . . . No, no. It was most likely one of her mother's miserable cats, those nasty little beasts that hid and darted throughout the property. Especially at night. Nothing to worry about and maybe nothing at all. Maybe she'd imagined it. After all, the T-Bird's windows had started to fog and—

Wait!

Something moved again.

She tried to focus.

Was that a shadow on the other side of the fir tree?

A human slinking in the thick shrubbery?

Or just the shifting of tree limbs casting shadows in the breeze?

She squinted as the car idled. Who would be skulking around in this nasty weather? Maybe kids out trick or treating, or older kids playing pranks like taking rolls of TP and throwing them over trees and cars or houses or leaving sacks of lit dog poop on a hated neighbor's porch. It wouldn't be the first time the gargoyles had been the target of some teenage skullduggery.

Anyway, the dark figure disappeared.

If it had ever existed.

She couldn't leave the damaged car in front of the gates blocking access to the bridge as she knew her mother and father were both out for the night, so she managed to swing the nose of her car around and parked awkwardly in front of the cottage's little garage.

Good enough!

On unsteady legs Anna climbed out of the car. She wobbled in her stilettos as the flagstones leading to the front door were uneven and slick. She caught her heel twice but managed not to fall. But she had to steady herself on the door frame as she unlocked the front door.

Once inside, she shed her coat, letting it pool on the floor. Her umbrella? Oh God, she'd left it in the car and hadn't noticed the rain as she'd walked to the porch.

She must be more wasted than she'd thought.

Catching a glimpse of her reflection in the mirror, she winced. Her French twist was beginning to fall, brunette strands straggling from her updo. Her lipstick had long faded, and her mascara had tracked down her face in unsightly rivulets.

"All for nothing," she whispered, pulling off her gloves.

She stole a cigarette from the pack Bruce had left on the kitchen counter, struck a match, and lit up. She should have listened to her mother. Olivia had never liked Bruce and had warned Anna about him.

"Looks like a huckster to me," she'd said after meeting Bruce for the first time. He had come bearing roses and chocolates and a big grin when he'd first met Olivia. "Way too smooth. And let me tell you, honey, you can't trust any man who's as slick as he is. They often turn out to be flimflam men."

But Anna hadn't listened.

What did her mother know?

Anna had fallen hard and fast for the handsome real-estate broker and she'd been set on marrying him. Despite her mother's reservations.

Even during the elaborate wedding ceremony at the huge church, Olivia had glowered at her daughter from beneath the broad brim of her hat. Anna, in her frothy dress with its sweetheart neckline and full skirt, had ignored her mother. She'd been in heaven as she'd nearly floated down the aisle.

Only later, after a few years of marriage, two kids, and the realization that Bruce had a wandering eye had she nose-dived off the soft, lofty perch of cloud nine and crashed onto the cold, hard stones of reality. Exactly where she had landed tonight.

In the bedroom, she kicked off her wicked-heeled shoes and, gripping the cigarette between her lips, slid out of her pencil skirt and silk blouse, letting them fall to the floor. Then she worked on her nylons, unhooking them from her garter belt and rolling them off her legs. God, how she'd worked hard so that the seam had been straight when she'd dressed to meet her husband for cocktails and dinner. Bruce loved seamed hose, and she'd wanted to please him, to seduce him, to rekindle the spark that had died between them.

And all the while, he'd been cheating on her.

A bitter taste rose in her mouth as she stubbed out her cigarette in a tray on the night table. What a fool she'd been. To trust him. To fall in love with him. To marry him. She should have listened to her mother.

Angrily, she stripped out of underwear and bra and threw on her nightgown. She reeled a bit. Was dizzy. Nonetheless, she padded barefoot into the kitchen and found a bottle of gin.

Her mother's favorite. And good enough for a nightcap.

But just one . . . well, make it two. No telling how long she'd have to wait up for the slimy bastard. She snagged a glass from the cupboard, poured the first drink, then left it on the counter while she went into the bathroom at the end of the hall. After using the toilet, she washed her hands and caught her reflection again, this time in the mirror over the medicine cabinet.

The image wasn't good.

She was thirty-six. Forty was staring her in the face, and after bearing two children in a rocky marriage, her age was beginning to show, or so it seemed tonight. She scrubbed her face clean, getting rid of the drizzles of mascara and eye shadow. Next up, she washed off her foundation, powder, and the rest of her lipstick. With her face clean, she did look younger, except for the fact that the whites of her blue eyes were red from her recent tears and recent drinks.

She turned off the water and heard something.

A movement in the front of the house?

She went to investigate. Maybe Evan was home, back from the

events of the night early, or maybe her lying, cheating, scumbag of a husband had returned.

But the living room was empty, the kitchen just as she'd left it.

Weird. She could have sworn . . .

She took a long swallow.

Had one of her mother's nasty cats somehow gotten in?

She opened the door to the garage and saw that Bruce's sporty little Aston Martin wasn't parked in its usual spot. But wait! She had blocked the drive with the crumpled T-Bird. So maybe he parked out front.

"Bruce?" she called unsteadily.

No answer. Just the whoosh of air through the ducts from the furnace and the hum of the old Frigidaire over the steady drip of the rain on the deck.

Of course he wasn't home.

She knew better.

"Hope springs eternal," she said and silently berated herself for being a fool. She took another big gulp and poured herself another drink. *But first*, she thought suddenly, *I need to check on Harper. What was I thinking?* But the house seemed so quiet. For the tiniest bit of a second, she wondered if Bruce had truly been worried about their daughter and called the doctor and begged him to look at Harper.

Probably wishful thinking.

But she should check.

Clinging to the railing, she made her way upstairs where she cracked open the door to her daughter's room. She knocked softly and pushed open the door. In the slice of light spilling from the hallway, she could just make out Harper's bed. She seemed buried under the covers, the dog at her feet. Bandit lifted his head, ears up expectantly, but Anna said, "Shh," and held a finger to her mouth.

Funny, she couldn't feel her lips.

And her tongue felt thick, as if it were twice its normal size.

Too much booze, she thought, stumbling against the door to her son's room.

It banged open to reveal a shadowy mess of clothes, books, records, and baseball cards. His bed was unmade, and she thought maybe his pillow was missing, but she didn't care.

Bump!

She started.

Did she do that?

Or had it come from downstairs?

God, she was drunk.

Wobbling, she eased down the steps, but at the base of the staircase, she said, "Bruce? Is that you?" Again, she waited, listening, but heard only her own heartbeat.

And yet, she couldn't shake the feeling that she wasn't alone. "Bruce?" Anna called, as she staggered into the kitchen and picked up her drink. Nothing here. Sipping from her glass, she walked unsteadily to the laundry room and flipped on the porch light. Peering uneasily through the window cut into the door, she had trouble focusing. Between the dark night, rain, and the combo of booze and pills, she saw nothing.

Opening the back door, she noticed that the lock wasn't latched. Not that it ever was, because of the kids coming and going at all hours. But tonight? Fumbling, she turned the latch.

"Huh." Steadying herself on the wall, Anna returned to the kitchen for "just one more." She teetered a little as she set the glass on the counter, ready to pour in the last of the gin. As she did, she noticed bits of powder in her empty glass. "What the hell?" Hadn't it been clean when she'd taken it from the cupboard?

Or—

Suddenly the lights went out.

Had they blown a fuse? Like a main one?

A spidery feeling tickled the back of her neck.

A warning.

And something rustled.

Just slightly.

Fear slid down her spine.

"Is anyone there?" she asked and started for the phone.

Something was wrong. Terribly wrong.

She reached for the receiver and heard a rush of footsteps.

Coming straight at her.

"What—?" She turned.

Smack!

Something hard and flat hit her full force. Across her face.

"Oh!"

Blood gushed from her nose.

Gasping, she staggered backward, her entire face throbbing.

What—?

Whack!

Another blow to the face.

Excruciating pain roared through her body.

Her knees crumpled.

She fell trying to save herself. Failing. The side of her head bounced off the counter's sharp edge to thud against the old linoleum.

The dark world spun crazily.

She couldn't move, and when she tried to speak, her voice was the barest of whispers. "Help," she murmured when she knew there was none.

She was only vaguely aware of being dragged into the garage and then hefted with difficulty into something that she thought was the wheelbarrow. Barely conscious, feeling every bump as the garden cart bounced down a trail behind the main house, she felt the cold drizzle of rain and heard herself moan. She blacked out momentarily, then came to.

Wake up, Anna. Wake up! She tried to force herself up and out, but her legs and arms wouldn't move and she kept losing her thin thread of consciousness.

Down, down, down she was rolled, her weight shifting to the front of the steel tray, the icy drops chilling her body. Her eyes wouldn't open, her hands flopped when she tried to move them, and she couldn't rouse herself. The whole world seemed to be whirling, spinning out of control.

All at once, the wheelbarrow stopped its downward descent.

The back end of the cart was lifted and pushed forward.

She was dumped into the floor of the tram. Seconds later its engine clicked to life. With a whine, it lurched forward.

Anna was aware of movement, ever downward.

She didn't notice when the tram stopped and was only thinly aware that she was being dragged across wooden planks.

Then she was hauled to her feet and forced to somehow stand.

Blinking, she managed it, barely. Swaying. Trying to get her bearings on the edge of the dock. Far in the distance, wavering, were the lights of Fox Point, she thought as she teetered in the rain.

For a second she thought she heard her daughter call out to her—the faintest of whispers.

Or was that her imagination?

Was this all a dream?

A painful, soul-jarring dream?

The black ever-moving water stretched out in front of her.

Lights on the far shore shimmered and winked.

And then in an instant, her balance gave way.

She slipped.

Off the dock.

And into the cold caress of Lake Twilight.

1988
The Present

Chapter 49

Sellwood had changed in the past twenty years.

Harper drove through the narrow streets lined with parked cars. The rain had stopped, a cold wind scuttling down the streets while shafts of sunlight broke through the clouds, shimmering against the wet asphalt.

She was surprised at how many antique stores, boutique shops, and cozy restaurants were in the area. In hooded jackets or carrying umbrellas or laden with backpacks, people crowded the crosswalks. Some walking dogs, others with children, a few couples strolling hand-in-hand as they window-shopped.

Carefully she maneuvered her Volvo through the clog of traffic while trying to locate the address for Levi's business.

"Thirteenth and what?" she muttered, glancing down at the map lying open on the passenger seat. His address was somewhere north of Tacoma Street and west of Moreland Park. She turned a corner and saw a newer cinder-block structure with storefronts and offices on the lower level, apartments above. "Gotta be it."

Screwing up her courage at the thought of seeing Levi again, she parked in a tight spot and climbed out of her wagon. "Emotional suicide," she told herself and felt her insides twist. But here she was, about to deliver all of Chase's high school memorabilia and the diamond necklace to his younger brother, a brother he never quite trusted. The exchange should only take a few minutes. That was all. Then she was done with it. Once and for all.

With renewed determination she grabbed her bag and hunched against the October breeze, walked back the two blocks to the building. Between a bistro and a boutique was a door marked only by a number. It opened easily, and she hurried down a short hallway that branched to another corridor leading to offices tucked behind the smaller street-facing shops. She found a windowless door marked 121, which sported a single plate: Levi Hunt Investigations. A telephone number was listed beneath Levi's name.

She tried the knob.

No luck.

Locked tight.

"Awesome," she whispered. She didn't know what she'd expected. A windowed suite of offices with a panoramic view of the street? A busy receptionist seated behind a mahogany desk, a headset in place, a computer keyboard at her fingertips? Maybe a large door with pebble glass and Levi's name engraved in gold leaf?

Well, this wasn't it. Definitely not.

This could only be described as a back-alley hole in the wall.

She knocked.

Waited.

Nothing.

So here she was with her bag of Chase's belongings and no one to give them to.

Looking down the hallway, she spied a staircase. Hadn't Beth said Levi lived above his office but was moving? She took the stairs to that second-story hallway, a duplicate of the one at street level. The whole setup reminded her of a cheap inner city hotel with a row of doorways on either side of the carpeted corridor, all numbered, no names and no way to tell which one was Levi's.

"Great. Mission not accomplished."

Once back at the main vestibule, she checked the listing for the mailboxes. Numbers only. She tried the door to his office once more, failed, and wrote the phone number listed on a notepad she found in her purse.

It was as if Levi didn't want anyone to find him, which was a weird way to run a business. Unless, of course, that business was somewhat secretive. And he'd told her about being a PI. "A long story," he'd said and hadn't elaborated. Hadn't Beth said he'd been a spy or something? Was that possible? She remembered him visiting her in the hospital and certainly hadn't immediately thought of clandestine meetings, smoky back rooms, or dark, puddled alleyways.

Get over yourself!

She was letting her imagination get the better of her. He had a small, cheap office and he wasn't in. No big deal.

But it was a frustrating way to spend a fall afternoon when she had a million and one other things to do. She slid inside her Volvo and reversed her course, noting as she crossed the river a few fishing boats scattered on the gray water and sunlight peeking through the cloud cover reflected in patches that shimmered.

Absently she switched on the radio, where a news reporter was talking enthusiastically about the Dodgers winning the World Series before he launched into a report that President Reagan was leveling the new American Embassy in Moscow because of suspected listening devices implanted in it.

Was that a surprise?

Spy vs. Spy, she thought, remembering the comic strip in *Mad Magazine* where espionage agents took on the images of masked birds. Evan had devoured every issue of that magazine while she had been more interested in *Seventeen* or *Tiger Beat*.

Such a long time ago. And now Levi was back, possibly had been a spy himself, and had opened up a small one-man investigation gig in Portland.

The newscast ended and the lilting tune and upbeat lyrics of "Don't Worry, Be Happy" by Bobby McFerrin played. "Sorry, Bobby." She snapped off the radio. "Not in the mood." Happiness was in short supply these days.

The rest of the drive she was lost in thought, mostly about Levi and what she was going to say to him. What she was going to admit. "Nothing," she said as she reached Almsville and drove along Northway. Through the trees she caught glimpses of the lake, dark and moody, the water choppy with the wind, the sun now blocked by clouds. As she turned into the short lane to the bridge, she spied the red pickup she recognized as belonging to Craig Alexander.

"Great." She wasn't really in the mood to deal with him.

The truck was empty, but as she parked, he rounded the corner of the garage. Wearing a bomber jacket and jeans, a baseball cap pulled low over his eyes, he was followed by Rambo, who tagged along slowly sniffing the wet shrubbery as they approached.

"Hey!" he said, greeting her with a smile. "I thought I'd missed you."

"No such luck," she half joked and wondered about him. If he had a key. If he'd put the threatening message on the dolls. If he had left the dead cat's skeleton. She glanced at the freshly turned soil in the rose garden where once Earline had been buried.

"Very funny," he said, but it wasn't, and as he reached into the cab of his truck, she noticed a rifle was mounted in the gun rack. Was he dangerous? *Not today*, she decided, but she was wary, watching as he withdrew a manila envelope. "I took a chance and brought over the estimate rather than send it through the mail," he explained, and she relaxed a bit. "Look it over, and we'll talk. I'm just finishing a job—it should take about three weeks, maybe four, but I could order materials and get started, say, uh, maybe around the middle of November?" He handed her the envelope, then squinted up at the upper story of the house. "Just as long as there's no major roof work or foundation issues—nothing serious that has to be done outside, the weather shouldn't affect us too much. Oh, and Beth said you really wanted to seal off the boathouse."

"Her idea."

"Well, she's right. It needs to be closed off, or maybe built out in that cave. That should probably be done sooner rather than later."

"I'll think about it."

"Great." Whistling to the dog and shooing the big Newfoundland into the cab, he added, "Just let me know. And if you make any decision on the cars?" He hitched a thumb toward the closed garage doors. "I'm interested. Very interested."

"Okay," she said and couldn't resist adding, "And the guns, right? You might be interested in a rifle or shotgun. What about the pistols?" she pushed, knowing she'd mentioned them before, but . . .

Did Craig flinch?

Just a bit?

Did an eyebrow twitch?

"Oh . . . well," he said, and he seemed suddenly more tense than he had been. "Sure. I'm into firearms, so if there's anything you've got, I might want to take a look." Then, as if suddenly remembering, said, "I might be interested in a shotgun, especially that old Parker Side by Side that I saw Dad cleaning a couple of times."

"But the pistols?"

He lifted a shoulder. "Sure."

"Okay. I'll look for them," she said, noting that his eyes narrowed just a fraction. "Funny thing. I found one pretty soon after I got here, but then, I don't know." She shrugged. "It went missing."

"You said there were two," he reminded her.

"Yeah, I know, but I only came across one and then . . . well, it's gone." Her gaze held his. "I know right where I left it and now, I can't find it. It's not there."

He snorted. "Guns don't just get up and walk by themselves."

"That's what I keep telling myself." She held his gaze, and she couldn't be sure, but it seemed like his jaw tightened just a fraction. "The other thing that I'm missing is my cat," she said. "I found his collar, but he's just gone."

"Cats wander off. It's what they do. He'll probably come back."

"He'd better," she said and couldn't keep the edge out of her voice. "If you see him—he's a tuxedo, black and white—let me know."

"I'll keep a lookout."

"Do that."

Craig made a big show of looking at his watch. "Look, I gotta run. Let me know about the estimate." He opened the door of his truck and slid behind the wheel next to his dog. "And don't forget about the guns and cars. Especially that Corvette. Man, I'd love to take that one for a spin."

"Who knows if it will even start."

"Not without keys," he reminded her. He forced a smile, climbed into the cab, and then he was off, driving his truck across the bridge and through the gate. As she headed back inside, she automatically scanned the undergrowth for Jinx.

Where the hell was that cat?

He had been wearing his collar when he disappeared with Harper's phone number on his tag. No one had called, though of course the number on the collar was for her home in Santa Rosa and, more importantly, someone had left his collar around the doll as a clear message.

Nonetheless, she decided to check her phone in California. She didn't expect to hear about Jinx, but there could be other important messages. She called her own number in California and used a numerical key to access her messages. There were half a dozen, including an offer for lawn service, a volunteer asking for support for Michael Dukakis's presidential campaign, and several hang-ups.

About what she expected.

She erased all the messages, then, screwing up her courage, called the number that she'd copied from Levi's office door. On the third ring, his answering machine picked up, and she hesitated about leaving a message about Chase's things and the diamond necklace. Instead, she just asked him to call her back, leaving her phone number.

Only then did she open Craig's estimate for repair work on the house.

She nearly choked. He'd broken the work down into what was necessary just to get the house functioning reasonably well and what it would take to bring it up to code, and then what he suggested to get it in "resale" condition. The numbers were staggering. And then there was the gatehouse, which in Craig's estimation was a total gut job. There was a note that it might be easier and more cost-effective to level the little house near the front gates and start over.

"Wow," she said. She'd inherited a fortune, true. But it had been significantly pared down over the years by Gram's attorneys, and her father and stepmother dipping in—ostensibly for Harper's care and education, but she still wasn't convinced of that.

She glanced over the figures and told herself she just had to get a second bid, despite Beth having once been her best friend.

Harper should think beyond the people she knew growing up. That might be smarter. More professional. Beth might be upset with her, but so what?

She was slipping the estimate into its envelope when the phone rang and she answered.

Her daughter was on the other end of the line.

"Hey, Mom, listen," Dawn said a little breathlessly. "It turns out I'm driving a friend to Portland today, so I thought I'd drop her off and swing by Grandpa's to check on him. He's okay, right?" She sounded concerned.

"I think so, as Marcia told me on the phone the other day, 'It's not his time.'"

"Not 'his time'? What was she talking about? Like, his time to die?"

"I guess."

"Gross," Dawn said. "Well, if I can't see him, I still need to check in with Dad."

"He's here?"

"In Portland at a hotel for now. But he's looking for a place."

"Hold on a second," Harper said at the mention of Joel. "As in looking for a place to stay?"

"To move. That's what he said."

"Where?" This was news and not welcome. "Your dad is planning to *move* to Portland?"

"I thought he told you."

"I haven't talked to him since I first got here."

Hadn't he said something about being in town for just a few days? Why the lie?

"He said he was moving to Almsville."

That was a sucker punch.

"Why?"

"I don't know. He and Melanie broke up *again* for like the kajillionth time."

Harper's heart sank.

Dawn said, "I think that for now he's in a hotel, but he's looking for a place to rent. But, you know, it's probably just temporary." Dawn sighed loudly, and Harper envisioned her rolling her eyes. "You know how he and Melanie are. Talk about on-again, off-again! Really, it's too exhausting to keep up with." Then she changed the subject. "Anyway, I should be at your place probably in the early evening, but maybe earlier. It depends on Gina—that's my friend— she may want to go back to Eugene tonight. Something about a super-late showing of *Heathers* at the theater here, like at midnight. But I'm not sure we could even make it, so we might have to crash at your place—that would be okay? Or maybe Gina would stay with her aunt, she said something about that. Anyway, I'm not really sure what the plan is, but I thought I'd give you a heads-up. Cool?"

"Cool," Harper agreed, though it was a lie. There was a lot of Dawn's plan that she was definitely not cool with. Most of it had to do with the intruder and his dark, twisted messages. How dangerous was he? No way would she knowingly put her daughter in any kind of jeopardy.

Then there was the matter of Joel Prescott. Why the hell had he lied? Now he was back, and according to Lou Arista, making noise about her inheritance. He'd known she'd had money when she'd married him, and it was probably some of the allure, a reason he wanted to marry her, pregnant as she was. He'd made mention of the fact that she was going to inherit several times during their marriage and was always eager to cash her quarterly checks from the trust.

It had bothered her, been in the back of her mind, that he'd known about her when they'd met. He had lived on the lake, in the house across from the island. Joel had been aware of Chase and her relationship with him. And he'd accepted oh so easily that she'd been pregnant.

Of course their marriage had never been solid. Not from the get-go. And then, midlife came and along with it came Melanie Jallet, his on-again, off-again girlfriend fifteen years younger than he.

Shrugging out of her jacket, she walked into the parlor and sat at the table near the telescope again. Then she looked through the eye-piece to the houses across the lake. This time she focused on the rental house, the place where Joel Prescott had spent half a year, including the winter of 1968.

Over the years she'd wondered why she'd never noticed him, if he'd lived so close to the Hunts. Then again, she'd been wrapped up with Chase. But what about Joel. Had he seen her? Had he witnessed her with Chase on Fox Point? Could he, as she was doing now, have looked across the lake to the island and seen her on the dock or the beach? Had he caught glimpses of her reading or sunbathing or swimming? No, not in winter. Still . . .

She fiddled with the focus. Remembered his first line. "You're Harper, aren't you?"

Had it been mere coincidence that he'd run into her in California so soon after she'd moved? At the time she'd thought so. He'd said as much. But she'd been young, naïve, and desperate.

Now, as an adult and not for the first time, she considered the fact that their first meeting hadn't been by chance and, more likely, been some kind of pre-planned plot.

1968

Chapter 50

Harper felt the weak winter sunshine against her crown as she walked across the quad to the deli. She was starving and yet slightly nauseous, her stomach as conflicted as she. She picked up a cheese bun and a Coke, then sat at a small outside table near a crepe myrtle tree, sparrows flitting through the branches. Famished, she took several bites before opening the schedule of classes she'd picked up. Spring term was due to start soon. Too soon. Though she'd passed her GED with flying colors, she doubted she could enroll in any of the classes she'd need. But summer term would be doubtful as well, because by then her pregnancy would be evident. For now, her abdomen was flat, but that wouldn't last for long, according to the doctor who had examined her and confirmed her pregnancy just two days earlier.

So she'd have to put off college.

Until after the baby was born. Or maybe she could take some correspondence courses. And get a job.

She picked at her bun, dropping some tiny pieces onto the sidewalk where some of the less timid birds fluttered down to peck at the crumbs.

"Excuse me. You're Harper, aren't you?" a male voice asked as a man's shadow spread across the table top and her open booklet. "Harper Reed?"

Her queasy stomach dropped.

Oh no!

On alert, she looked up. No one knew her here. No one. That's the way it was supposed to be.

Shading her eyes with one hand, she squinted up at him, a tall, lanky guy in jeans, T-shirt, Birkenstock sandals, and a string of love beads slung around his neck. His blond hair was unkempt, eyes an intense shade of blue, and just for a millisecond she thought of Chase.

However she didn't know this guy. Geez, was he yet another reporter who had tracked her down here, in California where her father and Marcia had insisted it would be safe, that she would be anonymous? No one was supposed to know about Chase's disappearance or Gram's death here.

She didn't want to talk to him. Didn't want to find out. In an instant she started wrapping the rest of her sandwich.

"You are, aren't you?"

She didn't respond, just gathered her things, knocking over her Coke and upturning her purse. "Oh crap!" she cried, as soda spilled all over her bag. She quickly turned to a nearby table and grabbed a handful of napkins from the dispenser. The guy actually tried to help clean up the mess, but she yanked her purse away and glared at him.

"Sorry," he said. "I didn't mean to surprise you."

"Well, you did." Who the hell was he?

"I'm Joel," he said as if reading her mind. "I've seen you around."

"I've got to go."

"Why?"

"I just do." She started to turn, but he grabbed her arm. "What're you afraid of?"

"Nothing!"

"Seems like."

She jerked her arm away and he didn't reach for her again. "I saw you at the lake."

Of course he did. Of course that was the connection. He was from

Oregon. Some kind of reporter dressed like a college kid to blend in. To make her trust him.

So much for anonymity.

He explained, "I lived right down the street from Chase Hunt."

Oh sure. "I don't think so." She was walking away, but he strode quickly to catch up to her.

"He was a friend of mine."

"What?" This wasn't making any sense. "Oh right." She didn't bother hiding her sarcasm as she reached into her purse for a pair of sunglasses and noticed that the inside of her bag was still wet from the spilled Coke.

"No, no, for sure," he was saying, keeping up with her. "Chase and I? We met at college."

"I thought you said you lived down the street from him." She shook soda off the sunglasses and slipped them on.

"I did. In Eugene. And then when I graduated and was moving up to Portland for a job, Chase told me about a cabin that was near his house in Almsville. He thought maybe I could rent a room there."

"What does this have to do with me?" She was walking toward the apartment her father had rented while he and Marcia started house hunting in Sonoma.

Joel had no trouble keeping up with her. "I just thought you might need a friend."

"A friend?" Speed-walking now, she said, "And why would you think that?"

"Because you don't know anyone here."

She turned on her heel to stare at him through shaded lenses still blurry from the spilled cola. "How would you know?"

"Because I've been watching you."

"Oh great. So you're what? A Peeping Tom? Well, no thank you." She was walking so fast she was nearly jogging. "I don't need any friends."

"Everyone does."

"Oh, save me!" Who was this guy anyway? She'd never heard Chase mention him and she didn't need any connections to her past. The whole idea of her family moving to California was for a chance at a new beginning.

She stepped off the curb, starting to cross the street.

A motorcycle roared around the corner.

"Watch out!" Joel grabbed her arm. He pulled her back to the sidewalk just as the biker glanced her way and sped off.

"Oh. Oh." Harper could hardly catch her breath. Adrenaline pumped through her blood. "That guy nearly ran me over," she said, feeling her knees going weak.

"'Nearly' is the important word."

"I think 'ran over' are the important words." She was still shaky.

Joel glared after the disappearing bike, then turned back to her. "Are you okay?"

"You mean other than freaked out of my mind?" She squinted up at him through the dark, blurry lenses. "Yeah. I mean . . . yeah." But she was quivering inside.

"Good." He nodded. "That's good. Don't suppose you got the guy's license plate?"

"Uh, no." She shook her head, letting out an unsteady breath.

"Me neither," he admitted. "It happened so fast."

She realized he was still holding onto her upper arm, and she moved away. "Look. Thanks. For—for saving my life, I guess, or whatever, but I've really got to go."

"Maybe I'll see you around."

"I—I don't think so."

But as she crossed the street, she hiked the strap of her purse over her shoulder and looked back to find him watching her. He held up a hand and she returned the favor before dashing along the tree-lined street to the apartment building and her new, if temporary, home.

She still didn't trust him.

These days she didn't trust anyone.

But he was right about one thing.

She could really use a friend.

More than that, she could use a boyfriend.

Not that her heart was mended.

She doubted it would ever be.

But she was going to have a baby and every kid deserved a father.

That night, alone in her twin bed, with her father and stepmother a paper-thin wall away, Harper started hatching a new plan. No longer was she constrained to helping Chase avoid the draft or getting pregnant for his benefit. Now she could concentrate on her own needs. And her child's needs. So maybe . . . her thoughts strayed to uncomfortable territory as she thought about her future.

She didn't see Joel the next day.

Nor the next.

She'd looked for him on campus and wished she knew his last name. But he'd never given it and with all the hubbub of the spilled Coke and nearly being hit by a crazed motorcycle driver, she hadn't asked for it.

Now she wished she had. She'd walked around the junior college buildings, hoping for a glimpse of him. So far, no luck.

Today she was back at the outdoor table near the deli where she'd first met him. Though she was ravenous, food still wasn't agreeing with her, so she picked at what she could keep down of an avocado and tuna sandwich, then tossed bits of bread, alfalfa sprouts, and lettuce to the pigeons and small birds that flocked nearby. All the while she was hoping for a glimpse of him. To talk to him. Someone near her age. Someone interested. Someone male.

Why hadn't she asked him for a number or address or if he had a job or was going to school? Didn't he say he'd already graduated from the University of Oregon?

All she had was his first name.

She'd about given up and had decided she wouldn't see him again, but she'd been wrong. Later that week she caught sight of him walking with three girls toward the quad where a protest rally was scheduled.

Harper's heart sank as she watched them.

A freckled redhead wore bell-bottoms and a midriff blouse. Her long hair was parted down the middle and held in place with a feathered headband. She was in deep conversation with a girl with a wild Afro who wore a sleeveless jumpsuit and bracelets that sparkled in the sunlight. All the while the third girl, a sun-streaked blonde in a suede miniskirt and peasant blouse, clung to his arm, rapt at whatever he was saying.

Ugh.

Harper felt a stupid pang of jealousy, which she told herself was completely out of line. She didn't even know the guy, not really, wasn't even sure that what he'd told her was the truth.

The group of four walked to the middle of the quad where the small protest was forming, clusters of students armed with placards and armbands and outrage. Harper could read a few: MAKE LOVE NOT WAR! and POWER TO THE PEOPLE! and HELL NO! WE WON'T GO!

For a fleeting second she thought of Rand Watkins, already in the jungles of Vietnam fighting a war these people were protesting. And she thought of Chase, still missing, who vowed never to go.

And here she was, an outsider again.

She concentrated on Joel. He and the girls sat cross-legged on the grass. A pipe was passed between them while a duo with acoustic guitars sang on the stage. Nearby a group of people she thought were the speakers were gathering. As the antiwar crowd grew, a group of protestors spread out on the lawn.

Her stomach turned over. Queasy again.

As the music died, a tall, bearded man took over the mic. His hair wild and curly, he started speaking vehemently, getting the crowd to respond.

Harper listened halfheartedly for a while, then started back to the apartment.

Just as she reached her front door, she heard footsteps running fast behind her.

"Harper!" Joel called.

She turned and found him jogging across the parking lot.

He was alone. The girls he'd been with minutes before not in sight.

His smile wide, he said, "Thought I saw you." He was breathing hard, his face flushed. "I've been meaning to stop by."

"Oh?" She was surprised, yet felt not only relief but a little thrill as well.

"Yeah, I found something you dropped the other day. When you spilled your Coke and your purse fell over?"

"What?"

He reached into the front pocket of his jeans, and she noticed the careful embroidery on the denim. Daisies winding up his leg by the side seam. "I went by the table where you were sitting on the way back and I found these." He handed her a small plastic bottle. Inside were her pre-natal vitamins, her name printed on the label. She hadn't even missed them.

"Oh." She let out a breath and felt her cheeks grow hot. She wanted to deny that they were hers but obviously couldn't. "Uh. Thanks." Embarrassed, she didn't know what to say.

"You okay?"

"What do you think?" she shot back.

He lifted a shoulder. "Don't know."

"Well, let's see, since you know my deepest, darkest secret," she said, "then you've probably figured out that I'm just fine. This is exactly where I thought I'd be at eighteen. Pregnant, having to get a GED, and all those universities that accepted me? Forget it. No college for me. Oh, and the father of my baby? Not in the picture."

His smile had slowly fallen from his face. "I'm sorry," he said. He actually looked like he understood.

"Yeah." She blinked against a rush of tears. "Me, too." Clearing her throat, she put up a brave front. "Look, thanks for finding these." She held up the vial of pills, shaking it so that it rattled. "I don't know how I could have explained losing them." Dashing the tears from her eyes, she blew out a long breath and pulled herself together.

An awkward silence ensued, and she finally said, "I'd better get go—"

"Would you like to go out?" he said suddenly, and she thought she hadn't heard correctly.

"What?"

"Yeah. You know. Go out. On a date."

"You want to take me out? Seriously?" He was being absurd, or felt sorry for her, which she definitely didn't need. She motioned to her abdomen. "Why would you want to do that?"

"I said before, you could use a friend."

"And I told you I didn't need one."

"But maybe I do." He appeared almost sheepish as a soft breeze passed by. Leaves on the branches overhead shimmered, casting shivering shadows across the walkway.

She laughed. "Looks like you've got plenty of friends to me." Gesturing to the intricate embroidery on his jeans, she said, "Someone who sews flowers on your Levis, unless you have hidden talents with a needle and thread."

"Hardly."

"And you have people to go to protests with."

He lifted a shoulder. "Maybe I want to meet someone new."

"A girl who's pregnant?" she said, shaking her head and laughing. "Oh sure."

"That has nothing to do with it."

"Come on." This was ridiculous.

"See you at eight," he said, not accepting "no" for an answer. Then he took off, jogging away, a tall man with an easy, loping stride.

"Wait!"

He slowed, looking over his shoulder.

"I don't even know your last name."

His grin widened. "Prescott," he said and then was off again.

She, still grasping the pill bottle, wondered what his game was.

Why was he interested in her?

And did he even know where she lived?

There was one way to find out.

Harper would take him up on his offer.

Chapter 51

Now that she was committed, Harper spent hours worrying about her upcoming date. What should she wear? Where would he take her? What would they do? How would she feel about being out with someone other than Chase?

"Quit being ridiculous," she chided herself as she stood in front of a full-length mirror, eyeing her still flat stomach. She'd tried on a short dress, then a pair of bell-bottoms and a loose-fitting blouse, both of which she tossed onto her bed. Thankfully her clothes still fit, though she knew that would be short-lived.

She couldn't understand her case of nerves. What did she care what she wore? Angry that it mattered at all, she settled on faded jeans and a crop top.

Marcia loudly disapproved. "Oh my God, Harper, what're you thinking?" she'd cried. "You're going to be a mother."

"Leave her be," Dad said before asking how she'd met Joel. Satisfied with her quick explanation, Dad met Joel at the door with Marcia hovering, pinched-faced, behind him. "Have a good time," Dad said. "Home by midnight."

Harper dashed out a little breathlessly, grateful to be out of the apartment.

Joel took her to a place he knew, a crowded café off campus that was filled with kids about her age. They shared a pot of cheese fondue while conversation and laughter buzzed around them. Afterward, because he knew the bouncer, Joel got her into a club though she was barely eighteen.

It was the first time she'd gone out in ages and it felt wonderful. Joel was funny, and though his sense of humor was a little on the sarcastic side, she liked it. She liked him.

She didn't get home until nearly two and Marcia was beside herself, but her father, thank God, understood and before her stepmother could light into her, Dad told Harper goodnight and she shot into her room.

The second she closed the door behind her she could hear the argument resonating through the paper-thin walls. Ear to the door, she closed her eyes and listened.

"She just needs to unwind a little," Bruce said. "Be a kid."

"You gave her a curfew."

"I know, but—"

"But she's going to have a baby!" Marcia wasn't about to be placated.

"I know, honey, but not for a while."

"It'll come sooner than you think. Really, I don't know if I can take this! You know, Bruce, this wasn't part of the deal! We had plans, remember? To travel? Once Harper was in college, we would be free to come and go as we please. To see the world! You promised!" Marcia's voice had risen an octave. "You—You told me we would move into the main house on Lake Twilight, didn't you? That we would live on the island. And you said, you promised that we would go to Hawaii and London and Paris and—"

"Shh, honey," Dad cut her off. "We'll still be able to do those things."

"Are you out of your mind? We're talking about another human being coming into the world. A *baby* with diapers and bottles and toys and colic and tantrums and—Oh dear God, I can't even think about it!"

"Then don't."

"But she's *here* with us! The baby will be *with us!*"

"Marcia, please."

"And what about your brilliant daughter, huh? She won't be going off to Stanford or USC or wherever now, will she? She'll be stuck here with us and we'll be babysitting around the clock while she goes out to God-knows-where and does God-knows-what!"

"Marcia, you're overreacting."

"Oh my God, Bruce, wake up and smell the coffee! We're going to be saddled with her and that kid for another twenty years! Do you know how old we'll be? Do you? Think about it!" She was starting to hyperventilate. "This is not what I signed up for!" And then there were a few quick, hard footsteps before the door to the next room banged shut.

Involuntarily, Harper jumped. The whole apartment seemed to shudder.

Everything Marcia said rang true. Slowly, leaning against the door, she slid to the floor. She placed a hand over her abdomen. "It's okay," she whispered, rocking back and forth, not knowing whether she was speaking to the baby or herself as tears drizzled down her cheeks. "It's going to be okay. I'll make it work out. Somehow."

The next day and those following were no better.

The argument between her father and Marcia still simmered, he trying to placate his wife and daughter and Marcia icing both of them out. Bruce spent some of his time at a branch office of the company he worked for, while Marcia glowered and barely spoke or spent days in her bedroom with the door shut.

Unable to stand the tension in the tight unit, Harper spent as much time out of the apartment as possible, at the college, in the park, or window shopping. And she saw Joel, either on a date her parents knew about or on the sly.

She learned he'd grown up in Southern California, gone to college at the University of Oregon where he'd gotten not only his BA but a Master's in English, spent half a year looking for jobs in Oregon before coming here, where he was hoping to land a full-time job at the junior college. Currently he juggled his time as a bartender at night while tutoring students during the day. He'd gotten out of the draft due to some medical issue.

She liked him more and more. He brought a little fun into her life. But she fought the ridiculous urge to think she was falling in love. Did he remind her of Chase? A little, she supposed, and her heart still ached for the boy she'd loved so fervently.

Joel seemed a bit of a dreamer and talked about everything he wanted to do in life. But then, didn't she have dreams as well, dreams a baby might put on hold but wouldn't destroy? And the more time she spent with him, away from the tension in that apartment, the more she wanted to spend with him. When he kissed her for the first time, she kissed him back. With more passion than she'd expected. When he touched her, she responded and found the feel of his hands on her body welcome and warm.

And the first time they made love, in an apartment he shared with two roommates, she cried for all the mistakes she'd made. He held her and she felt the ice around her heart begin to crack.

One night, three weeks after Harper met Joel, her father and stepmother were fighting again, a rehash of all the other spats they'd had—about Harper, about the baby, about finding a house, about being forced out of Oregon, about how unhappy Marcia was.

As the argument escalated, Harper left the apartment and waited in the parking lot for Joel. He picked her up, and they drove off in his old Rambler. "Bad?" he asked.

"The worst." In the passenger seat, she tapped her fingers on the edge of the open window, the recent fights between her father and Marcia swirling through her brain. Marcia thought Harper was ruining her life by spending time with Joel, and she wasn't afraid of telling her about it. She'd said, "One boy got you into this mess. Another one won't help!" It was as if Marcia expected her to be a nun. Well, a pregnant nun. If that was even a thing, which it wasn't.

Grimly Joel said, "I'm sorry."

"It's okay." But it wasn't.

They ate pizza at the local parlor, then, because his roommates were home studying, Joel drove them to the hills. The windows were down, music blasting from the speakers, warm air fanning her face and tangling her hair. He stopped in a spot where they'd parked before, on a quiet hill overlooking the city lights. He cut the engine and said, "You're obviously bummed. Wanna talk?"

Talk was the last thing on her mind. She just wanted to forget. "No." She reached out and pulled him close to kiss him and he responded, kissing her back, tugging her blouse from the top of her jeans, his hands finding her breasts as she arched upward.

They made love with a fevered passion that left Harper breathless. Joel, too, was gasping as he flopped back against the seat. "Man, what got into you?" he whispered.

"Don't know." But she did. She just didn't want to say how much she needed a release from all the bad karma at home. She didn't even want to think about living with her parents. She just wanted to escape. From their rules. From their fights. From everything about them. She saw the clock on the dash and blew out a long breath. "I have to get back." Another thing she wanted to escape from was her curfew. How dumb. She was going to have a baby and they were still bossing her around to the point of telling her when she could come home at night.

Marcia had said it earlier today. "You live in our house, then you live by our rules."

Bitch.

Joel was pulling on his jeans. He yanked them over his hips as she rehooked her bra. Glancing over at her, he said, "Let's get married."

"What?" Despite her mood, she almost laughed. "You can't be serious."

"I am. Dead serious."

"Are you crazy?" She looked up at the night sky, a crescent moon shining in a vast array of stars. "We can't just get married."

"Why not? You're eighteen now, right?"

"Yes, but—"

He twisted his key in the ignition, and the Rambler sparked to life. "We can drive to Nevada. Reno's not that far, and if we want to, we could drive all night and hit Vegas by morning."

She actually laughed then. "You're insane." She struggled into her jeans and buttoned her blouse as the car idled.

"I've been thinking about it. A lot."

"Oh, I get it. You don't want to be drafted," she said automatically.

"That's not it," he said confidently. "I'm not fit to join up. Asthma and bone spurs."

"Really?"

"Really." He slipped the car into gear and backed up. "This—you and me getting married—has nothing to do with that."

"Then why?"

"Because I want to be with you. All the time. Not just in bits and pieces. Not under your parents' thumb. Not with some stupid curfew dictating when we can see each other." He brushed a strand of hair from her cheek.

Her throat closed at his tenderness.

"I'm serious," he said quietly. "And face it, Harper, you're miserable."

"But the baby."

He reversed, then put the car into drive. "What about the baby?"

"You . . . would want to—?"

"I want you, okay?" he cut in. "You and the baby, you're a package deal. Don't you get it?"

She leaned against the door and watched his profile as he drove. As often as she'd fantasized about being Mrs. Chase Hunt, she hadn't gone there with Joel.

Joel had never once said that he loved her, nor had she uttered those fateful, fanciful words. And yet here he was driving into the night, seemingly dead serious. "Your baby needs a father," he said as they turned onto the main road.

"Chase is—"

"Never coming back," he said finally as the beams of an oncoming car washed over his face. A handsome face even in the harsh, moving light.

"You don't know that," she said, watching him as a worrisome thought came to mind. "Or do you?"

"Know what happened to him? Shit, no. Of course not. How would I?"

"You said you knew him."

"A little. It's not like we were all that tight," he said as he drove onto the main road. "And it's obvious, isn't it? If he was coming back, he would have shown up by now. Right? He left, Harper. Whether he intended to or not. I mean, maybe something happened to him."

"Like he's dead," she whispered.

"Whatever, the end result is he left you and the baby."

"He didn't know about the baby. I was going to tell him that night. The night he disappeared." She swallowed hard and looked out the passenger side window to the darkness beyond. "I just never got the chance." Then she turned to face Joel again. "And he didn't leave me. Something happened to him. Something in the middle of the lake."

She eyed him closely, looking for any tiny sign that he might lie. "Do you know what it is?"

"No!" He was emphatic. "Geez, Harper, get real. I wasn't even there when it happened."

She'd heard all the theories that Chase had left the boat running and then hitchhiked away, that the boat had been a decoy to give him time to reach the border. Or that he had a friend pick him up in another boat and left Tom Hunt's Triton to idle. Or that he'd swum to shore and found a ride or hopped a bus. Or whatever. But in her heart of hearts she couldn't believe that he would just leave her.

He'd said they would be married . . .

But that was before Uncle Sam had come calling.

Then everything had changed.

Joel swung wide for a corner, and the car skidded a bit, then settled back into the lane. There was more traffic now as they were heading back to the city, flashes of bright illumination as cars passed them. "Do you really want to live with your dad and stepmom?" he asked.

"No!"

"If you think it's bad now, how do you think it will be once the baby arrives?"

She didn't have to guess. "Marcia isn't happy about it. You know that. I don't think she's gonna be one of those hands-on grandmas." Not like Gram was. Warm and loving and always hoping to spend time with Harper and Evan. Her heart twisted. Oh, how she missed Gram, the woman who knew the answer to anything, it seemed, and who had loved her with all her heart. Clearing her throat, Harper ignored the pain and said, "I can't really see Marcia heating bottles and changing diapers."

"Me, neither."

"But you can see yourself doing that?" she asked. She didn't think he was being as up front with her as he'd like her to believe.

"Sure. How tough can it be?" He threw her a cocky grin.

She thought about it. Not buying it. Sensing there was something more going on here. "And what's in this marriage for you?" she finally asked.

"You."

"Got to be more," she said, drawing away so that she was leaning on the passenger door.

"My future," he said, elaborating. "Maybe it's time for me to settle down. A wife and kid. It could be cool."

"And if it's not?" she asked, hardly daring to believe that Joel Prescott was the answer to her prayers.

"If it's not?" He slid her a glance. "Let's just make sure it is." He smiled then and again, that hard, ice-cold part of her heart, the space where distrust dwelled, started to melt.

"I don't know," she said. "We barely know each other." And that was the truth. They'd been dating less than three weeks.

"So, we'll get to know each other after we tie the knot. Come on, Harper, what've you got to lose?"

She bit her lip. "If Chase comes back—"

"He isn't coming back, Harper."

"But *if* he did."

"We would figure it out," Joel insisted, and that's what she liked about him, his self-confidence.

Something she could use a little of herself.

"If he loves you as much as you think he does, then he'd fight for you, right?" Joel reasoned. "He wouldn't rest until you were back in his arms."

That stung.

Because, deep down, she wasn't sure.

She bit her lip. She was tempted. Why not throw caution to the wind?

"Look, Harper, I want to take care of you."

They came to a stop sign. Literally a crossroads. One way was to the security and tension of the apartment with her father and step-mother. The opposite direction led to the bright, shimmering lights of Las Vegas. Sin City. The unknown. Her heart thumped at the thrill, the daring of it all.

Was she going to be a scared, coddled little girl, hiding her pregnancy? Living with parents who didn't want her, didn't want her child?

Or was she going to step forward, live her own life, become a mother on her own terms?

And a wife.

Remember that, Harper. You'll be Joel Prescott's wife.

"What's it gonna be?" he asked, the car idling. "Do we go to Las Vegas and get married? Or do you want to go home?"

She thought again of the apartment.

Of her angry, irritable stepmother.

Of her despondent, miserable father.

They didn't need to be tied to her and her unborn child. She was an albatross around the neck of their marriage.

The seconds ticked off and headlights appeared in the rearview.

"Harper?" Joel prodded.

Her heart pounded in her head. She swallowed hard. "Vegas," she whispered.

He took the corner. "You're sure?" he asked, crooking an eyebrow.

She hardly dared to breathe. "Yes!" she finally said. Nodding, she felt more and more certain. "Yes. Yes." She bit her lip, caught up in the thrill of it all now that she'd agreed. "Let's go!"

"You got it!" He stepped on the gas. The Rambler took off, and he laughed. "On our way," he said as they drove toward the freeway. "Vegas, here we come! By this time tomorrow, you'll be Mrs. Joel Prescott and you can kiss your parents and all their rules good-bye!"

1988
The Present

Chapter 52

On the way to Camille Musgrave's home, Rand filled Chelle in on his conversation with his father. She listened from the passenger seat of his Jeep, for once not peppering him with questions.

They passed an accident, cops and ambulance already on the scene, a Toyota's hood and quarter panel crumpled, headlight dangling, a service van with smashed rear doors on the shoulder. Traffic was routed to one slow-moving lane while officers interviewed several agitated people.

Finally the snarl opened up and Chelle asked, "So you believe your dad, that Chase Hunt is dead, his body hidden by his father who killed him by accident."

"That's what Dad believes."

"And Tom Hunt committed suicide because the guilt finally got to him."

"Right."

"And maybe that happened when Cynthia finally discovered the truth."

"The time line fits."

"Huh." Chelle was digesting the information, turning it over in her mind. "So then here's a question: Why did Tom Hunt want the gun used to kill Evan Reed?"

"Don't know," Rand admitted, driving along a county road before he found the entrance to a sprawling 1970s subdivision of look-alike ranch homes. "But I think it might be tied up with Tristan Vargas or Larry Smith or whoever he is. He was blackmailing Tom, he was a known criminal, so I'm guessing there's a connection. Hopefully Camille Musgrave can help us."

"Or Janet Van Arsdale Collins. Moonbeam. She may have kept up with him."

"Let's see her later today," he said as he took a final corner, then parked on the curb in front of the tan Rambler with wine-red trim and a faded Ford Pinto parked in the driveway.

"This looks like my Aunt Zena lives here," Chelle remarked as they walked past a patchy lawn decorated with all kinds of yard art. Everything from pink flamingos to garden gnomes and ceramic frogs peeked out from overgrown vegetation.

They stepped onto a porch covered with gourds, pumpkins, and a scarecrow that had definitely seen better days.

Rand pressed on a doorbell and heard chimes pealing from within.

"Coming," a woman's voice called just before a chain clinked, and the door opened a crack. A slip of a woman with thick Coke-bottle glasses and a house coat peered through the screen door. Her gray hair was wrapped in rollers, and she wore a medical boot on one foot.

"I'm Detective Watkins, Almsville Police Department, and this is my partner, Detective Brown." He produced his ID, as did Chelle. "We're looking for Camille Musgrave."

"Well, you found her." She sized him up. "Your dad is Gerald, right? Man, oh man, you look just like him. I remember him. He was a cop, too. Lived down the street from our cabin." Her gray eyebrows drew together. "So, what's this about?"

"Chase Hunt's disappearance."

"Oh, that." She scoffed and waved a hand. "Yesterday's news."

Chelle said, "We'd just like to talk to you for a few minutes."

"Well, come in then. It's miserable out there."

She unlocked the screen and opened the door.

They followed her inside as she, using a cane, hobbled into the living area while the smell of roasting chicken emanated from the back of the house. Camille passed by a stone fireplace, flipped a switch, and flames immediately flickered over the gas logs in the firebox.

"Sit, sit!" she said, motioning to a couple of side chairs in the living room while she plopped onto a small floral recliner and cranked up the footrest. "Damn this thing," she grumbled, adjusting the boot. "Twisted my ankle last week, and this is what they gave me. A pain. That's what it is." She eyed them both. "I'm afraid you made the trip out here for nothing. I can't tell you anything about that Hunt boy. When it all happened, I told the police the same thing. Nothing has changed since."

Rand and Chelle sat in separate chairs in front of a large picture window overlooking the front porch. Between them was a bird cage on a stand, a little blue budgie jumping excitedly from one perch to the other.

Chelle took out a recorder and notebook and asked, "Do you mind if we record this?"

"Knock yourself out. It won't do any good. As I said, nothing's changed."

"Mom?" a female voice called. "Was that the door?" A fiftyish woman walked into the living room from the hallway. "Oh! Uh . . . who are you?" She, too, was short, but fuller-figured than Camille and twenty or so years younger. In jeans and a sweatshirt, her mop of brown curls held away from her face with a headband, she hesitated in the archway to the living room.

Rand got to his feet and pulled out his ID. Introductions were hastily made, she being Camille's daughter, Lynette Decker.

Lynette wasn't just surprised that there were cops in her living room, she was downright skeptical of why they'd come. "You think Mom can help you?" she asked, and before he could answer said, "It's been, what? Twenty years? I saw the write-up in the *Tribune* this morning because Mom still gets the Almsville paper, but really? She and Dad didn't even live in Almsville at the time. They rented out the cabin on the lake."

"To those hooligans," Camille interjected bitterly. "Hippie scum."

Lynette rolled her eyes and stepped in front of the fire to warm the back of her legs. "They ripped Mom off. Skipped out on the last month's rent and trashed the place."

"More than that," the older woman interjected as the bird whistled. "They were selling drugs and doing who knows what else down there. Ticked me off, let me tell you. My father built that cabin and that dock, the biggest on the damned point, and he'd be rolling over in his grave if he ever found out what had happened there!"

"Water under the bridge, Mom," Lynette reminded her.

But the older woman wasn't listening. Agitated, she said, "Renting the place out was Victor's idea, and if he wasn't already dead, I'd wring his scrawny neck!"

"Victor was my dad," Lynette explained with a sigh. "We probably should have sold that place ages ago, but—"

"Over my dead body! Didn't I just say that your grandpa, he built the cabin, and the boat slip and the damned dock? It's not leaving this family, not while I'm still kicking." Camille's chin jutted out, and she sent her daughter a warning glare.

"I know, I know," Lynette said, as if she'd heard it all a dozen times over. "Mom, just tell them what you know. Oh God, is the chicken burning? You were supposed to watch it and let me know if it was done."

"Well, I got busy now, didn't I?" With lips pursed, she hitched her chin toward Rand and Chelle.

"Holy crap!" Lynette was already hurrying around the fireplace, presumably in the direction of the kitchen.

"Anyway," Camille said, drawing out the word. "I can't tell you anything. And I'm surprised you're asking. Those other cops who were on duty then? They didn't care a lick about what went on down there, and if they questioned any of those hooligans, I didn't hear about it. As a matter of fact, they all tore out the day after that boy went missing. Just left the place a pigsty!"

"She's right," Lynette agreed, wiping her hands on a dish towel as she returned.

"The chicken?" her mother asked.

"Crispy. But it'll be okay."

Chelle brought the woman back to the topic at hand. "Were any of the people you rented to friends of Chase Hunt?"

"How would I know? Was he into drugs?" Camille asked, shifting her booted foot again. "If he was, then, by God, he was there with that lot."

"Mom, please." Lynette sighed and dropped the towel onto the raised hearth. "I think it was just pot and—"

"There is no such thing as 'just pot.' We're talking about marijuana, Lynnie! Have you ever seen *Reefer Madness*?"

"Oh, Mom, stop!" Lynette sat on the sofa next to her mother's recliner. She took Camille's hand. "The police are busy. So let's just keep to the topic." Turning to face Rand, she said, "It was a bad scene, and as I said, the people who lived there just took off."

"Scattered like leaves in the goddamned wind," Camille interjected as the budgie hung upside down for a second, before saying, "Pretty boy," clear as a bell.

"Mom taught Enos a few words. Right, buddy?"

He repeated, "Pretty boy," and Lynette went on, "I don't even know if they talked to the police. A lot of their things were just abandoned."

Camille interjected, "As I said, it was a frickin' pigsty!"

"She's right, a real mess." Lynette patted her mother's thin shoulder.

"Do you have forwarding addresses or phone numbers where they might be reached?"

"What do you think?" Camille snorted. "Those little sons of bitches left us with all the bills. Phone included. Electricity. Gas. All fell back on Victor and me. You think they'd leave us any way to contact them? Hell no, they didn't! Hippie scum, that's what they were!"

"Mom!" Her daughter warned.

"It's true." Camille shifted away from Lynette's touch, and her chin jutted more sharply.

"Fine, I know," Lynette conceded and explained. "Mom's right. We couldn't locate any of them, and we tried."

"Poof!" Camille threw open her palms "Vanished. You tell me they're not guilty!"

Lynette said, "The person who signed the lease was Tristan Van Something."

"No, no. That was the girl's name. The one he was with. Van Arsdale. Janet Van Arsdale," Camille interjected and scowled at her daughter. "You're as bad as your father with names. The person who signed the lease was Tristan Vargas." Camille's lips pursed. She took off her glasses and began cleaning the lenses with the cuff of her sleeve. "I'll never forget that little snake in the grass with his long hair and round glasses. Mr. Cool."

"That's right." Lynette was nodding. "He went by a nickname."

Rand nodded. "Trick."

Chelle asked, "Did you know him by any other name?"

"No. Just Trick. Dumb name if you ask me." Camille seemed certain.

"Like I said, we never heard from him again," Lynette interjected. "Oh, we tried. But Dad wasn't well even then. He had a stroke soon after and, well, we didn't rent the place for a while."

"Just locked it up." Camille was nodding, adjusting her glasses. "If you ask me, the police were in on it. That would be your father," she said, glaring at Rand. "They knew drugs were being peddled out of there. For the love of Christ, you'd have thought they'd do something about it. But did they? No. Just looked the other way."

"Mom," Lynette said in a cautionary voice, "Detective Watkins's father was on the—"

"I know who he was! Didn't I say so? Don't treat me like I'm a half-wit!" Camille snorted, then motioning toward Rand, said, "They came here poking the bear, asking questions, didn't they? Well, they're gonna get the truth from me. I'm not sugarcoating anything." She folded her arms over her chest defiantly.

"It's fine," Rand said.

"Okay." Lynette seemed mollified. "So, later, when it was obvious no one was coming back to the cabin," she explained, getting the conversation back on track, "we cleaned the place up and started renting it again."

Chelle asked, "What happened to their belongings?"

"Got rid of 'em," Camille said. "This was after Victor passed, mind you, but we junked everything. Well, except what was in that attic space."

"They left things in the attic?"

Lynette's eyes slid away, and she rubbed her chin nervously. "Well, yes, and . . . well, we just locked it up. Actually sealed the door closed. No one's been up there in years."

Rand asked, "Why?"

"Oh, I don't know. Mom was paranoid about it," Lynette said.

Camille chimed in, "Didn't really know what was up there."

Lynette nodded nervously. "She thought we might get in trouble."

"With?" Chelle prodded.

Lynette sighed. "The authorities, or possibly some drug kingpin, or even the renters themselves if they ever returned."

"About what? What's up there?" Chelle was leaning closer.

"Spy stuff!" Camille spat out the words. "And dope and who knows what else!"

"Spy stuff like what?" Rand asked.

"Cameras. Listening devices, you know 'bugs' like in the spy movies," Camille said, her eyebrows arching over her glasses. "Tape recorders and movie cameras and binoculars—like they have in the army, high powered." Camille picked at the lace at the edge of her sleeve, pulling at a loose thread. "Victor, when he was alive, he thought maybe it was some kind of government operation—a sting and that Trick or one of the others was a spy. Maybe even a Ruskie."

"On Lake Twilight?" Chelle asked but managed to keep the skepticism from her voice.

Still toying with the loose thread, Camille shot her a damning are-you-stupid look. "We're not that far from Portland. And don't you think there aren't spies there!"

Lynette explained, "When he was alive, Dad thought that the cops might be planning some kind of undercover drug bust or something. But he was into all kinds of conspiracy theories. And then his stroke." Lynette offered a weak smile. "It was a lot to deal with so . . ."

Chelle asked, "Any chance that stuff is still in the attic?"

"Don't see why not." Camille snapped the thread in her fingers. "I suppose you want to take a look, eh?"

Chelle was nodding. "Yes. It might help."

The budgie bird gave off another high-pitched whistle before pecking rapidly at his hanging mirror.

"Don't count on it." Camille winced as she moved her booted ankle again. "Damned thing. Weighs a ton."

Lynette was on her feet, ready to end the visit. "Okay. Good. The house is empty now. We're between renters."

"Because *you* want to sell it," her mother charged, a pissy look on her face.

"I can meet you over there in a couple of hours," she said.

Rand nodded. "That would be great."

"But you'll need a crowbar and possibly a hacksaw—something to get the door to the attic open. I've got a key, but it won't do much good." Nonetheless, she went into the kitchen area and returned with a key ring with two keys, one tarnished. She held the ring by the brighter-looking key. "We changed the locks again after the last tenants. This one is for the front door. And the other one is for the attic."

From behind her thick glasses, Camille skewered him with a knowing glare. "Big waste of time if you ask me. If you're looking for Chase Hunt, thinking he might be up in that attic?" She snorted and shook her head. "I hate to disappoint you, but he's not there."

Chapter 53

Traffic was sluggish, the sky ominous and dark, as Rand drove back to Almsville. At Chelle's request, they stopped at Wendy's for burgers and drinks. "I work better on a full stomach," she told him, "and that roasted chicken at the Musgraves' house was driving me crazy."

They ate in the near-empty break room, and by the time Rand was back in his office, he found a thick packet on his desk. Inside was a partially burned and water-soaked photograph album with a few pages still inside. Also there were dozens of dried-out photographs that had been collected from the lake after Cynthia Hunt's death. They were faded, most almost impossible to discern, but as he looked through them he caught images of Levi and Chase, their parents, and even a couple images of Rand himself. Of course there were a few of Harper. She'd nearly been a fixture in the Hunts' lives, first as a friend to Levi and then as Chase's steady. Until she wasn't.

"What're you looking at?" Chelle asked as she returned, her drink from Wendy's in hand.

"Pictures that belonged to Cynthia Hunt. Dredged out of the lake."

"Oh." She set her soda on her desk and looked at them. "Is that you?" she asked, and he squinted at a faded, slightly crumpled picture of three people in swimsuits standing on a dock, the lake shimmering behind them.

"Yeah," he said. Chase, tall and blond, was front and center as always. His arm was slung over Harper's shoulders with Rand on his other side.

"Who took the picture?"

He thought. "Levi, I think," remembering that vibrant summer day.

"Chase Hunt's brother?"

"Yeah. I think it was his camera. He was into all that stuff."

She held the photo closer to her face. "You look mad."

"I probably was." He glanced at her. "A way of life back then."

"Huh." Scanning several of the photos, she said, "I wonder why Cynthia took all this stuff with her?"

"Dunno," he said as she picked up her drink and sipped through the straw. "Obviously she wanted to make a statement."

"As if what she did to herself wasn't enough." She sat on the corner of her desk and took a sip through the straw. "You think she was triggered because Harper Prescott came back to town?"

"A distinct possibility."

"But how did she know she was back?"

"Good question," Rand said, and one he'd been asking himself. *I doubt I'll ever know*, he thought as he picked up his phone for his messages. He had one. From Janet Collins, the woman they knew as Janet Van Arsdale. Or Moonbeam.

"I know this was all a long time ago, but I read about what happened to Mrs. Hunt in the paper and then I saw that there was a story about tragedies on Lake Twilight, you know? And there was mention of Chase Hunt disappearing. I, um, I lived in a cabin on Lake Twilight years ago with a bunch of kids. It was at the dead end of Trail's End, the road on that point whatever it was called. And I remember on the night Chase Hunt went missing, I saw something. I was with Trick, uh, that's what he went by, but his name was Tristan Vargas and he had all kinds of equipment. Cameras. Recorders. Shi—stuff like that. Anyway, I saw Chase and his old man fighting on their dock. Really going at it. The father hauled back and clocked Chase, he fell back and went down. Trick, he got it all on camera." There was a pause in the recording, then she went on. "I know I should have told the police a long time ago, but Chase's father, he was a cop, so I thought what good would it do. And, to be truthful, I was afraid." She left her phone number.

They already had her address.

He hung up and returned the call.

It went directly to an answering machine. "Hi, you've reached Janet," she said, and then a younger male voice chimed in, "And Rory. You know the drill. Leave a message."

Rand left his name and the department's number, then asked her to call him back.

Chelle, too, had been returning calls, the most important one being to Matilda Burroughs, Olivia Dixon's caretaker. "She hasn't changed her tune," Chelle said after hanging up.

"The gist of it is she blamed—no, make that still blames—Harper Prescott for Olivia Dixon's death. Matilda claims she measured out Olivia's medication carefully, leaving the exact dose with implicit instructions before she left. She'd done it before. Matilda also insisted that Harper had been old enough to understand that no one should drink alcohol while on that medication. Then she went off on Harper."

"So no real help," Rand said.

"No." Chelle took a last noisy drink from her straw, then crushed the cup and dropped it into the trash. "I guess we'd better go meet the Musgraves."

"Then we'll head over to Janet Collins's place," he said, filling her in as he grabbed his jacket. "Do we have a work number for her?"

"Not yet."

"Let's get it. Maybe we can still get to the Musgraves' cabin before Lynette arrives. I'd like to beat her there. Poke around a bit. Get the lay of the land."

"Don't you know it? Being as you're neighbors and all?"

"Haven't been down there in years."

They made the short trip. Rand parked in his own driveway, then went into the small shed at the side of the A-frame. He slipped a couple of screwdrivers and a claw hammer into a pocket, then picked up his crowbar and ax and hoped that he wouldn't have to use either as he walked with Chelle to the end of the street.

The Musgraves' cabin was in need of paint, the porch sagged a little, and the roof was covered in fir needles from the tall trees dominating the yard.

Chelle eyed the place. "Could use a little TLC," she observed. "The attic access is on the outside, right?"

"Yeah, the west end. Near the woods." Conveniently out of sight of the neighbors.

He followed her to the narrow side yard where stairs ran up the exterior. He'd noticed them as a kid when he'd ridden his bike or hiked up the deer trails, but he'd never thought much about the rickety steps.

Until now.

Chelle was already halfway up when Rand spotted the orange Pinto rattling down the street to pull into the driveway. So much for getting something done before they arrived.

Lynette climbed out of the driver's side door, but Camille, hair no longer in rollers but styled into a helmet, was positioned in the passenger seat and didn't try to get out of the car. "Mom wouldn't let me come alone," Lynette explained as she walked up to Rand, who was standing at the corner of the house. "It's like she doesn't trust me. She seems to expect that I would sell the place out from under her."

"Why don't you pull up to the end of the street so she can watch what we're doing?" he suggested.

She eyed the ax and crowbar. "Try not to destroy the door," she warned. "Mom would have a fit, and I really don't want to buy a new one."

"Got it."

As she went back to the car, he mounted the steps. On the small landing Chelle was already attempting to open the door with the key, which when inserted turned, but the door didn't budge. She gave it a push with her shoulder, but still it remained. "Damn, they're right," she said with a sigh.

"Let's try this," he said, setting down the tool box and ax and hefting the crowbar. "Stand back." She took three steps down as the Pinto cruised to a stop at the end of the street.

Rand used the crowbar, wedging it between the door and frame. He applied all his weight and strength to it. It held for a second, then with a loud creak, the door gave. Nails popped. Bits of the door splintered. "We're in," he said. He pushed the door open wider and was hit by a wave of musty-smelling air. Leaving his tools on the small landing, he hunched slightly to get through the door. Inside he hit the switch at the side of the door, and the single dangling bulb flashed and then sizzled, the only illumination coming through a round window cut into the angle of the room.

"Got it," Chelle said, turning on her flashlight, sweeping its beam over the interior as she followed him inside. "What is this place? A crash pad?" The beam crawled over a mattress on the floor, stuffing blooming from it, a layer of dust and grime everywhere.

"And an observation post. Shine the light over here, under the window."

She did and exposed a long desk running beneath the grimy window, a telescope positioned near the nearly opaque glass. Two other sets of binoculars were close at hand, along with half-filled ashtrays and a lava lamp, which Rand turned on, a weak light emitting from its conical shape. Cameras and video equipment, circa 1965, microphones and transmitters littered the desk. Night vision goggles and scopes were tucked nearby. A lot of the equipment appeared to be military issue, technology developed during the war.

He remembered.

"It's a time capsule," Chelle observed.

She was right.

The lava lamp was heating and oil blobs started to rise and fall within, casting the attic in a weird blue light. Chelle bent over the telescope and peered through the eyepiece. "Weird," she whispered, adjusting the focus.

"What?"

"This is trained on the house on the island across the lake. Fixed in this position."

"Really?"

"Like it was left that way."

"For twenty years?" Rand asked.

"If what the Musgraves say is true." She scanned the sloped roof and bare beams where spiderwebs and bees' nests were in evidence. "It sure doesn't look like anyone's been up here. Just rats and yellow jackets and spiders."

"You're right," he said. "Let me take a look."

She stepped aside, and he leaned over to stare through the telescope. The magnification was powerful and indeed focused across the lake to Dixon Island. Through the lens he viewed the entire island, including the boathouse, dock, tram, and mansion. Or, intensifying the magnification, he was able to stare into individual rooms, with enough clarity as to make out the bottles in the liquor cabinet, some old doll on a divan, and a crucifix on the wall.

He froze as Harper passed by the window. She glanced outside, and she seemed to be staring straight at him, so visible that he saw the lingering discoloration on her face, the red area on her chin where there had once been stitches.

Harper blinked, her blue eyes intelligent and searching. He felt a tightening in his chest. Then, as if she'd heard something behind her, she turned quickly and disappeared from the viewfinder.

"You done being a voyeur?" Chelle prodded as Rand straightened from the telescope in the Musgraves' attic. She was smiling. "And you claim you don't have a thing for her."

"I don't—" He started to protest, then said, "She was someone I knew, a friend. When we were kids." *If that*, he thought. But certainly not after the interview. "She's not that crazy about me now."

"Uh-huh." Chelle didn't bother hiding her skepticism as she shone the beam of her flashlight over shelving on the far wall where movie reels and canisters of undeveloped film were stacked. On the shelf below were microphones, cameras with interchangeable lenses, batteries, and flashbulbs.

Rand picked up a Brownie movie camera. "Straight out of the fifties," he said, remembering that the Hunts had owned one like this. The second camera was a Kodak Instamatic M8. And the third he didn't recognize, but it looked expensive, more professional as it had interchangeable lenses. Possibly one allowing night vision? Rand didn't know enough about photographic equipment to make an educated guess, but the equipment looked state of the art for its era.

He heard footsteps on the stairs. As he replaced the movie camera, Lynette poked her head inside. "Oh. Gross," she said, looking around. "Holy . . . Was Dad right? Was this a spy ring? Or drug den?"

Chelle said, "We're still checking it out."

"And that awful smell—did something die up here?" Lynette's face twisted into an expression of disgust.

"Maybe a water leak, or mold. Haven't found any sign of it," Rand said. "But you might want to check it out with a contractor."

"Oh, great. One more expense." She clucked her tongue. "We should just sell this place. I think I'm making an executive decision here, with*out* Mom."

Rand said, "We're going to need to go through everything here."

"Oh sure." Lynette flipped a hand. "Anything you want up here, just take. It's been twenty years."

"We will," Chelle said.

"Good." Lynette started to leave and touched the splintered wood on the door with a finger. "If you want to see downstairs, I'll stick around for a while."

"Be right there," Chelle said and, once Lynette was out of earshot, shone her flashlight on the film canisters and reels. "I think we should go through all of these. Who knows what we'll find?"

"Right," he said and hated the creeping feeling of foreboding about dredging up the past again. But it was too late to turn back now.

Chapter 54

"Son of a bitch!" On a step stool, reaching onto the top of the closet in the master bedroom, Levi yanked the tiny microphone out of the wall and held the small device in his palm.

He knew exactly what he'd found. He'd used a similar one in surveillance for some of his clients.

It was small.

State of the art.

Easy to install.

And accurate. It could pick up whispers from several feet away.

Favored by spies and private investigators, a newer model.

Ironic that it had been used on him.

And Beth.

He didn't have to think too hard to know who had planted it. And, he bet, if he went into Craig's workroom at the Alexander house next door, he'd find earphones and a recorder. "Damn," he muttered, imagining Craig Alexander sneaking into this house and hooking it up. Craig had spent the past twenty-odd years of his life working in construction. He knew the trades. And he had the motive: Levi was sleeping with Craig's wife.

A mistake.

It had been from the get-go.

Levi hopped off the ladder and wanted to grind the damned microphone under his shoe but figured he needed a harder surface than the green shag carpeting that still covered the floor of his parents' bedroom.

Why hadn't he listened to his gut?

He'd had the feeling that he was being watched but had convinced himself that he was just being paranoid, had spent too many years in the spy business. Even as he'd begun the short affair.

He took the tiny listening device downstairs and walked outside. It was late afternoon, a chill in the air. The rain was holding off for the moment but was threatening in the slow-moving clouds easing across the sky.

He should never have gotten involved with Beth Alexander.

Angry at himself and the world in general, he hurled the microphone as far as he could throw it. The bug plunked into the water, immediately sinking. "Good riddance," he muttered, though it was really too little too late. The damage had been done.

Ramming his fists into his pockets, he looked farther across the lake to the island. Where lights glowed from windows in the darkening afternoon. Where he'd spent so much of his time as a kid. Where Harper now resided.

His jaw slid to the side and he wondered about her. She was divorced and had a teenaged daughter. And she'd tried to save his mother from a horrid, mind-numbing death. But what else was there about her that he didn't know?

Did she still like chocolate? He remembered Harper eating the chocolate layer first when his mother served slabs of Neapolitan ice cream cut straight out of the carton. Was Harper still a fan of the Beatles and have a crush on Paul McCartney? Had she followed Peggy Fleming's skating career with the admiration she'd shown as a girl? Did she ever get the horse she'd wanted—what was it? A cross-bred Arabian stallion like the horse in Walter Farley's *The Black Stallion*?

Most importantly, Was she still in love with Chase?

Annoyed at the turn of his thoughts, he kicked at a pebble on the deck, sending it flying into the distance.

Levi's relationship with Harper had once been innocent, then complicated, and now didn't exist. Except that she had called and left a message on his office phone, saying she had some things belonging to Chase and wanted to return them to him.

Too little too late. Whatever the items were, Levi didn't want them. Twenty-year-old mementos of a life that was long dead were of no use to him.

The past was long over.

And if his mother's note could be believed, Chase was dead.

Killed.

Or was the note Cynthia left him just the rantings of a crazy, grief-riddled old woman?

Who knew?

Hopefully Rand and the local police would figure it out.

One way or another, it was time to put what happened to his brother to rest.

He stretched, cracked his neck, and watched as a pair of ducks landed on the water, gliding across the surface, creating perfect wakes and quacking to each other while a bullfrog croaked from its hiding spot. The air had a chill in it, the promise of coming winter.

It could be peaceful here.

And it could be chaos. Another glance at the massive house on the island and he caught a movement. A woman backdropped by lamplight. *Harper's silhouette in the windows*, he thought. The distance between the point and the island was too great for details. He couldn't make out her features, but he assumed the slim woman appearing in one window and then the next was she. The way she moved brought back memories. Forbidden recollections. Taboo thoughts. He'd always found her attractive, not just physically but spiritually as well, if you believed in that crap.

Levi usually didn't.

But with Harper, he'd always bent the rules.

As he stared at her, a part of him twisted inside and yearned for a happier, less complicated time.

"Dreamer," he muttered, turning his back on the lake and all the memories that were better left forgotten.

He went inside to the cluttered kitchen, where boxes were still unpacked and his mother's things were everywhere. The coffeepot and blender on the counter, vases of dying plants in the windowsill, an ashtray near the burners of the harvest gold stove, magazines and newspapers piled near the back door. Vestiges of a life that stopped twenty years before.

He reached into the side-by-side refrigerator and yanked a beer from the six-pack he'd brought earlier. He cracked it open, then drank half the bottle before setting it on the counter and getting back to work unpacking the car.

As he pulled two boxes from his trunk, he saw Rand's Jeep parked in the drive of his A-frame. Also an old orange Pinto was sitting at the end of the street, someone inside.

He noted no vehicles were in sight at the Alexander house next door. He figured no one was home. The house was too still. No lights shone from the windows, and their dog wasn't in his usual spot on the front porch. No sign of their son Max, or anyone else. Though Beth usually parked her BMW in the garage, Craig's pickup was always front and center when he was home.

Not today. Not yet.

Good.

He carried the boxes inside, left them on the old couch, then spent nearly an hour sweeping the interior for more listening equipment, searching through the jumble of his things and his mother's furniture and household items. From the basement where the old Wurlitzer sat unplugged and gathering dust to the attic where he found more boxes of junk. He looked through old wire hangers, broken picture frames, and Christmas decorations from his youth, glass bulbs that glittered in what was then the new "Space Age" design. Straight out of the fifties.

But no more spy equipment.

Good.

Dusting cobwebs from his hair and grime from his hands, he returned to the chaos of the main floor. The only neat area of the house was one corner of the living room where he'd stacked the seven boxes he'd hauled from Serenity Acres earlier this week, days after Director Allison Gray had laid down her edict of when the unit had to be cleared.

Fuck that. His mother had just died a horrible death, and he hadn't been concerned with Serenity Acres' time line or Allison Gray's need to fill her room with another warm body.

Through the window, he saw the Alexanders' house.

Silently Levi berated himself for getting involved with Beth. What had he been thinking? When she'd approached him about selling this house, she'd flirted a bit and he'd resisted. He hadn't been interested.

She was married, for God's sake, and that's where he'd always drawn the line.

Before.

Hell, didn't he have enough clients on his books to know that getting involved with a married woman was the kiss of death? If not literally, then financially and emotionally?

He sipped his beer and thought back. They'd met several times, at her insistence, and as they'd had coffee or drinks, she'd let it slip that things weren't great between Craig and her. Money problems. She needed listings and sales, he needed new construction projects.

Levi had ignored her woes. She'd always been overly dramatic. Even in high school she got most of her news from tabloids at the check-out counter in the local grocery stores, so he'd discounted a lot of what she told him.

Even when she'd admitted that Craig had been unfaithful over the years but she'd stuck with him for the sake of their son, Max, Levi had only nodded and filed the information away.

Not his business.

Until it was.

Beth Leonetti Alexander was nothing if not persistent.

Once, when yet again they'd met and she'd tried to pressure him into listing the house, they'd had one too many drinks or possibly three or four too many. In her efforts to convince him to sell, she'd not only mentioned the profit he would make on the lakefront cottage but also how it would help her and her son. Max was a stellar student, but Beth had indicated she and Craig might not have any money to help Max with college. In fact she was afraid they would have to sell their house and were under water with it. They had borrowed extensively against their home on the lake in order to finance her purchase of the realty company and pump up Craig's fledgling construction business, which had never really taken off.

He thought about their conversation as he took his beer upstairs and walked into the room where he'd found the bug.

Beth had admitted their financial dilemma brokenly to Levi that night, and he had caught sight of a tear tracking down her cheek. She admitted that her marriage was over. She was sticking it out until Max left for the university, then she and Craig would split, her dreams of happily-ever-after shattered long before.

Levi had tried to console her, placing an arm around her. She'd turned into him and kissed him, then, her lips salty from her tears.

And, damn it, he'd responded, kissing her back, feeling his blood rise, desire sparking.

They'd ended up in bed together. *In this very bed*, he thought, casting an angry look at the king-sized mattress and springs and the hobnail bedspread with its tufted pattern his mother had loved. What had started out as solace had swiftly become passion and hot, raw sex, a physical release that had left them both breathless and gasping.

It had felt good, if tainted with a measure of guilt.

He should have ended it there.

Three weeks ago.

Before it had gone further.

But he hadn't.

Nor had she.

Though he'd regretted sleeping with her the very next day, he hadn't called and ended it. He had told himself it would never happen again, that it had just been a moment out of time. A mistake. One night.

But he'd been lying. Deep down, he'd known it at the time.

After all, his one night with Beth hadn't been the first time he'd stepped over that blurry line of a secretive tryst, but he hoped to God it was the last.

Now, it seemed, they'd been found out.

Recorded, for God's sake.

Today he would end their affair.

And if he ever did end up selling this place, he'd offer her the listing. *It's the least I can do*, he thought, draining his beer and leaving his empty on the cluttered kitchen counter.

He headed outside to his car and continued hauling boxes inside. It was time for a fresh start.

But first, he reminded himself as he carried in the final box and kicked the door shut behind him, he had to deal with Harper.

Chapter 55

"Wow. This is like sooo cool." Dawn stood in the foyer of the house and gazed at the split staircase, eyeing the way the steps ran up either side of the vestibule.

Harper was surprised to see her daughter. "I thought you were coming later."

"I know." Dawn lifted a shoulder. "Change of plans. Again. Grandpa wasn't home. I buzzed to be let into the penthouse, but no one responded. But it all worked out, I guess, because I'm kinda in a hurry. Gina wants to get back to Eugene earlier—something about when the movie is playing earlier, so I can't stay long. Sorry."

"It's okay." Harper felt a jab of disappointment that the visit would be short but also more than a little relief. Right now she wasn't certain the island was safe and she wasn't ready to explain about the dolls with their weird messages or the dead cat or the knowledge that an intruder had broken in. "I was thinking we could go to dinner," she said, locking the door.

"Next time, I guess. I should have just come up here myself, but Gina needed a ride and I have a car."

"My car."

"You've got the Volvo," Dawn said. "And it suits you better!"

"I don't know if that's a compliment."

"It means you're older. That's all." Dawn dropped her oversized purse on the marble floor before climbing up one side of the curved staircase. At the landing she paused to stare at the chandelier with its glittering bulbs and teardrop crystals. "Oooh, this is like thirties retro, right?"

"Probably." Harper craned her neck to look up at her daughter. "Maybe older. I think the house was built in the teens. I can't remember, but Gram's notes about the house are somewhere. I just haven't found them yet." Truth was, she hadn't looked. "Hey," she called up the stairs. "Are you hungry? Can I get you anything?"

"Nah. I'm good. Stopped at Mickey D's on the way up." Dawn leaned over the carved railing. "I feel like Juliet in the balcony scene up here," she said, and Harper was reminded that her daughter was now into Shakespeare, had been taking a class on The Bard. "Tell me again," Dawn said, "why I haven't been here before."

"We lived in California. Remember?"

"I know, but why didn't you and Dad move here?"

"Uh, maybe it was because we had jobs there and you were going to school."

"And you hadn't really inherited it yet, right?" Dawn started down the opposite side of the staircase, her Doc Martens ringing on the wooden steps, her fingers trailing along the railing. "And now you're moving in? Wow." She skipped over the last step and, grinning, picked up her bag again. "Awesome!"

"If I stay here."

"Why wouldn't you?" Dawn turned her doe-like eyes on her mother in wonder. "I mean this is almost like a castle."

"Or a haunted house."

"Even better. And I love those beasts hulking on the posts by the gate. They're beyond gnarly."

"The gargoyles?"

"Yeah!"

"Then you're probably a fan club of one."

"Really, no one likes them?" Dawn said. "Weird."

Harper wondered if that was a compliment, like bad is good and sick is cool and maybe weird meant out of sight or whatever. But calling something weird seemed odd coming from a girl who loved anything that was out of step with the norm. These days Dawn dressed in layered, uneven black skirts that sparkled and wore gloves without fingers, heavy boots, and umpteen necklaces and crosses, all at once.

There had been a time when she was in grade school when Dawn had worn T-shirts and hoodies, sweat pants and shorts. Like her mother before her, Dawn had been a tomboy. Naturally athletic, she had climbed any tree she saw, scrambling up to the highest branches. She'd ridden her skateboard all over Santa Rosa and had taken horseback riding lessons while earning a black belt in karate, one of the few girls in her class.

Then she'd turned fifteen.

Dawn had discovered boys, alternative music, punk culture, and the whole Goth scene as a sophomore in high school. She'd become sullen and withdrawn, found new friends, and tried to ignore her parents. Somehow, though, thank God, she'd managed to keep her grades up.

By the time she'd entered college, Dawn had dropped some of the moody oppressed-teen act. But even if now she was more borderline alternative, she still embraced the Gothic fashion sense as evidenced in today's all black outfit of torn tights, short lacy dress, and big hair. Today her lips were pale. She wasn't wearing the black lipstick that had been part of her makeup her senior year and aside from a line of silver studs crawling up one ear, she hadn't had any more body parts pierced. At least none that were visible.

"Are you okay?" Dawn asked, walking closer and poking an ebony-lacquered nail at her mother's chin. "This is where you had stitches, right?" She eyed the red line where the skin had been pulled together and the little dots on either side where the stitches had been pulled through. "Wow. Kinda looks like a caterpillar."

"It's fine. Seriously. I'm getting there."

"Will you have a scar?"

"God, I hope not."

Dawn actually seemed concerned. "What does the doctor say?"

"That I'm fine," she snapped, then hearing the harsh tone of her voice added, "Or that I will be. Maybe just a little worse for wear. It'll take a little time."

"Uh-huh." Dawn didn't seem convinced, but she let it slide.

Harper didn't want to further this particular discussion. "Come on," she suggested, "I'll show you around."

"Okay." Dawn dropped her purse again. "Let's go outside first! I want to see all around the island."

"All right. We'll start out back."

Harper walked Dawn through the overgrown trails where she'd played tag or war as a kid. They hiked beneath the fir trees with their sweeping, needled branches while fir cones littered the muddy paths. "I like it," Dawn said almost wistfully as she spied a great blue heron skimming the lake's surface, wingspan wide, his reflection visible in the water.

They took the steps to the dock and cavernous boathouse, where Dawn surveyed the rotting timbers with their bat droppings and the old, rotting boat creaked in its ancient straps. "Totally creepy," Dawn whispered above the echoing sound of the lapping water. "I *love* it!" Her enthusiasm didn't wane as they entered the tunnel and climbed the stairs to the terrace and the tram's garage.

Intrigued, Dawn wanted to test out the car. "Come on, Mom," she begged. "Show me how it works."

"Later," Harper said, "I'm not sure it would even start."

"Well, we could try. Isn't that what you always said, 'you'll never know until you try'?"

"But not today. If we were lucky enough to get it started, it's still not safe."

Even under its shelter, the car had collected dirt, grime, and fir needles. Who knew what condition the track was in? All of which didn't contribute as much to her aversion as the memory of Evan sprawled in the car. Even now, in her mind's eye, she witnessed him lying in the car, eyes wide, hair fanned around his head, blood dripping in red rivulets from the seat to the floor of the car.

Forcing the graphic image from her mind, she stepped back from the car's interior. "I thought you wanted to see the rest of the house."

"I do. For sure." Dawn pointed upward to the tower rising above the roofline. "Let's start up there. We can work our way down."

"Okay."

But as they reached the terrace, Dawn glanced around and asked, "Where's Jinx?"

Harper's heart nose-dived. She thought about admitting the truth but settled on, "He's around."

Dawn frowned and produced a rubber band from a pocket. "He could get lost here," she said, pulling her wild mane into a loose bun. "I mean, anyone could. Not just a cat."

"He's been gone for a couple of days," Harper admitted, stretching the truth a little. "But you know how he is."

"Yeah." But Dawn's brown eyes swept the area, taking in the beach, the dock, the trees and dense shrubbery on the island. "I bet he loves it here."

If only.

"This way," Harper said, to change the subject. As they went inside, Dawn eyed her surroundings and whispered, "I can't believe you actually lived here when you were growing up."

"Part-time. When I stayed with Gram."

"Which was a lot?"

"Yeah."

'Well, I think it's totally rad. I would have loved to have grown up here. Hey, what's this?" She pointed to the nearby wall covering the elevator shaft.

"The elevator," Harper said, thinking it was obvious. "It's not working."

"No, I see that, but what's the smaller doorway, er, cupboard? This." She knocked on the narrow wooden panel next to the elevator's entrance.

"Oh, that's the dumbwaiter. It's not working either."

"What's it for?"

"Originally hauling things from one floor to the next. It's not electric, was run on pulleys and cables, I think. It's never worked for as long as I can remember."

"Why would you need it if you had an elevator?"

"I don't know. I think it was installed first and, like I said, not electric, so servants could move linens or food or firewood or whatever from one floor to the next. It used to run from the basement all the way to the third floor."

"But no more?"

"No. I think it was dismantled when the elevator was installed. Or wasn't working or something. I don't really know."

Dawn tried the door. It didn't budge. "So someone nailed the door shut?"

"Right. I guess. Eons ago. It was a safety issue."

"I think you should get it going again. Along with the elevator." She inspected the closed door to the elevator shaft as well. "I mean how awesome would that be if it worked?"

"It was," Harper admitted. She remembered Gram being able to go upstairs after her stroke because of the lift. "I'm pretty sure we can get it working again. Don't know about the dumbwaiter."

"But you don't know until you try," Dawn reminded her.

"Riiight."

Satisfied, Dawn headed up the back staircase. "Let's go to the very top, okay?" she said and didn't wait for an answer. She just started clomping up the steps.

Once in Gramps's private room with its 360-degree view, Dawn mouthed, "Wicked." Spinning slowly, she said, "Holy shit, Mom, this is so damned awesome." She checked out the bathroom with its high windows and returned. "Retro, but fantabulous. Okay, okay, this is gonna be *my* room."

"I thought it might be my office. You might notice the computer and typewriter I carried all the way up here."

"Nah." Dawn shook her head, her loose bun starting to unravel. "I'm staking my claim. There are like a million rooms you can pick from, but I want this one. And I'll help move your stuff out of here."

"I don't know—"

"Oh wow." Spying the tripod and telescope near the windows facing the lake, Dawn grinned. She crossed the room in an instant and peered into the eyepiece. "How does this work?" Fiddling with the viewfinder, she said, "Oh. Got it. Oh my God! This is so awesome! You can see . . . wow, you can see everything that's happening across the lake in those houses over there."

"I guess."

"You *know*. Come on, Mom, you have to have looked through this. I mean, who wouldn't?" Adjusting the focus, she gasped. "Oh crap. You can see right into those people's bedrooms." Smothering a naughty smile, she said, "Don't those people ever shut their blinds?"

Rarely, Harper thought but said, "I don't know."

"You could be like a cool spy or something!"

"I think it's called a voyeur. And it's definitely not cool."

"Hey, there's something going on at that end house that kinda looks like a cabin."

"What?"

"Uh . . . People are moving out, I guess. Hauling stuff out of their attic."

Harper squinted through the window. "Are they? I guess you're right." She picked up the binoculars on a side table and trained the lenses on the last house on the lake. Sure enough, she saw a woman and a man taking bags of things down the outside staircase. At the base, they turned, their faces in profile and she recognized Rand Watkins, grim-faced, dark hair moving slightly as he walked, a younger woman with him.

She wondered what they were doing and remembered her short, pointed interview at the station and spying on him as he'd worked on the old files at his desk in the A-frame. Was it all tied together somehow? And what about the time she'd caught him on a night boat cruise around this island? Or was she making more of it than there was?

Or could it be that despite yourself, you've always found Rand Watkins more than a little bit intriguing?

That thought caught her up short.

Dawn, who had lost interest in the activity at the cabin, had moved the telescope, shifting the optical tube, swiveling it slightly on its mount. "Oh, and there's a guy two houses down not wearing a shirt. Kind of a hunk for an old guy."

"What guy?" she asked, then saw where the telescope was trained. On the Hunt house where Levi stood on the dock. "For God's sake, Dawn, he's my age. Not even forty."

"Like I said, old."

Harper trained her binoculars on the Hunt house, where she spied Levi in low-slung jeans and no shirt. His hair was damp, the muscles of his abdomen tight and visible until he pulled on a T-shirt.

For a second the back of her throat went dry.

Dawn asked, "You know him?"

"Uh-huh," she admitted, clearing her throat. "He was in my class in school."

"Yeah? Were you friends?"

"Yes," she admitted with a trace of sadness. They had been friends once upon a time when they were kids full of hope and innocence and a shared love for adventure. "A long time ago."

"Is he cool?"

"Sure." There was so much more she could say about Levi Hunt, so much she could tell her daughter, but she said only, "He's the son of the woman who died in the fire on her boat."

"That's the guy? And . . . wait, you dated her son. Is he the guy?"

"No, that one—Levi's older brother, Chase—went missing." She hesitated, on the cusp of divulging the truth, but was this the right time? No. She wondered if there ever would be a time that felt right.

But not today.

Harper set down her field glasses.

Dawn was squinting as she watched Levi.

Oh Lord. Something fragile inside of Harper broke. Time to end this. Harper started for the door. "Do you want to see the rest of the house?"

Dawn straightened. "Yeah, but remember, I claim this room."

"Okay, you've got it." Harper led the way down the narrow staircase. On the third floor, they stopped in Harper's bedroom.

"You picked this one? Really?" Dawn asked, eyeing the sparse belongings. "What's with the sleeping bag?"

"It's temporary. I wasn't sure how long I would be staying."

"Aren't there other beds here? With like sheets and stuff."

"Nothing that isn't twenty years old. I'll probably have everything moved from California, once I clean this place out."

They wandered through the servants' quarters on the third floor, and Dawn tested the dumbwaiter and elevator again. Neither responded. "I'm not kidding, Mom, you *really* have to fix these!"

"Got it. Duly noted."

"You know, this place is like a hotel."

"An old hotel," Harper said, leading the way down the stairs.

"Don't you love it here?"

Harper admitted, "Sometimes," but didn't add that often she hated it.

On the second floor, Dawn wrinkled her nose at the musty scent that the cleaning people hadn't quite eradicated. "It smells kinda funky up here."

"I know. I think I need to really air the place out."

"For sure."

They wended their way through the rooms. In the final guest room, she stopped short and stared within. "What's with all the dolls?" she asked. Harper had stashed most of Gram's collection here, out from underfoot. The bed and floor were littered with the dolls, while others spilled out from the closet. "There must be a hundred."

"Or more. They were Gram's," Harper said, eyeing the dolls she hadn't yet put in the trash. "I'm going to donate them."

"Why? I kinda like 'em. They add a creep factor. Especially the really old ones with the googly eyes." She walked inside and stepped on an old baby doll that cried out. "Oh shit. See what I mean?"

"I wasn't thinking about a creep factor motif," Harper said from the doorway. She thought about Maude and Toodles with their chilling messages, how someone had moved them around in the middle of the night. How that same sicko had left a dead cat in the house. What perverted son of a—

"Oh! Wait. What's this one?" Dawn wended her way through a pile of baby dolls to the bed. She pushed aside a brunette Bubblecut Barbie in a red swimsuit and tossed Midge in a two-piece out of the way to retrieve a pudgy doll with blond hair, freckles, and blue eyes, one half-closed.

"Chatty Cathy," Harper said, remembering how delighted Gram was to show it to Harper when she was around ten.

"Oh God, I've heard about these!" Dawn said. She turned the doll over and pulled the ring just below the doll's neck. "Does she talk?"

"She did. I don't know now if—"

"Please take me with you," Chatty Cathy requested in a surprisingly clear, high-pitched voice.

Dawn laughed.

"You can, you know. If you want the doll, she's yours. Any of them are," Harper said. "Take her. Take them all."

"Oh sure," Dawn said, smiling in amusement. Another pull of the string, and the doll requested a story. "These are all so cool. Mom, seriously, don't get rid of any of them! Your grandma loved them."

"That she did."

"You know what you could do?" Dawn asked, replacing the doll on the bed next to a blond Ken doll wearing only red swim trunks. "You could rent out rooms here. Everything is so retro and old. Creaky. Like if anyone wanted a 'haunted hotel' experience? Each room could have a doll or twenty in it. The house would pay for it-self."

"I'll think about it," Harper said dryly, though she didn't see her-self doing anything of the kind. An innkeeper she was not.

"Just don't sell it, please!" Dawn pleaded. "Come on, Mom, you can't!"

She could, but Dawn's supplication touched her. Despite the tragedies that were a part of the island and regardless of the silent in-truder who stalked the halls of the house at night, she did love it here, and with each passing day, she felt more connected to this is-land where she'd grown up. "It's a lot of house."

"So what? Make it work. Isn't that what—?"

"I always say. Yeah, I know. I said I'll think about it."

"That usually means no."

Harper didn't argue. She couldn't because it was true. She'd often promised to consider one of her daughter's ideas and then immedi-ately tossed it aside. Which is just what she was doing now. "Well, we're keeping some of these," Dawn announced, picking up Chatty Cathy, a black Ken, and a baby doll that Gram had probably named, but Harper couldn't recall. "I'm taking them to *my* room!"

"*My* room. Remember, it's *my* room," Harper argued as Dawn flounced up the two floors to the tower room and presumably left the dolls in the tower.

Once she returned with a smug smile pasted on her pale lips, they made their way down the back stairs to the main floor and the parlor with its dark drapes, settee, and collection of eclectic furniture, teacups, ashtrays, and even a couple of baby dolls that Harper hadn't yet rounded up.

"Geez, another telescope?" Dawn paused to look through the eye-piece and adjusted the focus. "What's the deal? This one's pointed at that Levi guy's house, too."

"Don't know," Harper lied.

"Well, he's gone now. Or at least not outside where I can see him."
As she straightened, Dawn noticed the wineglass Harper had left on
the table near the telescope. A slow grin lifted the corners of her
mouth. "You've been spying, Mom."

"No—" she started to argue, then admitted a partial truth. "Well,
okay, I have looked through it. Yes."

"Have you literally been scoping that guy out?"

"No. But I have seen him, and others." She decided to come
clean. "I know the guy in that A-frame, too. Next door to the Hunts."

"Oh yeah?" Dawn was moving the telescope slightly.

"He's now a detective with the local police department. Just like
his dad was when we were growing up."

"He went to school with you, too," Dawn guessed.

"Right. But he was a couple of years older."

"Doesn't look like he's home." Dawn straightened. "So this—"
She made a circular motion that Harper guessed included the house,
island, lake, and point on the far shore, "—is kinda like a high school
reunion for you?"

"Well, not quite, but the house on the other side of the Hunts'
was the Leonettis'. Beth Leonetti was my best friend in high school."

"You said that before."

"Right, well, she's a Realtor now. And *if* I decide to sell this house
once it's fixed up, I'd ask her to help me."

"Don't sell it!"

"Are you going to live here?"

"Well, yeah." Dawn nodded. "When I visit."

Harper cocked her head. "Realistically? And how often would
that be?"

"I don't know, but just don't put it on the market! Fix it up if you
want to, but keep it. For now," she said. "Don't I have some say in it?
Grandma says that once you die, everything goes to me, right?"

Grandma being Marcia. Every time she heard her daughter refer
to Marcia as her grandmother, she felt her skin crawl. "I'm listening
to you now. And Marcia doesn't have any say about what I—we—do
with this place." Harper didn't try to hide her irritation. Marcia's interest in the house and grounds, her proprietary attitude about
Dixon Island, had always been a source of friction to Harper. It had

been Marcia, not her father, who had doled out the trust fund checks and paid all the bills, along with that sleazeball of an attorney, Lou Arista.

She was so lost in thought, Harper actually started when she heard the doorbell chime.

"I'll get it," Dawn said, and before Harper could stop her daughter, Dawn was racing to the front door.

"Wait," Harper said, rushing after her, but it was too late.

Dawn unlocked the dead bolt and flung the door open wide.

Standing just outside was Levi Hunt.

Chapter 56

Joel straightened his tie and studied his reflection in the mirror. The lighting wasn't great in this hotel bathroom, and that was probably why he was looking older than his years, or older than he should have been.

His once-blond hair was graying slightly, and along with crow's feet fanning from the corners of his eyes, he noticed the beginning of bags under his eyes, bags that he didn't want to check out too closely.

Joel had a meeting scheduled with Lou Arista later this afternoon, and he was nervous. He was hoping the Portland attorney would understand that he had a good reason and case that he should receive a cut of his wife's—no, make that his *ex*-wife's inheritance. Joel and Harper had an unwritten agreement that when Harper inherited, Joel would receive a good share of it. Millions, he figured, though he wasn't sure of the figure and hoped the attorney would at least supply him with an estimate of what the estate was worth.

He saw dollar signs. Lots of them.

Unfortunately, though, he didn't have a prenuptial agreement.

A little fact he'd neglected to nail down.

But he'd married Harper, raised her child as his own, helped Harper through school, and aided her in finding employment. While it was true he really hadn't supported her financially, he'd been her emotional support for years. Harper was a trust fund baby, and her checks had done more than supplement the family income. Those quarterly installments had kept them afloat and made it possible to live a very nice, if not overly indulgent lifestyle.

No Ferraris or Porsches, but Volvos and Toyotas and Fords that were dependable if not flashy.

But now that she'd inherited . . .

Joel figured he was entitled to, if not half the value of the estate, then at least a third. He'd even settle for a quarter, though he wouldn't show his cards in his first meeting with Arista. But he would see how the lawyer reacted when he mentioned he might have to find his own attorney.

He checked the view of the city, late afternoon settling in, the day gloomy as he stared through the high-rises to the river and sprawling city beyond. So, if he didn't blow it, today was the day he'd been waiting for, the moment his ship would come in.

If he played his cards right.

Which he hadn't. Midlife had come along, bringing with it the requisite crisis in the form of Melanie Jallet, a student of his at the community college. She'd flirted, he'd responded, and though he cared for Harper, really cared for her, he'd strayed. His marriage to Harper had about played out anyway. Dawn had been nearly off to college herself. He considered her his child, and he'd been glad to do all the daddy things as she'd grown up, but now she was out of the nest.

Harper had divorced him.

Melanie was insisting on marriage and threatening to leave him for good. In fact they were currently broken up, and he wasn't sure that they'd get back together.

Either way, he needed the money.

Damn it, he deserved the money. Earned it. He'd bailed Harper out when she'd been at her lowest. From the first time he'd heard about the Dixon fortune from Trick in that little house in Almsville, Joel had set his sights on getting a part of it.

Now was the time.

With a final adjustment to his tie, he was satisfied. He had a little time and thought he'd stop off for one drink at his favorite rooftop bar, then walk the five blocks to the offices of Arista, Bartlett, and Connors.

After slipping into his coat, he grabbed his briefcase and took the elevator down to the lobby. Outside the day was cool, rain threatening again, but he didn't have to pop his umbrella.

Pedestrians crowded the rain-washed sidewalks, cars were parked nose-to-tail along the curbs, and the traffic was thick, tires humming, engines rumbling, conversation buzzing around him as he walked the few blocks. He was a little claustrophobic in the throng of bustling city-dwellers, and more than once he had the uncanny feeling that he was being followed.

He'd even looked over his shoulder a couple of times but had seen no one who was obviously tailing him. He was just uptight. That was all. His nerves about the meeting with Arista were getting the better of him.

He dashed into the lobby of the older building, pressed the call button for what had to be the slowest elevator west of the Mississippi, and waited impatiently, tapping the toe of one polished shoe.

Come on, come on.

He watched the elevator dial move at a snail's pace as the car slowly descended. Once it opened and a woman in a long coat and beret walked out, he was in. Alone, he rode the old car slowly to the rooftop without stopping at any of the floors in between, thank God.

Good. Maybe he was getting lucky.

As he expected, the small bar was nearly empty at this time of year. It was enclosed with sliding doors that opened to a wide patio. The tables that graced the area were now stacked to one side, awaiting summer and happy hours when he expected the rooftop would be alive with the after-work crowd.

Now two women were just finishing their glasses of wine and gathering their purses. They settled their tab with the bartender, a young guy Joel didn't recognize who seemed bored with his job.

Joel ordered a double bourbon, neat, and knocked it back.

Liquid courage consumed, Joel was about to leave when he saw a familiar face—older, but one he recognized—in the mirror over the bar. Trick Vargas, dressed in a gray suit and open collar, got off the elevator. His hair was darker and cut into a thick mullet. He wore oversized, wire-rimmed glasses with shaded lenses, a low-rider beard covering his jaw. But he was definitely Vargas.

"Hey, man," he said with a smile. "Long time, no see." He clapped Joel on the back. "What're you doing in Portland? I thought you moved away. Wasn't it somewhere in California? Maybe the Bay Area?"

"Moved back a while ago," Joel said, not elaborating.

"Me, too. I was down in Arizona. Scottsdale. Buy you a drink?"

"I'm in a bit of a hurry," Joel said. It wasn't really a lie. "Got a meeting."

"How about just one?" Trick offered. "For old times' sake. Come on. Let's catch up."

Joel checked his watch. He guessed he had ten minutes to spare. And he didn't want to get to the attorney's office too early. Didn't want to appear too eager or, worse yet, desperate. "Just one," he said, and Trick ordered another double for Joel as well as one for himself. They sat at the bar, and when the drinks came, they clicked glasses and took long drinks. Conversation flowed surprisingly easily, Joel thought, surprised because he'd always been a little wary of the drug dealer.

As he was finishing his drink, Trick said, "I heard you married Harper Reed."

"Divorced now. But how'd you know?"

Trick grinned, showing off that overlapping front tooth. "I've kept up. You scored big."

"As I said, divorced. I messed up." He left it at that, didn't want to think about how close he'd come to inheriting a goddamned fortune, only to have blown the whole deal by thinking with his damned cock. "But I'm going to see if I can get things right. Seeing the attorney today."

"That's the spirit. You gotta work for what you want, man. Hey, bartender, another round."

"Oh no," Joel said. "I've gotta run. And I can't be plastered."

"Just one more," Trick cajoled and leaned closer. "I hear you have a kid."

"I do." He was proud of her. Always had been. A stellar student and good athlete, Dawn was a great kid. Lately she'd stumbled a bit, gotten in with the wrong crowd and started dressing like she was going to her own funeral, but he figured she would snap out of it.

He had a picture of Dawn in his wallet and fumbled for it as two new drinks appeared. Where the hell was that photograph? "It's her senior photo," he explained, not looking up as he searched for it. "She's in college now. U of O. My old alma mater! Doin' great, too. Has her own apartment just off campus." He shuffled through the pictures and cards, absorbed in the process, and when he finally came up with the picture, he traded the head shot for a short glass in Trick's hands. "Oh, thanks. Here she is."

He slid the photo across the bar.

"Pretty," Trick said, eyeing the photo. "Real pretty. She's down in Eugene?"

"Yeah." He pointed at the picture where Dawn was looking seriously at the camera, her hair dyed black, her makeup pale, several necklaces draped around her neck. Her eyes were over-accentuated with black liner and mascara. "Dawn is kinda into the Goth thing, but hey, she's young. We were all into something at her age."

"Weren't we?" Trick agreed. "Speaking of which—" He lowered his voice but the bartender had stepped behind a curtain leading to a back room. "—I've got a little coke." His eyebrows arched over the rims of his shaded glasses. "Thought you might use a bump."

"Nah." Joel held up a hand. It was tempting but dangerous. "Those days are over for me."

"Seriously?" Trick wasn't buying it. "Maybe you could use a little something for the meeting you have to go to. You seem pretty uptight about it."

Joel considered. What could it hurt? Trick was right. He could use a shot of bravado in dealing with Arista. Besides, back in the day, coke had been his go-to drug.

"Uh, I don't know." He shook his head. "I should be clearheaded."

"You will be, man. When have I ever steered you wrong?" Again, the confident smile. Back in the day Trick had been a supplier, and the drugs he'd peddled had always been good. Trick reached into an inner pocket of his jacket and flashed a tiny packet.

"Okay, fine." Joel could use something to bolster him. And the added benefit would be that Trick would leave him alone. Joel could get rid of him.

"Outside," Trick said and pulled a pack of cigarettes from an inner pocket. "Let's go out for a smoke."

If the display was for the bartender who had reappeared, it didn't seem to matter. The guy was caught up in taking some kind of inventory, so Trick and Joel slipped outside and around the corner to a covered area where there were ashtrays and a few stools.

Joel felt a little off. His legs were a little wobbly. No, make that a lot wobbly. And he had trouble focusing. What the hell?

"Over here." Trick was shepherding him to the edge of the smoking area. "Want one?" Trick said, shaking the pack so a couple of Marlboros poked out.

"No. Gave them up, too. A long time ago. Oh wow." Joel stumbled over some electrical cords as Trick lit up.

Man, he was dizzy. "Maybe I . . . maybe I should sit . . ." His mind was spinning so fast, he grabbed onto Trick's arm to keep from falling. "What's the matter with me?"

"Nerves," Trick said, cigarette clamped between his teeth. He held Joel up with surprising strength.

"Not nerves. I just feel . . . feel bad." He had to steady himself on the railing. "Wow, what was in those drinks?" And the second the words were out of his mouth, he knew. He looked into Trick's eyes but couldn't see through the shades and curling smoke. His own vision was too blurry. "You little fuck," he whispered, just as Trick smiled again, his overlapping tooth exposed over the cigarette. "You did this!"

"You must've graduated summa cum laude from the university," Trick said with a humorless chuckle. Quick as a cougar striking, he lifted Joel off his feet.

"What? Hey, no!" Joel scrambled to right himself, but he couldn't control his limbs.

And it was too late. He was unable to stop Trick from hoisting him to the top of the rail. "Sorry, pal," Trick said. "But I gotta run. Got business in Eugene. And this is a helluva lot faster than the elevator. Adios."

He pushed with enough force to send Joel hurtling over the railing, headfirst down the fifteen stories to the crowded sidewalk below.

Chapter 57

Janet Collins didn't answer her doorbell.

Nor did she respond to several hard raps on her front door.

"Not home?" Chelle asked.

"Probably still at work."

"Let's see." Chelle checked her notepad. "I'll radio Suki and see if she can call and check. I know she works at a used car dealership on Eighty-second, but I don't have the name of the place." She radioed into the station while Rand walked the perimeter of the house, a daylight basement with a brick façade and fenced backyard with long grass and strewn with fallen leaves from the birch trees planted near the house. A basketball hoop stood on one end of a wide patio with a sliding glass door. He peered through the glass and found himself looking into a family room with an old plaid couch, a couple of bean-bag chairs, and a TV with wires snaking out of it, toward a gaming console on the braided rug.

No one in sight.

Slider locked.

As he rounded a corner to the front of the house, he caught a glimpse of the one room with lights. Through partially open blinds he saw the refrigerator and some cupboards, but no one visible. No movement within.

Chelle tried the door again.

Still no answer.

The garage door had a row of windows above the lower panels. Stretching, Rand was able to peer inside.

"See anything?" Chelle asked.

"Too dark. There's a flashlight in the Jeep. Glove box."

Chelle retrieved the flashlight and he shone the beam inside. A four-door Oldsmobile Cutlass was parked in front of a washer and dryer. Lying on the greasy floor next to the two steps leading into the house was a woman.

She wasn't moving.

Blood was smeared everywhere around her, staining the concrete steps and pooling beneath her head.

"Shit," he muttered. "I think we found her." He slipped the flashlight into his pocket and, using a handkerchief, grabbed the handle of the wide garage door and pulled it upward.

Groaning, the door rumbled upward, and he shot through, running straight to the woman and crouching near her.

She was lying face up, her features battered, bruised, and cut, her nose and possibly cheekbones broken, one eye swollen shut, the other fixed.

And she wasn't breathing.

"Radio in for an ambulance," he ordered over his shoulder, though he knew it was far too late. There was no pulse. Not even the tiniest breath escaping her cracked, bloody lips.

It looked like someone had pummeled her against the concrete steps, maybe smashed her face into the crumbling concrete edge, soaked as it was with blood, but then either her attacker or she had managed to turn her over.

He felt sick inside.

As used to violent death as he was, it still bothered him to think about what the victim had experienced.

He rocked back on his heels, surveying the garage with its washer and dryer and car in one bay.

Then he tried the light switch.

Nothing.

Odd.

Four panels of fluorescents hanging above and none worked?

If she'd come out here at night, the garage would have been completely dark.

She could have stumbled.

Standing, he swept the beam of the flashlight over the rest of the interior of the garage and noted the upturned laundry basket, lying on the dirty floor, and the rake that was nearby. An accident? She tripped in the dark when the lights didn't come on. She hit her head and had a brain bleed or something and her face got battered to a pulp?

No way.

From the looks of it, she was murdered in her own garage.

At the top of his list of suspects in her homicide was Tristan Vargas/Larry Smith.

Unless Janet had a violent husband, boyfriend, or son, Rand would bet dollars to donuts that Vargas was behind this killing. The lowlife was shutting her up and had moved from dealing drugs and blackmail to homicide.

Or maybe he'd always been a killer.

Could Vargas have decided to murder Janet not because of what she'd mentioned in the voice mail she'd left for Rand at the department, but because she knew of other crimes he'd committed? Rand thought of the unlikely deaths he was investigating, those near Lake Twilight, most having occurred years before.

What about the last couple of decades?

Where had Vargas lived, under what alias, and were there any unsolved homicides in his wake?

And why, after twenty years, had he chosen to strike now?

Did he know that the police were onto him? Had he somehow learned that evidence had been found in the Musgrave cabin? Or, more likely, had he read about Cynthia Hunt's death in the damned newspaper, the first of a series on mysteries and deaths surrounding Lake Twilight, and decided to take care of any loose ends he'd left dangling twenty years ago? Was Janet Collins's death an attempt by Vargas to clean up his mess from two decades earlier?

Or was Rand barking up the wrong tree? Even in the wrong damned forest?

He had lots of questions and only a few half-baked answers.

Chelle had joined him in the garage and was staring at the victim.

"Son of a bitch," she whispered under her breath as she crouched down for a closer look at the bruised and battered face. She studied Janet's hands. "No defensive wounds. No broken fingernails. She didn't fight back."

"He surprised her. Got the drop on her," Rand surmised aloud. "She didn't have a chance."

"Vargas." Chelle rocked back on her heels and glanced up at Rand. "That's my guess."

"You think he knew she put in a call to you?"

"Don't know." But it was a good guess that Vargas killed her because of what she knew about him in the past.

He wondered if they'd kept in contact over the years and she'd let it slip that she'd made the call, that for some reason she'd decided to tell the police what she'd seen. He wondered what that could have been and only hoped that the equipment they'd retrieved from the Musgrave cabin would tell the story that had now, with her death, been silenced.

As they waited for the ambulance and local police to arrive, Rand did a quick walk-through of the house. He was careful not to disturb anything but searching for any signs of forced entry or a struggle or anything he thought seemed the least bit out of the ordinary.

Nothing appeared out of place aside from the mess that was in her kid's room, where an explosion of clothes, books, CDs, candy wrappers, and soda cans littered floor, desk, and unmade bed. Posters of Iron Maiden, Def Leppard, and Michael Jackson along with Joe Montana and Michael Jordan covered the walls. This, he assumed, was probably the bedroom's normal state.

The other two bedrooms were as neat as the rest of the house.

From what he could glean, it appeared as if Janet had been interrupted the night before. A bottle of wine and box of crackers were open on the kitchen counter and a recording on the television was on pause.

Chelle found damp laundry in the dryer, though the timer had run out.

Rand wondered if Janet had gone into the garage to check on the wash and stumbled in the dark when the lights wouldn't snap on.

He checked.

And found that the circuit breaker had been tampered with.

All of which he told the local police when they, along with the emergency vehicles, arrived.

Janet Collins lived out of the Almsville Police Department's jurisdiction, so as a fire truck and ambulance, lights flashing, filled the driveway, Rand filled Officers Fuller and Washington in on what he knew, then repeated everything when the homicide detectives arrived.

By that time a portion of the street had been cordoned off and yellow crime scene tape strung around the house. The medical examiner and crime scene team arrived while neighbors gathered in doorways, driveways, and even inching down the street.

The detective in charge was a heavy-set woman with short graying hair and eyes that didn't seem to miss much. She introduced herself as Madge Hall and assured Rand and Chelle that she would take the investigation from that point forward but keep the Almsville department in the loop.

"Sad for the kids," Chelle said once they were inside Rand's Jeep again and he'd maneuvered through the knotted traffic clogging the neighborhood.

"Sad for everyone," he agreed.

"We need to nail Vargas."

"If he did it."

"Even if he didn't," she said from the passenger seat as Rand adjusted his windshield wipers for the mist that was collecting on the glass. "But I'll bet my next paycheck he's behind it all."

"Not gonna take that bet," Rand said, thinking about Vargas. All the evidence was pointing to his involvement. Rand's own father had said Vargas had been blackmailing Tom Hunt. And Janet Collins had called in to report what she'd seen with Vargas on the night Chase Hunt disappeared. He'd probably resurfaced because Cynthia Hunt's death had resurrected interest in Chase's disappearance.

Right now, Rand wasn't certain.

But he sure as hell was going to find out.

Chapter 58

"You're the guy from across the lake!" Dawn guessed, opening the door a bit wider so that Levi could step inside. "I saw you through the telescope!"

Oh dear God. Harper wanted to die a thousand deaths. "My daughter," she said, barely able to get the words out. "Dawn."

"Levi Hunt." His gaze didn't leave Dawn's.

Dawn was smiling. "I know. Mom said so."

Slowly Levi's gaze moved to Harper, and her heart dropped to the floor. He knew. Damn it, he knew. "What else did she say?"

"She said that you went to school together. Were classmates."

"That's right." His eyes narrowed just a fraction, but Harper knew him well enough to realize he was putting two and two together. No doubt he was coming up with three. "So why was I the topic of conversation?"

"Because we saw you. Across the lake. You were outside, near the water," Dawn answered. "Mom was showing me around, and up in the tower room there is this awesome telescope. I mean it's freakin' awesome. I looked through."

"And it was focused on my house?" he guessed.

"I guess, but really you can see all the houses across the lake."

"Is that so?" He was staring at Harper, and she felt her jaw tighten.

Dawn was nodding. "Yeah and—"

A sharp beeping sound interrupted her.

"Oh crap!" Dawn made her way across the foyer to her purse, picked it up, scrounged inside, and came up with a black pager. She checked the message. "Oops. Gotta go." She looked up at Harper. "I knew this would happen. It's Gina. She's such a flake!" Dawn rolled her eyes. "Listen, she's ready to go, and it gets intense with her aunt sometimes. Like really intense. Anyway, she really wants to see *Heathers*. Maybe since it's an earlier show, I can go with her. It's showing just a few blocks from my apartment, the theater by the Fifth Street Market. Really just around the corner and a couple of streets from where I live, so I could make it. But then, I really do have to study." She bit her lip, seemed torn. "Anyway, I have to go." She hiked the strap of her purse over her shoulder.

To Levi she said, "Nice to meet you."

"You, too."

She hugged Harper and said, "Later, Mom. I'll call." With that, she breezed out the door, dashing to her Acura which was wedged between Harper's Volvo and Levi's Ford.

"Drive careful," Harper called after her, just as she had since Dawn had first gotten behind the wheel by herself at sixteen. "Let me know that you got back safe."

Dawn just lifted a hand and slid into her car.

With Levi standing inches from her physically but miles away emotionally, she watched her daughter back out of the space, then put her little car into drive and speed across the bridge. The lump in her throat was immense.

Levi waited until the Acura had disappeared from sight, then turned to her and said, "Your husband isn't Dawn's father."

The world seemed to go quiet and fall away. If there were birds chirping nearby, or water lapping on the shore of the lake, or traffic passing on the street past the lane, she didn't hear any of them over the sound of her own heartbeat. She started to speak. Then stopped. The lie she'd been forming stuck in her throat. "Ex-husband," she forced out.

Levi waited, jaw set, lips razor thin, the temperature seeming to have dropped ten degrees.

"No," she admitted. "Joel isn't Dawn's father. I mean, her biological father."

"Does she know it?"

The question rang like a death knell.

"Dawn?" Harper cleared her throat. "I haven't told her. But . . . she may have guessed. She's smart and knows part of my history. But no, I never actually sat down and talked to her."

A breeze ruffled his hair and chilled her cheeks.

His brown eyes narrowed. "What about your ex? What did you tell him? He had to have known."

"Of course."

"So you told him that she was Chase Hunt's daughter and explained that he was missing and that you needed a father for your kid?"

Close enough, she thought, her throat as dry as desert sand. "Something like that. Yeah." But she saw the recrimination in his gaze. Her insides froze. *Oh dear God. He knows.* Her heart was thundering, her pulse pounding in her ears.

"So you lied," he accused quietly. "Again."

She closed her eyes for a second, gathering herself for the truth, this moment she had feared and dreaded for nearly two decades. "Yeah," she finally admitted, nodding. She wanted to look away, to avoid the truth, but as it was being laid bare, she met the condemnation in his gaze.

"You and I took biology together," he reminded her. "Sophomore year. Mr. Sandgren's class. We were lab partners."

"I remember."

"We studied genetics. Dominant and recessive genes."

She knew what was coming, could barely breathe.

"You and Chase—both blue eyes," he pointed out. "Recessive gene. But your daughter?"

"She has brown," Harper admitted, rubbing her arms to ward off a chill as her world imploded. All the lies she'd so carefully spun over the years were rapidly unraveling. It was an out-of-body experience. She felt she could look down and see Levi and her standing in front of the massive house, a fine October mist dampening their hair, cooling their skin, and the truth splintering the ground between them, causing the asphalt to rend and a bottomless abyss to separate them.

"I think you'd better come inside," she said. She didn't wait for him to respond, just walked through the open door to the parlor. She'd dreaded this day nearly as much as when she would have to explain the truth to her daughter.

She heard the door shut behind her, then his footfalls as he caught up with her in Gram's parlor. Levi. Once her childhood playmate. Her trusted friend. Her lover. And the father of her only child. Her heart felt as if it were being squeezed. Hard. "Maybe you'd like a drink," she suggested.

"Maybe I'd like the truth."

"Fair enough. But you're getting a drink anyway." With quivering fingers, she poured two short glasses of Scotch and handed one to him.

"Dawn looks enough like Chase that everyone who suspected the truth would just assume she was his kid," Levi guessed, having put the pieces together. "And you didn't do anything to discourage that."

She didn't disagree, just sipped from her drink.

"But they'd be wrong."

She licked her suddenly dry lips and pushed back on the feeling that the walls were closing in, that her whole world was crumbling. "Yes."

"Because," he said, stepping closer, so near that she felt his body heat and saw the differing striations of brown in his eyes, "that girl who just left here is my daughter."

The lump in her throat was so thick she had trouble swallowing, and there was a burning sensation behind her eyes that she fought with everything she had. She would not break down. Would *not*!

"Isn't she?"

"Yes," she finally admitted.

"Jesus H. Christ, Harper, why?" he asked, anger snapping in his eyes but his words surprisingly calm. "Why did you lie all this time?"

"Why do you think?"

"Because it was easy, the convenient thing to do."

"Oh right. Easy. Sure," she threw back. Who was he to judge her? Taking a sip from her glass, she looked past him, through the windows to the autumn day outside where leaves fluttered in the breeze. Lights were beginning to burn across the water at the houses on the point. *It's time*, she silently told herself, long past time to open the door to that dark, secretive chapter of her life.

Another sip.

Then she knocked the rest of her drink back and felt the Scotch warm a familiar path down her throat. Time to pull herself together. What had Gram always said when Harper had been faced with a tough problem and come running to her grandmother for comfort. There had been hugs and smiles and the wiping away of tears, but there had also been the simple advice: "Pull yourself up by your bootstraps, Harper girl." It seemed to Harper that she'd been doing just that all of her life and sure as hell was going to do it now. "Sit," she said. She expected from the hard angle of his chin that he would want to remain standing, but he took a seat in the chair next to the telescope.

She poured herself another drink.

Levi, she saw, hadn't touched his.

She said, "You remember Christmas break, when we were seniors?"

If possible, his jaw grew even harder. "Yeah."

"And you and I, we rang in the New Year together?"

Nodding, he set his untouched drink on the side table, his fingers brushing the end of the telescope. "Right."

"We—?"

"Got drunk and ended up in bed." It sounded so cold. Heartless. As if it was just a one-night hookup that happened all the time. Which wasn't the case. But it was the nuts and bolts of it. Just the facts.

Harper felt the heat climb up the back of her neck, but now that she'd started on this truthful journey, there was no turning back. "Right." She'd been disappointed and upset when Chase hadn't shown up to celebrate the new year, a special year when she would graduate and attend college, possibly with him at the university if she decided against Stanford and chose to go to Oregon, where they would be together without the confines of parental restrictions. And he was bagging out. He'd called and claimed that he needed to stay down in Eugene on that New Year's Eve, that the term was beginning and he needed to get a jump start on it.

"I'm sorry, Harper," he'd said from the other end of the line. "But you know that my grades aren't what they should be and I could lose my scholarship . . . I mean, maybe it's already too late, I'm already on probation. And if I'm not in school . . . shit, I could end up in the fuckin' army."

"Not if we get married," she'd argued and eyed the gleaming crystal glassware she'd set out, the bottles of liquor in the cabinet. She was alone. Even Gram had gone out with friends who'd picked her up for an overnight hotel party in Portland. A rarity. And an opportunity. She and Chase could have spent the night in her bedroom here in the manor, starting the new year off right. It would have been perfect. "You wouldn't have to go if we had a baby."

"I know, but that's got to happen really fast, now, doesn't it? You have to get pregnant. Immediately. I don't know why you haven't yet."

Like it was all her fault?

"Anyway, I've really got to go. I've got to figure this out," he'd said before hanging up.

She had whispered, "I love you," to the dial tone ringing in her ears and known that he'd lied. She'd heard noise in the background, music and voices, laughter and the clinking of glasses that he hadn't been able to muffle with his hand over the receiver. He wasn't studying. He was celebrating. Without her. Her heart had cracked more than a little, but she'd looked out the window and looked across the misty lake to see Levi outside, walking from the boathouse to the back door of the Hunts' house. Alone on New Year's Eve.

"Not for long," she'd whispered to Diablo, Gram's long-tailed gray cat. She picked up the receiver again, then dialed the number that she knew by heart. The Hunts' number. She'd have her own private party.

"You invited me over here," Levi said, abruptly bringing her back to the here and now. "And you got pregnant."

She nodded.

"And you didn't think to tell me?"

"Of course I thought about it, but by the time I knew the truth, that you were Dawn's father, I was already married."

"To a guy who thought Dawn was Chase's daughter!" he charged, his anger palpable. "He didn't think Chase was coming back and he assumed the role, right? And all the time you were living a lie."

"That's right, Levi," she said, her own temper sparking. He wanted the truth and now he was going to insult her with it? No way.

"So, do you want to know my story or would you rather just sit back and hurl insults at me and act as if you had no part of what happened? Because we can do it that way. But you were there, Levi. And as I remember it, an active participant. It didn't take a whole lot of persuading to get you into bed."

He looked about to argue but somehow stopped himself. "Point taken," he said, more calmly. "Just tell me what happened."

She took another bracing gulp from her glass, then explained everything she could. Harper told him that she was going to tell Chase she was pregnant the night he disappeared. She said that she had assumed he was the father and hadn't even questioned it until it was evident, several weeks after Dawn's birth, that her daughter's eyes were brown. By then, she explained, she thought there was no point to blurting out the truth and changing the course of their lives. "You were at school, Oregon State, right? And I was trying to get my life together, get accustomed to being a wife and mother. I had to get my GED and put off college until we could swing it. At that point, Dawn's paternity didn't seem important."

"Not important to you," he said sharply and climbed to his feet. He sighed and rammed stiff fingers through his still-damp hair. "Well, it sure was important to me. Still is." He looked at her and she read the shock in his expression. "Hell, Harper, I just found out I have a kid! And I didn't know about it for almost twenty damned years? And you expect me to keep calm, let it go? Is that it?" He stared at her as if she were some kind of monster.

"So what would you have had me do, Levi?"

"Tell the truth, damn it! Tell her! Tell me. For the love of God, Harper," he said, advancing on her. "Didn't you think for one second I would want to know?"

"Okay, fine. Let's play that out," she said angrily. "So, when I figured out that Dawn was your kid, I should have blown up my marriage and tracked you down at Oregon State? I think that's where you went to college, right?"

He didn't respond, but she plowed on. "So let's say I find you and I tell you the happy news and you—what? Drop everything because now you're a daddy at eighteen? Is that what you think should have happened? Chase was still missing and your parents were grief-stricken, still searching frantically for him. But they did know that you, their remaining son, was safe and off to college. Now keep in mind that they hated me and that your mom blamed me for her first-born son vanishing."

He seemed about to argue, but she cut him off. "That's what she thought. She told Alaina Leonetti, and Beth told me." Harper's voice was rising, her pulse ticking rapidly as she nailed him with the truth. "So—let's go back to our little pretend fantasy scenario—let's say I did show up—still married to Joel, mind you—and I informed you that you were the father of my baby. How do you think that would have gone down?"

Before he could say a word, she added, "I'll tell you what would have happened. It probably would have started with a paternity test. Right? No one, including you," she said, jabbing a finger in his direction, "would have believed me to start with, and just because Dawn's eyes are brown, no one would be convinced. God knows your mother thought I slept around anyway, that I was a slut. She would have come to the quick conclusion that I was trying to trap you, her precious baby boy."

"You don't know—"

"Oh, but I do." She arched an eyebrow, daring him to defy her. "I do know. And I did then. So don't come on all holier-than-thou, Levi. Just don't. You have no idea what I went through. That's what *you* don't know." She moved even nearer to him, angling her face upward, pushing her nose so close it nearly touched his. "And how would you have felt? Huh, Levi? Would you have felt good about it? Knowing that I'd been sleeping with your brother all along? Or would you have felt bad? Or maybe even trapped?" She was livid now, replaying the scene in her mind, remembering all of her own doubts at the time, all the guilt, all the fear. "Is that what I should have done?" she demanded. "Is that what you would have expected?"

"I didn't expect any of it!"

"But you were there, too, weren't you? That night when we got together?" she pointed out, though she didn't admit that when they got together that New Year's Eve a lifetime ago, she'd wondered if she might get pregnant. A little part of her had hoped so. Though she was loath to believe she was that manipulative, she surely hadn't done anything to stop making love with Levi from happening.

Nor had he.

Her motives had been different, of course, but she didn't want to examine them too deeply. That night, they'd both had too much to drink and thrown caution to the wind. He carelessly. She, though, with some degree of calculation. What had started out as a tentative kiss on his part had ignited fast. Hard. Soon he was kissing her feverishly and she kissing him back, feeling his hands on her body. She'd felt as if she were floating as he carried her up the stairs to her bedroom on the second floor, and there they'd made love. Not once. Not twice. But three times that she could remember.

Hot.

Wild.

Unbridled.

Even now, she felt a blush stain her cheeks.

So, this is where they'd ended up. Squaring off in Gram's house. Facing the consequences of what she'd kept secret for two damned decades. She finished her drink, then asked, "What do you want me to do?"

"Tell her the truth."

"Dawn? You want me to tell Dawn that you're really her dad? Just like that?" She snapped her fingers. "Don't you think it might come as kind of a shock?"

"We'll deal with it," he said, then clarified. "*I'll* deal with it."

"Oh no, no, no!" she countered. "You can't leave me out of it. Uh-uh. Besides, Dawn's just the beginning. We'll have to tell Joel. He thinks Dawn's father is completely out of the picture."

"He's your ex!"

"And Dawn is still his daughter. For all his faults, Joel is a good dad."

"He'll adjust. We all will. Now call her back," Levi said. "She's got a pager. Call her. Leave a message and get her back here." He finally picked up his drink and took a long sip from the glass. "I'll wait."

Harper saw her entire world colliding. Right here. Right now. It was happening whether she liked it or not. "Look, let's be sane about this," she said and heard him scoff. "We've waited almost twenty years. Another day or two won't make any difference."

"To you, maybe. But 'almost twenty years' is enough. Too many," he said. "It's been all of her life. When I think of the things I've missed." His jaw slid to one side, and he gripped his glass so tightly his knuckles showed white.

Oh, give me a break, she thought. Sure, he was having trouble dealing with the fact that he was actually a father. And he blamed her. Okay. Fine. She didn't fault him for that. But she sure as hell wasn't about to wallow in what-could-have-beens. Nor was she going to let him bully her into doing anything she didn't want to do.

"You might consider all of the things you didn't miss," she pointed out, thinking of dirty diapers, sleepless nights, bullies in preschool and first grade, and finally the rebellion in Dawn's teens. "It hasn't always been a bed of roses. There were tough times with Dawn."

"And I should've been a part of it."

"But you weren't, were you? You got to live your life the way you wanted to, with zero responsibility."

"Not my choice." He finished his drink and left his glass on the table near the telescope to stare through the window to the gray day beyond. Dusk was falling rapidly, the clouds dark and moody as they scudded across the sky. Two boats were cutting across the water, their running lights visible, wakes trailing after them as they raced eastward toward the town where, she saw, the first streetlights were winking on.

She knew he wasn't watching the boats. No, she decided, he was a million miles away, rolling back the years in his mind to their senior year when he'd not only lost a brother but also impregnated that brother's girlfriend.

"We were stupid," he finally said.

"Just kids."

He snorted, still had his back to her, his hands buried deep in his jacket pockets. "Stupid kids doing things with major, life-altering consequences."

She couldn't argue with that as she turned on several table lamps to chase away the gloom of the coming night. "Isn't that what all teenagers do? Take chances?"

He didn't respond.

"Look, Levi, we'll figure this out," she said and touched him at the crook of his arm.

He drew away sharply. As if her touch had burned him. When he turned around, his face was set. "Just let her know you want to see her. We can go to Eugene together, or she can come back here." Then as if the matter was settled, he changed the subject. "You called my office. Said you had some things for me?"

She didn't think their discussion about Dawn was over. Far from it. But for now, it was time to set it aside, for each of them to cool off.

"Right. I do. Just a sec." With their argument still echoing in her ears, she hurried up the stairs to the bedroom she'd claimed and found the box that she'd packed with the items belonging to Chase. She took several deep breaths. At least the truth was out. That, she told herself, was the first step. And it was massive.

Just handle this. You can do it.

By the time she returned to the parlor, Levi had poured himself another drink and was downing it. He didn't appear as tense, as if he, too, had cooled off a bit.

She handed him the box. "This is the stuff I found that I thought you might want. It's things Chase gave me. I'd forgotten about them, and they all got left here and locked up when Dad and Marcia and I went to California. We left in a hurry."

"Like thieves sneaking into the night," Marcia had complained as they'd loaded both cars before driving south to California.

"I remember." Levi set the box on a side table and opened the flaps to peer inside. The first item he retrieved was the necklace. He held the chain suspended by one finger, the diamond dangling and winking in the lamplight. "He gave this to you?"

"Yes." She remembered that hot summer night all too clearly. The thrill of Chase's vows of love, the pain of Evan's death.

Levi was frowning. "It belonged to my grandmother, and it went missing. Mom went out of her mind looking for it." His eyebrows slammed together as he thought. "I remember her and Dad fighting about it and tearing the house apart. He accused her of being careless and losing it. She insisted it had been stolen." He bit his lip. "I'm pretty sure they made an insurance claim for it." He fingered the diamond. "And Chase had it all the time?"

She shrugged. "I guess. It was kind of like a pre-engagement thing. He gave it to me in the summer before our senior year."

"He stole it." Levi was shaking his head. "That son of a bitch stole it and let Mom freak out. What a shit."

She remembered Chase had cautioned her not to wear it except when they were alone together. At the time she thought it was romantic, but now, belatedly, she realized he was just covering his tracks. Another disappointment.

"I'm sorry," she whispered, and it wasn't just about the necklace.

The doorbell chimed before she could say anything else. "To be continued," she said as she headed to the front door.

Her nerves were raw and she didn't want any company. She had enough to deal with as it was, and she figured only two people would be showing up on her doorstep unannounced, the first being Beth who had called several times, pushing Harper to fix the place up and sell. The second was Rhonda Simms who had left several messages on the phone insisting that Harper would want to add her "unique perspective" to the next installment of her series about Lake Twilight.

But Harper was wrong.

Neither woman was waiting for her on the other side of the door.

Instead she found Rand Watkins.

Detective Rand Watkins.

His expression was grim, lips flat in a beard-shadowed jaw, troubled eyes meeting hers in the window.

It was obvious he hadn't come bearing good news.

Chapter 59

Rand shouldn't have been surprised to find Levi with Harper at the Dixon estate.

Hadn't they always been linked in one way or another? Hadn't they been childhood friends? Gone through school together? Even come to his house together looking for Chase on the night he disappeared? The two of them had always shared a unique connection.

And right now it was more evident than ever.

From the moment Harper opened the door, he noticed the wariness in her eyes and a tightness in the corners of her mouth. Everything about her exuded tension.

"Levi's here?" he asked.

"Yes."

"Good."

She raised an eyebrow at that, and he explained, "I need to talk to both of you."

"Guess you're in luck," she said, but he knew she didn't mean it. Her gaze was too guarded. Whatever he'd walked in on, it was private and intense. And he was an interloper. Excluded.

Well, too bad.

She led him into a massive room in the back of the house filled with antiques and eclectic furniture from days gone by. He'd been here before, but not for years. Tonight there were no cats slinking through the shadows and only a few of the myriad of dolls he remembered. The whole house seemed somber and drab. Without the energy that had filled this home when he'd been here as a kid, visiting Evan.

Levi was standing near the windows, and he, like Harper, seemed wound tight.

Rand didn't care. Too much was at stake.

"What's going on?" Levi asked, looking from Rand to Harper.

"Sit down," Rand suggested, then to Levi, "It's good you're here. You need to hear this, too."

"Hear what?" Harper asked as she took a seat on the ottoman and Levi dropped into a wingback chair nearby.

"About Chase."

"Oh God," she whispered, hand to her throat.

"It's not official yet and I'm bending the rules by talking to both of you, but I figured you needed to know. So this is strictly off the record. For now." He held Harper's gaze. "He's dead."

"Oh. God." She went ghost white. "Oh God, you found him?" She blinked and looked at Levi.

"Not yet. But we know."

"How?" she said and looked about to fall apart.

Rand spoke directly to Levi. "Does Harper know about the note from your mother?"

"What note?" Harper demanded. "What's he talking about?"

Rand said, "Cynthia left a note with Edward Sievers before she died. She instructed him to give it to Levi."

"Edward Sievers? What's he got to do with anything?"

Levi said, "He's living at Serenity Acres. Across the hall from Mom's room." He explained about getting the embossed card with its strange message.

"Wait a sec," she interrupted as he relayed what was on the note. "Chase is dead? For real? And Cynthia knew it?" Her face drained of color and she took a deep breath before snagging a tissue from a box on a nearby table. Her eyes remained dry as she twisted the Kleenex through her fingers. "But you said you didn't find him."

"Right."

"I don't understand." Harper was shaking her head. "The note said '*They* killed Chase. Make *him* pay'?"

As Harper listened in horror, Rand explained about the fight between Tom and Chase, that Chase was accidently killed and Gerald Watkins was involved in the cover-up for his friend.

"Dad killed him," Levi said, nodding as if finally accepting the truth himself. He squeezed his eyes shut. "I remember he said he would kill Chase if he tried to dodge the draft. But who would do that? Who would even say such a thing?"

Harper sat still. Shocked.

"It was a tough time back then," Rand said, remembering. "For all of us." The country had been in chaos. He'd come back from war, not heralded as a hero but seen by some as a traitor, someone who had answered Uncle Sam's call to fight in a war in a far-off country, a war many in the U.S. despised. For Rand, it was water under the bridge. He'd done his duty and had memories that he'd rather forget, memories the shrapnel lodged in his shoulder wouldn't let him bury too deep.

And then there had been Chase. His best friend. Gone. No one knew where.

Until now.

"Tough times don't mean you kill your kid and cover it up. Even if it was an accident," Levi said, his voice cold.

"You're right," Rand agreed. "Absolutely." Then, as best he could, he briefed Levi and Harper on everything that Gerald had confided in him, confirming what Levi had already suspected.

Levi was stoic during Rand's explanation, taking in the information. The only sign of his emotion was the muscle in his jaw becoming tight.

Harper was silent on her tufted ottoman, her anxiety evident in her ever-moving fingers twisting the tissue until it shredded.

Levi said, "They didn't even call an ambulance?"

"No. According to my dad, Tom took Chase somewhere in his boat, he never said where, then he drove back to the middle of the lake where Dad picked him up. They left the Triton adrift in the middle of the lake."

Harper was nodding slightly, as if remembering.

"Dad swears he has no idea what happened to the body," Rand said.

Levi scowled. "Do you believe him?"

"Yeah, but I'm his son. So it doesn't count with the department. I'm stepping back. My partner is going to interview him again. I'm out of it. Dad won't like it, but that's too bad. He'll probably lawyer up, but at least we have an idea of what happened." He couldn't keep the bitterness out of his voice. His father hadn't been perfect, but all his life Rand had believed that Gerald Watkins was a straight arrow, a good, by-the-book cop.

Now he didn't.

"The case will be reopened? As a homicide?" Levi asked.

"That's up to the D.A., but I'm not sure. There's still no body, and the primary suspect is dead. All we've got is rumor and innuendo and the words of an ex-cop who was involved. We'll see."

Harper had gone quiet, her cheeks pale. "All this time he was dead?" she finally whispered, her throat thick as she got to her feet and let the flakes of the tissue drift to the floor. She rubbed her arms as if she'd experienced a sudden chill. "And we didn't know." Her gaze found Levi's. "We didn't know," she repeated, her voice cracking. "It's . . . it's just effing unbelievable."

"I know." Levi, too, got to his feet to stand near her.

"All the pain, all the worry, all the guilt, all the time wasted." Her voice cracked. "If we'd only known."

"But we didn't. Couldn't have." Levi folded her into his arms.

"If I had . . ."

"Shh," he said, his breath ruffling her hair. "You—we—had to expect that someday we would hear something. It just took a long time.

"Too long. And Dad knew. All along." Levi's voice was low and had a slight tremor. He shut his eyes for a second, just holding Harper, sharing their loss, consoling each other. Levi murmured that everything would be okay.

One more lie.

Things would never be okay.

Once again, Rand felt like the odd man out, the proverbial third wheel. He shifted on his feet and looked away, staring out the window and across the narrow portion of the lake to Fox Point.

The five houses along the shoreline were just visible in the shadowy light of dusk. Five homes that had each played a part in the drama that was their lives.

In the reflection he saw Harper drawing away, extricating herself from Levi's embrace. She brushed her hair out of her eyes and cleared her throat.

As Rand turned, she said, "At least we know what happened, even if we don't have his body, I guess."

Rand had little hope Chase Hunt, or what remained of him, would ever be found.

"My old man," Levi said. "He caused all this. But Mom? She knew and never told anyone? No, that doesn't make sense. She was always at the police department, insisting they dig further, and if she knew Dad was behind it . . . No, nuh-uh. I remember her making herself a nuisance at the station, and he was angry about it, accused her of not letting him do his job. He even said something to the effect that he more than anyone else wanted the case solved."

"I don't think Cynthia really knew what happened to Chase until after your dad died. Maybe he told her before he went out in the boat? Maybe she found some piece of evidence that convinced her, or maybe he told her. We may never find that out for certain."

"You think that's what pushed her over the edge? Finding out what he'd done? Do you think she snapped? Just mentally broke down?" Levi asked, his stoicism disintegrating.

"Maybe. Again, we'll probably never know. But what I do understand is that both your dad and mine didn't want to sully their reputations. Neither did their wives."

When Levi's head snapped up at the mention of more than one wife, Rand nodded.

"Yeah. Barbara knew, too. Or at least suspected. She came back to the house to say goodbye to me before I left for Vietnam. She saw that Dad was gone, the boat out, then learned in the next day or so that Chase was missing. She never said a word."

Levi said, "So they all kept their mouths shut."

"And let us believe there was a chance Chase was alive," Harper added.

"Son of a bitch," Levi said under his breath. "Son of a goddamned bitch. This is all such bullshit!"

Rand wouldn't argue that fact, but he wasn't finished. "There's something else."

"Oh great," Harper said, finally in control of her emotions. "The hits just keep on coming."

Rand ignored her comment. "You remember Janet Van Arsdale?"

Harper shook her head, so he added, "Janet married, so her name is Collins now."

Harper was still confused, but Levi was picking up on what he was saying. "She went by Moonbeam back in the sixties. She lived for a while in the house at the end of the street. With a bunch of college students."

Harper repeated, "Moonbeam," as if she'd heard it before.

"She's dead, too," Rand said.

"Dead?" Levi repeated.

"Looks like homicide," Rand said. "Still waiting for the ME to confirm the cause of death."

"What does she have to do with us?" Harper asked. "I mean it's sad and all, but I don't see how it affects us."

"Indirectly." Rand explained about finding her body at her home after she'd called in with information about the night Chase died. He left out details the police would want to keep from the public but did explain that though there were no official suspects, he was looking into Tristan "Trick" Vargas aka Larry Smith. The guy's name, or names, just kept coming up.

"Trick," Levi said, questions in his eyes. "You found him?"

"Wait—you know about this?" Harper said as she read Levi's reaction.

"Only that he was a scumbag drug dealer."

"And blackmailer, we think," Rand added, not bringing up the fact that, according to Gerald, Levi's dad had been on the take for years. "We're just scratching the surface of the crimes he might be involved in. He may be escalating."

"To murder?" Levi asked.

"Possibly. We think he was afraid that Janet would spill what she knew about him, dealing and blackmailing, that she was a liability. So we're looking for him, want to bring him in and see what he has to say." Rand reached into his pocket and withdrew the color print of the latest driver's license issued to Tristan Vargas. He handed the picture to Levi, and both he and Harper studied it. In the shot Vargas sported a dark blond mullet and oversized glasses, his slight smile showing off uneven teeth.

"Be on the lookout," he said. "And if you see him, let me know. Don't approach him."

"Armed and dangerous?" Levi asked.

Rand nodded. "Dangerous at the very least. Just give me a call."

Levi asked, "You think we'll see him?"

"I don't know. But there's a chance he might show up in the area. He left a lot of his cameras and equipment in the attic of the house at the end of the street." Rand pointed through the windows and across the lake to Fox Point. "He probably doesn't know what happened to it, but he might get nervous if he killed Janet because there could be evidence linking him to her."

"After all this time?" Harper asked skeptically.

"Right. The attic has been sealed for years. We're banking that he might panic and return. You and I," Rand said to Levi, "we live right down the street, so we can keep an eye out, and you?" He turned to Harper. "You've got this." He touched the telescope. "Looks high-powered. So if you see him or anyone around that cabin, let me know. It's empty, not rented currently, so no one should be there. Got it?"

"Right," she said.

"Good." Rand checked his watch, saw that he needed to get back to the station and promised, "I'll keep you posted."

Chapter 60

Rand's news about Chase had shocked her.
Why? Harper had no idea. She'd known that Chase was probably dead, that if he had been alive, he would have contacted someone somewhere or there would have been "sightings" of him.

Even though Elvis was dead and buried for over ten years, there was always a rumor that someone had caught a glimpse of him.

Of course Chase wasn't a music legend.

She could hold out hope, she supposed, as there was still no real evidence of Chase's death. Just a troubled mother's cryptic note and an ex-cop's side of an unconfirmed story.

Then there was Levi.

Now that he knew the truth about Dawn, everything had changed.

He'd left within minutes of Rand, and Harper was alone in this massive home. It seemed more cavernous than ever. As night descended, the rooms with their high ceilings, winding staircases, and long hallways felt empty and dark, shadowy and intimidating.

As she put together a tuna sandwich, she thought of how many people used to fill the hallways, stairs, dormers, and rooms. Her family, for starters. Mama and Daddy, Evan, Gramps and Gram, even the dour Matilda added life to the place, not to mention the servants that seemed to be on every floor. She even missed the cats slinking up the stairs or hiding beneath the tables or lounging like royalty on Gram's bed.

Thinking of the cats brought her back to Jinx.

She'd not seen hide nor hair of him, never heard him scratching or crying. Yet someone knew exactly where he was and what had happened to him. The damned intruder had left his collar on the doll as well as a rotting feline carcass under the chaise in the tower. Had he just found the breakaway collar on the grounds somewhere? Had Jinx wiggled out of it? Or did the intruder actually have her cat? In the back of her mind she hoped that if Jinx didn't come home, he'd found a good life by being adopted by another family, but she had worries as well, worries that something awful had happened to him.

"Don't go there," she reprimanded herself as she slapped butter on two slices of wheat bread, grated cheese on one side and the tuna mixture on the other. Then she added sliced pickles and chopped onion and turned on the stove.

As the sandwich toasted, sizzling in a pan, she listened to the phone messages that had come in while she was talking with Dawn, then Levi and Rand. She'd silenced the ring and let whoever called leave a message.

The first message was from the cable company, confirming their appointment in three days. The second was from the ever-present Rhonda Simms reminding her that the next installment of the series about the lake was due. "If you want to add your perspective, just give me a call," she'd said brightly.

"Next," Harper said in a flat tone, then let the following message play as she flipped her sandwich. Lou Arista's office. Not even the lawyer himself. An assistant asking she return the call and rattling off the number. "Fat chance," Harper said just as the phone rang, and for once she picked up.

"Hello?"

"Oh, hi, Harper," Marcia said, and Harper pictured her in the penthouse, walking around the living room and staring out the floor to ceiling windows while stretching the long phone cord. "Look, I just wanted you to know that we missed Dawn today and are devastated. We hope you saw her, and we're reporting Dad is feeling lots better."

"Right," her father said, sounding far from the receiver. And then more distinctly, "Don't list the house with Beth Leonetti."

"Her name is Alexander now," Marcia reminded him.

"I know, I know, but tell her, you tell her, Marcia, that I still have my license if she really wants to sell the place."

"You heard him, right?" Marcia said, then in a whisper, "He's very agitated at the thought of you putting the house on the market. So, just hold off, okay. I don't want him to get overly upset—"

"I heard that!" Dad cut in. "I've got a weak heart but damned good ears!"

"I'd better go," Marcia said without really stating the reason for her call.

Harper smelled butter burning and hung up, then flipped her sandwich, noting that the crust was pretty black. She paid more attention for the final side, then slid it onto a plate before scrounging in the fridge for a can of Diet Coke to wash down the meal.

"The dinner of champions," she mocked. She thought about watching TV, but the cable wasn't hooked up yet and the only television in the house was a small black and white relic from the sixties set up in Gram's bedroom. Harper doubted it worked and made a mental note to buy a new model so she could get lost in *The Wonder Years* or *Cheers* or whatever. Even the news or *Monday Night Football* would be welcome tonight after all the hard truths she'd had to face this afternoon.

I can't change the past, she thought, sitting in the wingback chair Levi had occupied earlier. All she could deal with was the here and now. For her future. And, more importantly for Dawn's. For the first time in years Dawn was more interested in being a part of the family, if her enthusiasm for living in this house were to be believed. That might change when she learned the truth about her biological father and that her mother had lied about him. *There are lies of commission and lies of omission*, she told herself as she bit into her sandwich. Yeah, it had a definite burned taste but was edible, so she ate over half of it and finished the Coke.

Time will tell, she supposed, but for now, she needed to make the house secure. Someone was intent on scaring her off. She didn't know why and she didn't know who, but whoever it was had found a way to get inside.

Despite the new locks.

She had to find a way to stop anyone unwanted from entering, and to do that she had to locate the point of entrance, a door she'd forgotten.

She remembered the set of keys she'd found in Gram's drawer. Maybe one of them would give her insight to another entrance to this old house. She snagged the ring off the kitchen counter where she'd left it after emptying her pockets the other day. She wondered what each key would unlock or if the locks even still existed.

Of course she recognized the car keys, one to Gram's Cadillac and the other to Gramps's Corvette. There were other keys as well of varying sizes—none, it seemed, for Evan's motorcycle. At least not on this ring.

She figured the cars wouldn't start. Surely their batteries were long drained. Did they have gas? Was it still good after twenty years?

But she decided to try anyway. *Nothing ventured, nothing gained*, she reminded herself and headed to the garage.

Once inside, she flipped on the overhead lights and opened the doors to each of the bays, just on the off chance the old engines actually sparked. She didn't want to fill the garage with exhaust.

She needn't have worried.

The Corvette was dead as a doornail, and as she sat in the driver's seat, she thought of her grandfather behind the wheel, driving way too fast, a driving cap tight on his head, white tufts of hair poking from beneath the brim. On a whim, she used one of the smaller keys to open the glove box. The catch stuck, but with a little effort it opened. She expected to find nothing, other than perhaps a second key. After all, Gram had had the car completely restored after it had been totaled in the wreck that had cost Gramps his life, so Harper assumed all of his personal items to have been removed.

She was surprised.

Inside the glove box she found a pair of Gramps's Wayfarer sunglasses. She remembered him sliding them onto his nose whenever he was "gonna take the Vette out for a spin."

Gram hadn't been impressed. Once she'd confided to Harper, "He thinks he's James Dean in them, you know. Like in that movie, *Rebel Without a Cause*." She had sighed and rolled her eyes. "If only."

Harper dug deeper and found an unopened pack of Lucky Strike cigarettes, two cigars, a pair of driving gloves, and Gramps's tweed driving cap. Gram must've retrieved them all from the wreckage and returned them to the glove box once the car had been restored.

Why?

As some memorial to Gramps?

That didn't seem likely considering their remote, often icy marriage. But maybe once he was gone, Gram had experienced a change of heart.

Harper turned the driving cap over in her hand and noticed something shiny and black within. Flipping the cap inside out, she discovered not one but two dead hornets caught in the lining.

"How weird." She stared at their slim little bodies and remembered the others she'd discovered in Gram's dresser. Then she looked over her shoulder to the nest still hanging by the garage window. It had been abandoned years before but still clung to the casing, a papery gray.

She replaced the cap, dead hornets and all, closed the glove box and climbed out of the low-slung sports car that Craig Alexander lusted after. She really had no use for it.

Nor the Caddy.

Nonetheless, she tried to start the big pink beast anyway. Why not?

It was an exercise in futility. Gram's Cadillac didn't so much as make a click or turn over when she twisted the key in the ignition.

She sat for a minute in the driver's seat, staring over the huge steering wheel and through the open garage door to the night beyond. Her Volvo was caught in the light that shafted from the garage and angled across the parking area to the rose garden with its macabre cat cemetery.

Someone had dug up one of Gram's cats and left it under the chaise in the turret room. Someone who wanted to terrorize her. Someone who knew where the cats were buried.

That narrowed the suspect list down a lot.

Even Beth, who had been at the cottage often while they were growing up, hadn't realized that Gram had interred her pets between her beloved rose bushes.

But someone knew. Someone who had helped bury a cat or two. Someone like the gardener, Martin Alexander, and maybe the son who had helped him with the pruning and raking and spraying?

"Craig," she whispered.

Harper adjusted the rearview mirror and caught a glimpse of the wide rear seat in the back of the Caddy. How many times had Evan and Harper ridden on that two-toned bench without seatbelts? Evan had fiddled with every button and knob he could while Gram eyed him from the mirror and cautioned him to stop. "Don't you be squirreling around back there," she'd said, stubbing out a cigarette in the ashtray as they cruised along Northway. "I can't very well drive and watch you two, now can I?"

Harper recalled how her grandmother had loved the behemoth of a car. "It's custom, you know," Gram said proudly, showing the car to Harper for the first time and admiring the pink color and white-walled tires. "Brand new. A 1960 DeVille. Isn't it just grand?" Her eyes had sparkled and she'd actually spun in front of the massive chrome grille, the skirt of her de Givenchy skirt flaring. "Your grandfather bought it for me," she added, but her smile had turned a little bitter as she'd whispered under her breath, "But, of course, he owes me."

Now Harper thought the car wasn't payment enough to assuage Gram's pain when it came to her philandering voyeur of a husband.

She started to climb out of the car but glanced into the side view mirror. In the reflection, just beyond the Caddy's pink tail fin, she caught the image of Gramps's locked gun closet. And she had a couple more keys that didn't have homes.

"Let's just see," Harper said, closing the Caddy's wide door.

She tried the smallest of the keys on the ring on the gun cabinet's lock and heard a satisfying click. With a creak of rusted hinges, the door opened to expose two rifles, three army-style handguns, and a shotgun—the Parker Side by Side.

The gun Craig Alexander wanted so badly. She reached inside the cabinet, withdrew the shotgun, and cracked it open.

A shell filled each of the chambers.

Perfect, she thought, snapping the shotgun closed.

Because she needed a loaded gun for what she was planning.

Chapter 61

Twenty years!

Twenty effin' years!

Levi stepped on the gas.

He pushed the speed limit heading south on I-5, his Ford's tires humming along the wet pavement, the wipers doing double time, the radio blasting. But no amount of soaring vocals by Whitney Houston or hard, driving beats from Madonna or gutsy working-class lyrics by Bruce Springsteen could bring him out of his dark thoughts. Or get him to Eugene faster.

Was he angry?

Oh yeah!

Was he frustrated?

For sure.

Did he blame Harper?

Yes and no. She could have, should have, come clean.

But mostly he blamed himself and Chase, of course. Even though it seemed his older brother—once his icon, later his nemesis—was truly dead.

At his own father's hand.

Christ, what a mess! He ground his teeth together and passed a semi pulling two trailers, its huge tires tossing up gritty water that the wipers couldn't swipe off the windshield fast enough.

His speedometer was showing he was going over eighty, the Fairlane flying down the interstate, but he risked the ticket. It was time to take his future into his own hands. Well past it. He wasn't going to wait for Harper. Fuck that. She'd had twenty years to spill the truth and hadn't.

So he would.

That thought gave him pause.

No doubt Dawn would freak out. The news about her paternity should come from her mother.

Well, it was too late for that.

Down the freeway he flew, passing cars and trucks, on the straight shot down the Willamette Valley. He took the off ramp before two hours had passed and eased off the accelerator as he crossed the gray Willamette River into the town. Winding his way through the city streets, he headed closer to the University of Oregon campus and located the little retro theater complete with ticket booth and a large marquee announcing the show times for *Heathers*.

From the looks of it, he had time before the next show, so he'd wait and in the meantime figure out how to approach Dawn and tell her he was her real father. Anything he came up with sounded lame, but, as he drove, he hoped inspiration would hit and he'd come up with something brilliant, something that wouldn't make him look like a nut case. At least they'd met already. He now wasn't a total stranger. He would ask her to phone Harper to confirm that he was indeed her dad.

Then hopefully they could spend some time together while she got used to the idea. He wasn't kidding himself. This wasn't going to be easy. In fact, she'd probably out and out reject him.

But at least it was a first step. There was no way he'd ever gain back trips to Baskin-Robbins for a kid's cone with sprinkles or her first bike ride. He would never hear her first word or see her take her first wobbly steps. She'd experienced her entire childhood without him, but that didn't mean he couldn't be there for her now or in the future. He'd missed a lot, didn't plan on missing any more.

If she accepted him.

"Pretty big 'if,'" he told himself, remembering that Dawn said she lived just a few blocks from the theater. He cruised the area and noticed several apartment complexes clustered together. As he turned a corner, he spied her Acura parked on the street by a newer L-shaped building. "Bingo."

Two blocks down, he parked the Fairlane under the nearly naked branches of a maple tree.

He left his car and jaywalked across the quiet street in the crisp autumn air. The sidewalk and streets glistened with the recent shower, but for now the rain had abated. He passed by the apartment buildings and a couple of alleys before reaching the area with a few bistros, shops, and the theater. There, under street lamps, pedestrians bundled in jackets and coats, carrying umbrellas or lugging backpacks, hurried along the sidewalks.

At a deli located across the street from the theater, he bought a cup of coffee and a newspaper, then took a seat at a table near the window. A few people were seated at the smattering of tables, a couple more at a long counter. At a nearby table a couple of students, textbooks open in front of them, were sipping coffee and picked at a shared monster cookie. A bell over the door tinkled as a young couple with a toddler entered, then picked up an order at the counter, where a chalkboard proudly announced the Soup of the Day and several sandwich specials.

From his table Levi had a view of the ticket booth across the street. He opened his newspaper and pretended interest in the columns of the *Register-Guard* while surreptitiously eyeing the activity at the theater.

The minutes dragged by.

He kept watching.

Finally a blond girl stepped into the booth, and people started buying tickets for the next show just as the doors opened and a crowd began streaming from the building.

He drained his coffee just as he caught a glimpse of Dawn in the same outfit she'd been wearing earlier. She was in the company of another, shorter girl with a big smile and wildly permed brown hair. They walked together, and Levi ditched his paper in a nearby trash can as he left the diner to follow at a discreet distance.

He was used to tailing a suspect and blending into the crowd, but never had he thought he would be using his private eye skills on his own daughter. Especially since he hadn't even known he had a kid.

He didn't want her to catch a glimpse of him so he hung back, and when the other girl peeled off at a side street, he quickened his pace. He'd formed a plan while sitting in the diner and decided he would wait until he was certain Dawn was home. Once she was inside, he'd phone her apartment. He'd already gotten the number from Directory Assistance at the phone company, but he wanted to assure himself that she would be able to answer. Leaving a message wasn't an option. Not for what he was going to say.

So he followed her as the crowd thinned, people leaving the main street to climb into cars or veer off to cross streets. By the time they'd left the business area, the sidewalk was nearly deserted.

He followed behind an older man walking a lumbering Basset Hound until the man and dog turned at the next corner.

Levi hung back a little farther, still keeping Dawn in sight as she walked swiftly along the tree-lined street, about fifty yards ahead of him.

How would he tell her that he was her biological father, that neither Joel Prescott nor Chase, his brother, had sired her? Would she believe him or think him a nut job? If he—

Something was wrong!

He knew it in an instant.

The second Dawn passed a darkened storefront, a man who had been loitering in the alcove stepped out to join her.

It didn't look right.

Maybe a friend?

A boyfriend?

He didn't think so.

Even though they seemed to be having a conversation. At first Dawn had seemed startled, but then she was talking to the guy. Whoever he was. But it didn't look right.

Levi quickened his pace, intent on closing the gap between them.

Too late.

As they reached the alley, the man struck. He grabbed Dawn around the shoulders with one hand while placing the other over her nose and mouth. She couldn't so much as scream. But she fought. As the attacker dragged her into the alley, she kicked and thrashed, then disappeared into the darkness.

Chapter 62

What the hell?

What was this freak doing?

Frantic, Dawn twisted wildly, trying to break her assailant's grip.

He'd come out of nowhere, some dude offering her weed.

When she told him no thanks, he said he knew her mother and mentioned Harper's name. She'd been surprised, turned to him to ask him how he knew her mom, and he'd jumped her. Shoved a sickening-smelling cloth over her mouth and nose and dragged her, fighting for all she was worth, into this dark alley with a tall building on one side, a fence on the other.

The sweet, sickly odor on the cloth was making her dizzy.

God, he was drugging her. Her mind was getting thick, the world fuzzy.

She held her breath, but it was too late. Whatever he'd soaked the cloth in was starting to work. She swung her purse at him, but it went flying, lipstick, pens, and wallet spilling out. She tried to kick and hit, but he was able to avoid her blows and she was dizzy, her blows not landing.

But she couldn't give up.

He was behind her, marching her toward the end of the alley, where she saw a single weak security lamp.

She twisted and writhed, but he was stronger than he looked.

If only she could break away and run. Or better yet land a karate kick to his nose and lay him flat.

She bit at his hand, but the cloth was thick and she tasted the awful substance saturating the cotton. If only she could scream. If only someone could hear her as she thrashed.

She had to break free! Had to! In desperation, she threw her body weight against him.

For a second he lost his footing.

They tumbled into metal trash cans, the clang of lids echoing down the narrow alley.

His hand slipped.

The cloth fell away.

She sucked in fresh air.

And let out an ear-piercing cry.

"Shut up!"

He was on her again, wrestling the sickening rag over her nose and mouth. His body pressed against hers.

But surely someone heard.

Tons of people lived in her apartment building, and it was only half a block away.

She tried to roll away, making more noise as a can toppled over, clattering loudly.

He yanked her roughly to her feet, drug-soaked cloth firmly in place. "Move!" he growled into her ear, pointing her toward the far end of the alley where just out of the security lamp's pool of light, a single vehicle was parked.

A black van.

No!

Whatever he was planning, it was not good. In fact, it would be deadly. Her insides turned to water, and for a second she couldn't move.

He pushed her roughly forward.

She redoubled her efforts.

Help! she screamed but the word was shouted only in her mind. Her attempt at yelling was muffled. Her knees wobbled and she knew she needed air. The world was spinning, her body not responding. *No one's going to come for you. You have to do this on your own! Fight, Dawn! Damn it, fight!*

Desperate, she threw her weight backward, against him, catching him off guard.

His grip broke.

The rag fell away from her face.

She screamed at the top of her lungs and started to run. If she could just get away—

He caught her by the arm. Spun her around.

Reached into his jacket.

And pulled out a gun.

A long-barreled pistol that he rammed against the side of her head.

"I really hoped it wouldn't come to this," he said, his glasses catching the light from the security lamp at the end of the alley. "Shut the fuck up!"

Chapter 63

Levi sprinted to the edge of the alley. Heart thudding, he saw the struggle.

No!

He raced forward.

Saw Dawn start to break free.

Her frantic scream echoed down the alley as the trash cans fell over with a loud crash.

"Hey!" he yelled, running and reaching into his jacket for his sidearm and coming up empty. His gun was tucked safely in the glove box of his car. But even without a weapon he was determined to save his daughter. "Stop!"

His voice was drowned by the clattering of trash cans.

The attacker caught her by the arm, pulled out a gun, and jammed it to her temple.

Oh. Jesus.

Levi stopped short, stunned. Afraid the assailant would shoot. He flattened himself against the side of the building and breathed deeply, trying to come up with a plan to end this madness.

Who would do this? Why? Not that it mattered at the moment. He couldn't let it happen. He couldn't let the daughter he'd just met be taken down by this monster.

As Dawn's assailant forced her toward the end of the alley, Levi followed, staying in the shadows, using trash bins and piles of junk as his cover but silently closing the distance. The attacker's attention was focused on Dawn, struggling, fighting despite the muzzle of the gun against her head.

Don't, he silently warned. He couldn't imagine watching his daughter die. Oh God, no!

He was accustomed to violent death, had seen it often enough in his line of work, but this was different. Gut-wrenching.

Ice-cold fear clenched his heart.

Moving stealthily, he glanced around his surroundings, trying vainly to come up with a weapon, something other than the element of surprise to gain an advantage.

He'd been in tight, dangerous situations before and lost those close to him.

Never again, he'd vowed when he left the government's service.

And not now.

He wouldn't lose his kid.

He'd save Dawn or die trying.

As he passed by the upturned trash can, he saw the glint of glass. A broken jar. He picked up the glittering piece, cutting himself as he did, but holding onto the shard just as he spied a small sharp rock near a fence post. He scooped it up in his free hand.

His weapons were rudimentary.

Useless against a gun.

But they were all he had.

Now it was his wits against those of the attacker.

Jaw set, he scurried forward, watching as Dawn was forced roughly toward a hulking black van parked in a corner of the empty lot.

Levi moved noiselessly faster, risking detection.

He had to get close to them, to somehow get the jump on the guy without the assailant pulling the trigger.

Dawn was still fighting, veering them off course, away from the van.

Cursing, her attacker forcefully wrangled her back toward the vehicle, his face caught in the lamplight.

Levi's blood turned to ice.

Trick Vargas.

An older version of the blond dealer he'd seen driving past his house when he was a kid. The blackmailing son of a bitch who probably killed Janet Collins.

Levi had no idea why the lowlife had chosen Dawn for his next victim, but it didn't matter. One way or another, Levi wouldn't let him get away with it.

At the back of the van Dawn still fought, despite the gun. It seemed as if Trick's grip on Dawn loosened a bit as he struggled to hold on to her while opening the door to the cargo area.

In a miraculous instant, she broke free.

Spinning, Trick took aim.

"No!" Levi yelled and raced forward. "Run, Dawn, run!"

Trick turned at the sound, his pistol trained toward the noise.

Without breaking stride, Levi hurled the rock, fast and hard.

Bam!

The gun fired.

Levi was knocked back a step, but the rock hit Trick square in his face, sending him stumbling backward against the van.

The gun went flying. Out of Trick's hands. Landing with a thud and scraping across the broken asphalt. Closer to Levi but out of his reach.

Just as Levi's knees buckled.

He went down.

Hard. Onto his knees on the uneven pavement.

Pain shot through his body and he collapsed, rolling onto his back, trying to keep his eyes focused, to stay conscious. To fight.

It was no use.

He blinked.

The world spun. "Run!" he yelled at Dawn again, his voice a croak. "Run!"

But Trick had recovered slightly. His glasses had flown off and blood covered his face, a gash splitting his forehead. He'd slid down the back of the van, his head bouncing on the bumper and was stunned. Yet he was attempting to stand, trying to get unsteadily to his feet.

He failed and fell forward. Then crawled toward Levi, his eyes hard with hatred. "You," he ground out, and Levi tried to force his legs to scoot him backward, his free hand scrabbling over the gravel-strewn pavement for the pistol.

If he could just reach—

Trick sprang.

He leapt onto Levi, his weight pinning Levi down, mashing his spine into the tarmac.

Levi groaned, pain radiating through his body. Still he stretched, reaching for the weapon, his fingertips brushing the butt of the gun and sending it spinning away.

Trick, too, grabbed wildly, straining to reach the pistol.

No way.

Despite his pain, Levi was not giving up. His fingers clenched around the jagged piece of glass. It cut into his flesh as he swung upward.

Connecting.

Smashing Trick's nose, then putting all his weight into the blow and gouging him in the eye.

With a squeal of agony, Trick rolled away. Off Levi. Flailing wildly for the gun. "You fucker!" He found the pistol. Grabbed it.

Just as Dawn leapt from the shadows.

She stamped hard on his hand with a heavy boot.

Bones crunched.

Trick screamed.

And Levi heard the sound of other voices.

Shouts. Running footsteps.

Trick, holding his injured hand with the other, rolled onto his back, then tried to stagger to his feet. "You little—"

She slammed her booted foot into his face, sending him sprawling backward.

"Get the gun!" Levi said, seeing the pistol on the ground. He tried to stand and failed. Then, unable to crawl, he inched forward, scooting, determined to get the weapon. "Run!"

Dawn didn't hear him or chose to ignore his words. Eyes laser-focused on Trick, she bounced on the balls of her feet, her hands curled into fists. "Don't move," she warned through clenched teeth.

The pistol was still ten feet away.

Trick dismissed the command. Tried to get up.

"Mistake," she said. She spun with amazing agility, cocked her leg, and landed a round-house kick to his face that sent him flying. Crying out, he landed with a thud, skidding on his back.

She wasn't finished. With a blood-curdling scream, she ran at him and jumped full force onto his crotch.

His scream of pain echoed through the alley, nearly drowning out the sound of the other voices and running feet. Was that the wail of a siren screaming in the distance? Or was Levi hallucinating? He tried like hell to hold on to consciousness, but the world was swimming around him, growing dark.

Through the blur he heard sharp voices.

Commands.

Screams.

"Stop!" a woman's voice ordered.

A male voice yelled, "Police!"

"Hands over your head!" The man again.

The woman said, "Shit, what the hell happened here?" Then, "This guy is out of it . . . we need an ambulance. STAT. Make that two! I don't think the other one's going to make it."

There was crowd noise, shuffling of feet, the buzz of excited conversation. "Get back," someone, another guy with a gruff voice, ordered. "Everyone back. Right now!"

"Would you look at that pistol?" the male voice asked. "Jesus, I haven't seen one of those cowboy guns in . . . well, maybe ever. Just in the movies as a kid."

The woman again. "Is anyone talking to the girl?"

Dawn.

Levi tried to speak, to make his lips move, but the words wouldn't pass his lips.

"Ambulance is coming!" someone yelled amid a muddle of comments, orders, and exclamations.

Nothing that made any sense.

Was someone kneeling over him?

"Oh God, this one's bad, too. Gunshot wound in the gut. Holy Christ, would you look at that. Could bleed out! We could lose him! Where the fuck are the paramedics?"

He blinked his eyes open.

Saw nothing but blackness . . . and a light. Weak but shining overhead.

He heard Dawn's voice above the din. "His name is Levi Hunt," she was telling someone, though her voice sounded far off, as if whispering through a tunnel. "Yeah, yeah, I think we're related . . . what? . . . Oh well, he doesn't know it yet, but I'm pretty sure he's my uncle."

Chapter 64

Harper found one key on the ring that was a mystery. The only one that didn't fit any lock she'd located. The key was old and tarnished and seemed original to the house, which was strange. All the exterior doors had been recently changed by the locksmith and were new, shiny, and bright.

Not this one.

But it had to go somewhere. Or at least had gone somewhere in the past.

She donned her rain jacket and walked around the exterior of the buildings, searching the boathouse, garage, a gardener's shed, and even the tram's carport for a lock she had missed.

Nothing.

Maybe it wasn't anything, just an old forgotten key to a lock long gone, but she was curious and couldn't help thinking the key might be important. It was a long shot, of course, but she thought maybe, just maybe, the key might help her figure out how the intruder had gotten into the house.

Since she failed on her perimeter check, she wondered if she were going about it the wrong way. Rather than start looking outside, maybe she could find the access point from the interior.

Earlier, Dawn had been fascinated by the elevator and dumb-waiter. Yes, they were unique, but they weren't functioning. Hadn't been for years, it seemed. She went to the elevator door on the main floor by the back stairs. She considered the elevator shaft. Was it possible that someone had been able to get inside and climb the shaft, forcing the doors open from inside? Starting from the top floor, she checked the doors for the elevator and dumbwaiter, but there was no way to get in, no scratches on either one, nor any other sign of someone forcing the doors open.

She worked her way down, and on each floor she found no indication that someone had used the lifts. As far as she could see, the shaft was impenetrable.

Except for a contractor who knew how things worked, someone who had tools.

Someone like Craig Alexander.

She didn't trust that guy, even though he was married to Beth.

Who, Harper reminded herself, was having an affair with Levi Hunt, so obviously Beth and Craig's marriage had serious problems.

As for the mystery key? She found no locks into which it fit.

"Forget it," she told herself. It could well be she'd put too much emphasis on it. So she'd discovered an old key in a house that had been built at the turn of the century. So what? Maybe she was barking up the wrong tree.

But right now it was the only tree she had.

In the parlor Harper held the key up to the light shed by one of Gram's Tiffany lamps and scrutinized the long piece of notched metal. She hoped beyond hope for some clue as to its identity. It didn't look like any of the other keys, not even the ones she'd replaced.

So where was the lock?

Maybe it didn't exist anymore.

Maybe it had been original to the house but replaced over the years and Gram had just kept the key.

"Give it up," she told herself, peeling off her jacket and draping it over a hook by the back door. The jacket slipped off and fell onto the boots that had been lined neatly under the coat rack—old boots that had sat in position for decades. As she picked up her coat, another image flashed through her brain. She remembered seeing the same row of boots on the night she freaked out searching for Chase.

One pair had been wet and puddling on the floor. They'd belonged to her father, and she recalled thinking how it had been odd to find them there as he'd been at the cottage with Marcia that night. Why had he left his boots at the main house? Where had he been, out sloshing through puddles?

However as soon as the questions flitted through her mind, she dismissed them.

Right now she needed to concentrate on the key.

She examined the key holder mounted on a shelf on the other side of the door. It was a small rack fitted with a tiny shelf and a row of cup holder hooks from which the keys to the car and outbuildings had always hung.

Had she ever seen this key dangling from one of the small hooks? Did it matter?

Either way, she couldn't remember.

She'd decided she was probably on a fool's mission when she remembered the blueprints for the manor that Beth had found in the tower room the other day. Maybe those yellowed schematics would provide a clue, if not for this key's lock, then possibly to an entrance to the mansion that she didn't know about. Like a sally port in an old castle. A secret entrance.

What were the chances?

"Good? None? Slim? Dream on," she said to herself but pocketed the key and rushed up the stairs, her hip reminding her that she wasn't completely healed. She didn't care. In the tower room, she turned on the only lamp that was working, then unrolled the plans on her grandfather's desk with as much enthusiasm as if she'd just discovered the Dead Sea Scrolls. She anchored one side with a heavy ashtray, then went through each page carefully, eyeing the fading lines. "Come on, come on," she urged, searching for anything that would tell her where there might be a hidden lock.

If there even was one.

On each page, floor by floor, Harper searched. She ran her fingers over the pages where they showed exterior doors, studying the elevator and dumbwaiter and the landing in the garage attic which had a locked door. They seemed the most likely hidden entrances.

"Where?" she said, the key in her pocket pressing against her leg, seeming to mock her. "Where?"

Once through the plans.

Twice.

A third time and nothing.

She shoved her hair from her face in frustration even though, she knew, deep down, this was probably a wild goose chase, a way for her to do something, no matter how far-fetched, to stop the intruder, and a means to keep her mind off of Levi and Dawn and the mess of their lives.

She reminded herself that the damned key wasn't the center of the damned universe. It might not even be a key to this house. She was just spinning her wheels, wanting to do something, anything to secure her home.

It had been an excruciating day.

Levi's recognition that he was Dawn's father and his insistence that Dawn be informed of that long-buried truth was wearing on her.

Rand's news that Chase was dead, killed by his own father decades ago, should have been expected but had drained her emotionally.

Janet Collins's murder, possibly by a drug dealer from the sixties and somehow connected to Chase's death, was a worry and ate at her.

It had all been too much to take in.

Giving up, she walked to the window and stared out. From this bird's eye view she saw the houses across the point, some with lights on, others dark. All with their own dark secrets, just like this old house.

She needed a drink.

No, no, no! She needed to be clearheaded.

But just one drink?

No!

Her eyes dropped to the blueprints with their yellowed pages, some ripped around the edges.

Maybe the key was meaningless. She fingered it and decided to give up, but as she started rolling up the pages, she caught a glimpse of the specs for the basement and stopped dead in her tracks. There on the drawings she saw the placement of the original furnaces, two huge wood-burning beasts with round, tentacle-like vents reaching upward to the myriad of rooms overhead. Next to the furnaces, lining two walls of the basement, were designated areas, huge open bins for storing and stacking firewood. Over the largest bin that encompassed one corner of the basement was the schematic for a chute that allowed the chopped wood, or coal, or anything else to be dumped into the basement as needed.

Like a storm cellar, it opened from the outside.

And it was locked.

She'd never seen it opened, not even as a child. In fact, shrubs and bushes had grown over the wing-like doors.

With a new sense of anticipation and urgency that could prove false, she ran out of the tower room, speeding down the stairs, the key in her pocket pressing hard against her thigh. In the kitchen, she grabbed a flashlight, then yanked her jacket from the coat rack near the back door and reminded herself that she could be wrong.

But it felt right.

Following the flashlight's bobbing beam, she jogged down the gravel path that wound around the side of the garage. The path that had once been wider to accommodate the carts that carried wood when delivering fuel. The path where she'd spied Craig recently, his big dog trailing after him.

After rounding the corner, she found the rhododendrons and hydrangeas that flanked the storm doors, nearly covering them with their dripping branches and effectively camouflaging the entrance.

"Son of a gun," she whispered, expecting that the old storm doors might be swollen or rotten from years of being exposed to the elements, but she fought her way through the tangle of limbs, extracted the key, and inserted it into the lock easily. It opened with a twist of her wrist. She pulled one heavy door open as far as the interlocking branches would allow and exposed the slide leading into the basement.

Access into the house.

Bending down, she shone her flashlight through the opening to examine the steel lining of the chute. It was free of dust.

As if it had been recently used.

Anyone who had a key could slide right in and bring with him a bat or a dead cat or anything else if he wanted to.

"You sneaky, slimy bastard," she said as the wind picked up and she shut the doors again and locked them.

She would bet her inheritance that the person behind the pranks was Craig Alexander. His father, Martin, could have been given a secondary key as he had been the groundskeeper when Gram was alive. Craig could have found it. And she knew he sneaked around in the dark. She'd seen evidence of that when he'd surreptitiously slipped into the Hunt house at night.

Why would he try to terrorize her?

To get her to sell?

To secure the expensive listing for his wife?

To make Harper so anxious to get out of here, she'd hire him to make all the necessary repairs?

Really? she asked herself but knew the answer.

It all came down to money.

And her best friend's husband.

She just had to prove it.

And the only way to do that was to catch him in the act.

Back into the house and up the stairs she went. Again, her hip started to ache, and again, she ignored the nagging pain.

In the tower room she didn't bother with lights but walked directly to the window to stare across the lake to Fox Point.

No lights glowed from Rand's A-frame, and even though Levi had moved into the house next door, the Hunts' cottage showed no signs of life. She hadn't seen a glimpse of Levi after their argument about Dawn and couldn't imagine what their next meeting would be like.

Closer to the swim park, lights were on at the Sievers' home. She saw people moving in and out of the kitchen in the back, but as time passed, most of the lights were turned off, although a TV with its shifting images was partially visible.

As usual, the house at the other end of the street, the Musgraves' cabin, was completely dark.

Not so the Alexanders' house, which was the one that held her interest tonight.

There was activity there, people moving about, so she took the time to reheat a cup of coffee and lace it with bourbon. Then she returned to the tower room and kept the lights off to ensure she wasn't backlit and couldn't be seen.

Propping herself up with pillows, she sipped her drink and kept her binoculars trained on the Alexanders' house.

As she sipped, Harper observed Beth, curly hair piled onto her head, dressed in an oversized sweatshirt and leggings. She moved about her kitchen making microwave popcorn and pouring a glass of white wine. After dumping the popcorn from its bag into a big bowl, she balanced the bowl and glass on her way to the living room. Then she put the popcorn on the table and plopped onto the couch to sip wine.

"Cheers," Harper said, holding up her cup in a toast where they would clink the rims of their drinks. As if Beth could hear her. As if Beth had any idea Harper was playing the part of the voyeur. On her best friend's family.

Harper did feel a little bad about spying but didn't stop. Not when she was certain Beth's husband, and possibly Beth herself, were involved in plotting to terrorize her.

So Harper kept watching as Beth picked up the TV remote to channel surf, eventually landing on MTV, where a black and white Guns N' Roses music video was playing.

Harper watched, found herself humming to the tune of "Sweet Child o' Mine," and kept drinking. She spied Max in the house, appearing from a hallway, their big dog tagging after him.

In pajama bottoms and a T-shirt, wearing headphones attached to his Walkman, Max went into the kitchen for a pint of Ben and Jerry's Chunky Monkey and bottle of Gatorade. He grabbed a spoon, took a couple of bites right out of the container, then wandered into the living room. Eyes on the television, he stopped by the couch to say a few words to his mom, then ambled off, disappearing into the hall. A minute later lamplight glowed in his room. His shades were drawn, she couldn't see what he was doing and didn't care.

How much of a creepy voyeur could she be?

Max was a kid.

And Harper's interest lay with Craig.

She found him in his office/workout room in the basement, shuffling papers, taking phone calls, so she sipped slowly, wondering about him. About Beth.

At eleven Harper reheated the last of the coffee, added a final shot of liquor, then returned to her post.

Max's room was dark.

Fifteen minutes later Beth retreated to her bedroom and shut off the lights.

But Craig was still up. He stood in front of the stationary bike and was throwing darts at his dartboard, three of which landed near the bull's-eye.

He was taking aim again, then stopped suddenly, turned, and walked to his desk. He answered the phone, cradling it next to his ear and pausing his game, as his attention was riveted to whatever the person on the other end of the line was saying.

She watched as his entire body grew tenser, muscles in his jaw bulging, his face becoming a deep red. His side of the conversation came in short answers, and Harper had no experience reading lips. But his body language indicated that he was angry as hell as he slammed down the receiver. He threw the darts he was still holding at the board, one at a time in rapid succession.

Zing!

The first dart went wild. Barely hit the board.

Zing!

The second was a better shot, sticking closer to the center of the board.

Zing!

The third dart was right on the money. A bull's-eye.

Visually calmer, he snatched all six darts from the board and pocketed them, then strode through the door to the hallway to the bottom of the staircase that led upward.

A few seconds later the kitchen was flooded with light and Craig appeared, his features hard and set but his face no longer flushed. As if his anger had given way to gritty determination. He beelined to the fridge, yanked out a bottle of beer, and twisted off the top. Taking a long swallow, he walked through the slider to the deck. He set his bottle down on the top rail and lit a cigarette, the flame of his lighter illuminating his grim face for a second.

He drew deep, then exhaled and didn't seem to notice that his dog had wandered through the open door and made his way down the exterior steps.

While Craig smoked, Rambo nosed around the lower deck where a kayak and patio furniture were stored. Nearby was a stack of firewood and a scarred stump that was obviously used as a chopping block. An ax had been buried deep into the stump. In her mind's eye Harper imagined Craig with an ax in his hand, throwing his shoulders into swinging the heavy blade downward to split chunks of fir. She imagined the split pieces spinning and flying across the deck and into the yard and Craig stacking them next to his house.

She thought about the empty bins in her own basement, where once firewood had been stored.

Craig knew this house like the back of his hand.

He and Beth had financial issues.

He wanted to renovate her house.

His wife wanted to sell it.

Both of them profiting if Harper hired Craig's construction company to fix up the place and then Harper sold it through Alexander Realty.

Still looking through the telescope, she watched as he drained his beer and flicked the butt of his cigarette into the air, its red tip arcing, then dying as he stalked into the house again. He made his way to the front hall where he picked up his jacket, then headed down the stairs to the basement.

Now what? she wondered, her gaze glued to the scenario playing in front of her.

Within seconds she saw him storming across the yard and into the boathouse.

Not a minute later the boat churned out of its berth and into the lake where Craig, at the helm, turned it, pointing the prow directly toward Dixon Island.

Harper smiled. "Well, come on then," she said aloud, her racing heart belying her calm words.

She headed down the stairs quickly, stopped on the first floor where she'd left the shotgun, and carried it down another flight to the basement even though she knew shooting it in a confined area was dangerous. Possibly deadly. Shotgun pellets would ricochet everywhere.

Threatening to fire the shotgun was a bluff at best.

Actually pulling the trigger, a last resort at worst.

For backup she grabbed the poker, then positioned herself so she could view the chute. Sitting on the gritty brick floor, her back propped against one of the old furnaces, she held the gun across her lap.

Then she waited.

Chapter 65

With Chelle looking over his shoulder, Rand stared at a new set of photographs laid out across his desk in his office. They had been at it for hours. It was late, the day shift having been replaced by the night crew hours before, the office illuminated only by overheads and desk lamps, the station quiet except for an occasional phone ringing or the undertones of a conversation, but at this hour, closing in on midnight, only a few officers were in the building.

The pictures they were viewing had been developed from the stash of old film canisters and cameras they had discovered in the Musgraves' cabin. The film was primarily black and white, the shots grainy, but he and Chelle had pored over the developed still pictures while the film from the old movie cameras was still being processed.

Though Trick might have had state of the art equipment in 1968, film technology had advanced in the past twenty years and it was taking a while to develop the 8mm film for what were, essentially, home movies. In the case of Trick Vargas, though, Rand expected the reels weren't of happy kids splashing in wading pools or marching in Fourth of July parades or opening presents on Christmas morning.

No, he expected the film from the movie cameras would prove to be moving images of what happened on the lake, the secrets of people in their private lives, secrets they would pay to keep hidden, secrets never meant to be exposed.

For now, though, until those movies were available, he and Chelle looked over the photographs.

There had been mountains of pictures to sort through, day and night shots, mostly of the activity on the lake. Nothing that meant anything. There were other photographs as well, of people who had come and gone to the Musgraves' home, shots taken from the peephole cut into the floor of the attic. Images of drug deals going down or couples or threesomes engaging in sex.

Rand figured some of the photographs were used for blackmail.

Others Trick might have seen as insurance so that no one would complain about activity at the house if they themselves realized they'd been caught on camera.

It had taken hours, but Rand and Chelle had sorted through them to come up with shots from the night Chase Hunt had disappeared. They had arranged them in sequence, according to the negatives, which showed each photo taken in succession.

Those photos were spread in a time line across the wide surface of his desk. The interesting thing, he noted, was that Trick had been busy that night. Many of the images were of the Hunts' dock, pictures snapped of the fight between Chase and his father. There had been just enough illumination from the street light and through the window of the Hunts' house to make out what happened, though some of the images on the pictures were blurry and useless. Those were set aside.

That night, Trick hadn't confined his spying to the Hunt family. His expensive equipment had captured images of people in houses across the lake and, more specifically, on Dixon Island.

And those images told a story.

It started with shots of the fight between Chase and Tom. Though some of them were blurred, there were photos of Tom and Gerald loading Chase's body into the boat, then leaving the boat adrift in the middle of the lake.

"These confirm your dad's statement," Chelle said, pointing to the pictures of Chase and Tom on the Hunts' dock. That much was true, and Rand only hoped that his father had truly and completely come clean. She said, "It's amazing that Trick got them."

"He was always on the lookout for something to use to get a buck ahead, and he was lucky that the Musgraves' dock was the largest so he could get an angle on the other houses on the point."

"Especially the Hunts' property as it sticks out farther into the lake," she observed. "The real point of Fox Point."

But there were other photos that bothered him. Photographs taken that night, most likely with a telephoto lens, possibly taken from a boat or some other watercraft. They were shots of Dixon Island, the manor house, and the people within.

He recognized Harper.

And her image was caught on the island's dock. Wrestling with a canoe.

Then another couple of pictures of her near Tom Hunt's empty boat in the middle of the lake.

"He was there," Rand said. "On the lake. He had to have been."

There were more pictures of the huge house on the island.

Images of someone in Harper's grandmother's room while Harper herself was in the canoe looking for Chase.

Someone who could have doctored the old woman's drink.

Someone he recognized.

And in that second the jagged pieces of what happened that night began to tumble into place. As he double-checked the time, an icy dread began to take hold. He was vaguely aware of the phone ringing but let Chelle answer it.

"That's right," she said after a short conversation, and when he started to reach for his jacket she held up a finger, her face going somber. ". . . the next of kin? I believe he has a daughter," she was saying, her gaze locked with Rand's as she reached for a pad and pen and held the phone between her ear and shoulder. ". . . No. Divorced as I understand it . . . Yes, we'll let her know. Where is the body?" she asked. "Mercy General? Yeah, Got it." She wrote across the top of the note so that Rand could read: HOMICIDE, JOEL PRESCOTT. "Okay, we're on it." She hung up and explained as she grabbed her coat. "Portland PD. It looks like Joel Prescott fell, jumped, or was pushed off a rooftop in Portland. He had ID on him and info with Harper Prescott's name. At first look, it was suspected suicide, but the bartender said he had a friend with him, someone he knew."

"Jesus." He felt sick inside. He picked up the phone and dialed a number he'd remembered, the number for the house on Dixon Island. He needed to tell Harper about her ex, and more than that, he felt an urgency.

Two people dead in as many days.

Who knew how far this would go?

And then there were the photographs of the intruder who, he believed, may have sent Olivia Dixon to an early grave and let Harper take the fall for it.

He waited, phone to his ear, sliding his arms into his jacket. "Come on," he said, willing her to answer.

Chelle, too, was slipping into her coat.

On the other end of the line the answering machine picked up.

"Shit!" He slammed the phone down. "Let's go!" he said to Chelle, who was zipping her jacket. "And bring your gun."

Chapter 66

Finally.

Sitting in the dark, Harper heard the key turn in the lock of the storm door.

She raised the shotgun to her shoulder, pointing its double barrel toward the chute.

With a creak the door opened, and she felt a rush of cold night air seep into the basement.

Finger on the trigger, nerves strung tight as bowstrings, she didn't move. Her heart was pounding, sweat collecting on the back of her neck.

Come on in, she silently welcomed, straining to listen as she heard him enter, pushing his legs through the opening, then with a soft nerve-wracking whoosh sliding his body down the chute.

His feet landed with a quiet thud.

Craig.

The back of her neck tensed, and she stared in the direction of the bin that he landed in. Though her eyes were accustomed to the darkness, she could barely make out his dark form, felt his presence more than saw him.

She sensed he was on his feet. Straightened.

"Hold it right there," she ordered.

"What—?"

She switched on her flashlight, aimed upward, right into his startled eyes.

Craig froze, his face a mask of confusion. He winced against the intense light and held up a hand to shield his eyes as he stepped backward.

"Don't move!" She dropped the flashlight and hoisted the shotgun to her shoulder.

"What the fuck?" he said, regaining some composure as she slowly stood, leveling the gun at his chest while the flashlight shone from the floor, illuminating his feet and legs but now leaving his face in shadow.

She steadied the gun.

"What're you doing here?" he asked.

"I live here."

"But here, with the gun? Put it down. It's me."

"I know who you are. I saw you coming. What're *you* doing here?" she countered. "Why the hell are you sneaking around in here?"

When he didn't respond, she pretended surprise. "What? Cat got your tongue? Oh, I mean *dead* cat got your tongue?"

"I don't know what you're talking about. Put the gun down, Harper. You're not going to shoot it down here. Shit, there would be buckshot everywhere. You'd kill us both!"

"I asked you a question. Why are you here?"

She saw the lie forming in the shadows of his face. "I came to the door. No one answered and I knew—"

"Bullshit, Craig. I saw you leave. You came in your boat tonight. Like you have before." She was watching him and in the feeble light noticed his face changing from surprise and thinking he could cajole her to a suppressed anger evident in the thin line of his lips, the way his eyes narrowed.

"Just give me the gun."

"No way. You tell me why you're trying to scare the living crap out of me! Ever since I got back here and maybe before, you've been sneaking into this house. Leaving me little surprises." Her anger was getting the better of her now. "Dolls with sick messages moving around the house? *ICU?* What the hell was that all about? Meaning I see you, like you were watching me, right? Kind of a sick joke." She could tell from his reaction, the blink, that she'd hit the nail on the head. Twisted bastard!

"I didn't . . . I wasn't . . ."

"You did! And you were! I caught you here tonight. For the love of God, Craig, do you think I'm a moron? I *know* you moved the dolls around in my house while I was asleep! I *know* you stole my cat and put his collar on one of the dolls. I *know* you dug up poor Earline and left her body for me in the tower room hoping I'd find it and freak out. Well, it worked! Mission accomplished!" she said, her fury mounting. "But what I don't know, what I can't for the life of me understand, is why."

"You're a smart girl," he said, and he was moving slightly, out of the flashlight's glow. "You figure it out."

"Stop!"

He didn't. He kept inching to her right, trying to avoid the light.

"Smart enough to get into Stanford, right? And tuition wouldn't be a problem because it would have been all paid for from this." He motioned upward, to include the massive house above them, and for just a second Harper thought she heard the floorboards overhead squeak, as if the house was protesting. "You never *had* to work a day in your pampered life. Everything handed to you on a silver platter." He snorted in disgust. "I didn't come here to hurt you, Harper. If I'd wanted to do that, I could have."

"You just wanted to terrorize me into selling. With your twisted, juvenile pranks. You thought you'd push me into moving out, hiring you to fix up the house, and then hiring your wife to list it and sell it."

"Because you weren't going to sell," he surmised, and she turned, keeping the gun trained on him. He was unstable. Desperate. "You were hesitating. Beth said so."

"She's in on this, too?" Harper felt a sharp jab of disappointment. She and Beth had been so close once.

"She doesn't know any of it," he admitted. "And she can't. She'd divorce me like that if she knew." He snapped his fingers. "I did it for her. And for Max. He's a smart kid. About to go to college, except there's no money."

So there it was.

"Without me getting a job like this," he said, motioning to the house again, "or one like it, Max can kiss Oregon State goodbye."

"Because?"

"Because we've got debts. Major debts."

"You gamble," she surmised, remembering his recent phone call and his anger.

"No—no. I just had to borrow," he admitted. "Personal loan. High interest rate and it's due. Beth doesn't know. She's already got one foot out the door," he admitted. So he knew about Beth and Levi. How desperate was he? She noticed by the lines creasing his forehead that he was weighing his options. "I need this job, Harper. It's for my family." He was too close now and his jaw had hardened.

"Stop right there!" she warned.

He didn't.

Instead he sprang and lunged for the gun.

She scrambled backward and tripped over the flashlight. The gun flew out of her hands to skitter across the grimy floor. She saw it all in the weird, moving light washing over the walls and floor as the flashlight rolled away.

No!

She leapt for the gun.

Craig caught her by the ankle and yanked hard.

Her hip screamed. She went down, cracking her knees, her head banging against the wall of the furnace. "Stop! Just stop, Harper," he said, but she didn't.

She kicked hard with her free foot, slamming her heel into his face.

He sucked in his breath.

His grip loosened for a second and she spied the poker. Within reach by the furnace.

She stretched.

Her fingers wound around it as he pulled on her leg, her hip screaming in pain. She swung the iron rod hard.

Downward.

Aiming for his head.

He shifted suddenly.

Thud!

The blow landed hard on his shoulder, sending him reeling, his grip on her loosening. "You fucking bitch!" He let go of her to grab the poker before she could swing again.

Frantic, she scooted closer to the shotgun.

He was bigger than she and stronger, more athletic. She'd been foolish to take him on, but here she was and now cornered. What had she said about this old house with its winding tunnels, various staircases, and dark corners? That there were a million places to hide in it. She'd better find one fast. Or better yet, get out of here completely and find help.

A phone.

If she could get to a phone.

She snatched the gun and threw herself behind a furnace. She had to get out of here. To hide somewhere. To save herself.

The flashlight moved, the beam shining over the walls.

He had it.

Damn, damn, damn!

"Where are you, Harper?" he said, his voice reverberating through the cavernous basement. She'd been an idiot to think she could take him, her anger getting the better of her. And now he was tracking her down as if she were prey.

But she had the shotgun.

If she had the guts to use it.

As he was between her and the stairs leading to the main house, she was forced to slink toward the door to the tunnel. Inching along the wall, watching as the flashlight's beam washed over the old walls, she crept silently.

He was getting closer, the beam nearly at her feet when she reached the door to the tunnel and quietly turned the knob, silently praying it wasn't locked. The door opened with a loud creak.

At the noise the beam of the flashlight moved swiftly, catching her in its glare.

She ran.

Fast as she was able, she slipped through the door and ran, tripping on the steps, but somehow managing to stay on her feet. If she could get to the boathouse, she could dive into the water, hide from him, and surface wherever she chose. She could swim to Rand's house or Levi's or even the Sievers'. It wasn't that far.

She heard him behind her.

Breathing hard, big footsteps speeding, the flashlight catching her. "Stop!" he yelled at her.

God in heaven, he was so close.

Frantic, she told herself she could use the shotgun if she absolutely had to. Even though she'd never shot a living creature in her life. The targets she'd practiced on years before were all clay pigeons, inanimate discs.

But things had changed.

And now, she realized, she could no longer threaten or intimidate him with the loaded gun. He wouldn't believe for a second that she would actually fire at him.

So she ran. As fast as she could. The boathouse was just ahead, the lake a few more steps. She could swim away. Or she could shoot him. She'd figure it out soon.

She heard him clambering behind her, his footsteps growing louder, though they echoed as if there were more people pursuing her, a host of assassins trailing behind him.

Run, Harper, run!

She was running blind, the tunnel ahead of her dark, the steps within causing her to stumble. The footsteps behind her got louder. Closer. The flashlight's beam piercing the darkness.

Zing!

A dart zipped past the side of her head.

Oh crap!

She redoubled her efforts, running in a zigzag pattern.

Zing!

Another dart flew past her shoulder to fall to the ground in the darkness ahead. The tiny little missiles wouldn't kill her, but they sure could wound her. Slow her down.

Her foot slipped on a step. She caught herself but glanced back.

Zing!

Zing!

One dart hit her on the shoulder.

The second pierced her cheek.

She cried out but kept stumbling forward, the watery smell of the cave closer. She ripped the dart from her cheek, felt a trickle of blood. Didn't care. In the wavering light, she saw the door to the storage room with the abandoned boating equipment.

And then a straight shot to the boathouse.

Finally!

If she could just get through—

Zing! A dart caught her in the arm, and she had to bite her tongue so she didn't cry out.

Another door.

Then she would have to cross the final storage room before reaching the boathouse. But she didn't have far now.

Zip!

A dart cut through the air, a hair's breadth from her ear.

That was the fifth, she thought. Right? Or the sixth. Did he still have one more?

She raced forward, the rank, fetid smell of the boathouse reaching her nostrils. She was close. So close.

And he was right behind her, breathing hard.

Another dart zipped past her.

Damn!

"Stop!" he yelled.

Oh God, he was almost on her.

"Harper! Stop!"

"Screw you!" She flung open the door, saw the yawning blackness of the boathouse, and raced through. A cloud of bats swirled around the old, rotting Chris-Craft hanging drunkenly above. It swayed and creaked on the moldering straps of its sling.

"Stop!" Craig yelled before she could jump.

He was too close.

He would catch her in the water.

Drown her.

She wouldn't have a chance.

"Harper! Stop!"

She spun, leveling the gun at the bobbing flashlight with its bright beam. If she pulled the trigger now, the shotgun blast would pepper him with pellets. But she backed up, her finger on the trigger, hearing his echoing footsteps. Could she do it? Could she shoot him? Kill him?

She yelled, "*You* stop!" Behind her the empty boat slip yawned, a black abyss. Above the slip, the old boat groaned. Carefully she edged toward the water, along the thin wooden decking, the rotting wooden boards slick with mold and bat dung.

"Harper?" His voice was like thunder.

Shotgun raised to her shoulder, she eased backward.

He emerged from the doorway.

He held the flashlight in his left hand.

In his right? The iron poker, raised as if he intended to thrust it at her like a javelin.

"Don't even think about it," she warned, sweat collecting at the back of her neck, her heart pounding as she squinted against the light. "Don't!" she warned. She was so close to the lake, but he was blinding her with the flashlight. Moving toward her.

Shoot! Pull the trigger!

He moved forward, taking his life in his own hands.

Shoot! Shoot him now!

Mouth dry, finger sweating on the trigger despite the cold, she tried to keep the distance between them so that he couldn't reach her. Only a few more steps and then . . . and then she would have to take her chances in the water.

"Put the gun down." His voice was low now, but the bright light was aimed right at her eyes.

Never. Pull the damned trigger!

Another step backward.

The timbers creaked, the musty water reeked, and the long-forgotten boat overhead hung drunkenly.

One more step, and there was nothing. She was at the entrance to the cave. From this point, she would have to drop into the water and he would be on her in an instant.

"You won't shoot," he said, his eyes focused on her, bats flying frantically in and out of the cave. "You wouldn't dare."

"Try me." Her finger on the trigger was moist. Her pulse pounding in her eardrums. She set her jaw.

He smiled then, a slash of white in the darkness. "Give me the gun, Harper, you're not going to pull the trigger."

He stepped forward but turned his head toward the open doorway.

Blam!

The blast shook the cave.

Echoing.

Reverberating.

Knocking Harper back.

Craig screamed.

The flashlight rolled against the wall.

Overhead the boat rocked wildly, one moldering strap unraveling.

Blood blooming on his torso, Craig hurled the poker, then fell, crashing into the dangling boat.

Dodging the poker, she lost her balance, tried to catch herself, and tumbled into the slip. Rank, cold water surrounded her.

The gun fell from her hands.

She came up coughing inside the cave, heard the ancient timbers creak ominously overhead. Saw Craig, attempting to swim out of the slip as bats flew crazily and the dark water turned murky with his blood.

Above, the Chris-Craft was hanging precariously by its stern.

As she tried to swim out of the boathouse, she was transfixed, watching as it spun slowly, spilling its contents into the water. An old thermos and life preserver fell, then a tattered, rolled tarp unwound as if in slow motion.

From within, bones appeared and to her horror, a skeleton tumbled out.

Craig let out a rumbling cry. "Jesus Christ! Oh shit! Oh shit! This is so fucked! So fucked!" Frantically he swam, away from the boathouse, from the horror within.

But Harper was frozen.

Couldn't move.

Her gaze glued to the skull with its haunting black eye sockets.

Those empty sockets seemed to stare straight to her soul.

No teeth missing in the skull, just a bit of blond hair, tattered shirt, and rotting jeans, and around its neck vertebrae a necklace of beads hung limply.

Love beads moving with the water.

Oh. Dear. God.

An arctic cold swept over Harper and she thought for a second that she might pass out.

She imagined him as he once had been. Tall. Blond. Athletic. Cocky. A bit of mischief in his blue, blue eyes.

Chase. She was staring at what remained of Chase.

Her heart stopped. Something inside of her broke, and a bubbling cry passed through her lips.

After twenty years of shadowy doubts, she'd finally found him.

Chapter 67

*D*on't panic.
Do not panic.

It's a dead body, yes. It's Chase. But, for God's sake, Harper, don't panic! Teeth chattering, her mind racing, Harper dragged herself out of the water. Cold night air surrounded her and she was shivering, shaking all over. All she wanted to do was run as fast and as far away as possible.

But she forced herself to get her bearings.

She remembered loving him, dreaming with him, wanting him so badly she physically ached. He hadn't loved her back, not the way she adored him, and he'd hurt her over and over again.

Because she let him.

Because she was eighteen.

Tears sprang to her eyes and she quickly dashed them away.

"I'm sorry," she said, not for what they had and lost, but for the fact that he never got the chance to grow up, to become a man. To break her heart again.

Coughing, she dashed her tears away. She wasn't that innocent, wide-eyed girl who would have done anything for him. Not anymore. She'd had the chance to live her life, to grow up, to become a wife and a mother.

And she had the scars to prove it.

She sat on the edge of the rotting decking in the boathouse and forced herself to stare at his skeleton. Never had she expected to find him, especially here.

How had no one known?

True, the house and island had been basically abandoned soon after he disappeared, but the smell alone would have been a dead giveaway. Unless Tom had wrapped him in the tarp with odor-suppressing chemicals and everyone had stayed away.

God, what a mess.

And what had happened to Craig?

She dragged herself to her feet and picked out the darts buried in her arm and shoulder. Damn that Craig. What a bastard. If he survived, she'd press charges against him, and if Beth didn't like it, well, she could just lump it.

Shivering, her teeth chattering, Harper found the flashlight resting against the wall of the boathouse. She cast one last look at the lapping water and wrecked boat and, of course, the bones that had been Chase, then she left, dripping, as she made her way through the tunnel and basement.

She'd call Rand when she got upstairs.

And Levi.

They both could deal with what remained of Chase, and Rand could round up Craig. Get the police and paramedics. Craig obviously wasn't hurt so badly that he couldn't swim. Maybe he would drown. Served him right! Her cheek still stung, as did her arm and shoulder where his damned darts had found her flesh.

And he would have killed her to keep her quiet, she decided as she made her way upstairs. Well, she wasn't going to keep quiet. Whether Craig lived, which she figured would happen, or died, which he deserved, the truth had to come out.

And Beth would hate her forever.

Well, too damned bad. A price she had to pay, she decided as she climbed to her feet and walked, dripping, through the tunnel and up the stairs to the veranda where the air was fresh. She was cold to the bone, her hip ached, and she'd have to attend to the pinpricks where Craig's darts had found her flesh.

Would he really have killed her?

It seemed so at the time.

He'd been like a cornered rat, ready to tear into her and damn the consequences. She tried the door, but, of course, it was locked. She had to go back the way she came as her keys were in the house.

At least now it was secure.

As she made her way into the boathouse, she cast one look into the water where she knew the remains of Chase now lay. "Rest in peace," she said brokenly, then headed through the tunnel.

The events of the excruciating day rolled through her mind as she walked, her sodden shoes squishing with each step.

Levi had come to the house and demanded to be named as Dawn's father. Well, that would have to be addressed, and everyone, including Joel, would have to deal.

Rand had showed up, too, telling them both about Trick Vargas and Janet Collins. Rand seemed to think Vargas and Janet's death were all tied into what had happened to Chase, that it was all somehow connected, but Harper didn't see how.

That was all just coincidence. Right?

Gram's voice came to her then. From a memory in late summer when Harper was only about five or six. "I don't believe in coincidence, Harper girl," she'd said as she'd watered her garden with a soft spray, then switched off the nozzle to watch a honeybee moving from one heavy rose blossom to the next, its tiny legs already covered thick with pollen. "But I do believe in God and Jesus Christ, of course." Her gaze had moved to a fuzzy bumblebee that was crawling on the pink petals of one of her favorite wild roses. "And I believe in karma," she said.

"What's karma?"

"Oh, let's see." Gram had looked upward, past the brim of her straw hat to the summer blue sky. "It's tit for tat, you know, meaning if you do something good, you'll be rewarded."

"And if you do something bad?" Harper asked.

"Oh, you wouldn't want to because then something bad will happen to you."

"Because God sees it?"

"Oh yes. He's definitely involved with karma. You can count on that, Harper girl."

She'd turned on the water again, and Harper remembered the

prism of light cast in the gentle spray, so soft it hadn't disturbed a spider's web, minuscule water droplets catching on the delicate threads.

Gram had added softly, "But coincidence? It just doesn't exist."

Now, in the tunnel, she was too cold, shaken, too damned disturbed to contemplate the existence of coincidence or anything else for that matter. Right now, she needed a stiff drink before making some important calls.

Some of her anger was dissipating, though, and she hoped to high heaven that Craig didn't die. Then she'd be a murderer. Even if she'd shot in self-defense.

As she reached the main floor, she went straight to the bar and poured herself a double shot of Scotch. Then she tossed the drink back, feeling the warmth hit her throat before settling in her stomach.

She let out a slow breath and went into the kitchen. She was still quivering from the cold, but her teeth had stopped chattering so she could make those phone calls. Then she would take a hot shower and find clean, warm pajamas and . . .

Did she hear something?

A soft scrape?

Did she feel a slight stirring in the house?

She paused to listen, then heard nothing. Her nerves were jangled, getting the better of her. Of course. That was it. Nothing more.

The nightmare was over.

Finally.

No longer would she have to fear finding any more dolls with cryptic messages or dead cats hiding in the shadows.

That was something to be thankful for. But then there was Jinx . . . Her heart twisted painfully as she thought she might never find out what had happened to him, that quite possibly his nine lives had finally run out.

She walked into the hallway and again thought she heard something.

A footfall?

No way.

She was imagining it, her anxiety getting the better of her.

She stood, listening, ears straining, but nothing seemed out of the ordinary and she saw no one.

In the bath downstairs she kicked off her shoes, toweled her hair, and caught her image in the mirror. "Still bad," she told her reflection. Though the red marks from her stitches had faded significantly and the bruising on her face was almost invisible, she now sported a welt on her cheek left from the dart. Worse and larger than a bee sting.

As she examined the mark, she remembered once telling her grandmother that she hated bees while Gram was applying a baking soda paste to the back of her knee where a hornet had nailed her.

"Oh no, dear," Gram had said in this very room. "All of God's creatures have a purpose."

Red-faced and crying, all of five, Harper had stomped her foot. "Not bees, Gram. Not that stupid black bee!"

"Oh, sweetheart, even hornets can be good and have a purpose. Just trust in God." Then she'd folded Harper into her arms, the smell of cigarette smoke and perfume heavy. "God has a plan always," Gram said, kissing the top of Harper's head. "And sometimes He asks us to help implement it."

"He even has a plan for hornets?" Harper had said, sniffling and disbelieving.

"Oh yes, Harper girl. Especially for hornets." Olivia had held her granddaughter at arm's length and winked at her. "Now, come along, I do believe I have some of that pineapple sherbet your mother likes so much in the freezer. Matilda bought some sugar cones last week, so I think I can rummage up a scoop of sherbet with your name on it!" She'd touched Harper on the tip of her nose with one finger. "Boop," she'd said, smiling and bustling Harper toward the kitchen. "Let's go see."

That was a long time ago, Harper thought as she walked barefoot into the kitchen to make the call.

Why the hell was she thinking of her grandmother now, when her whole life was falling apart?

Still freezing, she considered another drink but dismissed it. *Later,* she told herself. First the phone calls that had to be made. Then out of her wet clothes, through a hot shower—or maybe a bath.

She didn't bother with the lights as she listened to the two messages left on the phone's recorder.

The first, of course, was from Rhonda Simms giving her "one last chance" to weigh in on the next article about the island and Lake Twilight. "Oh, give it a rest," she said, erasing the call. Then she hit the Play button again, and this time Dawn's voice was audible. "Hey Mom, call me. I'm okay." Her voice trembled a little and there was a pause, then she cleared her throat. "Really, I'm fine. But I did run into some trouble."

What trouble? she thought, her heart in her throat.

"A guy attacked me tonight. But like I said, I'm okay," she repeated, either to assure Harper, who was now definitely not okay, or herself. "The police said his name is Larry Smith or Tristan Vargas or something. He's got lots of names—"

Harper stood frozen to the spot.

"—Anyway, he's in the hospital, and he's supposed to be okay. Eventually. And the other guy—"

"Other guy?" Harper whispered out loud.

"—that Levi Hunt? He came down here to see me, I guess, and he's hurt pretty bad. He was there. I don't know why, but I think he saved my life." Her voice had gone to a whisper, then she added, "Look, Mom, I *know* he's my uncle. Okay? You don't have to lie about it. I figured that out already."

Levi was there? Saved Dawn's life? Once more, tears formed behind her eyes and she felt weak inside, had to lean against the counter.

"But he keeps saying he is my dad," Dawn said. "Weird, huh? Like I said, he's kinda messed up. So, call me on my pager and I'll call you back. I'm at Valley General. The doctor wants to keep me overnight for observation or whatever. But I'm okay. Really, Mom, don't freak out. Okay?"

As if she wouldn't. Someone had attacked Dawn? Tonight?

"Oh God," she whispered. Could this night get any worse?

Just then a floorboard creaked behind her.

She looked over her shoulder and found Marcia standing in the archway leading to the foyer. In her hand, pointed straight at Harper, was the missing pearl-handled pistol.

Chapter 68

Harper dropped the receiver and stared at her stepmother. "What are you do—?"

"Your turn to die, Harper," Marcia said, taking aim. "It's your time."

"What?" She couldn't believe it.

"First Anna," Marcia explained, and Harper felt as if the earth had split.

Her mother? All those years ago? Marcia was talking about Anna's death? Is that what she was talking about?

"Then Evan."

"I don't understand," she said, but that was a lie. Marcia's deep-seated hatred was evident, the horror and depth of her plan spanning years. "Evan? But that was so long ago."

"Patience, Harper. Sometimes you have to play the long game."

"You killed them?" Harper whispered, stunned, her eyes on the gun. She had to get it away from Marcia or somehow escape.

"Then, of course, Dawn."

"No!" Not her daughter. No, no, no! Her eyes found Marcia's. What kind of a monster was she? "She calls you grandma," Harper charged, remembering all the times Marcia and Dad babysat her daughter, how Harper had entrusted her child to this murderous lunatic. "Don't you ever go near her again."

"Oh, I will. I have to, now. Unfortunately it seems the job was bungled. Yes, I heard her on the recording." Marcia's lips pursed as if she'd sucked on a lemon. "I guess she managed to get away. For now." Then, as if she wasn't holding a gun on Harper, as if all this horror and bloodshed wasn't her fault, she asked, "What can I say? I made a mistake, but I've learned my lesson: Never send a boy to do a woman's job."

"What boy? What are you talking about? Are you nuts? What does Dawn have to do with anything?" Harper said. But she was beginning to understand Marcia's twisted line of thinking and she felt sick inside. The "boy" was Trick. Marcia had hired him to kill her daughter.

"Then you. It should have been Dawn, then you, but I think this will work as well. If you die first, everything goes to Dawn and then if she happens to have a fatal accident before she's stupid enough to have a child, then your father will still inherit."

Anger boiled deep inside as everything fell together in Harper's mind. "You want this island."

"I was *promised* this island," she said with venom. "And everything that comes with it. This house, the gatehouse, the stocks and bonds. Everything." Marcia actually smiled as she thought about the fortune she'd plotted to inherit.

"And you would kill for it."

"Only if I had to," Marcia argued. "And, you see, I have to. Your father's got a bad heart. Won't last long, so I had to up my game. Besides, after all these years, that patience I told you about, it's growing thin."

"You're certifiable," Harper charged, trying to think of a way to get away from her, some avenue of escape. But the gun. In the semidarkness she saw the kitchen knives in a block on the counter. Butcher's knives. Chef's knives. A meat cleaver. They were dull with age but the best and only weapons available. And less than a foot away. She had to keep Marcia talking, stave off her inevitably pulling the trigger.

"Who promised you the island?" Harper asked, attempting to keep the conversation going, inching closer to the stove and the knife block. But she already knew the answer to her question, and it made her stomach churn.

"Who do you think?"

"Dad?" Harper whispered.

She was closer to the knife block now, mere inches away from reaching the cleaver.

"Of course your father," Marcia said as if it were obvious. "But he lied. What a do-nothing! I had to be the one who took care of Anna. He wouldn't do it."

Harper remembered the night her mother died, how she'd been sick and loaded with cough syrup and how she'd tried to meet Beth but was too woozy. She'd seen her mother on the dock and some dark figure with her, but all the time she'd thought she'd been hallucinating.

"Your father didn't have the balls. All he could do was dope you up so we could be together, but he screwed that up, too! Useless, useless man."

She was shaking her head, caught up in her own perceived misery.

Harper's fingers touched the block. "Dad wanted Mom dead?" She couldn't believe it.

Keep her talking. Just keep her talking.

"Well, no. But divorce wasn't an option, now, was it? If he divorced her, he would end up with nothing." Oddly, Marcia seemed to be enjoying letting go of her secrets by bragging about her plan. She went on. "Oh, I suggested she might have an accident, but he never caught on. Thought I was joking. Laughed off the idea. He had no idea what really happened that night. He just pumped you up with codeine and stood her up so we could get together. He thought her despondency had driven her to killing herself."

"And you let him think that."

The depth of Marcia's depravity was unfathomable. Harper's stomach turned sour.

"And Mom didn't OD and end her life. You ended it for her."

"Again, a few extra pills with her booze. Believe me, it didn't take much. She was well on her way."

The demon Harper had thought she'd seen and was told was part of her hallucinations was her stepmother. "You were there. I saw you." Oh. Dear. God. Marcia was evil. Pure, unadulterated evil.

"And everyone thought you were hallucinating from the fever and the cough medicine."

"Why?"

"Isn't it obvious? They had to be out of the way," Marcia said, as if Harper were thick. "For the damned inheritance laws. He promised me this island. Promised me! Once Anna was gone, he said you and Evan would inherit and that we could live here!" She gestured widely with her free hand. "In this house."

"But Gram lived here," Harper said, disbelieving, shifting her body slightly closer to the knife block.

"She was old. God, that stroke should have taken her out. That would have been perfect. And your dad, he was patient. So damned patient, content to stay in that broken-down cottage while the years were ticking away." She let out a sigh. "So I helped her along. I really had no choice. And you, so anxious to leave and meet Chase, took the fall. How perfect was that?"

"You poisoned Gram?" Harper whispered, horrified.

"Just added a few more pills to those in her tea. She was complaining about it anyway, and you'd thankfully screwed up the medication when you spilled those pills, so it all worked out."

"But Gram—"

"She didn't know what hit her."

"You're a monster," Harper bit out, remembering the wet boots in the hallway under the coat rack. They had been her father's boots, but Marcia had worn them, just in case any suspicion was cast on someone other than Harper.

"As I think I told you, she was old," Marcia said.

"And you let me think all these years—let the whole world think—that I did it?" Harper asked, her fingers inching toward the blades buried in the block, her eyes trained on the gun still pointed in her direction. "And you want me to believe Dad didn't know?"

Marcia snorted. "I don't care what you think. But the truth is, Bruce never suspected a thing. That's the thing about your father, Harper. So trusting. So naive." Marcia was proud of herself and went on. "That worked out well, I think."

And then, as her fingers brushed the knife block, Harper understood. Her father, not blood and not loved by her grandmother, would not get any of the Dixon estate. But his kids through Anna would inherit. If Anna was dead, leaving Bruce free to marry Marcia, they would have control of the fortune until Harper turned of age.

Harper thought she might be sick as she followed the natural trail in her mind. If Bruce and Marcia were married, and his children with Anna died . . . "You killed them all," she accused, her heart thundering in her chest as the depth of Marcia's depravity became evident. "Even Evan. He didn't commit suicide. You were there! I heard you."

Memories of that hot summer night when Chase had professed his love and given her the diamond necklace tore through her. Evan. In the tram. Blue eyes staring upward and fixed. Blood everywhere.

"He drew the short straw. Both of you had to die, so I chose. He lost."

Her stomach curdled.

"You're evil."

"Oh, hurt me some more. Funny coming from you when you got yourself pregnant and tricked another man into marrying you."

"I didn't trick Joel, and getting married isn't the same as murder."

"I suppose not. But did you know how greedy he was? That he was planning to go to the lawyer and demand part of the inheritance? He'd even called your father. Then Lou Arista. So, I knew he had to go."

"Had to go."

"Oh, didn't you know? He's dead. Took a leap off a tall building in Portland. Just recently. As if he deserved any of this." She let out a huff of disgust. "He had his sights on the fortune before he met you."

"Joel? You killed him, too." How far did this woman's venality stretch?

"Vargas took care of him," she said off-handedly, and let out a sigh. "But he was supposed to get to Dawn. Offer her drugs laced with something or other! Now I'll have to come up with Plan B."

"You cold, calculating bitch!" Bile rose in her throat. "You killed them all to get all this?" She motioned grandly as if to include the whole house and island, but as she did, she stretched, her hand touching the meat cleaver.

"Bingo! Give the girl a prize!" Marcia said without a grain of humor. "So you are a smart girl after all," Marcia scoffed. "But not smart enough not to get knocked up and ruin everything."

"Ruin everything?" Harper repeated. "Because Dawn got in your way?" Sick inside that her precious daughter was considered a stumbling block. It was all so twisted and dark.

"But you can't fire a gun and kill me. Everything has to look like an accident."

"You should have died when you fell through those stairs in Bend last summer!" Marcia charged.

"You did that?" Harper said, remembering how Joel had sworn they'd been repaired. "How sick are you?" She'd heard enough. She had to get away. Who knew what Marcia was capable of? And that was when she realized that Marcia was wearing gloves, so that the fingerprints on Gramps's pistol belonged to Harper. The last person to have handled the gun.

But she would have to get close to make it look like suicide. Or . . . she could say she walked in on the battle between Craig and Harper . . . either way, Harper had to get out. Now!

She gripped the cleaver.

"Uh-uh-uh!" Marcia chided. "Dumb move, smart girl."

Harper yanked the cleaver from the block.

Marcia fired.

Bang!

The bullet sizzled through the kitchen.

Glasses piled in the sink shattered.

Harper hurled the cleaver, and it spun wildly, whizzing end over end.

Marcia moved, but the cleaver nicked her shoulder. She cried out in pain. "You bitch!"

She fired again.

A cabinet near Harper's head splintered! Chunks of wood flew through the kitchen. Another wild shot.

Harper threw herself toward the foyer and the front door. If she could just get outside, she had a chance. She sped over the marble, skidding as she reached the door.

Bang!

Once more, Marcia pulled the trigger.

Pain exploded in Harper's shoulder and she stumbled, slipping past the door but flinging herself out of the foyer where she was an open target to the far side of the split staircase, taking whatever cover she could in the carved railing and spindles.

Marcia stepped into the foyer, blood staining her sweater, her face white, her expression deadly. Narrowing her eyes, her arm no longer steady, she took aim.

Bang!

Another shot.

Two spindles next to Harper burst, spraying her with splintered wood chips as she climbed.

Eyes trained on Harper, Marcia dashed to the opposite staircase and pointed the gun upward and across the foyer as Harper scrambled up the stairs.

Bang!

Glass and crystal exploded and the chandelier rocked, sending a shower of glass to crash on the marble floor below.

Harper didn't wait for the next shot. She raced up the final steps of the staircase and ran through the hallway to the stairs leading ever upward. She heard Marcia running behind her but there was nowhere to go but up.

Bleeding, leaving a trail of blood on the carpet, she forced herself forward.

Marcia had only one shot left. The revolver had six chambers. And Harper had counted five shots. But who was to say, her stepmother, having planned this for years, couldn't have more bullets?

"You can't get away!" Marcia called after her, but her voice wasn't as strong as it had been and she was breathing hard as she climbed the stairs. "You're doomed up there, Harper! There's no way out."

"Screw you!" she yelled back, hoping that Marcia would take another wild shot to even the playing field.

With each step her horror, fear, and anger prodded her on. Marcia had killed everyone she loved. The bitch deserved to die and to die a horrible, excruciating death.

And what about her father? Bruce Reed had to have known or suspected something. He couldn't be as naïve as Marcia had said.

Heartsick, her hip aching, her shoulder throbbing, she slipped into her room and reached into the sleeping bag for Evan's knife. Blood was running down her arm now, sticky and wet. She ignored it. What sweet vengeance it would be to slit Marcia's throat with the knife owned by the stepson she'd killed.

She heard the steady, slow sound of Marcia's footsteps still below.

Harper slid out of the room, leaving the door open, silently inviting her stepmother into the room, hoping the path of blood would direct her within. Then, hiding in the darkened curved staircase, she would get the jump on her.

Hardly daring to breathe, she hid in the shadows and saw the top of Marcia's head appear as she reached the landing.

Please, please, please.

Harper's grip on the knife tightened.

She counted her heartbeats, waiting.

Marcia paused on the landing, pushed open the door, and . . . snapped on the light.

A slash of illumination brightened the hallway, and Marcia caught a glimpse of the blood drops moving upward, so much that the trail was hardly interrupted.

She raised her weapon.

Crap!

Harper flew up the remaining stairs to the tower room. She locked the door. Breathing heavily, she went to the window and looked down to the terrace two full stories below. Even if the fall didn't kill her, she'd break something, a leg or arm or pelvis, and she'd be a sitting duck.

But maybe not a dead one.

Harper cranked open the window, the fresh cool air swirling inside. At least she had the option of jumping rather than giving Marcia the satisfaction of shooting her.

She glanced over at the far shore and saw the five houses on the point. Rand's house was dark. Levi's, too, showed no signs of life. A thin light shone from the Sievers' place, and the Musgrave cabin was dark. But there were lamps glowing at the Alexander house, and she didn't need to look through the binoculars or the telescope to see Craig sitting on the dock, Beth tending to him, the lights of an ambulance flashing through the trees in the swim park, its siren shrill and echoing across the water.

Craig was alive.

She hadn't killed him.

She remembered pointing the shotgun at him, her finger on the trigger, but she'd hesitated. Then the echoing, ear-splitting blast. He'd tumbled into the boat slip, hitting his head on the Chris-Craft as he fell. He hadn't been blown back, away from her but sideways. As if he'd been struck by a bullet coming from the tunnel. There had been no thunderous ping of dozens of buckshot pellets spraying on the walls of the boathouse or madly dappling the water.

She realized she hadn't shot him. She'd never pulled the trigger. Marcia had.

From a hiding spot in the tunnel.

She shot him with the first bullet of six, Harper realized suddenly. Was that right? Yes. Craig should have been blown backward if she'd shot him. Not sideways.

Since then, Marcia had fired five times.

So she was out of ammunition and possibly didn't realize it.

Hoping she was right, Harper unplugged the single working lamp in the tower room. Then she gathered her weapons, such as they were.

She heard the key in the lock.

Of course Marcia had a key.

The interior locks had never been changed.

But Harper was waiting, hiding just inside the open doorway to the private bathroom.

The door from the staircase swung open, and she heard Marcia's hands reach for the nonexistent light switch. "Where in the devil— oh shit."

Harper saw a shadow, the nose of the gun as Marcia advanced into the room.

Then she pulled the ring of the doll she was holding and Chatty Cathy's high voice said, "Please take me with you."

"What?" Marcia whirled, just as Harper hurled the Ken doll like a spear. It slipped in her hand but still whizzed through the air and hit Marcia square in the face.

"Ow! Shit!"

Click!

The gun didn't fire!

"Oh shit," Marcia said, her voice tight.

Click. Click. Click.

Marcia kept trying to shoot.

And over the clicking Harper heard the sound of frantic, loud pounding. Someone downstairs at the door.

"What?" For a second Marcia was distracted by the sound.

Harper leapt, hitting her full center. "Oof!" Marcia fell backward, Harper on top of her, knocking against the tripod holding the telescope upright. It wobbled but didn't fall.

The loud knocking suddenly stopped as Harper and Marcia wrestled, the gun tumbling away. They rolled against the chaise as Harper heard a thunderous crash of shattering glass as Marcia got a handful of Harper's hair and pulled her head back.

Harper swiped upward with the knife.

Marcia let go and in one swift motion, Harper flipped and pinned her stepmother to the floor.

"It's over," Harper said through clenched teeth as she glared down at her stepmother. "You fucking bitch, it's over." Then turned her head and shouted over her shoulder, "Up here! Rand, I'm up in the tower!"

"No!" Marcia reached out for the gun and grabbed it by the barrel. Then she swung upward. *Bam!* The pearl handle cracked against Harper's skull. The knife, slick with blood, slipped from her hands and the world started to tilt.

Footsteps pounded up the stairs.

With a fresh burst of adrenaline, Marcia swept up the knife and onto her feet. Bloody and breathing hard, she stood over Harper, ready to cut her to ribbons. "You've been the bane of my existence," she snarled, waggling the knife, taunting Harper. "But no more! No more!"

Frantic footsteps pounded up the final spiral stairs.

Harper's fingers curled around one leg of the tripod. She managed to get to her knees, but as she tried to stand, Marcia sprang.

"Die!" Marcia ordered, slashing wildly with the blade.

With all her might, Harper swung the huge telescope and hit her stepmother midair. Then she let go.

The door burst open just as Marcia let out a hideous scream. She and the spiraling telescope flew through the open window and into the dark night.

Still on her knees, Harper heard the sickening crunch of breaking bones on the terrace far below.

She winced at the sound, darkness closing in.

Rand was at her side. On his knees. Gathering her into his arms.

There was a single, gurgling moan and then silence.

"Radio for an ambulance," he said to someone—another person? Harper didn't know. Couldn't see.

"You're gonna be okay," he said to Harper, his breath warm against her cheek, his strong arms surrounding her. She almost laughed at how ridiculous it sounded. Being "okay" would be a long, if not impossible journey and she was fading. "You're gonna be okay," he repeated. "I'm here now."

"About effing time," she said before everything went black.

1965

Chapter 69

Beneath the broad brim of her hat, sweat trickled down the side of Olivia Dixon's face. For once, she was alone, not even babysitting her granddaughter, Harper, though truth to tell, Harper was long past needing a sitter.

Olivia fanned herself a bit as she sipped her gin and tonic on the terrace. This summer was one of the hottest on record in Oregon, and boats were scattered on the lake. People swimming and water-skiing or just cruising along the shoreline on this beastly hot day, a rare summer day in Oregon where the temperature had soared to the triple digits.

She watched as hummingbirds and butterflies flitted through the flowers. There were honeybees as well, and she even caught sight of a hornet. She wondered if she would have to catch a few of the shiny creatures, but maybe not. Maybe today would be the last that she would need them. She crossed her fingers as the black wasp crawled over the rim of a terra-cotta pot. With its white skull-like head and white rings on its tail end, it looked deadly. Aggressive. Able to sting through some cloth. Their sting was painful, and they defended their nests vehemently. Small. Fierce. Fatal.

She and the hornets had so much in common.

More than anyone knew.

Marilyn, her gorgeous calico, was sunning herself near the back door while that stinker Diablo was slinking through the shrubbery, on the hunt, his long gray tail twitching in anticipation. "Don't you dare," Olivia warned him as he eyed a hummingbird with its shiny pink crown. Oh, that cat was a devil and appropriately named.

Another sip and she heard the sound of a Corvette's engine.

So he was returning. And it was too hot of a day for him to have the top of the convertible down. Oh no, it would piss him off, but he'd have it up and the air conditioning blasting.

She knew.

She'd ridden with him enough to know.

And she hadn't been the only one. He'd had more than his share of floozies in that car with him doing God-only-knew-what. Her blood turned poisonous as she thought of his philandering and how shameless he'd been. How she had curdled inside when she'd learned of his flings. The distasteful gossip, usually from Louise Chilcote while playing a "friendly" game of bridge or gin rummy.

Louise, with her Lucille Ball red hair teased into a coiffed beehive, was a pathetic card player but had a keen mind for gossip and a sharp tongue for delivering it. Too often, Louise had offered kind, consoling words about George's latest rumored affair, trying to look sadly concerned for Olivia. However, Louise had never been able to hide the sparkle of nasty delight and satisfaction in her eyes at divulging a tantalizing secret she'd heard from her husband, Roger, the pot-smoking mayor of this tiny town, a damned druggie! It didn't matter that Louise would make a stupid card play. Oh no. What had been important was that her bit of scandal had hit its mark in embarrassing Olivia. And embarrassed her it had. Always.

Once teenage rivals, now superficial friends, Louise, a neighbor who lived in a modest home on the north shore, had always wanted to one-up the woman with her own private island.

Well, no more!

Olivia had seen to it that she would never be embarrassed by her randy, obscene husband again.

If not today, then tomorrow, or the next.

But soon. Very soon she'd be rid of the beast that made the gargoyles guarding the drive seem tame.

Listening and sipping, watching the ice cubes melt in her glass, she heard the roar of the Corvette's engine as he accelerated along the rim of the lake. He was driving recklessly. As he always did. Thinking himself impervious to any kind of catastrophe.

And he'd be wearing his cap despite the heat and the fact that the top was up. Incredibly vain, he kept his ever-growing bald spot covered at all times.

"Fool," she whispered, taking another swallow.

She listened.

Anticipating.

Knowing he would be approaching the S curve, two sharp twists in the road rimming the lake.

She felt her pulse elevate in anticipation.

The powerful engine revved more loudly.

Oh, he was driving fast. Too fast.

She waited. Held her breath.

The S curve was the most likely place for—

Brakes squealed.

Oh!

She perked up.

Heard the crash, a thunderous roar as if the entire earth were shaking. That unmistakable and horrible sound of groaning, twisting metal. The splintering of tree limbs. The shattering of breaking glass. Loud. Long. As, she imagined, the car tumbled off the steep slope, spinning end over end and bouncing against the sheer cliffs and towering firs.

Then the crashing stopped, but a horn began to sound in a steady monotone, like the sound of a heart monitor flatlining.

Perfect.

Slowly she sipped from her glass.

Swatted at a pesky mosquito.

It took several minutes. In fact, she was able to finish her drink before she heard the faraway wail of a siren.

The hornet buzzed around her head, and she smiled before lighting a cigarette.

"Not today," she told the pesky insect as it landed on the glass-topped table. "I won't be needing you today, and, if I'm lucky, never again." She smashed her glass down on the black and white creature before taking a long, calming drag.

Today, she hoped, she'd gotten rid of that scumbag she'd been married to for far too many years. Today, it seemed God, with the help of a hornet or two, had done her dirty work for her and that miserable son of a bitch she'd been married to—yoked to—for ages was finally meeting his maker.

"Good."

She figured it was really God's hand that had guided the hornets to George's bare face and neck, God's will that they had caused him to panic, had even stung him with their deadly venom. Because he was so allergic to them. Anaphylaxis. What a long exotic term for severe, even fatal, allergic shock. And he already had a weak heart, which, of course, was God's doing as well.

It wasn't murder.

It was diabolical. Well, maybe.

But murder?

Not really.

That would be a sin.

She sketched the sign of the cross over her chest and sent up a small prayer of thanks for what she believed to be the end of her torment, the end of her husband.

She picked up her glass, scraping the remains of the lifeless hornet off the bottom and finished off her drink.

Then she decided to pour herself another.

Just one, mind you.

To celebrate.

1989

Epilogue

The summer breeze caught in Harper's hair as she stood on the terrace and looked across the lake. She was healed, if not emotionally, at least physically. As she had predicted, it was a long, slow journey. Even now, standing on the flagstones, she couldn't look at the spot where Marcia had fallen without her skin crawling.

Maybe that's the way it would be for the rest of her life.

Staring across the water, she saw Rand, working on his boat, wiping it down with a towel. Her heart swelled a little, but she cautioned herself to tread slowly.

All the men in her life had ended up disappointing her.

Still . . . she wasn't going to stop living just because of past mistakes. She'd been seeing Rand this past year and was taking it slow, knowing she was falling in love and fighting it.

Trusting a new man, even an old friend, proved difficult.

She turned her attention to the house next door to Rand.

At the Hunts' cottage, Levi stood at a barbecue grill where Beth was serving drinks. He'd survived a gunshot wound in the fight with Trick Vargas, and Beth had been at his side as he'd healed. Harper, too, had visited and tried to mend the ripped fences between them, but it was still a very tentative work in progress.

As she looked at Beth, she noticed a sparkle, sunlight catching on the diamond at her throat. Beth, it seemed, was happy, Levi settled. Possibly for the first time in his life. The odd part about that little party was that on the picnic table nearby Dawn and Max were playing a game of cards. If Harper still owned a telescope, she could probably check out Dawn's hand, but she'd given up watching other people's lives through high-powered lenses and concentrated on her own.

For the most part.

Though it was still a thorny path. Dawn had accepted that Levi was her "next" father as Joel was gone. That had been a blow, and they both had wept at his funeral, but Dawn had been satisfied that she'd helped put his killer in prison for the rest of his life. Tristan "Trick" Vargas would never see the light of day as a free man again, and the gun he'd used to threaten Dawn was part of her grandfather's set, the very weapon Marcia had planted on Evan to make his death look like a suicide. Later, Trick, fascinated with the "cowboy" gun, had twisted Tom Hunt's arm into retrieving it from the evidence room.

And Tom had complied.

Did Gerald Watkins know that his partner had lifted the pistol from the evidence room? He claimed not. Harper would probably never know.

As for Craig, Beth's once-upon-a-time husband, he was living his own quiet hell. Harper hadn't pressed charges as she'd threatened, but Beth had divorced him immediately. Currently he was living in Central Oregon somewhere, working construction when he could get a job while Beth sold the family home and now lived with Levi and Max in the Hunts' cottage.

Now, it seemed, Levi was content with Beth. She had sold her family home to a young couple who were expecting their first child. "A new generation here on the lake," Beth had told her after lunch one afternoon in June. She'd also announced that she was listing the Musgrave cabin. "It's not your house, of course, and it doesn't come with its own private island," she'd pouted as Harper had told her she was definitely staying in Almsville. "But it's something and waterfront. But, Harper, seriously, if you ever change your mind about selling, let me know! Kisses!"

Harper wasn't going anywhere in the foreseeable future.

Dawn had made noise about moving back here permanently after graduation, and Rand lived just across the water.

Harper's own relationship with Levi was complicated.

As she watched him now, standing over a grill, looking like a suburban dad for the first time in his life, she wished they could be as they once had been, when they'd been childhood friends.

Unfortunately often the tension between them was palpable.

Even though they were trying.

Or at least she was.

They had a child.

And it was difficult.

Maybe someday they'd find the connection they'd lost over the years. Harper hoped so, but it would take time and a lot of forgiveness on Levi's part.

What were the chances? Too many years, too many doubts, too many lies had grown between them.

"You should live so long," she said, thinking that it was something Gram might say. God, she missed that woman. She probably always would.

She glanced down at the boathouse or what was left of it. Months before, Chase's body had been retrieved and the boathouse sealed off. There had been a small funeral and a splashy news story and reporters calling and asking questions as she'd healed from her wounds. Thankfully all the dart pricks had healed, and even the gunshot to her shoulder hadn't hit bone. She'd ended up with a scar and a brutal memory.

Of Marcia Reed.

Her stepmother.

Her father's wife.

Harper hadn't found it in her heart to forgive him.

She couldn't. Not yet.

He should have seen Marcia for what she was.

And Harper couldn't help but wonder if he'd been naïve as Marcia had claimed or had turned a blind eye to how mendacious she was, how cunning, and how evil. Harper couldn't really believe that Bruce would have gone along with his first wife's and son's murders, nor would he have condoned or been a part of the intended killing of his daughter and granddaughter.

But what did she know?

Just that she would never trust him again.

Nor forgive him.

"Too bad," she said now.

Bruce Reed was a widower. Again. And back on the market.

After suffering for several weeks after her fall, Marcia had finally died and now Dawn, who still kept in touch with him, reported that he was dating again.

Oh. Joy.

He'd sure put all the recent horror of their lives behind him. Had he ever realized that his death was a part of Marcia's plan? That's why she kept saying, "It isn't his time."

Because he could die only after he'd inherited the Dixon fortune.

It had taken months for news of the sensational events to die down. Rhonda Simms's series on the lake had expanded with the latest developments and had gained national attention. She was now reportedly writing a book about her experiences, again using Ned Gunderson, now retired from the Almsville Police Department, as her source.

At least Rhonda was actually writing a book. In that regard, she was ahead of Harper, who had put off her writing project until she'd healed from her wounds and renovations on the house were complete. She'd hired a local builder and architect to construct a new gatehouse and renovate the manor house after Dawn returned to school in the fall.

This summer they were living here together and Harper had relented, allowing Dawn to take over the tower room while she moved her office to Gram's old bedroom on the first floor. She had to admit, it did have a spectacular view of the lake.

And Rand's A-frame.

And sometimes, as dusk was settling as she sat at her desk, she imagined she smelled that unique blend of cigarette smoke and Chanel No. 5 and heard Gram sigh. *See, Harper girl, life isn't so bad. It's just exactly what you make it.*

As she leaned over the terrace railing, she watched an osprey soaring high over the lake before she let her gaze fall to Rand again.

He must've felt her watching him because she saw him look over at the house. He was wiping his hands on his towel and grinned, then waved.

She waved back, her heart beating a little faster as he climbed into his boat and headed across the water.

Rand had admitted to being with Chase on the night of his death. He'd admitted that Chase had talked about disappearing, a secret Rand had kept. He'd also confided to Harper that Chase had asked him to look after her.

And now he is, she thought, *twenty-odd years later*.

If she let him.

She heard a loud meow and turned to find Jinx at the French doors, inside the house. She walked in, and the cat greeted her by doing figure eights between her legs. "Hey, buddy." She picked him up, glad that his wandering days were over. Craig had admitted to having found the cat on the property in the days after Cynthia Hunt's tragedy on the lake. Already plotting to push Harper into renovating, then selling, the house, he'd taken the opportunity to steal the cat and had kept Jinx in a cage under the deck of his house, near the woodpile. Craig had sworn he never intended to hurt him, just "borrow" him. Beth supposedly never knew that Jinx was locked outside, she just wasn't home often enough to hear him cry.

Really?

It seemed wrong, but Beth assured her the catnapping had been all Craig.

Sick bastard, she thought, petting Jinx's sleek head.

She heard the motor of Rand's boat fast approaching.

"You stay here," she told the cat. "And don't get into any trouble." Then she slipped out the back door to the terrace again. Sunlight was shimmering on the surface of the lake, and she watched as Rand tied up at the dock.

Maybe this really was her home, this place Olivia Dixon loved.

"You were right," she said as if her grandmother could hear her over the sigh of the wind through the stately firs surrounding the house. "Life is what you make it."

And from here on, she was going to make it right.

She thought she heard her grandmother's voice in the rustle of the breeze whispering through the fir trees.

You do that, Harper girl, you do just that. And I'll be watching.